The Likes of Us

1928 - 2011

Stan Barstow was born in Horbury in the West Riding of Yorkshire in 1928, the only child of a miner. He attended Ossett Grammar School until he was sixteen, then went to work as a draughtsman at a local engineering firm. He married Constance Kershaw in 1951 and they had two children.

He was a novelist and scriptwriter; he won awards, including Baftas, for his TV and radio dramatisations. He is best known for his novel, A KIND OF LOVING (1960), which was subsequently made into a ground-breaking film. But his first sortie into writing was the short story. He started writing for money – 'certainly there was no question... of my thinking I had anything serious to say' – but he soon realised that 'writing insincerely rarely works'. 'The Search for Tommy Flynn', initially aired on BBC radio, was his first published work. In all, he produced three volumes of short stories, most set in his fictional town of Cressley. It was a form which fascinated him all his life.

In 2000, Stan Barstow left his native Yorkshire with his partner, the radio playwright Diana Griffiths, and went to live in south Wales. He died on 1st August 2011 at Neath. His work has been translated into many languages and is taught in schools and colleges all over the world. He was an honorary MA of the Open University, a Fellow of the RSL and a Fellow of the Welsh Academy.

Parthian
The Old Surgery, Napier Street
Cardigan SA43 1ED
www.parthianbooks.com

The Desperadoes first published in 1961
A Season With Eros first published in 1971
The Glad Eye first published in 1984
This edition published in 2013
© Stan Barstow
All Rights Reserved

ISBN 978-1-908069-67-2

The publisher acknowledges the financial support of the Welsh Books Council.

Cover design by www.theundercard.co.uk
Typesetting by Lucy Llewellyn and Elaine Sharples
Printed and bound by Gomer, Llandysul

The Desperadoes: Some of these stories have been broadcast by the BBC
'The Search for Tommy Flynn' first appeared in Pick 8 of *Pick of Today's Short Stories*, published by Putnam.

Some of these stories have been broadcast by the BBC. Acknowledgements for those which have been published elsewhere are made to: *Argosy*, *Flair*, the *Guardian*, *Today*, the *Sunday Citizen*, and *Weekend*.

British Library Cataloguing in Publication Data

A cataloguing record for this book is available from the British Library.

The Likes

of Us

Stories of Five Decades

Stan Barstow

PARTHIAN

Contents

THE DESPERADOES

For C.M.B.

The Human Element

a young man trapped into an engagement on a picnic in the country

Harry West's the name, fitter by trade. I'm working for Dawson Whittaker & Sons, one of the biggest engineering firms around Cressley, and lodging with Mrs Baynes, one of the firm's recommended landladies, up on Mafeking Terrace, not far from the Works. It's an interesting job – I like doing things with my hands – and not a bad screw either, what with bonus and a bit of overtime now and again, and taken all round I'm pretty satisfied. The only thing I could grumble about is some of my mates; but they're not a bad lot really. It must be because I'm a big fair bloke and the sort that likes to think a bit before he opens his mouth that gives them the idea I'm good for a laugh now and then. Some of them seem to think it's proper hilarious that I'm happy with my own company and don't need to go boozing and skirt-chasing every night in the week to enjoy life. And on Monday mornings, sometimes, when they're feeling a bit flat after a weekend on the beer, they'll try to pull my leg about Ma Baynes and that daughter of hers, Thelma. But they get no change out of me. I just let them talk. Keep yourself to yourself and stay happy – that's my motto. I'm not interested in women anyway; I've got better ways of spending my time, not to mention my money.

I've got something better than any girl: nearly human she is. Only she wears chromium plate and black enamel instead of lipstick and nylons. And she's dependable. Look after her properly and she'll never let you down, which I reckon is more than you can say for most women. Every Saturday afternoon I tune her and polish her for the week. There's no better way of spending a Saturday afternoon: just me and the bike, and no complications. All I ask is to be left alone to enjoy it.

Well, it's summer, and a blazing hot Saturday afternoon, and I'm down on my knees in Ma Baynes's backyard with the motor bike on its stand by the wall, when a shadow falls across me and I look up and see Thelma standing there.

'Hello, Arry,' she says, and stands there looking at me with them dull, sort of khaki-coloured eyes of hers that never seem to have any expression in them, so you can't tell what she's thinking, or even if she's not thinking at all, which I reckon is usually the case.

'Oh, hello.' And I turn back to the job and give one of the spindle nuts on the front wheel a twist with the spanner.

'Are you busy?' she says then.

I'm trying my best to look that way, hoping she'll take the hint and leave me alone. 'You're allus busy with a motor bike if you look after it properly,' I say. But even me giving it to her short and off-hand like that doesn't make her shove off. Instead she flops down behind me, coming right up close so's she can get her knees on my bit of mat and pressing up against me till I can feel her big bust like a big soft cushion against my shoulder.

4

'What're you doing now, then?' she says.

'Well,' I say, getting ready to answer a lot of daft questions, 'I'm just checkin' 'at me front wheel's on properly. I don't want that to come loose when I'm on the move, y'know.'

'You must be clever to know all about motor bikes,' she says, and I wonder for a second if she's sucking up to me. But I reckon she's too simple for that.

'Oh, I don't know. You get the hang of 'em when you've had one a bit.'

She gives a bit of a wriggle against my shoulder, sort of massaging me with her bust. She doesn't know what she's doing. She's like a big soft lad the way she chucks herself about. It'd be enough to give ideas to some blokes I could mention. But not me. It does nothing to me, except make me feel uncomfortable. I'm breaking a new pair of shoes in and I've cramp like needles in my left foot. But I can't move an inch with Thelma there behind me, else we'll both fall over.

She gives another wriggle and then gets up, nearly knocking me into the bike headfirst. And when I've got my balance again I stretch my leg out and move my toes about inside the shoe.

'We was wonderin',' Thelma says, 'if you'd like to lend us your portable radio set. Me mam wants to go on a picnic, but me dad wants to listen to the Test Match.'

Now here's a thing. I've got to go canny here. 'Well, er, I dunno...' I get up, steady, wiping my neck with my handkerchief, giving myself time to think of an excuse for saying no. I'm always careful with my belongings.

'Oh, we'd look after it,' Thelma says. 'On'y me dad's that stubborn about cricket, an' me mam won't go without him.'

I know Old Man Baynes and his sport. It's the one thing Ma Baynes can't override him on.

Thelma can see I'm not happy about the radio and she says, 'Why don't you come with us, then you can look after it yourself? We're goin' to Craddle Woods. It'll be lovely up there today.'

I know it will, and I've already thought of having a ride out that way when I've finished cleaning the bike. But this doesn't suit me at all. I haven't been with the Bayneses long and I've been careful not to get too thick with them. Getting mixed up with people always leads to trouble sooner or later. I always reckon the world would be a sight better place if more folk kept themselves to themselves and minded their own business.

But I see that Thelma has a look on her face like a kid that wants to go to the zoo.

'Well, I'd summat else in mind really,' I say, still trying my best to fob her off. 'I was goin' to clean me bike.'

'Clean it!' she says. 'But it's clean. Look how it shines!'

'It on'y looks clean,' I say. 'There's dozens o' mucky places 'at you can't see.'

'Well, it can wait, can't it? You don't want to waste this lovely weather, do you?'

I haven't thought of wasting it, not with that nice little ride all planned. But I'm concerned. That's how it is with people. They pin you down till you can't get out any way. I can see Ma Baynes taking offence if I don't lend them the radio now, and that's the last thing I want. No trouble. I'm all for a quiet life. So I give in.

'Okay, then, I'll come. When're you settin' off?'

Thelma's face lights up like a Christmas tree at this. 'About three, I sh'd think,' she says. 'I'll tell 'em to be...' And then she gets her eyes fixed on something behind me and forgets what she's saying.

6

'Look, there's Lottie Sharpe.'

I turn round and look over into the next yard, where a girl's walking by: a slim little bit, all dressed up in nylons and high heels and even a fancy little hat.

'I wish I looked like that,' Thelma says, sort of quiet and wistful like, and I can tell she's talking to herself, not to me. I take a good look at her, standing nearly as big as me, with that sort of suet-pudding face of hers, and I see what she means, but I say nothing.

'Lottie's gettin' married next month.'

There it is: they're all alike. Getting married and spending some poor feller's brass is all they think about. I say nothing.

Thelma watches right till Lottie turns the corner into the entry, then she gives a big sigh, right down inside herself.

'I'll tell 'em to be gettin' ready, then.'

She goes back across the yard. Her overall's tight and stretched across her fat behind and I can see the red backs of her knees.

I reckon I've had it for today and I begin to pick my gear up.

We go along the street to the bus stop. Ma Baynes is walking in front, wearing white holiday shoes and carrying the sandwiches in a tartan shopping bag. Old Man Baynes, in a new cap and cricket shirt, strolls along beside her sucking at his pipe and saying nothing.

I'm walking behind with Thelma, carrying the portable radio. Thelma's changed into a thin cotton frock that's as short and tight as the overall she had on earlier. I wonder if she has any clothes she doesn't look as though she's grown out of. Now and then I take a look down at my new shoes. They're a light tan, with long toes. I've had my eye on them for weeks, along with a

7

pair with inch-thick crepe soles, and I've had a lot of trouble making up my mind between them. But these are definitely dressier: a smashing pair of shoes. They'll be fine when a bit of the newness has worn off. Just now they've developed a bit of a squeak and once Thelma looks down and giggles. I give her a look and move away from her and try to look as if I'm not with them at all, and hoping like mad we won't run into any of the bods from the Works.

We sit downstairs on the bus. Just out of manners I have a bit of a difference with Old Man Baynes about who's going to get the fares. But I soon give in when I see one or two of the other passengers looking round. It's the Bayneses' treat anyway and I don't want to attract attention and have everybody taking me for Thelma's young man. She's sitting next to me, by the window. She's chattering all the time to her mother in front and bouncing backwards and forwards like a kid on a trip. Her skirt's getting well up past her knees and I can feel her leg hot when it rubs mine, so I move over to the edge of the seat and look at the barber's rash on the back of Old Man Baynes's neck.

In about twenty minutes we're well out in the country and we get off the bus and cross the road and take a path through a field of corn that's ready for getting in, it's so heavy and ripe, and as still as if we were seeing it on a photo. It's a real scorcher of a day. We go round the edge of the farmyard and down into the woods. The trees come over and shut the sun out and the path's narrow and steep. We walk in single file with Ma Baynes in front and every now and then one of us trips over the roots that stick out of the ground all hard and shiny like the veins on the backs of old people's hands. After a bit of this we come out into a clearing. Down the hill we can see the beck with the sun shining on it and on the far side there's a golf course with one or two nobs having a game. Past that there's fields stretching miles off and electricity pylons marching along like something out of a science-fiction picture.

'This'll do,' Ma Baynes says and drops her bag and flops down on the grass like half a ton of sand. Old Man Baynes shoots me a look and I pass the radio over. He takes it out of the case and switches on, stretching out on the grass with his ear stuck right up to the speaker as though he thinks the set's too little to make much noise.

Ma Baynes levers her shoes off and pushes the hair off her forehead. Then she clasps her hands in her lap and gives a satisfied look all round.

'We sh'd come here more often,' she says, 'stead o' stickin' in that mucky old town.' She gives Thelma and me a funny look. 'Me an' your father used to come courtin' here,' she says. 'Didn't we, George?'

Old Man Baynes just says 'Mmmm?' and Ma Baynes twists her head and pins him with a real sharp look.

'I hope you're not goin' to have your head stuck inside that thing all afternoon,' she says. 'If that's all you can find to do you might as well ha' stopped at home.'

'That's what I wanted to do,' he says, and gives the radio a tap with his fingers. 'I can't get no reception.' He picks the set up and gives it a shake.

'Here,' I say, 'let me.'

Ma Baynes gives a sigh. 'Here we are, next to nature, an' all they can find to do is fiddle wi' a wireless set!'

After a bit she sends Thelma up to the farm for a jug of tea. By this time me and Old Man Baynes between us have taken so many parts out of the radio it'd take a chopper to strip it down any more. All the guts of it are spread out in one of my hankies on the grass and

I'm looking at them in a bit of a daze, wondering if we haven't gone a bit too far.

Old Man Baynes has lost all interest. He's sitting by himself, looking out over the valley, chewing grass stalks and muttering to himself something like, 'I wonder how they're gettin' on.' He's worried sick about that cricket match.

Soon Thelma comes back with the tea and Ma Baynes sets the mugs out. 'Come on, you men, and get your teas.'

We get going on the fishplate sandwiches. Nobody has much to say now. It's all right going out into the country, but what do you do when you get there? It begins to get me down after a bit and I get to thinking about the bike and all I could be doing with her if I wasn't wasting my time sitting here.

When we've finished Thelma picks up the jug.

'I'll take that back, if you like,' I say. I think a walk might help to pass the time.

Ma Baynes looks up at us. 'Why don't you both go?'

I'd rather go on my own, but I give a shrug. 'If you like.'

We set off up the path under the trees. It's a bit cooler here but I'm still sweating a lot and my shirt's stuck to me. Thelma's the same. Her frock was tight to start with and now it looks as it it's been pasted on her. We get the full force of the sun as we leave the shade on the edge of the farmyard, and it's dazzling the way it bounces back off the whitewashed walls. Everything's dead quiet and there's no sign of life except for a few hens pecking around and a great red rooster strutting about among them as though he owns the place. I put my hand down on the flagstones as Thelma comes back from the house.

'Could fry your breakfast on here,' I say, just to help the conversation on a bit.

'It is hot, in't it?' she says, and flaps her arms about like an angry old hen. 'I wish we was at the seaside; I'd love to be in the sea just now.'

We go back into the wood and follow the path till we come to another one, narrower and steeper, leading off down through the bracken to the beck.

'Let's go down here,' Thelma says, and starts off before I can say yea or nay. She runs on in front and I follow, and when I come out on the grassy bank where the stream bends she's sitting down taking her sandals off.

'I'm goinna paddle,' she says. 'Comin?'

Paddling's nothing in my line so I shake my head and stretch out on the bank while she goes in. I chew a grass stalk and watch her bounce about in the water like a young hippo, holding her skirt up and giving me a good view of her legs above the knee.

Before long she's overdoing the jumping about a bit and I tell her to be careful of the stones on the bottom: but she just laughs and jumps right up out of the water. Well, it's her funeral, I'm just thinking, when her face changes and she starts to sway about and throw her arms out to keep her balance. I don't take this in for a second, and then I see she's not acting any more, and I jump up. The next thing I know my right leg's in water up to the knee and my arm's round her holding her up. I shift my hand to get a better hold and feel my fingers sink into her soft bust.

When I have her safe on the bank I take a look at my sopping trouser leg and shoe. But I'm not bothering about them somehow. It's my hand. Something's wrong with it. It's still got the feel of Thelma's bust in the fingers.

I look at her sprawling on the grass with her knees up. 'You've grazed your foot.' She's a bit short of wind and doesn't say anything, so I kneel down in front of her and dry her foot on my spare hankie and then tie the hankie round it in a makeshift bandage. 'That'll stop your shoe rubbing it till you get home.'

When I lift my eyes I find I'm looking straight along her leg to her pink pants and what with this and that funny feeling in my hand I look away quick and feel myself coming up brick red.

She puts her leg down and leans forward to feel at the bandage. I stand up out of the way.

'I don't know what I'd 've done if you hadn't been here, Arry,' she says.

'You'd ha' got wet,' I say, and give a short laugh. And all the time I'm looking down at her big bust lolling about inside her frock. She's got nothing much else on besides the frock and it looks as though if she leans over a bit further the whole flipping lot might come flopping out, and I can't keep my eyes off it, wondering what I'll do if it does. I don't know what's come over me.

Then all at once a funny thing happens. As sharp as if it was yesterday I remember the time we went with the school to the Art Gallery. It's the only time I've ever been but I remember clear as daylight all them naked women, big strapping women, lolling about on red plush, as brazen as you please. And it comes to me that Thelma would have been just right in them days: they must all have been like Thelma then. I shut my eyes and imagine her and then I begin to get excited. It's like a great bubble filling all inside me and then it goes down and leaves me all loose and wobbly where my guts should be. God! But I've never felt like this before. I put my hand out and I can't keep it steady.

'It's ever so nice havin' some'dy big an' strong to look after you,' Thelma's saying.

'I like looking after you,' I say. My throat's all clogged

up and I swallow hard to clear it. 'I... I'd like to look after you all along.'

Thelma stares and goes as red as fire. 'Would you, Arry? All along?'

I give her a nod because I can't talk any more, and sit down beside her. The way I'm feeling now I'd tell her anything.

'I allus knew you was a nice lad, Arry,' she says, and hides her face as I slide my arm round her waist and try to pull her over.

'Give us a kiss, then,' I say.

She doesn't move for a couple of seconds, then she turns her face round and turns it straight back again just as I'm making for her and I end up kissing her on the ear. We sit like that for a minute or two and then I try to touch her bust again. She gives a wriggle at this.

'We'd best be gettin' back, Arry,' she says. 'They'll be wonderin' where we've got to.'

She pulls her sandals on and we stand up. I grab her and plonk her one straight on the mouth. Her eyes flutter like bees' wings after that.

'You'll have to let me lean on you, Arry,' she says, all soft and melting like.

We get back to the main path and make for the clearing. Thelma limps along the path and I charge along through the bracken with my arm round her waist. As we get near the place where we left Ma and Old Man Baynes I begin to notice she's leaning on me fit for a broken leg, let alone a scratched foot. And I can feel my trouser leg all sopping wet and my foot squelching away in my shoe. The next minute I see Ma and Old Man Baynes sitting there waiting for us and all the feeling I had by the beck's gone and I just feel like turning round and running for it.

Thelma tells her everything and a bit more besides, nearly falling over herself to get it all out.

'An' guess what, Mam!' she says at the end. 'Me an' Arry's engaged!'

Even Old Man Baynes lifts his eyebrows at this and I feel myself go all cold at the glitter that comes into Ma Baynes's eyes.

When we get home Thelma offers to press my trousers. I reckon it's the least she can do, so I go upstairs and change and bring them down to her. She spreads them out on the kitchen table and sets about them with her mother's electric iron.

'That's right, love,' Ma Baynes says. 'Get your hand in.'

She's settled down with a box of chocolates and a woman's paper, and there's a variety show on the wireless. Old Man Baynes chucks his sports final down and takes his glasses off. 'Would you believe it?' he says. 'Rain stopped play. An' we haven't had a drop all day!'

I make some excuse and go up to my room where I can be on my own and think a bit and try to sort it all out. I sit down on the bed and look at my shoes standing under a chair. I've already polished them with a rag and one's bright and shiny, but the other one's soggy and dull. I can't see that one ever polishing up again. I really can't. Anyway, they'll never do for best again. New on at that. I think now that I could have reckoned the radio was bust when Thelma first asked me. I don't think fast enough by half, that's my trouble. It's bust now, though, right enough. A fiver that'll cost me, if a penny. The shoes and the radio. And on top of all that I've gone and got myself engaged! Fifteen quid for a ring, and Ma Baynes for a mother-in-law. How I ever came to do it I'll never know. But I'll have to get out of it somehow, even if it means finding fresh digs; which is a pity because

I've just nicely got settled here. I'll have to think about it. But not now. I can't concentrate now. I'll think about it later when I haven't got so much else on my mind. Just now I can't get over the shoes. I've had plenty of enjoyment out of the radio, but I've only worn the shoes today. A new pair of shoes like that; ruined first time on. A smashing pair of shoes, and they're done. It doesn't bear thinking about.

I sit there on the bed and I hear laughing coming up from the wireless in the kitchen. It sounds as though they're laughing at me. I begin to think what a nice life these hermit bods must have with nobody to bother them; and then I seem to go off into a sort of doze, because when I come to again it's dark and I can't see the shoes any more.

Freestone at the Fair

self-satisfied & humourless cuckold

*a gipsy's predictions came true —
a birth & a death*

comic satire

It was only afterwards that it occurred to Freestone to wonder why the gipsy should have picked on him rather than Emily or Charlie, and the thought that he might have looked the most gullible of the three never entered his mind. For when, after pondering the matter for a moment or two, he seemed to recall the woman's saying he had an interesting face, he was instantly satisfied with that eminently reasonable explanation. For there were deeper aspects of the matter concerning him by this time: aspects which might have had grave effects on the mind and reason of a lesser man.

She had stood in the opening of the tent and fixed on him a dark and lustrous eye. Her sultry stare did not perturb him and his natural inclination, when she offered to read his hand, was to walk on, ignoring the rapid mumbled persuasions. But to his surprise he found himself being pressed into acceptance by his companions.

His surprise contained more than a little irritation, for this was the third time that day they had formed an

16

alliance against him (but for them he would never have thought of visiting the fair in the first place, and only a few minutes ago they had failed to entice him to join them while they sampled the undignified thrills and delights of the Whip).

Mrs Freestone, her yellow-brown eyes and plump face shining with the unaccustomed excitement, urged him.

'Go on, Percy,' she said. 'See what she tells you.'

Since Emily was aware of his views on fortune-telling, as she was on most other subjects, Freestone considered this to be nothing less than wanton betrayal and his mind began instinctively to frame a future reprimand.

Charlie, fifteen stone of jovial, arrogant manhood, was, of course, all for it.

'Ye-es, go on and have a bash, Perce,' he said, giving Freestone a playful thump on the upper arm.

Freestone frowned at the unwelcome familiarity of the blow and the detestable abbreviation of his Christian name. He had for some time past regretted the generous impulse which had prompted him to offer Charlie accommodation while he looked for suitable rooms. He regarded it now as a lapse, a temporary mental aberration; whereas it had seemed such a naturally kindly thing to do at the time the Manager had introduced them and intimated that Charlie was the son of an old friend of his and was learning the business in preparation for higher things. Now the few days originally specified had stretched into several weeks and Freestone was finding Charlie's all-good-pals-together attitude to life simply too much at such close range. And the fact that he himself was manager of Soft Furnishings while Charlie, his supposed influence apparently not at all what it had at first seemed to be, was still a mere assistant in Hardware, loaded an already painful situation with an additional sting.

'Well really,' Freestone said now, with the intention of killing the matter with a few scornful words. 'There's absolutely no foundation to this fortune-telling business, you know. It's simply a catchpenny from first to last.'

But he seemed temporarily to have lost Emily, and Charlie was impervious to scorn in any shape or form.

'Oh, come off it, Perce!' he said with dreadful joviality. 'Let yourself go, man! Show a bit of holiday spirit! You'll get a laugh out of it if nothing else.'

And on to the camel's back of Freestone's resistance Charlie then blithely tossed the last straw.

'You're not scared of what she might tell you, are you?

Thus challenged, Freestone had no choice.

'Very well, then,' he said, with the lofty resignation of one who spends a large part of his life humouring the whims of the sub-intelligent. 'But it's nothing but foolishness to encourage these charlatans.'

With an instinctive gesture he lifted his hand to adjust the rim of his bowler hit, only to encounter instead the unfamiliar peak of the tweed cap which he had always hitherto considered a sufficient concession to the 'holiday spirit'. It was a psychological setback from which he recovered admirably, and with one hand resting lightly in the breast of his dirk blue blazer – rather in the manner of a certain deceased foreign dignitary of similar stature, but immeasurably greater significance – he marched with a firm and dignified tread into the dark interior of the tent.

There was a lot of what looked like black-out material draped about to add to the atmosphere of mystery, but a modern adjustable reading-lamp with a weak down shaded bulb occupied the place of the traditional crystal ball on the table in the middle of the tent. A voice from the shadows bade Freestone sit down and he obeyed, perching gingerly on the edge of a collapsible chair which sloped alarmingly in its stance on the uneven turf. A rather grubby hand appeared under the light. Freestone primed it with a two-shilling piece and replaced it with his own pink and well scrubbed palm.

The woman began by tracing Freestone's character, revealing all those sterling qualities, the possession of which he had never had occasion to doubt.

'I am looking into the future now,' the gipsy said at length. 'It is very hard. You are not responsive. You doubt my powers.'

Sighing at the waste of money, Freestone passed over another florin.

'You are a family man,' the woman said.

'Oh, but I'm not,' Freestone said.

'You will be, very soon. I see a child. A boy, I think. And a time of rejoicing. You have waited a long time.'

'And what after that?' Freestone said, smirking disbelievingly. 'Why not make it twins?'

'You are not sympathetic,' the woman said. 'You do not believe. It is not safe to scoff at those who have the power to pierce the dark mystery of the future.'

'Make me believe,' Freestone challenged her. 'Tell me more.

'I see,' the woman said. 'I see –' and with a gasp she thrust Freestone's hand from her.

He was immediately interested. 'What?' he said. 'What do you see?'

'It is nothing. I cannot tell.'

Recklessly, Freestone took a ten-shilling note from his wallet and laid it on the table. He extended his hand over it.

'Tell me what you see.'

The brown forefinger crawled over his palm and despite himself Freestone felt his spine chill as the woman said:

'Death. I see death.'

She set up a queer soft moaning under her breath and Freestone's flesh crawled.

'Is it the child's death you see?'

'No, not the child. The child is well, three months old. It is the father I can see –'

Freestone snatched his hand away. 'Are you trying to frighten me?' he said harshly. The woman grabbed the ten-shilling note from the table.

'You are unsympathetic.'

'You trek about the countryside,' Freestone said.

'Never do an honest day's work from one year to the next; preying on gullible people... Well let me tell you you've picked on the wrong man this time. I've half a mind to report you to the police.'

'I have said nothing,' the woman said. 'Please go.'

Freestone went out, bristling. He admitted to himself that she had given him quite a turn; but he was all right again when he had been out in the light and the fresh air for a few minutes: and he took pleasure in exacting a small revenge on Emily and Charlie by refusing to disclose anything but the few generalities from the beginning of the session.

Charlie felt for his loose silver. 'Here, let me have a go.' He disappeared into the tent and the Freestones stood and waited in silence. Ten minutes passed before he came out again.

'Well?' said Emily eagerly.

'Oh, the usual things,' Charlie said, dismissing it with a shrug. 'I'm to watch out for a tall dark man on a sea voyage.' He laughed. 'Come on, let's go knock coconuts down.'

'Pure poppycock,' Freestone said, enjoying the disappointment on Emily's face. He was thinking that there was at least one serious flaw in the gipsy's prophecy. Emily was a barren wife, which was the sole reason for their present childless state. It had rankled with him for years, and thinking of the gipsy's words renewed the irritation. He looked about him as they strolled along at the parents and children thronging the fairground and reflected bitterly on the unkind Providence which had given him such a colourless and useless mate. He stared irritably at the lock of mouse-brown hair which had come untidily astray from Emily's bun, and when she spoke to him he snapped her into a miserable silence.

In his constant pre-occupation with the smooth functioning of Soft Furnishings the incident became dismissed from Freestone's mind and he thought no more of it until some seven or eight months later.

He had just passed through a trying period culminating in the departure for fresh pastures of Charlie Lofthouse, when it had been made clear even to his thick-skinned self that his stay could not be indefinitely prolonged. No sooner, it seemed, had the Freestones resumed their placid and dignified pre-Charlie mode of living than Emily blushingly informed her husband that she was with child. Freestone was amazed and delighted, and it was not until the initial excitement had faded slightly that he remembered the incident at the fair. Resolutely he pushed it back into oblivion and managed to keep it there until after the birth of the child.

He was a boy, and the Freestones lavished on it all the obsessive affection of the middle-aged for their first-born. Congratulations were showered on them from all sides, not least from the staff of Soft Furnishings, who hoped with the coming of this new interest into his life for a mellowing of Freestone's personality and a relaxation of his iron rule.

21

It became obvious by the time the child was two months old that so far as physical resemblances were concerned Freestone ran a poor second to Emily. And there were those who, not knowing him well, were tactless enough to point this out. But Freestone dismissed physical likenesses as being of little importance and did not hesitate to assure the people concerned of his faith in the child's revealing, all in good time, its inheritance of his own intellect and general strength of character.

And then one day Freestone woke from his intoxicated state and remembered the child's age. Now, despite all his scepticism, he could not entirely erase the gipsy's words from his mind, and on the night the boy was three months old he slept badly, imagining strange pains in his chest and disturbed by unusual dreams. But he was at the store as usual the next morning and at five minutes to nine, after tidying himself up in the cloakroom, he took his usual stance in the middle of his domain in preparation for the first of the day's customers.

It was at half-past ten that the Manager summoned Freestone to his office, thinking that as he had known him best he should be the first to hear of the sad and sudden end of Charlie Lofthouse.

As the full significance of what his superior was saying smote Freestone he blanched visibly and put his hand on the desk as though for support.

'Did you know he had heart disease?' the Manager asked.

Freestone shook his head. 'He was such an athletic-looking chap,' he said weakly.

The Manager tut-tutted and pursed his lips. 'You never can tell,' he said profoundly. He looked up into Freestone's pasty face. 'It must have come as a bit of a shock to you,' he said. 'Perhaps you'd better go and sit down for a while.'

Freestone took the Manager at his word and for the next twenty minutes Soft Furnishings rubbed along without his guiding hand, while he sat locked in one of the cubicles in the cloakroom, alone with his thoughts. Nor did he show any of his usual sparkle and grip for the rest of the morning. His staff were quick to notice this and, though he was far from popular, sympathise once the news had got about.

At lunch, Freestone sat opposite Cartwright, who managed Men's Tailoring. Inevitably the conversation turned to the sudden end of Charlie, with added observations on the odd tricks of life in general.

Now Cartwright was a hard-headed, worldly type, Freestone thought.

'What do you know about fortune-telling?' he asked over coffee.

'You mean the crystal ball, playing cards, and all that?'

'Yes, reading the future in general. In a person's hand, for instance. I was reading something last night which set me wondering. Do you think a fortune-teller could read what would happen to one person in the hand of another?'

Cartwright stirred his coffee and thought about Freestone's question. 'If the prophecy were to have an effect on the life of the person whose hand was being read, I suppose it's feasible.' He tasted his coffee, added enough sugar to cover a sixpence, and tasted it again. 'Always allowing you believe in the business in the first place, that is,' he said. 'And ninety per cent of it's pure charlatanism, of course.'

'My own opinion exactly,' Freestone said. There was nothing like talking to somebody sensible for getting things into perspective.

'Though there are more things in heaven and earth...' Cartwright said. 'For instance, I have a cousin who once received a communication from a dead friend.'

'Spiritualism?' Freestone said disbelievingly.

'That's one name for it. Very interesting, you know, when you come to look into it...'

Freestone stood up. 'I'm sorry. I've just remembered something I must attend to.'

Well, well. Cartwright of all people. Who would have thought it? It shook him. And he remained shaken until towards the end of the afternoon when, at last, he seemed to come to a decision. At six o'clock, when he stepped from the store on his way home, he had the air of a man who has spent a long period looking deep inside himself and has emerged satisfied with what he has seen.

Emily's behaviour reassured him further. For when he told her of poor Charlie Lofthouse lying stiff and cold in his lonely room, his laughter silenced for ever in this world, she displayed what seemed to him to be no more than an appropriate interest and concern. People were born and people died. Life went on...

Especially did life go on, for as they sat by the fire after supper a cry from upstairs brought Emily to her feet with an exclamation of annoyance. 'Your son has been behaving badly all day,' she said. 'I've been able to get hardly anything done.'

They went up together and Freestone peered into the cot. The crying ceased.

'Ah!' said Freestone, 'he knows his father is here now and that he must be good. Yes he does, doesn't he? Yes he does. Tchk tchk, tchk...'

He bent over the cot and chucked dotingly to the child.

Later, sitting once more by the fire, Freestone paused in the act of reaching for the evening paper.

'You look to have something on your mind.'

'I was just thinking of poor Charlie Lofthouse,' Emily said.

'Oh?'

'Yes. You know, he wasn't really a bad sort of fellow.'

'No, no, not a bad sort,' Freestone said generously. 'Not our type, of course.'

'You remember that day we all went to the fair together,' Emily said, 'and you and he had your palms read?'

'Oh, yes, yes, I do recall it.' Freestone looked keenly at Emily.

'He mentioned afterwards that she'd told him he would have a long life, and children.' Mrs Freestone's eyes met her husband's. 'And the poor man didn't have either, did he?'

For perhaps five seconds their glances were locked. Then Freestone lifted his paper and shook it open.

'Haven't I always said that fortune-telling is poppy-cock?' he said.

The End of an Old Song

*Death of an old bandsman –
his wife's jealousy of the music
– Sentimental
+ war of the sexes*

He was already awake on Christmas morning when she went in to draw back the curtains. He watched her from the prison of his bed and his first words were: 'D'you think t'band'll call this mornin'?'

'I should think so,' she said in an off-hand tone as she admitted the grey half-light into the room and then came bustling over to tidy the bedclothes about his wasted form. 'They said they would, didn't they?'

'Aye,' her husband said. 'Aye, they said so.'

She stood by the bed, looking down at him with fretful concern in her eyes. 'Haven't you slept?'

He stirred sluggishly under the sheets. 'Oh, on an' off,' he said listlessly. His eyes wandered. 'I wonder what time they'll come,' he said in a moment.

Anticipation of the band's visit had been the only thing in his life during the last few days, outside herself and his bed and the four too familiar walls. But she no longer resented his pre-occupation: he was helpless now and this was all that was left to him of his lifelong passion. She was in command.

He had been in his uniform when she first met him, while strolling through the park on a summer Sunday afternoon. She was nineteen then and thought how handsome and military-like he looked in his scarlet tunic and shiny-peaked cap with its gold lyre and braid. But his playing had become a constant source of friction between them during the forty years of their marriage before the accident. What had first attracted her to him became anathema to her and she never grew used to taking second place to his music.

'But it i'n't a case o' taking second place,' he had said to her shortly after their marriage. 'You know I played wi't band afore you wed me.'

'I thought when you were married your wife 'ud be more important to you than your banding,' was her reply.

'But you don't want to look at it like that,' he said. 'Don't make it sound as though I don't think owt about you!' He told her that she should go with him and mix with the other bandsmen's wives; but she had notions of gentility and liked to choose her company.

'I can't stand that crowd wi' their drinkin' an' carryin' on,' she said.

He tried to persuade her that she would find grand women among them if only she would take the trouble to be sociable and get to know them. But she saw it as a test of strength and refused to give in. He went his own way and in the days and evenings without him she knew her defeat.

And then two years ago, twelve months before he was due to retire, a careless step on a muddy scaffolding had given him to her. She had devoted herself to his care, agonising for him with a feeling she had thought long dried up and finding a bitter satisfaction in the knowledge that he would be dependent on her for the rest of his days, and that the hated music could never take him away again.

Once more when she gave him his breakfast, and yet again when she went up to wash and tidy him for the day, the focus of his thoughts was revealed.

'Have you heard owt on 'em yet? Can you hear 'em anywhere about?' And at her negative reply: 'I wonder if they've decided to leave it till Boxin' Day.'

The excitement showed in two dull spots of colour in his pale cheeks. It was the only sign of spirit in him and it disturbed her.

'Nah don't you go gettin' all worked up about it,' she admonished him. 'They'll come all in good time. Why, they'll hardly have gotten out of their beds by now!'

He lay back weakly among the pillows while she sponged his face and hands and chest. He had been a big man once and quietly proud of his physique; but now the flesh was gone and the skin taut across the cage of his ribs. She wondered vaguely, as she had wondered so many times before, how long it could go on. The doctors could not tell her. He might last for years, they said; or he might go at any time. She must be ready for that. The only thing they were sure of was that he would never leave his bed again.

But she had a strange feeling about him lately. She felt that something was going to happen and she had prepared herself for the worst, which, she told herself, could only be a mercy for him. He had not been himself these past few days. He had no interest in anything but the band's expected visit and he made no effort to do even the small things he had always insisted on doing for himself, but rested passively, listlessly between the sheets while she hovered about him with brisk and dedicated efficiency.

'Don't you feel well?' she asked him as she put aside the bowl of grey, soapy water and drew the blankets up round him.

'I'm all right, I reckon.'

'You don't feel any pain anywhere, do you?' she said. 'No more than usual, I mean. You wouldn't like me to ask the doctor to call?'

He moved his cropped grey head against the pillows. 'No,' he said. 'I'm just tired, that's all. I feel tired out.'

He closed his eyes and she sighed and left him, going downstairs shaking her head.

It was almost half-past eleven before she heard from her kitchen the distant strains of the band as it played its first piece in the street. She wondered if her husband could hear it too and she went to the foot of the stairs and called out to him to listen. Some twenty minutes later there was the sound of voices and shuffle of feet in the entry, and when she peered out through the lace curtains she saw the score or so of musicians forming a circle in the yard.

They struck off with Christians, Awake! and followed with Hark! The Herald Angels Sing and Come, All Ye Faithful. They stopped then and during the ensuing mumble of conversation there came a knock on the door. When she opened the door the conductor, in mufti, was on the step. He leaned forward across the threshold, his breath like steam.

'Is he listenin'?' he said in a low, hoarse tone, as though he and the woman shared some secret kept from the man upstairs. His eyes swivelled skywards as he spoke.

'Aye, he's listenin',' she said, wiping her hands on her apron. 'He's been on edge all mornin', wonderin' if you'd forgotten him.'

The conductor's eyes opened wide with ingenuous surprise. 'Nay, Missis, he ought to know we'd never let him down.'

'I told him as much.'

The man leaned closer and she recoiled slightly from the smell of whisky that always awaited the band on Christmas morning at the mill-owner's house up the street. His voice sank to a hoarse conspiratorial whisper. 'Will you ask him if there's owt special he'd like us to play for him?' He nudged her arm. 'Go on, Missis. Nip up an' ask him. We'll give him a Command Performance.'

She went through the kitchen and up into the bedroom. He watched her come in with eyes that were brighter than before.

'I thowt they'd come,' he said. 'I thowt they wouldn't forget me.'

'Didn't I tell you so?' she said. 'Gettin' yourself all worked up like that...'

'How many on 'em?' he said.

She told him, about twenty, and he nodded. She could see it pleased him.

'A good turn-out.'

'They want to know if there's owt special you'd like 'em to play for you.'

He thought for a moment, then said slowly, 'I think I'd like 'em to play Abide with Me. That's all, I think.'

'All right.' She turned to go. 'I'll tell 'em.'

Then as she moved through the doorway he called softly to her, 'Ey!' and she stopped and turned back into the room. His expression was quietly eager and at the same time curiously bashful as he said, 'D'you think...'

He stopped. 'D'you think you could get me cornet?'

She was taken off balance and surprise put an edge on her voice. 'Whatever for?' she said. 'You can't play it.'

'I know,' he said. He looked away from her. 'I'd just like to have it.'

There was an expression in his pale eyes which she could not fathom, but it made her cross the room and rummage in the bottom of the built-in wardrobe till she found the instrument case. She took the cornet out of the case and put it on the bed beside him.

'Is t'mouthpiece theer an' all?'

She took the mouthpiece from its pocket and fitted it into the cornet, then watched him, suspicious and puzzled, and somehow disturbed.

'All reight,' he said then. 'That's all.'

When she had gone downstairs again he brought one arm from under the sheets and took hold of the cornet, his fingers feeling for the valves. He lay waiting and in a little while the band started the hymn in the yard below his window. He listened as the treble instruments followed the long-drawn-out and solemn melody, the soprano cornet adding its soaring sweetness to the melodic line, while below the bass instruments filled out the texture of sound with deep, rich, organ-like chords and the bass drum marked off the rhythm with its slow and ponderous beat. He thought of many things as he listened: of his days as a boy with the band; of the first world war and playing through French towns on the way to the front line. He thought of bright peacetime afternoons of concerts and on the march; and contests all over the country – Huddersfield, Leicester, Scarborough, and the finest of them all at the Crystal Palace and Belle Vue. It was as though his whole life, irrevocably bound up with music, passed through his mind as the music swelled and filled the yard and his room with a sound so noble and so moving that his eyes brimmed over and the tears rolled softly, silently down his cheeks.

Downstairs in the kitchen the woman hummed the hymn to herself as she peeled potatoes for the Christmas dinner. She thought as she worked of her husband and how many times he had 'played out' with the band at Christmas; and guiltily she savoured the bitter sweetness of her triumph.

When the music ceased she wiped her hands and took her purse before the knock came again.

'D'you think he'd like one'r two on us to pop up an' have a word with him?' the conductor asked.

Some of the old resentment stirred in her. She looked down at the man's dirty shoes and thought of them on her stair carpet and she said:

'No, I think not. He's not been too well these last few days. Best leave it a day or two.'

The man nodded. 'Just as you like, Missis. Well, I hope he liked it. It allus war his favourite.' He stood musing for a moment as the last of the bandsmen made his slow way out of the yard and down the entry. 'I got to thinkin' when we were playin' on how many happy times we've had together, us an owd John...' He sighed and shook his head. 'Ah, well, it comes to us all, I reckon. We'd best be gerrin' about us rounds. Wish him a happy Christmas thru all on us. An' the same to you, Missis.'

She felt in her purse as he moved away from the door. 'Here...'

He turned and recoiled, shocked. 'Nay, Missis, we don't want owt thru you! We didn't come here for that. This is a special call.'

She saw that she had offended him but she persisted, pressing the shilling into the mittened hand. 'We can pay for all we get yet,' she said. 'We're not in need o' charity.'

He avoided her eyes, the sympathetic friendliness gone from his face, leaving only a painful grimace of embarrassment.

'Just as you like, Missis,' he said.

She carried on with her work when they had gone and more than an hour passed by before she went upstairs again. There was something about the silence in the room which stopped her in the doorway. She knew at once that this was deeper than the silence of sleep and though she had thought herself prepared for it, the shock was like a blow to the heart.

She stepped into the room, her eyes falling on him as he lay there, his head deep in the pillows, the cold cornet under his hand. The moisture of his tears was gone from his cheeks and it was a new expression which stopped her short again. It was a smile, a smile of such happiness and deep contentment that it seemed to her that at that very moment he must be hearing down the rolling vaults of the Great Beyond the soaring of the cornets, the thunder of the basses, and the throbbing of the drum.

And she knew that to the very end she was defeated.

One Of The Virtues

*Grandfather's watch &
patience*

*the
watch* The watch belonged to my grandfather and it hung on a
hook by the head of his bed where he had lain for many
long weeks. The face was marked off in Roman numerals,
the most elegant figures I had ever seen. The case was
of gold, heavy and beautifully chased; and the chain
was of gold too, and wonderfully rich and smooth in the
hand. The mechanism, when you held the watch to your
ear, gave such a deep, steady ticking that you could not
imagine it ever going wrong. It was altogether a most
magnificent watch and when I sat with my grandfather
in the late afternoon, after school, I could not keep my
eyes away from it, dreaming that someday I too might
own such a watch.

It was almost a ritual for me to sit with my grandfather
for a little while after tea. My mother said he was old and
drawing near his time, and it seemed to me that he must
be an incredible age. He liked me to read to him from
the evening paper while he lay there, his long hands,
soft and white now from disuse and fined down to skin

34

and bone by illness and age, fluttering restlessly about over the sheets, like a blind man reading braille. He had never been much of a reader himself and it was too much of an effort for him now – possibly because he had had so little education, no one believed in it more, and he was always eager for news of my progress it school. The day I brought home the news of my success in the County Minor Scholarship examination he sent out for half an ounce of twist and found the strength to sit up in bed for a smoke.

'Grammar School next, then, Will?' he said, pleased as Punch.

'Then college,' I said, seeing the path straight before me. 'Then I shall be a doctor.'

'Aye, that he will, I've no doubt,' my grandfather said. 'But he'll need plenty a' patience afore that day. Patience an' hard work, Will lad.'

Though, as I have said, he had little book-learning, I thought sometimes as I sat with my grandfather that he must be one of the wisest men in Yorkshire; and these two qualities – patience and the ability to work hard – were the cornerstones of his philosophy of life.

'Yes, Grandad,' I told him. 'I can wait.'

'Aye, Will, that's t'way to do it. That's t'way to get on, lad.'

The smoke was irritating his throat and he laid aside the pipe with a sigh that seemed to me to contain regret for all the bygone pleasures of a lifetime and he fidgeted with the sheets. 'It must be gettin' on, Will...'

I took down the watch and gave it to him. He gazed at it for some moments, winding it up a few turns. When he passed it back to me I held it, feeling the weight of it.

'I reckon he'll be after a watch like that hisself, one day, eh, Will?'

I smiled shyly, for I had not meant to covet the watch so openly. 'Someday, Grandad,' I said. I could never really imagine the day such a watch could be mine.

'That watch wa' gin' me for fifty year o' service wi' my firm,' my grandfather said. "A token of appreciation", they said... It's theer, in t'back, for you to see...'

I opened the back and looked at the inscription there: 'For loyal service...'

Fifty years... My grandfather had been a blacksmith. It was hard now to believe that these pale, almost transparent hands had held the giant tongs or directed the hammer in its mighty downward swing. Fifty years... Five times my own age. And the watch, prize of hard work and loyalty, hung, proudly cherished, at the head of the bed in which he was resting out his days. I think my grandfather spoke to me as he did partly because of the great difference in our ages and partly because of my father. My mother never spoke of my father and it was my grandfather who cut away some of the mystery with which my mother's silence had shrouded him. My father, Grandfather told me, had been a promising young man cursed with a weakness. Impatience was his weakness: he was impatient to make money, to be a success, to impress his friends; and he lacked the perseverance to approach success steadily. One after the other he abandoned his projects, and he and my mother were often unsure of their next meal. Then at last, while I was still learning to walk, my father, reviling the lack of opportunity in the mother country, set off for the other side of the world and was never heard of again. All this my grandfather told me, not with bitterness or anger, for I gathered he had liked my father, but with sorrow that a good man should have gone astray for want of what, to my grandfather, was a simple virtue, and brought such a hard life to my mother, Grandfather's daughter.

So my grandfather drifted to the end; and remembering those restless fingers I believe he came as near to losing his patience then as at any time in his long life.

One evening at the height of summer, as I prepared to leave him for the night, he put out his hand and touched mine. 'Thank y', lad,' he said in a voice grown very tired and weak. 'An' he'll not forget what I've told him?'

I was suddenly very moved; a lump came into my throat. 'No, Grandad,' I told him, 'I'll not forget.'

He gently patted my bind, then looked away and closed his eyes. The next morning my mother told me that he had died in his sleep.

They laid him out in the damp mustiness of his own front room, among the tasselled chairback covers and the lustres under their thin glass domes; and they let me see him for a moment. I did not stay long with him. He looked little different from the scores of times I had seen him during his illness, except that his fretting hands were still, beneath the sheet, and his hair and moustache had the inhuman antiseptic cleanliness of death. Afterwards, in the quiet of my own room, I cried a little, remembering that I should see him no more, and that I had talked with him and read to him for the last time.

After the funeral the family descended upon us in force for the reading of the will. There was not much to quarrel about: my grandfather had never made much money, and what little he left had been saved slowly, thriftily over the years. It was divided fairly evenly along with the value of the house, the only condition being that the house was not to be sold, but that my mother was to be allowed to live in it and take part of her livelihood from Grandfather's smallholding (which she had in fact managed during his illness) for as long as she liked, or until she married again, which was not likely, since no one knew whether my father was alive or dead.

It was when they reached the personal effects that we got a surprise, for my grandfather had left his watch to me!

'Why your Will?' my Uncle Henry asked in surly tones. 'I've two lads o' me own and both older than Will.'

'An' neither of 'em ever seemed to know their grandfather was poorly,' my mother retorted, sharp as a knife.

'Young an' old don't mix,' Uncle Henry muttered, and my mother, thoroughly ruffled, snapped back, 'Well Will an' his grandfather mixed very nicely, and your father was right glad of his company when there wasn't so much of anybody else's.'

This shot got home on Uncle Henry, who had been a poor sick-visitor. It never took my family long to work up a row and listening from the kitchen through the partly open door, I waited for some real north-country family sparring. But my Uncle John, Grandfather's eldest son, and a fair man, chipped in and put a stop to it. 'Now that's enough,' he rumbled in his deep voice. 'We'll have no wranglin' wi' the old man hardly in his coffin.' There was a short pause and I could imagine him looking round at everyone. 'I'd a fancy for that watch meself, but me father knew what he was about an' if he chose to leave it young Will, then I'm not goin' to argue about it.' And that was the end of it; the watch was mine.

The house seemed very strange without my grandfather and during the half-hour after tea, when it had been my custom to sit with him, I felt for a long time greatly at a loss. The watch had a lot to do with this feeling. I still admired it in the late afternoon but now it hung by the mantelshelf in the kitchen where I had persuaded my mother to let it be. My grandfather and his watch had always been inseparable in my mind, and to see the watch without at the same time seeing him was to feel keenly the awful finality of his going. The new position of the watch was in the nature of a compromise between my mother and me. While it was officially mine, it was being held in trust by my mother until she considered me old enough and careful enough to look after it. She was all for putting it away till that time, but I protested so strongly that she finally agreed to keep it in the kitchen where I could see it all the time, taking care, however, to have it away in a drawer when any of the family were expected, because, she said, there was no point in 'rubbing it in'. *grammar school*

The holidays came to an end and it was time for me to start my first term at the Grammar School in Cressley. A host of new excitements came to fill my days. I was cast into the melting pot of the first form and I had to work for my position in that new fraternity along with twenty-odd other boys from all parts of the town. Friendships were made in those first weeks which would last into adult life. One formed first opinions about one's fellows, and one had one's own label stuck on according to the first impression made. For first impressions seemed vital, and it looked as though the boy who was lucky or clever enough to assert himself favourably at the start would have an advantage for the rest of his schooldays.

There are many ways in which a boy – or a man – may try to establish himself with his fellows. One or two of my classmates grovelled at everyone's feet, while others took the opposite line and tried systematically to beat the form into submission, starting with the smallest boy and working up till they met their match. Others charmed everyone by their skill at sports, and others by simply being themselves and seeming hardly to make any effort at all. I have never made friends easily and I was soon branded as aloof. For a time I did little more than get on speaking terms with my fellows.

One of our number was the youngest son of a well-to-do local tradesman and he had a brother who was a prefect in the sixth. His way of asserting himself was to parade his possessions before our envious eyes; and while these tactics did not win him popularity they gained him a certain following and made him one of the most discussed members of the form. Crawley's bicycle was brand new and had a three-speed gear, and oil-bath gearcase, a speedometer, and other desirable refinements. Crawley's fountain pen matched his propelling pencil and had a gold nib. His football boots were of the best hide and his gym slippers were reinforced with rubber across the toes. Everything, in fact, that Crawley had was better than ours. Until he brought the watch.

He flashed it on his wrist with arrogant pride, making a great show of looking at the time. His eldest brother had brought it from abroad. He'd even smuggled it through the customs especially for him. Oh, yes, said Crawley, it had a sweep secondhand and luminous figures, and wasn't it absolutely the finest watch we had ever seen? But I was thinking of my grandfather's watch: my watch now. There had never been a watch to compare with that. With heart-thumping excitement I found myself cutting in on Crawley's self-satisfied eulogy.

'I've seen a better watch than that.'

'Gerraway!'

'Yes I have,' I insisted. 'It was my grandfather's. He left it to me when he died.'

'Well show us it,' Crawley said.

'I haven't got it here.'

'You haven't got it at all,' Crawley said. 'You can't show us it to prove it.'

I could have knocked the sneer from his hateful face in rage that he could doubt the worth of the watch for which my grandfather had worked fifty years.

'I'll bring it this afternoon,' I said; 'then you'll see!'

The hand of friendship was extended tentatively in my direction several times that morning. I should not be alone in my pleasure at seeing Crawley taken down a peg. As the clock moved with maddening slowness to half-past twelve I thought with grim glee of how in one move I would settle Crawley's boasting and assert myself with my fellows. On the bus going home, however, I began to wonder how on earth I was going to persuade my mother to let me take the watch out of doors. But I had forgotten that day was Monday, washing day, when my mother put my grandfather's watch in a drawer, away from the steam. I had only to wait for her to step outside for a moment and I could slip the watch into my pocket. She would not miss it before I came home for tea. And if she did, it would be too late.

I was too eager and excited to wait for the return bus and after dinner I got my bike out of the shed. My mother watched me from the kitchen doorway and I could imagine her keen eyes piercing the cloth of my blazer to where the watch rested guiltily in my pocket.

'Are you going on your bike, then, Will?'

I said, 'Yes, Mother,' and, feeling uncomfortable under that direct gaze, began to wheel the bike across the yard.

'I thought you said it needed mending or something before you rode it again...?'

'It's only a little thing,' I told her. 'It'll be all right.'

I waved good-bye and pedalled out into the street while she watched me, a little doubtfully, I thought. Once

41

out of sight of the house I put all my strength on the pedals and rode like the wind. My grandfather's house was in one of the older parts of the town and my way led through a maze of steep cobbled streets between long rows of houses. I kept up my speed, excitement coursing through me as I thought of the watch and revelled in my hatred of Crawley. Then from an entry between two terraces of houses a mongrel puppy darted into the street. I pulled at my back brake. The cable snapped with a click – that was what I had intended to fix. I jammed on the front brake with the puppy cowering foolishly in my path. The bike jarred to a standstill, the back end swinging as though catapulted over the pivot of the stationary front wheel, and I went over the handlebars.

A man picked me up out of the gutter. 'All right, lad?'

I nodded uncertainly. I seemed unhurt. I rubbed my knees and the side on which I had fallen. I felt the outline of the watch. Sick apprehension overcame me, but I waited till I was round the next corner before dismounting again and putting a trembling hand into my pocket. Then I looked down at what was left of my grandfather's proudest possession. There was a deep bulge in the back of the case. The glass was shattered and the Roman numerals looked crazily at one another across the pierced and distorted face. I put the watch back in my pocket and rode slowly on, my mind numb with misery.

I thought of showing them what was left; but that was no use. I had promised them a prince among watches and no amount of beautiful wreckage would do.

'Where's the watch, Will?' they asked. 'Have you brought the watch?'

'My mother wouldn't let me bring it,' I lied, moving to my desk, my hand in my pocket clutching the shattered watch.

42

'His mother wouldn't let him,' Crawley jeered. 'What a tale!'

(Later, Crawley, I thought. The day will come).

The others took up his cries. I was branded as a romancer, a fanciful liar. I couldn't blame them after letting them down.

The bell rang for first class and I sat quietly at my desk, waiting for the master to arrive. I opened my books and stared blindly at them as a strange feeling stole over me. It was not the mocking of my classmates – they would tire of that eventually. Nor was it the thought of my mother's anger, terrible though that would be. No, all I could think of – all that possessed my mind – was the old man, my grandfather, lying in his bed after a long life of toil, his hands fretting with the sheets, and his tired, breathy voice saying, 'Patience, Will, patience.'

And I nearly wept, for it was the saddest moment of my young life.

A Lovely View
of the Gasworks

an unnamed couple
buy a house together

'Well,' he said after a silence, 'what d'you think to it?'

She answered him from the tall sash window where for several minutes she had been standing gazing out across the town in a dreamy, pre-occupied sort of way. 'Lovely view of the gasworks,' she said, stirring now and rubbing slowly at her bare upper arm with her left hand.

He had been keenly aware of her absorption of mind ever since meeting her that evening and it had created uneasiness in him. Now he said, with the suggestion of an edge to his voice, 'It doesn't matter what's outside; it's what's inside 'at counts,' and some deeper significance in his words made her glance sharply at him and seemed to bring her back from wherever her thoughts had carried her to the room and him.

'D'you think it might be damp?' she said, rubbing gently now at both arms together. 'It's none too warm in here.'

'The sun's gone,' the man said. 'And the house has been empty for weeks. You'd soon notice a difference when we'd had fires going a bit.'

44

She was quick to notice his choice of words, as though he himself had already accepted the house and now awaited only her acquiescence for the matter to be settled.

'You're a bit set on it, aren't you?' she said, watching him.

'I don't think it's bad,' he said, pursing his lips in the way she knew so well. 'I've seen plenty worse. Course, I've seen plenty better an' all, but it's no use crying after the moon.'

'It seems all right,' she said, looking round the bedroom. And now, strangely enough, it looked less all right than it had when they first came in. Then, lit by the evening sun, this room in particular had seemed charmingly airy and bright; but now the sun had gone she could see only the shabbiness of the faded blue wallpaper and feel how bleakly empty it was. She paced away from the window, a dark girl with a sallow complexion and pale bloodless lips, wearing a home-made yellow frock which hung loosely on her bony body. And suddenly then all the feeling the man had previously sensed in her seemed to burst and flood out as her features lost their control, and she threw up her hands.

'Oh, I don't know,' she cried. 'I don't know if it's worth it or not.'

'You mean the house?' he said, hoping she did, but knowing more.

'All of it,' she said with passion. 'Everything.' And she turned her face from him.

As he watched her his own face seemed to sag into lines of hopelessness and his nostrils quivered in a heavy sigh. 'I didn't think you'd come,' he said. 'I didn't think you'd do it in the end.'

'I haven't said I won't, have I?' she snapped over her shoulder.

'Well, what's wrong, then?' he said. 'What is it?'

'It's her,' the girl said. 'I saw her this afternoon. She followed me all round town. Everywhere I went, she followed. I thought about stopping and giving her a piece of my mind, but I knew she wouldn't mind a scene.'

'You did right not to speak to her. She enjoys feeling badly done to. She always did. God!' he said with feeling. 'Why can't she leave us alone? She gets her money regular, doesn't she? What more does she want?'

'You,' the girl said, turning to look at him.

'She never wanted me when she had me,' he said. 'A home, kids, the sort o' things everybody gets married for – she never wanted any o' them things.'

'You don't know much about women, do you?' the girl said.

'Not a thing. Not one damn thing.'

'She's your wife,' the girl said. 'And that's more than I'll ever be.'

She was near to tears now and he crossed the bare floorboards between them to take her in his arms and draw her to him.

'I'd marry you tomorrow. You know that.'

'I know, I know. But she'll never set you free.'

'Who knows?' he said past her shoulder. 'One day, p'r'aps.'

'And till then?'

'That's up to you. You're the one with everything to lose. You've your people to face, an' your friends. Folk'll talk three times as much about you as me. They won't blame me: they'll blame you. They'll say you're a fool for risking everything for a bloke like me. They'll say I can't be much good anyway: I couldn't keep steady with a woman when I was wed to her, so what chance have you to hold me without even your marriage lines.

They'll tell you I could leave you flat any time and you'd have no claim on me. She's got all the claims. You'll have nothing.'

'Oh, stop it,' she said. 'Stop it.'

He turned away from her and felt for his cigarettes. The packet was empty and he crushed it and hurled it into the fireplace.

'Who the hell am I to ask you to do this? he said. 'You could be lookin' round for some lad your own age. Somebody 'at could marry you, all decent an' above board.'

She looked at him, thinking how different love was from the way she had always imagined it would be, and she came again to the verge of tears before his thin balding figure in the ill-fitting sports coat and creased flannel trousers, and the baffled way he took life's blows on the face.

She ran and clung to him. 'I want you to ask me,' she said; 'because I want you. I want to give you peace and love and a home, and, someday, kids. Everything a man should have from a woman. Everything you've never had in your life.'

'You're a grand kid,' he said, stroking her hair. 'So sweet and good and grand. I keep telling myself, if only I'd met you earlier, and then I remember that you were only a nipper then. You're not much more now really.'

'I'll be all the woman you'll ever want,' she said fiercely, clinging to him. 'You'll see.'

They came apart with a start as the woman's voice hailed them from the foot of the stairs. 'Hello, are you there?'

The man crossed the room to the door and called down, 'Yes, we're just coming.'

He looked back at the girl and she joined him at the head of the uncarpeted stairs. They went down, the girl twisting the signet ring on the third finger of her left hand, to where the woman was standing in the living-room.

'Well,' she said, watching them keenly, her hands folded under her clean pinafore, 'have you seen everything?'

'I think so,' the man said.

'It seems very nice,' the girl said.

'It's not a palace,' the woman said bluntly; 'but of course, you're not looking for a palace, eh?'

'No,' they said, and smiled.

'Six hundred, you said, didn't you?' the man asked.

'Six hundred cash,' the woman said. 'Six-fifty otherwise.'

'Oh, we'd pay cash, but we'd have to see about a mortgage first.'

'No need to do that,' the woman said briskly. 'That's what I mean by otherwise. My solicitor can draw up an agreement. You pay me a hundred and fifty down and the rest at thirty shillings a week. That's fair enough, isn't it?'

'I think that's very decent,' the man said. 'We were a bit worried about the building society. They're getting very choosy about their loans nowadays.'

'Aye, and putting their interest rates up every other week,' the woman said. 'Well, we've no need to bring them into it at all. I'm selling all my houses the same way. It gives me a bit of capital and a regular income. That's my offer, and you won't get better anywhere else.'

'I'm sure we won't,' the girl said, and she and the man exchanged glances.

The man said, 'We'll have to talk it over.'

'Yes, have a talk about it. But don't wait too long if you want it. Would this be your first home?'

'Yes, the first.'

'With your in-laws now, is that it?'

'Yes, that's right,' the man said, and the girl found

herself wondering what change there would be in the woman's brisk friendliness were she to tell her that he had left his wife and they wanted somewhere to live in sin. She thought it would come out eventually anyway. You wouldn't hide much from this woman for long.

'Well you think it over,' the woman said, moving across to the door.

'Yes, we'll let you know either way,' the man said.

Walking away from the house, up the long street, the girl with her arm through his, the man seemed suddenly full of hope and high spirits. 'Just right,' he said. 'Not too big, and no messing about with building societies. That's a stroke of luck. I think I know where to scrape up the deposit, and we'll manage nicely after that.' He squeezed her arm. 'Just imagine,' he said, 'living there together all nice and snug. All our troubles 'll be over then.'

How easy, she thought, for her to dim the optimism in his voice and extinguish the bright hope on his face. She shuddered as she felt the shadow of a third person walking between them. But echoing his eager tones, she said, 'Yes, all our troubles 'll be over then,' while in her heart she wondered if after all they might be only just beginning.

'Gamblers Never Win'

A miner wins the pools — then dies

(a) exposition - *apathetic family quarrel*

In the dusk of the winter afternoon Mrs Scurridge stirred from her nap by the fire as she heard the light movements of her husband in the bedroom overhead, and she was already on her feet in the firelight and filling the soot-grimed copper kettle at the sink when he came into the big farmhouse kitchen, his thin dark hair tangled on his narrow skull, his sharp-featured face unshaven, and blurred with Saturday-afternoon sleep. He crossed the room to the fireplace without a word or a glance for her and ran his hand along the mantelshelf in search of a cigarette-end. He wore a striped flannel shirt, without collar, the sleeves rolled up above his elbows, and over it an unbuttoned navy blue waistcoat. Besides braces he wore a heavy leather belt buckled loosely about his thin waist. He was a shortish, bandy-legged man and he had to stretch up on his toes to bring his eyes level with the mantelshelf. After a moment's fumbling he found the partly smoked Woodbine, and pushed a twist of paper into the fire to get a light. The first mouthful of smoke

50

started him coughing and he was helpless for some moments, bending over and supporting himself by the palm of his hand on the tall, old-fashioned fireplace while the phlegm cracked and gurgled in his throat. When the attack had passed he spat into the fire, straightened up, wiping the spittle from his thin lips with the back of his hand, and spoke:

'Tea ready?'

His wife pushed him aside and put the kettle on the fire, pressing it firmly down on the glowing coals.

'It can be,' she said, as soon 'as you know what you want.'

She picked up the twist of paper that Scurridge had dropped in the hearth and lit the single gas mantle suspended directly over the table. The gas popped and flared, then settled down to a dim, miserable glow which revealed the heartbreaking shabbiness of the room: the square table with bulbous legs hacked and scarred by years of careless feet; the sagging chairs with their bulging springs and worn and dirty upholstery; the thin, cracked linoleum on the broad expanse of damp, stone-flagged floor; and the great brown patch of damp on the wall – as though someone had spilt a potful of coffee against the grimy wallpaper – in one corner of the room. The very atmosphere was permeated with the musty odour of damp decay, an odour which no amount of fire could drive from the house.

Scurridge reached for the morning newspaper and turned to the sports page. 'I fancy a bit o' bacon an' egg,' he said, and sat down beside the fire and placed his pointed elbows in the centres of the two threadbare patches on the arms of his chair.

His wife threw a surly glance at the upraised newspaper. 'There is no eggs,' she said, and Scurridge's pale, watery, blue eyes fixed on her for the first time as he lowered the paper.

'What y'mean "there is no eggs"?'

'I mean what I say; I didn't get any,' she added with sullen defiance. 'I couldn't afford 'em this week. They're five-an'-six a dozen. Something's got to go – I can't buy all I should as it is.'

Scurridge smacked his lips peevishly. 'God! Oh! God. Are we at it again? It's one bloody thing after the other. I don't know what you do with your brass.'

'I spend it on keeping you,' she said. 'God knows I get precious little out of it. Always a good table, you must have. Never anything short. Anybody 'ud think you'd never heard of the cost of living. I've told you time an' again 'at it isn't enough, but it makes no difference.'

'Didn't I give you another half-crown on'y the other week?' Scurridge demanded, sitting forward in his chair. 'Didn't I? It's about time you knew how to spend your brass; you've been housekeepin' long enough.'

She knew the hopelessness of further argument and took refuge, as always, behind the bulwark of her apathy. She lit the gas-ring and put on the frying pan. 'You can have some fried bread with your bacon,' she said. 'Will that do?'

'I reckon it'll have to do, won't it?' Scurridge said.

She turned on the upraised newspaper a look in which there was nothing of hatred or malice or rebellion, but only a dull, flat apathy, an almost unfeeling acceptance of the facts of her life, against which she only now and again raised her voice in a token protest; because, after all, she was still capable, however remotely, of comparing them with what might have been.

She laid a place for Scurridge on a newspaper at one corner of the table and while he ate there she sat huddled to the fire, nibbling at a slice of bread and jam, her left hand holding the fold of her overall close over her flaccid breasts. The skin of her face was sallow and pouchy; her hair, dark and without lustre, was drawn back in a lank sweep and knotted untidly on the nape of her neck. Her legs, once her best feature, were swollen in places with ugly blue veins. Only in her eyes, almost black, was the prettiness of her youth ever revealed, and this only momentarily when they flashed in an anger now rare. For most of the time they were like dirk windows onto a soul lost in an unmindful trance. Little more than forty-five years old, she had become already worn and aged before her time in the unending struggle of her life with Scurridge in this bleak and cheerless house which stood alone on a hillside above Cressley, an eternity from lights and noise and the warmth of human laughter.

Scurridge pushed away his plate and ran his tongue across his greasy lips. He drank the last of his tea and set the pint mug down on the table. 'Been better wi' an egg,' he said. His forefinger groped into his waistcoat pocket, searching absently for another cigarette-end. 'You want to economise,' he said. He smacked his lips, seeming to savour the word along with the fat from the bread. 'Economise,' he said again.

'What on?' his wife asked wearily, without hope of a reasonable answer. She had been whittling down her own needs for years, pruning where he would feel it least, and now there were only the bare necessities left for her to give up. It was a long time since any little luxuries had cushioned the hard edges of her existence.

'How the hell should I know?' Scurridge said. 'It's not my job to know, is it? I've done my whack when I've worked an' earned the brass.'

'Aye, an' spent it.'

53

'Aye, an' haven't I a right to a bit o' pleasure when I've slaved me guts out all week, eh? An' how do other folk manage, eh? There's many a woman 'ud be glad o' what I give you.' He got up to search on the mantelshelf once more.

'Nine out o' ten women 'ud throw it back in your face.'

'Oh, aye,' Scurridge said, 'I know you think you're badly done to. You allus have. But I know how t'men talk in t'pit an' happen you're better off than you think.'

She said nothing, but her mind was disturbingly alive. Oh! God, he hadn't always been like this: not at first: only since that demon had got into him, that demon of lust, lust for easy money and a life of idleness. She had never known the exact amount of his wages but she had once caught a glimpse of a postal order he had bought to send off with his football pools and the amount on it had horrified her, representing as it did the senseless throwing away of a comfortable, decent life.

As Scurridge straightened up from lighting his cigarette he peered at her, his eyes focusing with unaccustomed attention on one particular feature of her. 'What you don wi' your hand?' he said. He spoke roughly, without warmth, as though fearing some trap of sentiment she had laid for him.

'I caught meself on the clothes-line hook in the back wall,' Mrs Scurridge said. 'It's rusty an' sharp as a needle.' She looked vaguely down at the rough bandage and said without emotion, 'I shouldn't be surprised if it turns to blood poisoning.'

He turned away, muttering. 'Aw, you allus make the worst of anythin'.'

'Well, it's not the first time I've done it,' she told him. 'If you'd put me another post up I shouldn't have to use it.'

'Aye, if I put you another post up,' Scurridge sneered. 'If I did this, that an' the other thing. Is there owt else you want while we're at it?'

Goaded, she flung out her arm and pointed to the great stain of damp in the corner. 'There's that! And half the windows won't shut properly. It's time you did summat about the place before it tumbles round your ears!'

'Jesus Christ and God Almighty,' Scurridge said. 'Can't I have any peace? Haven't I done enough when I've sweated down yon' hole wi'out startin' again when I get home?' He picked up his paper. 'Besides, it all costs brass.'

'Aye, it all costs brass. The hens cost brass so you killed 'em all off one by one and now you can't have any eggs. The garden cost brass so you let it turn into a wilderness. The sheds cost brass so now they're all mouldering away out there. We could have had a nice little smallholding to keep us when you came out of the pit; but no, it all costs brass, so now we've got nothing.'

He rustled the paper and spoke from behind it. 'We'd never ha' made it pay.' This place 'ud run away wi' every penny if I let it.'

The mad injustice of it tore at her long-nurtured patience and it was, for a moment of temper, more than she could bear. 'Better than it all going on beer an' pools an' dog-racing,' she flared. 'Making bookies an' publicans their bellies fat.'

'You think I'm a blasted fool, don't you? You think I'm just throwin' good money after bad?' His hands crushed the edges of the newspaper and the demon glared malevolently at her from his weak blue eyes. 'You don't see 'at I'm out for a further fetch. There'll be killin' one o' these days. It's got to come. The whole bloody kitty 'ull drop into me lap an' then I'll be laughin'.'

55

She turned her face from the stare of the demon and muttered, 'Gambling's a sin.' She did not really believe this and she felt with the inadequacy of the retort surprise that she should have uttered those words. They were not her own but her father's and she wondered that she should clutch at the tatters of his teaching after all this time.

'Don't mouth that old hypocrite's words at me,' Scurridge said without heat.

'Don't tell you anything, eh?' she said. 'You know it all, I reckon? That's why your own daughter left home – because you 'at knew it all drove her away. Well mind you don't do the same with me!'

This brought him leaping from his chair to stand over her, his face working with fury. 'Don't talk about her in this house,' he shouted. 'Damned ungrateful bitch! I don't want to hear owt about her, d'you hear?' He reeled away as the cough erupted into his throat and he crouched by the fire until the attack had passed, drawing great wheezing gulps of air. 'An' if you want to go,' he said, 'you can get off any time you're ready.'

She knew he did not mean this. She knew also that she would never go. She had never seriously considered it. Eva, on her furtive visits to the house while her father was out, had often asked her how she stood it; but she knew she would never leave him. Over the years she had found herself thinking back more and more to her father and she was coming now to accept life as the inevitable consequence, as predicted by him, of the lapse into the sin which had bound her to Scurridge and brought Eva into the world. Eva who, as the wheel turned full circle, had departed without blessing from her father's house, though for a different reason. No, she would never leave him. But neither could she foresee any future with him

56

as she was. She had come to believe in the truth of her father's prediction that nothing good would come of their life together and she was sometimes haunted by an elusive though disturbing sense of impending tragedy. The day was long past when she could hope for a return to sanity of Scurridge. He was too far gone now: the demon was too securely a part of him. But she too had passed the point of no return. For good or for bad, this was her life, and she could not run away from life itself.

They sat on before the fire, two intimate strangers, with nothing more to say to each other; and about six o'clock Scurridge got up from his chair and washed and shaved sketchily in the sink in the corner. She looked up dully as he prepared to take his leave.

'Dogs?' she said.

'It's Saturday, in't it?' Scurridge answered, pulling on his overcoat.

All the loneliness of the evening seemed to descend upon her at once then and she said with the suggestion of a whine in her voice, 'Why don't you take me with you some Saturday?'

'You?' he said. 'Take you? D'you think you're fit to take anywhere? Look at yersen! An' when I think of you as you used to be!'

She looked away. The abuse had little sting now. She could think of him too, as he used to be; but she did not do that too often now, for such memories had the power of evoking a misery which was stronger than the inertia that, over the years, had become her only defence.

'What time will you be back?'

'Expect me when you see me,' he said at the door. 'Is'll want a bite o' supper, I expect.'

Expect him at whatever time his tipsy legs brought him home, she thought. If he lost he would drink to console himself. If he won he would drink to celebrate. Either way there was nothing in it for her but yet more ill temper, yet further abuse.

She got up a few minutes after he had gone and went to the back door to look out. It was snowing again and the clean, gentle fall softened the stark and ugly outlines of the decaying outhouses on the patch of land behind the house and gently obliterated Scurridge's footprints where they led away from the door, down the slope to the wood, through which ran a path to the main road, a mile distant. She shivered as the cold air touched her, and returned indoors, beginning, despite herself, to remember. Once the sheds had been sound and strong and housed poultry. The garden had flourished too, supplying them with sufficient vegetables for their own needs and some left to sell. Now it was overgrown with rampant grass and dock. And the house itself – they had bought it for a song because it was old and really too big for one woman to manage; but it too had been strong and sound and it had looked well under regular coats of paint and with the walls pointed and the windows properly hung. In the early days, seeing it all begin to slip from her grasp, she had tried to keep it going herself. But it was a thankless, hopeless struggle without support from Scurridge: a struggle which had beaten her in the end, driving her first into frustration and then finally apathy. Now everything was mouldering and dilapidated and its gradual decay was like a symbol of her own decline from the hopeful young wife and mother into the tired old woman she was now.

Listlessly she washed up and put away the teapots. Then she took the coal-bucket from the hearth and went down into the dripping, dungeon-like darkness of the huge cellar. There she filled the bucket and lugged it back up the steps. Mending the fire, piling it high with the wet gleaming lumps of coal, she drew some comfort from the fact that this at least, with Scurridge's miner's allocation, was one thing of which they were never short. This job done, she switched on the battery-fed wireless set and stretched out her feet in their torn canvas shoes to the blaze.

They were broadcasting a programme of old-time dance music: the Lancers, the Barn Dance, the Veleta. You are my honey-honey-suckle, I am the bee... Both she and Scurridge had loved old-time dancing a long time, a long long time ago: and, scorning the modern fox-trots, how often they had danced so in the first years of marriage while some kind friend looked to the baby, Eva! Oh, those wonderful early days: that brief era of glorious freedom, with the narrow restrictions of her father's house behind her and the mad decline of Scurridge in the unknown future! Oh! Those times... There seemed to be a conspiracy afoot tonight, set on making her remember, and she sat there while the radio played, letting the old tunes wash the long-submerged memories onto the shores of her mind; and later on she took a candle and went up into the cold, barn-like bedroom and climbing on a chair, rummaged in a cupboard over the built-in wardrobe and eventually unearthed a photograph album. Rubbing the mildewed cover on her overall, she took the album down to her chair by the fire. It was years since she had looked into the album and slowly now she turned the pages and went back across the years to her youth.

(e)
Eva's
visit

She was asleep when the knock came at the back door to startle her into sudden wakefulness, and consciousness that the gaslight had failed and the room was lit only by the flicker of the big fire in the grate. She thought for a bemused moment that she had imagined the sound, and then it was repeated more insistently this time, and she got up and after picking up and placing on the table the photograph album which had slid from her knee while she dozed, went into the passage.

She stood a few feet from the door and called out, 'Who is it? Who's there?' It was a lonely house and, though she was not normally nervous, being awakened so abruptly had disturbed her a little.

'It's me,' a woman's voice answered; 'Eva.'

'Oh!' Mrs Scurridge stepped forward and unbolted the door and swung it open. 'Come in, love, come in. I wasn't expecting you tonight. You must be near frozen through.'

'Just a minute,' her daughter said. 'I'll just give Eric a shout.' She walked to the corner of the house and called out. A man's voice answered her and then there was the coughing splutter of a motor-cycle engine, from the road at the front of the house.

'I thought you mustn't be in when I couldn't see a light,' Eva said when she came back. She kicked the snow off her boots against the step before coming into the passage. 'What're you doing sitting in the dark? Don't tell me you haven't a penny for the gas now.'

'It went out while I was having a little nap.' They went along the stone-flagged passage and into the fire-lit kitchen. 'I'll just find me purse and see if I've any coppers.'

'No, here.' Eva took out her own purse. 'I've a shilling here: that'll last longer.'

'Well, I've got some coppers...' her mother began. But Eva had already crossed the room and her heels were clacking on the steps to the cellar. Mrs Scurridge put a twist of paper into the fire and when she heard the shilling fall in the meter, lit the gas-mantle.

'Isn't Eric comin' in then?' she asked as Eva returned.

'He's got a football club meeting in Cressley,' Eva said, 'He's callin' back for me. He might pop in for a minute then.'

Her mother watched her as she took off her headscarf and gingerly fingered her newly permed mouse-brown hair.

'A busy young man, your Eric.'

'Oh, here, there an' everywhere.' Eva took off her heavy tweed coat. Under it she had on a dark-green wool dress. Round the high neck of the dress she was wearing a necklace of an imitation gold finish with a matching bracelet round her wrist. She brought an air of comfortable prosperity and well-being with her into the shabby room.

'They made him a foreman at the Works last week,' she said, with a faint note of complacent pride in her voice.

'Ah, promotion, eh?'

Eva lifted her skirt from the hips to avoid 'seating' it and sat down in her father's chair. She levered off her fur-lined winter boots and put her nylon-stockinged feet on the kerb. 'He'll be manager one day,' she said. 'Everybody says how clever he is.'

'Well, it's nice to hear of a young man getting on,' her mother said; 'especially when he's something to you.'

Eva ran her palms up and down her calves then pushed back the hem of her skirt to expose her knees to the fire. She was a thin young woman, easily chilled, and she could not remember ever being able to keep warm in this house in winter. She stretched out her hands and leaned towards the blaze.

'Brrrh! What weather... It's freezing like anything outside.'

'I hope your Eric'll be safe on his bike.'

'Oh, he'll be all right. He's a careful driver: and it's better with the side car on, weather like this... Have you been cutting yourself?' she asked, noticing her mother's hand for the first time.

Mrs Scurridge told her what had happened and Eva said, 'You want to look after it. Don't let it turn septic.'

Mrs Scurridge dismissed the injury with a shrug. 'It's only a scratch. I've put some salve on it. It'll heal up in a day or two...'

'I like your frock,' said Mrs Scurridge after a moment. 'Is it new?'

'Well, nearly. I've only worn it two or three times. I got it in Leeds when we were looking at furniture. It was in Creston's window – y'know, in Briggate – an' it took me eye straight away. Eric saw me looking at it an' he bought it me. I knew we couldn't afford it, what with all the expense of movin' an' everything, but he talked me into it.' She gave a short laugh of feminine pleasure, at this thought of her husband's indulgence.

'You've got moved and everything, then?'

'Yes, we're in, thank the Lord. It'll take a bit of making comfortable, what with it being so new in' all that, but it's like heaven after livin' in digs.'

'I dare say it will be. But you got on all right with the folk you lodged with, didn't you? You never had any trouble or anything?'

'Oh, no, nothing like that. Not that there hasn't been times when I could have said a thing or two, mind. But Mrs Walshaw's much too reserved an' ladylike to ever have words with anybody. She had a way of looking down her nose at you 'at I never liked. She'd taken quite a fancy to Eric, y'know, what with her an' Mr Walshaw not havin' any child of their own, an' I believe she thought he'd never find a lass good enough for him. No, you can't quarrel with Mrs Walshaw. Quite the lady, she is. You'd never think to meet her she'd made all her money keepin' a fish and chip shop an' taking lodgers in.'

'Aye, it takes all sorts... You'll have been kept busy for a bit, then?'

'Oh, You've no idea. What with cleanin' an' paintin' and buying furniture an' making curtains, we've had a real month of it. But it's such a lovely house, Mother. I walk round sometimes when Eric's at work and tell myself it's really ours. An' I still can't believe it. I'm always thinkin' I'll wake up one morning and find we're back in Mrs Walshaw's back bedroom.'

There was a short silence while Eva gently rubbed her legs in the heat of the fire. Then Mrs Scurridge said diffidently, 'You're not... You don't think you're over-reaching yourselves at all, do you? You know what I mean: taking on a bit more than you can manage.'

'Oh, no,' Eva said; 'we're all right. We've been saving up ever since we were married. Both of us working. An' Eric was always careful as a single lad, y'know. He never threw his money around like a lot of 'em do. No, we'll be all right. We shall have to pull our horns in a bit from now on; but we'll manage nicely, thank you.'

'Well then,' said her mother, satisfied. 'You know your own know best. An' I'm right glad 'at you're settled in a home of your own at last.'

'An' you can come an' see us any time you like now,' Eva said. 'It's not far – just half an hour on the bus from Cressley.'

'Yes, I'll have to see about it now. I'll be poppin' over one o'these fine days. Just let's get a bit o' better weather here.'

Eva toasted her knees. 'Well,' she said, 'an' how are you keeping?'

Mrs Scurridge gave a faint shrug. 'Oh, so so. A touch of lumbago now an' again; but I can't grumble. I'll be happier when we have a bit better weather. You feel so cut off here when there's snow on the ground. Half a mile from the nearest house and hardly any traffic on the road at night.'

'You should get out more,' Eva said, 'stead o' sittin' in night after night.'

'Aye, I suppose I should. You get out of the habit, though. And besides, this weather–'

'No need to ask about me father,' Eva said. 'Seems this weather doesn't keep him in. Where's he gone tonight? Down town?'

Her mother nodded, looking into the fire. 'Dogs, I suppose.'

'Leaving you here on your own, is usual.'

'There's no pleasure out on a night like this.'

Eva nodded. 'I know all about it.' She drew in her breath. 'I don't know how you stand it. I don't, honestly.' Her gaze flickered round the room and the dinginess of what she saw seemed so to oppress her that she barely restrained a shudder. 'Thank God I got out when I had the chance.'

'It was different with you,' her mother said. 'You'd have gone anyway, sometime.'

'Not if he'd had his way. It just suited his book having two women about the house to wait on him. An' with my money coming in he could hang on to more of his own.' She stopped, then burst out in angry impatience, 'I don't see it. I just don't see it. A husband should be somebody like Eric, who considers his wife an' looks after her. An' when he stops being like that your duty stops as well. You don't owe me father a thing. You could walk out of here tonight an' nobody could blame you. An' you know

64

there's a place waiting for you any time you want it now. You've somewhere to go now.'

Mrs Scurridge threw a shrewd glance at her daughter's profile, flushed pink now from the heat of the fire and her outburst of indignation. 'Is that what Eric thinks too?' she said. 'What does he think about it?'

'Well... he thinks like I do. He doesn't know why you stick it.'

'But that doesn't mean he'd be happy to be saddled with his mother-in-law as soon as he's settled in his first home. Especially a mother-in-law like me.'

'Why especially like you?'

'Well, I don't suppose he thinks I'm the smartest woman he's ever seen.'

'But you could be smart,' Eva cried. 'You could if you got away from here. What's the use of bothering here, though, livin' week in an' week out miles from anywhere with a husband who spends all his money on gamblin' an' drinkin'? How can anybody take a pride in conditions like that?'

'Well, my place is with your father, Eva, and that's all there is to it.'

'But you don't–'

'That'll do,' her mother said quietly.

Eva said, 'Oh!' and stood up with an impatient gesture.

The radio was still playing. 'Do we have to have this thing on?'

'You can switch if off if you like. I was listening to some old-time dance music, but it's over now.'

Eva went round the back of the chair and turned the knob. In the silence that followed she remained standing there, one hand resting on top of the wireless cabinet, her back to her mother.

'Mother,' she said suddenly, and turned round, 'am

I illegitimate?'

Her mother started. 'No, you're not.'

'But you an' me dad had to get married because of me, hadn't you?'

'No, no. It wasn't quite like that. We did get married when we knew you were coming; but we should have done anyway. We weren't forced into it.' She met her daughter's eyes. 'How did you find out?'

'Oh, it's something I've hid in the back of me mind for a long while now,' Eva said, still standing behind the chair. 'It was just a matter of checkin' a couple of dates to make sure.'

'Have you said anything to Eric?'

'No.'

'Are you going to?'

'I don't see why I should.'

'Neither do I,' Mrs Scurridge said. 'But you don't think he'd mind, do you?'

'I don't know,' Eva said frankly. 'He... Well, he's a bit straitlaced about some things, is Eric. I don't see any point in spoiling anything...'

'But nobody can call you illegitimate, Eva,' Mrs Scurridge said. 'We were married months before y...' She turned her gaze to the fire. 'I'm sorry, love. I never saw any reason to tell you.'

'Oh, don't you be sorry.' Eva's mouth set. 'It's him, not you.

'You shouldn't hate your father so much, Eva.'

'How can I help it when everything he touches turns rotten? He's spoilt your life an' he'd have done the same with mine if I hadn't stood up to him. He couldn't even get married in a right way. He had to get hold of you by getting you into trouble.'

'It wasn't like that at all,' her mother said intensely.

'He was different in those days. You'd never credit the difference.'

'So you tell me. But I can't remember him like that. The only father I know is a tight-fisted, mean-hearted old rotter who can't live decent for gamblin' everything away.

'Oh, Eva, Eva.'

'I'm sorry,' she said; 'but it just makes me boil.'

'Look,' her mother said. 'Just look in that album on the table and you'll see your father as he was.'

Eva moved to the table and opened the cover of the album. 'I don't remember seeing this before.'

'I might have shown it to you when you were little. I haven't had it out meself for years. It was that old-time dance music on the wireless that made me remember it. It started me thinkin' back...'

Eva pulled out a chair and sat down at the table. 'He wasn't bad-looking as a young man...'   *her father*

'A little wiry dandy of a man, he was,' Mrs Scurridge said. 'Honest, hardworking, full of fun. I was twenty-two when I met him and I'd hardly spoken to a man except to pass the time of day. I'd never been out to work because your grandfather wanted me at home to look after the house. It was stifling in your grandfather's house because there wasn't any joy or life. It was all God. God, God, God, from morning till night. Not a God of joy and love, but your grandfather's God. A God of commandments. Thou shalt not. Your grandfather was a man with God in his mouth and ice in his heart. I once heard somebody say that about him and I never forgot it. He had a saying for every occasion. "Gamblers never win" was one I keep remembering now. "They might seem to do", he used to say, "but be sure their sin will find them in the end". A stiff, unbending man, he was. I never in my life saw him soften at anything.

67

'The only time your father came to call on me your grandfather turned him off the step because he wasn't suitable. He came from a poor family and his father had been in prison for assaulting his employer. If there was anything your grandfather couldn't abide it was a work-man who answered back. He had half a dozen of his own and he ruled them with a rod of iron. Jobs weren't so easily come by in those days, so they didn't dare to complain. I took to meeting your father in secret whenever I could slip out of the house. It was the happiest time of my whole life. He brought sunshine and laughter into my life and I'd have gone to the ends of the earth with him...

'We were married in a registry office when we knew you were on the way. Your grandfather had done with me by that time. We were never married at all in his eyes – just living in sin because of the sin that brought you into the world. We didn't mind, though. We were very happy for a while...'

'But what changed him?' Eva asked. 'What made him like he is now?'

'All kinds of things help to change a man. Bad luck, weakness of character. When your grandfather had the stroke that finished him your father was out of work. We were struggling to make ends meet. All your grandfather's money went to the chapel and various other worthy causes. We didn't get a penny. He went to his grave without forgiving me, and your father never forgave him. He grew bitter. They were bitter years for a lot of people. He saw nothing in front of him but a life of slaving in the pits and nothing at the end of that but broken health or p'raps a quick end underground. So he began to crave for easy money. He wanted to get rich quick without working for it. It was like a demon that got into him,

68

ruling his life. Nothing else mattered. Everything else could go to the wall. Now it's too late. He'll never change again now. But I made my vows, Eva. I said for better or for worse and you can't believe in principles when it's easy and forget 'em when it's hard. I chose my life and I can't run away from it now...'

Suddenly overcome, Eva fell down beside her mother's chair, grasping her roughened hand and pressing it to her face in the rush of emotion that swept over her.

'Oh, Mother, Mother; come away with me. Come away tonight. Leave it all an' have done with it. I'll make it right with Eric. He's a good man; he'll understand.'

Mrs Scurridge gently withdrew her hand and touched her daughter's head. 'No, love. I thank you for what you've said; but my place is with your father as long as he needs me.'

Scurridge at the d) Pub – checking his pools

Carried along in the crowds that swarmed from the greyhound stadium, but alone, was Scurridge, richer tonight by six pounds. But it give him little joy. He knew that next week or the week after he would lose it again and probably more as well. His ultimate aim was not centred here; these small prizes were of only momentary satisfaction to him and it was only the constant urgings of the demon, the irresistible pull of something for nothing, which brought him here week after week. He turned right at the opening of the lane and walked along the pavement with his slouch-shouldered gait, chin sunk into the collar of his overcoat, hands deep in pockets, a dead cigarette butt between his lips. His pale eyes were brimming with tears, his thin features pinched and drawn in the biting wind which scoured the streets, turning the slush on the pavements and in the gutters to ice. He still dressed as he had in the lean thirties, in shabby overcoat and dirty tweed cap, with a silk muffler knotted round his neck to hide lack of collar and tie. The new prosperity had left no mark on Scurridge.

He was making for the Railway Tavern, one of his customary Saturday-night haunts, and as he neared the pub he heard himself hailed with joviality and beery good-cheer by two men approaching from the opposite direction.

'Fred! Ey, Fred!'

He stopped, recognising the men. He nodded curtly as they drew near. 'How do, Charlie. Do, Willy.'

They were better dressed than Scurridge though they were, like him, colliers – coal-face workers: the men who earned the big money, the elite of the pit. The one called Charlie, the taller of the two, came to a halt with his arm thrown across the shoulders of his companion.

'Here's old Fred, Willy,' he said. 'Ye know old Fred, don't you, Willy?'

Willy said Aye; he knew Fred.

'I should bloody well an' think you do,' Charlie said. 'Everybody knows Fred. The life an' soul of the party, Fred is. Here every Sat'day night; an' every other night in t'week he's at some other pub. Except when he's at t'Dogs. When he in't in a pub he's at t'Dogs, an' when he in't at t'Dogs he's in a pub. An' when he in't at either, Willy – where d'you think he is then, eh?'

Willy said he didn't know.

'He's down t'bloody pit wi' t'rest on us!' Charlie said.

Wheezy laughter doubled Charlie up, the weight of his arm bearing Willy down with him. Willy extricated himself and carefully straightened his hat. Scurridge, at this moment, made as if to enter the pub, but Charlie, recovering abruptly, reached out and took his arm.

70

'Know what's wrong wi' Fred, Willy?' he said, throwing his free arm back across Willy's shoulders. 'Well, I'll tell you. He's got a secret sorrer, Fred has. That's what he's got – a secret sorrer. An' d'you know what his secret sorrer is, Willy?'

Willy said no.

'No, ye don't,' Charlie said triumphantly. 'An' no bugger else does neither. He keeps it to himself, like he keeps everythin' else.'

Feeling he was being got at, and not liking it, Scurridge tried to free his arm: but Charlie held on with all the persistence of the uninhibitedly drunk.

'Oh, come on now, don't be like that, Fred. I'm on'y havin' a bit o' fun. I allus thought you'd a sense o' yumour. I like a feller with i sense o' yumour.'

'Come on inside,' Scurridge said. 'Come on an' have a pint.'

'Now yer talkin', Fred lad,' Charlie said. 'Now yer bloody well an' talkin'!'

They followed Scurridge up the stone steps and into the passage, where he would have gone into the taproom but for the pressure of Charlie's hand on his back. 'In 'ere's best,' Charlie said. 'Let's go where there's a bit o' bloody life.' He pushed open the door of the concert room. Beyond the fug of tobacco smoke, there could be seen a comedian on the low stage, a plump man in a tight brown suit and red tie. He was telling the audience of the time he had taken his girlfriend to London and some laughter broke from the people seated there as he reached the risqué punchline of the story. 'Over there,' Charlie said, pushing Scurridge and Willy towards an empty table. As they sat down the waiter turned from serving a party nearby and Charlie looked expectantly at Scurridge.

'What yer drinkin?' Scurridge said.

'Bitter,' Charlie said.

'Bitter,' Willy said.

Scurridge nodded. 'Bitter.'

'Pints?' the waiter said.

'Pints,' Charlie said.

The waiter went away and Charlie said, 'Had any luck tonight, Fred?'

'I can't grumble,' Scurridge said.

Charlie gave Willy a nudge. 'Hear that, Willy? He might ha' won fifty quid tonight, but he's not sayin' owt. He tells you what he wants you to know, Fred does, an' no more.'

'He does right,' Willy said.

'O' course he does, Willy. I'm not blamin' him. Us colliers, we all talk too much, tell everybody us business. Everybody knows how much we earn. They can all weigh us up. But they can't weigh Fred up. He keeps his mouth shut. He's the sort o' feller 'at puts a little cross on his football pools coupon – y'know, no publicity if you win. Wha, he might be a bloody millionaire already, for all we know, Willy.'

'Talk some sense,' Scurridge said. 'Think I'd be sweatin' me guts out every day like I am if I'd enough brass to chuck it?'

'I don't know, Fred. Some fellers I've heard tell of keep on workin' as a hobby-like.'

'A fine bloody hobby.'

The waiter put the drinks on the table and Scurridge paid him. Charlie lifted his glass and drank deeply, saying first, 'Your continued good 'ealth, Fred me lad.'

Scurridge and Willy drank in silence.

'Well,' said Charlie, putting the half-empty glass back on the table and wiping his lips with the back of his hand, 'Is'll be able to tell me mates summat now.'

'Tell 'em what?' Scurridge asked.

'At I've had a pint wi' Fred Scurridge. They'll never bloody believe me.'

This continued reference to his supposed meanness angered Scurridge and he flushed. 'You've got yer bloody ale, haven't yer?' he said. 'Well, you'd better sup it an' enjoy it, 'cos you won't get any more off me.'

'I know that, Fred,' said Charlie, in great good humour, 'an' I am enjoying it. I can't remember when I enjoyed a pint as much.'

Scurridge turned his head and looked sulkily round the room. The entertainer had come to the end of his patter and now, accompanied by an elderly man on the upright piano, was singing a ballad in a hard, unmusical pseudo-Irish tenor voice. Scurridge scowled in distaste. The noise irritated him. He hated music in pubs, preferring a quiet atmosphere of darts and male conversation as a background to his drinking. He lifted his glass, looking over its rim at Charlie who was slumped against Willy now, relating some anecdote of the morning's work. Scurridge emptied the glass and Charlie looked up as he scraped back his chair.

'Not goin', are yer, Fred? Aren't you havin' one wi' me?'

'I'm off next door where it's quiet,' Scurridge said.

'Well, just as yer like, Fred. So long, lad. Be seein' yer!'

Relieved at being free of them so easily, Scurridge went out and across the passage into the taproom. The landlord himself was in attendance there and seeing Scurridge walk through the room to the far end of the bar, he drew a pint of bitter without being asked for it and placed the glass in front of Scurridge. 'Cold out?' Scurridge nodded. 'Perishin''. 'He pulled himself up onto a stool, ignoring the men standing near him and the noise coming faintly from the concert room. Close behind him, where he sat, four men he knew, colliers like himself, were gathered round a table, talking as the dominoes clicked, talking as all colliers talk, of work...

'So when he comes down on t'face, I says, "I reckon there'll be a bit extra in this week-end for all this watter we're workin' in?" An' he says, "Watter! Yer don't know what it is to work in watter!" "An' what do yer think this is seepin' ovver me clog tops, then," I says: "bloody pale ale?"'

Scurridge shut his ears to their talk. He never willingly thought of the pit once he was out of it; and he hated every moment he spent down there in the dark, toiling like an animal. That was what you were, an animal, grubbing your livelihood out of the earth's bowels. He could feel the years beginning to tell on him now. He was getting to an age when most men turned their back on contract working and took an easier job. But he could not bear to let the money go. While there was good money to be earned, he would earn it. Until the day when he could say good-bye to it all...

He drank greedily, in deep swallows, and the level in his glass lowered rapidly. When he set it down empty the landlord came along and silently refilled it, again without needing to be asked. Then with the full glass beside him Scurridge prepared to check his football pool forecasts. He put on his spectacles and taking out a copy of the sports final, laid it on the bar, folded at the results of the day's matches. Beside the newspaper he put the copy coupon on which his forecasts were recorded, and with a stub of pencil in his fingers he began to check his entries. If was a long and involved procedure, for Scurridge's forecasts were laid out according to a system evolved by him over the years. They spread right across the coupon, occupying many lines, and could only be checked by constant reference to the master plan, which was recorded on two scraps of paper which he carried in a dirty envelope in an inner pocket. Consequently the glass at his elbow had been quietly refilled again before he came near to the end of his check and a gradual intensification of his concentration began to betray in him the presence of growing excitement. And then the movements of the pencil ceased altogether and Scurridge became very still. The noises of the taproom seemed to recede, leaving him alone and very quiet, so that he became conscious of his own heartbeats.

(e) Eva goes to bed

Mother and daughter heard at the same time the low growl of the motor-cycle as it approached the house.

'That'll be Eric now,' said Eva, glancing at her wristwatch. 'He said about ten.' She reached for her boots and slipped her feet into them.

'Won't you have a cup o' tea before you go?'

'No, thanks, love.' Eva stood up. 'We really haven't time tonight. We promised to call an' see some friends.' She reached for her handbag and felt inside it. 'Before I forget... here, take this.' She held out her hand, palm down. 'It'll come in handy.'

Her mother had automatically put out her own hand before she realized that it was a ten-shilling note she was being offered. 'No,' she said. 'Thanks all the same; but it isn't your place to give me money.'

'I can give you a present, can't I?' Eva said. 'Take it an' treat yourself to something nice. You don't get many treats.'

'How should I explain it to your father?' Mrs Scurridge said. 'He thinks I squander his money as it is. And I couldn't tell him you'd given it to me.'

Eva put the note back in her bag. 'All right. If that's the way you feel about it...'

'I don't want you to be offended about it,' her mother said. 'But you know how it is.'

'Yes,' Eva said, 'I know how it is.'

The sound of the motor-cycle had died now at the back of the house and there was a knock on the door. Eva went out into the passage and returned with Eric, her husband. He said, 'Evenin' to Mrs Scurridge and stood just inside the doorway, looking sheepishly round the room, then at his wife who had put on her coat and was now adjusting her headscarf over her ears. He was a big fair young man, wearing a heavy leather riding-coat and thigh-length boots. A crash helmet and goggles dangled from one end.

'It'll be cold riding your bike tonight, I expect?' Mrs Scurridge said. She felt awkward with her son-in-law, for she had had no chance of getting to know him.

His eyes rested on her for a second before flitting back to Eva. 'It's not so bad if you're well wrapped up,' he said. 'Ready, love?' he said to Eva.

'All about.' She picked up her handbag and kissed her mother on the cheek. 'I'll pop over again as soon as I can. An' you'll have to make an effort to get over to see us.'

'I'll be surprising you one of these days.'

'Well, you know you're welcome any time,' Eva said. 'Isn't she, Eric?'

'Yes, that's right,' Eric said. 'Any time.'

She wondered vaguely what would be their reaction were she to walk in on them unexpectedly one evening; when they had company, for instance. Then she pushed the thought from her mind and followed them out to the back door where she and Eva kissed again. Eva walked across the crisp, hardening snow and got into the side-car. Mrs Scurridge called good night and watched them coast round the side of the house. She waited till she heard the sudden open-throttled roar of the engine before closing the door and going back into the house.

She sat down and looked into the fire and in a moment a flood of misery and self-pity had swept away the uncertain barrier of her indifference and was over-flowing in silent tears on to her sallow cheeks. For the first time in years she allowed herself the luxury of weeping. She wept for many things: for the loneliness of the present and the loneliness of the past; for that all too brief time of happiness, and for a future which held nothing. She wept for what might have been and she wept for what was; and there was no consolation in her tears. She sat there as the evening died and slowly her sorrow turned to a sullen resentment as she thought of Scurridge, away in the town, among the lights and people; Scurridge, struggling through the Saturday-evening crowds to stake her happiness on the futile speed of a dog in its chase after a dummy hare. Leaning forward some time later to stir the fire she was suddenly transfixed by a shocking stab of pain. The poker clattered into the hearth as the pain pierced her like a glowing spear. Then with an effort that made her gasp, and brought sweat to her brow, she broke its thrust and fell back into the chair. Lumbago: a complaint with a funny name, that lent itself to being joked about. But not in the least funny to her. It could strike at any moment, as it had just now, rendering her almost helpless. Sometimes it would pierce her in the night and she would lie there, sweating with the agony of it, until she could rouse Scurridge from his sottish sleep to turn her on to her other side. She looked at the clock on the mantelpiece. It might be in hour or more before Scurridge returned. She longed for the warmth of her bed and with her longing came a fierce desire to thwart Scurridge in some way.

It was then that she first thought of locking him out for the night.

It was a pathetic gesture, she knew; but it was all she could think of: the only way to show resentment and defiance. She foresaw no benefit from it and her imagination, dulled by the pain which hovered across the threshold of every moment, could not stretch even as far as Scurridge's rage in the morning. The immediate horizon of her thoughts contained only the warm bed and the oblivion of sleep. It could neither encompass nor tolerate Scurridge's drunken return and the possibility of a demand for the satisfying of flesh that was a mockery of their first youthful passion.

She boiled a kettle and filled a stone hot-water bottle and hobbled with it upstairs. Then she made some tea and searched the cupboard where she kept the remains of old medicinal prescriptions and bottles of patent remedies accumulated over the years, until she found a round box of sleeping pills once prescribed for her. The label said to take two, and warned against an overdose. She took two, hesitated, then swallowed a third. She wished to be soundly and deeply asleep when Scurridge came home. Standing there with the box in her hand it occurred to her to wonder if there were enough tablets to put her into a sleep from which she would never awaken, and she thrust the box out of sight among the bottles and packets and returned the lot to the cupboard. She poured herself some tea and sipped it before the fire, her hands clasped round the warmth of the mug. At eleven o'clock she raked the ashes down from the fireback and went into the passage and shot the bolts on the back door. Even as she stood there in the act she felt the insidious creep of the old apathy. What did it matter? What good would it do? She turned away and went back into the kitchen where she doused the gas. By the light of a candle she made her careful way upstairs. She undressed and lay shivering between the clammy sheets, moving the hot-water bottle round and round, from one part of her cold body to another, until eventually she became warm, and in a short time after that, fell asleep. *his drunken return*

Scurridge stared from the pools coupon to the newspaper. A man came in and stood next to him at the bar counter. He ordered his drink and said to Scurridge, 'A real freezer out tonight, isn't it?' Scurridge made no answer; he was hardly aware that he had been addressed. His mind was a maelstrom of excitement and he put his hand to his forehead and by an effort of will forced himself into sufficient calmness to recheck the column of results. It was right, as he'd thought. No mistake – he'd forecast seven drawn games and he needed only one more to complete the eight required for maximum points. One forecast only remained to be checked and that was a late result printed in blurred type in the stop press column of the newspaper. He peered at it again. It could be a draw or an away win, he thought. If it was an away win he would be one point down and eligible for a second dividend. That one point could mean the difference between a measly few hundred pounds and a fortune.

'Here – can you make this out?'

He thrust the paper at the man who had spoken to him, pointing with his forefinger at the blurred print. 'That last result there. Is it two all or two, three?'

The man put his glass on the counter and took the paper out of Scurridge's hands. He turned it to the light. 'It's not right clear,' he said. 'I dunno. I'd say it's more like two, three. An away win.'

'It can't be,' Scurridge said. 'It's got to be a draw.' He

79

turned to the domino-playing miners. 'Anybody got an Echo?' The excitement was plain in his voice and the big miner who passed the newspaper said, 'What's up, Fred? Got a full line?' Scurridge grabbed the paper. 'I dunno yet,' he said. 'I dunno.' He ran his finger down the column to the result in question. It was a draw, completing his eight.

'It's a draw,' Scurridge said. He crushed the paper in his hands and let it fall to the floor.

'Hey up!' the big miner said. 'That's my paper when you've done wi' it.'

'I'll buy you a dozen bloody papers,' Scurridge said. 'I've got eight lovely draws. Eight bloody lovely draws. Look!' He snatched the coupon from the counter and thrust it at the group of miners. 'I've got eight draws an' there's on'y eight on the whole coupon!' The one sitting nearest took the coupon and scanned it. 'See,' Scurridge said, pointing. 'Seven on there an' this one here.'

The collier looked at the coupon in stupefaction. 'By God, but he's up. He's up!'

'Here, let's look,' said another, and the dominoes were laid face down while the coupon passed round the table. 'Lucky sod,' one of the men muttered, and Scurridge took him up with an excited 'What's that? Lucky? I've worked years for this. I've invested hundreds o' pounds in it, an' now it's up.'

'It'll be a tot this week, Fred,' the big miner said. 'There's on'y eight draws altogether so there won't be many to share the brass. Wha, it might be a hundred thousand quid!'

A hush fell over the group at the mention of this astronomical sum from which the interest alone could keep a man in comfort for a lifetime. A hundred thousand pounds! Somehow Scurridge's mind, occupied with the fact that the prize was in his grasp, had not yet put it into actual figures. But now excitement flamed in his face and his eyes grew wild.

'It's bound to be,' he shouted. 'There's nobbut eight draws on the whole coupon, I tell yer!'

He snatched his glass from the bar counter and took a long drink, slamming it down again as he came to a decision. 'I've won six quid on t'dogs tonight,' he said. 'I'll stand drinks all round. C'mon, drink wi' me. Have what yer like – whisky, rum, owt yer've a mind for.'

They passed up their glasses, needing no second invitation, and soon the news spread across the passage to the concert room, bringing people from there to slap Scurridge on the back and drink the beer he was paying for as he stood flushed and jubilant, pressed up against the bar.

Shortly after closing time he found himself on the street with a full bottle of rum and an empty pocket, in company with Charlie and Willy.

'An' I allus say,' Charlie said, 'I allus say a man shouldn't let his brass come between him an' his pals.'

'What's money?' Scurridge said.

'That's right, Fred, You've hit the bleedin' nail right on the head. What's money? I'll tell you what it is – it's a curse on the whole yuman race, a curse... An' I wish I had a cellarful. If I had a cellarful I'd lay in a nine-gallon barrel of ale an' I'd go down every night an' sup an' count it. An' I'd let you come an' help me, Fred. I wouldn't forget you. Oh no, not me. I wouldn't forget me old pals. What's money worth if it comes between a feller an' his pals?'

Willy belched stolidly. 'Friendship's the thing.'

'You never spoke a truer word, Willy,' Charlie said. He threw his arm across Willy's shoulders and leaned on him. 'Your heart's in the right place, Willy lad.'

81

They parted company on the corner and as Scurridge moved away Charlie called after him, 'Don't forget, Is'll want a ride in that Rolls-Royce.'

Scurridge waved the bottle of rum over his head. 'Any time. Any time.'

As he passed along Corporation Street on his way through the town he was suddenly arrested by the thought that he should send off a telegram to the pools people claiming his win. Wasn't that what you did? You sent a telegram claiming a first dividend and followed it with a registered letter. But the post office was closed; he could see its dark face right there across the street from where he stood. It baffled him for a moment. How could he send a telegram when the post office was closed? Why hadn't the pools people thought of that? And then a dim glow of light by the door of the post office building reminded him of the telephone and he made his way unsteadily across the deserted street. Inside the call box he stared for some time at the black shape of the receiver before putting out a slow hand and lifting it to his ear. He had never before in his life used a public telephone and when a small voice spoke right into his ear he took sudden fright and slammed the receiver back into its cradle as though it had burned hot in his hand. Not until then, as he stood, breathing heavily, in the call box, did it occur to him that he would need some money. He began to rummage through his pockets. The search produced only two coins – a sixpence and a penny – and he looked at them where they lay in his palm, with mingled relief and regret. Regret that he could not, after all, make sure of his money, and relief that he would now have to put off the complex business of sending the telegram till tomorrow.

Outside on the pavement once more he was struck by the irony of having a hundred thousand pounds yet not having enough in his pocket to pay for a taxi home. He looked about him, getting his bearings; then he turned towards home. On the way he began to think of his wife. Christ! This would be one in the eye for her. She'd never believed he could do it. No bloody faith. All she wanted was brass for fancy foods and for keeping hens. Hens! God! And still more brass to throw away on that great barracks of a house. Well now she could have brass, all she needed. She'd see that Fred Scurridge didn't bear grudges. She'd see what sort of man he was. And they'd get right away from this God-forsaken district to somewhere where there was life and plenty of sun, and no more dropping down into that dark hole to sweat his guts out for a living. He'd done it now. He was free... free...

Somewhere along a back street on the outskirts of town he lurched into the doorway of a newsagent's shop, failing against the door and sliding down into a sitting position. He uncorked the bottle of rum and took a deep swallow. He shook his head then and shuddered, making a wry face and breathing out, 'Aagh!' A moment later through the pool of light shed by the street-lamp opposite the doorway there slid the lean shape of a mongrel dog, its rough coat yellow in the dim light. It came into the doorway and pushed its cold muzzle into Scurridge's hand. He began to fondle it under the ears, talking to it as he did so: 'Nah then, old feller, nah then.' And the dog responded by licking his hand. 'Yer shouldn't be out on a night like this,' Scurridge said. 'Yer should be at home, all nice an' cosy an' warm. Haven't yer gorra home, eh, is that it?' He felt for a collar. 'Yer don't belong to nobody, eh? All on your ownio... all on yer own.' The dog sat down close to him, all the while nuzzling his hand. 'I used to have a dog once,' Scurridge said. 'Looked summat like you, he did. A long time since, though. He was a lovely dog... grand. He used to come an' meet me from t'pit. He got run over one Sat'day mornin' just as I wa' comin' out. A coal lorry got him. A full 'un. Rotten mess. I couldn't even pick him up and take him home to bury him. The driver shovelled him up an' took him off somewhere. I don't know where. I wa' that sluffed about it. A real pal to me, that dog was. I called him Tommy. An' eat! That dog wa' t'best eater 'at I ever saw. Scoff a beefsteak while you wa' lookin' at it.' He ran his hand along the dog's spare flanks and over its ribs. 'Long time sin' you had a beefsteak, old lad... Aye, well never mind. Happen yer'll get yer bit o' luck afore long. I've had a bit o' luck tonight, I'll tell yer. Best bit o' luck I ever had, on'y bit... never had any afore. Except maybe marryin' my missis. I didn't do bad there. She's not been a bad wife to me. An' now I'm goinna make her rich. Rollin' in it, she'll be. One in the bloody eye for that skinflint father of hers. Left all his brass to the chapel when we were near starvin'. Said I wa' no good an' never would be. Well I wish he was alive to see me now. I hope he's watchin' where ever he is. Never had a good word for man nor beast, that old devil. Not like me. I allus had a soft spot for animals. Like thee. Tha're a grand old lad even if tha are a stray 'at nobody wants. What's it feel like when nobody wants thee? Lousy, I'll bet. Here!' he said suddenly, lifting the dog's jaw on his hand. 'I'll tell thee what – here's thy bit o' luck. Tha can come home wi'me. How'd yer like that, eh? How'd yer like that?'

He put his hand to his forehead and mumbled to himself. It occurred to him that he was not feeling well; not well at all. 'Time we were off home, lad,' he said to the dog. 'Can't stop here all night.' He tried to get to his feet and fell back with a thud that shook the door. He sat there for a minute before making another effort which took him reeling out into the street. 'C'mon, lad,' he said to the dog. 'C'mon, boy.'

He was a long time in coming to the path through the wood, for he walked slowly and unsteadily, staggering about the pavement and making occasional erratic detours on to the crown of the road, and sometimes stopping altogether while he slouched against a wall, the rum bottle tilted to his mouth. The steep path under snow was like narrow frozen rapids – difficult enough to anyone sober, and next to impossible to Scurridge, in his condition. After falling on his hands and knees several times in as many yards he left the path and made his way up the slope through the black, twisted, snow-frothed shapes of the trees, the dog, with infinite patience, following at his heels. Near the top of the slope he caught his foot in a hidden root and sprawled headlong, striking his head heavily on the trunk of a tree before coming to rest face down in the snow. For several minutes consciousness left him; and when it returned he was mumbling to himself and shaking his head in a dazed manner as he got up off the ground and went unsteadily upwards and out of the trees.

He was almost at the back door before he realised that the house was in darkness. He groped for the latch and pushed at the door, thinking at first that it was stuck, and then realizing that it was locked. What the hell was she playing at! He knocked, and then, in a spasm of temper, drove the side of his clenched fists at the door panel. 'Hilda!' he shouted. 'Open up an' let me in!' But there was no sound from within and in a few minutes he wandered round to the front door and tried that. As he had expected, that was locked too. It was always locked: they had not used the door in over fifteen years. He came back along the side of the house, swearing softly and thickly to himself. She hadn't locked him out on purpose, had she? She couldn't have locked him out! She wouldn't do a thing like that to him. Not tonight, after he'd been so clever. The dog stood some way off and watched him as he stood there in the snow, his head bowed as though in deep thought, wondering what next to do. He felt ill, terribly ill. It was a fit of sickness that hammered in his head and made him sway on his feet. He put a cold, shaking hand to his brow, remaining like that in a coma of illness, during which time his memory seemed to cease functioning. So that when at last he stirred himself again he could not remember what he was doing there alone in the darkness and the snow.

He slumped down on the doorstep, huddling into the corner to get as much protection as possible from the wind, and took out the bottle of rum. He drank deeply, feeling the spirit sear his throat and spread in a warm wave inside him. For a moment it seemed to revive him, and then all at once the sickness came back to him, worse than ever this time, almost engulfing him in a great black wave. He dropped the bottle and put his head in his hands and moaned a little. What was it? He wanted to get in. He had to get in to Hilda. He had something to tell her. Something good. Something she would be pleased to hear. But he couldn't get in. Couldn't get to her to make her happy. And now he couldn't remember what he had to tell her. He only knew that it was something good, because he could recall being happy himself, earlier on, before he came over badly. He couldn't remember ever feeling as bad is this... Suddenly he reared to his feet and bawled it the top of his voice, 'Hilda! Hilda! Let me in!' and the dog, startled, ran off into the trees.

There was only silence. Perhaps she'd gone, he thought. Hopped it. She'd said she would, many a time. He'd never believed her, though. He'd never wanted her to go. She was his wife, wasn't she? He'd never wanted any other woman. He couldn't live by himself. Who'd look after him? How would he manage? And if she'd gone he wouldn't be able to tell her. Tell her what?...Something good. Something to make her happy... He turned and rambled off across the patch of unkempt land that had been the garden and looked with aimless curiosity into the mouldering outhouses with their damp and rotten timbers. The thought came to him that he might shelter there. But it was too cold and he was very ill. He had to get into the house where it was warm. He returned across the snow and looked at the house which stood out plainly in the sharp, clear light shed by the new moon. And after some moments he thought of the window.

He lurched across to the wall of the house and put fumbling hands on the stones. With some difficulty he managed to get one knee onto the sill, his fingers feeling for holds in the interstices of the weathered stonework. He pulled himself up till he was standing upright and felt for a gap across the top of the window. He moved his foot and it slipped away from him across the icy stone of the sill and he lost his balance and fell sideways, his hands clawing at the wall. His right hand described an arc against the wall and the wrist hit the rusted needle-sharp point of the clothes-line hook jutting out some inches from the stone, and his falling weight pulled him on to it, so that for a few seconds he hung there, impaled through the arm. He felt the indescribable agony of the hook as it tore out the front of his wrist and he cried out once, a cry that ended in a choking, sobbing cough, before falling in a huddled heap on the snow, to crouch there, moaning and gibbering senselessly, his good hand clawing feebly at the gaping wound and feeling the warm gush of blood spouting from the severed arteries. And then the pain swamped his already befuddled senses and he rolled slowly sideways and was still.

As he lay there the dog returned to nose, whimpering softly, about him before turning again and loping away to the wood. A few minutes later snow began to fall, swirling down in fat feathery flakes all across the valley and the town and the hillside. It fell soundlessly on the roof of the house, over the room where Mrs Scurridge lay in her drugged sleep, and on Scurridge, melting at first and then slowly, softly, drifting and falling, covering him from sight.

his night of triumph ends in death

The Drum

Comic band story
Old Sam's ambition to play
the drum

'I allus reckon you can't judge by appearance,' said Sam Skelmanthorpe, apropos of a casual remark I'd just made about someone we both knew slightly. He pushed his glass across the bar counter. 'Gimme the other half o' that, George lad. Don't know why they ever invented gills. Gone in a couple o' swallows...'

'Now you take Fred Blenkinsop,' he said, turning to me again.

'Who's Fred Blenkinsop?'

'Y'know – our librarian. I must ha' mentioned him afore.'

'Oh, yes. The chap who works on the farm.'

'That's him. Now you'd never ha' thought there was any more to him than you could see...'

With his replenished glass before him, Sam began to talk about Fred, sketching in his background. They called him Short Fred in Low Netherwood, Sam said, because he stood no more than five-feet-three drawn up to his full height; and if the name came off their lips with dry familiarity it was because he'd lived in the village for the best part of his sixty-odd years and they naturally thought they knew all there was to know about him. But most men have little dreams and secrets locked away in the private corners of their hearts, and Fred was no exception. With him, Sam said, it was an ambition: a small enough ambition at that, but one that had troubled and pestered him for years, sometimes lying dormant for long periods, only to spring into life again without warning, like the itch comes to the born gambler, or the thirst to a man with drinker's throat.

'Aye,' Sam said pensively, 'an ambition.' He took a drink and licked his lips, then looked down at the tobacco pouch I'd slid across as I saw him reach for his pipe as though wondering where it had come from.

'An ambition,' I said, prodding him, but gently. 'It's a curious thing, ambition –'

'Aye,' Sam said. 'He wanted to play the big drum.'

'You mean in the band? But why didn't he, then? Surely all he had to do was –'

'Ask?' said Sam. 'Aye, I suppose so. He'd have had to ask. He was our librarian an' there was allus some strappin' great lad tackling the drum. He'd have had to ask; an' he couldn't bring hisself to do that because, y'see, in his heart of hearts he thought that wantin' to play the drum was a bit daft – more for a lad than a grown man of his age. So he never did ask.

'A good lad, Fred is; we'd be lost without him. He was our librarian when I joined the band, an' he'll be handing out music when I'm under t'sod, I'll bet. On'y one time he ever let us down and that was one night in Cressley Park. Trombones found they had the parts for 'Poet and Peasant', while t'rest of us were crackin' through Lists's Hungarian Rhapsody.'

90

Fred had been a miner, Sam told me, but since retiring from the pit he'd done odd jobs for Withers, who kept the farm on Low Road. There was a bench in a garden at the end of High Street – the traditional gathering place of old-age pensioners. But this was not for Fred. And Withers, knowing a good worker, had been only too happy to relieve Fred of the miseries of idleness. And in addition to his natural zest for work, Fred was of value to Withers in another way. He was one of the few men in the district who could handle Samson, Withers's valuable pedigree Friesian bull. Samson was a vicious and bad-tempered beast with as much love for the human race as a boa constrictor. Withers had considered getting rid of him until Fred came along; and it was with surprise and relief that he found, after a time, a positive affection springing up between the little man and the bull. To see Fred stroking Samson's nose and whispering in his ear while the great beast stood in something approaching ecstasy was a sight that, until the novelty wore off, brought the hands from the fields to stare in wonder.

This then was the uneventful pattern of Fred's life: the days on the farm, the evenings in the Fox and Ferret with a glass of ale, and his duties with the band.

'And then one day,' Sam said, 'he got his chance. Day o' the Sunday-schools' Whit-walk, it was. I remember it well. Boilin' hot. We were all sittin' round in the band-room chatting and smoking, and Fred had his head in the cupboard sortin' the march sheets out. All at once in comes Thomas Easter, our solo euphonium player. His face is as red as his tunic, an' he goes straight to Jess Hodgkins, our conductor.

'"Jess," he says, "we're without a drummer. Young Billy Driver's tum'led off his delivery bike this mornin'.

I've just seen his mother in t'street. It looks like a broken arm, Jess."

'Well, Jess's conducted our band for nigh on fifty year an' he's grown used to misfortune, as you might say. So this bit o'news didn't bowl him over.

"'Well now," he says, when Thomas is catching his breath. "You'd ha' thought he'd ha' done it yesterday an' given us time to get another man." An' he sighs. "I don't know," he says. "If it in't a cornet player wi' a split lip, it's a drummer wi' nobbut one arm." He looks at Thomas. "Wes'll have to do wi'out drummer, Thomas, that's all, lad."

"'Nay, Jess," says Thomas, "wes'll sound awful." Thomas, y'see, has played engagements with some good bands in his time, an' he's allus particular about fieldin' a full side.

"'Then some'dy else'll have it to do," says Jess. An' he has a look round the room. He can't spare any of us, an' his eye falls on Short Fred, still busy with the music. He hasn't heard a word of this an' when Jess gives Thomas the wink an' calls him over he comes up as innocent as you please.

"'Tha's been servin' thy apprenticeship in t'music-sortin' department o' this band for forty-five year 'at I can remember, Fred," he says, his face never slippin'. An'

Fred, mystified, says, "Aye, Jess?"

"'Well I've been thinkin'' 'at it's about time tha made a noise, just to let fowk know tha're still with us," Jess goes on. "An' to make sure everybody hears thee, I'm goin' to give thee t'biggest noise in t'band. Does tha think tha could play t'big drum for us this afternoon?"

'Fred's heart must ha' taken a crotchet rest then. Here's his big chance, straight out of the blue. But not a sign of this shows on his face. "I'll do me best for thee, Jess," he says.'

They rolled the drum from the cupboard, Sam said, and adjusted the straps to suit Fred's short stature. He looked down at the drum, an eager light beginning in his eyes. It was a beautiful instrument, painted in glossy scarlet and gold, with white cords, and the words LOW NETHERWOOD SILVER BAND inscribed on it in gold letters.

'Tha're sure tha can carry it, Fred?' asked one of the players, in mock anxiety, and Fred said scornfully, 'Carry it? Give us ho'd on it an' I'll show thee!'

So they hoisted the drum into position on Fred's chest and fastened the straps. He had a little difficulty in seeing over it, but there was no doubt of his ability to carry it.

'Just give us a steady beat, lad,' Jess instructed him as they formed up in the lane. 'No fancy work, an' tha'll be all right.'

At a blast from Jess's whistle a few stragglers emerged, fortified for the afternoon, from the Fox and Ferret and filled the gaps in the ranks. Fred moved to his place at the rear of the band and made a few practice swings with the drumsticks. He hitched the drum up higher on his chest and as Jess sounded the whistle for off he wielded the sticks with all the enthusiasm of a schoolboy. This was the life!

One two three – boom boom boom. They were off down the lane.

'We joined the procession at the bottom of the lane in High Street,' Sam said. 'A lovely sight, it was: all the kiddies in their new clothes and the banners. We get to the head of 'em an' wait till they're in order. Then Jess blows his whistle an' we're off up High Street, with all the fowk watching, and the banners flying and us blowin' fit to burst. I allus did like a schoolfeast. And there's Fred havin' the time of his life, hitching the drum up higher an' higher an' leaning over backwards to balance it, till he can't see in front of him at all an' he has to rely on his view to either side to tell him where he's goin!'

'We were on the way to Withers's big meadow an' it was just on the corner of the lane that it happened. Only the day before the council had dug a deep trench in the road, to check if the water pipes were still there. There's red flags an' lamps all round it. We swung out an' made a detour; but Fred, not seeing a thing in front of him, marches straight on, knocking the tar out of the drum an' generally havin' the time of his life.

'They shouted to warn him, but it was too late. He put one foot into fresh air an' so they say as saw it, sort of pivoted round on his other foot an' fetched up on his back in the bottom of the trench with the drum sittin' on his chest like a great playful dog.'

And he lay there, Sam said, swearing feebly, while the band, unconscious of his plight, marched on and into the meadow. Anxious faces appeared over the rim of the trench and strong arms reached down to haul him to the surface. The drum was unstrapped and Fred examined for injury. Finding that he was only shaken, he sat on the edge of the trench under the laughing eyes of the village folk and waited for his breath and composure to return.

'How much for t'drum, Fred?' somebody called, and Short Fred writhed with discomfiture. They'd be laughing over this in the sewing circles and the pubs for evermore. The devil take the drum! Why he'd let himself in for this he'd never know.

Meanwhile, the procession had entered the meadow. The children, bursting from restraining hands, ran free on the grass, the girls in their pretty frocks, and straw bonnets, the boys in their stiff new suits. The uniforms of the bandsmen were a bright splash of colour against the more sober dress of the rest of the throng, and perhaps it was this that caught the eye of Samson as, disturbed by the noise, he nosed his way out of his unlocked stall and stalked peevishly across the yard.

'They say bulls are colour blind,' said Sam. 'Well, mebbe they are. But they can tell a bright colour from a dull 'un and they can hear noise. An' if it's a bull like Samson that's enough to get its rag out. You can nearly imagine him thinkin' to hisself, "Who do they think they are, these fowk, all dolled up an' makin' their noise in my field? Time they had a lesson."'

Short Fred was, by this time, coming down the lane by the meadow, carrying the heavy drum (he'd curtly rejected all offers of assistance), and wishing himself anywhere else in the world. His thoughts ran on in miserable confusion, the predominant theme being the folly of childish fancies in the old.

'Summat then – some sixth sense – made him turn his head and look up towards the farm. He stopped then as though he'd turned to stone as he saw Samson there, working hisself up to do murder.

"Heaven help us!" he whispers.

'He sizes up the position at a glance. There's the bull at one end of the field, and a crowd o' fowk – mostly kiddies – at the other. And even if he yells they've to come half-way up the field to reach the gate. He didn't think for a second 'at there being all these fowk 'ud put the bull off. Not Samson!

'Well, Samson stirs and Fred lets out an ear-splitting yell. Then he throws the drum over the hedge and jumps after it, his bruises playing merry hell with him. From where he's standing now the ground slopes away fairly sharp, and he's looking straight across Samson's line of attack.

'Samson launches hisself and charges breakneck down the field. Fred gives a hasty prayer and stands the drum on its rim and gives it a mighty old push, sending it bumping and rolling down the slope. Has he mistimed it? Is it going wide? And just when it seems Samson's gone by, the drum bounces right between his legs and brings him crashing down.'

I looked over my shoulder. The audience had grown during the telling of Sam's dramatic tale and now they were all agog for more, though surely several of them must have known the facts of that day.

'What then, Sam?' asked a thin-faced man on the other side of Sam. 'What happened then?'

Sam, conscious that he had them, took a pull at his beer and nonchalantly pressed down the dottle in his pipe. 'Anybody got a match?' he said, and several boxes were thrust towards him. He fumbled in his waistcoat pocket and found one of his own. He lit up in a leisurely manner, timing their patience to a nicety.

'Well,' he went on, his head in a cloud of smoke, 'Fred dashes across the field afore Samson can get his legs out o' the drum. And then he puts the old charm on him, stroking his nose and whispering sweet nothings in his ear, his heart in his mouth all the time, wondering if Samson'll turn nasty again. And when he thinks Samson's calmed down a bit he cuts a length o' cord off the drum and passes it through the ring in Samson's nose.

'Then he gets him up, ever so easy like, stroking and talking to him all the time. And Samson gives a few snorts and shakes his head a bit, and lets hisself be led up the field. When he's safely shut away, and the stall locked this time, Fred goes into the house with Withers, telling him he's right sorry about what's happened. He can't imagine, he says, what made him act so careless as to leave the stall unlocked. A proper day of it, Fred had had.

"'Nay, there's no need for you to apologize, Fred," Withers tells him. "Cause you weren't to blame, lad." And he pulls his seven-year-old nephew out from behind his chair. "Here's the culprit," he says. "Just confessed to me. He thought it'd be a lark to let Samson out. Well he's had the fright of his life for it anyway."

'Well, Short Fred's the village hero after this. An' now he can play the drum any time he likes, cause when Withers presents a new 'un to the band they feel sort of obliged to offer Fred the job.

'But he's finished with that sort of ambition, and he never wants to see another drum. Old Jess nods when he hears Fred's decision. "Happen tha're right, Fred lad," he says. "Tha're not much of a musician, lad." An' then a twinkle slips into his old blue eyes. "But I reckon," he says, "'at wes'll never see any musician put this 'ere new drum to a better use than tha put our old 'un!'"

One Wednesday Afternoon

a young wife injured & disfigured in an industrial accident the husband's moving, inarticulate response –

Excitement boiled in the woman and overflowed in an almost incoherent torrent of words in which the gatekeeper's puny inquiry bobbed for a second, unheeded, and was lost.

'An accident, y'say?' he asked again as the woman caught at her breath. 'Jack Lister?'

Her vigorous nod set heavy flesh trembling on cheeks and chin. 'His wife... I'm his mother. They've taken her to hospital.'

'Just a minute, then.' The gatekeeper went into the gatehouse and the woman watched him through the dusty side-window as he lifted the receiver of the telephone and spoke to someone inside the low sprawl of factory buildings. In a few minutes he came out again. 'He'll be out in a minute,' he said. He eased the peak of his uniform cap, then clasped his hands behind his back and rocked backwards and forwards, almost imperceptibly, on toes and heels as he looked down at the woman.

She said, 'Thank you,' repeating the words absently a moment later. Then suddenly, as though a tap had been turned on inside her, the gush of words started again. The gatekeeper listened placidly until she touched on the nature of the accident, when his face screwed itself into a grimace.

'Ooh, that's nasty,' he said. 'That's nasty.'

At first when the foreman spoke to him the man did not appear to understand. 'Somebody wanting me?' he said, knitting his eyebrows in perplexity.

'Aye, up at the gate. There's been a bit o' trouble or summat. I should go up an' see what's doin', if I were you.'

The man wiped his hands with slow, puzzled thoroughness on a piece of wool waste, then brushed the dark forelock off his brow. He was near his middle forties, of medium height, and thin, with a dark, gaunt, high-cheekboned face. His short black hair with its forelock helped to give him a curiously old-fashioned appearance, as though, once out of the faded boiler-suit and dark workshirt, his choice of leisure garments would be a stiff wing collar, high-fronted jacket, and narrow trousers with piping down the seams.

'I reckon I'd better, then,' he said in his soft, troubled voice; and laying aside the piece of waste, he made as if to walk away.

'I should take me coat,' the foreman said, and the man stopped. 'An' look – gerrit cleared up, whatever it is, afore you bother comin' back.'

More baffled and puzzled than ever, he said, 'Oh, aye, right, thanks.' He reached for his jacket and cap on the hook behind the machine and with troubled perplexity still creasing his forehead, strode away among the clamour of the shop, passing along the walk through the ordered chaos of machines and the jungle-like growth of compressed-air pipes to the door at the far end.

His mother hurried to meet him as he came out of

the building into the yard, pulling on his jacket as he walked.

'It's Sylvia, Jack,' she blurted. 'She's had an accident.'

He stopped and stared at her, seeming to be wrested from his troubled absorption by her words and the sight of her, hatless and with the flowered apron visible under the unbuttoned coat. He gripped her by the upper arm, the flesh soft and yielding under his fingers. 'What's she done?' he said. 'What's happened?'

'They came to tell me, Jack. They've taken her to the infirmary. It's her hair – she's had her hair fast in a machine.'

'Oh! God,' he said.

She ran clumsily alongside him as he started for the gate. 'All that hair, Jack... She wouldn't have it cut short an' sensible. An' I bet she never even wore it fastened up like other women. She never should ha' gone out to work again anyway, but she wanted too much brass for lipstick an' donnin' up in fancy clothes... Your wage wouldn't do for her. Any decent woman would ha' been content to stop at home an' look after her bairn... I told her it wasn't right, an' she knew you didn't like it... It's a judgement on her, that's what it is... a judgement.'

They were outside the gate now and still her voice went on and on, clamouring at the edge of his mind and driving him deeper into confusion. Until he turned on her suddenly. 'Shurrup! Shurrup! I can't hear meself think.' He stood at the pavement-edge and rubbed his hand across his face. 'God,' he said in a whisper. 'Oh! God.'

'What time did it happen?' he said. 'Will they let me see her, d'you think? Did they say how bad it was?'

'Just after dinnertime, it was,' his mother said. 'They couldn't have above got started again... It sounded bad to me.'

He set off down the road to the bus stop. 'I'll go straight away. I'll get there as soon as I can... Surely they'll let me see her.'

They had to wait five minutes for a bus. The mother stood by the signpost while her son paced restlessly about by the bill-hoarding behind, his stoutly nailed working boots rasping on the flagstones. When at last the bus came he stepped quickly past her and onto the platform, looking back in vague surprise as she followed him.

'Are you comin' an' all?'

'Course I am.'

They took seats on the lower deck. It was early-closing day in Cressley and the bus was almost empty. There was something that rattled with the vibration of motion and he tried with a part of his mind to locate it. Was it a window, or the back of a seat?

'What about t'bairn?' he said, as he remembered.

'I took him next door. I had to. He'll be all right. Mrs Wilson'll see to him while we get back.'

He nodded. 'Aye, she's not a bad sort.'

He became conscious as they drew near the town of his greasy overall and that he needed a wash and a shave. As his mother, unable to keep silent, broke into the quiet with her sporadic bursts of talk he fretted quietly about going to the hospital in such a state. And slowly then, after the initial shock, real consciousness of the accident began to fill his mind and he stiffened in his seat, coming rigidly upright beside his mother's stout form and staring straight ahead, the big adam's apple jerking convulsively in the slack skin of his neck as he tried to swallow with a throat gone dry with fear. Until, as they alighted from the bus, everything was lost in an overwhelming panic that his wife would die before he could reach her, and he started towards the hospital with long urgent strides, stopping occasionally to mutter with soft, frantic impatience as his mother climbed the hill breathlessly behind him.

Inside the hospital they had to wait again, but the house surgeon, when he came, was young and very gentle.

'Are you her husband?' The man nodded dumbly, cap in hand. 'And you're her mother?'

The woman said, 'No, her mother an' father are dead. I'm his mother. They live with me, y'see.'

The doctor nodded and the man blurted, 'How is she, Doctor?'

'It was a nasty accident,' the doctor said carefully. 'I'm afraid a good deal of her scalp has gone.'

'Will it disfigure her?' the woman asked, her eyes fixed on the doctor's face.

The doctor frowned. 'I shouldn't worry about that,' he said evasively. 'It's really amazing what can be done nowadays.'

The man brought his eyes up from the floor. 'I... I'd like to see her if...'

'Well, perhaps for a minute, if she's out of the anaesthetic, but no longer.' He left them and returned with a young nurse. 'She's in Victoria Ward. The nurse will take you up.'

When the woman made as if to follow her son, the doctor restrained her. 'Just one now. He won't be long. You can sit down in the waiting-room.'

Going up in the lift he began to feel faint. He had always hated hospitals. He realised the foolishness of his dislike; hospitals were places of healing and mercy. But his aversion was to physical suffering in others and here he felt surrounded, overwhelmed by it. The characteristic smell of the building seemed to grow stronger the farther

102

they were carried from the outside world, and his stomach seemed empty of everything except nausea. At the door of the ward he was handed over to the sister, who led him down the triple row of beds to the screened-off corner, where she said, 'Just a minute,' and left him exposed to the eyes of the occupants of the ward who, to his furtive glances, seemed every one to have an arm or a leg raised and secured in some agonisingly unnatural position.

The sister reappeared. 'She's awake. Now no noise or excitement. I'll come back when your time's up.'

He tiptoed, ponderous in his heavy boots, behind the screen. She was lying there, her lips pale and bloodless, her face a dead, pasty white against the crisp skull-cap of bandages and the pillow under her head. Her eyes flickered open. 'Jack.' He swallowed painfully. 'Aye, it's on'y me, Sylvia. It's only Jack.' He pulled forward a chair and sat down, fiddling uneasily with his cap for a time before letting it slip to the floor between his knees.

She watched him, her eyes dull and heavy-lidded. 'It's a mess, Jack, in't it?' she whispered then.

He groped for something to say. 'How did it happen?'

'I don't know really. It was so sudden. I was just reachin' over for somethin' an all of a sudden me hair was fast round the spindle an' it was pullin' me in...' She closed her eyes and her body trembled under the sheets. 'It was awful...'

'It's about time they had t'Factory Inspector round that place,' he said in an angry whisper. 'I've heard some tales about 'em.' He looked at her. 'Does it pain you much?'

She moved her head feebly. 'Not now... It did at first, but they give me somethin' to stop it a bit.' The beginnings of a bitter little smile touched her lips. 'This is one up for you an' your mother, in't it? It's your turn to crow now.

'No,' he said urgently. 'No, it's not like that.' He stopped, wringing his hands in helplessness. He wanted to say more but he did not know how. There was so much that he should say to make her understand. The fifteen years difference in their ages had never seemed so great. But words had never come easily to him and now he was bogged down again in inarticulateness: lost, with all the wordless misunderstanding of their marriage between him and her. He made a little movement of his arm. If only he could touch her... But the sheets were drawn right up to her throat and his hand with its dirt-ringed nails and the grease ingrained in every line was like a sacrilege hovering above their spotlessness.

The sister returned silently. 'You'll have to go now.' He sighed in mingled relief and despair.

The girl in the bed opened her eyes again as he stood up and replaced the chair. He made a last desperate attempt. 'I'll come again, as soon as they'll let me,' he said. 'An' look, don't worry yerself about it, lass. It'll be all right. It won't make no difference. No difference at all.'

'Look after Peter,' she said, and tried to smile. 'So long, Jack.'

There was horror in the sunlight outside, and in the normality of the traffic passing along the main road at the bottom of the hill, and in the people going about their business, not knowing or caring that she lay helpless in that great building with half her scalp torn away. A young girl rode by on a bicycle, her long hair blowing out behind her. A picture came to him then of his wife's beautiful red-gold hair entwined in the oil-blue steel of the spindle and he closed his eyes and clutched at the wall as his senses swooned and the world spun about him.

His mother took his arm. 'Come on, Jack. You'll be all right now you're out in t'fresh air.'

She said little going down the hill, but on the bus she started to talk again. 'She won't be the same again, Jack. You could tell the doctor didn't like to say. But I knew... This'll cure her vanity. She'll not be wantin' to do much gallivantin' again...'

He only half-heard her, his attention held by a view across rooftops where a factory chimney poured out smoke, thick and dark against the sky, like a woman's hair...

'Now'll be your chance to put your foot down,' his mother was saying. 'You should ha' done it long since. Now'll be your chance to show her who's boss –'

He put his hands to his face beside her. 'No,' he broke in. 'No, now's me chance to show her...'

'Show her what?' his mother said. 'Show her what, Jack?'

He dropped his hands and clenched his big-knuckled fists on his knees'. 'Nowt,' he said, and the ferocity and anguish in that one word made her gape. 'Nowt... you wouldn't understand.'

The Actor

*comic, sad tale
of amateur dramatics*

He was a big man, without surplus flesh, and with an impassivity of face that hid extreme shyness, and which, allied with his striking build, made him look more than anything else, as he walked homewards in the early evening in fawn mackintosh and trilby hat, like a plainclothes policeman going quietly and efficiently about his business, with trouble for someone it the end of it.

All his adult life people had been saying to him, 'You should have been a policeman, Mr Royston,' or, more familiarly, 'You've missed your way, Albert. You're cut out for a copper, lad.' But he would smile in his quiet, patient way, as though no one had ever said it before, and almost always gave exactly the same reply: 'Nay, I'm all right. I like my bed at nights.'

In reality he was a shop assistant and could be found, in white smock, on five and a half days of the week behind the counter of the Moorend branch grocery store of Cressley Industrial Co-operative Society, where he was assistant manager. He hid been assistant manager for five years

106

and seemed fated to occupy that position for many more years to come before the promotion earmarked for him would become fact. For the manager was a man of settled disposition also, and still comparatively young and fit.

But Albert did not apparently worry. He did not apparently worry about anything; but this again was the deception of his appearance. Quiet he might be, and stolid and settled in his ways; but no one but he had known the agony of shyness that was his wedding day; and no one but he had known the pure terror of the premature birth of his only child, when the baby he had longed for with so much secret yearning was dead and had almost cost the life of the one person without whom his own life would hardly have seemed possible – Alice, his wife.

So it was the measure of his misleading appearance and his ability to hide his feelings that no one ever guessed the truth, that no one was ever led from the belief that he was a taciturn man of unshakeable placidity. 'You want to take a leaf out of Albert's book,' they would say. 'Take a lesson from him. Never worries, Albert doesn't.'

Thus Albert, at the age of thirty-seven, on the eve of his small adventure.

Amateur drama was a popular pastime in Cressley and varied in standard from rather embarrassing to really quite good. Generally considered to be among the best of the local groups was the C.I.C.S. Players – the drama group of Cressley Industrial Co-operative Society. They restricted their activities to perhaps three productions a year and worked hard to achieve a professional finish. It was about the time of the casting for the Christmas production, perhaps the most important of the year, since at this time each group was shown in direct comparison with all the other bodies who joined together in the

107

week-long Christmas Festival of Amateur Drama in the Co-operative Hall, that the rather fierce looking lady from General Office who was said to be the backbone and mainstay of the C.I.C.S. Players, happened to visit the shop. Seeing Albert on her way out as he towered over a diminutive woman customer, she stopped abruptly and, waiting only till he was free, crossed over to him and said, 'Tell me, have you ever acted?'

As it was the oddest thing anyone had ever asked him, Albert simply stared at the woman while a colleague said, 'He's always acting, Albert is. Make a cat laugh, the antics he gets up to.'

'Take no notice of him,' Albert said. 'He's kiddin'.'

'What I mean,' the lady said, 'is, have you had any experience of dramatics?'

'Dramatics?' Albert said.

'Taking part in plays.'

Albert gave a short laugh and shook his head.

'There's a chap coming from M.G.M. to see him next week,' the facetious colleague said. 'Cressley's answer to Alan Ladd.'

Ignoring the irrepressible one, the lady continued her interrogation of Albert with: 'Has anyone ever told you you look like a policeman?'

'I believe it has been mentioned,' said Albert, wondering if the woman had nothing better to do than stand here asking him daft questions all morning.

She now looked Albert over in silence for some moments until, unable to bear her scrutiny for another second, he bent down and pretended to look for something under the counter. He had his head down there when she spoke again and he thought for a moment he had misheard her.

'Eh?' he said, straightening up.

'I said, would you be interested in a part in our new

production? You know, the C.I.C.S. Players. We're doing R. Belton Wilkins's *The Son of the House* for the Christmas Festival and there's a part in it for a police constable. We've no one in the group who fits the role nearly so well as you.

'But I can't act,' Albert said. 'I've never done anything like that before.'

'It's only a small part – about a page. You'd soon learn it. And you'd find it great fun to be part of a group effort. There's nothing quite like the thrill of the stage, you know.'

'Aye, happen it's all right if you're that way inclined,' Albert said, and was relieved to see a customer at the lady's elbow.

'Well, I won't keep you from your work,' she said; 'but think it over. We'd love to have you, and you'd never regret it. We start rehearsals next week. I'll pop in and see you again later. Think it over.'

'Aye, aye,' Albert said. 'I'll think it over.' Meaning that he would dismiss it from his mind for the nonsense it was as soon as she was gone. Acting! Him!

But he did not dismiss it from his mind. A part of his mind was occupied with it all morning as he attended to his customers; and at lunch-time, when the door had been locked, he went over to one of the young lady assistants from the opposite counter.

'You're mixed up with this acting thing, aren't you?'

'The Players?' the girl said. 'Oh yes. It's grand fun. We're doing R. Belton Wilkins's latest West End success for our next production.'

'Aye,' Albert said, 'I've been hearin' so. I've had yon' woman on to me this morning.'

'You mean Mrs Bostock. I saw her talking to you. A real tartar, she is. Terrifically keen and efficient. I don't know what we'd do without her.'

'She's been doin' a bit o' recruitin' this morning,' Albert said. 'Been on to me to take a part in this new play. Don't know what she's thinkin' about.' All morning a new feeling had been growing in him and now he realised that he was pleased and flattered by Mrs Bostock's approach, nonsense though it undoubtedly was. 'I always thought you wanted these la-di-da chaps for play-actin',' he said; 'not ord'nary chaps like me.'

'I don't know,' the girl said, unbuttoning her overall. 'What part does she want you for?'

'The policeman.'

'Well, there you are. Perfect type-casting. You look the part exactly.'

'But they'd know straight away 'at I wasn't an actor, soon as I opened me mouth.'

'They don't want to know you're an actor. They want to think you're a policeman.'

'But I can't put it on.'

'Policemen don't put it on, do they? You'd just have to be yourself and you'd be perfect.'

'And I've no head for remembering lines,' Albert said.

'How do you know if you've never tried?'

'Hmmm,' Albert said.

'Look,' the girl said, 'I'll bring my copy of the play back after dinner and you can have a look at the part. As far as I remember, it's not very long.'

'Oh, don't bother,' Albert said. 'I'm not thinkin' o' doin' it.'

'No bother,' the girl said. 'You just have a look at it and see.'

That afternoon, in the intervals between attending to customers, Albert could be seen paying great attention to something slightly below the level of the counter; and when the shop had closed for the day he approached the girl who had lent him the book and said, 'Will you be wantin' this tonight? I thought I might take it home an' have a look at it.'

'It's getting you, then?'

'Well, I've read it about half-way through,' Albert said, 'an' I've got interested like. In the story, I mean. I'd like to see how it ends, if you can spare the book.'

'You can borrow it,' the girl said. 'You'll find it very gripping near the end. It ran for over two years in London.'

'You don't say so,' Albert said. 'That's a long time.'

'Of course, we're only doing one performance,' the girl said, 'so you needn't get the wind up.'

'What d'you think happened at the shop today?' Albert asked Alice after tea that evening.

Alice said she couldn't imagine.

'We had that Mrs Bostock down from General Office an' she asked me if I'd like a part in this new play they're getting up.'

'You?' Alice said. 'She asked you?'

'Aye, I knew it,' Albert said. 'I knew you'd think it was daft an' all.'

'I don't think it's daft at all,' Alice said. 'I'm surprised, but I don't think it's daft. What sort of part does she want you to play?'

'Guess,' Albert said. 'She took one look at me an' offered me the part.'

Alice began to laugh. 'Why not? Why ever shouldn't you?'

'Because,' Albert said, 'there's a difference in walkin' the streets lookin' like a bobby an' walkin' on to a stage an' reckonin' to be one. I don't think I could do it, not with maybe hundreds o' people watchin' me.'

'Oh, I don't know. They tell me you forget the audience once you start saying your lines.'

111

'Aye, an' supposin' you forget your lines? What then?'

'Well, you just have to learn them. And you have rehearsals and what not. I don't suppose it's a long part, is it?'

Albert fingered the book. 'Only a page. I have it here.'

'Oh, ho!' Alice said.

'Well, young Lucy Fryer would bring it for me, an' I started readin' it and got interested. It's a real good play, y'know. They ought to do it on the telly. It ran for two years in London.'

Alice took the book and looked at the title. 'Yes, I've heard of this.'

'It's all about a young feller and his dad's ever so rich and dotes on the lad. Thinks the sun shines out of him; an, all the time this lad's a real nasty piece o' work. A proper nowter.'

'Where's the policeman's part?'

'In the second act. Here, let me show you. This lad an' his brother are havin' a row, see, because he's run some'dy down in his car and not stopped, because he was drunk. An' right in the middle of this I come in an'–'

'You come in?' Alice said. 'I thought you weren't interested in the part?'

Albert looked sheepish. 'I haven't said I am,' he said. 'I sort o' tried to imagine meself as I was reading it, that's all.'

'I see,' Alice said.

'Aye, that's all... What you lookin' at me for?'

'I'm just looking,' Alice said.

It was two days later that Mrs Bostock came in again.

'Well,' she said with ferocious brightness, 'did you think it over?'

'He's read the play, Mrs Bostock,' Lucy Fryer said, coming over. 'I lent him my copy.'

'Splendid, splendid.'

'Yes, a very entertainin' play indeed,' Albert said. 'But I haven't said owt about playin' that part. I don't think it's owt in my line, y'see. She thinks so, an' my missis; but I'm not sure.'

'Nonsense,' Mrs Bostock said.

'Y'see I'm not the sort o' feller to show meself off in front of a lot o' people.'

'Rubbish,' Mrs Bostock said.

'Oh, it's all right for you lot. You've done it all before. You're used to it.'

'Come to rehearsal Monday evening,' Mrs Bostock commanded.

'Well, I don't know.'

'My house, seven-thirty. I won't take no for an answer till you've seen us all and given it a try. Lucy will tell you the address.' And she was gone.

'A bit forceful, isn't she?' Albert said.

'A tartar,' Lucy said.

'Oh, heck,' Albert said, 'I don't like this at all.'

But secretly now he was beginning to like it enormously.

At seven twenty-five on Monday evening he presented himself, dressed carefully in his best navy blue and shaved for the second time that day, at the front door of Mrs Bostock's home, a large and rather grim-looking Victorian terrace house with big bay windows on a long curving avenue off Halifax Road, and was joined on the step by Lucy Fryer.

Mrs Bostock herself let them in and showed them into a large and shabbily comfortable drawing-room furnished mostly with a varied assortment of easy chairs and settees, and more books than Albert had ever seen at one time outside the public library. He was introduced to a thin, distinguished-looking, pipe-smoking man who turned out to be Mr Bostock, and then the members of the drama group began to arrive.

There were only seven speaking parts in the play but several people who would be responsible for backstage production turned up too and soon the room was full of men and women whose common characteristic seemed to be that they all talked at the top of their voices. Albert was bewildered, and then smitten with acute embarrassment when Mrs Bostock, standing on the hearthrug, clapped her hands together and saying, 'Listen, everybody; I'd like you all to meet our new recruit,' directed all eyes to him.

'I'm trying to talk Mr Royston into playing the policeman in *Son of the House* and I want you all to be nice to him because he isn't completely sold on the idea yet.'

'But my dear Effie,' said a stocky young man in a tweed jacket and yellow shirt, 'you're a genius. You really are. Where on earth did you find him?' And Albert stood there feeling very uncomfortable while everybody looked at him as though he were an antique which Mrs Bostock had uncovered in an obscure shop and was now presenting for their admiration.

'Mr Royston is the assistant manager in Moorend Grocery,' Mrs Bostock told them. 'I took one look at him and knew he was our man.'

To Albert's relief attention turned from him and he was able for a time to sit in his corner and watch what went on without being called upon to do or say anything. But not for long. A first group-reading of the play was started upon and Albert followed the action in his copy, amazed at the way the actors let themselves go in their parts, delivering the most embarrassing lines without the least sign of self-consciousness. 'You know I love you,' the young man in the yellow shirt said to a pretty dark girl sitting next to Albert. 'Do you love me?' she replied. 'Or is it just that you want to go to bed with me?' Albert blushed.

At the entrance of the policeman a silence fell upon the room and Mrs Bostock, still directing operations from the hearthrug, said, 'Now, Mr Royston, this is where you come in.'

Oh, it was terrible. His heart thumped sickeningly. He found his place, put his forefinger under the line, swallowed thickly, and said in a faint voice:

'Is one of you gentlemen the owner of that car standing outside?'

'Weak,' Mrs Bostock said. 'Come now, Mr Royston, a little more authority. Can't you imagine the impact of your entrance?...'

'Just imagine it, Alice,' Albert said, getting up out of his chair with the book in his hand. 'Here's this rotter of a bloke, who's had one too many an' been drivin' like mad an' hit somebody an' left 'em in the road. He's scared out of his wits an' now he's telling his brother an' pleadin' with him to help him, when the maid comes in and says there's a policeman come – and I walk in.

'"Is one of you gentlemen the owner of that car standing outside?" An' this 'ere young chap nearly passes out with fright, thinkin' they're on to him. And really, y'see, all I'm doin' is pinchin' him for parking without lights. Just imagine it. It's... it's one of the dramatic climaxes of the play.'

'It's ever so thrilling, Albert,' Alice said. 'Did you say it like that tonight?'

'What?'

'Is one of you gentlemen the owner of that car outside?'

'Well, happen not quite like that. It's not so bad when

there's only you listening to me, but it sort o' puts you off with all them la-di-da fellers there. You're scared to death you'll drop an aitch or say a word wrong... It'll be easier when I'm a bit more used to it.'

'You're really taking it on, then?'

'Well,' Albert said, scratching his head, 'I don't seem to have much option, somehow. She's a very persuasive woman, that Mrs Bostock. Besides,' he went on, 'it sort of gets you, you know. If you know what I mean.'

Alice smiled. 'I know what you mean. You do it, Albert. You show them.'

Albert looked at her and in a moment a slow grin spread across his face. 'I think I will, Alice,' he said. 'I think I will.'

Once committed, Albert sank himself heart and soul into the perfecting of his part. Attendance at Mrs Bostock's house on Monday evenings opened up a new vista of life to him. It was his first contact with the artistic temperament varied in inverse ratio to the amount of talent. He was fascinated.

'You've never met anybody like 'em, he said to Alice one night.' They shake hands to feel how long the claws are an' put their arms round one another so's it's easier to slip the knife in.'

'Oh, surely, Albert,' said Alice, a person of sweetness and light, 'they're not as bad as all that.'

'No,' he admitted; 'some of 'em's all right; but there's one or two proper devils.' He shook his head. 'They're certainly not sort o' folk I've been used to. Three-quarters of 'em don't even work for t'Co-op.'

'How is it coming along?' Alice asked.

'Pretty fair. We're trying it out on the stage next week, with all the actions an' everything.'

116

On the night of the dress rehearsal Alice answered a knock on the door to find a policeman on the step.

'Does Albert Royston live here?' a gruff official voice asked.

Alice was startled. 'Well, he does,' she said, 'but he's not in just now.'

She opened the door a little wider and the light fell across the man's face. Her husband stepped towards her, laughing.

'You silly fool, Albert,' Alice said indulgently. 'You gave me a shock.'

Albert was still chuckling as he walked through into the living-room. 'Well, how do I look?'

'You look marvellous,' Alice said. 'But you've never come through the streets like that, have you? You could get into trouble.'

'It's all right,' Albert told her. 'I had me mac on over the uniform and the helmet in a bag. I just had to give you a preview like. An' Mrs Bostock says could you put a little tuck in the tunic: summat they can take out before it goes back. It's a bit on the roomy side.'

'It must have been made for a giant,' Alice said as she fussed about behind him, examining the tunic. 'Ooh, Albert, but isn't it getting exciting! I can't wait for the night.'

'Well, like it or lump it,' Albert said, 'there's only another week now.'

He was at the hall early on the night of the play and made up and dressed in the police constable's uniform by the end of the first act. As the second act began he found himself alone in the dressing-room. He looked into the mirror and squared the helmet on his head. He certainly looked the part all right. It would be a bit of a lark to go out in the

117

street and pinch somebody for speeding or something. He narrowed his eyes, looking fiercely at himself, and spoke his opening line in a guttural undertone.

Well, this was it. No good looking in the book. If he didn't know the part now he never would. Out there the second act was under way, the players doing their very best, revelling in a hobby they loved, giving entertainment to all those people; and in return the audience was thrilling to every twist and climax of the plot, and not letting one witty phrase, one humorous exchange go by without a laugh. A good audience, Mrs Bostock had said: the sort of audience all actors, professional or amateur, loved: at one with the players, receptive, responsive, appreciative. And soon its eyes would be on him.

He was suddenly seized by an appalling attack of stage fright. His stomach was empty, a hollow void of fear. He put his head in his hands. He couldn't do it. How could he ever have imagined he could? He couldn't face all those people. His mouth was dry and when he tried to bring his lines to memory he found nothing but a blank.

A knock on the door made him look up. He felt panic grip him now. Had he missed his entrance? Had he ruined the performance for everybody by cringing here like a frightened child? The knock was repeated and Mrs Bostock's voice said from outside, 'Are you there, Mr Royston?'

Albert took his script in his hand and opened the door. She smiled brightly up at him. 'Everything all right?' She gave him an appraising look. 'You look wonderful. You're not on for a little while yet but I should come and stand in the wings and get the feel of the action. You look a bit pale about the gills. What's wrong – stage fright?'

'It's all a bit new to me,' Albert said feebly.

'Of course it is. But you know your lines perfectly and once you're out there you'll forget your nervousness. Just remember the audience is on your side.'

They went up the narrow steps to the level of the stage. The voices of the actors became more distinct.

He caught the tail-end of a line he recognised. There already? Recurrent fear gripped his stomach.

He looked out on to the brightly lit stage, at the actors moving about, talking, and across to where the girl who was acting as prompter sat with an open script on her knee. 'Shirley hasn't had a thing to do so far,' Mrs Bostock murmured. 'The whole thing's gone like a dream. She took the script from Albert's hands and found the place for him. 'Here we are. Now you just follow the action in there and relax; take it easy. You'll be on and off so quick you'll hardly know you've left the wings.'

'I'm all right now,' Albert told her.

He realised to his own surprise that he was; and he became increasingly so as the action of the play absorbed him, so that he begin to feel himself part of it and no longer a frightened amateur shivering in the wings.

Two pages to go. The younger son was telling his brother about the accident. The row was just beginning and at the very height of it he would make his entrance. He began to feel excited. What was it Mrs Bostock had said? 'From the second you step on you dominate the stage. Your entrance is like a thunder-clap.' By shots! He realised vaguely that Mrs Bostock had left his side, but he didn't care now. He felt a supreme confidence. He was ready. He'd show them. By shots he would!

One page. 'You've been rotten all your life, Paul,' the elder brother was saying. 'I've never cherished any illusions about you, but this, this is more than even I dreamed you were capable of.'

119

'I know you hate me, Tom. I've always known it. But if only for father's sake, you must help me now. You know what it will do to him if he finds out. He couldn't stand it in his condition.'

'You swine. You utter swine...'

The girl who was the maid appeared at his side. She gave him a quick smile. No nerves about her. She'd been on and off the stage all evening, living the part. Albert stared out, fascinated. Not until this moment had he known the true thrill of acting, of submerging one's own personality in that of another.

'Where are you going?'

'I'm going to find that man you knocked down and get him to a hospital. And you're coming with me.'

'But it's too late, Tom. It was hours ago. Someone's sure to have found him by now. Perhaps the police...'

Any minute now. They were working up to his entrance. Like a thunder-clap. Albert braced his shoulders and touched his helmet. He glanced down at the script and quickly turned a page. He had lost his place. Panic smote him like a blow. They were still talking, though, so he must be all right. And anyway the maid gave him his cue and she was still by his side. Then suddenly she was no longer at his side. She had gone. He fumbled with his script. Surely... not so far...

He felt Mrs Bostock at his elbow. He turned to her in stupid surprise.

'But,' he said, 'they've... they've –'

She nodded. 'Yes. They've skipped three pages. They've missed your part right out.'

He was already at home when Alice returned.

'Whatever happened, Albert?' she said anxiously. 'You weren't ill, were you?'

120

He told her. 'I went and got changed straight away,' he said, 'and came home.'

'Well, isn't that a shame!'

'Oh, they just got carried away,' Albert said. 'One of 'em lost his place and skipped and the other lad had to follow him. They did it so quick nobody could do owt about it.' He smiled as he began to take off his shoes. 'Looks as though I'll never know whether I'd 've stood up to it or not,' he said.

He never did anything of the kind again.

A long time after he was able to face with equanimity his wife's request, in the presence of acquaintances, that he should tell them about his 'acting career', and say, 'No, you tell 'em, Alice. You tell it best.' And the genuine smile on his honest face during the recounting of the story of the unspoken lines, which never failed to provoke shouts of laughter, always deceived the listeners. So that never for one moment did they guess just how cruel, how grievous a disappointment it had been to him at the time.

The Fury

The rage of a passionately jealous wife.

There were times when Mrs Fletcher was sure her husband thought more of his rabbits than anything else in the world: more than meat and drink, more than tobacco and comfort, more than her – or the other woman. And this was one of those times; this Saturday morning, as she looked out from the kitchen where she was preparing the dinner to where she could see Fletcher working absorbedly, cleaning out the hutches, feeding the animals, and grooming his two favourite Angoras for the afternoon's show in Cressley.

She was a passionate woman who clung single-mindedly to what was hers, and was prepared to defend her rights with vigour. While courting Fletcher she had drawn blood on an erstwhile rival who had threatened to reassert her claims. Since then she had had worse things to contend with. Always, it seemed to her, there was something between her and her rightful possession of Fletcher. At the moment it was the rabbits. The big shed had been full of hutches at one time, but now Fletcher concentrated his attention on a handful of animals in which he had a steady faith. But there were still too many for Mrs Fletcher, who resented sharing him with anything or anybody, and the sight of his absorption now stirred feelings which brought unnecessary force to bear on the sharp knife with which she sliced potatoes for the pan.

'Got a special class for Angoras today,' Fletcher said later, at the table. He was in a hurry to be off and he shovelled loaded spoons of jam sponge pudding into his mouth between the short sentences. 'Might do summat for a change. Time I hid a bit o' luck.' He was washed and clean now, his square, ruddily handsome face close-shaven, the railway porter's uniform discarded for his best grey worsted. The carrying-case with the rabbits in it stood by the door.

Mrs Fletcher gave no sign of interest. She said, 'D'you think you'll be back in time for t'pictures?'

Fletcher gulped water. He had a way of drinking which showed his fine teeth. 'Should be,' he answered between swallows. 'Anyway, if you're so keen to go why don't you fix up with Mrs Sykes?'

'I should be able to go out with you, Saturday nights,' Mrs Fletcher said. 'Mrs Sykes has a husband of her own to keep her company.'

'Fat lot o' company he is Saturday night,' Fletcher said dryly. 'Or Sunday, for that matter... Anyway, I'll try me best. Can't say fairer than that, can I?'

'Not as long as you get back in time.'

Fletcher pushed back his chair and stood up. 'I don't see why not. It shouldn't be a long job today. It isn't a big show. I should be back by half-past seven at latest.'

'Well, just see 'at you are,' she said.

She stood by the window and watched him go down the road in the pale sunshine, the carrying-case, slung from one shoulder, prevented from jogging by a careful hand. He cut a handsome, well-set-up figure when he was dressed up, she thought. Often too handsome, too well-set-up for her peace of mind.

By half-past seven she was washed, dressed, and lightly made-up ready for the evening out. But Fletcher had not returned. And when the clock on the mantelshelf chimed eight there was still no sign of him. It was after ten when he came. She was sitting by the fire, the wireless blaring unheard, her knitting needles flashing with silent fury.

'What time d'you call this?' she said, giving him no chance to speak. 'Saturday night an' me sittin' here like a doo-lal while you gallivant up an' down as you please.'

He was obviously uneasy, expecting trouble. 'I'm sorry,' he said. 'I meant to get back. I thought I should, but there were more there than I expected. It took a long time...' He avoided her eyes as he went into the passage to hang up his overcoat. 'Didn't win owt, either,' he muttered, half to himself.' Not a blinkin' sausage.'

'You knew I specially wanted to see that picture, didn't you?' Mrs Fletcher said, her voice rising. 'I've been telling you all week, but that makes no difference, does it? What does your wife matter once you get off with your blasted rabbits, eh?'

As though he had not heard her Fletcher opened the case and lifted out one of the rabbits and held it up to him, stroking the long soft fur. 'You just wasn't good enough, was you, eh?' The rabbit blinked its pink eyes in the bright electric light. 'Nivver mind: you're a beauty all t'same.'

His ignoring of maddened Mrs Fletcher was almost more than she could bear. 'I'm talking to you!' she stormed.

'I heard you; an' I said I'm sorry. What more do you want?'

'Oh, you're sorry, and that's the end of it, I suppose. That's all my Saturday night's worth, is it?'

'I couldn't help it,' Fletcher said. 'I said I couldn't help it.' He put the rabbit back in the case and sat down to unlace his shoes. She watched him, eyes glittering, mouth a thin trap of temper.

'Aye, you said so. You said you'd be home at half-past seven an' all, and we've seen what that was worth. How do I know what you've been up to while I've been sitting here by myself?'

He looked quickly up at her, his usual full colour deepening and spreading 'What're you gettin' at now?'

'You know what I'm getting at.' Her head nodded grimly.

Fletcher threw down his shoes. 'I told you,' he said with throaty anger, "at that's all over. It's been finished with a long time. Why can't you let it rest, 'stead o' keep harping on about it?'

He stood up, and taking the carrying-case, walked out in his slippers to the shed, leaving her to talk to the empty room. He always got away from her like that. She grabbed the poker and stabbed savagely at the fire.

On Sunday morning she was shaking a mat in the yard when her next-door neighbour spoke to her over the fence.

'Did you get to the Palace this week, then, Mrs Fletcher?' Mrs Sykes asked her. 'Oh, but you did miss a treat. All about the early Christians and the cloak 'at Jesus wore on the Cross. Lovely, it was, and ever so sad.'

'I wanted to see it,' Mrs Fletcher said, 'but Jim didn't get back from Cressley till late. His rabbits y'know.' She felt a strong desire to abuse him in her talk, but pride held her tongue. It was bad enough his being as he was without the shame of everyone knowing it.

'Oh, aye, they had a show, didn't they?' Mrs Sykes said. 'Aye, I saw him in the bus station afterwards. He was talking to a woman I took to be your sister.'

Mrs Fletcher shot the other woman a look. What was she up to? She knew very well that her sister had lived down south these last twelve months. Her cheeks flamed suddenly and she turned her back on her neighbour and went into the house.

Fletcher was lounging, unshaven and in shirt sleeves, his feet propped up on the fireplace, reading the Sunday papers. She went for him as soon as she had put the thickness of the door between them and Mrs Sykes, who still lingered in the yard.

'You must think I'm stupid!'

'Eh?' Fletcher said, looking up. 'What's up now?'

'What's up? What's up? How can you find the face to sit there with your feet up and ask me that? You must think I'm daft altogether: but it's you 'at's daft, if you did but know it. Did you think you could get away with it? Did you really think so? You might ha' known somebody 'ud see you. And you had to do it in the bus station at that – a public place!'

'I don't know what you're talking about,' Fletcher said, but his eyes gave him away.

'You'll brazen it out to the very end, won't you?' she said. 'You liar you. "Oh, I've made a mistake", he says. "I'll never see her again", he says. And what do you do but go running back to her the minute you think you can get away with it!'

Fletcher got up, throwing the newspaper to one side. 'I tell you I don't –' Then he stopped, the bluster draining out of him. 'All right,' he said quietly. 'If you'll calm down a minute I'll tell you.'

'You'll tell me!' Mrs Fletcher said. 'You'll tell me nothing any more. It's all lies, lies, lies every time you open your mouth. Well, I've finished. Bad enough your rabbits, but I draw the line at fancy women. You promised me faithful you wouldn't see her again. You said it sitting in that very chair. And what was it worth, eh? Not a row o' buttons. What d'you think I feel like when me own neighbours tell me they've seen you carryin' on?'

'If you wouldn't listen so much to what t'neighbours say an' take notice o' what I have to tell you –' Fletcher began.

'I've done listening to you,' she said. 'Now I'm having my say.'

'Well, you'll say it to yourself, and t'rest o' t'street mebbe, but not to me.' He strode across the room and dragged down his coat. 'I'll go somewhere where I can talk to somebody 'at's not next-door to a ravin' lunatic.'

'And stop there when you get there,' she told him. 'Go to her. Tell her I sent you. Tell her I've had enough of you. See if she'll sit at home while you traipse about t'countryside with a boxful o' mucky vermin.'

He was at the door, pulling on his coat.

'And take your things,' she said. 'Might as well make a clean sweep while you're about it.'

'I'm goin' to our Tom's,' he said. 'I'll send for 'em tomorrow.'

'I'll have 'em ready,' she said.

When the door had closed behind him she stood for a moment, eyes glittering, nostrils dilated, her entire body stiff and quivering with rage. Then suddenly she plucked a vase from the mantelshelf and dashed it to pieces in the hearth. She clenched and unclenched her hands at her sides, her eyes seeking wildly as the fury roared impotently in her.

At half-past ten she was in the kitchen making

127

her supper when she heard the front door open. She went through into the passage and her hands tightened involuntarily about the milk bottle she was holding as she saw Fletcher there.

'Well?' she said. 'Have you come for your things?' Her voice was tight and unnatural and Fletcher took it as a sign of her lingering anger.

He closed the door and stood sheepishly behind it, his eyes avoiding hers. 'I just thought I'd come an' see if you'd calmed down,' he said.

'I thought we'd heard the last of that this morning?' Her eyes were fixed, bright and unmoving, on his face, and Fletcher caught them with his own for an instant and looked away again.

'We were both a bit worked up like,' he said. 'I know how it is when you get mad. You do an' say a lot o' things you don't really mean. Things you regret after.'

There was silence for a second before she said, the same tight, strained note in her voice, 'What things?'

'I mean like me walkin' out,' Fletcher said. 'All it needed was a bit o' quiet talkin' an' it wouldn't ha' come to that. It'd ha' been all right if only you'd listened to me.'

'I never expected you to come back,' she said, and moved almost trance-like across the room to the fire, still watching him intently, almost disbelievingly, as though she had expected that with his slamming of the door this morning he would walk off the edge of the world, never to be seen again.

He came over to the hearth to stand beside her. He started to put his hand on her shoulder, but as she moved away slightly he dropped his arm again and looked past her into the fire.

'What I said before, I meant,' he said, speaking quietly, earnestly, with the awkwardness of a man not

128

used to expressing the finer feelings. 'I could ha' told you about it last night, only I didn't see any point. It was all forgotten as far as I was concerned. Finished. But she was waiting for me when I came out o' the show. I told her I didn't want to see her again. There was never owt much between us anyway. But I couldn't get rid of her. She hung on like mad. An' when I looked at her, all painted an' powdered up, I found meself thinkin' what a great fool I'd been ever to risk losing all that mattered for a brazen baggage like her. It took me a couple of hours to get rid of her. She got proper nasty towards the end. Started shoutin' and swearin', right in the street. It was awful.' Fletcher sighed and shook his head and a shudder seemed to run through Mrs Fletcher. 'I had to jump on a bus in the end and just leave her standing there. There was nowt else I could do bar give her a clout or summat...'

As he finished talking something seemed to snap inside Mrs Fletcher and she began to cry softly. He put his arm round her shoulders, tentatively at first, then, when she offered no resistance, with pressure, drawing her to him.

'Now, lass. Now then. Cryin' won't do any good. We've had our little bust-up, an' now it's all over in' done with.'

'Oh, why didn't I listen?' she sobbed. 'None of this would have happened then.'

He drew her down into an armchair and held her to him. 'Never mind now, lass. No harm done. Don't cry any more.'

After a time, he said, 'I'll just nip out an' see to the rabbits, then we can get off up to bed.'

She held him to her. 'No, leave 'em. Come to bed now.'

He smiled quietly, indulgently. 'Still a bit jealous, eh? Well, I reckon they'll manage till morning.'

Later still, in the dark secret warmth of the bed, she clung to him again. 'Did you mean it?' she said. 'When you said you loved nobody but me?'

'I did,' he said.

'Say it, then,' she said, holding him hard.

'I love you, lass,' he said. 'Nobody but you. It'll be better in future. You'll see.'

She could have cried out then. Better in future! Oh, why hadn't she listened? Why, why, why? If only she had listened and heard him in time! For now this moment was all she had. There could be no future: nothing past the morning when he would go out and find the rabbits slaughtered in their hutches.

The Living and the Dead

Sad tale - the prodigal son returns to visit his father's grave - ~~visits~~ meets his sister

He picked his way gingerly between the graves like a man stepping through a pit of snakes. Yet the only serpents he feared to disturb were those from his own distant past, and surely they were fangless after all this time...

He found now that memory had played him false. The cemetery had changed. It was bigger, for one thing; the gravestones that, seen from the station entrance on the other side of the river, had seemed to him like litter on a park slope, were set out now almost to the boundary fence, and it occurred to him that soon another field must be purchased. Waste, he thought. He himself believed in cremation, when he thought of death at all. Or, better still, burial at sea: no memorial, no mess.

So he went on, putting his feet carefully into the long wet grasses until he reached the asphalt avenue on the other side; and as he stood there, looking uncertainly about, trying to reorientate himself, the sexton came up the slope, walking with long easy strides, clay-streaked spade over his shoulder. As he drew abreast the man spoke to him.

'I'm looking for William Larkin's grave,' he said. 'He'd be buried ten days or a fortnight ago.'

The sexton swung the spade down and leaned on it, wiping his neck with a dark blue handkerchief.

'New grave?'

'No, family. I thought I could go straight to it, but the place has changed.'

'Larkin... aye.' The sexton was an elderly man. He glanced at the other now, but without recognition. 'Aye... up here.'

He shouldered the spade again and they strolled up the slope together, exchanging commonplaces about the weather. And when they had gone only twenty yards the man's memory cleared and he found the grave without further direction.

He looked at the marble headstone, resting one foot lightly on the kerbstone until he realised and stepped off it. It was this same unexpected but unignorable sense of propriety that, a few moments later, arrested his hands as they fumbled for cigarettes and matches. There were two inscriptions on the stone, the upper one more than twenty years old: 'In memory of Jane Alice Larkin, dear wife and mother...' and below this, newly chiselled into the marble: 'and of William Henry Larkin, husband of the above... a beloved father, greatly missed...' 'Greatly missed...' That was a good one. He wondered which of them had thought of that. Still, it would never do always to put the truth on a gravestone. Imagine seeing it: 'Not before time' or 'Glad to see him go...'

So they perpetrated the last sham.

He stood there looking at the stone, not seeing the inscriptions now, his mind looking back over fifteen years and more. And so she found him, the woman who hurried down the path between the laurels from the water-tank near the sexton's cottage, brimming flower-holder in hand, red and yellow heads of tulips bobbing at the rim of her shopping-basket. She stopped, seeing him so, and watched him for several minutes unobserved. In his navy-blue raincoat, shabby blue serge suit, and roll-necked blue jumper he carried an unmistakable tang of the sea. He was a tall man, but thin, fined down, the brown skin taut over the high-cheekboned face, with the big fleshy nose and slightly protuberant blue eyes. He had changed since last she saw him, but she knew him for her younger brother.

'Well,' she said, and her voice startled him half-round to face her, 'you came after all!'

Her sudden appearance threw him off-balance for a moment, so that when he spoke it was with a note of gently patronising amusement which was, however, more of a defence than anything else, for there was real affection and pleasure in his slow smile.

'Well,' he said, his voice echoing hers; 'well, well, well – Annie; little Annie.'

'I thought you weren't coming,' she said as she came between the graves towards him. 'We broadcast for you...

'I was at sea,' he said. 'I was surprised. I wondered why you'd bothered.'

'It was Henry's idea.'

'I should have thought I'd be the last person Henry wanted to see.'

'It was Father... He wanted to see you.'

'Him – see me!'

She knelt and pressed the flower-holder firmly in place among the marble chips and began to insert the long stems of the tulips.

'There's no need for bitterness, Arthur. We've got past all that... Anyway, you've had the last satisfaction of knowing he went without you being here.'

'Bitterness!' he said. 'Satisfaction! He cursed me out of the house... stood on the doorstep and told me never to cross his threshold again. You know what happened, Annie. You were there. Anyway,' he went on when she did not answer him, 'I was at sea. Coming back from Cuba. I couldn't charter an aeroplane.'

'How did you know he was dead? How is it you didn't come straight to the house?'

'A feller down in town told me. I didn't know him, but he remembered me. He told me, so I came straight here.'

He stood with his hands deep in the pockets of his raincoat and watched her arrange the flowers, breaking a stem here and there until they were balanced to her satisfaction.

'You look after it?' he asked. 'Is it your job?'

'It's always been my job,' she said. Then, without malice, 'The others come at Easter: I come all the year round. I've looked after it for Mother all this time and it's no more hardship now there's two of 'em here.'

'There's room for another, isn't there?' he said. 'What about it then? Will you enjoy looking after Henry or Cissie?'

'It might be me,' she said. 'What then?'

'You'll outlive those two.'

'Perhaps,' she said. 'Then it might be Lucy: she's the oldest.'

'Lucy?'

She gave a quick glance up at him. 'Father's second wife, I mean.'

'You mean he married again?'

'Eight years ago.' She got up and looked at him across the grave. 'You wouldn't know about that, never having let anybody know where you were.'

He shrugged, uneasy under her direct gaze. 'Ah.

You know how it is. I've been all over the place: Canada, Australia, Singapore. South America now... Besides, why should I make excuses? There's never been anybody I wanted to hear from; or who wanted to hear from me. Except you, Annie. I've often wondered about you.' His gaze fell to her naked, virginal left hand, then lifted again. 'It is nice to see you again, you know, Annie.'

Her eyes on him had softened. 'And you, Arthur,' she said. 'I didn't know what could have become of you. I thought when you didn't come that perhaps you were –'

'Dead?' He laughed. 'Not me, Annie. You know what they say – only the good die young.'

'And you're not good, is that it?'

Her picking up of his lightly spoken words put him on the defensive again.

'I've never pretended to be better than I am.'

'Like some you could mention, eh?'

'I didn't say it.'

'But you meant it.'

'Look' – he stirred uneasily – 'what is this? First you accuse me of being bitter, and now you put the words into my mouth. I haven't seen you for fifteen years, Annie; let's not be like this.'

'No, you're right.' She picked up the basket and slid it along to her elbow. 'I'm sorry, Arthur. I was just so disappointed when you didn't get here in time.'

'What was it?'

'Bronchitis. The old complaint. Been troubling him for years. The last cold spell finished him.'

They made their way back to the avenue and turned up the slope, walking towards the gate.

'Well,' she said after a silence, 'what did it feel like coming back to the place after all these years?'

'A bit queer...' He frowned. 'I couldn't see that it had

135

changed much – a few estates about – but it was sort of different somehow.'

'That'll be all the years away.'

'Aye, everything seems different when you've been away a time.'

She looked at him with a swift sideways and upwards glance. 'Everything?'

'Well, no,' he said, hesitating, 'perhaps not everything.'

She sighed audibly and his voice when next he spoke had sharpened slightly with irritation. 'We're all the same people, y'know, Annie. Did you think when you saw me of Henry and Cissie killing the fatted calf? I've been away and they've stayed here – but we're still the same people.'

'He wasn't the same.'

'Who?'

'Father... You'd never have believed the change in him. You couldn't credit what the woman did for him, not having witnessed it. But I saw it all. I watched it happen, month by month; day by day, even.'

'How did she change him?'

'She softened him, Arthur. Mellowed him. He was a different man when he'd been married to her a few years. All that hard sourness and bitterness seemed to drain steadily out of him. And he wanted to see you again. It was his dearest wish that he might make his peace with you before the end.'

'I was at sea,' he muttered. 'What could I do?'

'But you did come,' she said, 'as soon as you could.'

'Aye, as soon as I could.'

He did not tell her that it had taken him a week after the ship docked to make up his mind, but he felt somehow that she guessed the truth. Anyway, he would have been too late. He felt for and lit now the cigarette he had denied himself earlier and they walked on in silence to the gates.

'You'll be coming –' she began as she made to pass straight out into the street. But he took her arm and restrained her.

'Let's sit down for a minute,' he said. 'Let's talk for a while.'

She allowed him to lead her to a near-by bench where they sat down together, he leaning back, legs crossed, pulling at his cigarette, she sitting straight-backed, hands resting on the handle of the shopping-basket on her knee.

Now it seemed that neither of them had anything to say, and they sat in silence for some minutes until he shivered suddenly and pulled up the collar of his raincoat.

'Cold?'

'It is a bit chilly up here.'

'I thought it was quite warm,' she said. 'A nice spring day.'

'Spring!' he said with a scoffing laugh. 'English weather! Every time I come back from a trip I'm half-frozen.'

'You'll be used to used to hotter parts, I reckon?'

'I love the warmth and the sunshine,' he said. 'It can't be too hot for me. Some blokes I know can't stand South America, but I just lap it up. I reckon I'll end up there for good, or some place like it, before I've done.'

She was silent for a moment before she said, 'You've never thought of coming back, I suppose?'

'What,' he said, 'here? What is there here for me?'

'Same as there is anywhere else.'

'Ah, I'm all right as I am for a bit: going places, seeing things. Deck-hand. No responsibility; no trouble. Sign on for wherever suits me.'

137

'And then?'

'What?' he said.

'When you've been everywhere and seen everything. What then?'

'Well, like I said: South America, or somewhere else far off.'

'It's the same all over, Arthur,' she said. 'There's people and things, just as there is here.'

He threw the end of his cigarette across the path. 'I had all I wanted of this place a long time ago.'

'And you got out.'

'Yes, I got out. And not before time.'

She started to speak again, then stopped and turned her head.

'That's half-past eleven striking,' she said. 'I shall have to be off. It's half-day closing and there's one or two things I must get.'

They stood up and moved out together into the street.

There she said, 'Anyway, there's no need for you to trail round the shops with me, unless you want to. You can go and wait for me at the house. Lucy's out, but you can take my key.'

He shook his head, 'No, Annie. The visit's over. I've seen all I want to see now. I was too late for anything else.'

'But you've only just got here... You can't go now. Lucy'd be ever so pleased to see you.'

'Why barge in on her?' he said. 'She doesn't know me. Why bother her now?'

'And there's Henry and Cissie.'

'Ah, dear old Henry and Cissie. How are they these days, by the way?'

'Oh, doing well enough. Henry has his own plumbing business and Cissie's husband's manager of the Co-op grocery. Henry's thinking of standing for the council this time.'

138

'All nicely settled and going steady. All good sober industrious citizens. No, they've nothing for me, Annie. And I've nothing for them. They've no need ever to know I've been here at all if you don't tell 'em.'

'But, Arthur –'

'No,' he said, 'I mean it. I want you to promise me you won't tell 'em you've seen me. Let 'em think of me as they always have. Don't have 'em trying to reckon me up all over again.'

'Oh,' she said, 'but, Arthur –'

'Promise,' he said, and suddenly smiled. At her puzzled look, he said, 'I'm just thinking of a long time ago. Remember how Father used to make us go to bed early, and I used to slide down the coal-house roof so's I could get out to see that lass over Newlands way?'

'I remember. And I remember the last time you did it, that night in December, with a fall of snow on the ground.'

'And I lost control and shot clean over the edge into the yard and brought Father out to me. You stuck up for me, and Henry spilled the beans.' He looked reflectively past her shoulder. 'He leathered me black and blue, and I leathered Henry. That was the night I finally made up my mind to get out. I told nobody of my plans but you. You didn't give me away then, and you won't now, will you, Annie?'

She looked at him long and steadily. 'I'll never give you away, Arthur,' she said.

'Gentle Annie,' he said, taking her hand. 'Sweet little Annie... Why has no man ever married you?'

She coloured faintly. 'I'm all right. What about you?'

'Oh me... you know me. Like I said – no ties: no responsibility.'

'And now you're off again?'

'Now,' he said, 'this minute.'

He kissed her lightly on the cheek and released her hand. 'So long, Annie' he said. 'Take care of yourself.'

She did not move from the spot as he walked away from her. After a few yards he turned and waved, then turned away again. His steps suddenly became jaunty, and several more yards brought a shrill whistle to his lips. Why, he could not have said. Not to deceive the passers-by, for why should he want to deceive them? Perhaps to deceive himself, then? Certainly not to deceive her, for the one he had never been able to deceive was the one who stood now and watched him go.

The Search for Tommy Flynn

Sad story
– his pov

a war-shocked man
loses his mind & his money
to a tart

On a December evening just three weeks before Christmas after an uneasily mild day that had died in a darkening flush of violet twilight, Christie Wilcox came down into Cressley to look for his long-lost pal, Tommy Flynn.

His mates at the factory said Christie was only elevenpence ha'penny in the shilling, and had been ever since the war; but like the management, they tolerated him, because he was able-bodied and harmless, and for most of the time as near normal as hardly mattered. For most of the time – except on the occasions when this blinding urge came over him, this unswervable obsession to find Tommy Flynn, the pal he had not seen since the night their ship was blown from under them. And then he would leave the little house on Cressley Common where he lived with his widowed mother and go down into the town to search. Sometimes he would stop someone on the street and ask, 'Have you seen Tommy Flynn?' and the questioned would perhaps mutter something, or just pass by without a word, only a look, leaving Christie standing on the pavement edge, looking after them with helpless stupefied loneliness and dejection on his face and in the droop of his head and shoulders. But mostly he bothered no one, but simply scanned the features of people on the streets and opened the door of every pub he passed, searching the faces in the smoky taprooms and bars. Tommy Flynn had been a great one for pubs.

But he never found him. He never found him because They wouldn't help him. They all knew where Tommy Flynn was but They wouldn't tell Christie. They just looked at him with blank faces, or nodded and grinned and winked at one another, because They knew where Tommy Flynn was all the time, and They wouldn't tell.

Some of Them had tried to tell him that Tommy Flynn was dead; but Christie knew otherwise. He knew that Tommy was alive and waiting for him to find him. Tommy needed him. The last words he had ever said to him were, 'For Christ's sake get me out of this, Christie!' And Christie had not been able to help. Why, he could not remember. But now he could help. Now he could help Tommy, if only he could find him.

He had walked the mile and a half from his home, letting the lighted buses career past him down the long winding road; and on the edge of town he began to look inside the pubs he passed, sometimes startling the people there by the sudden intensity of his face, all cheekbones and jaw and dark burning eyes, as it appeared briefly in the doorway, then vanished again. And when, after more than two hours, he came to the centre of town, he was, as usual, no further in his search. He stood on a street corner and watched the faces of the people passing by. He even stood lost in contemplation of the suited dummies in the lighted window of a tailor's shop, as though he hoped that one of them might suddenly move and reveal itself as his lost pal. And all the while the yearning, the terrible yearning despair in him grew into an agony, and he muttered hopelessly, over and over again, 'Tommy, oh, Tommy, I can't find you, Tommy.'

He wandered along a line of people queuing outside a cinema for the last show, looking at every face, his own face burning so oddly that it provoked giggles from one of a pair of girls standing there; and a policeman standing a little way along looked his way, as though expecting that Christie might at any moment whip off his cap and break into an illegal song and dance.

They laughed. They laughed because he could not find Tommy Flynn. Everybody against him: no one to help.

Oh! If only he could find just one who would help him. He stopped and gazed at, without seeing, the 'stills' in the case on the wall by the cinema entrance, then turned away.

Some time later the dim glow of light from a doorway along an alley took his attention. It occurred to him that this was a pub he had never been in before. A new place to search. He went down the alley, pushed open the door, and stepped along a short corridor, past the door marked 'Ladies', and into the single low-ceilinged L-shaped room of the pub. It was quiet, with only a very few people drinking there. Two men stood drinking from pint glasses and talking quietly. The landlord had stepped out for a moment and there was no one behind the bar. One of the two men knew Christie and greeted him.

'Now then, Christie lad.'

And almost at once he saw that Christie was not himself.

'Have you seen Tommy Flynn?' Christie asked him.

'Can't say as I have, lad,' the man said, and his right

143

eyelid fluttered in a wink at his companion, who now turned and looked at Christie also.

'Tommy Flynn?' the second man said. 'Name sounds familiar.'

'You don't know him,' the first man said. 'He's a pal of Christie's. Isn't he, Christie?'

'A pal,' Christie said.

'Well, he hasn't been in here tonight. Has he, Walt?'

'That's right. We haven't seen him.'

'How long is it since you've seen him, Christie?'

'A long time,' Christie mumbled. 'A long time ago.'

'Well, I'll tell you what,' the man said: 'you go on home, and we'll keep an eye open for Tommy Flynn. And if we see him we'll tell him you were looking for him. How's that?'

'What about a drink afore you go?' the man called Walt said good-naturedly.

'He doesn't drink, Walt,' the first man said.

'Don't you smoke, either?' Walt asked.

Christie shook his head. He was beginning to feel confused and he looked from one to the other of them.

'But I'll bet you're a devil with the women.'

The first man laid a hand on his companion's arm. 'Easy, Walt.'

'Oh, I'm on'y kiddin',' Walt said. 'He doesn't mind, do you, lad? Take a bit o' kid, can't you, eh?'

But the film of incomprehension had come down over Christie's eyes and he just stood and looked at each of them in turn.

'I've got to go now,' he said in a moment.

'Aye, that's right, Christie lad. Off you go home; an' if we see Tommy Flynn we'll tell him. Won't we, Walt?'

'Course we will,' Walt said.

Christie had turned away from them before he

remembered about the money, and he wondered if he should tell them so that they could tell Tommy Flynn. Tommy had always been so short of money. He put his hand into his pocket and took out some of the notes. Then, at once, he changed his mind and went out without saying anything.

The two men had already turned back to their glasses and only one person in the bar saw the money in Christie's hand: a middle-aged tart with greying hair dyed a copper red, a thin, heavily powdered face and pendant ear-rings, sitting at a corner table with a tall West Indian, his lean handsome features the colour of milk chocolate, wearing a powder-blue felt hat with the brim turned up all round. As Christie went out she got up, saying something about powdering her nose, and left the bar.

Outside the alley Christie walked away from the pub, then stopped after a few paces, to stand indecisively on the cobbles. Always he came to this same point, the dead end, when there was no sign of Tommy Flynn, and nowhere else to look. He bowed his head and furrowed his brow in thought as his mind wrestled heavily with the problem.

Light sliced across the alley as the door of the pub opened, then banged shut again. The woman paused on the step, looking both ways, before stepping down and clicking across the cobbles to Christie.

He took no notice of her till she spoke at his side.

'Did you say you were looking for somebody?'

And then Christie's head jerked up and his eyes, level with the woman's, blazed.

'Tommy Flynn,' he said. 'I'm looking for Tommy Flynn. Have you seen Tommy Flynn?' he asked with breathless eagerness in his voice.

'What's he look like?' the woman asked, playing for time.

But Christie only mumbled something she did not catch and then, the light gone from his eyes, 'I'm looking for Tommy Flynn.'

A man entered the alley from the far end and walked along towards the pub. The woman took one step back into shadow. When the door of the pub had closed behind him the woman said: 'I know a Tommy Flynn.'

And Christie came alive again as though a current of power had been passed through him.

'You do? You know Tommy Flynn? Where is he? Where's Tommy Flynn?' His hand gripped her arm.

'I think I know where to find him,' the woman said. 'Only... you'd have to make it worth my trouble like. I mean, I've left my friend an' everythin'...' She stopped, realising that Christie was not taking in what she said. 'Money, dear,' she said, with a kind of coarse delicacy.

'Money? I've got money. Lots of money.' He thrust his hand into his pocket and dragged out a fistful of notes. 'Look – lots of money.'

Startled, the woman covered Christie's hand with her own and looked quickly right and left along the alley.

'Just keep it in your pocket, dear, for the time being.'

She put her arm through his and turned him towards the mouth of the alley.

'C'mon, then,' she said. 'Let's go find Tommy Flynn.'

Once across the lighted thoroughfare beyond the alley the woman led Christie into the gloom of back streets, hurrying him under the sheer dark walls of mills; and he followed with mute eagerness, sometimes doing more than follow as in his excited haste he pulled away so that he was leading, the woman occasionally having to break into a trot to keep pace with him.

'Not so fast, dear,' she said several times as Christie

146

outpaced her. She was breathless. 'Take it easy. We've plenty of time.'

And all the while she was thinking how to get the money away from Christie. He was simple, there was no doubt about that. But often simple people were stubborn and stupid and untrusting. She would have taken him into a pub on the pretext of waiting for this Tommy Flynn and got him to drink; only she did not want to be remembered afterwards as having been seen with him. So she led him on, her mind working, until they came to a bridge over the dark river. She pulled at his arm then and turned him onto a path leading down the river bank.

'This way, dear.'

To the right the river ran between the mills and warehouses of the town; and to the left the footpath led under the bridge and beyond, where the river slid over dam stakes and flowed on through open fields. In the darkness under the bridge the woman stopped and made a pretence of looking at a watch.

'It's early yet,' she said. 'Tommy Flynn won't be home yet. Let's wait here a while.'

She kept hold of Christie's arm as she stood with her back to the stonework of the bridge.

'What d'you want Tommy Flynn for?'

'He's my pal,' Christie said, stirring restlessly beside her.

'And haven't you seen him lately?'

'No... I can't find him. Nobody'll ever tell me where he is... We were on a ship together... an'...' His voice tailed off. Then he said with a groan. 'I've got to find him. I've got to.'

'We'll find him,' the woman said, 'in a little while.' And she looked at Christie in the darkness under the bridge.

For a moment then she stood away from him and fumbled with her clothes. 'Why don't you an' me have a nice time while we're waiting?' She took him and drew him to her, pressing his hand down between her warm thighs. 'You like a nice time, don't you?' she said into his ear.

'What about Tommy?' Christie said. 'Where is he?'

'I know where Tommy is,' the woman said, her free hand exploring Christie's pocket, where the money was.

'Why aren't we going to him, then?'

'Because he's not at home yet.' The woman kept patience in her voice. 'I'll tell you when it's time to go.'

The thought had already come to her that he might be dangerous, and she recalled newspaper reports, which she read avidly, of women like herself being found strangled or knifed in lonely places. But there was always an element of risk in a life such as hers, and Christie seemed to her harmless enough. There was, too, the feel of all that money in her fingers, and greed was stronger than any timidity that might have troubled her. So she played for time in the only way she knew how.

'Why don't you do something?' she said, moving her body against his. 'You know what to do, don't you? You like it, don't you?'

The feel of her thighs moving soft and warm against his fingers roused momentary excitement in Christie, causing him to giggle suddenly.

'I know what you want,' he said. 'You want me to –' and he whispered the obscenity in her ear.

'That's right,' the woman said. 'You like it, don't you? You've done it before, haven't you?'

'Me an' Tommy,' Christie said. 'We used to go with women. All over the world. All sorts of women.'

'That's right. You and Tommy.'

148

'Tommy,' Christie said, and, his excitement with the woman broken, tore his hand free. 'Tommy,' he said again, and looked away along the path.

He stepped away from her and her hand, pulling free of his pocket, retained its hold on the notes. She hastily adjusted her clothes as he moved away along the path.

'Wait a minute,' she said. 'It's early yet. It's no good going yet.'

'I'm going now,' Christie said, walking away. 'I'm going to find Tommy.'

Stepping out of the shadow of the bridge into moonlight, he stopped and threw up his arms, uttering a cry. Beside him now, the woman said, 'What's wrong?'

'Tommy,' Christie said, trembling violently. 'Look, look, look.'

And following the wild fling of his arm the woman saw something dark bobbing in the greasy water by the dam stakes.

'Tommy!' Christie shouted, and the woman said, 'Quiet, quiet,' and looked anxiously all about her.

'It's Tommy,' Christie said, and the next instant he was free of her and bounding down the rough grass bank of the water's edge.

'Come back,' the woman said. 'Don't be a fool. Come back.'

'I'm coming, Tommy,' Christie bawled.

For a few seconds the woman hesitated there on the bank then she turned and fled along the path, away from the bridge, stuffing banknotes into her bag as she went. Behind her she heard the deep splash as Christie plunged into the river, and she quickened her pace to a stumbling run.

Standing in the middle of the room, his shoulders

hunched, Christie said, 'I found him, Mam. I found Tommy Flynn, an' he's drowned, all wet an' drowned. I couldn't get to him...'

There was something of resignation in his mother's dismay. She looked past him to the police sergeant who had brought him home.

'Where...?' she said, in a voice that was little more than a movement of the lips.

'The river.'

'He's dead,' Christie said. 'All wet an' drowned.'

'Well then, Christie lad, don't take on so. He's happy, I'm sure he is.'

But as she spoke Christie began to cry helplessly, collapsing against her. She held him for the second of time it took the sergeant to spring across the room and get his hands under Christie's armpits.

'We'd best get him upstairs,' the mother said, and the sergeant nodded. He swung Christie up like a child into his arms, and Christie wept against his chest as he was carried up the stairs to his bedroom.

The sergeant laid Christie on the bed and stood aside in silence while the widow swiftly stripped her son and set to work on his cold body with a rough towel. There was admiration in the sergeant's eyes by the time the woman had pulled the sheets over Christie and tucked him firmly in. She struck a match then and lit a night-light standing in a saucer of water on the chest of drawers. Christie was weeping softly now.

'He doesn't like the dark,' she explained as she picked up the wet clothes and ushered the sergeant out of the room. 'I think he'll go to sleep now.'

In the living-room once more, the sergeant remembered to take off his helmet, and he mopped his brow at the same time.

'Wet through,' the woman said, feeling her son's clothes. 'Absolutely sodden. Whatever happened?'

'He must have been in the river,' the sergeant said. 'My constable said he'd run up to him, dripping wet, and shouting that this Tommy Flynn was in the water; but when Johnson went with him all he could see was a dead dog. Seems that was what your son had taken for his Tommy Flynn.'

The woman bowed her head and put her hand to her face.

'Anyway, the constable didn't take much more notice of it. He said he'd often seen your son about the town, and he knew...' The sergeant stopped and grimaced.

'He knew that Christie wasn't quite right in the head.' the widow said.

'That's about it, Missis.' The sergeant shifted his weight from one foot to the other; then, as though he had only just thought of it, he took out his notebook.

'I know it's upsetting,' he said, 'but I shall have to put in a report. I wondered if you'd give me a bit of information on your son...'

'What do you want to know?'

'Well, where this Tommy Flynn comes into it; and what makes your boy go off looking for him.'

'During the war, it was, when he met him,' the widow said, raising her head and looking somewhere past the sergeant. 'He was in the Merchant Navy. He was all right till then: as normal as anybody. This Tommy Flynn was his special pal. He used to write home about him. He hardly mentioned anything else. His letters were full of him. It was all Tommy Flynn had said this, or done that. And what they were going to do after the war. They were going to start a window-cleaning business. Tommy Flynn said there'd be a shortage of window cleaners, and all they needed was a couple of ladders and a cart and they could make money hand over fist. I don't know whether there was anything in it or not... Anyway, Christie had it all planned for Tommy Flynn to come and live here. He was an orphan. I didn't mind: he seemed a nice enough lad, and he looked after Christie, showing him the ropes...'

'You never met him?' the sergeant asked.

The widow shook her head. 'I never saw him, but Christie thought the world of him. He could hardly remember his father, y'know, and this Tommy was a bit older than him. He sort of took him in hand.

'Then towards the end of the war their ship was hit by one o' them Japanese suicide planes and got on fire. Christie was on a raft by himself for ages and ages. He was near out of his mind by the time they found him, and all he could talk about was Tommy Flynn. They reckoned Tommy must have gone down with the ship, but Christie wouldn't have that. He raved at them and called them liars.'

'But they'd treat him?'

'Oh aye, they treated him. They said he'd never be quite the same again; but of course you can't hardly tell unless he's in one of his do's, and he didn't start with them till he'd been home a while.'

'How often does he have these... er – attacks?' the sergeant asked.

'Oh, not often. He's all right for months on end. Anybody 'ud just take him as being a bit slow, y'know. An' he was such a bright lad...'

'Why don't you try and get some more advice?' the sergeant suggested. 'Y'know he might do himself some damage one of these times.'

'I did ask the doctor,' the widow said; 'and I mentioned

it to Christie – when he was his usual self, I mean. He begged and prayed of me not to let them take him away. He broke down and cried. He said he'd die if they shut him up anywhere... It wouldn't be so bad, y'see, if he was one way or the other; then I'd know what to do...'

She swallowed and her lips quivered, then stilled again as she compressed them before looking straight it the sergeant.

'You'll look out for him if you see him about, Sergeant, won't you?' she said.

'I'll look out for him,' he assured her, frowning a little. 'But I'd get some more treatment for him, if I were you, Missis.'

'I'll see,' she said. 'I'll have to think about it again now.'

The sergeant picked up his helmet.

'It'll be all right about tonight?' she asked. 'There'll be no trouble?'

'I shouldn't think so. I shall have to report it, o' course; but it'll be all right. He hasn't broken the law.'

Not yet, he thought, and put his hand into his tunic pocket. 'By the way, you'd better have this. It came out of his pocket.' He put the wet notes on the table. 'Four quid.'

He caught the startled look fleetingly in her eyes before she hid it.

'Do you let him have as much money as he likes?' he asked, watching him.

'Well, not as a rule... I like him to have a bit in his pocket, though, and then he's all right... If anything happens I mean.'

The sergeant nodded, his eyes remaining on her face a moment longer before he reached for the latch.

'Well. I'll get along.'

The widow seemed to stir from thought. 'Yes, yes... all right. And thanks for taking so much trouble.'

153

'Just doing me job, Missis.' The sergeant bade her good night as he opened the door and stepped out onto the pavement.

When the door had closed behind him the widow looked at the money on the table. She picked up the notes and fingered them, the thoughts tumbling over in her mind, before going to the dresser and taking her purse from the drawer. She examined its contents and then put it away, closing the drawer, and went quietly upstairs to her room.

She took a chair and stood on it to reach into the cupboard over the built-in wardrobe for the shoe-box in which she kept all her and Christie's savings. She knew almost at once by its lightness that it was empty, but she removed the lid just the same. Her heart hammered and she swayed on the chair. Nearly a hundred pounds had been in the box, and it was gone. All the money they had in the world.

She put the box back in the cupboard and stepped down, replacing the chair by the bed. She put her hand to her brow and thought furiously, pointlessly. Christie was quiet in his room. She went out and stood for a few moments outside his door. Then she went downstairs and felt in every pocket of the wet clothing on the hearth. Nothing. She sank into a chair and put her head in her hands and began to sob silently.

When Christie woke next morning she was at his bedside.

'What did you do with the money you took out of the box, Christie?' she said. 'Where is it?'

'He's drowned,' Christie said. 'Tommy's drowned. All wet and dead.'

She could get no other response from him and in a little while she went away. He showed no sign of wanting to get up and at intervals during the day she returned, hoping he had recovered from the shock of last evening, and asked him, speaking slowly and carefully, as to a child, enunciating the words with urgent clarity, 'The money, Christie, remember? What did you do with the money?'

But he stared at the ceiling with dark haunted eyes and told her nothing.

He never told her anything again. The search for Tommy Flynn was ended; and shortly after she let them come and take him away.

The Little Palace

*told from a woman's viewpoint
a young couple leave their
first home – her affection for
it – the man's thoughtless
defacement.*

We both knew at once when the removal van arrived, at ten o'clock, on the Saturday morning because there were no curtains at the windows and it was so big that it shut out almost all the light as it stopped on the damp cobbles outside the house. I said, 'Here they are, Tom,' and got up from my knees beside the tea-chest into which I'd been carefully packing the most fragile of our crockery.

Tom looked down from where, standing on a chair, he was dismantling the cupboards over the sink: the cupboards he had intended leaving behind had the new tenants not turned out to be the sort of people they were. The first thing anyone noticed about Tom, I suppose, was his size. He wore his fair hair cut short and he had blue eyes in a guileless, pug-nosed face. The numerous mishaps, small, thank God, sustained in his work as a coal miner were recorded in the faint blue scars on the backs of his hands: hands that were big and calloused and rough to the touch: hands that could be so unbelievably gentle and tender when touching me.

'I reckon everything else is ready, Janie,' he said now. 'I'll be done here in a jiffy.'

I often wondered when people glanced at us when we were out together what they made of Tom and me. Tom so big and so obviously a man of toil and sweat, and me so petite, with looks that Tom thought so pretty and lady-like and I'd always considered insipid; Tom with his voice heavy with the West Riding, and mine from which my mother and the elocution teacher she had sent me to had coaxed all trace of locality in my childhood. I'd heard one of Tom's sisters refer to me as 'The Duchess' when I wasn't supposed to hear, but I'd learned to hold my own with them, and Tom, when I told him about it, said it was a compliment, and if I wasn't proud of it, he was.

I opened the door as one of the men knocked.

'Manage it in one trip easy,' Tom said as the two men stepped over the threshold and looked around with experienced eyes. There wasn't a lot. We had been married only a year, and the house was very small: one room up, one down.

As the men started to carry out the furniture I slipped on a coat and went outside; partly to be out of their way, and partly to watch that they did not mishandle anything as they packed it into the gaping interior of the van. And as I stood out there on the pavement I felt a hidden audience watching from the cover of lace curtains. I knew I had disappointed and antagonised some of our neighbours by not encouraging them to run in and out of my house as they did one another's; and now the more inquisitive would be snatching a last look at what they had merely glimpsed as it came into the house a year ago. Mrs Wilde from the next house below came out onto the step. Her face was unwashed; her hair uncombed. She stood with her arms folded across her grubby pinafore, her bare toes poking out of worn felt slippers. When I thought about it I could not remember ever having seen her in a pair of shoes.

'Well, off you go to leave us, Mrs Green,' she said amiably.

'Yes,' I said, 'off we go, Mrs Wilde.' She had been into the house several times, and there was little strange for her to see.

'Don't seem hardly two minutes sin' ye got here,' she said, relaxing into her favourite stance against the door jamb.

'No, time flies.'

'It does that,' she said. 'It does that! You'll know a bit more about that when you get to my age... Aye. Thirty year I've lived in Bridge Street. Sort o' settled down, y'know. Nivver wanted to go nowhere else, somehow. Brought six kids up in this house an' all, little as it is. Course, young fowk nowadays wants summat better. Got bigger ideas na we hid in our young days... Bought your own place over t'new part o' town, so I hear?'

'Yes, that's right, Mrs Wilde. A semi-detached on Laburnum Rise.'

She nodded. 'Aye, aye. I reckon that'll be more your quarter like than over here. I mean, this is nowt new to yer husband. I've known his fam'ly for years, an' they've allus been collier-fowk. But I knew straightaway 'at you were used to summat better. You can tell fowk 'at's had good bringins up. Leastways, I allus can.'

I made no reply to this. I didn't know what to say. For what Mrs Wilde said was true: I hadn't been used to this kind of neighbourhood until my marriage; but I'd become accustomed by now to at least one small part of it – the house Tom and I called home. The first home we had ever had.

'You certainly made t'best on it, though,' Mrs Wilde was saying. 'I wouldn't ha' recognised t'place if I hadn't lived right next-door. A proper little palace you made on it – a proper little palace. That's just what I said 'to my husband when I first saw inside. Such a shame an' all 'at you've to leave it in one way: after all t'work you put into it. All them lovely decorations. Must break your heart to leave it all to some'dy else.' She paused and cocked an inquisitive eye at me. 'Course, anybody fair like 'ud be only too willin' to make it right with you I mean, it's only proper an' decent, in't it?'

I did not respond to her probing, but merely remarked, 'Yes, you can usually come to some agreement.' I did not feel inclined to summon up her rather dubious sympathy by telling her that the new tenants, a cold-faced elderly couple, had refused even to consider the question of compensation. And of course there was nothing to be done about it: we had no legal claim for improvements done to someone else's property. It had made Tom very angry and he had almost quarrelled with the elderly man.

'Perhaps they aren't very well off,' I'd said afterwards. 'Or why should they want a poky little place like this at their age?'

'Oh, you're too soft by half, Janie,' Tom had said. 'You'd let anybody put on you... No, it's meanness, that's what it is. I could see it in the way their faces sort o' closed up the minute I mentioned the valuation. You can bet your life they're not short o' brass. They're not sort to spend any ''less they're forced to.' He had stopped speaking then to consider the situation. 'Well, we can take the cupboards an' shelves I put up, I suppose. A bit o' timber allus comes in handy. But we can't take the wallpaper an' paint. They'll have the benefit of that, damn their stingy souls!'

'Yes, it's only right an' proper,' Mrs Wilde said.

We had arranged that I should go with the van and direct the unloading of the furniture, then come back for Tom, who had one or two last jobs to do, when we would go on for lunch with his family. When the loading was finished, then, I gave the driver the address of our new house and climbed up into the cab, where they made room for me between them. It was only a ten-minute drive across town, but it was to me like a journey into another world: my own world of neat houses along tree-lined backwaters and the Sunday-afternoon quiet of sheltered gardens. It was the sort of district that people in books and plays scoffed at as dull and suburban. But people like that, I thought, had never lived in a place like Bridge Street. But though it was my own world, and the thought of living there again was very pleasant, there was yet no place in it I could call home: not as I regarded the Little Palace (as we called the house, after Mrs Wilde) as home. I thought as the men begin to unload at the end of the short drive, of how that once strange and dirty place had become almost like a part of me, so that ever since waking that morning, and before, there had been in me a vague melancholy at the prospect of leaving it. I had chided myself for my foolish fancies, but it was almost as though I felt that the house was a part of our luck, and that in leaving it we might also leave something of our happiness within its walls.

For we had been happy there – gloriously happy. And not much more than a year ago I had not even seen the house. A little over two years ago there had been nothing – not even Tom. And what was there in life now without him? Tom, who had appeared and shattered the cocoon which my parents' genteel, middle-class way of life had spun about me and taught me to live as I never had before. It seemed to me that I had hardly been alive at all until that strange, disturbing afternoon when I first noticed him from the office window as, tired and dirty, he crossed the yard from the pit-hill at the end of the shift...

I tipped the two men when they had finished, and then walked through the house from room to room, seeing how lost our furniture looked in it, and noting with my woman's eye all the things that needed to be done. And then I left the house and walked to the bus stop at the end of the avenue. It was well past noon now, and the sky, overcast all morning, had cleared and showed great patches of blue behind the big pillows of cloud. As we ran into town by a stream which flowed into the river I looked out of the bus at the black water and saw the breeze-ruffled surface shimmer, as though someone had thrown handfuls of sunlight onto it from behind the willows which, just there, seemed to me to crouch like big green shaggy dogs by the water's edge. But despite the sunlight and the blue sky there was a sneaking chill in the air and I felt in its touch the end of the glorious but all-too-short summer.

The sun was shining, the sky blue, the day I had met Tom. Two days after my first noticing him he came into the big new building, with its many area control offices, to see the manager and blundered into the wrong office, and so into my life. It was like nothing I had ever known before, that feeling which possessed me from then on; it flushed my cheeks at the thought of him, brought tremors to my hands and knees, and filled me with a breathless, delightful excitement. And from that first brief contact, when I came into the corridor to show him the door he wanted, grew Tom's awareness of me. His eyes began to seek me out as he crossed the yard at the end of the day shift, and soon we were openly exchanging smiles. Even though we did not speak to each other again for some time a kind of intimacy seemed to grow between us through the medium of those daily smiles; so that one day when I had occasion to leave the office early, not long after the change of shifts, it seemed very natural when he came roaring up the yard behind me on his motor cycle that he should offer me a lift into town, and that I should at once accept. That was the day he asked me, with almost painful diffidence, to go out with him one evening, and the day I became hopelessly lost. Three months later, to his open astonishment, I accepted his halting proposal of marriage.

And all this was what the Little Palace had come to mean to me. More, much more, than cleanliness and shining paint had emerged from the squalor of flaking plaster and peeling wallpaper that had been the house when first we took it. A marriage had been made there, had come through its first vital year; a marriage that had received little but discouragement because of the differences between Tom and me. I was too good for him, they had said. I was throwing myself away on a boy from the back streets whose rough-shod nature and way of living would sooner or later break my heart. But they had been wrong; only the walls of the Little Palace knew how wrong. Those walls had held our year of hope and happiness, our little failures, and, above all, our success. It was because of this that I knew I should remember it for the rest of my life.

I alighted from the bus in the station into a swarm of shoppers and home-going workers and decided it would be quicker to walk the rest of the way. I was soon out of the teeming shopping centre and plunging deep into the back streets on the old side of town: the district in which Tom had lived all his life, and which I had not been in more than twice before meeting him. I walked along the cobbled river of Gilderdale Road, with its noisome tributaries, each with its twin banks of terraced houses, ceasing abruptly by the blackened upright sleepers of the railway fence, and, turning the corner by the little newsagent's, came into Bridge Street. A year of it had not changed my sense of being alien and conspicuous and now, walking along its uneven pavement for what, for all I knew, might be one of the last times in my life, I felt even more acutely self-conscious than usual – as though in every house along the way the occupants had put aside what they were doing to watch me pass – and I was glad when I reached the cover of the entry which broke the terrace and gave onto the communal backyard behind the houses. As I came through, my heels echoing on the brick paving, I could hear Tom whistling inside the house. He was happy today. He had never reconciled himself to my living here. It had been I who insisted on our taking the house when Tom's mother heard of it, rather than wait in the hope of something better turning up. We could not afford to buy at that time. My father's offer of help would have solved the problem, but only at the expense of Tom's pride; and I had seen the Little Palace as a challenge to me, to be faced boldly, without fear. We had won through, and now it made Tom happy to be able, after only a year, to take me out of it and across the town.

Absorbed in these thoughts, I had walked right into the living-room before I saw what awaited me there. And then I stood and gaped in staggered disbelief. The room was as though emblazoned with warnings of a terrible plague; for on each of the walls, stretching diagonally from ceiling to floor across the pale blue wallpaper, and on each of the doors, Tom had painted a huge scarlet cross. And now, brush in hand, he spoke to me over his shoulder as he heard me come in.

'Janie? Little surprise for you. An' a damn big 'un for them two stingy old codgers when they turn up again.'

I turned without answering and ran out of the room and up the uncarpeted stairs into the bedroom. He had done that room first. I came slowly down again. My heart hurt as though a great hand was kneading it brutally, and I couldn't speak.

'Thought of it yesterday,' Tom said. He was putting on his jacket now and he wore a grin which slowly faded as he saw the expression on my face. 'Well, I mean, damn it, we couldn't let 'em get away with it altogether, could we?'

I shook my head. 'No, Tom.'

'Damn it,' Tom said again, 'it serves 'em right for bein' so flamin' mean!'

He wrapped the paint-brush in a piece of rag and put it in his pocket. 'They can have the paint.' He looked at me. 'C'mon, then, let's be off. Take your last look at this place. You won't be seein' it any more.'

We went out, he closing and locking the door behind us, and walked away together. It was about half-way down the street, that, to Tom's confusion and distress, I began to cry.

'What's up, Janie?' He stopped and peered down at me. 'What's wrong, love?'

But I could only shake my head in reply. It was going to be all right. I just knew it was. But I couldn't help but cry.

The Years Between

A man returns from Australia to his first lost love

At fifty-three, when nostalgia could be borne no longer, Morgan Lightly turned his back on the sheep-farming land of his adoption and returned to Cressley, sick for the sight of his native county, which he had not seen for thirty years, and of the woman who had jilted him all that long time ago. With no more announcement than a brief letter to his brother Thomas, his only surviving relative, with whom he had corresponded spasmodically over the years, he came back.

He came in winter and for several days he curbed the impatience that would have hid him rush off at once to find her whom he had loved and lost, and wandered the dark town and the countryside, drinking in the sight and sound and smell of all that which, though changed, still held the savour of his youth. And then, when nearly a week had passed, he decided that if he were not to allow the prosaic reporting of the weekly Argus to rob his reappearance of its drama it was time for him to appease his other yearning.

Driving up out of the town he felt as nervous as a boy on his first date and on the crest of the hill he stopped the hired Ford and relit his dead pipe. He sat there for a little while, with the window down, enjoying the tobacco in the keen air. Before him the road fell into the narrow valley of the stream, then twisted upwards to the village which, not much more than a double row of stone-built cottages in his youth, now carried a pale fringe of new corporation houses and several architect-designed bungalows and villas sited in such a way that, through a deep cleft in the hillside, they commanded a view of the town. Above the village was the winter-brown sweep of the moors and beyond, in the west, pale sunlight touched the thin snow on the Pennine tops.

Morgan got out of the car and walked across the road to look back the way he had come, at the town. His town. How often had memory conjured it up thus when he was thousands of miles away! There were changes visible – the twin cooling towers of the power station by the river were strange to him – but the hard core of it was the same. And it satisfied him to note that most of the changes were for the better. 'Muck and brass', they had said in his youth; 'they go together'. But not everyone accepted that now. Light and space and clean untrammelled lines were what they went in for nowadays. The new estates, covering the playing fields of his youth on the fringes of the town, with their wide streets and well-spaced houses; and the lawns and gardens in the public squares and streets that had known no colours but grey and soot-black. The smoke was still there, fuming from a thousand chimneys, but when you planted grass it came up fresh and green every spring. He liked that. It was good. It was good too to see well-dressed people thronging the streets, and the market and to notice the

166

profusion of goods behind the plate-glass windows of the new shops: for he had left the town at a time when men hung about on street corners, their self-respect as worn and shabby as their clothing, idle, eating their hearts out for want of work to keep them occupied and feed and clothe their families decently.

He returned to the car, the feeling of nervousness and apprehension returning to him as he reached the floor of the valley and changed gear for the climb into the village. He turned the green Consul into the steep main street where the windows of the parallel terraces of cottages winked and glinted at other across the narrow cobbles, and he noticed lace curtains flutter in some of them as the car moved along, taking up almost the entire width of the roadway and darkening the downstairs room of each house in turn. An elderly woman, standing in a doorway with a shawl over her shoulders, stooped and stared with frank curiosity into the car. He stopped and lowered the window.

'I wonder if you can tell me where Mrs Taplow lives – Mrs Sarah Taplow.'

The woman directed him farther up the hill, still gazing intently at him as he thanked her and moved on. He had a feeling of knowing the woman and he wondered if she had recognised him. Down in Cressley he could walk about largely unknown but here in the village some of the older people were sure to recall him – and the details of long ago. And standing on the pavement outside Sarah Taplow's house he hoped that no one had stolen his thunder and deprived him of the pleasure of surprising her as he had looked forward to doing. But when she opened the door to his knock and faced him, gaping at him with all the astonishment he could have wished for in her blue eyes, he could only shuffle his feet like a bashful boy and say sheepishly, 'Well, Sarah?'

Without speaking she ran her eyes over him and he felt them take note of every detail of his appearance: his tanned cheeks, his hair – greying fast now and cropped shorter than when he was young – and the good thick tweeds on his heavy, solid frame. And when at last it seemed there could be no doubt left in her mind, her eyes returned to and rested on his face and she said, 'It is you, then, Morgan Lightly?'

Morgan chuckled, but a little uneasily, 'It is indeed, Sarah. I didn't think I'd startle you quite as much as that; but you'd not be expecting me to pop up at your door after all this time, eh?'

'I never thought I'd see you again,' she said. She took a deep breath as if to take control of her startled self, and turned to go into the house. 'You'd better come on inside,' she said. 'No need to fill the neighbours their mouths.'

'You've given me a turn,' she went on as they entered the living-room through the in-door. 'I never thought to see you again,' she said once more. She turned and faced him, standing by the square table which was laid for a solitary dinner, and her eyes, still disbelieving, roved ceaselessly over his face.

'You've come back, then,' she said. 'After all this time.' The words were spoken half-aloud and seemed more of a statement to herself than a question addressed to him.

'Thirty years, Sarah,' Morgan said. 'It's been a long time.'

She nodded and echoed him softly. 'A long time.'

He noted the changes of that time in her, but saw with approval her smooth, clear complexion, the soft, still-dark hair, the full mature curve of her bosom, and

168

the proud straight line of her back. He knew her: she was Sarah. He felt warmth and hope move in him, as though only now had he reached the end of his journey, and for a moment he forgot his earlier doubt and uncertainty.

She stirred, seeming to come to, and motioned him to one of the armchairs by the fireside. 'Well, sit you down, Morgan. I was just getting my dinner onto the table. You'll join me in a bite, I suppose?'

In this swift transition from astonishment to what seemed like a calm acceptance of his presence it seemed to Morgan that the years fell away almost as though they had never been, and he was relieved. The reopening of their acquaintanceship had been easier than he had expected.

'Don't put yourself out for me, Sarah,' he said. 'I can get lunch at my hotel.'

But it was a token protest, for it had been comparison of hotel meals with his memory of Sarah's cooking that inspired him in his choice of this rather odd hour for visiting her.

'It's no trouble,' she assured him. 'It's all ready.'

She went off into the kitchen and Morgan looked round the little room: at the well-worn but neatly kept furnishings and the open treadle sewing machine against one wall, with a half-finished frock over a chair beside it. They told their own story. His eyes fell on two photographs in stained wood frames on the sideboard and he left his chair to look more closely at them. One of them, a portrait of a thin-faced balding man, he recognised as being of Sarah's dead husband. And the other, a young army officer, remarkably like Sarah, could only be her son. He turned to her, the photograph in his hand, as she came back into the room with cutlery for him.

'Is this your boy, Sarah?'

There seemed to be something of reserve, a barrier, in her glance, then it was lost in pride as she looked it the photograph.

'Aye, that's my boy, John. He's in Malaya with the Army.'

'He's a fine-looking young chap, Sarah. How old is he?'

Again that unfathomable flash of something in her eyes. 'Going on thirty. He's a doctor, y'know. He wanted to be a doctor and he wanted to travel, so he joined the Army and got a commission.'

'A doctor, eh?' Morgan replaced the picture, impressed. 'You must be very proud of him.'

'Aye, he's a grand lad and a good son. He wanted to resign his commission when Mark died but I wouldn't let him.' She shot him an inquisitive look. 'Have you no children, then?'

Morgan shook his head. 'No, I've none.'

'But you did marry, I expect?'

'Aye, when I'd got settled a bit, I married.'

He returned to his seat in the armchair and looked into the fire. Strange, but even after all this time he did not find it easy to look at her and speak of marriage.

'She was a fine lass, Mary was,' he said at length. 'But not one of the strongest, you know. The hard times seemed to take all the strength she had and she didn't live to enjoy many of the better years.' He looked up at her now. 'And you lost your man, Sarah.'

She looked away and he sensed in her a similar discomfort to his own. 'I've been a widow this past five years,' she said briefly, then left him to return to the kitchen, reappearing in a few moments with two plates of steaming food.

'Here it is, then. There isn't a lot because you caught me unawares. Just as well I had the stew as well. It'll stretch it a bit further.'

170

'A mite o' your cooking was always worth a deal of anybody else's, Sarah,' Morgan said as he took a seat at the table. A faint flush coloured Sarah's cheeks and he looked down at his plate.

They ate in comparative silence. There seemed so much to say and at the same time so much to be wary of speaking of. At length Morgan laid down his knife and fork and sat back. Sarah had already finished for she had given him by far the bigger portion of the pudding and stew. Now she watched him and smiled faintly.

'You haven't lost your fondness for Yorkshire pudding, I see,' she said dryly. 'Nor all your Yorkshire talk, for that matter.'

'Do you know how long it is since I tasted a pudding like that?' he asked her. 'It's half a lifetime, Sarah. I'm still a Yorkshireman, y'know, even if I have been away all that time. I always had an idea I'd come back one day.'

'It seems like no time at all, seeing you sitting there,' said Sarah, watching him as he felt for pipe and tobacco. 'Though I'm sure I never expected to see you again.'

He glanced at her as he fiddled with his pipe, trying vainly to read her thoughts. He became aware that no matter how quickly now the time might seem to both of them to have passed there still was thirty years of unshared experience between them; and those years could not be bridged by the sharing of a meal and a few scraps of conversation.

He felt suddenly slightly ill-at-ease and he pretended to sigh, laying one hand flat on the front of his waistcoat in what, considering the amount of food they had shared, was an exaggerated gesture of repletion.

'It was worth coming home just to taste that meal,' he said. 'You were always the best cook for miles around, even as a lass.'

171

Her expression darkened without warning. 'And as I remember you always had the smoothest tongue.'

He pressed tobacco into his pipe, frowning, dismayed at this sudden antagonism. Surely, after all this time, she could forget, if he could?

She brought in the pot and poured tea. 'How long have you come for?'

'For good, Sarah.' He put a match to his pipe. 'I've sold up and come home to stay. Australia's a fine country, but this is my home. I want to settle where I can see the hills and feel the wind and the rain come down off the moors.'

'You didn't talk like that thirty years ago,' she reminded him, and he shook his head.

'No, but times change, and a man changes in some ways.' He looked into her face. 'In some ways he never changes though.'

She did not hold his look but sipped tea from her cup, looking past him through the lace-curtained window into the narrow street. He wished once again for the power to read her mind.

'So you must have made that fortune you were always talking about?' she said abruptly and Morgan smiled at her bluntness.

'Hardly that, lass,' he said. 'But enough to live on quietly for the rest of me days.'

They talked on in a desultory manner for another hour, until Morgan became aware that she could not work properly with him there. He left her then, promising to call again soon, and he went away still uneasily aware of the undercurrent of antagonism which had showed itself in that one remark of Sarah's. He visited her several times in the next few weeks and took her for drives in the country and once to dinner and a theatre in repayment for her hospitality. But always he was conscious of the barrier of reserve through which he could not seem to break.

At last he could stand it no longer. He was sure now of what he wanted. He had known it before starting for home and it had needed only the sight of her to confirm it. She was still the same lass he had courted all those years ago, and he was still the same chap in his feelings for her. This thrusting and parrying which continued through their every meeting was getting them nowhere. If memories of thirty years ago still rankled they must be brought out into the open and examined and given the importance due to them and no more. And he knew the way to bring that about.

Yet when he came to broach the subject he did not find it easy. After all, he thought, she had preferred someone else before, and why should she feel differently now?

Sitting by her fireside, he made a great show of cleaning his pipe, screwing himself all the while to the point where he could say what he wanted to say. Abruptly, but with a studied casualness, he said, 'I've bought Greystone Cottage, Sarah. You remember the place. We used to fancy it in the old days when old Phillips lived there. Well his son's been occupying it apparently and now he's dead – he wasn't married – and the place was put up for auction. I bought it yesterday... gave 'em their price...'

He waited for her to say something now that the first direct reference to their past relationship had been made. But she looked into the fire as though she had not heard him and made no reply.

'It's in pretty bad shape,' he went on. 'It'll want a bit of brass spending on it to make it comfortable. I had a good look around. I fancy extending it a bit besides

modernising. I reckon I'd as soon live there as anywhere…
I can't stop in a hotel for the rest of my life…'

She had resumed her hand-sewing and she went
on with her work, not looking at him and not speaking.
He was suddenly seized with the idea that she knew
exactly what he was leading to and was only waiting
for him to get to the point. But what would her reaction
be? He glanced at her, uncertainly. Should he, so
quickly? Perhaps he should wait until she had grown
more used to having him about again? But time was
slipping by. Neither of them was young and each of
them was avoiding talking about the important things
that concerned them both.

'Of course,' he said carefully, 'I shall need somebody
to look after it for me… keep it tidy and cook…' He
stopped for a moment, then went doggedly on. 'I know
it'll seem a bit sudden-like after all this time, Sarah, but
you know there's nobody I –'

He stopped again, alarmed this time, as Sarah stiffened
in her chair, then stood up her eyes flashing and all
the smouldering antagonism he had felt flaring openly.

'So it's housekeeping you're offering me after all
these years, Morgan Lightly. Well if that's what's in your
mind I'll tell you now that I need neither you nor your
money. I wonder how you can find the face to come here
as you do and expect me to fall in with your plans. I
managed very well without you thirty years ago, and I
can do the same now!'

'But, Sarah,' Morgan said, getting to his feet. 'You
don't understand –'

'I understand well enough,' she said in a low, furious
voice; 'and I want no part of it.' She turned her back on
him and picked up the blouse she was sewing. 'Now if
you don't mind, I've got work to do.'

174

Morgan stood there for a moment, frowning helplessly. He could not make her out at all; and when she took no further notice of his presence he said good-bye and left.

Driving back to town he cursed himself for being a hasty fool and shook his head in wonder at the ways of women.

'I made a mess of it, Thomas,' he confided later, when sitting in the living-room over his brother's grocery shop in one of Cressley's dingy back streets. 'I should have bided my time. You can't step over thirty years as easy as all that.' He pulled thoughtfully at his pipe. 'But I can't understand why she flared up like that. I think she nearly hated me just then; as though I'd done her a wrong.'

'You touched her conscience, turning up like you did,' Thomas said. 'And I'm surprised at you, I must say, running to her of all people as soon as you get home. After what she did to you... Running off and marrying that chap the minute your back was turned, and you with it all fixed up for her to join you as soon as you got settled down a bit.'

Morgan sighed. 'Aye, but she was a grand lass, Thomas – and still is! A fine, proud woman. That's what's wrong with her – pride. If I could get round that I might do it yet. A fine woman... Just the comfort for a chap like me in the twilight of his days.'

'Twilight of your days!' Thomas scoffed. 'You want to go talking like that it your age! How old are you – fifty-two-three? And a fine upstanding chap with a bit of brass behind you. You shouldn't go short of comfort. There'll be plenty ready to see 'at you're comfortable. And a fat lot o' comfort she was to you. I never knew her well but I heard tell 'at you never knew which way she'd jump next.'

175

Morgan shook his head and smiled reflectively. 'I thought I knew, Thomas,' he said. 'I thought I knew, lad.'

Christmas came, and then the new year, bringing with it weeks of dry, biting winds; until February arrived, ferocious with driving snow and ice: a month when it did not rise above freezing point for days together. And at last, when it seemed that the long grim winter was without end, the earth softened to the coming of spring. Catkins flickered like green light in the dark winter woods and crocuses appeared, white and mauve and yellow, in the public gardens of the town.

Morgan filled his days with the leisurely pleasures of looking up old friends and renewing old acquaintanceships, and with his plans for making Greystone Cottage his home. His solitary home, it seemed now. For in all this time he had not seen Sarah once; but she was never far from his thoughts.

On a bright Sunday morning early in May he went as usual to Thomas's house for Sunday dinner. He found Meg, Thomas's wife, preparing the meal in the kitchen over the shop.

'Thomas is up in the attic, Morgan,' she told him. 'He's taken it into his head to sort out some of his old belongings.'

Morgan climbed up into the top of the house and found his brother bending over a tin chest, looking through a collection of dusty books. He paused for a moment in the doorway and watched him. In the crouching attitude of that slight figure he saw for an instant the dreamy, bookish lad of long ago. Then, almost immediately, the spell was broken as Thomas straightened up and looked round.

'Oh, it's you, Morgan. Come in, come in. The sunshine shafted down through the skylight and Thomas screwed up his eyes behind his glasses. 'I just bethought me to look at some of these old things of mine.'

Morgan sat down on a rickety chair and Thomas resumed his inspection of the dusty books, lifting them out one by one from the trunk, dusting them over, and peering at the titles. Occasionally he would stop and flip over the pages, reading a passage at random.

'I had a look at some of these the other week,' he said. 'First time I'd touched 'em in years.' He sat down on a box facing Morgan, a heavy, well-bound volume in his hands. 'Remember how I scraped and saved to buy these, Morgan? I did all manner of jobs.' He read out the title on the spine: '*A History of England and its People*, in ten volumes. I reckoned there couldn't be much history I wouldn't know if I read these.'

Morgan nodded. 'You were a rare lad for learning, Thomas.'

Thomas weighed the book in his hand. 'And now these books are a history in themselves, Morgan. My history: the history of a failure.'

He removed his glasses and cleaned the lenses on his handkerchief. 'It's funny the tricks life plays on you. When we were lads I was the one who was going to set the world on fire – me – Thomas, the scholar. Instead, I wind up keeping a backstreet grocery shop, while you, the rough and ready lad, come back from the other side of the world with your fortune made, just like somebody in a book.'

In their youth the brothers had felt their dissimilarity too keenly for real closeness, but now Morgan felt a surge of affection for Thomas. 'You're too hard on yourself, lad,' he said gently. 'There's all kinds of failure and all kinds of success. You've been happy, haven't you? You've made Meg happy, I can see that. All I have to show for everything is a few quid in the bank. I'd be a liar and a hypocrite if I said that didn't matter. It's a great comfort, Thomas. But there are things I'd rather have had.'

177

Thomas smiled and touched Morgan's knee. 'I'm all right, Morgan. It's just you coming home that started me off thinking back. I'd not have had it any different – not if it had meant not having Meg.' He put the book aside and bent over the trunk.' She'd skin me alive if she heard me talking like that.'

In a few minutes Meg came to the foot of the attic stairs and called them to lunch. Morgan put his pipe away and stood up to go.

'Just a minute, Morgan, before you go.'

Morgan turned and looked at his brother. Thomas, with a strange half-embarrassed expression on his thin face, was fumbling in his pocket. 'I've got something belonging to you that I think you should have.' He produced an envelope. 'It's been lying up here for years. I thought it was no good posting it on to you after all that time; but I couldn't bring myself to throw it away.'

He handed the envelope to Morgan, who took it and turned it over to look at the writing on it. There was no stamp, just his name in dried and faded ink.

'Well, what on earth is it?' he said.

'It's probably nothing much at all,' said Thomas. 'But it is yours and I think you should have it. Don't you know whose writing that is?'

'No.'

'It's hers – Sarah's. I reckon it was to tell you she wouldn't be coming out to you after all.'

Morgan made no move to open the envelope. 'Tell me, Thomas, just how you came by it.'

Thomas sat down again on the box.

'It was after you'd gone down to Southampton to see about your passage. I was coming down to see you off and visit Uncle Horace, remember? Well, you'd been gone a few days and Sarah gave me this to give to you.

She was hanging about one night at the end of the street, waiting for me. I reckon she didn't know your address.' He shook his head and looked penitently at the floor. 'I don't know how it happened, Morgan, but what with one thing and another, I clean forgot it. I remember I wasn't too fit about that time. It was the year I cracked up and had to go into the sanatorium. Anyway, it wasn't till months later that I came across it again in a book. I reckoned if it had been all that important Sarah would have surely seen me to ask if you'd got it. As it was, by that time she was married to Mark what's his name and had a kiddy too. I saw no good reason for bothering any more. I know I'd no right to keep it back, but I reckoned you were well out of it.'

Morgan's eyes were fixed on his brother's face. 'And you mean you've hung on to it for thirty years?'

'Well, not exactly. I couldn't bring meself to burn somebody else's letter, you see, so I shoved it in a book again and I didn't come across it again till a week or two ago when I was rummaging about up here. I've been turning over in my mind ever since whether to give it to you and own up or destroy it and let sleeping dogs lie.'

Morgan ripped open the envelope and read the letter inside. Thomas stared at him as the colour drained from his face.

'For God's sake, Morgan, what is it, man?'

Morgan shook his head. 'Nothing, Thomas, nothing. It just brought it all back for a minute, that's all.'

He refolded the letter and returned it to the envelope which he put carefully away in an inside pocket. Of what use was it to rant and foam at Thomas now? As he had said, he was ill at the time, seriously ill and not to be held responsible for a careless mistake. And nothing would be gained by telling him now that this letter, delivered at the right time, could have changed the course of two people's lives.

'I... I am sorry, Morgan,' said Thomas, peering anxiously at his brother.

Morgan turned abruptly to the door. 'Forget it, Thomas,' he said. 'It was all a long time ago.'

They went downstairs as Meg called again. Throughout the meal Morgan was withdrawn and silent and it was not long after when he took his leave. Back at his hotel he sat down and wrote a note to Sarah. He thought for some time before putting pen to paper, and at length he wrote:

'My dear Sarah, the enclosed letter has only just come into my hands. It has explained many things to me and the fact that owing to a series of mischances my brother Thomas delivered it thirty years too late may help to ease what must have embittered you for so long...'

He put the note and Sarah's letter to him together in an envelope, and walking along to the corner by the hotel, he posted them in the pillar box there.

In the fine warm afternoon of the following Sunday Morgan visited Sarah for the first time in several months. There was a short pause before she answered his knock, and they regarded each other in silence for a long moment as she stood in her doorway.

'Well, Sarah,' Morgan said at last. 'I thought it was a nice day for a drive out.'

Her eyes were unfathomable as she said, 'I'll get a coat.'

He followed her into the house and was instantly drawn to the sideboard and the photograph of the young officer, Sarah's son. She returned suddenly to the room and her glance flickered briefly on his face as he stood there with the photograph in his hand.

'I'm ready.'

'Righto.' He replaced the picture on the sideboard and preceded her out of the house. Once clear of the narrow main street of the village, Morgan put on speed, heading straight for Greystone Cottage on which the work of conversion was now progressing. The hillside here was drenched in fresh green that was still untouched by the grimy smoke-fingers of industry which curled up out of the valley. In the orchard behind the house blossom sprang pink and white among the neglected trees. They walked in silence up the path and Morgan unlocked the door and stood aside for Sarah to enter. There was a new strangeness in their manner together now and they had spoken little in the car. From the cardboard tube he carried Morgan took out a copy of the architect's plan for the conversion. As they walked from room to room, striding over rubble and builders' materials, he explained to her all that was being done. She listened to him, nodding now and then, but making little comment. They came to the kitchen last of all and Morgan pointed to the tall cast-iron range and fireplace.

'That's going, Sarah. I'm knocking this wall right out and extending four feet back. There'll be all built-in units along that wall there. It's wonderful the things they make for kitchens nowadays.' He talked on, flourishing catalogues with shiny illustrations of gleaming kitchen equipment. 'It'll be fair dinkum when it's done.'

'Fair dinkum?'

'Australian for proper champion.'

'Oh.' She looked about her. 'Well, it sounds very nice.'

He watched her face with eagerness. 'Aye, it'll be labour-saving; and I reckon just enough for one woman to manage – with a bit of help for the heavy work, y'know.'

Sarah did not meet his eyes. 'You've got somebody in mind to look after it all for you, then?'

He gazed steadily at her. 'I think so, Sarah,' he said quietly. 'I'm thinking of getting married again. I know just the lass. She needs somebody to look after her.'

'Well, don't you think you should talk it over with her before you get it all settled? Especially the kitchen. Every woman has her ideas about kitchens.'

'Well, Sarah,' he said, 'let's have your ideas, then.'

'My ideas?'

'Whose ideas do you think they should be?'

She turned away from him, hiding her face and walking to the window which looked out on to the unkempt stretch of orchard.

'You know – you don't owe me anything, Morgan.'

'But look, Sarah –'

'He isn't yours, y'know.'

He was baffled now. He looked back at her with puzzlement in his eyes. 'I don't understand.'

'John, I mean,' Sarah said. She stood quite still, looking out of the window, both hands clasping her bag. 'He's not your boy, Morgan.'

'I... I don't understand, Sarah,' he said again. 'The letter...'

'Oh, that was true enough.' She turned and walked aimlessly across the gritty floorboards, not looking at him. He watched her, his eyes never leaving her as she said, 'It never came to anything. I was mistaken. John is Mark's boy, Morgan, not yours.' She looked at him now, watching for his reaction as he lifted his hands in a gesture of helplessness.

'I don't know what to think now, Sarah. For a week I've believed I had a son.' He smiled wanly. 'It wasn't a bad feeling.'

'And what about Mark? You married him just the same.

'I was panic-stricken,' Sarah said. She gazed past his shoulder with the look of one who sees not great distances but over the long passage of years. 'I didn't know which way to turn. I thought you'd let me down. I told Mark. He'd always wanted me.'

Morgan nodded. 'I know.'

'And he still wanted me after I'd told him. I was afraid and lost. I didn't know what to do. Mark seemed the only way out.'

'But you found you were mistaken?'

'Yes, soon enough. But I couldn't give Mark up then, not after he'd stood by me. So we were married. I didn't love him – not the way I'd loved you – but I respected him. He was such a good man, such a kind and gentle man that I couldn't help but come to love him in time. We had a good life together: a good marriage. And we had John.'

'And all these years you've been thinking that I'd let you down?' Morgan said.

She smiled dryly. 'And you've been thinking the same of me.'

'Oh, what a waste,' he burst out. 'What a wicked, wicked waste!'

'No, Morgan, not a waste. We both brought happiness to someone else. It wasn't a waste.'

He rolled the plans in his hands. 'No, you're right.'

She straightened her back and strolled across the room again. 'So you're not obliged to me after all, Morgan. You don't owe me anything.'

'No, we're quits,' Morgan said. 'We're back where we started.'

'Except we're both thirty years older,' Sarah pointed out; and we've both been married.'

183

'Which is no reason for not having another go.'

'It's not everybody that wants another go,' she said. 'Some people are satisfied with what they've had.' She turned to face him. 'I don't have to get married. I'm quite comfortable as I am. I have my pension and my sewing and John sends me money. I'm self-sufficient, y'know.'

Morgan nodded. 'Aye, it'd take more than being widowed to get you down.'

'But it's not that nobody wants me. I'm young enough, y'know, and not bad looking. I've had my chances.'

Morgan began to smile. 'I don't doubt it lass. But don't you think it was a happy providence that kept you till I'd come right round the world for you?'

'Right round the world for me? To your old Yorkshire, you mean!'

'But only a Yorkshire with you in it, Sarah. If I hadn't known you were a widow I don't think I'd have come at all.'

She tossed her head suddenly and in the coquettish gesture he saw quite clearly the girl he had loved and lost so long ago.

'Nay,' she said, 'you'll have to convince me of that.'

He slapped the cardboard tube down in his hands, laughing out loud. His heart sang. 'I will, lass,' he said. 'By God, but I will!'

And he did.

The Desperadoes

4 teds on a night of increasing violence

What started it that night was the row Vince had with his father. He couldn't remember just what began the row itself, but something like it seemed to blow up every time the Old Man saw him, and started using expressions like 'idle layabout', 'lazy good-for-nothing' and 'no-good little teddy boy'. The Old Man never talked to you – he talked at you: he didn't carry on a conversation – he told you things. When Vince stormed out of the house he hardly knew where he was going he was so full of bottled-up fury. Violence writhed in him like a trapped and vicious snake. He felt like kicking in the teeth of the first person who might glance twice at him and he thought that perhaps the easiest way of relieving his feeling would be to find the boys and go smash up a few chairs at the Youth Club. Except that that might bring a copper to the door and he got on the wrong side of the Old Man easily enough without having the police to help along.

He had no trouble in finding the gang: they were

obstructing the pavement at the end of Chapel Street, making the occasional passer-by get off into the road. He watched them sourly as he descended the hill – stocky Sam, little Finch, and big surly Bob – and his mouth twisted peevishly as he heard one of them laugh. They were watching something across the road that he could not see and they did not notice his approach till he was upon them.

'Now then.'

'What ho!'

'How do, Vince.'

Sam said, 'Get a load of that,' nodding across the junction.

Vince looked. He might have known. It was a girl. She was straddling a drop-handlebar bicycle by the kerb and talking to a thin youth who stood on the edge of the pavement. She was a dark blonde. She wore very brief scarlet shorts which displayed her long, handsome thighs, and a white high-necked sweater stretched tight over her large shapely breasts.

Finch was hopping about as though taken bad for a leak and making little growling noises in his throat.

'D'you know her?' Vince asked.

'Never seen her before.'

'Who's that Sunday-school teacher with her?'

'Don't know him either.'

Vince felt a spasm of gratuitous hatred for the youth. There was no one about; the street was quiet in the early evening. He said, 'Well, what we waitin' for? Let's see him off, eh?'

'An' what then?' Bob said.

Vince looked at him where he lounged against the lamp-post, his hands deep in the pockets of his black jeans. He was becoming more and more irritated by Bob's habit of making objections to everything he suggested. He had a strong idea that Bob fancied taking over leadership of the gang but lacked the guts to force the issue.

'What d'you mean "what then?"?' he said.

There was no expression on Bob's long sullen face. 'When we've seen him off?'

'We'll take her pants off an' make her ride home bare-back,' Finch giggled.

'Aye,' Vince said; ''an if laughing boy has any objections we'll carve his initials round his belly button.'

He brought his hand out of his pocket and pushed the handle of his knife against Bob's shirt front just above the buckle of his belt. He pressed the catch and let his relaxed wrist take the spring of the blade. He wondered if anyone had ever made a knife with a spring strong enough to drive the blade straight into a man's belly.

'You want to be careful wi' that bloody thing,' Bob said, eyeing the six inches of razor-sharp steel, its point pricking one of the pearl buttons on his black shirt. 'Don't you know there's a law against 'em?'

'I'll have to be careful who sees me with it, then, won't I?' Vince said. Looking Bob in the eye he inclined his head across the street. 'Comin'?' he said.

Bob shrugged with exaggerated casualness and eased his shoulders away from the lamp-post as Vince retreated the blade of the knife. 'Okay, may as well.'

They crossed the road in a tight group, fanning out as they neared the opposite side to approach the girl and the youth from two sides. The youth looked more startled than the girl to see them coming.

'Hello, sweetheart,' Vince said. 'Been for a ride in the country?'

Finch rang the bell on the bike's handlebars. 'Your mam's ringing for you,' he said to the youth. 'Time you were off home.'

The youth looked confused and startled. His smooth, unshaven cheeks flared with a brilliant flush of red as he looked at the faces of the gang.

'What's all this about?' the girl said, and the youth, finding voice, said, 'Why don't you go away and leave people alone?'

'Why don't you go away an' leave us alone?' Vince said. He waved his hand at the youth. 'Go on, sonny, get lost. Beat it.'

Sam, Finch and Bob closed round the youth and began to hustle him away along the street. 'Let me alone. Who d'you think you are?' he said as they moved him along. They turned a corner with him into a side street and his voice died away. Vince held the handlebars of the bicycle with one hand to prevent the girl from leaving.

She flashed blue eyes at him. 'Who d'you think you are?' she said, echoing the youth, 'pushing people around like this?'

'Vice squad,' Vince said. 'Cleaning the streets up.'

'Well, you want to start by staying at home yourselves.'

'Now that's not nice, is it?' Vince said. 'After we've protected you from that creep.'

'He's not a creep.' The girl's eyes flashed over him, taking in the long pepper-and-salt jacket, the exaggeratedly narrow black trousers, the black shirt, open-necked, with stand-up collar, and the white triangle of sweat shirt at the throat. Vince in his turn was examining her with appreciation: the spirited blue eyes in a lightly tanned face, the shapely breasts taut under the sweater, the long bare legs.

'He's a creep,' he said. 'You're the best-looking piece of crackling I've seen in a fortnight. What you want to waste your time with a drip like that for?'

'It's a question of taste,' the girl said coldly. She

188

looked back over her shoulder at the empty street. 'What are they doing to him? I'm warning you, if they hurt him I'll report you all to the police. Don't think you can frighten me.'

'Oh, they won't hurt him,' Vince said. 'They'll just see him on his way.'

As he spoke, Sam and Finch and Bob reappeared round the corner. Finch was laughing and saying something to the others.

'Where is he?' the girl said. 'What have you done to him?'

'We didn't lay a finger on him,' Sam said. 'All done by kindness.'

'He's remembered he's got to do an errand for his mother,' Finch said with a snigger.

'And I've got to go as well,' the girl said. 'Would you mind taking your hand off the handlebars?'

'What's the hurry,' Vince said, 'just when we're gettin' friendly?'

Finch was prowling round the bike, pretending to examine it. He crouched beside the front wheel and fingered the tyre valve.

'Is this where the air goes in an' out?'

'Don't you touch that!' the girl said.

'No, leave it alone, Finch,' said Vince.

'Thank you for nothing.'

'Isn't she polite?' Vince asked the others. 'She must have been to a good school.'

'Where d'you live, love?' Sam asked.

'Not far from here. And you'd better let me go if you know what's good for you. My father's a sergeant in the police force.'

'An' my old man's the chief constable,' Vince said; 'so they'll know one another. What's your name?'

'None of your business.'

'That's a funny name,' said Finch, and the gang hooted with laughter that was mostly forced.

Vince was wishing the others had stayed away longer, because he was sure he could have made some progress with her, given more time. All this defiance – it was mostly show. She was just keeping her end up and he wondered what she was like behind it, when you got to know her.

'P'raps we'd better introduce ourselves,' he said with a little bow. He pointed to Sam: 'That's Sir Walter Raleigh'; to Finch: 'Field Marshal Montgomery'; to Bob: 'Marilyn Monroe in disguise; an' I'm Sammy Davis, junior.'

'Very funny,' the girl said. 'Now I'll thank you to let me go.'

'Tell us your name an' then we'll see.'

'I've told you, it's none of your business.'

'I used to know a lad called nobody's business,' Finch said, pursuing his joke. 'Was he your brother? Then there was one called dirty business – the black sheep of the family.'

Vince was watching the girl's face closely. Was that really the faintest flicker of humour in the depths of her eyes, or was he imagining things?

'Well, if you won't tell us, we'll have to keep you a bit longer. Can't let you go when you're feeling so unfriendly.'

'Look,' she said, 'if you don't let me go I'll call out to that man over there.'

Vince smiled. 'He'd probably run like hell the other way. You read every day in the papers about people gettin' hurt through not minding their own business.'

'Proper young gentlemen, all of you,' the girl said. She gave a quick backward look over her shoulder. 'Well, I don't think you'll scare two policemen.'

They all fell for it. Vince said, 'What...?' and as he momentarily relaxed his grip on the handlebars she sent Finch reeling from a swift push in the chest and pressing down on the pedals, was away.

She swayed uncertainly for a moment as she forced the speed, and then she was gone, head down, scarlet shorts brilliant in the drab street.

'Fancy fallin' for that one,' said Sam.

Vince watched until she turned the bend and disappeared from sight. 'She's a real smart piece,' he said. 'You've got to give her that... A real smart piece.' He found himself hoping he would meet her again in more favourable circumstances and he let his mind dwell briefly on her remembered charms.

'I could shag it from supper to breakfast-time,' said little Finch, and Sam laughed and punched him tauntingly on the shoulder.

'Aagh, she'd make mincemeat o' two your size,' he scoffed. 'It takes a man, mate, a man.'

'Just gimme the chance,' Finch said. 'I'd risk it.'

'Here,' Bob said all at once, 'what did you mean by sayin' I was Marilyn Monroe in disguise? You tryin' to make out I'm a puff or summat?'

'I just said the first thing 'at came into me head,' Vince said.

'Well why didn't you say it about Finch or Sam? Why me?'

There was a dangerous little smile lurking in Vince's eyes as he looked at Bob. 'I just didn't think of it till I got to you.'

'Well I didn't like it. You want to be careful.'

'Or else what?' Vince said nastily, his temper flaring again. 'Are you tryin' to make summat out o' summat?'

'I'm just tellin' you,' Bob said.

'That's your trouble: you're allus tellin'. What's up –
don't you like runnin' around with this gang, or what?'

'I like it okay.'

'Well why don't you shurrup allus tellin' an' objectin'
every time anybody says anythin' or suggests anythin'?'

'I'm just sayin' what I think,' Bob said. 'Seems there's
only one what does any suggestin' round here.'

Vince felt himself go tense. There, it was out, it was
said. 'Meanin' what?' he said.

'Meanin' everything you say goes an' nobody else
has a look in.'

Vince kept his eyes levelled on Bob's face and slowly
slid his hands free of his pockets.

'I haven't heard anybody else objectin'.'

'Oh no, they'll fall in with owt you say.'

'Well that makes you the odd man out. You're out-
numbered, three to one.'

'Why don't you belt up, Bob?' Sam said. 'What you
want to start all this for?'

'I'm only sayin' what I think,' Bob said, his heavy
face flushed now.

Vince, watching him, knew that the moment, if there
was to be one, was not now. 'Well now you've said it.'

'Aye... well... I can say what I think, can't I?'

'Course you can,' Vince said. 'Any time.' He clapped
Bob on the shoulder and threw his other arm round
Sam's neck.

'Well, now Bob's said his piece, what we goinna
do, eh?'

'Let Bob suggest summat,' Sam said. 'He's grumbled
enough.'

'That's it,' Vince said. 'What we goinna do, Bob?'

Bob looked surly. 'I don't know.'

'There's that stripper on at the Tivvy,' Finch said,

prancing round from behind them. 'I've seen the pictures outside.' He drew a voluptuous torso in the air with his hands. 'Grrr.'

'We could go up to the Troc or the Gala Rooms after an' find some women,' Sam said.

'They mebbe won't let us in at the Gala Rooms after last week,' Vince said, referring to a fight they had been involved in on the dance floor.

'An' there's Jackson at the Troc,' Bob reminded them.

'Aw, he's got nowt on us,' Sam said. 'He won't keep us out.'

'That big, stupid, brussen, show-off bastard,' Vince said. 'One o' these days somebody'll walk all over his stupid face, an' I want to be there when it happens so's I can have a good laugh.'

'Well what say we go to the Tivvy first an' then the Troc?' Sam suggested, and Vince nodded.

'Aye, let's go to the Tivvy first an' give Finch a thrill.'

'Here, why me?' Finch said. 'Anybody 'ud think you lot didn't like tarts.'

'As I says to the vicar the other night, over our glass of dandelion wine,' Vince began. 'I says, "Vicar," I says, "I don't know what we're goinna do about young Finch. He's got women on the brain, Vicar, an' he keeps his brains in his trousers, y'know..."'

'Come off it,' Finch said.

Vince grinned and winked at Sam and they seized Finch and turned him upside down, holding him by the ankles, his head six inches from the pavement. Coins fell out of his pockets as he wriggled furiously.

'Lay off, you bloody fools. Stop yer bloody clownin'!'

'Have we to get it out an' cool it off, Sam?' Vince said, pretending to fumble at Finch's flies.

'You bloody dare!' Finch roared.

193

'He might catch cold in it,' Sam said; 'an' that'd never do.

Finch put his hands flat down on the pavement as they lowered him. They released his legs and stood by laughing as he righted himself and then scurried about the pavement retrieving his loose change. Vince clapped him on the shoulder and pulled him in between Sam and himself.

'C'mon, then; let's go an' have a belly laugh an' a look at this tart.'   music hall

They caught a downtown bus and sat in a noisy group on the upper deck. They got off at the corner of Market Street. The Tivoli theatre stood in an alley near the centre of town. It was very small and, now that the Alhambra had closed its doors, the only live theatre in Cressley. It boasted, along with the City Varieties, Leeds, of being one of the oldest music halls in the country and in its time it had played host to all the legendary names of variety. But its hey-day was far behind it. It could not compete with the mass audiences and huge fees available on television and it was fifteen years since any important name had appeared on its playbills. The fare it offered now was a series of fifth-rate touring shows composed of those who had never made the top, the pathetically hopeful, and strip-tease artistes and semi-nude performers of varying ages, talent, and physical charm. The gang paused to examine with lewd and vociferous admiration the photographs of Paula Perez, the Peruvian Peach, displayed in the foyer.

'Four on the stage,' Vince said to the woman in the box.

She glanced at the seating plan. 'Four orchestra stalls, row G, at four-and-six,' she recited, without smiling. 'First house just starting.'

194

They paid and went in, ignoring the programme-seller just inside the door, and marched down the side aisle of the narrow red-plush auditorium. The hall was almost full near the front, but the audience thinned out noticeably towards the rear. They stumbled without apology over the feet of the people already seated as the five-piece pit band struck up, the steely tone of the violin characteristically dominating the sound. The curtains parted and five young women with frozen smiles went through a lackadaisical routine of slipshod precision dancing.

'Cor,' Finch said, 'lamp that elephant on the end.'

'Must be the producer's daughter,' Vince said.

'Looks more like his mother,' Sam said.

They began to clap loudly and shout "'Core, 'core,' as the dancers tripped in line off the stage.

Their place was taken by a perky, broadly smiling young man in a light grey suit, blue polka-dot bow tie and a soft hit with the brim turned up all round. He peered over the footlights, pretending to look for the audience.

'Is anybody there?'

'There's only thee an me,' Vince called out.

The comedian responded with a quick professional grin. 'An' there'll awnly be thee in a minute,' he retorted in an imitation Yorkshire accent.

Finch nearly fell out of his seat laughing at this. He leaned forward and thumped the back of the seat in front, causing the little nondescript man in glasses sitting there to turn and give him a glare.

The comedian was also the compere. He told a couple of stories to warm up the audience, then introduced the first act: a saxophone and xylophone duo.

The first half of the show moved on through an acrobatic trio, a young singing discovery from Scotland, a brother-and-sister tap-dancing act, interpersed with quips, stories and lightning impersonations from the compere, and came to its climax with Paula Perez the Peruvian Peach. Peruvian or not, she was black-haired, dark-eyed and brown-skinned. She performed against a pale mauve back-curtain, with a dressing-table, a cheval mirror and a double divan bed as props. She began in a dark mauve cocktail dress, and elbow-length white gloves which she peeled slowly off and held at arm's length before dropping them in turn onto the stage. To the music of the orchestra she turned her back and unzipped her frock. She stepped gracefully out of it with a coy backward glance at the audience and performed a few steps about the stage in a transparent nylon slip. The gang were still and absorbed now, except Finch, who fidgeted restlessly in his seat as though impatient for each succeeding move in the sequence of disrobing. The slip went, followed by the stockings, which were shed with much waving of long legs from the depths of a bedside chair. Miss Perez now went into an extended dance routine in which her long legs flashed and the mounds of her breasts quivered and trembled above the low line of her white brassiere. She turned her back to the audience once more and unhooked the brassiere, throwing it away from her onto the bed. Turning again, she continued the dance with her arms crossed over her breasts, finally turning her back yet again while she ridded herself of her transparent pants. The act was almost over. The audience waited for the climax that would reveal all. The Peruvian Peach moved a few steps each way, her dimpled buttocks quivering, then stopped in the middle of the stage. For a long moment she did not move. A side-drum rolled in the orchestra pit. Suddenly she spun round, flinging her arms wide. The pale rose of her nipples and the triangle of diamante-studded cloth in the vee of her thighs were visible for a split second before the stage lights were doused.

She stepped between the curtains in a lilac-coloured nylon négligée to receive the applause of the audience, blowing kisses and flashing her dark, mascara-ed eyes into every corner of the house.

Finch thumped the back of the seat in front in his excitement, and the little man turned his head.

'Do you mind?' he said. 'I've paid for this seat.'

Finch gave him a blank look and went on applauding wildly until the Peruvian Peach had disappeared from the stage.

They made their way out to the stalls bar and extolled the charms of Paula Perez while they drank bottled beer.

'Does she come on again in the second half?' Finch asked.

'They usually do,' Vince said.

'I wonder what she'll do this time.'

'Ask for a volunteer to go up an' unfasten her clothes for her.'

'Gerraway!' Finch said, his eyes popping at the thought.

They had a second bottle of beer apiece, the quick intake of alcohol loosening in them a pleasant sense of irresponsibility and a desire for some mischief to add spice to the entertainment offered.

'See that little bloke in front o' me gettin' an eyeful?' Finch said.

'What did he say when he turned round?' Vince asked.

'Oh, summat about me keepin' to me own seat.'

Vince raised his eyebrows. 'Did he, then? We might have a bit o' sport with him before we've done.'

They returned to their seats as the band struck up. The show sagged in its second half and Vince soon became bored and restless through the repeat sequence of acts.

197

As the acrobats bounded onto the stage he snapped open his knife and pushed the blade through the red plush upholstery between his thighs. He ripped open a slit six inches long and probed for the stuffing, pulling out a handful and passing it to Finch on his left. 'Here, hold that for me, will you?' Finch dropped the wadding onto the floor, consumed by a fit of giggling. There was an empty seat immediately in front of Vince and to the right of the nondescript man who had spoken to Finch. Vince put the knife away and lit a cigarette and leaned forward to expel smoke about the little man's ears. The man coughed and looked around. Vince showed his teeth in a smile and the little man turned away in some confusion. Eventually, after repeated references to it by the comedian-compere, it was the turn once more of Paula Perez. She assumed the role of a slave-girl, with a loin cloth and a strip of matching material across her breasts, dancing before a painted wooden idol which stood at the back of the stage. The curtain fell when she had prostrated herself in an attitude of abandon before the idol, and rose again almost immediately to show the Peruvian Peach concealed behind two large ostrich-feather fans. She had disposed of the garments worn during the slave-girl act and as she danced now the manipulation of the fans allowed the audience momentary glimpses of her naked, made-up body.

Vince leaned forward and spoke into the ear of the little man:

'You're a dirty old man comin' here to look at women's tits when you should be at home puttin' the kids to bed. Look at her, though – she's got a lovely pair, hasn't she? Isn't she a teasing bitch the way she gives you just a look an' no more? I bet you're wondering what she's like in bed, aren't you, eh? Wouldn't you like to fondle 'em, eh? Run your hands all over her...'

The little man eased over to the far side of his seat, his gaze fixed on the stage and the Peruvian Peach. Vince went on talking, his suggestions becoming more and more obscene, and the little man began to sweat, small beads of perspiration breaking on his forehead and running down his fleshy cheeks. Until, as Paula Perez reached the climax of her act, where she retired to the back of the stage, dropped the fans and froze into a nude pose, his nerve broke and he left his seat and stumbled along the row to the aisle.

Vince waited for a moment before nudging Sam on his right. 'Go on, get out, quick!' Sam, not knowing quite what Vince was up to, did as he was told and with Finch and Bob following they left the theatre and paused in the brightly lit foyer.

'What's all the rush about?' said Bob. 'It wasn't over.'

'All bar the shoutin'. C'mon.' Vince led the way to the end of the cobbled alley and stopped, looking right and left along the street. 'He's there.' The little man was crossing the road, walking fast, about twenty yards away.

'C'mon, we're goinna have a bit o' sport.'

They crossed over the street, following the man but keeping some distance behind him. Once he glanced back as though expecting to be followed, then hurried on, his pace not slackening. In a short while he had left the main thoroughfares and was striking up the hill into the back streets. They saw him turn a corner and, turning it after him, found him thirty yards away, alone in a dimly lit street running between two sheer-sided blocks of mill offices. Vince called after him:

'Ey, you there; wait for us!'

The man stopped only to look back: then he began to run.

'C'mon,' Vince said.

'What we goinna do?' Bob said.

'We're goinna have some fun.'

He broke into a fast run, the others following. They easily outpaced the little man and overtook him well within the confines of the lonely street. He backed against a wall as they reached him.

'What's wrong?' he said. 'What d'you want?'

'We just wanted to talk to you,' Vince said. They faced him in an arch and he fought for breath, his chest heaving, as his frightened glance flickered from face to face.

'What about? I'm in a hurry.'

'Dashin' off to tell the missis all about Paula Perez an' her marvellous tits,' Vince said.

'There's no call for mucky talk like that,' the man said.

'Don't tell me,' Vince said. 'I know – you're an art lover. I bet you like mucky photos an' all. Have you any on you now? C'mon, show us your mucky photos.'

'I don't know what you're talking about.' The lenses of the little man's glasses flickered dimly as his eyes turned to look at each face in turn. 'Can't a man have a quiet evening at the theatre on his own without being molested by hooligans?'

'Hooligans? Hear that, lads? He says we're hooligans.' Vince took hold of the man's coat. 'Let's see them mucky pictures.'

'I haven't got any mucky pictures. Now let me go or I'll shout for help.'

'I wouldn't do that if I were you,' Vince told him. 'That wouldn't be friendly at all.'

'Well let me go, then. I don't know what you want. I haven't done anything to you.'

'Who says you have?'

200

'Nobody, but –'

'Well, what you bindin' about, then?'

'Look, all I want is to get on about my own business, that's all.'

Vince let go of the man's coat and appeared to consider this. He looked at his friends in turn. 'He wants to get on about his business. Shall we let him?'

'Yes, let's let him,' Sam said.

'Even though he's called us hooligans?'

'Well, he doesn't know us,' Sam said. 'Anybody can make a mistake.'

'We don't want to take it out of him over a little mistake, do we?' Vince said. He stepped away from the little man, allowing him to move clear of the wall. Vince extended his hand. 'No hard feelings, eh?' The little man looked at Vince's hand before putting out his own to meet it. As Vince grasped, he pulled, jerking the little man forward so that he staggered against him. 'Been drinkin' and all,' Vince said. 'A bit unsteady on your feet, aren't you? Mebbe a spot o' shut-eye 'ud do you good.'

With no more warning he smashed his fist into the man's face, sending him reeling backwards to fall over Sam, who had taken up a crouching position behind him. The man rolled over, face down, and groaned, his hands moving feebly. Sniggering, Finch danced on the fallen spectacles, the lenses crunching under his shoes. As the man moved and made as if to lift himself on his hands, Bob moved in and drove his foot into his ribs. He collapsed again and lay still.

'Let's blow,' Vince said.

Bob looked round from where he was bending over the man. 'What about his wallet? He might have some brass on him.'

'Leave it,' Vince said sharply. 'We don't want pinchin'

for robbery with violence. Not unless it's big enough to make it worth the risk.'

They left the scene, cutting out of the street by way of a ginnel and returning to the middle of town by a roundabout route. They went into the saloon bar of a public house, ordered pints of bitter and sat down at a corner table. As he drank, Vince relived the moment when the sight of the little man's stupid face had become unbearable and felt again the violent uncoiling of tension in the smash of his fist. The violence had given them all a sense of release and now they talked animatedly about the show and Paula Perez, and women in general. Another two rounds of drinks increased their feeling of well-being and they decided it was time to go to the Trocadero and try their luck. They felt ready for anything, even to face the arch-enemy, Jackson.

He was standing in the foyer, eyeing everyone going in, his hard, square-jawed face expressionless. He wore a light-blue, double-breasted suit which hung easily on his big muscular body. He moved across to the pay-box as Vince and the others stepped in from the street.

'Hello, hello. What's up – won't they let you in at the Gala Rooms?'

'Why, what d'you mean?' Vince asked blindly.

'Don't come the injured innocence with me,' Jackson said. 'You know there was a scrap there last week.'

'Nothin' to do with us, Mister Jackson,' Finch said.

'Well, I'm paid to keep order here,' Jackson said stonily; 'and the first sign of trouble here tonight and you lot are out. Just bear it in mind.'

He nodded to the girl in the box and she took their money and issued tickets. He watched them bleakly as they filed past him into the hall.

'Bastard,' Vince said as they passed through the doorway and out of earshot.

They edged their way through the press of people standing just inside the doors and stood on the edge of the floor to watch the dancers with cool, dangerous insolence on their young faces. An archway on the left led through the trellised wall to the coffee and soft drinks bar. Vince said, 'We'll meet over there between sets.' It was routine to them to have a gathering-place as they liked to know where support lay in case of trouble. Before they could separate now Finch grabbed Vince's arm in excitement.

'Ey, look who's there.'

'Where?' Vince said. 'Who?'

'That tart on the bike. Christ, look at her! What a dish! Over there, see, dancin' with that tall lad in the blue sports coat.'

Vince found her and as his gaze fell on her something in him seemed to turn over. She was wearing a wide, blue-flowered skirt topped by a sheer nylon blouse through which was visible the lace edging of her slip. He rubbed his hands together. His palms were already hot and moist from the heat of the hall.

'That's for me.'

'Ey up!' Finch said. 'I saw her first, din' I?'

'Get lost, laddie,' Vince told him. 'Go find somebody your own measure.'

He began to edge along the perimeter of the floor, formed at this end of the hall by the people standing, and farther down towards the bandstand by the green cane chairs set out along the wall under the curtained windows. The set ended, the floor clearing, and he found the girl standing with her partner, the tall youth in the blue sports coat and grey slacks. Vince took his measure as he approached, decided he did not constitute any serious threat, and greeted her boldly:

'Well, well, well! Fancy running into you here! Got home all right, did you? No punctures or anything?'

The girl's glance was momentarily startled, then cool. 'Yes, thank you very much.'

'Good,' Vince said, smiling broadly now. 'Good.' He looked into the eyes of the tall youth. 'What's your name, might I ask.'

The young man's eyebrows came together. 'Colin Norton. Why?'

'I thought it was. There's somebody askin' for you at the door.'

'Oh? Who is it?'

'Dunno. Young bloke; wavy hair.'

The tall young man pondered this for a moment. 'I'd better go and see...' He looked uncertainly from Vince to the girl. 'Excuse me.'

'Sure,' Vince said.

He watched Norton walk up the hall, then turned back to the girl. 'You with him?'

'No, not particularly.'

'Did you come with anybody else?'

'I've one or two friends here.'

'Boy friends?'

She shrugged faintly. 'Nobody special.'

Vince grinned. 'Good.'

'Was there really somebody asking for him?'

Vince's smile broadened. 'You never know.'

She began to smile in turn. It broke through first in her eyes, then moving her mouth.

'You're a proper devil, aren't you?'

'That's me,' Vince said. 'Right first time.'

He was pleased when the band struck up again. He

wanted to be away from this spot before Norton realised he had been hoaxed. Not that he couldn't take care of him if it came to that, but he didn't want any trouble to complicate matters now. He jerked his head in the direction of the floor, which was filling up again.

'Care to?'

She hesitated, her glance flickering up to his face. 'All right.'

It was a slow foxtrot. He took her lightly in his arms, keeping the correct distance, and steered her with easy confidence through the moving throng of dancers. When they had made one circuit of the floor she said, 'You're a very good dancer, you know.'

Vince nodded. 'I know. It comes easy. If you're light on your feet and have a sense of rhythm there's nothing to it. Practice helps... You're not so bad yourself, anyway.'

'I'm better if I have a good partner. Half these lads can hardly dance a step. They grab hold of you like a sack of potatoes and walk all over your feet...'

'No style,' Vince said, 'that's their trouble.'

She gave him a quick speculative look, but said nothing. He pulled her in a little closer.

'I don't even know your name.'

'I know yours; you're Sammy Davis, junior.'

'That's only my professional name. Vincent Elspey's my real name.'

'I like that. It sounds a bit distinguished.'

'My friends call me Vince.'

'Do they? How nice for them.'

He didn't know what to make of this so he said nothing for a minute, waiting.

'Well?'

'Well what?'

'What's your name? I can't talk to you all night without knowing your name, can I?'

'Are you thinking of talking to me all night?'

'That and other things.'

She pulled away and looked at him. 'Just a minute! Not so fast, friend. I think you've got your lines crossed somewhere. Don't be getting ideas.'

'What ideas?'

'You know what ideas.'

'Cross my heart,' Vince said.

'And what?'

'I mean every word I say.'

She laughed again, as earlier, almost despite herself, the light coming to her dark blue eyes, the smile lifting the corners of her red mouth.

'Come on,' Vince said. 'What's your name?'

She shook her head.

'Come on. What's wrong?'

'I don't like it.'

'...What?'

'My name'

'Well, what is it?'

She hesitated. 'Iris.'

'Well what's wrong with that, for Pete's sake?'

'I don't know. I just don't like it.'

'It's okay. What's wrong with it? I thought you were goinna say Aggie or Clara or summat right horrible.'

'Oh, no. I just don't like it, though. I've always wished I was called something else.'

'Such as what, for instance?'

'Well, Audrey, or something like that.'

'Well then, we'll reckon you never told me your real name an' I'll call you Audrey. How about that?'

'All right.'

He saw Sam standing alone on the edge of the floor and caught his eye, lifting his hand from the girl's back to form an 'O' with forefinger and thumb. He winked over the girl's shoulder and Sam gave him an approving wink in return and the thumbs-up sign. Sam was the one Vince was closest to in the gang. He had known him longer than the others and he was a good lad to have beside you in a tight corner. Little Finch was okay but his size meant that he couldn't throw much weight into a fight and Bob, big enough and tough when it came right down to it, spent half his time sulking because somebody had hurt his feelings.

When the second of the three dances in the set ended he asked the girl if she would like a cup of coffee. She said she didn't mind and they went through into the snack bar adjoining the floor.

'Where are your friends tonight?' she asked when they were seated, with cups of coffee on the green Formica-topped table between them.

'Here.'

'Do you always run around with the same crowd?'

'Usually. You have your own mates, y'know.'

'Do you always go about looking for trouble?'

'What d'you mean?'

'Oh, come on,' she said. 'You know the way you hustled John Sharpe off on the street earlier.'

'Was that his name?'

'Yes. Do you always do just what you want like that?'

He didn't like the question. He felt a lack of the power of argument necessary to defend his position. And anyway, all that had no part in this, sitting here with her. He remembered again the moment when he had driven his fist into the face of the man in the back street and felt no shame, because that part of him, the

207

part keyed to violence, was separate from the part which sat here enjoying being with her. She was waiting for him to say something.

'We like a bit o' fun,' he said reluctantly.

'Fighting as well?'

'We have a scrap now an' again.' He glanced at her face. 'Well, you can't back down if somebody starts throwin' his weight about, can you?'

'But you never pick fights with anybody? You don't start trouble?'

'Look,' he said, 'you've got to have a bit o' fun. You've got to break out now and again. You'd go barmy if you didn't. You spend all day workin' to fill somebody else's pockets with brass, an' everybody allus onto you: the Old Man callin' you a layabout an' a ted, an' the coppers watching you when you cross the road because your hair's cut a bit different. They're all alike: they want everything their way. Just be quiet an' don't get under the feet. Don't get in the way. An' what sort of a mess have they all made of it, eh? Wars an' bombs 'at'll kill everybody if they let 'em off. An' they say, "Keep quiet; don't cause trouble. Just keep out of the way till we're ready to polish you off."'

His fist clenched itself on the table-top. 'Sometimes you feel you just can't rest till you've smashed summat; till you've shown 'em all you don't give a bugger for any of 'em, an' they can't boss you around.'

She sat very still, listening to him, her eyes on his face.

'Suppose everybody thought like you?' she said. 'What sort of world would it be then?'

'Couldn't be much worse than it is now, could it? Nobody trusts anybody. Everybody's out to get what he wants. Countries as well as people. Well I haven't got

208

it upstairs – what it takes to make myself a nice little pile, like some of 'em do; so people look at me as if I'm dirt an' say, "Look at him, a ted, goin' about making trouble." So I make trouble when I feel like it.'

'But what about the ordinary decent people?'

'You mean the stupid ones, the ones everybody puts on? They're the ones the coppers an' politicians push around. Suckers. They're okay till nobody wants 'em. Like our old feller. He goes an' gets himself all shot up in the war an' now he's got one arm what's practically useless. So he gets a bit of a pension an' does jobs nobody else wants and walks about with it all twisted up inside him, hating everybody, including me, because I've got two good arms an' I can earn more brass than he does. An' he calls me a layabout!'

He drained his cup and pushed it moodily aside. 'What you want to start all that for? Why d'you want to bring all that up?'

She looked down into her own cup. 'I just wanted to know about you.'

They sat in silence for a time, then he said abruptly, 'C'mon, let's go dance some more.'

He stood aside at the door to let her precede him and as he followed her he noticed for the first time a small wart on the back of her neck, just below the hair-line. The lights were down in the hall for a slow waltz, and curiously touched by the blemish he had just noticed, he tightened his hold as they moved away together and brought her closer until her hair was touching his cheek. He wondered where she lived and if she would let him see her home when the dance finished. He wanted this very much. He wanted to see her again afterwards, too, and knew he would ask her for a date before long. She wasn't like the girls he and the gang usually went for:

she was a few rungs higher up the ladder than them, and sharper, more intelligent. No other girl had ever had him in a corner explaining himself. He wouldn't have stood it from another girl. They were usually interested only in how good a time you could give them and how far they were prepared to let you go in return. They were easier to deal with: they took you for what you were and you didn't need your wits about you all the time as you did with this one. But they were none of them as attractive as she and not one of them had caused him to feel as he did now, dancing with her in his arms, quiet, at peace, the need for violence drained out of him so that he wished the music would never stop.

It was now after licensing hours and the hall had filled up with the latecomers from the closing pubs. The air, despite the open windows behind the long curtains, was thick and stifling and several times used. When the set ended they found themselves near the door. The girl pretended to fan herself with her open hand.

'I feel is if I'll never draw another breath. How much warmer can it get in here?'

'Let's go outside for a bit,' Vince suggested, 'an' get some air.'

He wondered what she was thinking as she looked at him.

'C'mon,' he said. 'I'll look after you. We can have a walk up the street an' back.'

'All right, then. This is getting a bit too much.'

They got pass-outs at the desk and stepped out into the street.

'Sure you'll be warm enough?' Vince asked, thinking of her thin blouse.

'Oh, yes: it's a mild night.'

She linked her arm through his as they walked up

the quiet street and he glanced at her, feeling uplifted and happy. He knew nothing about her and began to ask her about herself. She lived in a street off Bradford Road, she told him, not far from where they had encountered her earlier that evening. She had an older sister who was married and a young brother still at school. Her father was an insurance superintendent and she was a typist in the main Cressley office of her father's company. She liked dancing, the cinema, records of Frank Sinatra, and swimming.

'Swimming?'

She told him how many lengths of the public baths she could swim and he was impressed.

'I should ha' thought with a figure like yours you'd be one o' them 'at never went in the water.'

She laughed. 'Swimming's good for the figure.'

'You're a good advert. I can't swim a stroke mesel. I have to wear a lifebelt in the bath at home.'

'You'd soon learn with a bit of practice. It's like riding a bike – once you know how you can't imagine why everybody can't do it.'

'Oh, I can ride a bike. A motor bike an' all. I'm goinna get a motor bike. Next year mebbe.'

'A scooter?'

'Naw, a right bike. A six-fifty Norton, or summat like that. Summat with some power.'

'They're expensive. Have you been saving up?'

'I've got enough for a good deposit. It's a question of gettin' the old feller to sign the hire purchase papers, only he can't make his stupid mind up. He likes to act bloody awkward.'

'What do you do for a living?'

'I'm a motor mechanic. Why?'

'I just wondered.'

'You could tell I hadn't an office job by me hands, couldn't you?'

'What's wrong with your hands?'

'They show me trade. Grease an' stuff you can't get off.'

'They're a nice shape,' she said. 'I noticed. I always notice people's hands. There's nothing to be ashamed of in working with your hands. Do you like being a motor mechanic?'

He shrugged. 'It's okay. I like knackling with engines an' that. It's like every other job, though – you're just makin' brass for somebody else.'

'You're young. You can't do everything at once. Perhaps you'll have your own business one day.'

'Aw, I haven't got the brains for that sort o' thing. Messin' with books an' all that. An' anyway, where'd I get the capital?'

'Well you never know,' she said.

They made a circuit of the block and approached the Trocadero from the other side. As they walked along between the parked cars and the wall of the building Vince stopped and turned her round with his hands on her shoulders, feeling smooth warmth through the blouse.

'Don't get panicky,' he said. 'I'm just goinna kiss you.'

'Who's panicky?' she said as his mouth came down on hers.

She was quiet at first, acquiescent but passive, her mouth cool and unresponsive under his. Then she parted her lips and put her arms about him. He felt a thrill of pure clear joy shoot through him as they broke away and stood close together in the shadow of the wall.

'I bet you never thought you'd end up like this when I saw you earlier on.'

She laughed. 'No, I didn't.'

'Neither did I, for that matter. I never expected to see you again... But I hoped I might.'

She was quiet.

'Will you let me see you again?'

'Do you really want to?'

'Yes, I do. I mean a proper date, where we arrange to meet each other an' there's just the two of us. Will you?'

'We'll see,' she said.

He dropped one hand from her shoulder to rest lightly on the swell of her breast and she lifted her own hand to remove it.

'Steady now.'

'Honest,' Vince said huskily. 'I'm not startin' anything. I'm not gettin' fresh. Honest. I wouldn't. I... I like you too much.'

The tenderness that overcame him as he held her was something new to him and appalling in the way it left him defenceless, drained of all violence, weak at the knees. She could do just what she liked with him, that was the way he felt about her. And under the joy it was frightening the way it made him think of things he had always scoffed at: things like steady courtship, marriage, a little home with someone to share it and be waiting for him at the end of the day.

'Oh, Christ!' he said as her mouth drew him again.

The beam of the flashlight picked them out as they stood embracing, mouth to mouth, body to body, against the wall. The shock of it was like cold water on them both. The girl hid her face but Vince turned his full into the beam of the torch, his eyes narrowing with fury as Jackson's voice said:

'I thought so. I thought that was what you were up to, you mucky little bugger. Bringing lasses out an' getting them up against the wall.'

Vince's heart pounded sickeningly. 'What the hell's up wi' you?' he said furiously. Hatred of Jackson scorched

213

through him in a hot flood. 'Why can't you leave people alone? We're not doin' any harm.'

'I'm not having this sort o' work here,' Jackson said. 'You can either get back inside or clear off an' do your dirty work somewhere else. Come on, now, let's have you.'

He held the beam of the torch steadily on them as they walked to the corner of the building, the girl with her head bowed and Vince looking straight before him, biting his lips to restrain his wild rage.

Jackson walked away through the car park, leaving them in the light of the foyer. They went in, Vince showing the pass-outs.

The girl's face was scarlet with humiliation. Vince said, 'The swine; the lousy stinkin' swine.' He looked at her. 'God,' he said, 'I don't know what to say...'

She turned away from him, avoiding his eyes. 'It doesn't matter.'

'But look, I –'

'Leave me alone,' she said. 'Just leave me alone.'

He tried to take her arm. 'Look, Audrey...'

She shook herself free. 'My name's not Audrey.'

She hurried away from him into the cloakroom. He stood there for some moments until he became gradually aware of people watching him. His own cheeks burned as he went into the gents' cloakroom and shut himself in a cubicle. He was almost crying now with anger. He clenched his fists and beat them on the air, cursing Jackson silently through clenched teeth. He stayed there several minutes until he felt he could face returning to the hall. As he came into the foyer he caught a glimpse of a girl who looked like Audrey hurrying out through the street door with a coat over her shoulders. He made a movement as if to follow her, then checked it and turned and went into the hall to find Sam and Finch and Bob. This was one thing Jackson wasn't going to get away with.

He found Sam first, alone, which was as he wanted it. He told him what had happened outside and how the girl had reacted.

'I don't know now if I'll ever see her again, Sam, or if she'll speak to me if I do. She's a chick with some class, Sam, see. It made her feel cheap being caught up against a wall like that. I know just how she feels, an' I'll allus remind her of it. Oh, that bloody lousy stinkin' pig Jackson.'

'He's a bloody maniac,' Sam said. 'Sex-mad. Where's the bird now?'

'I think she's hopped it. I thought I saw her goin' out just now.'

'An' where's Jacko?'

'He stopped outside playin' the bloody Peepin' Tom with his flashlamp.' Vince gripped Sam's arm. 'Listen, Sam, I'm goinna get that bugger for this. He's not gettin' away with it this time.'

'What you goinna do?'

'Wait for him on his way home an' do him. Are you with me? You'd like to have a go at him, wouldn't you?'

'Too bloody true I would,' Sam said. 'I haven't forgotten that night last winter when he picked on me an' threw me out of here. But it's no good just the two of us. Two of us can't manage him.'

'No, but we can if we have Finch an' Bob to back us up. We can bash the bugger till his own mother won't know him.'

Sam looked doubtful. 'Think they'll come?'

'Why not? They don't like Jacko any more than we do.'

'An' they don't like gettin' their earholes punched, either.'

215

'Oh, Christ Almighty, Sam, if the four of us can't manage him, I don't know who can. Where are they, anyway?'

'I think they're sittin' down the other end.'

'You get 'em. I'll go an' get a table in the coffee bar.'

A few minutes later the four of them were sitting round a corner table and Vince was telling the others what he had already told Sam. Bob appeared to find it amusing.

'What the hell you grinnin' at?' Vince demanded.

'Well, it's funny, in't it?' Bob said.

'I don't see owt bloody funny about it.'

'Well, there's a funny side to it, in't there?' Bob said. 'I mean, there's you standin' up against the wall with this tart an' along comes old Jacko an' shines his lamp on you.'

'You'd ha' thought it wa' funny if it'd been you, I suppose?' Vince said angrily. 'You'd ha' burst out laughin', I suppose?'

'No, I'd ha' been as mad as you,' Bob said. 'Only it wasn't me, it wa' you.'

'An' that makes all the bloody difference, eh?'

'Well, I mean...' Bob subsided in the face of Vince's furious glare.

'I'll bet you could ha' killed him,' Finch said.

'If thoughts could kill he'd be lyin' out there stone dead this minute.'

'Let's get down to business,' Sam said. 'Time's gettin' on. They'll be slingin' everybody out of here afore long.'

'What's up?' Finch said.

'We're goinna do Jackson on the way home,' Vince told him; 'that's what's up.'

'Who's we?' Bob wanted to know.

'Me an' Sam; an' you an' Finch if you're game.'

Finch said nothing but gave a quick startled glance at the faces of Vince and Sam sitting opposite him.

216

'You an' Sam...' Bob said. 'Think you can manage him?'

'If we have to,' Vince said grimly. 'But it'll make it easier if you an' Finch join in.'

Still Finch remained silent.

'I dunno,' Bob said. 'He's a big bloke... fifteen or sixteen stone. An' he can use his fists. You've seen how he handles blokes he doesn't like.'

'Aye, tackling him'll be a bit different from kickin' a bloke in the ribs up a back alley,' Vince said.

Bob flushed. 'You know I'm not scared of a scrap. You know I allus hold me corner up.'

'I know you do, Bob.' Vince's voice was now conciliatory, but under it he wished furiously that he could upturn the table on them all in contempt and go and do what he had to do alone. 'You're a good lad in a scrap. That's why we want you with us. You don't like Jacko, do you? You'd like to have a hand in doin' him, wouldn't you?'

Bob looked at Sam, then at Vince.

'What's your plan?'

'Well, you know the skinny bastard won't pay for a taxi an' he allus walks home except when it's chuckin' it down with rain. I've been thinkin', if we go first an' wait on the edge of the common, just by the wood, we can jump him before he knows we're there.'

Sam nodded. 'That's a good idea. It's the best place, an' he'll never know who we are in the dark up there.'

'He won't even know how many of us there is,' said Vince. 'We can make mincemeat of the bastard an' drop down into town an' be home in bed by one.'

'Suppose he doesn't go that way tonight?'

'He allus does. An' if he doesn't we'll have to call it off till another time. But he'll be there; it's a nice night for a walk.'

217

'An' a good scrap,' Sam said, smiling.

Vince warmed to him. 'Good old Sam,' he said, putting his arm round the other's shoulders.

'Suppose he recognises us?' Bob said.

'Oh, Christ, suppose, suppose. He's got nothin' on us, has he? He can't prove anythin'. We can think of a story an' back one another up.'

Sam glanced at his watch, a large gold one with a gold strap that he had picked up for a pound late one night from a young National Service soldier who was too drunk to walk home and hadn't a shilling in his pocket towards a taxi fare. 'We'd better be off if we're goin'. They'll be finishing here any time now.'

Vince looked at Finch. 'What about you, Finch? You've said nowt so far.'

Finch hesitated before speaking. 'I reckon I'm game,' he said in a moment, 'if Bob is. Not if there's only three of us though.'

'Good lad, Finch. You're a bloody trouper, you are. Now then, Bob, what about it?'

Bob played with a dirty cup which had not been cleared off the table before they sat down. He said nothing before Sam burst out impatiently:

'Oh, come on. What the hell's everybody ditherin' about? He's only one bloke against four of us. Let's get the bugger done. He's had it comin' to him for long enough.'

Bob decided, and pushed the cup away from him. 'Okay,' he said, 'I'm on.'

'That's the style,' Vince said exultantly. His eyes glittered in a face now flushed with excitement. He scraped back his chair. 'We'll half-kill the bastard. We'll give him summat to think about.'

The drums of the band were rolling for the National Anthem as they pushed a way through to the door. The dance was over. Jackson, they guessed, would be leaving in about fifteen minutes, which gave them time to approach the common by a roundabout route. Midnight struck from the clock tower of the Town Hall as they left the steep streets and took to an unsurfaced track along which they walked for a few minutes before leaving it for a narrow path across the rough grassland. They were quiet, speaking only occasionally and then in subdued voices, though the chance of their being seen or overheard here so late at night was remote. They were high up now above the town. Before them the path led on over the common to the Calderford Road and behind the darkness of the valley was pricked in a thousand places by the sparkle and glitter of streetlights. They left the path, swinging back in an arch towards the small wood on the town side, and now, for some time, no one spoke at all as they went on, lifting their feet high on the tussocky grassland.

Vince realised a few moments later that they had lost one of their number. 'Where the hell's Finch?' They stopped and turned, looking back the way they had come, as Finch came up after them at a run.

'Where the hell you been?'

'Stopped for a leak,' Finch said. 'I couldn't wait.'

'Thought you'd dropped down a rabbit hole,' Bob said, and Finch said, 'Ha, ha!'

'For Christ's sake, keep with us,' Vince told him. 'We're nearly there.'

'I've never been up here in the dark afore,' Finch said. 'Glad I'm not by meself. It's a lovely spot for a murder.'

'Quiet,' Vince said. 'Don't talk 'less you have to.'

They reached the wood, which was no bigger than a large copse, and made a quick reconnaissance. They decided then to stick to Vince's original plan of lying in wait for Jackson just where the path entered the trees.

219

Anyone using the path must surmount a small rise before dropping into the wood.

Vince said, 'I'll go up here an' keep a lookout. What time is it?'

Sam consulted the luminous face of his watch and said it was nearly a quarter past twelve.

'He shouldn't be long now.'

'If he comes at all,' Bob said.

'Course he'll come,' Vince said impatiently. 'He allus comes this way. It's his quickest way home when he's walkin'.'

He went forward to the summit of the hillock and as he stretched himself out on the cool grass the Town Hall clock struck the quarter hour. The moon was rising, lightening the sky. He hoped Jackson would not be too long or it might be light enough for him to recognise them. And too long a wait might rob Finch and Bob of their taste for the job. He wasn't worried about Sam. He would stick. He was a good mate. Vince felt that he could trust Sam as much as possible in a world where, when it came right down to it, you could trust nobody; where you depended on nobody but yourself and you relied on people and used them just as much as you only had to, and no more. He, if he admitted the truth, was using the gang tonight for the purpose of wreaking his personal revenge on Jackson. They none of them liked Jackson, true; and each had his reasons for not being sorry to see Jackson beaten up. But in none of them did the pure hatred burn as fiercely as it did in Vince and none of them would ever have made an attempt on Jackson if he hadn't screwed them up to it tonight. It was a performance he knew he could not repeat. It was tonight or never. If Jackson chose this one night to change his routine and go home another way, revenge was lost. And if he didn't come in the next few minutes it might be too late because already Vince could sense impatience in the wood behind him as a voice murmured and he heard the scrape of a match and saw its glow as some fool lit a cigarette. He wanted to shout at them, but dared not. He could only lie there waiting, hoping that Jackson would come soon.

He looked out across the valley. The starless sky seemed to be lifting and growing paler. He could make out the shape of buildings, the looming bulk of mills and the clock tower of the Town Hall. A car's headlights swooped on Halifax Road. He heard the gear-change in the valley bottom and the labour of the engine as it pulled away up the hill. In the quiet that followed a man coughed in the street beyond the fence and Vince's heart jumped. He lay very still, his muscles tensed ready for flight to the wood. But there was no other sound, not even a footstep.

Finch came up beside him. 'Isn't there any sign of him?'

'Not yet. He'll come, though; there's still plenty of time.'

'Happen he's gone another way.'

'He allus comes this way.'

'He might have got himself a woman to take home.'

'He's wed. Got a couple o' kids, I believe.'

Finch grunted. He was crouching and Vince said, 'Keep yoursen down, can't you?'

Finch crouched a little lower. 'How much longer are we waitin'?'

'We'll give him a bit longer. He might have had a bit o' clearin' up to do, or summat.'

'Bob says he doesn't think he's comin' now.'

'Who the bloody hell cares what Bob thinks?' Vince hissed. 'Is that him smokin' that fag?'

221

'Yeh, he lit up a minute or two sin'.'

'Well get back to him an' tell him to bloody well put it out,' Vince said.

Finch disappeared and Vince lifted himself on his elbows. That Bob. He was more and more trouble every time they met. The time was coming fast when they would have to settle it once and for all. And one swift hard punch into Bob's face would do the trick. If Jackson didn't turn up it might be a way of relieving his feelings tonight, because Bob was sure to have something to say about their having spent all this time on the common for nothing.

'Come on, Jackson,' he murmured. 'Come on, you big, stupid bastard, and get what's comin' to you.'

He began to think about the girl and he wondered if he would ever see her again. He remembered holding her and kissing her under the wall of the Trocadero and a lingering memory of tenderness touched his heart. Surely she wouldn't hold it against him for ever? Surely when she had calmed down and got over the humiliation she would realise that he, Vince, had not been able to help it? He had to see her again to find out. The Trocadero would be out after tonight because there would always be the fear that Jackson had known them.

And Cressley was a big place. He could go for years and never run into her again. But perhaps she too would avoid the Trocadero now and go to the Gala Rooms, because she had said she liked dancing. She had also said she liked swimming, so he could always look for her at the baths. He would go to the baths every evening after work for a month if necessary, because he had to see her again, no matter what. He just had to.

His heart lifted then with sudden excitement as he became aware of somebody whistling down the hill.

222

Jackson was coming, and whistling to keep himself company in the dark. He knew it was Jackson because he could recognise the whistle anywhere: light and musical and full of little runs and trills. He waited till Jackson's head and shoulders appeared at the stile, then slid down out of sight and ran back to join the others.

'He's comin'. Can you hear him whistlin'? We'll give the bastard summat to whistle about!'

They crouched on both sides of the path, hearing the scuff of a shoe-sole on a stone, then seeing Jackson's figure silhouetted against the lightening sky as he topped the rise.

'Remember,' Vince whispered. 'Don't talk.'

They closed with him as he came off the open common and into the shadow of the trees. Vince had visualised the attack as being quick, concerted and silent. As it was, there was a moment's hesitation as they became visible to Jackson, as though no one knew who was to lead the assault.

Jackson stopped and stepped back. 'Now then, what's this?'

'You'll find out in a minute, Jackson!' Finch said, and Bob said quickly, but too late, 'Shurrup, fool!'

Jackson came for them, his fists at the ready. His first blow swung little Finch off his feet and sent him crashing helplessly into the bushes. Vince yelped as the toe of Jackson's shoe cracked against his shin. Then Jackson went down with Sam and Bob hanging on to him and Vince held back, rubbing his calf and waiting to see where he could help to best effect. He watched as the three bodies rolled about on the ground and heard the grunts and curses that came from them. Then the sound of someone crashing through the dry bracken diverted his attention and the next moment he saw Finch

223

break clear of the wood and scurry up the path over the hillock. He opened his mouth to shout for Finch, then checked himself, muttering under his breath, 'The miserable little shit. The yellow little bleeder.'

Two of those struggling on the ground came to their feet, leaving the third bent almost double, holding his belly and moaning. Vince thought it was Sam. It wasn't going right. Jackson was too much even for the four of them. With Finch gone and Sam out of the fight it was time he looked to himself. But it was already too late. Jackson broke free of Bob's hug, felled him with a blow, and turned to Vince.

'Now you,' Jackson said. His voice was thick, as though he was swallowing blood. He was breathing heavily too and he was unsteady on his feet. He had taken a lot of punishment from Sam and Bob but he was far from finished.

Vince cursed Finch again as he backed away. He knew that once Jackson closed with him he was done for. Before he hardly knew it the knife was open in his hand.

'Hold it, Jackson, or you'll get some o' this.' He flourished the weapon in an attempt at bravado and the blade glinted dully in the moonlight filtering down through the trees.

Jackson stopped for a second, then came on more slowly, his arms wide apart, his body poised ready to jump at the lunge of the knife. 'Don't be a bloody fool. Put that thing away before you hurt somebody.'

There was no reason left in Vince, only a sobbing rage and hatred for Jackson, who would beat him unmercifully if he once got in close enough. It had all gone wrong and it was Jackson's fault. Hatred seemed to swim in a hot wave before his eyes. He felt then the trunk of a tree behind him and knew he could retreat no farther without partly turning his back on Jackson. A trickle of warm liquid ran down the inside of his leg and he thought with stupid anger that he should have stopped when Finch had. His voice raised itself, shrill with fear and the knowledge that he was afraid.

'It'll be you 'at'll get hurt, Jackson. I'll carve the bloody tripes out of you, you dirty stinkin' bastard, if you come any nearer.'

Jackson came warily and steadily on, his eyes fixed on the blade of the knife.

'I've warned you. Keep back!'

There was a movement from behind Jackson. In the same second he sprang, Bob jumped him from the rear and Vince drove forward and upward with the knife, the force of the blow taking his fist hard against Jackson's belly. They all went down together in a heap.

Vince and Bob extricated themselves and got up together. They looked down at Jackson. There was blood on the fingers of Vince's right hand. He moved them and felt its sticky warmth. In a kind of daze he half lifted his hand to look.

'That's settled him,' Bob was saying. 'Now let's get out of here.' A second later he saw the knife. 'Christ, what you doin' with that?'

'I told him,' Vince said stupidly. 'I warned him he'd get it.' He touched Jackson's leg with the toe of his shoe. 'Jackson! Come on, now.'

'You've finished him,' Bob said. There was raw panic in his voice. 'Oh, Christ! Oh, Christ!'

Sam came up behind them, still rubbing his belly. 'God, me guts... What we hangin' about here for?'

'He's knifed him,' Bob said. 'The bloody fool's finished him.'

'Don't talk daft,' Vince said. 'He's okay. He's just

reckonin'. We only roughed him up a bit, didn't we? That's all we said we'd do, in't it? Nobody said owt about killing the stupid bastard, did they?'

'Jesus,' Sam said. 'Oh, Christ Jesus. I'm not in this.'

'Me neither,' Bob said. 'I didn't do it. They can't touch me for it.'

He turned and blundered to the path, breaking into a run over the rise.

'Jackson!' Vince said. 'Give over reckonin', you lousy sod.' He pushed at Jackson with his foot. 'Jackson!'

He heard Sam say something from behind him but did not take in the words. He dropped the knife and went down on his knees beside Jackson.

'Jackson. Come on. Jackson, wake up. I know you're actin'. You can't kid me. C'mon you lousy dog, c'mon. Stop reckonin'!'

His hand came in contact with the mess of blood on the front of Jackson's shirt and he recoiled and stood up, staring in horror at the dark smear across his palm and fingers. It was as though this finally released in him a tremendous force of uncontrollable fury and hatred. He began to kick Jackson's body in a frenzy, assaulting it with savage blows of his feet and swearing in a torrent of words. And when, at last, he stopped, exhausted, his body suddenly sagging from the hips, his arms hanging limp at his sides, he raised his head and looked round. The moon rose from behind a ragged edge of cloud and the pale light fell on his upturned face. It was quiet. He was alone.

A SEASON
WITH EROS

A Season with Eros

Ruffo had waited a long time, kept at bay through his two-year courtship of that girl whose body turned men's heads in the street by the discipline imposed by her cold-eyed watchful mother. A certain amount of boy-girl contact was expected, even approved of: holding hands while watching television in her front room; kisses and tight straining cuddles when the parents were absent; but any attempt to get closer to Maureen than the clutching of her resilient flesh through her clothes was met with an automatic and persistent response: 'No, I can't.' 'Why not?' 'Me mam says I've to wait till I get married.' Beyond this Ruffo found it impossible to go. At best she was stupid, childlike in her reiteration of 'Me mam says...'; at worst Ruffo wondered whether in her he had found that most sexually maddening of combinations – a girl whose body yelled promise but whose mind and emotions had no real interest in the subject at all. Exasperated, he drew away from her until his continual casual excuses for not seeing her made his neglect obvious and she, ingenuous in her directness, faced him with it.

'I don't see much point.'

'Oh...What's made you change your mind?'

'Your mother. She runs your life for you.'

'She's only trying to do her best for me. Anyway, if that's all you want me for...'

'If that's all I want you for I've been seeing you a long time for bugger-all, haven't I?' Ruffo said. 'If you want the truth, I can't stand it any more.'

'I've told you, I don't think it's right when you're not married.'

'You mean your mam doesn't.'

'Well, I've always taken notice of what she says.'

'I'm not talking about going the whole hog,' Ruffo said.

'But one thing leads to another, doesn't it?'

Ruffo might have looked at the mother and discerned, more than the person who was keeping him from what he wanted, the woman the daughter could become. But he saw only, behind the canteen buildings where they had met, the creature of his long-repressed desire, the pout of her lips, the rise and fall of her breasts under the thin nylon overall, and he knew that he must have her.

'We'd better get married, then.'

'Oh!' She took it with apparent surprise as though she'd been prepared to go on as they were indefinitely. 'Well, we'd better get engaged first.'

'I don't want any long engagements dragging on. We've been seeing each other for two years now.'

'But we've nowhere to live. And no stuff collected.'

'I'll find somewhere.'

'I suppose me mam 'ud let us live at our house for a while.'

'No,' Ruffo said. 'We want to be on our own. I'll find somewhere.'

He began scanning the property columns of the evening newspaper and asking round among the men in the engineering shop. In the meantime, Maureen broke the news to her mother, who said that Ruffo ought to make his intentions public by buying her a ring. The thirty pounds that this cost Ruffo he parted with grudgingly, feeling that it was money he could ill-afford. Houses were expensive and whatever they found they would need all the cash they could scrape together to put in it even the necessary minimum of furniture. He worked all the overtime offered him, cut out his weekly drinking night with his mates, and stopped taking Maureen anywhere it cost money. He didn't smoke, so there was no saving to be made there. Thinking that he should have a clear idea of their combined resources, he asked Maureen about her savings, only to find to his dismay that was she still giving her wages to her mother, who returned her a weekly sum of pocket money which she spent on make-up and small luxuries.

'Me mam always said I could start paying me own way when I was twenty-one,' Maureen said. 'And, of course, that's still a couple of months off.'

'So you're coming to me empty handed.'

'I've a few sheets an' pillow-cases 'at me mam's giving me.'

'That's bloody generous of her.'

'An' of course they'll be paying for the wedding.' Ruffo thought with some regret of the passing of the dowry system. 'What we need is brass,' he said. 'Hard cash, to pay the deposit on a house and furnish it.'

'They're building some lovely ones up Lime Lane,' she said.

'You must be out of your mind. They're a four-and-a-half thousand quid touch. That means at least five hundred deposit.'

Which Ruffo hadn't got. And as he went on looking and making enquiries he came to see the nature of the trap he had laid for himself. Marriage to Maureen had seemed an obvious way of getting what he wanted; but marriage was not, it seemed, a state easily achieved. And now he was worse off than before: still deprived, but robbed by that engagement ring of the freedom to come and go which he had held in reserve and thought of as a bargaining counter.

Then he struck lucky, hearing from a workmate about a house occupied by an old lady who had just been taken into hospital with what looked like a fatal illness.

'You want to get round there. Put your word in afore anybody else does.'

'I'll bet there's five hundred after it already.'

'You never know. You'll lose nowt by trying.'

And gain nothing if I don't, Ruffo thought.

He went straight to the owner, a wholesale grocer who received him in the hall of his grand new bungalow.

'A house? I don't know that there's one coming vacant.'

Ruffo saw the delicacy of the situation and chose his words accordingly. 'An old lady lived there. I heard she'd died in hospital.'

'It's news to me if she's dead.' The man eyed him shrewdly. 'You mean you want to be first in line if she does pop off? By God, you're quick off the mark, some of you. You don't let the breath leave the corpse.'

'I expect there's plenty before me, anyway,' Ruffo said. 'You don't stand much chance of dropping across a house to rent nowadays.'

'Why don't you buy one?'

232

'Because I haven't got the money. If I could find a place in the meantime it'd give me a chance to save up. Everybody's got to start somewhere.'

'Otherwise it's in-laws, is that it?'

Ruffo shook his head. 'I'm not having that.'

'No, happen you're wise there. What did you say your name was?'

'Billy Roughsedge.'

'Did they call your father Walter?'

'Aye, that's right.'

'I knew him. Played bowls with him many a time in days gone by. Dead now, though, isn't he?'

'Aye, me mother as well. I live with me married sister.'

'Well, like I say, I don't know that there's anything coming vacant, but I'll keep you in mind. Give us your address.'

Ruffo thought little more of it; but a fortnight later he got a note through the post to say that the house was now empty and if he still wanted it would he go to see the agents.

It stood in a terrace on a back street; two rooms down, two up; no hot water, and a lavatory – shared with another family – in the long communal yard. Everything in that area was probably due for demolition during the next few years, Ruffo thought. But programmes like that had a way of being put back and before then he and Maureen would have got out; or if they hadn't the Corporation would be compelled to offer them alternative accommodation, along with everyone else. It was a start, a place to live, on their own; nothing to shout about but no worse than either of them had known before at some time in their lives. And it could be made cosy enough.

They fixed a date for the wedding and Ruffo went through the house stripping paint and wallpaper and redecorating from top to bottom. Before that, with the help of a friend, he pulled out the black old range and replaced it with a tiled fireplace. He also fitted over the corner sink an electric water-heater which he'd bought second-hand through the small ads in the evening paper. For their furniture they went to sale rooms. Maureen would have liked more new pieces, but Ruffo showed her the balance in his Post Office Bank book and made it clear that he did not intend to start out with a load of hire-purchase debts.

Marriage

Marriage suited Ruffo. He had lived for too long in someone else's house; and though the people involved were his sister and his brother-in-law there had been occasional small points of friction. Their children were growing up, needing more space, and he'd had for some time the feeling that he was beginning to get in the way. Now he had his own place and a wife: a home where he could do as he liked, and as much sex as he wanted with the girl he'd always wanted it with. Any lingering fears that she might not find pleasure in it were quickly dispelled. With the wedding over, and a ring on her finger, she became willing and compliant, following wherever he led with no more protest than an occasional indulgent 'Ruffo! Whatever will you think of next?'

For Ruffo, in possession of her at last, had thrown himself from the cliff of frustrated deprivation into a protracted sexual binge. Impossible for him to have too much of her, he liked her to go without pants and bra in the house so that at any moment he could catch at her, one hand into her blouse to knead at a breast, the other under her skirt where, to her coy whinnies of delight, his probing fingers would draw the juices of her instant response. His fondling of her like this in the early evening, sometimes by the sink as she washed-up after their meal, would often lead to his taking her there and then, she standing, back arched, legs apart and braced, panting to the electric contact of his flesh. On other evenings, with the fire built high and the television picture flickering silently in the corner, she would dress for him in items of exotic underwear and lingerie which he bought through the post to accentuate or semi-conceal the objects of his never-ending desire: briefs whose flimsy transparency held like a dark stain the tufty triangle of her crotch; brassieres cut low to lift those already splendidly jutting breasts and thrust them up and out, rampant-nippled, like great pale tropical fruits. Nor did any of this tire them for later when, in bed together, his earlier spending gave him a restraint which could carry them through an hour of intertwined limbs, bringing her time after time until it seemed to her that each night was one long moan of love.

He was confident, in command. His ego strutted and he carried himself with an assurance which bordered on the insolent. It was not lost on other women: Ruffo felt their awareness. One who served behind the counter of the canteen watched him as he stood in line for his meal. When he got to the head of the queue she put a double portion of cabbage on his plate.

'There y'are. That'll put some lead in your pencil.'

'I've got plenty, thanks.'

'You could run short, the way you're going on.'

Ruffo's head came up. 'What d'you mean by that?'

'Nay, lad, I'm only kidding you. If you've any to spare you can bring it round to my house. My old man's forgotten what it's all about.'

Ruffo grinned. 'Sorry. It's all spoken for.'

'Aye, well,' the woman said with mock regret, 'you can but try.'

Ruffo challenged Maureen that evening.

'What have you been saying to them women in the canteen?'

'Oh, you know how they kid about things like that, Ruffo. They got on at me and somehow or other it came out that we do it every day. Sometimes more. They're only jealous.'

'Aye,' Ruffo said, his hands on her. 'I look after you well, don't I?'

'Mmm, you do. It's lovely.'

'It's better than that,' Ruffo said. 'It's bloody perfect.'

He was happy. He worked hard, saving all the money he could; but beyond this he did not worry about the future. Today was what mattered. Yesterday was gone; tomorrow would come when it came. They were both young; there was plenty of time for everything. He lived for the present; for each evening when, secure and warm in their own home, they could indulge in their sexual games. Maureen was his now; he moulded her to his desire, was masterful in the way he took her. She seemed to want it that way, content in being the focus of most of his waking thoughts. A knowing little half-smile would often appear momentarily in her eyes when he touched her, as though she knew very well the power her compliance gave her over him.

One evening they were lying together on the hearthrug when Maureen's mother came unexpectedly to the door. Ruffo grabbed his clothes and went upstairs while Maureen put on her dressing-gown and let her in.

'I was just getting washed and changed,' Maureen explained.

Her mother glanced round the room, her nostrils

Mother's visit
— case of illness to bring
the people's change of attitude

dilating, as though she could smell their passion in the air. Ruffo, coming down the stairs a few moments later, heard a part of their conversation.

'He's not, er, asking too much of you, is he?'

'What do you mean?'

'Well, some men, you know, they're greedy. They never leave a woman alone.'

'Oh, I see! No, it's not like that at all.'

'As long as you're all right. There are other things in life, you know.'

Tell her you love it, Ruffo thought. Tell her to mind her own business. He opened the door and walked into the room.

It was a few evenings later that Maureen said, 'Ruffo, I think we ought to save it till we're in bed.'

'Eh?'

'Well, you know the other night, when me mam came; I didn't know where to put meself for a minute or two. Suppose we'd forgotten to slip the latch and she'd walked straight in?'

'Oh, now...'

'I mean, she knew what we were doing, Ruffo. I know she knew.'

'Well, what about it? Come o-on...'

He got his way, but for the first time he felt in her submission an unspoken reproach. There was little response: she was acquiescent, no more, and he was alone, with her as the passive instrument of his pleasure.

He had no time to resolve this before she went down with a heavy cold which turned into influenza and confined her to bed for a week. Her mother came every day to tidy the house, do their washing, and attend to Maureen while Ruffo was out at work. Then there came an evening when she was fully recovered and Ruffo thought it was time he broke his sexual fast. He went upstairs to look in her lingerie drawer and came back down again to ask her:

'Where's your black sling bra?'

'Which one do you mean?'

'You know which I mean. The one I sent away for.'

'Oh, that one.' She wasn't looking at him. 'Ruffo, me mam found it when she was sorting out the washing.'

'Oh, did she?'

'She said she didn't know how I could wear a thing like that. She said it was the sort of thing a prostitute wears.'

'How does she know what a prostitute wears? And what's it got to do with her, anyway?'

'Nothing, I suppose. But still...'

'And where is it, then?'

'I... I burned it. I put it on the fire the other day.'

He was incredulous. 'You did what? What the hell made you do that?'

'I wanted to be rid of it, I just didn't fancy wearing it any more.'

'Nobody was asking you to go out in it. It was for me.'

'I know. All the same...'

Ruffo went back upstairs and had another look in the drawer.

'You've made a clean sweep, haven't you?'

Still she couldn't meet his eyes. 'I... I felt... well, sort of dirty.'

'Oh, you did!' Ruffo said, irate now. 'Did I make you feel mucky when I bought 'em for you and you put 'em on for me?'

'Well, no, not then.'

'But you would now?'

'It was all right, Ruffo. I knew *you* liked it. But we can still make love without that sort of thing.'

238

'You'll be bloody getting undressed in the dark next,' Ruffo said, the anger bursting out of him.

'There's no need to exaggerate.'

'Look,' Ruffo said, 'haven't we had a good time since we got married? You and me. Haven't we had a good time?'

'Of course we have.'

'Well, why let somebody else stick their nose in?'

'It's not that...'

'Well, what is it, then?'

'Give up, Ruffo. Stop getting on at me. I've got a headache.'

Ruffo carried his anger to bed with him. For the first time they lay back to back, not touching.

He was surly and uncommunicative during the next few days, speaking only when necessary. He ate his evening meal in silence then looked at television for three or four hours before going early to bed. One night he went down to the local pub, something he'd done only a couple of times since they were married, and came back uncertain in his movements. Maureen began to stay in bed another half an hour in the mornings, leaving him to get himself off to work. It was less retaliation on her part than a wish not to provoke him, to let him work off his mood in his own time. For she had something to tell him and when the weekend arrived without any change she forced herself to speak.

'Ruffo, I know you're out of sorts with me, and I'm sorry. But there's something you'll have to know. I think I'm pregnant.'

'Well, that's bloody marvellous,' Ruffo said.

'Is that all you've got to say?'

'I thought we were going to wait till we'd moved to a decent house and settled down a bit.'

'I know, but—'

'We're only... we're only kids our*selves*! What do we want a baby yet for?'

'That's all very well. But if I'm having one, I am. You can't always plan these things, can you?'

'Course you can,' Ruffo said. 'Ninety-nine times out of a—' He stopped and, for the first time in days, looked directly at her. 'You didn't do it on purpose, did you?'

'What makes you think—?'

'You did,' Ruffo said. 'You bloody did. I can see it written all over your face.'

'Look, Ruffo,' she said eagerly, 'the younger you are when you have your family the more time you have together when they've grown up and you're on your own again.'

It was like a doctrine she had learned. He stared at her, aghast. 'Who cares about what happens *then*? We might all be bloody dead by then. I want my time now, while I'm young.'

'You don't want a family at all, do you?'

'In a year or two,' Ruffo said, 'when we're better placed and we've enjoyed being together, just the two of us.'

'But we've had that, haven't we?'

'Aye, we have,' Ruffo said. 'We've had it, all right.'

It was all going, vanishing before his eyes. He looked at Maureen as though he'd never really seen her before. He had thought he was moulding her but now, in a flash of intuition, he perceived his fate as a function of the phases of her life. He was too young for a glass case marked 'husband'.

He brooded on it for a couple of days; then one morning he turned over in bed when the alarm clock rang and said he wasn't feeling well. When Maureen had gone out to work he got up, shaved and dressed, packed his personal belongings in a case, wrote a note for her, and left.

The note said that he would not be coming back, but that when he had settled down elsewhere he would write again and arrange to pay maintenance for the child. Maureen's mother wanted her to put the police on his trail so that she could sue for maintenance for herself, but Maureen refused to do this. She had her job and she gave up the house and sold its contents and moved back in with her parents. Six months later she heard from Ruffo who was now in Australia, working on a hydroelectric power scheme. He said he would be willing if she wanted to divorce him, since she was still very young and would no doubt want to marry again. There were times when she felt a vague yearning for Ruffo's loving, but she came to accept that as a stage of her life which had passed; that, and the earlier one of the young unmarried girl single-mindedly keeping herself untouched for her future husband. With the child big in her now she was absorbed in her new role of mother-to-be. And to this she added the unexpected one of deserted wife without too much apparent strain.

acceptance of stages in life

She accepts the traditional role society pushes at her
He rejects it

Twenty Pieces of Silver

[handwritten annotation:] a good religious women is tested by temptation of a pound # a small drawer of religion (asked)

When the Misses Norris, in pursuance of their good works, called on little Mrs Fosdyke at her tiny terrace house in Parker Street she answered their discreet knock dressed for going out. They apologized then in their quiet, genteel way and said they would call again. But Mrs Fosdyke beckoned them into the house. 'I've just come in,' she said. 'A minute or two earlier and you'd have followed me down the street.' It was then that the Misses Norris realised that Mrs Fosdyke was dressed in black, the hat shop-bought but the coat probably run up on her own machine, and, as if reading their minds, she said, 'I've just been to a funeral,' and the Misses Norris murmured 'Oh?' for no-one of their acquaintance had died during the past week.

They sat down when asked to, the elder Miss Norris on the edge of the armchair by the table, legs tucked neatly away behind her skirt; the younger Miss Norris upright on a chair by the window. Mrs Fosdyke slipped off her coat and occupied herself with kettle and teapot at the sink in the corner.

'You'll have a cup o' tea?' she asked, the spoon with the second measure poised over the pot.

'Well...' the younger Miss Norris began, and her sister said, with the poise and grace of her extra years, 'You're very kind.'

'I hate funerals,' Mrs Fosdyke said conversationally as she poured boiling water into the pot. 'If it's anybody you thought anything of they upset you; and if it's somebody you didn't like you feel a hypocrite.'

She took two more cups and saucers from the cupboard over the sink, wiping them thoroughly on the tea towel before setting them out alongside her own on the oilcloth-covered top of the clothes-wringer under the window.

'Was it a relative?' the younger Miss Norris ventured.

Mrs Fosdyke shook her head. 'No, a friend. A good friend. Mrs Marsden from up Hilltop. Don't know if you knew her. A widow, like me. Her husband died five or six years back. He used to be something in textiles over Bradford way. Quite well-to-do, they were. Poor dear... She had cancer, y'know. It was a happy release for her.'

She poured the tea, handing the Misses Norris a cup each and passing the sugar bowl and milk jug to each in turn. She herself remained standing, between the wringer and the sink, the late-morning sun lighting her grey hair below the little black hat.

'Funny,' she said reflectively, between sips. 'Fifteen years I'd known Mrs Marsden and it might only have been a month or two. Funny how friendships start...'

'I answered an advertisement in the *Argus*, y'know. That's how I came to go in the first place. Jim was alive then and he'd just taken to his wheelchair. I was looking

243

for work but I couldn't take on a full-time job because of having him to see to. So I got a few cleaning jobs that kept me busy six mornings a week. Mrs Marsden's was one of them. Three mornings, I went to her.

'I didn't think I was going to stick it at first. There was nothing wrong with the job or the money, mind; but they hadn't started running buses up to Hilltop at that time, and it was a mile and a half uphill from town. A rare drag, it was, and it seemed to get longer and steeper and harder every morning I went there. Anyway, I needed the money, and that was that.

'I knew when Jim first went down it wouldn't be easy, but I told meself we'd manage. Just so long as I could keep going.'

The Misses Norris, neither of whom had ever done anything more strenuous about a house than vacuum a carpet, murmured in sympathy and understanding and sipped their tea.

'Well, it wasn't too bad when I'd got used to it – the going out and cleaning, I mean. We managed. Mrs Reed next-door kept her eye on Jim in the mornings, and I did my own cleaning and my shopping in the afternoons. We'd always been ones for simple pleasures. We liked the chapel. There were the services on Sundays and the Women's Bright Hour on Wednesday afternoons, and I used to park Jim's chair in the porch where he could hear the singing and watch what was going on in the street. And then there were the Saturday-night concerts in the schoolroom – though they don't have so many of them nowadays – and anybody who was willing did a turn. I can see Jim's face now, all flushed and cheerful, his head nodding to the music...'

'He was a brave and cheerful man, Mrs Fosdyke,' said the elder Miss Norris. 'We all admired his courage.'

'Aye, aye. Well, of course, you know all about the chapel and the Bright Hour, an' that.

'Well, Mrs Marsden made me realise you could be well off and still unhappy. That you could be lacking in peace and quietness of mind even with no money worries, and a husband in good health.

'I remember the first time we talked as woman to woman. It came up because it was a Wednesday and I wanted to finish prompt on twelve so's I could get done at home in time for the Bright Hour. It was my first week with Mrs Marsden and I had to explain the position.'

'"I don't mind stopping a bit extra on Mondays and Fridays, if you need me," I said, "but I shouldn't like to miss my Bright Hour on a Wednesday."'

'"I'm sure I shouldn't like to be the one to keep you away," she said, and there was something a bit odd in her voice that puzzled me. But nothing more was said till the Wednesday after, and then she brought it up herself, and this queer something in her voice was there again, and I asked her if she didn't go to a place of worship herself, then.

'"I used to," she said, "a long time ago. I was brought up in the Church. I was on several committees. I worked like a slave for it."

'"And whatever made you give it up, then?" I said. "I lost all reason for going," she said.

'I was a bit shocked then. "You mean," I said, "you lost your faith in God?"

'As soon as I'd said it, of course, I was sorry I'd pried. It was none of my business, after all.

'And then, after a minute, she said "Yes." Just like that: straight out.

'I remember clearly as if it were yesterday, knocking off the vacuum cleaner and looking at her. I knew lots of people who never went to either chapel or church, but I'd never come face to face with one who said straight out she was atheist. Because, that's what it amounted to.

'So I said to her, "Well, I mean, it's none of my business, but what ever did that to you?"

'And she rolled her duster up and her face went all hard. "I had a boy." she said. "He died."

'I could feel for her. "That's terrible," I said. "But lots of people—"'

"'But this was *my* boy," she said. "For ten years we prayed for a child. We prayed and prayed, and then eventually he came. He was an imbecile. He died when he was three. Have you ever had an idiot child, Mrs Fosdyke?" she said, and she was so twisted up with bitterness inside her I could hardly bear to look at her.

'So I said, no, I hadn't. "But I've seen a fine God-fearing man struck down in his prime and condemned to spend the rest of his days in a wheelchair," I said. "I can sympathize with you, Mrs Marsden."'

"'And yet you still believe," she said, and she was full of impatience and anger. "How can you believe in a God of love who allows these things?"

"'Wouldn't it be easy to believe if everything in the world was fine and grand?" I said. "Anybody could believe with no trouble at all. But that's not God's way. He has to send suffering to try us, to steel us and purify us."

"'Oh, stuff and nonsense," she said. "I've heard it all before. What does a little child know of these things?"

"'I know, I know," I said. "It's hard to understand. But how can he make an exception for children? There has to be danger for them, just like grown-ups."

'So she just turned her back on me then and polished away at the dresser. And then she spun round on me in a second. "But how can you reconcile yourself to it?" she said. "How can you accept it?"

"'It's one of those things you can't argue out, Mrs Marsden," I said. "You can talk about it till Domesday and get no forrader. It's something you've got to feel. And I reckon you either feel it or you don't. How can I accept it, you say. Why, what else can I do? If I lose that, I've nothing else left." And I looked at her and I said, "But you do miss it, don't you, you poor dear?"

'I'd gone a bit too far there. She drew herself up and went all chilly. She was a very thin woman, you know, and she could look very proud when she set herself. "I don't need your pity, thank you," she said. "What you believe is your own business... You can finish the carpet now," she said, "if you don't mind."

'I was sorry afterwards that it had happened. I was beginning to find in this business of going into other women's homes that a friendly but respectful relationship was the best on both sides, and I didn't want to spoil anything...

'Another cup? Oh, go on; it'll just be wasted if you don't... That's right.'

The two Misses Norris allowed their cups to be refilled, and since they had nothing else to do that morning which could not be done later, settled back in comfort to hear whatever else Mrs Fosdyke would tell them of her relationship with the late Mrs Marsden.

'She wouldn't leave it alone, though,' Mrs Fosdyke said. 'She seemed to be waiting for chances to bring it up again. She seemed to have to let out that sourness and bitterness inside her. I didn't like it, and I did think of leaving her. But I decided I could stand it. She wasn't a bad employer, and I needed the money. Pride has to take a bit of a back seat when you're in a position I was in then.'

'Anyway, I'd been working for her for six months, and one Wednesday I went up there as usual. The mornings passed quickly, and it seemed like twelve o'clock came almost before I'd gotten started. As I was putting my things on to go, Mrs Marsden remembered two things at once. She wanted me to leave one of her husband's suits at the cleaners, and she had to nip out to see a neighbour who'd be going out at any minute.

'So she came into the kitchen with the suit draped all any-old-how over her arm. "Here we are," she said. "He hasn't worn it for some time. I'd like to see if it will clean up decently. Now if I don't hurry I shall miss Mrs Wilson. You'll find paper and string in that cupboard; and you might just go through the pockets before you wrap it up. I haven't time, myself." And with a last reminder to drop the latch as I went out, she was off.

'I had a look at the suit then. It looked nearly new to me, and I thought to myself. "Fancy being able to cast aside a suit like this." I hadn't got to the stage of begging clothes, but I was tempted at times. Jim had never had a suit like that in his life.

'Well, I took each part of it in turn and brushed it down with the flat of my hand and went through all the pockets. When I got to the waistcoat I more felt than heard something crackle in one of the pockets, and when I put my fingers in I pulled out a pound note, folded in two. So from thinking about Mr Marsden discarding good clothes I got to thinking about a "carry on" that could allow a pound note to be lost without being missed.

'I popped it down on a corner of the kitchen cabinet and wrapped the suit in brown paper. I found myself glancing sideways at the note. Who knew about it but me? A pound... twenty shillings. What was a pound to the Marsdens? And what was a pound to Jim and me? There were few enough ever came our way, and every one was hard earned, every shilling to be held on to till I couldn't help spending it. Things had been tighter than usual lately, as well. We'd had a lot of expense. I took the note into my hand and thought of all it could buy. Fruit for Jim, and a bit of tobacco – always a special treat. And he needed new underclothes. And I'd planned to get him a bottle of the tonic wine that seemed to buck him up so.

'So, I stood there in Mrs Marsden's kitchen with her husband's pound note screwed up in a little ball in my hand where nobody else could see it; and it was just as though there was nothing else in the world but that note and my need of it.'

Mrs Fosdyke's voice had grown softer and now it died away altogether as she stopped speaking and gazed out through the window. The two sisters exchanged a swift glance before she stirred and turned to put her empty cup on the draining board.

'Well, that was a Wednesday, like I said. And on the Friday I went up to the house again. I was there at nine, my usual time. I remember distinctly that it was a rainy morning. Not heavy rain, but that thin, fine stuff that seems to wet you through more thoroughly than an out-and-out downpour. Anyway, I was soaked by the time I got there, and when I'd changed into my working-shoes, I took my coat upstairs to let it drip into the bath. Then I helped Mrs Marsden with the few breakfast pots and we got going on the downstairs rooms, like we always did on a Friday.

'She was a bit quiet that morning, Mrs Marsden was, and I thought perhaps she wasn't feeling too well. At eleven we knocked off for five minutes and went into the kitchen for a cup of tea and a biscuit. And then Mrs

Marsden said, just casual like, "By the way," she said, "Mr Marsden seems to think he left some money in that suit you took to the cleaners. Did you find anything when you looked through the pockets?"

'I'd clean forgotten about it till she mentioned it. I put my cup down and got up and felt under one of the canisters on the shelf. "You didn't see it, then?" I said. "I popped it up there on Wednesday. I meant to mention it, but I get more forgetful every day. That's all there was: just the odd note." I wondered she didn't notice the tremble in my fingers as I handed it to her.

'She spread the note out by her plate and said she'd give it to Mr Marsden when he came home. And I said it was funny that he'd bethought himself about it after all that time. I remembered she'd said he hadn't worn the suit for some while.

'"Well," she said, "you see -er-er..." And she got all sort of tongue-tied, and then I knew there was something wrong somewhere. I didn't like the look on her face, for a start. And then it came over me, all at once.

'"Why," I said, "I believe you put that money in your husband's suit. I don't think he knows anything about it. You put it there deliberately, hoping I'd take it and say nothing."

'She went red then; her face coloured like fire. "I have to test the honesty of my servants," she said, sort of proud like, but uneasy under it.

'And it got my rag out, that did. I was blazing mad. "Well you tested mine," I said. "And if it's any joy to you, I'll admit I was sorely tempted. Isn't it enough that you should lose your way without making me lose mine? A pound, Mrs Marsden," I said. "Twenty pieces of silver. Is that my price, d'you think? They gave Judas thirty!"

250

'She got up. "I don't have to take this kind of talk from you," she said, and brushed past me and ran upstairs.

'I sat down at the table and put my head in my hands. I was near to tears. I couldn't understand it. I just couldn't understand what had made her do it. And I said a little prayer of thanks. "O God," I said, "only You knew how near I was."

'In a few minutes I got up and went and listened at the foot of the stairs. I went up to the bathroom and got my coat. I stood for a minute then. There was no place for me here in the future. I felt like leaving straight away: walking out without another word. But I was due to a week's wages and I couldn't afford pride of that sort.

'So I called out softly, "Mrs Marsden."

'But there was no reply. I went across the landing to her bedroom door and listened. I could hear something then, but I wasn't quite sure what it was. I called again, and when nobody answered I tapped on the door and went in. She was lying on one of the twin beds with her face to the window. I could tell now it was sobbing I'd heard and her shoulders shook as I stood and watched her. There was something about her that touched me right to the quick, and I put my coat down and went to her and put my hand on her shoulder. "There, there," I said, "don't take on so. There's no harm done." I sat down behind her on the bed, and all at once she put her hand up and took mine. "Don't go away," she said. "Don't leave me now."

'I remember just the feeling I had then. It was like a great rush of joy: the sort of feeling you get when you know you're wanted, that somebody needs you.

'"Of course I won't leave you," I said, "Of course I won't."

Mrs Fosdyke sighed and turned from the window. 'And I never did,' she said. 'I never did.'

She looked at each of the sisters in turn. 'Well,' she said, a bashful little smile coming to her lips. 'I've never told anybody about that before. But this morning sort of brought it all back. And she's gone beyond harm now, poor dear.'

She glanced at the clock on the mantelpiece. 'Gracious, look at the time! And me keeping you sat with my chatter.'

'But what a lovely story,' said the younger Miss Norris, who was of a romantic turn of mind. 'It's like something out of the Bible.'

'Well, that's as maybe,' Mrs Fosdyke said briskly. 'but I'm sure you didn't call to hear me tell the tale.'

'As a matter of fact,' the elder Miss Norris said, drawing a sheaf of papers from her large handbag, 'we're organising the collection for the orphanage and we wondered if you could manage this district again this year. We know how busy you are.'

'Well' – Mrs Fosdyke put her finger to her chin – 'I suppose I could fit it in.'

'You're such a *good* collector, Mrs Fosdyke,' the younger Miss Norris said. 'Everyone gives so generously when you go round.'

'Aye, well, I suppose I can manage it,' Mrs Fosdyke said, and the Misses Norris beamed at her.

'Oh, we know the willing hearts and hands,' Mrs Fosdyke,' the elder sister said.

'I suppose you do,' said Mrs Fosdyke, with a hint of dryness in her voice.

'There'll be a place in heaven for you. Mrs Fosdyke,' gushed the younger Miss Norris.

'Oh, go on with you.' Mrs Fosdyke said. 'Somebody's got to look out for the poor lambs, haven't they?'

Principle

*Argument between a
miner - man &
a Strike breaker
in the family*

Mrs Stringer had a hot meal ready for the table at twenty-five past five when the click of the gate told her of her husband Luther's approach. His bad-tempered imprecation on the dog, which was lying on the doorstep in the evening sun, told her also what frame of mind he was in.

With the oven-cloth protecting her hands she picked up the stewpot and carried it through into the living-room. 'Your father's in one of his moods, Bessie,' she said to her daughter, who had arrived home a few minutes before and was laying the table for the meal. 'For goodness' sake don't get his back up tonight. I've had a splittin' head all day.'

There was the sound of running water as Luther washed his hands under the kitchen tap, and in a few minutes the three of them were sitting together round the table. Luther had not spoken a word since his entrance and he did not break his silence now until Bessie inadvertently went almost to the heart of the trouble when she said casually:

'Did Bob say anything about coming round tonight?'

Luther was a thickset man of a little above medium height. He had a rather magnificent mane of iron-grey hair which in his youth had been a reddish-blond colour and of which he was still proud. It topped a lean and rather lugubrious face with blue eyes and a thin-lipped mouth which had a tendency to slip easily into disapproval. He loved to argue, for he had opinions on all the topics of the day. But he was also a man who never saw a joke and this, with his baleful, ponderous way of making a point, made him, unconsciously, a source of amusement to the younger of his workmates, among whom he was known as 'Old Misery'.

He chewed in silence now and swallowed before attempting to answer Bessie's questions. Then he said briefly, 'No, he didn't.'

'Didn't he mention it at all?' Bessie asked.

'I haven't spoken to him all day,' Luther said, and blew hard on a forkful of steaming suet dumpling.

'Well, that's funny,' Bessie said, 'an' him working right next to you. Is there summat up, or what?'

'You might say that.' Luther took a mouthful of water. 'They've sent him to Coventry.'

'They've what?' Bessie said, and her mother, taking a sudden interest in the exchange, said, 'But that's miles away. Will he be home weekends?'

'What d'you mean they've sent him to Coventry?' Bessie said.

'Just what I say.'

'But whatever for?'

Luther put his elbow on the table and looked grimly along his fork at Bessie. 'I didn't work yesterday, did I?'

'No, you didn't. But—'

'I didn't work,' Luther said, 'because we had a one

-day token strike in support o' t'union wage claim. I didn't work an' none o' t'other union members worked – bar Bob. He went in as usual.'

'And you mean none of you's talking to him just because of that?'

'Aye,' Luther said with heavy sarcasm. 'Just because of that.'

Bessie drew herself up indignantly. 'Well, it's downright childish, that's what it is. Nobody talking to him because he worked yesterday.'

Luther put down his knife and fork.

'Look here. What do you do wi' a lass when you've no room for her?'

'Well, I...'

'Come on,' Luther said. 'Be honest about it.'

'Well, I don't have owt to do with her. But–'

'That's right,' Luther said, picking up his knife and fork and resuming eating now that the point was made for him. 'An' when a lot o' men feels that way about one chap it's called sendin' him to Coventry.'

'You don't mean to say *you've* fallen in with it, Luther?' Mrs Stringer said.

'I have that,' Luther said, shaking his head in a slow gesture of determination. 'I'm wi' t'men.'

'But Bob's my fiancy,' Bessie wailed.

'Aye, an' my future son-in-law, I'm sorry to say.'

'I must say it does seem a shame 'at you should treat your own daughter's fiancy like that,' said Mrs Stringer, and Luther gave her a look of resigned scorn.

'Now look,' he said, preparing to lay down the law, 'Bob's a member o' t'union. When t'union negotiates a rise in wages Bob gets it. When it gets us an improvement in conditions, Bob gets them an' all. But when t'union strikes for more brass – not just at Whittakers, not just in Cressley, but all over t'country – Bob goes to work as usual. Now I don't like a chap what does a thing like that. An' when I don't like a chap I have no truck with him.'

'I'll bet nobody give him a chance to put his side of it,' Bessie cried.

'He has no side. There's only one side to this for a union member. He should ha' struck wi' t'rest on us.'

'Well, that's a proper mess,' Bessie muttered. But her mind was now on the more immediate problem. 'I don't know whether I've to go and meet him, or if he's coming here...'

'I shouldn't think he'll have t'cheek to show his face in here tonight,' Luther said.

But half an hour later, when the table was cleared and Luther had his feet up with his pipe and the evening paper, and Bessie, now made-up for the evening, was still dithering in distress and confusion, there came a knock on the back door and Bob's voice was heard in the kitchen.

Bessie ran out to meet him and Luther raised his paper so that his face was hidden. To his surprise, Bob came right into the living-room as Bessie told him in great detail of her uncertainty about the evening's plans.

'Your dad's told you, then,' Bob said.

'Oh, aye,' Bessie said, 'an' I told him how childish I thought it was. Like a pack o' schoolkids, they all are.'

'A flock o' sheep, more like,' Bob muttered. 'All fallin' in together.'

This brought Luther's paper down to reveal his flashing eyes. 'Aye, all together. How else do you think a union can work?'

'Oh! You'll talk to him now, then?' Bessie said.

'I'm askin' him a question,' Luther said. 'How else does he think a union can work?'

'I don't know an' I don't care,' Bob said. 'I'm fed up o' t'union an' everybody in it.'

'That's a lot o' men, an' there's a fair number on 'em fed up wi' thee, lad. Anyway, happen tha'll not be bothered wi' it for much longer.'

'How d'ye mean?'

'I mean they'll probably call for thi card afore long.'

'Well, good riddance. I never wanted to join in the first place.'

'Why did you, then?'

'Because I couldn't have t'job unless I did. I was forced into it.'

'An' for why?' Luther said. 'Because we don't want a lot o' scroungers an' wasters gettin' t'benefits while we pay t'subscriptions.'

'Who's callin' me a scrounger?' Bob said, with a first show of heat. 'Don't I do as good a day's work as t'next man – an' better?'

'Well, tha can work,' Luther admitted. 'But tha hasn't common sense tha wa' born wi'.'

'Sense! I've enough sense to think for meself an' make up me own mind when there isn't an independent man among t'rest of you.'

'That's what I mean,' Luther said blithely. 'All this talk about independence an' making up your own mind. They like it, y'know. It's playin' right into their hands.'

'Whose hands?'

'T'bosses' hands, I mean. They like chaps 'at's independent; fellers 'at don't agree wi' nobody. They can get 'em on their own an' they haven't as much bargaining power as a rabbit wi' a ferret on its tail.'

'Ah, you're fifty year out o' date,' Bob said impatiently. 'Look, here we are with the cost o' livin' goin' up and up. We've got to stop somewhere. It's up to somebody to call

257

a halt. But what does t'union do but put in for another wage increase. What we want is restraint.'

'Like there is on profits an' dividends, you mean?'

'What do you know about profits an' dividends?'

'That's it!' Luther cried. 'What do I know? What do you know? Nowt. We don't see hardly any of it where we are. We have to take t'word of somebody 'at knows, somebody 'at's paid to study these things. T'union leaders, lad, t'union leaders. An' when they say "Look here, lads, these fellers are coalin' in their profits an' dividends and t'cost o' livin's goin' up an' up an' it's time we had a rise," then we listen to 'em. An' when they say "Strike, lads," we strike. At least, some of us does,' he added with a scornful look at Bob.

'Look,' Bob said, 'I believe in a fair day's work for a fair day's pay.'

'No more na me.'

'An' if t'boss is satisfied with me work he gives me fair pay.'

'He does if t'union's made him.'

'He does without that, if he's a fair man. Look at Mr Whittaker.'

'Aye, let's look,' Luther said. 'I've worked for Whittakers now for thirty years. I know Matthew Whittaker and I knew old Dawson afore him. Neither of 'em's ever had cause to grumble about my work an' by an' large I've had no cause to grumble about them. When t'union's put in a wage claim they've chuntered a bit an' then given us it. But they wouldn't if we hadn't been in force, all thinkin' an' actin' together. There's fair bosses an' there's t'other sort – that I'll grant you. But then again, there's bosses an' there's men. Men think about their wages an' bosses think about their profits. It's business, lad. It's life! I'm not blamin' 'em.

258

But you've got to face it: they're on one side an' we're on t'other. An' when we want summat we've got to show 'em we're all together an' we mean to have it. That's what made us all so mad at thee. Everybody out but thee. We listened to t'union an' tha listened to t'bosses callin' for wage restraint.'

'I don't listen to t'bosses,' Bob said. 'I listen to the telly an' read the papers an' make up me own mind.'

'Well, tha reads t'wrong papers, then,' Luther said. 'Tha'll be tellin' me next tha votes Conservative.'

'I don't. I vote Liberal.'

Luther stared at him, aghast. 'Liberal! Good sainted aunts protect us! An' is this t'chap you're goin' to wed?' he said to Bessie.

'As far as I know,' Bessie said, putting her chin up.

'Well, he'll be a fiancy wi'out a job afore long.'

'Why? He worked, didn't he? It's you lot they should sack, not Bob.'

'But you see,' Luther said with enforced patience, 'they can't sack us because there's too many of us. We've a hundred per cent shop up at Whittakers an' t'men'll not work wi' a chap 'at isn't in t'union. An' your Bob won't be in t'union for much longer, or I'm a Dutchman.'

'Well, if that isn't the limit!' Bessie gasped.

'I do think it's a cryin' shame 'at a young chap should be victimized because of his principles,' said Mrs Stringer.

'You keep your nose out,' Luther said. 'This was nowt to do wi' women.'

'It's summat to do wi' our Bess,' his wife said. 'Your own daughter's young man an' you're doin' this to him.'

'Nay, don't blame me. There's nowt I could do about it if I wanted.'

'Which you don't,' said Bessie, her colour rising.

'I've said what I have to say.' And Luther retired behind his paper again.

'Well, I've summat to say now,' Bessie flashed. 'It doesn't matter what your flamin' union does to Bob. He's headin' for better things than t'shop floor an' bein' bossed about by a pack o' tuppence ha'penny workmen.'

'Shurrup, Bessie,' Bob muttered. 'There's no need to go into all that.'

'I think there is,' Bessie said. 'I think it's time me father wa' told a thing or two. Who does he think he is, anyway? I don't suppose you know,' she said to Luther, who was reading his paper with a studied show of not listening to her, 'at Bob's been takin' a course in accountancy at nights. An' I don't suppose you know that Mr Matthew Whittaker himself has heard about this an' that he's as good as promised Bob a job upstairs in the Costing Office if he does well in his exams. What do you think about that, eh?'

The paper slowly lowered to reveal Luther's face again. 'I'll tell you what I think about it,' he said. 'I think you'd better take that young feller out o' my house an' never bring him back again.' His voice began to rise as his feelings got the better of him. 'So he works because he doesn't agree wi' t'union policy, does he? He thinks we ought to have wage restraint, does he? He stuffs me up wi' that tale an' now you tell me he's anglin' for a job on t'staff. It wasn't his principles 'at made him go in yesterday, it wa' because he wanted to keep on t'right side o' t'management.'

'Calm yourself, Luther,' Mrs Stringer said. 'You'll have a stroke if you get so worked up.'

'I'll have a stroke if ever I see that... that blackleg in my house again,' Luther shouted.

'I shall marry him whether you like it or not,' Bessie said.

'Not at my expense, you won't.'

'C'mon, Bessie,' Bob said. 'Let's be off.'

'Aye, we'll go,' said Bessie. 'You'd better see if you can control him, Mother. He's yours. This one's mine.'

Bessie and Bob left the house and Mrs Stringer went to wash-up, leaving Luther pacing the living-room, muttering to himself. In a few moments he followed her into the kitchen, in search of an audience.

'Wage restraint,' he said. 'Think for yourself. Don't be led off like a flock o' sheep. Oh he knows how to think for hisself, that one does. You know, I half-admired him for sticking to his principles, even if I did think he was daft in the head. But that one's not daft. Not him. He's crafty. He's not botherin' hisself about wage restraint an' principle. He's wonderin' what Matthew'll think if he strikes wi' t'rest on us. He's wonderin' if Matthew mightn't get his own back by forgettin' that job he promised him. That's what he calls a fair boss. He knows bosses as well as' t'rest on us. Principle! He's no more principle than a rattlesnake...'

Mrs Stringer said nothing.

'Well, our Bessie can wed him if she likes. She'll go her own road in the end, an' she's too old to be said by me. But there's no need to plan on bringin' him here to live. They'll have to find some place of their own... An' what's more, I won't have you havin' 'em in the house when I'm out. You hear what I say, Agnes? You're to have no more to do wi' that young man.'

It was at this point that Mrs Stringer, who had not said much so far, suddenly uttered a long drawn-out moan as of endurance taxed to its limit. 'O-o-oh! For heaven's sake, will you shut up!' And bringing a dinner

261

plate clear of the soapy water she lifted it high in both hands and crashed it down on the tap.

Luther's jaw dropped as the pieces clattered into the sink. 'Have you gone daft?'

'I shall go daft if I hear you talk much longer.'

'That's a plate from t'best dinner service you've just smashed.'

'I know it is, an' I don't care. You can pay for it out o' that rise your union's gettin' you. As for me, I've had enough. I'm havin' my one-day strike tomorrow. I'm off to our Gertie's first thing an' I shan't be back till late. You can look after yourself. Aye, an' talk to yourself, for all I care.'

'You're not feelin' badly, are you?' Luther said. 'What's come over you?'

'Principle,' Mrs Stringer said. 'Twenty-seven year of it, saved up.' And with that she walked out of the kitchen and left him.

Luther went back into the living-room and picked up his paper. He switched on the radio for the news and switched off immediately when he got the amplified roar of a pop group. He tried for some minutes to read the paper, and then threw it down and wandered out into the passage and stood at the foot of the stairs, looking up at the landing as though wondering what his wife was doing. He remained in that attitude for several minutes, and then, as though reaching a decision, or dismissing the problem as not being worth the worry, he reached for his cap and coat and left the house for the pub on the corner where he was sure to find someone who spoke his language.

Closing Time

Contrast of 2 marriages
- one untidy + happy
- the other neat + unhappy
A man has a heart-attack
in a pub while watching a
horse-race where his outsider
wins

By the time Halloran had backed his fancy and got out of Mulholland's Betting Shop and gone along the road, the landlord of the Greyhound, Jack Marshall, was shutting his front door. Halloran shouted, 'Ey! Ey, Jack!' Marshall looked round the door as Halloran crossed the road in a stiff-legged run.

'Am I not in time for one?' Halloran asked, catching his breath.

'Nay, Michael, it's gone twenty past three.'

'I was hoping to see Tommy Corcoran,' Halloran said.

'He was up and away half an hour ago. They've all gone. And I'm closing.'

Halloran pulled at his long thin nose, his brow wrinkling in thought.

'There's no harm in me comin' in for a minute. If I could just see the telly for the three-thirty.'

The landlord hesitated, then stood aside. 'Come on, then, before t'bobby sees you.'

'Sure, they can't object to a man lookin' at the telly.'

'They object to all sorts o' things on licensed premises.'

Halloran went into the big lounge bar where the television set stood high up on a shelf at one end of the long counter. He watched as Marshall switched on and the screen flickered into life. In a moment his eyes fell and passed over the pump handles. His seeming to catch everything in the tail of his gaze, as though his brain were a fraction slow in registering what his eyes moved across, gave him an appearance of slyness.

'Ah, you've got the... the towels on.'

'I have,' Marshall said. 'And they're not coming off.'

'Ah!' Halloran nodded several times. Then he held up a tentative hand, the thumb and forefinger an inch apart. 'Perhaps a...?'

'You'll get me shot,' the landlord said. 'I expect you've spent all dinnertime at the Black Horse.'

'No, no.' Halloran shook his head. 'I haven't had a drop today. Honest.'

'I'll believe you, where thousands wouldn't,' Marshall said. 'All right. What's it to be?'

'A rum an' pep. You're a decent man, Jack... Did Tommy Corcoran ask after me at all?'

'Not that I know of. Was it summat special you had to see him about?'

'He thought there might be the chance of a job on the site.' Halloran took the glass the landlord placed on the bar counter and felt for his money. 'Will you, er...?'

'No, thanks all the same, Michael. I've had me ration for this dinnertime.'

He put the coins in the till and gave Halloran his change.

'A job, eh? You're not going back to carryin' the hod at your age, are you?'

'Oh, I've still plenty of life in me,' Halloran said.

'Oh, aye, I don't doubt that.'

At fifty-five, Halloran, with a wife ten years younger than himself, had just fathered his eleventh child. With the dole and family allowances, plus various supplementary benefits, they managed to live in the periods when Halloran was out of work – periods which were now longer than those in which he was employed. Sometimes he would be technically in work but playing sick with one of his recurrent disabilities: his back, his chest, or his legs. His contempt matched that of others when discussing the work-shy who lived off social security and were kept by the dues and taxes of more conscientious men.

The landlord washed and polished glasses as the runners lined up for the three-thirty race.

'You've got summat on this, have you, Michael?'

'I have.'

'And what is it you fancy?'

Halloran held up a quietening hand as the commentator began to speak. Marshall shrugged and went back into the private quarters to have a word with his wife.

'Is there anybody still through there?'

'Only Michael Halloran. He popped in to watch the three-thirty.'

'He's not drinking, is he?'

'Only a small rum and pep.'

'You're daft, Jack, risking trouble with the police for a feller like Michael Halloran.'

'It's all right. If they come in, he's with me.'

'You'd think some of them had no homes to go to.'

'His must be a bit crowded.'

'Whose fault is that?'

'Aye, all right, then, don't get on. He'll be away in a minute.'

'You're the wrong type to keep a pub, Jack. You lean too much to your customers.'

'Don't talk so daft. How much drinking after time have you seen here? I run this place as well as anybody else could. A bit more interest from you 'ud be a help.'

'You know how I feel about it. You've never done. It's after half-past three now. You'll be open again at six and you won't get to bed till one. What kind of life is that?'

'It's a pity you didn't say all this before we came.'

'I did, but you wouldn't listen.'

It was true. He'd known he was persuading her against her real wishes, but he'd persisted, hoping she would take to the life in time. Instead, she had become more bitter and dissatisfied than she had ever been. With their children grown up and gone away, Marshall had looked for something they could tackle together, which they could build on towards better things. His idea was to acquire experience here for the time when they could have their own business – perhaps a small hotel, or in some branch of catering. But to his wife they had gone from the voluntary bondage of the family to the enforced one of licensing hours and regulations, the need to be pleasant to people they didn't care for, and all the endless comings and goings of pub life. She had never cared for pubs. It was all beneath her.

Marshall looked at his watch. 'The race'll be over now. I'll get him out and finish clearing up.'

When he went back into the bar there was no sign of Halloran. Marshall switched off the television set and washed out Halloran's empty glass. He waited a while for Halloran to come back from the gents, then went to look for him. He was not there; nor, with the front door still bolted, was there any indication that he had left.

'Now, where the hell's he gone to?' he said out loud.

He took cloth and bucket and went round into the lounge to empty the ashtrays and wipe the tabletops. It was when he turned in the process of doing this to face the bar counter that he saw Halloran slumped there on the floor. Marshall went and crouched over him.

'Now then, Michael, what's all this about?'

His first impulse was to lift Halloran under the armpits and get him on to a chair; but when he saw that the man was unconscious and breathing in an odd, strained way, he straightened up and called along the passage to his wife.

'Nora! Nora! Come here, will you?'

'What's wrong?'

'Come here. Quick!'

She came at her own speed. 'What is it?'

'It's Halloran.'

She stretched up and leaned over the counter. 'Oh God! Is he drunk?'

'No, he's badly. He's collapsed. I think it's his heart.'

She came round. 'Has he complained about it at all?'

'He's complained about all manner of things. Half the time I didn't believe him.'

'Can't you bring him round?'

'Nay, I don't know how to deal with this. He needs expert attention.'

'Shall I ring for a doctor?'

'Better dial 999 for an ambulance. That'll be quicker.'

'They don't like that unless it's an emergency.'

'It is an emergency. He could be dying, for all we know. And bring me that travelling-rug and cushion out of the living-room. I daren't move him but I'd better wrap him up and keep him warm.'

The ambulance was at the door in six minutes, diverted from a scheduled call in the district by a wireless message.

'It looks like a coronary,' one of the two men said as they got Halloran onto a stretcher. 'Have you got his name and address?'

'Aye. Where will you take him?'

'The General. Has he got a wife?'

'Yes. I'll go round and tell her as soon as you've gone.'

He saw them out through the front door and watched the ambulance move off. His wife was in the lounge again when he went in. She held up a piece of paper.

'Is this anything important?'

'It's a betting slip. Where did you find it?'

'On the floor, where he'd been lying.'

'I'll see to it.' He folded the slip and tucked it into his waistcoat pocket.

'Are you going to see the wife now?'

'I ought to. Isn't it that stone-built cottage at the far end of Furness Street?'

'Don't ask me. You'd better watch out for a horde of kids.'

'Aye. Will you finish off in here for me while I'm gone?'

She looked round reluctantly.

'There's not much to do,' he said.

'All right.'

Don't bloody force yourself, he thought in a spasm of temper. Always, in everything, working against the grain. He went out through the back door to the car in the yard.

Passing Mulholland's Betting Shop on the way he remembered the slip and stopped. He went in and showed it to the clerk.

'Is there anything to draw on this?'

The clerk looked it up in his ledger. 'I'll say there is. Didn't you hear the result?'

'No. It's not mine, you see.'

'Oh. Wait a minute. Wasn't this bet placed by Michael Halloran?'

'That's right. He was taken ill in my pub and I found it afterwards. I'm on my way to see his wife.'

'I'm sorry to hear that. Is he bad?'

'We won't know till she phones the hospital.'

'They've taken him away, then?'

'Yes. If you'd rather I got his wife to come herself.'

'No, that's all right. You've got the slip. It'll be a nice surprise for Michael, when he hears about it.'

'You mean it's a sizeable win?'

'He had a fiver on "Rocky Road", an outsider. It came in at 33 to 1. A damn good job we laid it off.'

'Good heavens!'

'It'll maybe cheer his missis up as well.'

'I should think so!'

He found the Hallorans' house on a stretch of unmade road at the dead end of Furness Street. It stood on a patch of ground, littered with old sheds and a wired-in enclosure full of hens, by a now disused railway line. There were slates missing from the low sagging roof and it was possible only to guess what colour the last coat of paint had been. The woman who answered his knock had lingering signs of prettiness in her dark, nearly black eyes, and the set of her cheekbones. She carried a baby in her arms as she looked at him.

'Mrs Halloran? I'm Jack Marshall from the Greyhound. I've got a message about your husband.'

'Yes?'

'I'm afraid he's been taken ill.' He saw the fear spring at once into her eyes.

269

'Ill?'

'He collapsed in the pub. I thought it best to call an ambulance. They've taken him to the Infirmary.'

Two children had appeared in the doorway now. They tugged at her skirt. 'What's wrong, Mam?' She spoke to them with a surprising gentleness, her gaze never leaving Marshall's face.

'This gentleman's come with a message about your father. He's not...?' She shook her head slowly as though willing him to give a favourable answer.

'No, no. If you just give 'em a chance to see to him, and then ring up, you'll very likely find he's all right... There was something else... If I could come in for a minute...'

'All right.'

He followed her through the door into a big unkempt all-purpose room. The reek from some badly washed nappies drying on the brass rail of the guard round the hot fire caught at his throat and he swallowed hard, controlling a desire to retch.

'Your husband had a bet on a horse this afternoon. It came in at 33 to 1.' He took the bundle of fivers out of his pocket and put it on the table. 'A hundred and fifty-nine pounds, and some silver. Perhaps you'd like to count it.'

She barely glanced at it. He didn't think she could understand.

'It's a lot of money,' he said.

'I can't get out of the house just now,' she said. 'Maybe when my bigger ones get in from school... But there's still the baby. He has to be fed regular, and I'm givin' him the breast, y'see.' She bit her lower lip fretfully. 'Will I be able to see him, d'you think?'

'I'd telephone first,' Marshall said, 'just to see how he is.'

270

He suddenly realized that she was finding the problem insuperable.

'Would you like me to ring up myself a bit later on, then come back and tell you how he is?'

'Would you do that? It sounds like an awful trouble.'

'It's no trouble.'

One of the children, a boy of about three, pulled up one side of his trousers and began to urinate on the flagstone floor in a corner.

'Kevin!' his mother said, softly reproachful. 'Don't you know better than that? What will the gentleman think? Go and get a cloth and wipe it up, now.'

'Oh, poor Michael,' she said then. 'I thought there was something wrong with him this morning, when he hardly touched the breakfast I cooked for him. He's not strong, y'know.'

Marshall turned at the door. 'I'll pop back later, then, and tell you the news. And I'd put that somewhere safe.'

'What?' She glanced over her shoulder. 'Oh, yes.'

The bigger of the children had climbed onto a chair and was setting out the notes singly in rows across the top of the table.

'D'you think you could pass on a message to him when you telephone?'

'I'll see.'

'Will you tell him he's not to worry, an' I'll be over to see him as soon as I can.'

'I'll do that.'

Marshall took several very deep breaths on his way back to the car, filling his lungs with cold fresh air.

His wife was vacuuming in one of the bedrooms. She came down when she heard the car, and the back door slam.

'Did you find her, then?'

271

'Aye, I found her. You know that betting slip you picked up? Halloran had backed a 33 to 1 winner. I called in at Mulholland's and took the money round to his wife. A hundred and fifty-nine quid.'

'Good gracious! Wasn't he watching the racing when he collapsed?'

'Yes, he was.'

'You don't think the shock could have done it to him?'

'Nay, I don't know.'

'I expect his wife would be pleased to see all that money.'

'She took no notice of it. She was more bothered about Halloran.'

'Oh? Well, that's fitting, anyway.'

'All the same, it's a lot of money.'

'Yes. It'll come in useful with all that lot to feed and clothe. Twelve, is it?'

'Eleven.'

'What's one more or less when you've got so many? How do they manage with them all? He hardly ever works, yet he drinks and gambles. I'll bet it's a right muckhole. Isn't it?'

'Oh, aye,' Marshall said.

'And him. What she'll have to put up with him.'

Marshall gave a short exasperated snort of laughter. He looked at her, throwing out his hands.

'They're as happy as pigs in shit,' he said.

'Such language!' his wife said.

272

Estuary

*A man recovering from illness +
mother's death at the seaside —
Sexual encounter with a bored exotic
woman.
Settles down into a routine, constructed life*

café

'It comes in fast, doesn't it?' Parker said. He sat with his large soft-skinned hands holding his coffee cup at a table in the window of the café over the confectioner's shop and watched the rippling grey line of the bore as it swept silently up the channels between the low muddy sandbanks in the river-mouth.

It was the first time that one of his mid-morning visits to the café had given him such a good view of the tide at the most impressive stage of its sweep into the estuary. The first time, also, since he plodded up the lino-covered stairs three days ago, that he had addressed any words of conversation to the grey-haired, bespectacled waitress who stood beside him now with ballpen poised over her bill-pad.

He was a hefty young man, crouching bulkily, shoulders hunched, over the flimsy table. But his skin had the pallor of a recent illness and he looked as though he had lost some weight.

'There won't be a bit of land to be seen in half

an hour,' the waitress said. 'It fills up quickly once it starts.'

Parker saw how the bore, its sweep broken by the concrete feet of the railway viaduct, encircled and isolated the smooth mounds of dark river sand.

'It'd be an easy thing to get cut off, I reckon.'

'They've to fetch people out every year,' the waitress said.

'Don't they see the danger?'

'Some people never see danger till it's too late,' the waitress said. 'Of course, it isn't all that bad at this time of year. But you should see it in the spring. We get some real tides then. If anybody gets in then they don't stand much chance, I can tell you. They get caught in the current under the bridge and you can't get to them in time. We had a man drowned there this year.'

There was unconscious satisfaction in her voice: an involuntary touch of pride in this dangerous phenomenon on her doorstep.

Parker drained his cup and felt for some money.

'It was two vanilla slices, wasn't it?'

'Yes, two.'

He was reminded once again, with a pang, of his mother as the waitress made out the bill and laid it by his plate.

'Pay downstairs at the desk, sir, if you please.'

He had always had a sweet tooth and every day when the local baker had delivered his tray of cakes and pastries to the little general shop, Parker's mother had kept her sharp eyes and tongue on guard. 'You just keep your hands off them vanilla slices, Bernard my lad. I'm watching you and they're all accounted for.'

He put a threepenny bit on the table and went downstairs. When he had settled his bill at the counter

274

he walked across the narrow promenade to the river wall and sat down on a bench to watch the tide.

A few small boats, grounded on the shore, moved and eventually floated as the water curled under and lifted them. A train rattled across the viaduct and Parker saw the anonymous faces of the passengers as they were carried over the deepening water swirling about the legs of the structure. The sun glistened on the water, and down on the narrowing shore a child laughed in a sudden spasm of joy. The menace of the tide fascinated Parker and held him there while the sandbanks slowly submerged and the estuary became an unbroken stretch of water, calm enough on the surface but current-corrupted beneath, from a few yards below his feet to the distant line of the far shore; and it was not until the noon sun clanged brassily off the water into his eyes and he stood up to walk back to his lodgings that his mind sank again into contemplation of the emptiness of his life.

It was a small and cosy life he had lived with his mother in the years since his father died. Unlike his father he had felt no pull from the world outside the little shop with the house behind it. He had never much cared for his father, whom he vaguely felt had held him in some contempt, and when his father died he had drawn closer than ever to his mother in an understanding where monosyllables and gestures conveyed almost all they wished to say. And he was content. There seemed no reason why anything should change. He never thought about it. But then he had contracted pneumonia and while he was in the period of crisis, fighting for his own life, his mother had two strokes in quick succession, the second one finishing her. They told him nothing until they felt him strong

275

enough to take the news, and even so it was not until he went back to the closed shop and the empty house that full realization of it all broke into his stupefied mind.

He would be wise to go away for a while, the doctor said. Have a complete change; go somewhere quiet and stroll in the sun; sort himself out and come to terms with his new life. So he had come here to sit on the narrow promenade or drink coffee and eat vanilla slices in the café over the shop while the tide ran into the estuary from the sea.

Every day Parker came down the hill from his lodgings to watch the tide. He would have liked to explore the country inland but he still tired easily, and only during the second week did he venture along the river path that led off the promenade and gave onto a tree-lined stretch of shore out of sight of the village. Here he found that he could sit, away from people, in an almost mindless contemplation of the river in which the pain of the change in his life was curiously dulled. And here, on the third day, he saw the swimmer.

Men quite often bathed inshore off the promenade, but this head bobbed far out where the sea ran at its strongest into the basin. Parker stood there for some time, watching the tiny distant movements of the swimmer in the waste of water. Then he crunched slowly across the shingle to the pile of clothing which lay just above the high-water line. There seemed to be only one garment there: a bathrobe of soft red-and-white striped towelling. He could also see now, through the trees, a white-stuccoed house with a flat parapeted roof. When he turned back to the river it took him a moment to locate the swimmer and he saw that the man was making for the shore, swimming with strong sure strokes. Some

276

minutes later he became aware that the swimmer wore a bathing cap and was not a man but a woman.

He wanted to move away but curiosity kept him there until she reached the shallows and stood up to walk out. Then it was too late to go without speaking. As she came towards him, removing the rubber cap and shaking her head to free the short dark hair, he said awkwardly, 'I was just thinking you might be in trouble.'

Black, expressionless eyes met his briefly. 'No, no trouble.'

'They said it was dangerous to swim any way out.'

'It's all right if you're a strong swimmer,' the woman said.

Though older than himself, she was still young: about thirty, Parker thought. As she dropped the cap and lifted her hands to her hair she stretched herself tall, rising slightly on her toes. Her whole body gave an impression of flatness in its width of hips and the smooth hardly developed curves of her breasts, which reminded Parker later of the gentle mounds of sand in the estuary, the cold rigid nipples like pebbles under the wet clinging skin of her black one-piece swimsuit. Her face was dark and sallow-skinned, and her black eyes seemed never to lose that constant inscrutable stare.

She took cigarettes from a pocket of the robe, offering them to Parker and, when he refused, lighting one for herself. Then she put on the robe and began to rub herself dry, the smoke from the cigarette between her pale lips making her narrow her eyes.

'It's the only exciting thing round here,' she said suddenly. 'Everything else is half dead.'

'I was wondering if I ought to go for help,' Parker said.

'It would have been too late,' she said. 'They couldn't have got a boat to me in time.'

277

He looked after her when, a few moments later, she walked away with an easy, graceful swing of her body towards the trees, and she came into his mind from time to time during the rest of the day. Until, when he was undressing for bed, he found himself wondering why he should think of her. He had never needed women in his little world and, apart from a momentary flicker of sexual curiosity about some girl in the shop or a face glimpsed briefly on the television screen, thoughts of them had not troubled him. Yet he thought of this one, the flat body, the undeveloped breasts, and unfathomable black eyes coming to him time and again. Always he saw her lifting herself out of the water as he had seen her that morning, and it seemed to him that she had become inextricably associated with his thoughts of the tide and its fascination for him.

He drifted into a heavy, dream-laden sleep in which he found himself down in the estuary, walking on one of the sandbanks at night. He became aware of the bore, silver in the moonlight, sweeping silently along the channels on either side and in sudden fear he turned one way and another, to find water all round him. He began to run across one of the channels, feeling the water deepening round his legs until all at once there was nothing under his feet and he was thrashing madly, in panic, trying to keep his head and shouting at the top of his voice, 'I can't swim. I can't swim.' The woman's voice answered him. 'It's all right if you're a strong swimmer.' He had a sense of someone near him, and then he began to shout again as a terrible pressure forced him under the surface. The water flooded his lungs and the blood beat in his head until he thought his brain would burst.

He was crouching near the foot of the bed when

278

he woke, the clothes spilling over on to the floor. He dragged them up round him and lay shivering in the dark, his body clammy with sweat, his heart beating with sickening force.

Behind the house where Parker was staying were fields *walk* trailing off into common land which ran up into the wooded headland that cut off the view of the bay and the open sea. For some time he had felt a desire to watch the full sweep of the tide as it rolled in across the sands. The rim of the headland looked to be no more than a mile and a half away, and on a hot afternoon towards the end of the second week he set out to walk up there.

Crossing the common, climbing steadily all the time, he felt the sun on his back and he took off his jacket and carried it over his arm. By the time he reached the edge of the trees he was tired and thirsty. His thighs ached and his armpits were soaked in sweat. The distance to the headland, foreshortened in the view from his bedroom window, was twice his original estimate and it was only the thought that it would be cooler under the trees which kept him going forward. The paths he had seen seemed to lead away from his objective and he had ignored them, climbing in what he judged to be a direct line to the headland across the rough tussocky grass. Now, at the edge of the wood, his view of the higher ground cut off, he faced the way he wanted to go and walked straight in under the trees.

Five minutes later he seemed to be lost, and looking back he could not make out the way he had come. He was entirely alone and even the occasional bird-calls seemed a part of the silence which surrounded him. When he saw two sets of initials cut into the trunk of a silver birch he reached out to them as if for reassurance. RF-GL: friends

279

who had been this way, stood on this same spot, ten years ago. Or, more likely, lovers, welcoming the solitude of the wood. Parker gazed pensively at the letters as his relaxed fingers traced their outline.

He went on, hoping for some break in the trees which would allow him to get his bearings, and came presently into an open space that turned out to be a trap of grass-covered brambles into which he blundered and entangled his legs, falling forward and slashing his hands and face before he pulled himself clear and lay flat on the ground, his heart hammering, his breath coming in short painful gasps.

As his body relaxed he closed his eyes and slept for a time, waking with dry hard lips and a raging desire for water. He got on to his feet and clutched at a tree as the wood reeled before his eyes in a blur of sunlight and shadow. When he felt steadier he began to move down through the trees. It was rough going: he clambered down steep banks and skirted impenetrable thickets, not knowing where he was going but always heading downhill, his throat parched, his head swimming from over-exertion. He had done too much, he kept telling himself; a lot too much. He was a fool for having taken it on. His mother would—no, not his mother. He stopped abruptly in his thinking at the inescapable fact that his mother would never rebuke him again. There was no-one to rebuke him. He could do as he liked. His behaviour and his welfare were matters for himself now. He was on his own. 'Are them shoes wet, Bernard? Changed your clothes? You're asking for pneumonia delivering orders in them wet things.' Never again. She'd always said he had a stubborn, foolhardy streak that he'd inherited from his father...

280

Ten minutes of downhill stumbling and scrambling brought him, almost exhausted, first to signs of tree-felling and then a vehicle-width track with the impressions of heavy tyres in the soft black earth. Now the going was easier. He caught glimpses of the river through the trees and then the glare of sunlight on the white walls of a house. The sun caught him again as he emerged from the shade of the trees and he wondered if he dare ask at the house for water. He shrank from it, but he had never known such a thirst. Still thinking of it, he went along under a tall cedarboard fence until he came to a gate. He was standing there in indecision when the woman he had watched swimming in the estuary two days before came up the lane from the direction of the shore. *Seemd*

weeky

Her feet were bare except for rope sandals. She wore a pale blue cotton beach-dress, tied at the waist and reaching halfway down her thighs.

Parker saw as she came nearer that her hair was damp, and he knew she had been swimming. For some reason the knowledge started small fluttering tremors of excitement in the bottom of his stomach.

She looked at him without recognition. 'Was there something you wanted?'

'I was up the hill,' Parker stammered. 'I got lost... I was wondering if I could have a drink of water.'

He stood aside as she reached for the latch of the gate. Her gaze rested on him and he felt a flush of colour spreading up from his neck.

'You'd better come in.'

He followed her to the kitchen door and waited while she ran a tumbler of water and brought it to him on the step. He drank it straight down without stopping. It took his breath away and he gasped as he lowered the glass from his lips.

'I was ready for that.'

She took the tumbler from him. 'Don't you feel well? You look pale, and there's blood on your face.'

'I got lost,' Parker told her again. 'Up the hill, there. Then I fell head first into some brambles.'

'You look done in,' the woman said. 'Look, why not come in and sit down for a while?'

'Oh, I'll be all right now,' Parker said. 'I feel better already.'

She asked him if he was staying in the village. Then, 'You really ought to come in and sit down. You don't want to walk any more till you've had a rest.'

He was uncomfortable under her direct expressionless gaze. He said, 'Well, just for a minute, then. I don't want to put you out.'

'Don't be silly,' she said, turning into the house. 'Come on.'

He was conscious again of the grace of her movements as she led him through the kitchen and into a long, airy lounge with big windows looking out towards the river.

'Sit down,' she said. 'You'll feel better after a rest.'

Parker lowered himself onto the edge of an armchair.

'I don't want to get in your way.'

'I'm not going anywhere,' she said. She put her hand on his shoulder and pressed him back into the soft upholstery.

'Sit back,' she said. 'Be comfortable.'

Her complete self-possession astonished Parker. He had never met anyone quite like her before. But he rested his head back gratefully and looked round the room, hearing the chink of a glass behind him, then her voice saying, 'Here, drink this. It'll set you up.'

He took the glass she held out to him.

'It's brandy,' she said as he looked at it. 'More pep in it than water.'

'I don't reckon to–' he began, and she said, 'Drink it up. It'll do you good.'

She sat on the arm of a chair opposite him as he sipped from the glass.

'Better?'

He nodded, feeling the fire of the brandy in his throat.

'Have you walked a long way?'

'I set off for the top,' Parker said, 'but I got lost and came down again.'

She nodded. 'It's easy to lose your sense of direction round here.'

'I wanted to watch the tide coming in,' Parker said. 'But I took too much on.'

'Too much? It's not far if you know the way. Aren't you used to walking?'

She made statements and asked questions in the same flat, incurious voice, as though she was concerned only in asking and not with the answers he gave her. And the black eyes seemed to support this; for though they never left him for more than a few seconds, they rested so dispassionately on him they seemed to be occupied with some aspect that was of him yet somehow not of him. It struck him that she was regarding him with the withdrawn composure of someone contemplating an object.

'I've been poorly, you see,' he told her. 'I'm supposed to be resting and getting myself well again, not knocking myself up.'

'You've been ill?' Her eyes moved again to his face.

'I had pneumonia.'

'Bad?'

'I nearly died,' Parker said. 'I was lucky.'

283

Surprisingly now, she began to admonish him, as though she had some personal interest in his welfare... 'You need somebody to stop you doing silly things. Are you married?'

Parker shook his head. 'No. I lived with my mother, but she died.'

He was ill at ease again. He looked into his glass, then lifted it to take another sip of the brandy. It was doing him good. He felt a lot better already.

'What made you come to this place? Have you been before?'

'No, but I wanted somewhere quiet and it was recommended to me.'

She was at the window now, looking out, her back to him. He felt easier.

'It's quiet, all right,' she said. 'I've lived here for three years. Since I got married. I was on the stage before that.' She spun round to face him. 'Did you guess I'd been on the stage? Could you tell?'

'I thought there was something about you,' Parker said.

She nodded. 'You can always tell. It stamps you, being on the stage.'

She went into a long story about herself, about her career before her marriage, telling him of the shows she had appeared in, the towns she had visited, the people she had met.

Until, in a break in her monologue, Parker said, 'What made you give it up if you liked it so much?'

'Liked it?' She gazed at him as though looking straight through him to something beyond him. Then she shrugged. 'I suppose it's all right if you've got what it takes. But there was no future in the kind of stuff I was doing. It was cheap-jack stuff. It's all right if you

284

can get on, but I knew I never could. I hadn't got what it takes. I hadn't the figure, for one thing.'

Parker looked at her in the short beach-dress, at the light tan on her limbs. He said diffidently, 'I think you've got nice legs.'

'Oh, they're all right,' she said indifferently. 'But I've no bust.' She ran her hands down over her flat breasts, posing in the sunlight flooding through the big window. 'And I'm not pretty. And my skin's sensitive. You might not think so, but it is. I couldn't stand all that make-up.'

Parker drank off the last of his brandy.

'Do you want another drink?' she asked him. 'Some more brandy, or some whisky?'

'No, thanks. That was all right.'

'A cigarette, then?'

Parker said no. 'I don't smoke.'

'Haven't you ever smoked?'

'No, I never got the habit.'

She took a cigarette for herself from a chrome-plated box on the low occasional table and lit it before sitting on the cushioned window-seat and swinging up her feet to stretch full length her long flat body and graceful legs. She puffed inexpertly on the cigarette, without inhaling.

Anxious not to outstay his welcome, Parker was gathering words of leavetaking, when she spoke again. 'I left the stage for security,' she said. 'That's what everybody wants, isn't it?'

'I suppose so,' Parker said.

'Yes, but it's dull,' she said. 'It's so dull I could scream.' She turned her head towards him for a moment. 'I'm talking a lot, aren't I?'

'I don't mind,' Parker said. 'I think mebbe I should be going, though.'

'Miles was married before, you know,' she said. 'He'd been married a long time. He's nearly sixty. They don't like me round here. They remember his first wife. She was in on everything. Miles is disappointed that I don't mix more. But I've tried to be friendly and they don't like me. I can feel it. They think I hooked Miles, but they're wrong. He was mad about me. He begged me to marry him. I was quite a time making up my mind.'

Parker sat forward in his chair and put down the empty glass. He took his mind off the woman by concentrating on the effect of the brandy. It had done him a power of good. An early night tonight and he'd be all fixed up.

'We don't go out much,' the woman was saying. 'There's nothing to do here: no shops or theatres. But Miles doesn't mind. He plays the gramophone when he's at home.' She reached down and slid open a cupboard under the window-seat, revealing a neat row of records in their sleeves. 'Look at all those. That's all he does besides fishing. All he does: play records. Nothing lively, though; all dull stuff: Beethoven, Handel, Mozart. The duller they are, the more Miles likes them...'

'Is that why you swim in the river?' Parker said.

'It's the only exciting thing round here,' she said. 'And I can only do that when Miles isn't at home. He's furious if he knows I've done it. He lost a boy in the bay once. He's never got over it. It was his only child. He talks about it sometimes when he's feeling sentimental. Then it makes me feel good to know I can beat it.'

Parker got up. He didn't know where to put his hands.

'I ought to be going.'

She went out with him and at the gate he thanked her again. 'Saved my life, I reckon,' he said, forcing a tight grin.

'You can come again, if you like,' she said. 'You could sit out in the garden and rest. You're too pale; you need sun.'

'I go home Saturday,' Parker told her.

'Well, come tomorrow. See if you can get your face red to go home with. You can't go back looking so pale.'

There was nobody to notice, anyway, Parker thought. He said, 'I could come in the afternoon, I suppose.'

'Yes, do that. Come after lunch.'

She showed him the shortest way back to the village and he left carrying with him the image of her running her hands over her body in the sunlight, the excitement fluttering in him as he thought of this and the flood of talk released in the extremity of her boredom. There was no need to go back, he told himself. He could decide tomorrow.

second visit — third meeting

'Would you like another drink?' she asked, and Parker started. The silence since either of them had spoken had been so long that, dozing himself, he had thought her asleep. There was a tray with tumblers and a vacuum jug of iced lime-juice in the shade of the trees nearby.

Parker said, 'No, thanks,' and lifted himself onto his elbows on the rug. He had been in the garden for nearly an hour now. The sun was hot again and his shirt clung damply under his arms.

After lunch he had sat for a time in the garden of the cottage before setting out across the village. He entered the grounds of the house by the main gate, walking up the driveway and mounting the shallow steps to press the bell by the front door. There was no reply and he rang again, wondering if she had forgotten her invitation; forgotten him, even, as soon as he had gone from her sight.

The house was quiet in the strong sunlight; deeply quiet, as though life had abandoned it, leaving it clean, preserved, but dead. It would be like one of those fantastic stories you sometimes read, he thought, if somebody else came to the door and told him they'd never heard of the woman. It struck him then that he did not know her name, and she had never asked his. He came down the steps again and walked with an increasing feeling of unreality round the side of the house to a gate in the tall cedar fence which shut off the garden and the back of the house. He opened it and went through, starting across the flagged area to the kitchen door before he saw her, lying face down on a travelling-rug by a border of flowering shrubs at the far end of the lawn.

She became aware of him before he was halfway to her.

'I thought you'd decided not to come,' she said. She raised herself on her elbows as he approached. The dark look flickered onto his face, then away again as she relaxed as before, with her face on her arms.

She was wearing a bathing costume: not the one he had seen her swimming in, but a very brief two-piece of soft dark red wool.

'I rested for a bit,' Parker said.

'Isn't that what you were supposed to do here?' she said, and Parker thought she sounded like a petulant lover who had been kept waiting; not someone whom he had known only a few days; with whom he had exchanged only a few casual words before yesterday.

'I suppose so,' he said.

He stood looking down at her, at the sallow skin of her neck and the broadness of her back with the straight spinal gully between firm pads of flesh. When she didn't speak again he dropped his jacket and sat down beside her on the rug, resting his weight on one arm.

'I was just thinking how nice a cold drink would be,' she said then. 'I'll get some in a minute...'

Now, after the long silence, she said. 'I don't know how you can bear all those clothes. You should have brought some trunks and changed in the house.'

'I haven't got any,' Parker told her. 'I can't swim.'

'I could teach you in a week,' she said. 'But you're going home tomorrow, aren't you?'

'Yes,' Parker said. 'Tomorrow.'

'What do you do at home?'

'I've got a little shop: grocery.'

'Does it pay its way?'

'It does pretty fair... Course, there's only me to keep out of it now.'

There in the hot sunlight he was all at once mourning for his mother again, knowing that he was near the time when he must go home and face day-to-day existence without her. He had avoided making plans, as though unable to face the inevitable. Now he would be forced to think about it: about the housework and help in the shop; about the loneliness.

'You'll have to find yourself a girl,' the woman said. 'Get married.'

Just like that, Parker thought. It was the obvious thing. But the very thought of taking a wife into his life filled him with dread. And who could it be?

She had turned her head so that she could see him.

'Don't you bother with girls much?' she said, and Parker made an awkward, bashful movement of his hand without speaking.

'Somebody will take you in hand,' she said. 'There'll be somebody with her eye on you now.'

'I don't think so,' Parker said.

'You don't know much about women.'

'You're right there,' Parker said.

Her eyes were on him in one of those long moments of contemplation that so filled him with awkwardness and a feeling of inadequacy. He plucked at the cropped grass. What was he doing here, anyway? After nearly two weeks of being alone, looking at the river, thinking about home, he was here in a private garden with this strange, bored, restless woman. And she was leading the way at every step, spinning out of her boredom a web of excitement which gripped him now as it had from the first.

'The sun's moving round,' she said, taking her gaze off him. 'We ought to be up on the roof.'

'The roof?' he said stupidly.

'Yes. We can lie in the sun longer up there. That's what it's meant for.'

She sprang up and held out her hand. 'Come on.'

Parker allowed himself to be led across the lawn and into the house. The way to the roof lay up thickly carpeted stairs and along a corridor with closed white-painted doors. At the end of the corridor Parker followed the woman up another short flight of steps to a door which opened out into the sunlight.

At once he felt acutely exposed standing there on top of the house. He looked at the woman, who was at the rail surmounting the low parapet, gazing out at the river. She beckoned him and he went and stood beside her.

'Look,' she said, 'it's coming in.'

The view was better than any he had had before. From here he could see part of the bay and the low grey line of the sea, thrusting its foaming fringe before it deep into the river channels, and as he watched he felt the woman's fingers entwine themselves in his. There was a surprising strength in their grip, but it seemed to Parker that she was hardly conscious of him, all her concentration focused on the sweep of the tide. He wondered what was in her mind as she looked out there minute after minute, and all at once it came to him that she was afraid of the sea and he trembled slightly, feeling the heat and tension of her body against his forearm.

At last she released his hand and turned away to sink down on a large airbed which lay inflated on the flat roof. She lay with her face hidden from him. It was as though she had forgotten him.

Parker got down beside her in a silence that grew into minutes. He said at length, 'Are you asleep?'

'No... There's a bottle of suntan lotion somewhere about. Will you rub some into my back?'

Parker found the lotion and poured some into his hands. He held them poised over her back, unable to touch her until she said, 'Can't you find it?'

'Yes, I've got it.'

'Go on, then,' she said. 'Don't be shy.'

Parker flushed. He knelt beside her and laid his hands on her back. He began to work the lotion into her skin, the movement of flesh and muscle under his hands transmitting itself to him in slow mounting waves of excited feeling. When his fingers touched the string holding the upper half of her costume she said, 'Unfasten it.'

He pulled at the bow and parted the two halves of cord.

'You have smooth strong hands,' the woman said, 'I could fall asleep with you doing that.'

She stretched her limbs indolently, then relaxed again under the pressure of his touch. Again, a feeling of being exposed came over Parker.

'Can't anybody see us up here?'

'Nobody,' the woman said. 'We're as private as if we were inside four walls. Sometimes I sunbathe in the nude up here, but Miles doesn't like it. He's very prudish, really. When he sees me like that it reminds him of when I was on the stage. He was on a night out with some business acquaintances and he came back three more times in the same week. He wanted me to leave the stage straight away, but I wouldn't throw up everything for him. I told you I was a long time making up my mind. He followed me to other places. He told me I'd the most exciting body he'd ever seen. But he forgot about his heart and that he wasn't a boy any longer.'

'You can't stay young for ever,' Parker said.

'You don't know anything about it, do you?' she said. 'You live your own life in your own little world, among people you've known for years...'

'I know what it's like to be lonely,' Parker said.

'What is it like?'

'I reckon it's something you've got to get used to.'

'You never get used to it,' the woman said. 'The most you can do is find moments when it goes away.'

Parker was looking at her right hand which rested, fingers slightly open, on the blue airbed, and noticing for the first time that the little finger was curiously malformed. The sight of that twisted finger on the small and otherwise well-shaped hand aroused in him a feeling he had never known before. He did not know how to deal with this strange compassionate feeling except by putting his hand on her back again and moving it over her skin as though lightly applying more oil. But there was a difference in its touch, and under its new tender urgency the woman shuddered, then turned over without speaking in a quick movement that exposed to him for a moment the naked front of her body before she reached out to pull him down into the bruising ferocity of her kiss. The nails of one hand dug into his shoulder and the light fluttering gasp of her breath was on his face as she drew away to speak to him.

'Now,' she said, 'Be very quick.'

He was nothing. He knew it through the flare of his response. Something the sea would use and discard. He thought it in the fleeting second before she took him, unresisting, plunging down with her into the vortex of her frenzy.

departure

In the morning, his bag packed, Parker went back to look at the house. He had no words for the woman: no more than yesterday when he had left her as she slept in the sun. But something drew him back there. A car stood in the driveway, a large black saloon with dusty bodywork. He looked at it as he passed and went on without stopping.

The train was not busy and he found an empty compartment and settled himself by the window. As they swung out on the viaduct, the village falling away behind, Parker looked down the shoreline for the last glimpse of the white house through the trees. But there was nothing to see: nothing but the estuary, empty now, the smooth sandbanks drying in the sun, the river and its minor channels winding placidly out into the bay; free for a time of the deep dark treachery of the tide... *denovement*

He thought about the woman often in the months that followed, and the memory of her brought a vague half-longing that sank him in moods of dreamy discontent. It was in one of these periods that he became engaged to the small plump slow-moving girl with the deep, tolerant laugh who had answered his advertisement for help; and since there was no reason to wait, he married her quickly and took her to live in the little house behind the shop. She was a good wife to him, and as the warmth and solid contentment of his new life enfolded him, the woman became increasingly dreamlike and remote until there came a time when he did not think of her any more.

Love and Music

Comic tale —
Jealousy between friends
in a brass band

Popping into the lounge bar of The Wheatsheaf just before lunch that Saturday morning, I was surprised to see Sam Skelmanthorpe sitting behind the bottom half of a pint and lighting up the room with the full glory of his scarlet tunic.

'Chalk that up to me, George,' he called to the landlord as I ordered my own half-pint of bitter; and once served, I went over, glass in hand, to join him.

'Contest today?' I asked him after a brief exchange of greetings.

'Wedding,' Sam said. 'Just got back.'

'Somebody important?'

'Important to us,' he said. He took a pull at his glass. 'Have you never seen a full brass band at a wedding?'

I said no, I hadn't. 'A lovely sight,' Sam said. 'And when they play it brings tears to your eyes. Better than any organ. Lovely.'

If there's a man who likes to tell the tale it's Sam Skelmanthorpe; but you have to work him round to it

295

gently. And a little while later, when he was comfortably settled behind a fresh pint, with his pipe drawing well, he began to tell me all about it.

I don't suppose you know Dave Fothergill and Tommy Oldroyd, do you? Sam said. Well, they're two lads in the band. Young chaps; real pals. They've known one another right from the time their mothers took 'em to the clinic together as bairns; and before that, even, because their families lived on'y three doors apart down Royd's Lane and there wasn't much more than twenty-four hours between them being born. You might say they were thrown together right from the start, and that's the way they carried on. They went to school together – and when you're young, y'know, you can change your pals as easy as changing your shirt.

But not Dave and Tommy. They stuck like glue.

We allus used to say it'd take a woman to come between 'em, and that's how it happened. Even then we were a bit surprised.

They took an interest in the band very early on, and soon they were nattering their dads to get 'em an instrument apiece. So their dads brought 'em to see the committee. We have one or two instruments that we lend out to learners and we said we'd fix 'em up, seeing as how they were so keen. We allus try to encourage young lads, y'know. Brass banding isn't what it used to be when I was a lad. What with all this television and radio, all this entertainment laid on, there isn't the interest in learning an instrument, some road.

Anyway, they both had to have the same instrument, o' course, and they picked the cornet as being to their liking. And old Jess Hodgkins, our conductor, offered to give 'em a few lessons just to put 'em into the way o' things.

Now they soon showed a bit o' capability and Jess used to talk about 'em at practices. 'I've two right good lads yonder,' he used to say, 'and do ye know, I'm blessed if I can tell which is t'best between 'em!' They kept on getting better, and when they could hold their end up a bit, we took 'em into the band. By the time they were sixteen or seventeen they were sharing the solo parts between 'em and we knew that we'd two o' the best young cornet players in Yorkshire. An we began to get a bit windy, I can tell you, because by the time young lads start working these days they're pining for the bright lights and pastures new, as they say. And we were a bit scared that one o' the big bands, like Fairey or t'Dyke might be hearing of 'em and snapping 'em up. Not that we'd have stood in their way, mind you; but they were two such grand players that they all but made our band, and we couldn't bear the thought o' losing 'em.

But as it turned out, they seemed well settled. When they left school they took to farming with old Withers, as keeps that place on Low Road, and this seemed to suit 'em nicely. They played engagements round about with any band that was short o' men, and they even had offers to go and play with jazz bands in Cressley and suchlike places. But they weren't having any o' that. No jungle music for them, they said. They were stopping where they could play some real stuff.

Well, all this was fine for us. But we all knew that one thing was sure to take 'em away and split 'em up, and this was their National Service. But you know, they went up together, they served together, and they came back together. And when we asked 'em how they'd managed it, they just grinned in that quiet way they both have and said it'd take more than the Army to split *them* up.

Well, I reckon you've guessed, it did. It took a lass. And a town lass at that.

Seeing as they wouldn't be away all that long, Withers had decided not to hire another man. He set a landgirl on. And no sooner had Dave and Tommy got back to work than the trouble started. Give credit where it's due – it was Short Fred, our librarian, who first spotted what was going on; and he used to come up to the band-room and tell us how both Dave and Tommy were making sheep's eyes at this lass; and how she was making up first to one then the other.

What I should tell you here is that neither of 'em to our knowledge had ever shown any interest in lasses afore; but this Cynthia was a sly bit. She made out she was a music lover, and that she'd heard 'em play. Find a man's weak spot, they say, don't they? Well, she found both Dave and Tommy's there. She had 'em danglin' straight away. Not satisfied with one, she had to set one off against the other by telling each of 'em, when the other wasn't there, that he was the finest player she'd ever heard.

One of the nicest things about Dave and Tommy up to this time was that there'd never been a breath of jealousy between 'em; but after a bit of Cynthia's tactics they started giving one another funny looks. In the end they gave up coming to practices, and word got about that they weren't speaking.

Well, this was a bit of a caper. I mean, it was the last thing anybody expected. And here we were with a full programme of summer concerts and our two best men behaving like bairns. We couldn't reckon it up at all. We studied it all roads, and we spent a lot o' time talking about it when we should have been practising. We sent Jack Thomas, our secretary, down to see 'em, and he came away with a flea in his ear. So there was nothing else we could do. I mean, folk have been getting into that kind of trouble ever since the Garden of Eden and the best thing to do is leave 'em to come round on their own. But that didn't alter the fact that we shouldn't sound so good without 'em, and we brooded about it.

Then one Thursday night both Dave and Tommy rolled into the band-room and sat down in their places. They didn't say much to nobody and not a word to one another. And when the practice was over they packed their instruments and walked off without stopping for a dust-slaker in the Fox and Ferret like they'd allus done before. We couldn't reckon this up, either. It left us with summat else to speculate about.

The same thing happened Sunday morning. In they walked, said nowt to nobody, did their playing, and walked out again. But after, Fred gave us a bit of news. Cynthia was leaving the farm. We were sure this had some bearing on it, and before long, what with odd bits of talk and gossip, we'd pieced it together, and the idea was this. They were both fed up with one another interfering with their courting, and still this Cynthia wouldn't plump for either of 'em. Well, it was being a music lover, like, that had first attracted her to 'em, so she said, and they both knew they'd be doing a bit o' showing off at our first concert, so they'd fixed up for her to come and hear them and make up her mind between them after.

In the week or two left before the concert they practised like mad, and folks used to hear music coming from down Royd's Lane at all hours of day and night. It got so bad towards the end that the bobby had to have a walk down and tell 'em that all this midnight triple-

tonguing constituted a public nuisance, and they'd
better tone it down – or else!

I remember that the Sunday after Whit was a lovely
day. We hadn't another like it all summer. We hired
a bus as usual to take us and the tackle down to the
park, and when we got there the place was packed to
the tree-tops with folk in their Sunday best. A record
gate we had that day, as a matter of fact.

The afternoon concert went off grand, and we had
a very nice boiled-ham tea, I remember, before setting
about the evening programme. This was when Dave and
Tommy were going to do their stuff. You know, I've been
in brass banding for nigh on forty year and I've heard
some stock o' cornet players in me time; but I've never
enjoyed owt so much as hearing them two lads play that
night. They played like angels: they were like somebody
possessed. One of the pieces we did was *Alpine Echoes*,
and we had Dave on the platform and Tommy up a tree
in the park, echoing him. Wonderful! And the clapping! I
didn't know park audiences had it in 'em. But you know,
I shouldn't have liked to pick between the two lads.

Well, when we'd played *The Queen* the lads hopped it
and the rest of us went across the road to The Weavers for
a sneck-lifter before going home. We'd be in there about
three-quarters of an hour, I should think. And when
we got back to the bus who should be there but Dave
and Tommy; Tommy sitting inside on his own and Dave
prowling about outside, reckoning to look how the bus
was put together. We all climbed in, reckoning that we
thought nowt of it, though we could see from their faces
that all wasn't well. And in the end we couldn't hold it any
longer and we gave Short Fred the nudge, seeing as how
he knew 'em best, and he asked 'em what was wrong.

Well, Dave looks down at his feet, then sneaks a

glance at Tommy, who's begun to colour up a bit. Then he says, 'She's gone.' Just like that. 'She's gone.'

'Gone?' we says. 'How d'you mean, gone?'

'I mean what I say,' Dave says, a bit short like. 'She's gone with another chap.'

And then Tommy finds his voice, and he was all choked up he was so mad. 'Aye,' he says, 'I know him an' all. He's a blitherin' accordion player from Bradford.'

Well, we just gaped at 'em for a minute, and then somebody started to laugh, and in a second we were all at it, fit to bust. And all of us rolling about helpless seemed to bring the lads round; because in a minute Dave gives a sheepish grin and looks at Tommy, and Tommy grins back. And before we're home they're sitting together and chatting away as though they'd never heard of a lass called Cynthia.

'And that's how it's been ever since,' Sam said. 'They just got married this morning. Both of 'em. Double wedding.'

'To two girls, of course,' I said.

'Oh aye,' said Sam. 'But twins. Lasses from down in Cressley. Alike as two peas, they are. Nobody but Dave and Tommy seems to be able to tell 'em apart.'

He lifted his glass and drank. I looked up in time to catch a broad wink directed at me over the rim.

'Course, now we're all wondering what's going to happen next.'

Travellers

A choir in a station —
old man jokes in after
a funeral —
his joyless daughter as contrast

Pathos

Who they were, where they had come from and where
they were going, I never did find out. There were times
afterwards, in memory, when they seemed unreal;
though they were real enough and welcome that night
as they filed into the waiting room out of the November
fog which had clamped down on the country from coast
to coast, disrupting my planned journey by bus and
sending me to the little out-of-the-way junction to wait
for the last train to the city, fifteen miles away.

There were about twenty of them; a nondescript
bunch of sober, respectable men and women of varying
ages. They crowded into one end of the narrow room,
surrounding and hiding the heavy bare table as they
huddled in their topcoats and made wry jokes about the
weather outside. One man stood out from the rest by
virtue of his dress as well as his general demeanour. He
seemed to be in a position of authority or responsibility
towards the others: in some way their leader; and they
regarded him with restrained amusement as well as

respect. He had already spoken to me as they came in, making some conventional remark about the state of the night, and now I looked at him with interest.

He was a small man with a red fleshy face and pince-nez perched on his fat little nose. He wore a dove-grey homburg hat tipped back from his forehead and his navy-blue double-breasted overcoat hung open to reveal a blue polka-dot bow tie and a fawn waistcoat. But what really took my eye were the felt spats which showed below the turn-ups of his grey-striped trousers. It was a long time since I'd seen a man in spats. He had altogether rather an air about him; a presence and a sense of dash exemplified by his clothes and the expansiveness of his gestures, which latter were no doubt heightened by the contents of the flat half-bottle of whisky whose neck protruded from one of the pockets of his overcoat.

I'd not been alone the entire time before this invasion. One would have expected any infusion of extra human warmth to alleviate the cheerless atmosphere of that bare room, but the entry of these earlier people, ten minutes after my arrival, had seemed to lower the temperature rather than raise it.

There were three of them: a middle-aged couple and an old man, tall and lean as a garden rake, who walked between them. The younger man had answered my good evening but the woman's response was to pierce me with a gimlet look, as though she suspected me of being an exponent of the three-card trick out to fleece them of their money, or a salesman who would spend the waiting-time unloading onto them fifteen volumes of an expensive and unwanted encyclopedia.

Since then there had been no communication between us, not even the crossing of a glance. At the entrance of the little man's group they were still sitting motionless on the bench near the fireless grate, the couple like sentinels, one on each side of the old man, who seemed to be sunk in a coma, totally unaware of his surroundings, his gaze fixed on the floor some distance beyond the polished toes of his black boots. A narrow band of black material encircled the grey herring-bone tweed of his left arm. The woman was looking disapprovingly towards the crowded end of the room from behind round spectacles. I guessed she was a woman who looked disapprovingly at most things.

It had struck me a few minutes after their appearance that the group must be a choir, for they all carried bound copies of what looked like music. And as if to confirm my guess the little man now lifted his voice and addressed them all.

'We've got a while to wait, so what about a song to keep us warm?' There was a general murmur of assent followed by good-humoured groans and jeers as the little chap went on, 'Not that any chance to practise comes amiss, eh?'

He stood before them, his shoulders thrown back, regarding them with an almost comical assurance. He could handle them, I thought. He might be a slightly humorous figure but he knew how to deal with them.

'Well, sort yourselves out, then,' he said. 'Let's not get sloppy, because an audience is an audience, however small.' He half-turned and bowed his head in acknowledgement of our presence as the members of the choir reshuffled themselves and waited for his signal to begin. He pondered for a moment, then announced a piece whose name I didn't recognise, and the choir fell silent as he raised his arms.

It was as they burst into song that the old man's

head lifted and turned. Something came to life in his eyes and the long fingers of each hand slowly clenched and unclenched themselves. The music was open-throated and stirring, designed to display the blend of the full choir, and the conductor guided it with flamboyant but accurate sweeps of his hands, his head cocked back and an expression of ecstasy on his plump shining face.

The old man suddenly stirred and got up, and before his companions had realised it he was striding down the room to stand at the end of the line of tenors. His head came up and his throat vibrated as he joined his voice to the singing.

The couple exchanged surprised glances and the woman said something to the man, her mouth snapping peevishly shut at the end of it. The man glanced uncertainly at the body of singers and the woman gave him a dig of the elbow which brought him to his feet. He crossed the room and took the old man's elbow and tried to lead him away. The old man was now singing at the pitch of his voice and the sound carried clear and wavering above that of the other singers. He shrugged the younger man off and the other said something to him and took his arm again.

Just then the conductor noticed the little scene and called out over the choir, 'Let him alone. He's all right. Singing does you good. It's a tonic.'

This seemed to nonplus the younger man and he stood for a moment looking uncomfortable before returning to his seat. The woman gave him a furious look as he sat down, and made as if to rise herself. But he restrained her with his hand and his lips formed the words, 'Leave him alone. He's all right.'

The woman went off into a long muttered harangue during which the man looked sheepishly at the floor.

Then she nudged him as though to prod him into action again as the choir came to the end of their piece and the conductor applauded vigorously, shouting, 'Bravo, bravo! Lovely, lovely!' He took the whisky bottle out of his pocket and tilted it to his mouth.

'Now then,' he said. 'What about another one, eh. What this time? I know, I know. An old one. A real old favourite. *Love's old sweet song.*'

A moment later, before the little conductor could gather his importance round him and lift his arms, the old man had started the song in the still true, still sweet, but weak and quavering relic of what must, years before, have been a telling tenor voice:

"'Oft in the dear dead days beyond recall...'"

And the conductor, recovering from his momentary surprise, gazed fondly at the old man, holding back the choir until the chorus and then bringing them in, deep and sweet and rich:

"'Just a song at twilight, when the lights are low, and the flickering shadows softly come and go...'"

I watched and listened, my spine cold. For the old song had associations with my life, bringing memories of my mother's contralto voice and the gaiety and fun of family parties, so long ago...

"'Comes love's sweet song, comes lo-oves old swe-et song...'"

The music died into a hush. No-one spoke or moved for several moments. The old man stood absolutely still, staring somewhere before him. Then the woman nudged her companion again and he went over and touched the old man's arm. The old man came this time, unresisting, and as he turned fully towards me I saw that his face was livid with emotion, his eyes bright and shining in the waiting-room lights. He was two steps from his seat

306

when it all left him in a sudden draining of life and energy that took the use from his limbs and sent him slumping to the floor. At that moment too there was the clank of the loco outside and the porter stuck his head in at the door.

'This is it. The last one tonight.'

The choir broke their ranks and moved out in a body. As the little choir conductor brushed by some instinct made me reach out and lightly lift the whisky bottle from his pocket. The couple had got the old man on to the bench but he hadn't come round. I went over to them.

'Come on,' I said, 'I'll help you to get him onto the train.'

With his arms round our shoulders the younger man and I carried him between us to the waiting train and struggled him into a compartment where we laid him out on the seat. The woman got in behind us, clucking with exasperation. The porter slammed the door, a whistle sounded and the train jerked into motion.

'I knew we never should have come,' the woman said. 'I knew from the start 'at it was foolish; but he would have his way. And now look at him. It might be the end of him.'

I got the whisky bottle out. 'Hold his head up,' I said to the man, who was gazing helplessly at the prostrate figure on the seat. He put his arm under the old man's head and raised it.

'He's teetotal, y'know,' the woman said, looking at the whisky. 'He never touches strong drink.'

'He's ill too,' I said. 'It won't do him any harm.'

I put the bottle to the old man's lips and let a few drops of whisky trickle into his mouth, at the same time slipping my other hand inside his coat to feel for his heart.

'Wrap your overcoat up and put it under his head,' I said to the younger man.

The woman leaned forward from the opposite seat, the lenses of her glasses glinting in the light. 'Are you a doctor?' she said.

I said no, letting a few more drops of whisky trickle into the old man's throat. His breathing was becoming stronger.

'Will he be all right?' the man asked and I nodded. 'I think he's coming round now.'

We sat in a row and looked at the old man.

'I knew we never should have come,' the woman said again, and the man rubbed the palms of his hands nervously together between his knees.

I put the whisky away to give back to the little choir conductor when we got off the train. I imagined he'd be missing it by now.

'All that way,' the woman said. 'Thirty mile there and thirty mile back. And a cemetery on the doorstep! I told him, but he wouldn't listen. Stupid. Stubborn.'

'He's her father,' the man said to me. 'We've been to bury his wife. Not her mother; his second wife. She came from up Clibden. Happen you know it.'

'A little place, up on the moors, isn't it?'

'That's right. Miles from anywhere. He met her while he was out hiking one day. They used to laugh about it together and say how near he'd come to missing her. He'd reckon he wished he'd taken another turning. "I never knew what wa' waiting for me up that lane," he used to say.'

His voice sank to a confidential whisper. 'The wife, y'know, she didn't approve of the trip. She said we should've buried her nearer home, in the family grave. But he said he'd always promised to take her back there if she went first. We never thought he'd go through with it, it being winter an' all that. But we couldn't budge him. We never should've humoured him, though. The wife's right: we should've made him bury her at home. It's been too much for him. I don't suppose he'll ever be right again now... An' all that singin'... Whatever made him do a thing like that, d'you think? After he's been to a funeral, eh? I thought the wife 'ud die of shame when he got up like that and sang at the top of his voice.'

I looked at the old man as his son-in-law's voice droned fretfully on and thought of him in the waiting-room, singing the old songs... 'Just a song at twilight, when the lights are low...'

Then the woman spoke up suddenly from the other side of her husband. 'The trouble with old people,' she said, 'is they've no consideration.'

'No,' I said.

Holroyd's Last Stand

A middle-aged man is punished by his wife & daughter for his last attempt at philandering

Comic tale

Mrs Holroyd first gets wind of it when she finds a small lace-edged handkerchief in the pocket of her husband's best suit one morning when he is down the pit. She wonders, of course, as any wife would, and realises there could be, and no doubt is, a perfectly reasonable explanation for its presence there. He could have picked it up on the street or found it in a bus. After all, he has never given her cause to suspect him before. True, Holroyd was a ladies' man at one time, but that was years and years ago and marriage has long since cured him of the urge to wander. That and age. Or so she has always thought. For the brash cockiness of the well-built florid youth has long ago changed into the dour taciturnity of a middle-aged man who works hard in a man's world. He neglects her, of course; but how many women in the village could say otherwise? To a miner there is a man's world and a woman's, and the two make contact only at the table, in bed, and sometimes on weekend evenings in the pubs and clubs. But all the same, there is a code, and Holroyd has never carried on with other women, she is sure. At least, she always has been sure because she has never given the idea a moment's thought. But now? Who knows what he really does on his many nights out?

Mrs Holroyd leaves the handkerchief where she found it and says nothing. The morning after Holroyd has worn the suit again she looks for it and finds it gone, which makes her wonder still more and prompts her to begin examining his clothes regularly. What she hopes to find she is never quite sure but her watch is rewarded a week later when she finds in another pocket of the same suit a partly expended packet of an article she and Holroyd have never used in their married life. And then she wonders in silence no longer but calls her two married daughters to her side and divulges all.

The person concerned being their father, they are at first shocked and then, more naturally, angry.

'The old devil,' says Gladys, the elder daughter.

'After you've given him the best years of your life,' says Marjorie, who reads a great many romantic novelettes and held out for some time against the local lads, waiting for the coming of a tall, dark, pipe-smoking man with expensive tastes in fast sports cars, only to wind up married to a young collier from the next street, who smokes the cheapest fags and can afford nothing more dashing than a pedal cycle against the competition of a new baby in each of the first five years of their marriage.

'This is the thanks you get,' Marjorie goes on, 'for working your fingers to the bone for him.'

'Well, what are we going to do about it?' says Gladys, the practical one.

'Aye, you can't let him get away with it.'

311

dialogue Mrs Holroyd, after revealing the evidence of her husband's guilt, feels mildly inclined to his defence. 'I would like a bit more proof,' she says uncertainly.

'Proof!' Marjorie exclaims. 'What more proof do you want than them things? Ugh! Mucky things. I wouldn't have one in my house.'

'Where d'you think he meets her?' Gladys asks, and Mrs Holroyd shakes her head.

'Nay, you know as much as I do now. Sheffield, I suppose. I shouldn't think he'd do it too near home. He'd be too frightened o' being seen.'

'It'll be when he goes to t'Dogs,' Gladys says. 'Happen he doesn't go to t'Dogs at all, but meets her, whoever she is.'

'Happen he takes her to t'Dogs,' Mrs Holroyd says.

'The cheek of the old devil,' Marjorie says.

'We'll soon find out,' Gladys says with determination. 'Next time he goes I'll be on the bus before him an' waiting. I'll soon fathom his little game.'

'Suppose he sees you?' her mother says. 'An' what will you tell your Jim?'

'He won't see me,' Gladys says. 'An' I'll think of summat to tell Jim. An' not a word to Harry, Marjorie. We don't want them getting ideas.'

A fortnight later mother and daughters hold another conference.

'There's no doubt about it, then,' Mrs Holroyd says. 'He's carrying on.'

'The same one every time,' Gladys says.

'A fast-looking piece, I suppose?' her mother says.

'A bit simple-looking, if you ask me,' says Gladys. 'All milk an' water and a simpering smile. Just the sort to suck up to me dad an' make him think he's a big man.'

'Aye,' Mrs Holroyd says, 'he allus liked lasses

312

sucking up to him as a lad. But I thought he'd grown out of that years ago.'

'They never grow out of it,' Gladys says.

'I wouldn't ha' classed all men alike before this,' her mother says. 'But now...'

'Now we know,' Marjorie says.

'Aye,' Gladys echoes, 'now we know. And we've got to decide what to do about it... Put the kettle on, Mother.'

the surprise invitation

'Is that a new tie you've got on?' Mrs Holroyd is asking her husband one evening a few days later.

'This? Oh, aye, aye. I saw it in a shop winder in Calderford t'other Saturday afternoon an' took a fancy to it.'

'Very smart,' Mrs Holroyd says. 'Your shoes are over here when you want 'em. I've given 'em a rub over.'

'Eh? What? Have you?' Holroyd glances at her in the mirror where he is combing his thinning black hair.

'Aye. You don't want mucky shoes when you've got a new tie on, do you?'

'No, that's right. Thanks very much.'

'I don't like to see a man become careless with his appearance as he gets older,' Mrs Holroyd says, stirring the fire with the poker. 'When a man's smart it shows he's got an interest in life.'

'Aye. I suppose you're right.'

'Dogs tonight, eh?'

'Aye, that's right – t'Dogs.'

'Does your lady friend like t'Dogs?' Mrs Holroyd asks, and Holroyd, suddenly very still, shoots her a startled look in the mirror.

'Eh?' he says. 'What's that?'

'Your lady friend,' Mrs Holroyd says. 'That young woman friend of yours in Sheffield.'

313

'Well, I, er...'

'Now don't tell me you didn't think I knew,' Mrs Holroyd says. 'Though you have kept pretty quiet about her, I must say.'

Holroyd turns from the glass and bends for his shoes, saying nothing.

'You're not ashamed of her, are you?' Mrs Holroyd asks. 'She's not deformed, is she?'

'Oh, no, no,' says Holroyd, darting perplexed looks at her now, which is easy enough to do since she doesn't once meet his eyes.

Only when he is on the point of leaving, and showing signs of wanting to get away without further conversation, does she transfix him at the door by looking him straight in the face and saying:

'Well, why don't you bring her and let's have a look at her?'

He gapes, flabbergasted. 'Bring her here?'

'Aye, why not? Bring her to tea sometime.'

He looks at her for several moments during which the frown on his face gives way to a glint in his eyes.

'All right,' he says finally, a half-embarrassed but defiant note in his voice, 'I will. I'll bring her o' Sunday.'

'Aye,' Mrs Holroyd agrees, turning away. 'Sunday. That'll be nice.'

Tea with Ellen

'Come in, then,' Holroyd says. 'C'mon, don't be shy.' He takes the young woman by the arm and pulls her off the dark step and into the kitchen.

'What d'you want potterin' about at back door for?' Mrs Holroyd says. 'T'front door's for visitors. Anyway, come in, don't hang about in t'doorway.'

'Dyed hair,' is Mrs Holroyd's first thought as the young woman steps into the light.

314

'Well, er... Holroyd says, 'this is Ella, er, Miss Fairchild. And this is my, er, Alice.'

'How d'ye do, Miss Fairchild,' says Mrs Holroyd.

'Pleased to meet you, I'm sure,' says Miss Fairchild, blinking in the strong light of the kitchen bulb. Her eyes are very blue in a doll-like face and though her features give her an appearance of youth she won't, Mrs Holroyd is sure, ever see thirty-five again.

'I've heard quite a lot about you from William,' Miss Fairchild says.

'Oh, have you now? You've told her a lot about me, have you?'

'Well, I, er...' Holroyd says.

'Oh, yes, he's often spoken of you. And always with the most gentlemanly respect.'

'Well, that's nice to know.' Mrs Holroyd gives a sidelong glance at Holroyd, who avoids her eyes.

'Yes, I said to him once, I said, "Now see here, William, you must tell me about your wife. What sort of woman is she? I want to know all about her."'

'Oh, did you now?'

Holroyd clears his throat noisily.

'Of course, I never thought I'd meet you.'

'No, I don't suppose you did.'

'No. Not all wives would understand a relationship like mine and William's.'

'You don't think so?'

'No, you see—'

'Er, let's go into t'other room, shall we?' Holroyd says. 'Out of Alice's way.'

'Aye, you go on,' Mrs Holroyd says. 'I really can't do with you standing on top of me when I'm trying to make the tea.'

They go through into the living-room and Mrs

Holroyd gets on with preparing the tea while their conversation mumbles through to her. Miss Fairchild seems to be doing most of the talking.

'Asked him all about me, did she?' Mrs Holroyd thinks. 'Wouldn't understand their relationship. Mmm. Well, well!'

Twenty minutes later Mrs Holroyd is asking their visitor how she takes her tea when the front door opens without ceremony and Gladys walks in.

'Oh,' she says, 'I didn't know you had company.'

'Come in, come in,' her mother says. 'This your father's lady friend, Miss Fairchild... My elder daughter, Gladys.'

Miss Fairchild says she is pleased to see Gladys and blushes. 'I'm sure I didn't think I was going to meet all the family.'

'Oh, don't mind me,' Gladys says. 'I'm allus popping in like this. I live just up the street, y'see.'

'I do think it's nice when families don't split up and drift apart,' Miss Fairchild says.

'Oh, we're big family people round here, y'know,' Gladys says. 'We stick together. Have you got no family, then?'

Miss Fairchild says with momentarily downcast eyes that she is all alone in the world, which is why she values friendship so much.

'Aye, well,' Gladys says with a laugh, 'you know what they say: you can pick your friends but you're stuck with your family. Happen you're luckier than you think.'

'Oh, I wouldn't say that,' Miss Fairchild says. 'But life has its compensations.' This with a quick fluttering glance at Holroyd, who is gazing rigidly at his plate and does not respond.

'Have a cup o' tea love?' Mrs Holroyd asks.

316

Gladys says she ought to be going and making Jim's tea, but she won't refuse. She takes off her coat and settles into a chair by the fire.

'You're quiet, Dad,' she says then, and Holroyd starts and says, 'Oh, aye, well...'

'Too many women about the place for you, is that it? Me dad was glad when me an' our Marjorie got married, y'know, Miss Fairchild. Can't stand a crowd o' women jabberin' round him.'

'Oh, I know he's a man's man,' Miss Fairchild says, casting another glance at Holroyd, who hunches a little farther down into his collar, as though to hide his head.

'You think so, do you? We've allus thought of him as a ladies' man, haven't we, mother?'

'Nay, look here...' Holroyd begins.

'Now you can't deny you had all the lasses on a string when you were a young feller,' Gladys says. 'I've heard 'em talk about it.'

'But that's thirty year ago.'

'There's no need to deny it for my benefit, William,' Miss Fairchild says, and Gladys suppresses a giggle into something that sounds like a sneeze.

'Have you caught a cold, Gladys?' her mother enquires.

'No, just a bit o' dust up me nose.'

'Nay, there's no dust in here. I had a right good clean down when I knew your father's friend was coming.'

'You know,' Miss Fairchild says, 'you shouldn't have gone to all that–'

'Oh, I have me pride, Miss Fairchild, even if I have been married thirty years come next Easter. I like things to be clean and tidy. Particularly on special occasions like this.'

'Eeh, you know, I wish our Marjorie 'ud pop in,'

317

Gladys says, 'She'll be wild if she knows she's missed you. She doesn't get out all that much, y'know, with five bairns to see to. Did you know me dad was a grandfather seven times over, Miss Fairchild?'

'So many,' Miss Fairchild murmurs. 'And I dare say he's proud of them all.'

'Oh, aye, aye. My eldest is a bit too big to bounce on his knee now, but he's proud of 'em. An' they're proud of him. There isn't one of 'em 'at doesn't come running the minute they see him.'

The fire is burning low and Mrs Holroyd piles more coal onto it. Then, tea finished, they move away from the table and sit round the hearth while Gladys keeps up a cheerful monologue punctuated by remarks that she really will have to go, she only called in for a minute, and isn't it a pity that Marjorie hasn't popped in to see her father's friend. She is just saying that she'll call on her way home and tell Marjorie to come round when her sister comes into the house through the back door. Like Gladys, Marjorie expresses surprise at the presence of 'company' and says she is only staying a minute. Like Gladys also she takes a cup of tea from the replenished pot and joins the group round the fire. Gladys changes her mind about leaving and she and Marjorie carry on a conversation occasionally added to by Mrs Holroyd, while Miss Fairchild sits with a bemused little smile on her face and looks now and again at Holroyd who is keeping quiet and still, like a man who has walked into a patch of attractive forest and suddenly wonders about the presence of wild animals.

He has not spoken for half an hour, nor even drawn attention to himself by lighting a cigarette, when Marjorie says suddenly, 'What a lovely frock you've got on, Miss Fairchild. I've been admiring it ever since I came in.'

Miss Fairchild's soft mouth purses with pleasure. 'Oh, do you really like it?'

'It shows off your figure lovely,' Gladys says. 'I reckon he'll like it for that, eh?'

Miss Fairchild turns a delicate pink. 'As a matter of fact,' she says, 'he chose it.'

'O-hoh!' Gladys says, while Holroyd gives a startled glance from his eye corners. 'And paid for it, I'll bet!'

'Well' – Miss Fairchild stifles a little giggle – 'he's very generous, you know.'

'Oh, aye, he always was free with his money,' Mrs Holroyd says, adding as though in casual afterthought, 'outside the house.'

Again Holroyd seems to shrink in his chair, as though wishing to hide inside his clothes. Still he says nothing.

'Course, I couldn't wear a frock like that,' Marjorie says frankly. I'm too fat. But I bet our Gladys 'ud look well in it.'

'D'you think so?' Gladys says.

'Aye, I do.'

'I wonder, Miss Fairchild,' Gladys says eagerly, 'would you let me try it on? Such a lovely frock.'

'Well, I...'

'We can pop into the bedroom. It'll only take a minute.'

Miss Fairchild looks at Holroyd as though for guidance, but he is gazing fixedly into the fire and will not meet her glance. She stands up, her hands fluttering uncertainly at the waist of the frock, and Gladys and Marjorie take her out of the room and up the stairs. Now Holroyd lights a cigarette and draws on it deeply. Mrs Holroyd pours herself another cup of tea. They sit without looking at each other.

319

the attack on Ella

Upstairs in the front bedroom Gladys is pulling the dress down over her head and shoulders while Miss Fairchild shivers in her slip.

'Mmm,' Gladys says, turning one way then the other in front of the wardrobe mirror and smoothing the frock over her hips. 'Not bad.'

'A bit on the long side, though, isn't it?' Marjorie says, standing back and examining her sister.

'Ye-es. It'd need a couple of inches off the hem for me.'

'Well, that's easy.' Marjorie opens a drawer of the dressing-table and takes out a pair of scissors. Before the horrified eyes of its owner she bends and sticks the blades through the hem of the dress.

'Stop it!' Miss Fairchild shrieks.

She starts towards them but is abruptly stopped short when Marjorie turns and straightens up, giving her in the same movement a slap that sends her backwards on to the bed.

Marjorie sprawls across her with her full weight, turning a corner of the eiderdown over Miss Fairchild's head to muffle her cries.

'All right. I can hold her.'

Gladys takes off the dress, slips into her own jumper and skirt, and picks up the scissors.

Holroyd turns his eyes to the ceiling. 'What's going on up there?'

'They're havin' a woman to woman talk,' his wife says. She reaches for the poker and balances it in her hand as though deciding whether or not to stir the fire.

It is the sight of Miss Fairchild as she bursts into the room uttering little shrieks of near-hysterical anger, the remnants of her dress clutched in her hands, that brings Holroyd to his feet, his mouth agape.

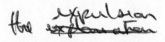

'What's up?' Mrs Holroyd says. 'Don't tell me you've never seen her in her underwear afore.'

'My dress,' Miss Fairchild cries. 'Oh, look what they've done to my lovely dress!'

'What you done?' Holroyd demands as his daughters come into the room. 'What you been up to?'

Miss Fairchild is sobbing noisily now as she looks at the frock. 'It's ruined,' she says, 'completely ruined.' She turns a distorted face on Holroyd. 'This would never have happened if you hadn't brought me here.'

'Get him to buy you another,' Gladys says, 'if he's gormless enough.' She has Miss Fairchild's coat now and she thrusts it into the woman's arms. 'Now hoppit!'

She and Marjorie push her through the kitchen, open the door and propel her into the darkness of the yard, and at the same time Mrs Holroyd places her hand squarely in the middle of her husband's chest and pushes him back into his chair. The girls return to the room and Holroyd cowers away as he sees the expression in the three pairs of eyes levelled at him.

'Now for you,' Marjorie says.

Five minutes later, kicked, scratched and bruised, he is on his hands and knees in the backyard. The door slams behind him and the bolt shoots home.

There is no sign of Miss Fairchild. Holroyd himself does not come home for three days. But Mrs Holroyd does not mind. She spends a very interesting time discussing with her daughters new ways of making his life miserable when he does return.

A Casual Acquaintance

A young man pursues a dream girl seen on a bus — her unhappiness offers no hope — his friend marries her, but it goes wrong.

seeing the girl + tracking her

I was twenty that autumn. It was quite simple the way it happened. I noticed her for the first time on the bus on the journey home from the office one Friday afternoon and fell in love with her on the spot. I pointed her out with studied casualness to my friends Larry and Peter, but neither of them knew her.

I thought about her all weekend and looked out for her every afternoon of the following week. But it wasn't until Friday that I saw her again; for although this was the only afternoon my office closed at five, she evidently travelled at the same time every day. So I watched for her on the one day only and a Friday without my seeing her left me downcast for days, my spirits rising only when the weekend was well behind and another Friday approaching fast.

For weeks I was content just to look at her: to get onto the bus, my heart racing with excitement at the possibility of seeing her and, if it was a lucky Friday, taking a seat from which I could observe without being

322

noticed and gazing at her all the way into town. In the bus station, where we both alighted, I'd stand and watch her cross to her connection, small, straightbacked, with a poise that singled her out from her contemporaries, and a slight haughtiness in the set of her head and the cool glance of brown eyes in a heart-shaped face that chilled in me any notion of a brash approach, a high-handed sweeping aside of the formalities that stood between us.

One Friday afternoon she was talking to another girl as I boarded the bus and brushed past her. I heard her addressed as Joyce. It excited me to have a name by which to think of her. It identified her and made me determined to find out still more about her.

That same afternoon I followed her across the bus station and got onto the same bus. It took us out to the other side of town. An acute fear of appearing conspicuous stopped me from following her to her door, but I watched where she alighted, and at the next stop I jumped off myself and caught a bus back into town. Now I knew her first name and roughly where she lived, and as I rode home I thought that with this increase in my knowledge of her the time was surely approaching when we should meet and really know each other. As it was now, I thought with sudden gloom, she was probably not even aware of my existence, let alone my feeling for her.

As the weeks passed by with no progress made I began, on the evenings when I could leave my studies, to take long walks into the district where she lived. I'd get off the bus and stroll up the road which wound away over the hill and into the next valley. On the brow of the hill I'd stop for a while, leaning on the wall and looking out over the dark forest of chimneys at the lights of the town.

Away in the distance, on my left, I could see the lighted windows of a huge mill working the night shift. It seemed to me like a great ship floating on a sea of night; full of souls, hundreds of people, whom I would never see and never know. I thought then of the wonderful chance that had singled Joyce out for me; and it seemed to me in some way preordained that that same chance would eventually bring us together. I was sure of it.

From the top of the hill I wandered back through side-streets and looked at the curtained windows of strange houses and wondered if she was inside, living her life. On all these rambles through the lamplit streets, which though strange at first soon became familiar to me, I cherished vague dreams of suddenly coming face to face with her and having the right words to say. But I didn't see her once. I went on, living in a kind of suspense, loving her from a distance, waiting for the miracle that would bring us together. Until Christmas was only a fortnight away. And then it happened.

the weekly

On that Saturday, two weeks before Christmas, I was in town, pressing through the throngs of shoppers to choose presents for my family. I was looking at socks in a department store when she turned her head and showed me her dear face, three counters away. I forgot my own errands at once and made my way towards her. I had no idea of accosting her but as she moved on, absorbed in her own shopping, I followed behind. She was by herself.

I kept her in sight all round the store until, at last, with her shopping bag and basket both filled, she made for the door. Alarmed then at the thought of losing her on the busy street, I pushed forward until I was immediately behind her.

I was so close I could have reached out and touched her at the moment the handle of her bag broke and half

324

the contents spilled out on to the floor. She gave an exclamation of annoyance, and before I realised it I was down on my hands and knees picking up packages and putting them back in the bag.

'There.' We looked at each other as I straightened up, and I was chilled by the lack of recognition in her eyes and in a curious way astounded that she couldn't tell simply by looking at me that I'd been yearning for her all those months.

She thanked me and held out her hand for the bag, which I was holding under my arm.

'Please let me carry it for you.' I motioned to her basket. 'You can't manage them both; this handle's useless now.'

'It's very kind of you.' Her voice was doubtful, and I said, 'I can see you don't know me. But I know you. I've seen you nearly every Friday on the bus into town.'

Was it politeness or a genuine glimmer of recognition in her eyes now, as she said. 'I thought there was something familiar about your face.'

It was enough for me for the moment. We moved by common consent out of the store and onto the teeming pavement. There I looked at her. 'Which way?' I asked, and she smiled at my persistence.

'I've finished my shopping, so if you wouldn't mind walking to the bus station...'

'I was going that way myself,' I lied.

'I'm not taking you out of your way, then.' She gave me another of those smiles which seemed to turn my heart right over. 'But it really is very good of you.'

We walked along in comparative silence. I had the reputation among my friends of being something of a wit; but now I was almost tongue-tied and could think of only the most commonplace remarks. And soon we'd be in the bus station and it would all be over.

'This is really lucky for me,' I said all at once.

She glanced up at me. 'Oh?'

'Yes. I've seen you quite a lot these past few months and I've wanted an excuse to speak to you.'

'Oh?' she said again.

'I couldn't simply walk up to you and start talking, could I? You know with some girls you could, but not you.'

We had stopped on a corner now and she was gazing at me with hazel eyes full of bland sophistication that made me feel fourteen years old. I felt that I was on the verge of a blush; but I was determined to see it through. I might never have another chance. She glanced at her watch and I blurted out, 'Well, you see, the idea was that I should ask you to come out with me some evening.'

'But I don't know you,' she said.

'That's the trouble,' I said, feeling smaller and more foolish with every second she went on gazing up at me. 'But how else can we get to know each other?'

'No,' she said, freeing me from her direct gaze at last. 'I see your point. But I'm afraid I couldn't. My boy friend wouldn't like it, you see.'

'Oh! Your boy friend.' What a fool I was! Seeing her always alone, I'd never considered the most obvious point – that someone else might have a prior claim on her.

She went on, blasting all my hopes and driving me deeper into confusion. 'He doesn't live round here and we only see each other at weekends; but he wouldn't like me to go out with anybody else during the week.'

'No,' I babbled. 'No, of course not.' All I could think of now was what a fool I must look to her. I gave her back her shopping bag. 'I'm sorry I said anything.'

Going home, I thought that these things worked only in books or on the films; in real life you were just made to look silly. And it was pride that was really uppermost in my mind now. So long as she didn't turn the incident into a joke to tell to her friends, it mightn't be too bad. I'd told nobody about her; not even Larry and Peter; and I was even less inclined to take them into my confidence now.

But when that confusion had left me I realised that the setback had not changed my feelings about her. I abandoned my evening walks but still watched for her on Friday afternoons. And now the ice was broken; we could greet each other as acquaintances, and she did at least acknowledge my existence by letting me ride with her into town and talking with me while we waited for our connections. Sometimes Peter, who lived out in my direction, would be with us, but more often we were alone. All the rest of the winter my mind was full of her, and the idea that, if only I were patient, she might one day turn to me. This became the great impossible dream of my life. My feeling for her deepened steadily, strengthened by the very absence of encouragement, until it seemed to me that all the wonder and delight of Woman was contained in her sweet and gentle self. And, sustained by my dream, I went on wooing her passively by my presence on those short homeward journeys on the one afternoon in the week.

On an afternoon in March, with the days lengthening into spring, we stood together chatting idly in the bus station. I was talking about a film I'd seen at the weekend. She mentioned then that she'd spent the weekend indoors and, wondering at this, I mentioned my unknown rival for the first time.

'He's neglected you for once, then?' I said, trying to keep my voice light.

'For always,' she said. 'It's over. It has been for weeks.'

327

dialogue

My heart gave a tremendous leap of joy. Over! Then there was nothing to stop her going out with me.

'Are you still thinking about that?'

'Of course.' Oh, God, wasn't it all I'd been able to think about since I first saw her!

'But why?' she said, and it seemed to me that there was a great weariness in her voice. 'We're friends, aren't we? Isn't that enough for you?'

'It can never be enough.'

'But why?' she said again.

'Because... because I like you too much.' No, it wasn't good enough. I had to say it, even here in broad daylight, among streams of people. I must say it. 'Because I love you.'

She shook her head. 'It's no use. I'm sorry, Clive, but it could only lead to disappointment. People never live up to expectation, you know.'

It needed only one word from her to make my world a place of life and joy and laughter; and I was shocked by the disillusionment in her voice. 'Why... that's defeatism! Look, maybe you are a bit cut up just now, but you can't look at life in general like that.'

'It's the way things are,' she said with quiet finality. 'It's the way it goes.'

I could only think she had loved him very much, and envy him for that. Whatever had happened between them had hurt her badly. Frantically, I searched for something else to say, then gave it up as I realised that it was no good. I knew with miserable certainty that it never had been.

I saw her several times more before summer came, bringing with it the end of my deferment and a summons to serve a postponed period of National Service.

I took a job in Wales when I came out of the army

and it was only on infrequent weekends that I went home to see my family. As time went by I lost touch with Larry and Peter and I saw neither of them for several years until I ran into Larry quite accidentally while on a visit home. It was lunchtime and we went into a pub to talk over a glass of beer. Larry had been working away too – in London – but he'd married now and returned to settle in his home town.

'And Peter,' I said when we'd gossiped for a while. 'What's he doing nowadays?'

'He's in the Merchant Navy. Third Engineer. Or is it Fourth? I forget now.'

'I seem to remember hearing he'd got married too.'

'Lord, yes!' Larry's ugly mobile face screwed itself into a grimace of disgust. 'Bought himself a real packet there. He signed on to get away from it all.'

'As bad as that, eh? Who did he marry? A local girl?'

'Called Joyce Henryson. Used to work up the road from us. That's how he met her. On the bus.'

'Joyce Henryson?' Could it be? I tried to analyse the feeling the name evoked in me. How long since she'd been in my thoughts? I could almost feel myself blushing now at my past folly. But trouble?

'That's right,' Larry said. 'You knew her. You used to ride down into town with her, didn't you? I remember thinking at one time that you'd a fancy for her yourself.'

'And you say old Peter went to sea to get away from her?'

'He certainly did, mate. What a so-and-so she turned out to be! He always knew she liked a good time, mind. He was mad about her, but after they were married he just couldn't keep up with her. He wrote to me and I got him a job with my firm in London. The money was better but she wouldn't move and he was no better off,

329

trying to keep both ends going and seeing her only once every few weeks.'

I drank from my glass, listening to him.

'A sorry tale, Clive. Then... well, he eventually found out that she was carrying on with a bloke she'd known years back. A married man. Seemed she'd had an unhappy affair with him then, and now he'd left his wife and there was nothing standing between them but poor old Peter. She seemed to blame him for that. I tell you, she got him so he didn't know what he was doing. And you know what a steady lad he always was.'

I nodded. 'It'll be divorce, then?'

'The sooner he gets rid, the better.'

We drank in silence for some minutes.

'No signs of you getting hitched, then, Clive?'

'No... I haven't found the right one, I suppose.'

'Yes, it's fine if you get the right one; and hell if you pick a wrong 'un.'

'You know,' I said in a moment, 'she never struck me as being that sort.'

'Nor Peter, evidently. Still, you never did know her well, did you?'

I looked at the amber dregs of my beer. Of course I was thinking – would it have been different with me? Could I have held her or would I have got the same rotten deal as Peter? And how rotten did the deal seem to her? They were things I'd never know.

'No,' I said at length. 'No, she was just a casual acquaintance.'

Waiting

An old man waiting to die
while his houseproud daughter-in-law
hovers, eager to change his house

Old Thompson was seventy-four the winter his wife *death*
died. She was sixty-nine. They would have celebrated *g wife*
their golden wedding the following summer and they
were a quiet and devoted couple. It was bronchitis that
finished her, helped along by a week of November fog
poisoned by Cressley's industrial soot and smoke. In
ten days she was gone.

His wife's death nearly finished Thompson too. He *effect*
was a changed man. Always active and vigorous, carrying
his years lightly, and with a flush of ruddy good health in
his face, he now seemed to age overnight. He seemed to
shrivel and bend like a tree from whose roots all nutrition
had been drained. His hands were all at once uncertain
and fumbling, where they had grasped surely. The world
about him seemed to lose interest for him. He became
silent and withdrawn. He would sit for long hours in his
tall wooden-backed armchair by the fire, and what he
thought about in his silence no-one knew. *Bob +* *Annie*

Bob, the Thompsons' younger son, and his wife

Annie were living in the house in Dover Street when Mrs Thompson died. The Thompsons had had four children. The elder son was lost at sea during the war; a daughter married and emigrated to Australia, and a second daughter, Maud, fifteen years older than Bob, lived with her family in another part of the town.

Bob and Annie had not known each other long before they became eager to get married: Bob because he wanted Annie and she (though she was fond of Bob in her own way) because she could at last visualise a life away from her roughneck family. When Mrs Thompson suggested that they marry and live with them in Dover Street until they could get a house of their own, Annie hesitated. Her ideal of marriage had been a process whereby she acquired a husband and an orderly, well-furnished home in one fell swoop. But she soon saw the advantages in this arrangement. She would, first of all, escape from her present life into a house which was quiet and efficiently run, if not her own; and she would be able to go on working so that she and Bob could save up all the more quickly for their own house. She would also get Bob, a good enough husband for any working-class girl: good-natured and pliable, ready to be bent her way whenever it was necessary for her ends.

In time Bob became used to the silent figure in the house: but Annie, who since her mother-in-law's death had given up her job and was at home all day, began to find the old man's constant presence a source of growing irritation.

'He gets on me nerves, Bob,' she said one night when they were alone. 'Just sitting there all day and me having to clean up round him. And he hardly says a word from getting up in a morning to going to bed.'

'Well, I reckon he's a right to do as he likes,' Bob

said mildly. 'It's his house, not ours. We're the lodgers, if anybody.'

But to Annie, now looking after the house as if it were her own, it was beginning to seem the other way about.

On Wednesday afternoons Annie took the bus into Cressley to shop in the market. For an hour or so she would traverse the cobbled alleyways between the stalls, looking at everything, buying here and there, and keeping a sharp lookout for the bargains that were sometimes to be had. And then, with all her purchases made, she would leave the market for the streets of the town to spend another hour in her favourite pastime: looking in furniture-shop windows. There were furniture shops of all kinds in Cressley, from those where you had to strain your neck to see the prices on the tickets to others where you could hardly see the furniture itself for the clutter of placards and notices offering goods at prices almost too tempting to be true.

One Wednesday she found a new shop full of the most delightful things, with a notice inviting anyone to walk in and look round without obligation. Annie hesitated for a moment before stepping through the doorway where, almost at once, she stopped entranced before a three-piece suite in green uncut moquette. There was a card on the sofa which said: 'This fine 3-piece suite is yours for only ten shillings a week', and very small at the bottom, 'Cash price eighty-nine guineas'. Ten shillings a week... Why, she could almost pay that out of her housekeeping and never miss it!

A voice at her shoulder startled her. 'Can I help you, Madam?' She looked round at the assistant who had come softly to her side.

'Oh, well, no,' she said, flustered. 'I was just looking.'

'Was it lounge furniture you were particularly interested in?' asked the young man.

'Well, no... All of it, really.'

'I see. You're thinking of setting up house?'

'Well, yes, as a matter of fact, I am. I'm just looking round, y'know, seeing what there–'

'We can supply everything you need.' The assistant took her by the elbow. 'If you'll just come up to the showroom you'll see what I mean...'

'Well, I...' Annie began, panicking a little at the thought of getting involved; but she was already being led to the rear of the shop and up a few wide steps.

In the entrance to the showroom she stopped and gaped. There before her, filling every corner of the vast room, was furniture of all shapes, sizes and uses; lounge furniture, dining-room furniture, furniture for bedroom and kitchen, and even television and wireless sets.

'You know we can furnish a complete home for only a few pounds a week...'

Half an hour later Annie was on the bus, going home, with pictures of beautiful rooms floating through her intoxicated mind. All that, and for just a few pounds a week. Why, there was no reason why they couldn't have their home tomorrow. No reason except they hadn't got a house.

'Bob, when are we going to have a house of our own? We've been hanging about for three years now and we're no nearer than when we got married.'

'Oh, I don't know,' Bob said easily. 'There's not a lot o' point in trying to get another place with things as they are. Besides, who'd look after me dad?'

'Your Maud might think about doing her share.'

'Aye, aye, I know,' Bob mumbled. 'Happen she'd buckle to if it came to it. She's not a bad sort at bottom, our Maud. But anyway, it hasn't come to that. Where would we go if we did move? You can't get a house to rent any more than you could three year ago.'

'What about buying one, then?' Annie said.

'We'd better wait till we've enough brass for a good deposit.'

'We've over three hundred pounds in the bank,' Annie said. 'What did we save it for?'

'You could spend all that on furniture. That wouldn't go far.'

They were walking home from the cinema after seeing a film set partly in an American house with an open split-level living-room where there was lots of space and all the furnishings looked smart and well made. Annie knew the limitations of her life and did not yearn for the impossible; but she was becoming avid now to reach out and take what was there awaiting her grasp.

'There's always hire purchase. I was talking to a feller in a shop today and he told me you could furnish a house for just a few pounds a week.'

Bob laughed. 'Had one o' them chaps on to you, have you? They'll tell you owt. No, we can do wi' out debts like that. Someday you'll have all you want.'

'Someday...' Annie muttered. 'Stopping at home after working all that time has got me wanting a place of me own.'

'Well, I mean this place is as good as yours, isn't it? You do pretty well as you like in it, don't you? And it'll really be yours one o' these days. After all, me dad can't last–' He stopped.

Annie glanced quickly at him. 'You mean he can't last for ever.'

'Shurrup,' Bob muttered. 'We shouldn't be talking like that.'

There was a light on in the house and they found Bob's father sitting in his chair by the fire.

'Still up?' Annie said. 'I thought you'd have been in bed long since.'

The old man lifted his face to them, though his eyes seemed hardly to take them in. 'I wa' just going.'

He pulled himself up and went out without another word.

No Sunshine

They went on as they were for some time. And then summer came and with the warmer days old Thompson stirred from his chair and began in the afternoons to stroll down the hill to the park where he could sit on a bench in the sun.

It was a great relief for Annie to be without him for a while each day, and she found new zest for her life as a housewife, the life she had always craved for from being a girl in a rough, overcrowded home. She tackled the work with great spirit, scrubbing and polishing until the house was always faultlessly clean.

But still there was something lacking. It wasn't like caring for her own possessions, for she was surrounded by furniture that was heavy and dark and old-fashioned and which never gave her a true reward for all the effort she applied to its care.

'This old furniture gives me the willies,' she complained to Bob. 'It's like living in a museum. All them chinks and crannies just harbour dust. I don't know how your mother put up with it all them years.'

'She was used to it. It's the furniture they got when they were married. It was all the fashion at one time.'

'It's out o' fashion now, all right,' Annie said.

'Aye, well, we'll have some good stuff when we get a place of our own.'

336

'Look, Bob,' she said, 'why don't we get some new furniture now? Think how nice this place could look with a new carpet and a three-piece suite, and–'

'Hold on a minute,' Bob said. 'What about me dad? This is his house, y'know, and he might like it as it is.'

'You can ask him. I don't think he'd mind. You know how he is these days.'

'But what could we do with his stuff?'

'Oh, we could sell it. Somebody on the market 'ud take it off our hands.'

'We can't just sell the old feller's home up round him,' Bob said. He sounded shocked at the thought. 'Dammit, what would he do when we left?'

'I don't know as there'd be any need for us to leave if we had some decent furniture,' Annie said.

Bob saw her smooth round face set stubbornly in the expression which always frightened him a little. He was still surprised she had ever married him and anxious to please her in any way he could.

'I suppose – that's to say, if me dad doesn't mind – I suppose we could put it into store. Then if he ever needed it it'd be there.' *tht change*

In the event they sold the furniture, the old man offering no objection. They gave him the money, a pitifully small number of notes which he gazed at in silence for some time before closing his hand round them and putting them away.

They redecorated the living room, using a light modern paper which seemed to push the walls back, and hung new curtains. Then when the furniture came – the carpet, the dining-suite and the three-piece – the transformation was complete and startling. Annie was ready to hug herself. Here was something worth looking after, that rewarded dusting and polishing, something that was her own. The only jarring note was struck by the old man's tall-backed chair, empty more often now in the long warm afternoons when he was sitting on a bench in the park.

For a time she was at peace. And then she could not help speaking to Bob about an unfairness that had rankled before but which seemed more obviously unjust now that the house had her own stamp on it at last. She suggested that Bob's sister be approached with a view to her taking the old man.

'We've had him for nearly a year now,' she pointed out. 'I don't see why your Maud shouldn't take her turn. She's got as much room as we have.'

'But this is his home,' Bob said. 'He won't want to go.'

'What's the difference between one place and another?' Annie said. 'He hardly knows where he is anyway.'

'I dunno,' Bob said. 'There's summat not–'

'Look, just promise you'll see her and mention it.'

'Well... I don't suppose there's any harm in sounding her out.'

He came into the house a few nights later to find Annie and the old man sitting on opposite sides of the hearth, his father with his hands resting on the stick between his legs as usual, but perched on the edge of one of the new armchairs. Bob looked round.

'Where's your chair, then, Dad?'

The old man's voice was stronger than he'd heard it for a long time now. 'Ask her,' he said.

Annie was blushing a fiery red. 'I... I let it go this afternoon,' she said. 'I sold it to a chap at the door for five bob. Your dad won't take the money.'

'You did what?' Bob said incredulously.

Annie was obviously regretting her impulse, but it was too late now.

338

'It was out of place here... And I knew your Maud wouldn't want it.'

Taken off balance as he was, Bob spoke without thinking of the old man sitting there.

'It's not the only thing our Maud doesn't want.'

No-one spoke for several moments and in the silence a quiver ran through old Thompson's body. He got to his feet, drawing himself erect as he faced the two of them.

'You've been round there, haven't you? Trying to get rid o' me.' His voice, pitched high and thin, cracked with his anger. 'I know what it is. You're wantin' me to die. Well, I'll tell you – I'm wantin' it an' all. There's nowt left for me sin' my Mary went. I'm waitin', just bidin' my time till the good Lord sees fit to take me to her again.' His stick rose and fell with a mighty crack against the skirting board. 'And you'll just have to bide your time an' wait anent me.'

He turned his flushed face and glittering eyes from them and went through the door. They heard his slow feet on the stairs. Neither of them spoke. In a moment they looked at each other and then they looked away.

Madge

A woman obsessed with her own dignity — saved from the shame of abandonment & divorce by her husband's death.

Madge

If there was one thing all who knew Madge Collins were agreed upon it was that she was a lady: she had grace, charm, poise. Most people acknowledged her qualities with approval; in some, conscious of being lesser mortals, they aroused feelings of rancour. She was too perfect for this life, and pride went before a fall.

It had always been so with her. As a child she was a 'little madam', wilful, used to getting her own way, but without the passions, tears and sulks others found inseparable from the attaining of their ends. At twenty-nine, the eldest of the three Greenaway girls, she was still single. Her youngest sister, Angela, had got herself pregnant while still at university and married with unfortunate haste at nineteen. You couldn't imagine Madge Greenaway in a situation like that; and it was less the moral aspect of it that one saw as sitting incongruously on her personality than the simple untidiness of it; the mess. At twenty-nine she seemed to be placidly biding her time (and leaving it a touch late, some thought). Though her name had never been closely connected with any man's, no-one doubted that she'd had her chances. She was handsome, intelligent, and she would have money from her father. Potential suitors came and went. One came and stayed long enough to transfer his attentions to the middle sister, Catherine, and marry her. Nor was there any feeling in this that Madge had lost a husband, that Catherine had stolen a man from her. She was hardly aware that her future brother-in-law had come to woo her before all the attractions he thought he'd found in her were more piquantly displayed to him in the person of Catherine. Madge, who hadn't wanted him anyway, gave them her blessing and went on living her own well-ordered life. 'The man isn't born who's good enough for Madge Greenaway,' said an observant, concerned, and somewhat irritated friend at this time. *Edgar*

Edgar Collins changed this notion. It had been said that Madge did not meet enough eligible men because she had never gone out to work. Adam Greenaway became a widower while Madge was in her last year at school. She showed no interest in continuing her education and, at eighteen, she chose to stay at home and keep house for her father and younger sisters. Adam Greenaway was the managing director of a family motor sales and repair firm which he ran with a brother and a nephew, and there was plenty of money to pay for help for Madge. A woman came to the house every day and relieved her of all the menial tasks, leaving her free to supervise the shopping and household expenditure and to cook, all of which she enjoyed doing and showed an aptitude for. When her father, who for several years had been a Conservative member of the town council, came to serve his term as mayor, Madge became his mayoress and discharged her duties with such grace and ease she might have trained for the purpose all her life. On the occasions when she spoke in public she did so in a manner which, while not controversial, was lucid and piquant and avoided the shabby clichés so many of her predecessors had relied upon. Madge Greenaway didn't flap easily; not even when the chairman at one of the functions she opened became himself so controversial as to describe her as the most charming mayoress the town had had for many a year to an audience containing two recent holders of the office. One of them who had already despised the other for owning all the faults Madge Greenaway was so free of now found that she detested Madge Greenaway more. The second woman was honestly pleased to see someone function so admirably in a role she herself had feared and fumbled in, to the extent of tripping on the stairs at the mayor's ball and sending sprawling the first citizen of a neighbouring town. It was at the mayor's ball held during her father's year of office that Madge met Edgar Collins.

He was introduced to her across an arbitrarily come -together circle in the bar, a shortish, stocky, sandy-haired man whom she smiled at and took no more notice of until a few moments later when, Tommy Marshall having launched into a risqué story he'd been awaiting an audience for all evening, she felt a touch on her elbow and realised that Collins had edged his way round the outside of the group and was asking her to dance.

'Or would you like another drink?'

'Thank you. I think I'd prefer to dance.'

He had green eyes. His colouring wasn't of a type she had thought she cared for. She handed him her empty glass and he got rid of it before they walked together along the passage to the ballroom.

'I hope you didn't mind, but I thought a rescue ~~dialogue~~ operation might be in order.'

'He can be very funny at times.'

'It didn't strike me as being one of those times.'

'Perhaps you're right.'

'The dignity of the office, and all that,' he said.

'Even if the holder doesn't care...'

'Ah, now, I didn't say that. I was thinking about the dignity of your sex as much as anything.'

'Thank you.' She was amused.

'And somehow I turn out to sound pompous and stuffy.'

'No, I wouldn't say that.'

'I'm neither, really. And as a matter of fact, it is a very funny story.'

'Then why take me away?'

'There's a time and place for everything. If you like, I'll tell it you myself, when we get to know each other better.'

She said, lying, 'I'm sorry. I didn't catch your name.'

Collins was an architect who had a junior partnership with the ageing head of a firm in a nearby town. Some work for the Corporation had given him his connection with the Town Hall, hence his invitation to the mayor's ball where he met Madge.

He telephoned her three days later to say that he had to run out on Saturday afternoon to take a quick look at a site in Harrogate and would she like to go with him and then spend the evening in Leeds, where they could have an early dinner and go to see the touring production of a West End musical, for which he had tickets. It was the odd make-up of the invitation that stopped her from putting him off till another time. Why had he not suggested just dinner and the theatre? Why should she go all the way out to Harrogate with him?

But she went, and sat with cold feet and a mounting irritation as the warmth drained out of the stationary car and Collins and his client tramped about, pointing and talking interminably in the rapidly fading light. She tried not to show her impatience as Collins finally shook hands and came back to the car. He was himself in a mild temper.

'Idiot,' he muttered as he slammed the door and pressed the starter.

'What's the matter?'

'Oh, I'd hoped to have a quick look at the site without seeing him; but he turned up and I was forced to listen to his cockeyed ideas.'

'I thought the man who paid the piper called the tune.'

Collins grunted. 'That, if I may say so, is a typical client's attitude. He's got a nice sloping site there, with a view. He wants his sitting-room to both overlook the view and catch the afternoon sunlight. Unfortunately, I can't give him that without rearranging the order of the sun's coming up and going down.'

'What will you do?'

'We'll talk about it and promote a bit more bad feeling on both sides, then settle for the inevitable compromise.'

He glanced at her as he took the car round a big island on to the Leeds road. 'I'm sorry. I didn't intend to keep you hanging about for so long.'

She looked out at the coloured lights in the trees. 'I was wondering why you'd brought me out here with you.'

'I knew I shouldn't have time to go all the way back to pick you up.'

'Couldn't we have met in Leeds?'

344

'That would have meant you making your own way there.'

'I'm quite capable of doing that.'

'Yes, you'd either come in by bus, or in your own car. The first method is inconvenient and the second would have meant an incomplete evening: parting in Leeds instead of my driving you home.' He flicked on his headlights as they left the street-lamps on the edge of the town. 'Now I've spoiled the beginning of it by leaving you bored and cold.'

The warmth from the heater began to move round her calves and feet as they drove down the hill. Headlights swung and lifted in the sudden intense darkness as ascending cars overtook a slow-moving bus.

She said, 'All right. I'll forgive you.'

He was a logical man, who organised his life. She must overlook the small occasions when circumstances upset his plans. She leaned forward as far as the safety belt he'd insisted she wear would permit and gently rubbed her legs below her knees. He glanced at what she was doing and asked, 'Feeling warmer now?'

'Yes.' Now, she found, she was pleasantly expectant about the evening ahead.

He parked in a street off Briggate and led her round the corner to a pub in a narrow yard which was reached through an alley between two shops.

'Is this where we're going to eat?'

It wasn't what she had expected. She looked at the late-Victorian interior as they stepped inside: a low ceiling, black wood, brass rails, grey mirrors – some carrying chipped and faded advertisements for products forgotten since the First World War – and caught a glimpse past the heads of the standing drinkers of joints of roast beef and ham on a marble-topped counter. She

345

thought, 'Oh, no, not a cold sandwich in this crush!' before feeling Collins' hand on her arm as he made way for her to follow him through to the restaurant area beyond the bar.

He gave the waitress his name and she pulled out a table so that they could sit side by side with their backs to the wall.

'Are you hungry?'

'Famished.'

'The steak and kidney pie's good. So's the fillet steak, for that matter. And to start with I can recommend either the pate or the whitebait. They're both delicious.'

They ordered, and Madge sat forward to lean on her elbows and scrutinise her surroundings from this new vantage point.

'This is a quaint place.'

'You've never been before?'

'I didn't even know it existed.'

'It can't have changed much since the turn of the century. A real old music-hall pub. Can't you imagine it full of gents with mutton-chop whiskers and ladies of doubtful reputation with low necklines, too much make-up, and big hats?'

Their drinks came. Collins lifted his glass and turned his head to look into her face. 'Cheers!'

Madge echoed him. She had speculated earlier about where he would take her if he wanted to impress her on this first evening out. The Metropole? The French restaurant at the Queen's? But she saw now that he was not the man to establish false precedents. He might indeed take her to such places sometimes, but she would know now that it was a special occasion. Impress her? She was just a little irked to realise that he had succeeded in doing that simply by not at all trying to do so.

Had her father lost his wealth Madge Greenaway would have missed what it bought, but – providing there were no attendant disgrace – she would have coped with her changed circumstances. For Madge's life was conditioned not by considerations like happiness and fulfilment, but by a sense of the fitting, and it was a sense she would have applied in whatever drawer of the social cupboard she had found herself. Not that she thought much about this. It was in instinct for the way she wished to appear to other people; and it had more to do with respect – hers for herself as she felt it reflected in the eyes of others – than with anything as obvious as popularity and being liked.

When it became clear, as it soon did, that Edgar Collins was more than casually interested in her, she began to think about the matter of marriage to him.

She wasn't in love with Collins but she was fond of him. As the junior partner in a small firm of architects he wasn't the most obviously desirable match; but he was young enough and ambitious enough to better himself, and Madge was not averse to pushing him where it might seem needed. She was nearly thirty. Opportunities for marriage were bound to become fewer. Spinsterhood, however proud, had no place in her scheme of things. She *ought* to be married.

She made up her mind; not so much that she would say yes when he asked her to marry him, but that she would lead him into a position where he would ask. For she sensed that behind the smiles, the jokes, the cool banter, Collins was a little in awe of her. Perhaps it was the enormous respect many men had for the woman with whom they were newly in love; or maybe it was simply the strength of her personality which kept him at a distance. She thought that she was, anyway, the stronger of the two; that she would lead the way here as she would, no doubt, on so many occasions in the future.

She began to charge their meetings with small intimacies: borrowing a handkerchief which she returned washed and ironed; giving him cigarettes from her own lips while he was driving; letting him turn when others were there to find her watching him; and gazing at his mouth while they were alone and he was talking, in a manner that suggested a preoccupation less with what he was saying than with him himself. She wanted him to try to make love to her, to put himself into a situation over which she had full control. She didn't doubt her ability to control it. But something held him back. He took her hand in a cinema and kissed her briefly when they parted, but that was all. Collins would come to the moment in his own time, she was sure, and patience was a quality which, in maturity, she had never lacked. But there was satisfaction in controlling the pace and pattern of events, and pleasure in the thought that she might engineer the time and place herself.

the door But not foolishly. She went to see her doctor. He was an elderly man who had known Madge all her life.

'I know I can't expect you to approve,' she said. 'And the best precaution of all is to say no.' She was appealing in her apparent frankness. 'But you see, I can't guarantee to do that.'

He waved his hand. 'The fact that you're sensible about it is something.' He paused. 'You are a virgin?'

'Yes.'

'You've played tennis, ridden a little, led an active life... You should be all right in that respect. As to the other matter, I'm afraid there's not much I can suggest.' He coughed. 'At this stage, it should be up to him.'

348

'But I can't broach the subject till it happens. And if he hasn't–'

'Do you know anything about the so-called safe periods?'

'A little.'

'All I can say is rely on that until you can discuss the other ways with him.'

'But how do I know it will happen during...?' Madge stopped. She knew he'd seen through her. She didn't care. It was her business.

'It's a risk, though, isn't it?' she said.

He swung round in his swivel chair and looked directly at her.

'I take it you intend to marry the young man?'

'Oh, yes. When he asks me.'   *the seduction*

It happened some weeks later, when Adam Greenaway was absent on business and Madge had the house to herself. They came back from a cinema and sat drinking gin and tonic on the sofa in front of the fire. They held hands and Collins kissed her. Before long, he put aside his glass, took Madge's from her, and pushed her back into the cushions.

In a few moments Madge said firmly, 'No!'

Collins drew away at once. 'What's wrong?'

'This sordid fumbling. It's like kids with mum and dad in the other room.' She got up and stood by the fire. 'Do you seriously want me, Edgar?'

'I've wanted you for ages.'

She turned and looked at him levelly before speaking again.

'Will you give me five minutes and then come up? It's the door facing the stairs, at the end of the corridor.'

She went quickly up to her room and took off her clothes. She stood then before the full-length glass in the wardrobe door and looked at herself. Her body was one she need not be ashamed of. She wondered if she should let Collins see it now. But that, she thought, was altogether too brazen. She shivered and, turning back the sheets, got into bed, leaving only the bedside light.

Collins tapped on the door before coming in. She did not look at him and he said nothing. The rustle of his undressing was followed by a long pause because she felt his weight on the bed. Then he slid down beside her and switched off the light. He felt for her in the darkness, his hands soft and light in their touch. 'Oh, Madge, Madge, you're so very beautiful.' His breath on her face smelled of pipe tobacco and gin.

'Am I?'

His mouth felt for her breasts. It was a gamble for her. It could go wrong now in the worst possible way, make her a conquest, available again. It wasn't comfortable, either. There must be more to it than this. She stiffened under him and caught her breath.

'I'm hurting you.'

'No, it's all right. It's just that I've never...'

'Never?' Collins asked.

She shook her head against the pillow. 'No.'

'Darling Madge. I love you.'

'Oh, do you, Edgar?'

'Madge... will you marry me?'

Her mouth curved as she smiled in the darkness.

'Yes, Edgar. Oh, yes.'

Some time later she felt the shaking of his body beside her.

'Edgar... what's the matter?'

He was laughing!

'Oh, God,' he said at last. 'I was beginning to think I'd never find the nerve to ask you.'

They were married in the parish church. Edgar *wedding* Collins' parents and other members of his family came up from the Midlands. Madge's sisters, Catherine and Angela, were matrons of honour, and she had three bridesmaids as well. Women shoppers stood in their dozens along the churchyard railings while photographs were taken on the sun-dappled lawn. Afterwards, a string of hired limousines and private cars drove fifteen miles to Beech Hall Country Club, which was known for the skill with which it handled private functions such as this. The champagne flowed without stint and those guests who, having travelled some distance, had eaten early or not at all sat down to the wedding breakfast in a fuddled but happy state of mind. Adam Greenaway had spared nothing in giving his firstborn, the last-to-be-married daughter, a splendid send-off. *honeymoon in France*

In the late afternoon, Madge and Edgar Collins drove to London where they stayed the night. The next morning they went on to Lydd and flew with their car to Le Touquet. From there they motored south, staying single nights in towns which took their fancy along the route: Troyes, Dijon, Valence and finally Arles. They had intended to go right down on to the Côte d'Azur, but Arles charmed them and thinking of the crowds they would find on the coast they decided to stay there until it was time for them to go north again. Apart from excursions into the countryside and to nearby towns the pattern of their days was quiet and leisurely. In the mornings they walked about the town, looking at the Roman remains and the shops, Edgar talking a lot about Gauguin and Van Gogh; in the evenings they ate dinner in a small but admirable restaurant they had found by the Rhône bridge, then drank liqueurs and coffee sitting at a pavement table outside one of the

351

cafés along the Marseilles road. During the afternoons, in the fiercest heat of the day, they stayed in the hotel near the Place du Forum, lying naked on one of the two wide beds in their room, making love then sleeping, with the shutters open onto a small sunlit courtyard.

Observing the sensuality that frequent lovemaking had kindled in her after all the years of abstinence, Madge was both involved and detached. She knew that Collins was madly in love with her body, living in a state of heightened sexual awareness that the tautening of the line of her breast or the movement of her thighs under her light skirts could explode into urgent desire; and if she were to be proficient in satisfying him it was as well that she should enjoy it also. Yet even in the moments when they were most closely locked together there was a part of her which stood outside and observed it all as a performance. She observed and judged and found it satisfactory.

The old man Collins worked with died and Collins took over the business. His affairs began to prosper. He had for a long time chafed under the restrictions the old man's conservative attitude had imposed on the firm; now he began to strike out after more ambitious jobs, and get them. He designed a new bus station for the town where his office was, and a small shopping precinct with flats. He found bigger premises, hired more staff, and was called in as consultant to the Borough Surveyor's department when several blocks of multi-storey flats were planned for a slum-clearance area. Madge's judgement in marrying him was vindicated. Collins was known as a coming man, and, what was more, one who was getting on through his own energy and ability. Madge encouraged him at every step, and when it was advantageous for his professional

352

and private lives to overlap she was there with her direct support, ever the courteous and discerning hostess. If some of their guests felt a certain abrasiveness behind her charm, it was a not unfitting complement to Collins' own quiet unassuming warmth. Others succumbed without reservation. 'A delightful couple.' 'He's lucky to have a wife like that. It's hard luck when a man starts to climb and his wife can't keep up.' 'They're so very polite to each other, too. I wonder if they're like that in private.'

They were. For by this time what the world saw of them together was virtually all there was to be seen.

Two years after their marriage, Madge Collins lost a child through a miscarriage in her third month. The bad time she suffered then and the warning of a specialist about the dangers of another pregnancy were enough to kill her already failing sexual appetite. It had been pleasant enough for a time, but even in those very early days when she had most enjoyed the act some fastidious side of her nature had recoiled from so blatant an offering of herself. Once – just once – when Collins had reached and exposed a nerve she had not known she possessed, what she remembered afterwards was not the ecstasy but, with shame, the moment when she had yelled, and reared under him, and he had seen her lost. So, little by little, during the subsequent years she discouraged their intimacies, and without encouragement Collins' desires, too, seemed to die.

But in this assumption she was mistaken, and the revelation of her error shook her as nothing ever had before.

When their guests had left on that evening Collins stood looking into the sitting-room fire while Madge plumped up cushions and emptied ashtrays before

dialogue

sinking into a chair and lighting the last cigarette of the day.

'What would you say if I told you I had a mistress?' Collins turned as he spoke.

She didn't think she could have heard him properly. She looked at him. Her heart had quickened its beat to an uncomfortable rate.

'Are you serious, Edgar?'

'What would you say?'

'I take it it is a hypothetical question?'

'Would you mind? I mean, we haven't been lovers for years now.'

'I certainly wouldn't share you with anyone.'

'Not even though she wouldn't be taking anything you want for yourself?'

'I'm your wife, Edgar. I want, and expect, my due.'

'You mean you must own all of me so that the parts you're not interested in you can accept or reject as you like.'

'You're talking in riddles, Edgar.'

'Was it really the fear of becoming pregnant that turned you away from me, or did you just never enjoy it as I did?'

'We had our... our time of passion; I thought we'd both settled happily into a relationship of affection and mutual respect.'

'I'm sorry,' Collins said. 'It's not good enough. And it's much too late to remedy it now. Perhaps at one time, if I'd been a bit more persistent... But I hated to think you were doing anything against your will. Humouring me. "Being nice", they call it, don't they?'

'So you're trying to tell me you've found consolation elsewhere?' She must keep calm; not let him suspect the panic growing in her.

354

'The question was – would you mind?'

'And I believe I answered that by saying I wouldn't share you.'

Collins rattled a box of matches on the mantelshelf with the tips of his fingers. 'No,' he said eventually. 'Neither will she, not any longer.'

'You mean there really is somebody? What are you telling me this for? Are you trying to punish me for something?'

'I'm coming round to telling you that I want to leave you.'

She was proud of herself. It was really admirable the way she held herself in, taking this bombshell with no more sign of distress than a deep sigh.

'Is she someone I know?'

'No.'

'How old is she?'

'Twenty-five.'

'Pretty?'

He shrugged. 'So-so.'

'Prettier than I am?'

'It's not the point.'

'Younger, anyway.'

'That's not the point, either. I love her.'

'You used to say you loved me.'

'Oh, yes, I did.'

'But not any more?'

'I'm not satisfied with the way our marriage has gone, Madge. There was a time when I thought that if only I could get you there'd be nothing I couldn't do. But it's sterile – all surface show, appearances.'

'You miss not having children?'

'I do, of course I do, but that wouldn't have mattered so much if I'd still had you.'

'You've got me. I'm not the one who's talking of leaving.'

'Madge, we don't live together, we live side by side.'

'I just don't know how we've come to this, Edgar. I never realised, not for one moment, that you were so... so unhappy.'

'It happened gradually,' Collins said, 'through all the years when you pulled away from me and into yourself. Even before that; even in the very early days when just some little unconscious movement would make me tremble with wanting you. Even then I knew there was a part of you holding back. As though you felt you'd lose something absolutely vital to yourself if you ever really gave yourself up to me. Marriage to you is a social convenience. I don't think you were ever capable of the kind of relationship I hoped for and needed.'

'Thank you for telling me. What do you intend to do?'

'Leave here, give you the evidence you need, and ask you to divorce me.'

'Where will you go?'

'I have a flat. I've had it for some time. It's furnished and ready for me to move into.'

'My God, Edgar, you have got it all worked out, haven't you? Well, go and live in your little love-nest and take her with you; but if you plan to marry her you'd better tell her she'll have to wait a long time, because you'll get no divorce from me.'

'I hoped you'd see it more reasonably than that.'

'Did you expect my blessing?'

'Madge, you're like a selfish child with a cupboard full of dolls. You don't play with most of them but you wouldn't dream of giving them to someone more needy than yourself.'

'I need you. Does that satisfy you?'

356

'You need me for what? Look, I'm a living, breathing human being. I want someone I can cling to, who'll cling to me. I want *warmth*, Madge, and tenderness. I want *love*, not a social contract, an arrangement for the eyes of the world. I'm stifling, Madge, and I want *life*.'

'And what about me? What do I get?'

'You've got yourself,' he said. 'You've taken good care of that, and it's all you've ever needed.'

Collins left the house early next morning to drive to a business appointment in Birmingham. Madge stayed in bed until he'd gone. She had slept only fitfully, coming awake after each shallow spell to a shocking awareness of the catastrophe which faced her. Always, at every stage of her life, she had felt herself capable of controlling matters to her satisfaction. What she could not mould or shape to her image of what was fitting and proper for her she had avoided with an unerring instinct. And now, to be led to this pass... The humiliation of it seared her. She coloured up, her cheeks flaming, as she pondered the implications of it. She was supposed to lunch with a friend but she telephoned and cried off, giving a bad headache as her excuse; she did not, for once, feel herself capable of getting through the occasion without betraying something of what she was feeling. And no-one must know. Not a soul must entertain the slightest suspicion that all wasn't well, until she had had time to think what she could do.

Sometime about mid-morning she went into her husband's study. There was a drawing-board on a flat table, a couple of filing cabinets, and a divan bed that Collins had often slept on when working late at night. He had slept there last night and the rumpled sheets were thrown back as he had left them. She looked at the roll-top desk where he kept personal papers. It was locked. She was consumed with curiosity about the girl.

357

Would she, if she broke open the desk, find something she could defend herself with? No, she would not be seen to lose control in that vulgar way.

Collins would not be back until late. There was nothing she could do until she could talk to him again, try some different approach, make promises, get him to see reason. Plead with him, if it came to that. Yes, she would *plead*. Would he realise then, when she begged him, that she too was a human being with needs outside herself? And what would be left of her then, when she had so humbled herself? She clenched her fists and beat them at the air in her exasperation.

She tried to read. Then she sat before the television set during the afternoon's schools' programmes, smoking incessantly. Later, she did a little desultory housework. She had not been out of the house, feeling that her dilemma was written across her face for all the world to see. She had made lunch of an apple and a glass of milk; now she cooked herself an omelette and ate it at the kitchen table.

She didn't believe it; that was her trouble. She just didn't believe it was happening to her. *the accident*

At seven the doorbell rang. There was a police sergeant on the step.

'Mrs Collins?'

'Yes.'

'Mrs Edgar Collins?'

'That's right.'

'I wonder if I could come in for a minute, Mrs Collins. It's about your husband.'

She led the way into the sitting-room, then turned to face him. 'What it is?' It came to her as she spoke. 'Has there been an accident?'

'I'm afraid so, Mrs Collins. Nottinghamshire County Constabulary came through to us just now. A pile-up on the M1. Eight cars involved, one of them your husband's.'

'You've no idea how–?'

'I have a number for you to ring. It's the hospital they took him to.'

'And you've no idea whether he's badly hurt?'

'You ring that number, Mrs Collins. I'll hang on a minute while you do.'

She went to the telephone. Collins was gravely ill, a woman's voice told her. Yes, she could go down if she wished but she would be able to look at him for only a minute or two, and he would not know her, because he was unconscious.

She rang off and 'phoned her father. Adam Greenaway came straight over to pick her up.

They spoke little as they went south down the motorway, except for one exchange when Adam Greenaway said:

'I heard it on the six o'clock news. Listened to 'em and thought nothing of it. Eight cars. Rain after a dry spell. Greasy road. Somebody going too fast and can't pull up in time. Then you've got a pile-up. People get hurt in cars every day, yet you somehow never think of it happening to someone close.' He grunted. 'No, that's not right. You always think of it happening to someone close; never to yourself. I remember when you and Catherine were still at home, how on edge I'd be when you were out in the car in doubtful weather. But Edgar's such a damned good driver. Fast, but as safe as houses.'

'You can't always account for the other person,' Madge said.

'No, that you can't. Too many damned maniacs on the road nowadays. There was a time when driving was

359

a pleasure. Not any more. D'you know, I've been on the motorway and actually had chaps pass me on the inside?'

An hour later they stood in turn at the porthole window of an intensive care room and looked at what they could see of Edgar Collins lying inside the shiny transparent skin of an oxygen tent. He could have been anybody. He had multiple injuries, the sister said, and they couldn't deny the gravity of his condition. Had they driven far?

Madge told her.

'It's a long way. Of course, you can visit when you like, but there's not much you can do until he recovers consciousness.'

'I shall come,' Madge said.

'Of course,' Adam Greenaway said. 'I shall bring you. Don't worry about that.'

'I should telephone in the morning and see if there's any change.'

Madge asked about Collins' personal effects. 'His keys in particular. They'll be needed for his business.'

'Yes, of course.'

The sister brought Collins' things and Madge signed for them.

'You're sure you'll be all right on your own?' Adam Greenaway asked when he drew up at her door. 'Wouldn't you rather come home for a day or two?'

'I shall be all right,' Madge said. 'In any case, I gave them this phone number to ring if there's any news.'

She went in, took off her coat, and smoked a cigarette before going upstairs with the keys and into Collins' study. She opened the roll-top desk and went through the papers. Most of them concerned matters she already knew about: Collins had kept no business secrets from her and they had regularly discussed the

360

contracts he was working on. Then she found what she was looking for: a large square envelope containing letters from a woman, addressed to Collins at his office and marked 'personal'. She expressed regret that when she had fallen in love it had to be with a married man. It was up to him. If he said go away, leave him alone, she would; but not before he said it. Another letter was from a seaside town where she was on holiday. She was missing Collins badly, imagining him there, their having dinner together, then walking on the beach in moonlight... Madge's mouth curled. How the girl had thrown herself at him, blatantly, without reservation. Where was her pride? How had she known he wasn't just using her for a brief period of amusement? And then, once she was sure of him, the screw was turned: ...if there were children involved I wouldn't say these things; but there's only you and her, and she can more than take care of herself. How long are we to go on like this, wasting our chances of happiness together while the years slip steadily by? I want to give you children and I don't want to leave it too late. You say you'll speak to her. Do it. Settle it. Come to me and I'll be everything you'll ever need...' There was a photograph too; it showed the face of a reasonably good-looking dark-haired girl who smiled slightly at the camera. Madge put everything away and had a hot bath. Then she drank some whisky and took a couple of sleeping-pills and went to bed.

There was no change in Collins' condition when she rang the hospital in the morning. He was still unconscious, and seriously ill. She drove down with her father again in the evening. The sister they had seen before brought a doctor to speak to Madge. He took her to one side.

361

'I'm sorry to have to tell you, Mrs Collins, but the situation is very grave.'

'He's not improving at all?'

The man shook his head. 'There's damage to the brain as well, you see. We might relieve that a little if we operated, but it's major surgery and in his condition he just couldn't stand it.'

'I see. So...'

'He's slipping; losing his hold. We're doing everything we can, but...' He shrugged regretfully.

'How long?'

'Now that's hard to say. He could surprise us all and–'

'Twenty-four hours?' Madge said. 'A couple of days?'

She went back to her father. 'Bad?' She nodded.

'You can take me home tonight, but first thing in the morning I shall pack a bag and drive back and book in at an hotel. I want to be near.'

'As bad as that?' Adam Greenaway said.

The telephone was ringing as Madge let herself into the house. She ran to it. A young woman's voice asked:

'Mrs Collins?'

'Speaking.'

'Could you tell me how Mr Collins is, please?'

'Who is that?' Madge said.

'I don't think it... I'm a friend of his. They told me at his office which hospital he was in, but when I rang them they were rather evasive.'

'They don't hold out any hope,' Madge said clearly. 'They think he's going to die.'

Madge heard a long shuddering sigh on the line. She waited. In a moment the girl said:

'I wonder if... You see, I don't think they'll let me–'

362

Madge cut her short. 'I'm afraid that's out of the question.' She replaced the receiver.

death

Edgar Collins died twenty-seven hours later, early in the morning. Madge was in the room when it happened. There was no change that she could discern and she recognised the moment only when the sister, who was checking apparatus on the other side of the bed, suddenly peered intently at Collins then hurried out to get the doctor. He came in, looked at what the sister had seen, then lifted up the side of the transparent tent to lean over the bed. He straightened up and turned to Madge.

'I'm sorry, Mrs Collins. I'm afraid he's gone.'

Madge got up off the chair in the corner and approached the bed. 'Can I look at him now?'

Adam Greenaway took over the arranging of the funeral in consultation with the friend whom Collins had named as executor of his estate. Before giving this man access to Collins' papers Madge took out of the desk the letters and the photograph of the girl. She tore them into small pieces and burned them on the sitting-room fire. She informed the managers of both of Collins' offices that they were to close on the day of the funeral. Then she took her address book and wrote and posted a large number of black-edged cards.

On the funeral morning Madge, dressing alone in her room, looked out of the window at the many cars standing in the drive and along the street. The voices of people calling to pay their respects before the coffin left the house had been heard in the hall for an hour or more. Adam Greenaway was receiving them but soon now she would have to go down and face them herself.

She sat down at her dressing table and applied just a touch of almost colourless lipstick to her mouth. She wore no other make-up. Her hairdresser had visited the house yesterday, as had her dressmaker three days before. Now Madge took her hat and placed it on her head. Composedly, she looked at herself in the glass.

It was odd, she thought, how appropriate to one's nature the turns of life could be. Not that she was glad of Edgar's death. She would miss him a great deal. But she had been about to lose him anyway. And she could never have seen herself as a divorced or deserted woman. Everything in her recoiled from the picture. It cast doubt upon her, put her into an area of fallibility, in which she could be judged and possibly found wanting. Divorced? they would have said, their minds speculating. No matter that she would have been the innocent party; people would accept the legal apportioning of blame while nevertheless wondering how much and in what way she herself had been at fault. But bereavement and widowhood... these she could bear, and earn the admiration of her friends for her fortitude in the face of a blow from a malign providence. And her dignity.

She got up, made a last appraisal of herself in the full-length glass, and went out of her room and along the landing to the head of the stairs. She paused then, looking down at the people in the hall. Her presence communicated itself to most of them and they turned to watch her as, steadily, she began to descend. It came to her clearly then, in a thought too private – too harsh even – ever to be revealed. But she could not hide its precise expression from herself, for every face turned up to her was evidence of its truth. She was saved.

A Bit of a Commotion

*an oafish lazy worker
sees an accident
– row with wife
– twist ahead*

the accident

There was a bit of a commotion in the bus station this morning. An old woman, crossing between two islands, got herself knocked down by a double-decker swinging in from the street. I was near enough to it but I didn't actually see anything, standing there reading the paper, hunched into the collar of my coat against the cold. Soon enough there are people bending over her and others craning their necks to see. An inspector makes his way across from a bus he's just boarded and he's joined by a second one from the office. They push their way into the middle and in a few seconds the one from the office is out again and going back where he came from, at a trot.

I watch a chap in overalls leave the scene and come over to join the queue I'm in.

'What's going on?'

'It's an old woman. Got knocked down.'

'You'd think they'd have more sense than to wander about out there.'

'Nay, some of them buses come in at a rare lick.'

'Is she hurt bad?'

'They can't tell. She's unconscious. They're debating whether to move her or leave her there till the ambulance comes.'

'Them buses come round that corner too fast,' a woman says.

'Well, you know that, so you've to take care.'

'She's nobbut an old woman.'

'So if she's short-sighted or hard of hearing, and not so nimble, she ought to take more care.'

'You'll be old yourself one day,' the woman says to me. 'Aye, happen so.'

'She's somebody's mother,' the woman mutters, which strikes me as a bloody silly thing to say. After all, it's the old woman herself who's laid out there, not her son or her daughter.

delay 'Let's hope it doesn't throw the services back,' I say, and I wish I hadn't then because I catch a couple of looks which show they're thinking I'm a right hard case. But I was just speaking my thoughts aloud. Because it would be just my luck that it's happened this morning, when I've turned over a new leaf. I'll get no mercy from Etherington, old woman or no old woman. He's told me about being late often enough and yesterday's was his final warning.

'One more time this month, Gravener, and you're out. Five minutes or half an hour won't make any difference. You'll be finished. I mean it. Absolutely and positively. Out.' He walks away, and turns back. 'And don't think you can get round it by taking the day off. I shall be satisfied with nothing less than a doctor's note.'

So one day means taking a week and convincing a doctor that I'm badly. And no money except a couple of days' sick pay.

Phyllis is no help, the idle cow. No getting up for her half an hour before me and chivvying me about and sending me out with a good hot breakfast. Turning over for another hour's kip is all she's good for; that and queening it down at the pub every night. Still, I was the one who fell for her sharp tits, her long legs, and that 'come and get me if you're big enough' look. I shan't get another job with as much money as this one; and we need every penny we can get, believe you me, the way she can spend it.

So I'm standing there getting more and more worked up while the crowd's still gathered in the middle of the station and the buses are held up outside until the ambulance arrives. I know I should have come for an earlier bus still, and given myself twenty minutes to spare; but it's too late to think about that now. It's too late for everything except going back home and collecting my money and cards on Friday. We're not on the clock at our place but there's no getting past Etherington standing in that yard at eight sharp and seeing that everybody's in.

There's nobody downstairs when I get back home. Phyllis turns over in bed to look at me when I've stamped up the stairs.

'Don't you ever get out o' bed till dinnertime?'

'What you doing back here?'

'There's been an accident in the bus station. Everything's running late.'

'Well, couldn't you go, and tell 'em?'

'You know I told you I'd had my last warning.'

'What are you doing now, then?'

'I've come back. I'll fetch me money and cards on Friday.'

'You an' your turning over new leaves,' she says.

'A lot of bloody help you've been. A right wife 'ud have been up to send me off right. Anyway, I've told you; it's not my fault.'

'You're old enough to look after yourself. Only you can't do owt right, can you?'

'I did the first thing wrong when I wed you, you useless cow.'

'You know what you can do if you don't like it.'

'Aye! An' I'll start now.'

I grab the bedclothes and uncover her with one heave; then as she starts to struggle up I lace into her, slapping her about the bed till her yells and curses give way to tears. Then I stop and stand back, looking at her, half satisfied, half sorry at what I've done.

In a while she stops crying, twists on the bed, and gets up.

'No man does that to me, Harry Gravener.'

'One just has.'

'Aye, and it's the bloody last time.'

I leave her and go downstairs where I put the frying-pan on the ring, thinking that now I've the time I might as well at least have a right breakfast. I've got everything nicely sizzling and popping and a pot of tea on the brew when Phyllis comes down, dressed to go out and with a little case in her hand.

'Where d'you think you're going?'

'Out. And I shan't be back.'

'If you can find a better hole than this, get off to it. There isn't another feller who'd put up with your ways for a week.'

'Thanks. We shall see.'

I turn back to the cooker and hear the door shut behind her, which takes me aback a bit because I didn't expect her to go without a bit more argument. If she went at all. I sit down and get on with my bacon and eggs, thinking she'll be back.

There's no sign of her by eight o'clock. But I've already decided that I'll give her a day or two to cool down and come to her senses before I make any move to look for her.

I go down to the pub for want of something better to do and one of the first people I see is Walt Henshaw from the yard.

'What's been up with you today, then? Badly?'

'Oh, I didn't feel so well this morning so I laid in.'

'You'd better have another couple, then, and get a sick note for Etherington.'

'Bugger Etherington, and his job an' all.'

'I thought you were late again when you didn't turn up at eight.'

'I expect Etherington thought that an' all. I can just see him standing there rubbin' his hands an' waiting to finish me.'

'No, he wasn't there to watch for latecomers today. He no sooner got there than he was called away again, by a phone call.'

'Oh?'

'Aye. It was his mother. Seems she got knocked down in the bus station this morning.'

369

The Assailants

Brian a lorry-driver & Leonard the tailor/typographer duel for the love of Joyce

Brian repairing the lorry

The ten-tonner with the man working under it by the glow of the wire-caged inspection light stood, parked pretty, on the almost empty patch of waste ground.

Brian had left Aberdeen late yesterday, after a half-day's search for a return load, and limped into here in the small hours, to spend what was left of the night in searching for the fault in his engine and repairing it as best he could with the tools to hand. Now he was done. He pulled himself out with a grunt and stood upright, wiping his hands on a piece of rag. The sky had lightened quite quickly while he was under the vehicle and he glanced about him at the shabby streets of silent houses and wondered whether he should break the quiet with a trial start of the engine.

He decided against it. Let them have the rest of their sleep till the early traffic began. The engine would get him home. He was good with engines and he would never have left the motor repair shop had his boss, Nevinson, not driven him beyond the limit of his good nature and Joyce, in temper, persuaded him to stick up for his rights. The lorries were something that came his way almost immediately and Joyce had got him to take them as a temporary measure while he looked round for another place. But he'd been driving for a couple of years now; he was a steady man and he didn't like to chop and change.

There was a raw dampness in the air and it chilled him as, the concentration and effort of his task over, he stood there beside the lorry, thinking about what he ought to do, the rag working in the almost unconscious movements of his hands. Finally he closed the cowling over the engine and took his donkey jacket out of the cab before locking the door and walking with steady strides, a big man, out of the park. The sodium lights on their tall, bird's-neck standards of concrete were switching off in batches all the way down the long main road into the city, the pink glow of the fading filaments lingering against the pallid dawn sky. Brian crossed over towards a house next to a small general shop. He had his hand on the doorknob when an approaching motor bike cleaved the quiet he had been reluctant to disturb with a bandsaw rasp of brutal unsilenced sound. He stood for a moment and watched it go by, the black-clad rider crouched low over short swept-back handlebars, and his mouth moved with mild derision to frame the one word 'cowboy' before he opened the door and went into the house.

The sound of the door brought Mrs Sugden out of the bathroom and down onto the half-landing, a thick blue dressing gown over her nightclothes.

'Good heavens, it's you, Brian. I thought you were in bed and asleep hours since. Have you been out there all this time?'

'It took longer than I expected.'

'I should think so. And me lying up there half the night with the door unlocked for anybody to walk in that fancied.'

'I was only across the street.'

'With your head stuck in that engine and taking no notice of anything else.'

She came down and passed him to go into the kitchen. He followed and watched her move the draught regulator on the coke-burning stove in the fireplace.

'I shouldn't ha' thought you'd be so timid,' he said. 'I mean, all the fellers 'at sleep here...'

'I can size them up before I let 'em in,' Mrs Sugden said. 'But I can't do owt about somebody who walks in off the street in the middle of the night.'

Brian's lips moved in a faint smile. He didn't take her complaint seriously. He knew she was more concerned that he should have spent all that time across there in the cold when he could have been in a warm bed. She was like that with him; she thought that his nature saddled him with more inconvenience and discomfort than was necessary.

'Sit yourself down and get warm. I'll cook you some breakfast as soon as I've got dressed.'

He moved across the room and sank into a fireside chair, which had a loosely draped shroud-like cover over it to protect the upholstery from greasy overalls, and stretched out his legs towards the stove as Mrs Sugden left the room and went back upstairs. His presence in the kitchen made him the privileged of the privileged; for Mrs Sugden gave food and shelter with care, selecting only those she liked the look of, and most of the men she took in ate in the bare dining-room across the hall, with its formica-topped tables and easily scrubbed lino-covered floor. She had to be careful: he understood that. There were loudmouths in any pull-in, ready to brag about the extra comforts to be found along the road, and as a widow still, in her forties, handsome and well set-up, her motive in offering beds to men here today and gone tomorrow would, to some of them, appear more than the simple one of augmenting the living she made from the little general shop next door.

You had, indeed, Brian found, to be careful yourself as you moved about the country. Some men courted trouble in their readiness to accept casual pleasure. There was the place in Liverpool where that simple-faced teenaged girl rubbed her breasts against any man she could get close to, going with some of them behind the vehicles in the lorry park when she had a few minutes free from waiting on tables. He'd an idea she was younger than her well-developed body and the sly carnality of her glance suggested. Sooner or later somebody would knock her up, or the police move in and start asking questions. So Brian had taken warning and not gone back. Then there were the birds you met along the road, hanging about the cafés waiting for lifts. Brian left them to the men who liked the possibility of a bit on the side in exchange for a ride, or the others whose only motive in helping them on their way was good nature. Singly or two together, they were all potential trouble and he kept clear of them.

His eyelids drooped in the rising heat from the stove and he woke some time later to the sizzle and smell of bacon frying on the cooker. Mrs Sugden was looking at him.

'Now then. You've just saved me from having to wake you. Your breakfast's nearly ready.'

'How long have I been asleep?'

'Oh, three-quarters of an hour, maybe. I did think

at one time of leaving you; but when you've got some breakfast into you you can get off up into a comfortable bed.'

He sat up and knuckled his eyelids.

'I've just been thinking. I'll have me breakfast and get on me way.'

She stared at him. 'But you've had no sleep, man.'

'It's all right. I'll make it up later.'

'They're poor employers 'at won't allow a man some leeway when he's had a breakdown. It's not your fault you had trouble with your lorry, is it? Now you're going to drive all that way with no more than a cat-nap. You're not safe on the road, man.'

'I shall be all right. I was thinking, y'see. It just occurred to me, if I set off now I can cut across and drop me load in Carlisle and get back down home before Joyce goes out tonight. Then Gloria won't have to go next door to Mrs Miles's.'

Mrs Sugden's head tilted back so that she seemed to aim the disapproval of her glance along her nose.

'Oh, that's it. She's still messing about with the Houdini feller, is she?'

'Leonardo, he calls himself,' Brian said. 'That's his stage name. His real name's Leonard. Leonard Draper.'

Mrs Sugden turned to the cooker and spoke over her shoulder: 'Leonardo, Houdini, or Uncle Tom Cobleigh. I don't know as his name makes any difference.'

'She enjoys it. It gets her out and meeting people. What with me being away so much.'

'Aye, with that bairn pushed from pillar to post, and when you are at home you've got to sit on your own while she's out cavorting on a stage with a conjuror... You'd better get your hands washed. It's ready.'

He got up and went to the sink, standing next to her as he ran water, and fingered grease-remover out of the tin she kept there. 'He's a hypnotist mainly. That's his big thing.'

'He seems to have hypnotized your wife all right. All I can say is, some women are lucky to have husbands 'at'll stand for it. My Norman wouldn't have had it. He thought a woman's place was in the home and I was content to abide by that. We were never lucky enough to have any kiddies, and I didn't take boarders in in them days, either; but I'd plenty to keep me occupied in making a nice home for him.'

He moved his shoulders in embarrassment. He regretted having told her about Joyce and Draper in that quiet conversation some months ago. It was from this that she had made her quick summing-up of him, fixing him immediately as a man who could be put upon. And, that lesson learned, he should have held his tongue just now and left without giving her more ammunition to fire at the wife she'd never met in her self-appointed role of defender of him, who was too soft for his own good. For she didn't understand, couldn't know. She was, in her own way, like some of the drivers he heard talking, men who were always bragging about some point scored, some small victory won over the missus; as though marriage were a never-ending battle in which any concession was a weakness to be exploited. It wasn't like that with him and Joyce.

'Anyway,' Mrs Sugden said, 'I'd 've thought she'd see enough people working in the shop all day.'

'That's not the same thing. She likes being on the stage. It's... it's glamorous to her.'

'I'd give her glamorous. Showing herself off in front

of all manner of folk. Her with a husband and a growing bairn.'

'Aw, you're old fashioned, Mrs Sugden. You think everybody should be like you.'

'Aye, I talk like your mother might, don't I? When there's less than ten years between us.' She put the plate of bacon and eggs on the table and clamped the fingers of one hand onto a loaf of bread, the knife poised in the other. 'Still, I like to think I've picked up a bit of sense over the years.'

'I suppose you'd have me stop her going out to work as well wouldn't you?'

'Why not? It'd make sense. Working for that feller during the day and going all manner of places with him at night. She must see ten times more of him than she does you.'

'It's not every night. And you can't be suggesting there's–'

'I'm suggesting nothing. I'm just seeing a carry-on that isn't all it should be. Come on, get it down before it goes cold.'

'Maybe I'm not all I should be,' Brian said.

'You what?' Her gaze came directly onto him again, the knife arrested this time halfway in its cut through the bread.

'Well, if I can't earn enough to keep us in all we want, and I'm only at home half the time, can you wonder she has to go out to work and wants a bit of... of excitement in her life?'

'Why, there's many a woman 'ud...' She stopped, as though on the verge of saying too much, and severed the slice from the loaf with two heavy strokes of the knife. 'What are you always underselling yourself for, you big daft lump?' Her voice fell as she turned away, and what she said came in a dismissive mutter, as if to end the conversation: 'You must be a daft lump or you'd have told me to mind my own business by now.'

Yes, he would have to do that – or stop coming here. Which would be a pity, because it was a fine place, the best he knew. He glanced at her back briefly but she said nothing more. He took the slice of bread and dipped a corner of it into the soft yolk of the egg on his plate and began to eat.

brian & family

'You'll be all right, then, Gloria, now your daddy's here.'

The little girl sat up close to Brian on the sofa, her eyes fixed on the bluish square of the television screen. A sudden loud burst of music made the picture tremble, the figures on it wavering as though seen through disturbed water.

'Oh, it's always doing that,' Gloria said. 'It spoils all the best parts. Can't you twiddle a knob or something, Daddy?'

'I've adjusted it all I can,' Brian said. 'It must be the aerial.'

'It's the set that's clapped out,' Joyce put in. 'It's time we had a new one.' She was looking distractedly round the room. 'Where did I put my hairbrush? You haven't had it, have you, Gloria? I'm talking to you, Gloria.'

'No, Mummy.'

Joyce began moving cushions. 'Here it is.' She stood on the hearthrug and brushed her hair in the glass over the fireplace. Among the pale gold were some strands that shone like silver as the light caught them. They were the lingering tints of childhood, not a sign of advancing years, but she was self-conscious about them and sometimes spoke of dyeing the whole to a uniform blonde. Brian was against it.

377

'I can't see, Mummy.'

'You'll have to do without for a minute. I'm late as it is.'

'Where is it tonight?' Brian asked.

'Forest Green Club.'

'Have they a good audience?'

'I don't know. If it's like most of the other workingmen's clubs all they want is singers and comedians.'

'Can I look at your costume, Mummy?' Gloria said.

'Oh, Gloria. It's every time I go out. You've seen it many a time, and I'm late, love.'

'Oh, come on, Mummy, just let me see it.'

'Well, if I do you'll promise to be good and not give your daddy any trouble about going to bed?'

'She's never any trouble. Are you, poppet?'

Joyce slipped off her skirt to reveal the glitter-finish stage costume, cut high up each groin to display the full length of her splendid legs in nylon mesh tights. She put one hand on her hip, throwing up the other one and turning slightly on one foot. 'Ta-rah!' At the same time she shot a quick sideways glance at Brian's face as though to detect any sign of disapproval. It was odd how the costume always seemed more excessive here in the confines of the house than it ever did on stage, making her self-conscious about this private display of limbs which, later, she would show without qualms to an audience of strangers.

'You do look lovely, Mummy.'

'Yes, I'm not wearing too badly, love. I can still make their heads turn.' She glanced down at her legs. 'A few pints and a look at them and Leonard can get away with murder.'

The flippancy of her remark compensated for that silly twinge of guilt. There was nothing brazen in what she did. And Brian didn't care, anyway. His face was impassive as his gaze ran briefly over her then switched back to the television screen. She reached for her skirt and finished getting ready to go.

the hypnotism act

By nine-thirty 'Leonardo' had run through the first part of his act – the routine with coloured silks and steel rings which mysteriously linked themselves and came apart again – and, timing the audience's patience for this run-of-the-mill conjuring to a nicety, culminated in producing Joyce from the interior of a dolls' house which he had just demonstrated as being empty. Now he came to his speciality, in which the audience would participate through identification with one or more of its members. Occasionally people quizzed Joyce about the secrets of Leonardo's act, ending, when she refused to be drawn, with the exclamation: 'Oh, well, we know they're all tricks'. Of course they were tricks! It was the skill with which he hid the trickery which made the routine. All that was, except the hypnotism. That was proved to be genuine every time he did it. Joyce had seen him put half the people in a room under, their fingers locked foolishly behind their necks until he released them. She herself had never seen her part of the routine they did together and could only believe it when, during their first rehearsals, he had taken a photograph and shown it to her afterwards. She'd not been able to suppress all feeling of uneasiness, but tried to cover it with a little laugh. 'There's no knowing what you could get me doing when I'm under,' she said. 'Oh, basically the subject won't do anything against his nature,' Leonard explained. 'On the other hand, who knows what urges are bottled up inside people? I once had a young woman on stage who showed an irresistible desire to take all her clothes off. I had to snap her out of that pretty quickly, or we'd have all been in trouble.'

379

'And now, ladies and gentlemen, for the next part of our performance, which is a demonstration of the power of mind over matter, I need the assistance of a volunteer from the audience. A muscular young man... Have we a handsome specimen of British manhood who is willing to come forward and help me?'

There was a stir in the audience as people looked at their neighbours. Joyce picked out a table down front at which a young woman was nudging her companion with her elbow while he made grimaces of resistance. Leonard had spotted them too.

'Do I see someone down there trying to make up his mind? Come along, sir. Don't be shy.'

He turned his head and nodded to Joyce, who went down off stage to a greeting of shouts and whistles and held out her hand with a smile to the young man. The girl put both hands on his back and pushed. 'Go on with yer. What yer scared of?'

The boy shrugged in an elaborate attempt at casualness and let Joyce lead him up off the floor of the hall, Leonard starting a round of applause as, still held by Joyce's hand, he followed her onto the stage. She eyed him discreetly as he faced Leonard; not tall, but broad-shouldered and deep-chested: no waster.

'Now, sir,' Leonard began, 'let me first of all assure you that you'll be perfectly safe up here with us. Tell me, have you ever been hypnotised?'

'Not by a feller,' the boy said, and Leonard responded with his quick stage grin.

'Quite so. But have you any objection to my hypnotising you now?'

'Not if you can.'

'You don't think I can? By the way, will you tell me your name?'

'Ted.'

'Right, Ted. You say you don't think I can put you under hypnosis.'

'Yes. I mean, no.'

'That's a pity. Hypnotism, you know, does rely a great deal on the willing cooperation of the subject. However, we'll do our best.' Leonard raised his right hand, the forefinger extended. There was a thimble on the end of it which flashed brilliantly in the lights. 'Would you keep your eyes fixed on the charm, Ted. I shall count to six. On the count of six I want you to close your eyes. I shall continue counting to twelve. On the count of twelve you will be under my influence. You will be able to hear what I say and acknowledge by nodding your head. Keep your eye on the charm...'

Ted's eyes closed on six and at twelve, when Leonard asked him if he could hear what he said, his head dutifully nodded.

'I want you to put your hands on top of your head and link your fingers.' As Ted obeyed Leonard turned away from him. 'I think he'll be quiet till we need him again.'

He waited till the laughter subsided. 'Now, ladies and gentlemen, to demonstrate further the marvellous power of mind over matter I am going to put my assistant, the charming Joyce, into a trance...'

She went under easily and, at Leonard's bidding, walked to where three straight chairs stood in a row and lay down across them. Leonard made sure that her head and heels were in position.

'I am now going to remove the middle chair but you will remain supported in the same position.'

There was applause as Leonard took out the middle chair, leaving Joyce stretched rigid, supported only by her heels and the back of her head.

'We can leave her for a moment, ladies and gentlemen. I assure you she is quite comfortable and can rest like that indefinitely. Now back to our young friend.' He stood before Ted. 'On the count of three you will wake up but you will not be able to unlock your hands. One – two – three.'

Ted blinked as he came awake. He tried to lower his arms, but he couldn't. 'Here, what you done?'

'Can't you unlock your fingers?'

'No, I can't.'

'When I snap my fingers twice you will be able to.'

The girl Ted had left at the table laughed delightedly as he was released.

'Now,' Leonard said, 'I want you to observe my assistant.'

'Any time.'

'Yes, I know what you mean. Observe her, balanced between those chairs, supported only by her head and her heels. Do you think you could rest like that?'

'I expect you could make me.'

'I see we have a convert here, ladies and gentlemen. Tell me, Ted, how much do you weigh?'

'Thirteen and a half stone.'

'Do you think Joyce could support such a weight in the position she's in?'

'No, she'd collapse.'

'Shall we try it?'

'You mean me?'

'Yes, Ted, you.'

'I don't want to hurt her.'

'I can assure you that I'll take full responsibility... Ladies and gentlemen, such is the nature of the trance I've imposed on my assistant she can do things she would not normally be capable of. This is the power of the prepared mind over the inadequacies of the body. Our friend tells me he weighs thirteen and a half stone. I shall now demonstrate that, under my influence, Joyce can support this weight. Now, Ted, come along with me. I want you to sit on Joyce.' Ted looked at Joyce then Leonard. 'It's all right; don't be shy. Give me your hands. Now, gently down onto her midriff... There. Are you comfortable?'

'More or less.'

'You won't fall over if I let go of your hands?'

'No.'

'Righto, then. When I let go of you I want you to lift your feet slowly off the floor until your full weight is resting on Joyce. All right.'

He released Ted's hands and the boy uneasily raised his feet.

'No wires and no invisible aids, ladies and gentlemen. Joyce is now carrying thirteen and a half stone on her unsupported body. Try it when you get home, ladies and gentlemen. But put some cushions on the floor first... Thank you, ladies and gentlemen. Thank you, Ted. A round of applause for Joyce, ladies and gentlemen, as I free her from her trance.'

He replaced the third chair and snapped his fingers. Joyce opened her eyes and sat up, swinging round to stand on her feet. Ted said something to Leonard, who stepped closer to him and listened.

'Ladies and gentlemen, our young volunteer has asked me if I can stop him smoking. Do you really want to stop?'

'Yes, I do.'

'And have you tried to do it for yourself?'

'I've had one or two goes.'

'But without success?'

'The trouble is, I like it too much.'

'Ah, yes, quite so. Well, since you've helped me so splendidly this evening I'll see what I can do. I shall put you under my influence first. Please look closely at the charm again. Again, when I've counted to six you will close your eyes. At the count of twelve you will be under my control...' Leonardo put him under and glanced at his watch. 'At ten-fifteen you will light a cigarette. That cigarette will taste revolting and you will put it out. Cigarettes will continue to taste revolting and you will lose all desire to smoke them. Now when I snap my fingers twice you will awake. You will not remember what I've said but you will act upon my commands.'

'Is that it?' Ted asked a moment later.

'That's all, sir. Thank you very much. A big hand for a good sport, ladies and gentlemen.'

A man in the passage lurched into Joyce's path as they went down off the stage. 'That was lovely, darlin'. Just lovely.' Her reaction as his hands fell on her shoulders was to push him away so hard that he lost his balance and reeled back against the wall.

'That's not part of the act, mister.'

The man blinked his eyes several times in something like surprise. 'My sincere apologies, darlin'. No offence meant. Absolutely not.' He straightened up and walked towards the door, still talking. 'Wouldn't dream of it...'

'Stupid devil,' Joyce said. She turned to see the sardonic amusement in Leonard's eyes.

'You don't give them much change, do you?'

'Ah, you show them your legs and they think they can maul you.'

'You're a little puritan. I've told you before.'

'Maybe I am. It's my privilege, though.'

384

He smiled. 'Go and get your clothes on and we'll go round for a drink.

Brian & daughter

"'... the little girl was very frightened as she went along the dark corridor. Then suddenly she turned a corner and saw a light coming through a doorway. She made her way towards it and, lo and behold, there she found herself looking into a magnificent room. There was an enormous polished floor, paintings on the walls, and beautiful silk curtains at the windows. And all this splendour was lit by the light from six huge blazing crystal chandeliers which hung from the painted ceiling. The little girl gasped at the wonder of it all. Where could she possibly be? And who could this magnificent room belong to?'"

Brian closed the book. 'Do you know who it belonged to?'

'No,' Gloria said.

'Well, we'll find out tomorrow night.'

'Oh, Daddy, read me a bit more.'

'No. If it was on the telly you'd have to wait to find out, wouldn't you? And it's long past your bedtime. You'll be too tired to go to school in the morning.'

'Mrs Miles lets me stop up.'

'Well, she ought to know better.'

'What time will Mummy be coming home?'

'Not for a while yet.'

'Will you ask her to come and tuck me up?'

'I'll tell her. But if you're not asleep by then I shall be cross with you.'

'She's a lovely mummy, my mummy is.'

'Yes.'

She reached up and encircled his neck with her arms. 'And you're a lovely daddy as well.'

'I'm glad you think so. Now snuggle down and shut your eyes. I want you to be asleep in five minutes.'

Leonard glanced at his watch when he'd ordered the drinks. He touched Joyce's elbow as they stood at the long bar and indicated Ted sitting at his table. The boy took out a packet of cigarettes and said something to the girl he was with as he became aware of her and the people round them watching him. He lit a cigarette and took one pull before making a face and reaching for the ashtray. There was audible laughter from those sitting nearest to him and when the girl had spoken to him Ted looked over to where Leonard was standing and grinned, lifting his hand in a thumbs-up sign. Leonard acknowledged him and the small ripple of applause with a nod of the head and a slight smile as the club's entertainments secretary, a stocky grey-haired man with scarred thick-fingered hands, came to them.

'On the house, Mr... er...' he said as the barman placed their drinks on the counter.

'Thank you.' Leonard poured tonic water into Joyce's gin and added water to his own scotch.

'That was very good,' the secretary said. 'Very successful, I thought.' He handed Leonard an envelope. 'I think you'll find that right.'

Leonard took the envelope with some distaste at being paid in public and pocketed it without looking inside. 'Thank you.'

'They don't usually go for conjurors and suchlike,' the man said.

'I'm a hypnotist and illusionist,' Leonard said.

'Eh? Well, you know what I mean. And the young lady helped a lot. They all understand that kind of thing.'

'I know what you mean,' Leonard said. 'Any bunch

386

of lads with a couple of guitars and a lot of cheek can hold them better than I can. It's too much trouble for them to watch a real artiste at work.'

'We're very selective in our bookings, y'know. We don't engage rubbish.'

'You certainly haven't in my case. Quality is still quality, even in these days when we seem to have less and less sense of real values.'

The man was beginning to look flustered. 'Yes, I'm sure we all appreciate–'

'No, I'm sorry,' Leonard said, 'but I don't think you do. What you've had tonight is as good as you'll get in the profession. I have a reputation, built up carefully over the years, and I'm proud of it. I don't care to expose it to those people who can't appreciate what they're seeing. Perhaps you've never heard of the W.C.M.?'

'No, I, er...'

'The World Conference of Magicians. It's to be held in Brighton in a few weeks' time. When you get on the stage there you're performing for your peers, not for an audience with one eye on you and the other on the waiter bringing the drinks. I hope with the help of my young lady assistant to come away with a few honours myself this year.'

'We must wish you luck, then, Mr, er, Leonardo. Excuse me. There's somebody over there I've got to talk to.'

His smile was strained as he left them.

'You went for him a bit hard, didn't you?' Joyce said.

'I will not be patronised by little runts like that.'

'He meant well enough.'

'So did that chap in the passage. We're all touchy in our different ways.'

'All right.'

'Would you like another drink?'

'I've got enough with this one, thanks. Anyway, I mustn't be late.'

'Don't worry. I can't see me sticking round this place for long.' He spoke to the barman. 'Another scotch, please.'

Joyce poured the rest of the tonic water into her glass and said, 'It's not on, you know, Leonard.'

'What isn't?'

'Brighton.'

'You mean he's put his foot down?'

'No.'

'Oh, my God, there's only three weeks to go and here you are, backing out on me.'

'I never said I'd go.'

'No, but I did think–'

'I'm a married woman, Leonard. I've got a husband and a child, I can't just slope off to Brighton for three or four days.'

'Look, I'm depending on you. I can do big things this year. I know I can. But not without you.'

'Can't you get somebody else?'

'Find somebody and train her in three weeks? Talk sense, love.'

'I'm sorry, Leonard. But you knew when I started what the position was.'

'I thought this was the middle of the twentieth century, not the nineteenth.'

'He puts up with a lot, you know.'

'And so he should. Look, would you like to go?'

'Of course I would. Three or four days at the seaside. And you know I like being in the act.'

'Ask him, then. Ask him tonight.'

'Look, it's–'

Leonard's fingers gripped her elbow and his eyes looked directly into hers. 'Ask him.'

~~Brian & Joyce~~

He was asleep when she got home, sprawled in the chair in his working-clothes, his mouth slightly open. She switched off the television set and shook him by the shoulder.

'I just shut my eyes for a minute,' he said as he came awake. 'What time is it?'

'A quarter past eleven. Did Gloria go off all right? She wasn't fretful, was she?'

'No. Why?'

'I'd a feeling she might be sickening for something earlier today. Might have been my imagination. Have you had any supper?'

'No.'

'Do you want some now?'

'I don't know.' He rubbed his eyes and pulled himself up in the chair. 'Let's have a cup of tea while I think about it.'

She took off her coat and laid it across a chair and went into the kitchen. He followed her and stood in the doorway, stretching, as she filled the kettle.

'Ugh! It feels more like a quarter past three.'

'You should have gone to bed.'

'Ah, it gets till it's all bed and work. I don't see anything of you.'

'I know you hate it,' she said.

'What?'

'Me going out like this. Helping Leonard.'

'I've never said so, have I?'

'I know it, without you saying anything.'

'If it gives you a bit of pleasure, excitement. I mean, I'm away so much... It's no fun for you.'

389

'Are you going up north again tomorrow?'

'No, he's putting me on local runs for a day or two, till he gets the wagon properly seen-to.'

The kettle was on the gas. She put tea into the pot and set out two cups. 'Do you want something to eat, then? I might as well see to it while I'm here.'

'Go on, then,' he said. 'I'll have a bacon sandwich.'

Joyce put the frying pan on another ring and took bacon out of the cupboard. She kept her eyes on her hands trimming off the rind as she said, 'Leonard's talking about the World Conference now.'

'What conference?'

'World Conference of Magicians. Didn't I mention it? I knew it was out of the question, anyway. Brighton, in three weeks' time. He reckons he can sweep the board if I'm there to help him.'

'Brighton?'

'Yes. Isn't it silly? Three or four days away. I told him, what did he expect? Me, a married woman, with a husband and a little girl to think about.'

'You're not going, are you?'

'Well, of course, I told him.'

'You want to go, though, don't you? You'd like to go with him?'

'What do you mean "with him"? Have I asked you?'

'You're asking me now.'

'Look. I–'

'You're not going.'

'Look, Brian, don't come the heavy husband with me. There's no need for you to lay the law down.'

'I want him to know,' Brian said. 'I want you to tell him.'

'Tell him what he knows already? Or that you've put your foot down?'

the argument

'I don't care. Just tell him.'

'Look, Brian, just who the hell do you think you are?'

'I'm your husband.'

'And how long do I have to go on being grateful for that?'

'I don't know what you mean.'

'You should. I was grateful when you married me. Not every man would have done what you did, would they? You took me and made me respectable. You got me out of trouble. Why shouldn't I have been grateful?'

'I married you because I loved you.'

'Because you wanted to go to bed with me and I was carrying somebody else's kid.'

'There's no need for talk like that.'

'Would you like to forget it? Don't you think about it every time you look at her? She's upstairs now, asleep. She doesn't know, but we do. When shall we tell her, Brian?'

'It was a long time ago. She's eight years old now and she's ours – yours and mine. Why do you want to start on all this?'

'Because I'm sick of it. Sick of everything.'

'You wouldn't tell her, would you?'

She faced him. 'Why not? Hasn't she got a right to know the truth?'

Leonard & Joyce in his tailoring shop

'There we are, sir. And your receipt. Your suit will be packed up and waiting for you when you call back. I hope you'll find it satisfactory in every respect.'

Leonard's customer smiled. 'I'm sure I shall. I must say it's a pleasure to shop where there's still some service.'

'It's very kind of you to say so, sir. Quality and courtesy are the cornerstones of any good business.'

'There's a lot of people forgotten that, though.'

'There are indeed, sir. There are indeed.' He opened the door for the man. 'Good day, sir.'

He picked up the suit from the counter and went into the back room where Joyce, with cups and teapot ready, was waiting for the electric kettle to boil.

'Nicely timed. I'm just brewing up.'

'I'll just pack this and we'll have a nice cuppa.'

'He seemed very pleased, the man who's just gone out.'

'We're both pleased. That makes for a satisfactory transaction.'

'You're a good tailor, aren't you, Leonard?'

Leonard brushed the suit down with the flat of his hand, holding it up for a last scrutiny before folding it into a large square box which he then tied round with string. 'The best in this town.'

'Haven't you ever thought of expanding? You know, opening another shop?'

'I did consider it at one time. But I couldn't be in two places at once and I didn't fancy the idea of putting my reputation into the hands of somebody who might not care for it as I do. So I settled for one shop and that run well. It works. I'm well known to a good clientele and I make a comfortable living. Personal service from the man who actually cuts the cloth – that's what they expect and what they're prepared to pay for.'

Joyce poured boiling water into the teapot. 'Leonard, about the conference.'

'Yes?'

'It's still no go.'

'You asked him, then?'

'No, I didn't actually ask him. I told him it was coming off. He jumped on it straight away. We had a row.'

'I'm sorry.'

'It was my fault, I suppose. I lost my temper and said some awful things.'

'He never...' Leonard hesitated. 'He doesn't strike you, does he?'

'Brian?'

'He's a big strong ox of a man. They do lose themselves sometimes.'

'The trouble with Brian is he won't argue or row. That's what makes me so mad sometimes. The way he stands there so bloody good and patient.'

'And stupid,' Leonard said.

'What?'

'Yes, I'm sorry, Joyce – stupid. Doesn't he realise what sort of woman you are? That you deserve something better than being tied to the house, cooking and cleaning for him?'

'Don't all women think like that sometimes?'

'There are plenty of women who are happy with that. They're ten a penny. But you're special; something different. You're like a lovely tropical bird that loses its colours and dies when it can't spread its wings and fly.'

She suppressed her desire to laugh at this sudden fanciful flight of talk.

'A bird in a gilded cage. Except the cage isn't gold. It's all very well, but–'

'No, Joyce.' He came round the table and took her hands. There was something in his eyes that she'd never seen before. 'It just won't do.'

She was so surprised then, when he kissed her, that she rested passively and without resistance in his arms. Until the pressure of his embrace increased, when she pulled free with a light laugh.

'Why, Leonard, I never knew you were one for kissing and cuddling in the back room.'

He held her hands. 'Joyce, I've never said anything before. I thought I'd no right. But I can't stand around and watch it any longer. You, grubbing for extra money, living a life with no beauty or refinement in it. I'm not a wealthy man but I could give you at least something of what you ought to have. A better life than you'll ever have with him.'

She withdrew her hands and tried to hide her surprise and confusion by pouring the tea. 'You've given me a shock,' she said eventually.

'I've always hidden it before,' he said. 'As I say, I didn't think I'd the right. You should know as well that I... I shouldn't make any demands that you weren't prepared to accept.'

It had gone far enough. She said with a little dismissive laugh. 'Don't talk silly.'

He stiffened, not answering.

'I'm sorry, Leonard. You just don't understand.'

'I can understand misplaced loyalty. I know what sort of woman you are; I wouldn't want you if you were any other way.'

'It's loyalty, Leonard, but it's not misplaced. And it's something more than that.'

'You can't tell me you still love him.'

'I said some things to him last night, and afterwards, when I saw the look on his face, I could have killed myself.'

'You don't like to hurt people. What you don't realise is that it's not you but the truth that does the damage.'

'I did a terrible thing. I threw it in his face that Gloria isn't his child. After all these years.'

'What? What do you mean?'

394

'She isn't his. You didn't know that, did you? I had an affair with a married man. I was young and silly, I suppose. Anyway, I'd finished it just before I met Brian and not long after I'd started going out with him I realised I was pregnant. It would have been easy enough to let Brian have me and pretend it was his. But I couldn't. I told him the truth. And do you know what he said? He said he wanted to marry me and this way he could have me all the quicker. I never even told him who the other man was.'

'The child doesn't know?'

'Nobody knows. You're the first person I've ever told. Brian worships Gloria as though she were his own. And last night I threw it all in his face. I even practically threatened to tell Gloria the truth.'

'It makes no difference. You can't live on gratitude for ever.'

She picked up a cup and held it out, looking steadily at him.

'Oh, but you can, Leonard. That, and what it leads to.'

Brian sat in the cab of his lorry, parked opposite the doors of the school. It was an old building, inadequate for today's needs, with a patched tarmac playground between it and the iron railings along the road. In a couple of years Gloria would leave here for the new secondary modern school set in green fields on the edge of the town. From thinking of this it took no great stretch of the mind to imagine her finished with school and in her first job. The years passed with increasing speed and with every one now she would become less dependent upon him and Joyce and more capable of making her own decisions.

Her birth had been a difficult one and the

395

complications were finally resolved by an operation which made it impossible for Joyce to conceive again. No matter though, that Brian could not have a child of his own; Gloria was as good as his and he loved her fiercely, seeing no necessity for her ever to know the truth about her parentage. It was only Joyce who kept that issue alive, resurrecting it in spasms of fierce and, to him, inexplicable resentment during her attacks of discontent. There was no reason for her to feel gratitude towards him. He had made no sacrifice in marrying her. He'd wanted her and was himself grateful for the circumstances which made her accept him. He doubted that he would have got her otherwise and he had never quite been able to believe his luck. Now he was beginning to wonder if he could hold her. He brooded incessantly on their most recent quarrel and his apparent inability to make her happy.

The doors swung back and the first of the children appeared. He watched for Gloria and got out of the lorry to call her when he saw her.

'Gloria! Over here, love.'

She broke away from her friends and ran to him and he took hold of her and swung her up through the open door of the cab. He climbed in beside her and started the engine.

'Your mummy wants me to take you to her at the shop. You can stop with her till closing time; then she'll take you home.'

'Oh, goody!'

The child was used to spending the last part of the afternoon with neighbours, and this visit to the shop was a treat. Brian pondered on the chances of his getting a job with more money so that Joyce could stay at home. And then he wondered whether, even if he doubled his wages, she would ever settle down to the day-to-day routine of the house.

Draper was arranging a stand of ties when they went into the shop.

'Ah, Brian, and little Gloria. Not so little now, though, eh?'

He always addressed him as Brian, but Brian, hesitating at the familiarity of 'Leonard', yet not wishing to be so formal as to call him 'Mr Draper', managed to avoid the use of any name at all.

'Joyce said to bring her round. She said she'd look after her till closing time.'

'Yes, that's all right. Your mummy's gone on a little errand for me, but she won't be long. Come into the inner sanctum.'

'Well, I haven't much time. I'm skyving as it is, you see.'

'You can spare another minute or two, can't you? Don't you want to see Joyce?'

'I suppose I could wait a minute till she comes back.'

'That's right,' Draper said. 'Come through.'

Brian touched Gloria's arm, guiding her ahead of him into the back room where suits hung, shoulder-on, to the wall, and there was a partly unrolled bolt of cloth on the square table.

'I haven't any pop or anything for you to drink,' Draper said. 'Perhaps your mummy will bring you something. I'll tell you what I have got, though.' He reached up and took a box of biscuits off the shelf, opening it and offering it to Gloria. 'I expect you'd like one of these, wouldn't you?'

'Say "thank you",' Brian said as Gloria took a biscuit, and the girl dutifully repeated the words.

Draper patted her on the head. 'That's all right, my

sweet. We don't stand on ceremony here. They're nice, those, aren't they? They're your mummy's favourites as well. Did you know that? I keep telling her she'll spoil her figure but she goes on eating them and it doesn't seem to make any difference. Aren't you glad you've got such a pretty mummy?'

Gloria nodded and said yes.

'And you're going to grow up just as pretty. I can see that. You favour your mummy. Anybody can see whose little girl you are. But I can't see much of your daddy in you.' Draper glanced at Brian as though to confirm his judgement, then looked back at Gloria, his head bent forward and a little to one side as he spoke to her. 'But that's on the right side, isn't it? Your daddy's a big strong man, but you're going to grow up into a pretty lady like your mummy.' Brian frowned as the words brought back once more the pain of his quarrel with Joyce. 'What will you do then? Go on the stage and dance and sing, or act? Your mummy's very good when she's helping me, but she's got your daddy to look after...' He stroked her hair once more before looking at Brian.

'I'm afraid I've got nothing to offer you, Brian. Unless you'd like a cup of tea.'

'No, no,' Brian said. 'I shall have to be off.'

'Daddy, can I have a comic?'

'Of course,' Draper said. 'You'll want something to keep you amused while your mummy and I are looking after the shop.' He took a shilling out of his pocket. 'Watch carefully.' He palmed the coin and held out his closed fists to Gloria. 'Which hand do you think it's in?'

'That one.'

'This one?' The hand was empty. 'It must be in the other one, then, mustn't it? No, it's not there, either. I

398

wonder where it can have got to? Do you know? Well, let's try here, shall we?' He put his hand to the side of Gloria's head and pretended to take the shilling out of her ear. 'There it is! Who'd have thought that? Here you are. It's all yours. There's a shop on the corner.'

'Ooh, thank you!' Gloria turned and ran out.

'It must be very satisfying to watch a child like that growing and developing as the years go by.' Draper spoke reflectively, his gaze on the open doorway through which Gloria had disappeared. 'Mrs Draper and I never had any children. She wanted to wait. And then she fell ill and died and it was too late. Perhaps she wouldn't have made a good mother. She was a neurotic woman and we weren't happy together. It may sound cruel, but it was a merciful release for me when she died. Some men look for consolation outside their marriage, but I found that sort of thing wasn't enough.'

'Why didn't you get married again?' Brian asked.

'It's not as easy as all that. You're frightened of making another mistake and you don't meet anyone who can overcome that fear in you. Or if you do, perhaps she's already committed elsewhere.'

Brian shrugged as Draper's gaze slid round to his face. He neither liked nor understood him and he was always vaguely uneasy in his company.

'I shall have to be off.'

But Draper came forward in a quick movement before he could leave the room. 'Look, I wanted to tell you. You mustn't be too hard on Joyce, you know.'

'I don't know what you mean.'

'You mustn't judge her too harshly. She was only very young.'

Brian said, 'What're you—?' then stopped as Draper fixed his eyes on something behind him. He turned and saw Gloria was already back and standing in the doorway, a garishly coloured comic in her hands.

'Gloria, just run out for a minute and see if your mummy's coming.'

'Oh, Daddy, I've just been out.'

'Do as you're told.' He watched her go, heard the shop door open and close, then faced Draper. 'Look, tell me what you're talking about.'

Draper's gaze was still fixed in the same direction, holding there so steadily that Brian turned his head again with the momentary thought that Gloria must have deceived him and returned to the doorway. Then he felt the first touch of an inexplicable fear which quickly, as Draper stood motionless, refusing to speak, resolved itself into a conviction that this man knew something which could harm him and the child.

'I want to know what you're talking about,' he said, the edge of his voice roughening.

Draper turned, his head thrust forward as he looked at Brian. As he spoke he moved his hands as though to weave patterns of communication in the air between them. 'It was all over when she met you. I can understand about Brighton, but you mustn't be hard on her. There's nothing between us now.'

Brian stared. Incredulity robbed him for a moment of the power to speak. '*You*? You mean... you and her?'

'I tell you she was young. It was just one of those things.'

'And Gloria's...?' He couldn't take it in. 'She's not yours,' he said. 'She's mine.'

'How do you think it feels to me?' Draper said. 'Seeing them deprived of things. I could give them a better home and a fuller life.'

'But you can't have them. You can't have either

400

of them.' Something was rising in him, screaming to a point where he could not contain it. He held himself rigid. His body shook and he found that he could discern only the outline of Draper's face as it was thrust at him and the lips moved, letting out words that now had venom in them.

'She's ready to come. She's sick and tired of being grateful to you. Tired of living with you because of what you did for her. How will you stop her if she wants to come? What will you do when she tells you she's leaving?'

'You bas-tard!' The roar of his cry filled the room. He hit Draper in the face, sending him reeling back against the hanging clothes, and sprang after him as he dragged them with him. He took him round the neck and squeezed, his fury uncontainable. 'You'll not have 'em. You'll never take 'em away. They're mine. Mine, I tell you, mine.'

A moment later he realised that he was holding Draper's full weight in his two hands and he let him slip to the floor as Gloria said from the doorway, 'Daddy, what are you doing?'

He ran and crouched and embraced her.

'Daddy, what's wrong?'

'It's all right,' he said. 'He had a dizzy spell. He'll be all right in a minute.' He stood up and took her hand, turning her round. 'We're going for a ride.'

'Aren't we waiting for Mummy?'

'No,' Brian said, 'we're going on a trip.'

Before she could say anything else he swept her up in his arms and carried her out.

He had been driving for some time before he became aware that Gloria was not well. He put his hand on her

401

forehead where she lay curled up, sleeping, on the seat beside him and felt it hot to his touch. Food and a hot drink might help her but he dared not stop at any of the cafés along the road and so mark his route for anyone looking for him. The alarm had probably already been raised. Joyce would be too shocked to cover up for him, even if she wanted to, and the police would quickly discover that he'd been due to call at the shop and now he and Gloria were missing from home.

He had no chance. His flight had been instinctive, an act of panic rather than one containing the possibility of escape. They would get him; but before then he needed somewhere to be quiet for a time, so that he could think. There was only one place he knew.

He drove steadily northwards through lashing rain, his eyes straining to see the road ahead of him. Occasionally he put out his hand and touched the face of the sleeping child, fretting now not about his own predicament but about her having seen what he'd done to Draper; wondering how much of it she had taken in and how deeply into her mind it had gone.

Brian & Mrs Sugden

He woke her to get her out of the lorry but she stood with heavy eyelids, as though drugged, while Mrs Sugden made noises of concern over her head. She appeared to need restful sleep more than food or drink and Mrs Sugden urged him to take her upstairs and put her to bed. There were no questions until he came back down into the kitchen.

'Well?' When he made no answer, Mrs Sugden went on, 'You didn't just bring her for the ride, did you?'

'I've killed him,' Brian said. It had to be like that, quickly, brutally, or he would never have found the courage to tell her.

She caught at her breath, her eyes widening, as Brian moved to the table and pulled out a chair, slumping heavily into it.

'He taunted me. Said he'd take them away from me and give them a better life than I could. There... there was somebody before I met Joyce, y'see. Gloria's his. He said it was him. I suddenly saw him, after all this time, stepping in and taking everything... I hit him, then I got hold of him.' Brian turned his hands up on the table. 'I got hold of him. I couldn't think of anything except what he said, what he could do to me.'

There was no need to ask whom he was speaking of. She said, 'Oh, my God!' under her breath and took a bottle of scotch out of the cupboard, pouring some into a glass and handing it to him. He gulped at it, downing it in one, shivering suddenly and pulling a face.

'What're you going to do now?'

He shrugged. 'I don't know. All I could think of was to come here for a bit, somewhere I could be quiet and work something out.'

'But why the little girl? You can't–'

'I just picked her up and brought her with me. I couldn't leave her there with him.'

'You mean to say she saw what happened?'

'Part of it. I don't know how much she really took in.' He lifted his eyes for a moment. 'She's all I've got now.'

'But what are you going to do?'

'I don't know. If I can just rest and be quiet for a while.'

'Do you want something to eat or will you go up to bed?'

He got up and crossed to the fireside chair with the cover over it. 'I'll just put me head down here for a bit.'

She let him be and he slept for a time, waking to find her sitting across from him, very still, her hands in

her lap, her gaze in sombre contemplation of his face.
For a second it was as though there was nothing out of
the ordinary in it; then it all came to him and he said,
'What time is it?'

'It's getting on.'

'Is Gloria all right?'

'Yes. Let her have her sleep out. Does your wife
know where you are?'

'I don't suppose so.'

'What will she do?'

'What can she do except call the police? There's
nowhere I can go. They'll find me inside twenty-four hours.'

'They can't call it... murder, Brian. Not after what he
said.'

'Who's to know what he said?'

'You'll have to make 'em believe you. Get her to tell
the truth. She's the one who's led you into all this.'

'There's you and him, isn't there?' Brian burst out.
'And us in the middle.'

'What do you mean?'

He subsided, unable to carry the thought through.
'I don't know. There's always somebody onto you. They
won't leave you alone.'

'You're not without friends, y'know.' She looked at
him as he got up without answering. 'D'you hear what
I say, Brian?'

He wrested his mind back to her. 'What?'

'You're not on your own.'

'What do you know about it?'

Her gaze wavered then fell. She half-turned her
head.

It was the first time he had ever seen her outfaced.
For the first time it also occurred to him that she might
want him. But not simply: in other circumstances she

404

would have contained him in *her* mould, shaped him to her design. For his own good.

'I should have thought you'd be glad of anybody who could speak for you,' she said in a moment.

'What could you say?'

'I could tell 'em what sort of man I think you are. I could tell 'em all you've told me about what kind of a dance she's led you.'

'That's your own idea, what you think. You never did understand about us.'

She was recovered now and she faced him with the old assurance. 'It doesn't look like it, does it?' she said.

He stood in silence for a time, then shrugged. 'It's no use talking.'

'No. You should be thinking about what you're going to do.'

'There's nothing I can do.'

Whatever Mrs Sugden was going to say then was cut off by the sound from upstairs: a cry that trembled on the edge of becoming a scream.

'That's Gloria.' Brian hurried out. A pair of small metal ornaments danced on the mantelshelf as he pounded up the stairs.

Joyce was in the hospital corridor when the trolley came through the double doors. The doctor walking beside the trolley took her arm as she moved forward.

'I've got to talk to him.'

'Are you the one who brought him in?'

'I got the ambulance yes.'

'Are you a relative?'

'No, I work for him. I found him.'

'Do you know what happened?'

'No, that's why I want to talk to him.'

405

'He's in no state to talk to anybody. He's been very severely manhandled.'

He let her forward sufficiently to lean over the trolley and look at Leonard's face. It was heavily swathed in bandages and the eyes were closed.

'If I waited till he woke up...'

'He won't talk to you even then,' the man said. 'His jaw's broken.' He nodded to the porter who pushed the trolley on and into a lift. Joyce turned away as the grille was pulled across. 'Have you spoken to the police?'

'Yes. It wasn't robbery, though. There was nothing missing.'

She had rung the police after calling the ambulance. It was between her putting down the telephone and their arrival a few minutes later that, wondering where Brian and Gloria had got to, she began to connect Brian with what had happened. She telephoned his firm, phrasing her enquiry so that they would have no cause for alarm, and found that he'd not been there since lunchtime.

There was nothing to do now but go home and wait. She had been there for nearly an hour, smoking one cigarette after another in short nervous puffs, her eyes on the television screen but taking in hardly anything, when she remembered that Brian had once written down for her the address and phone number of his lodgings up north.

She found the slip of paper among some letters in the rack on the fireplace and, putting on her coat and counting her loose change, she went out of the house again and walked to the telephone kiosk on the corner.

Brian's farewell to Mrs Sugden

Brian got Gloria settled in the cab of the lorry, with the help of the rug and the cushion which Mrs Sugden had loaned him, then went back into the house.

406

'She's all right now she knows she's going home.'

'It's goodbye for a bit, then?' Mrs Sugden said. She grasped his hand. 'You're a good man, Brian. They must see that.'

'I'd better be off,' Brian said. 'If she starts getting upset again...'

'You won't forget, will you? What I said about friends.

Perhaps it won't be long...' She reached up and kissed him on the mouth then let go of his hand and turned away.

She heard the door close behind him and the engine start. She had gone out and was watching the tail lights of the vehicle moving away along the road when the telephone began to ring in the hall.

Brian & Joyce

'I thought I'd killed him.'

He had said it before, in the same slow disbelieving way, and the stupid wonderment of it angered her.

'You bloody fool, Brian, for believing what he said.'

'It wasn't true, was it?'

'Of course it wasn't true. I've told you it wasn't.'

'Why should he say a thing like that? Why should he make it up?'

'How do I know? To cause trouble. Because he's evil-minded. He made a pass at me; said he wanted me. When I turned him down all he could think of was making trouble.'

'And I thought I'd killed him.'

You didn't even get that right, did you? Taking Gloria and running away like that, and all for nothing. You're a fool, Brian, a bloody useless fool.'

'Don't keep saying that, you selfish bitch. I spent nearly twelve hours thinking he was dead; thinking I'd

407

have to do ten years for him. And all you can say is "you bloody fool". Well, you're right: I am a fool, a fool for putting up with your rotten, selfish ways. I did it for her. It was her I was thinking about. If I thought I could keep her he could have you tomorrow.'

'Who the hell do you think you are, talking to me like that?'

He reached out and took her by the wrist, dragging her to her feet. 'I know who I am, and you'll listen when I talk – bitch.'

It was the first time he had ever laid a finger on her in anger and for a moment the shock of it took her voice.

'God! I hate you, you big useless–'

'And I hate you, so what are you going to do about it?' She swung her free arm, aiming to strike him across the face, but he caught that wrist too and held her there in the grip of both his hands. The glare of outrage in her eyes was akin to that of desire. She was beautiful in her anger. He knew that to bear her down and take her now, on the floor, quickly and without tenderness, would be a greater satisfaction to him than striking her, and a more searing humiliation to her.

The moment held. She stared him out, defying him to do what he liked. Another thought slid into his mind and was expressed before he could decide its wisdom.

'Do you ever think about him?' Brian asked. 'The one who did give you the kid?'

Her eyes narrowed as though she did not instantly understand. Then, 'Yes,' she said. She threw her head back as she saw his face, and screamed. 'Yes. Bloody yes!'

He pushed her away from him on to the sofa and went across to where he had left his donkey jacket on a chair. She watched him put it on.

'Where are you going?'

'I'm taking the lorry back to the yard and leaving a note for the boss.'

'Will you want anything to eat when you come back?'

'No.'

'Are you going to work today?'

'No.'

'What are we going to do?'

'What about?'

'Us.'

'What do you want to do?'

'Go on living.'

'That's all we can do, isn't it?'

He went out, closing the inner door after him. She stared for a long time at the fire and then went upstairs and brought down her clothes, turning on the radio before she left the room. She had undressed once she had known he was on his way back. Now she slowly began to dress again, uncovering and reclothing one part of her body at a time as a voice read the early morning news bulletin... *news*

'...Miss Forrest is one of the most sought-after stars in the film world today. Travelling with Miss Forrest was her husband, Mr Ralph D. Packenheimer, whose business interests in the United States include motels and drive-in cinemas. They were married a month ago and London is their last stop on a round-the-world honeymoon tour which has taken in seven countries. Mr Packenheimer is Miss Forrest's fourth husband.

'Arriving on the same flight at London Airport was the Prime Minister of the newly independent African state of Kandaria, Mr Walter Umbala, who is here on an unofficial visit. Our reporter asked Mr Umbala about recent unrest and disturbances in Kandaria. He said that in a nation of mixed races and religions there were bound to be disagreements from time to time, but they only became serious when exploited by outside agencies for their own ends. "We must be ever vigilant and resist these outside elements with all our might," Mr Umbala said. "Only then shall we go forward, united and strong, to our destiny among the free nations of the world–'"

Joyce gave a small exclamation of impatience and turned the tuner till she found some music. She lit a cigarette and sat down, looking at the fire and hearing under the sound of the wireless the soft shift of the hot coals, as she waited for Brian to come back.

This Day, Then Tomorrow

(title of her novel)

A young teacher gets her first realist novel accepted for publication — a record of her first love affair

family reaction to the acceptance of the novel

Something out of the ordinary had happened in the Hatton household. Ruth, at twenty-two the youngest of the Hatton girls, had got a novel accepted for publication. The publisher's letter was on the breakfast table when she came down, and the sudden joyful spring of colour to her cheeks as she opened and read it betrayed her to Mrs Hatton, so that she was forced to break the news not at a moment of her own choosing, but there and then.

'Two hundred and fifty pounds advance on royalties!' Mrs Hatton said. 'And what's this novel about, ever?'

Ruth made a movement of her hand. 'Oh...'

'Two hundred and fifty pounds?' Mr Hatton took the letter in his turn. 'I didn't know you were writing a novel, Ruth.'

'She's been going to that literature class in the evenings for nearly two years,' Mrs Hatton said, as though he were somehow more remiss than herself in.

411

not knowing what their daughter was up to. 'And she's always scribbled in her room.'

'I thought she was studying people like Shakespeare and Dickens,' Mr Hatton said, 'not writing books of her own.'

'Why ever shouldn't Ruth write a novel, Bernard?' Mrs Hatton said. 'She's had a good education.'

Mr Hatton was too used to his wife's instant allotting of their roles in any situation – her own one of perception and concern, his that of a neglectful obtuseness – to become irritated.

'We study literary composition,' Ruth said, 'and we're expected to do some original writing.'

'But a novel!' Ruth's older sister Celia said. 'You can't deny you've kept it quiet, Ruth. It must have made a fair-sized parcel to put in the post.'

'Well... I didn't know whether it was any good or not, so there was no point in saying anything yet.'

'But we're here to share your disappointments as well as your successes, surely, Ruth,' her mother said.

Some of them, anyway, Ruth thought. She had prepared herself for their knowing if the manuscript were returned, but she could not have endured the initial waiting period except alone. Once her mother had seized on such an event outside the normal life of the household she would not have let it drop. There would also have been the necessity of letting her read and comment on the book. Now, of course, when it had acquired a cachet of a publisher's acceptance, it was different. Or was it? The contents were still the same, and soon now they would become public property. For the first time Ruth felt a tiny tremor of anxiety.

Her father was more concerned with the business aspects of the matter. 'They say they'll send you a

412

contract to sign,' he said. 'Perhaps you ought to get legal advice on that.'

'It's a standard procedure.'

'Yes, but you don't want to sign your rights away.'

'Dad, they're among the most reputable publishers in London.'

'You don't think they're going to cheat the girl, do you, Bernard?' Mrs Hatton said.

'Of course not. But they're businessmen and it's their job to make a profit.'

'Perhaps you can let Mr Astley glance at it, Ruth,' her mother suggested.

Mr Astley had acted for Mr Hatton in the purchase of their house and in a number of other routine matters. Ruth didn't think that he, or any other solicitor in the district, would know much about authors' rights in a literary agreement.

'I'll show it to my tutor at the class,' she said. 'He's had poetry published, and some stories.'

Mrs Hatton's mouth pursed in an expression that was almost a smirk. 'What a feather in your cap when you walk in and tell them about it!'

Mr Hatton, leaving first, patted Ruth's head and twinkled at her from the doorway. 'Well done! It looks as though we're going to have a celebrity in the house.'

She was called to the telephone in her free period that morning. The male voice at the other end of the line belonged to a reporter on the local weekly newspaper.

'I understand you've had a novel accepted for publication.'

'Well, yes. How do you know?'

'Your mother rang the editor, I believe.'

Ruth felt a spasm of irritation. She had wanted to

413

savour the good news privately for a while; to ponder this development in her life and come to terms with it before speaking of it to anyone. But already she was being pushed along at someone else's pace.

'I wondered if I could come along and talk to you about it. It'll make a very interesting item for our readers.'

'Our readers.' Everybody. Common knowledge. That Hatton girl's written a book. She suddenly became acutely conscious of how many people who didn't read a novel from one year's end to the next would read this one because she was its author. And how, of course, they would presume to judge it. With that thought came a keen desire to put this man off, to make any excuse to avoid having to talk to him. But wasn't all this part of the process? She had written a book and offered it for publication. So now the public would read it, and what they made of it and her were factors over which she had control. She ought to be flattered and pleased by this instant opportunity of publicity, but instead she felt something more like fright. Oh, Lord! Why had she done it?

'Well, then?' she asked.

'I thought I might call round this evening. We go to press tomorrow.'

'But it'll be months before the book's published.'

'Oh, we can do a follow-up piece nearer the time, but we'd like to be first with the original story.'

First? Who else could be interested?

She said, 'All right. Will seven o'clock be convenient?'

'Righto, seven. I have the address.'

Arthur Debenham, who taught Senior English, passed by as she left the telephone cubicle. He glanced at her and nodded. Ruth turned her head and watched him stroll along the corridor with his long slow stride and curious swing of the shoulders. Debenham was in his fifties and given to occasional caustic denunciations in the staff room of contemporary trends in the arts. What usually provoked him were newspaper reports of a new play or novel by 'the latest back-street genius from Bradford' or 'Bermondsey'. 'We're living in the age of the literate illiterate,' was Debenham's line. Everybody's writing novels or plays. They've none of them anything to say, and they don't know how to say it anyway, but they're so full of their own insignificant – and usually grubby – feelings, they have to share them with the world.'

What would he make of her adding to the number? Because soon he would know. Everybody would know.

'A few biographical details first, I think.' The reporter was a young man about Ruth's age. It was raining outside and his gingerish suede boots were darkly wet on the toes, but he had gauchely declined to remove the blue anorak which he wore over a grey roll-neck sweater and Mrs Hatton glanced at him from time to time as though apprehensive that he would lean back and stain with damp the lime-green cover of the chair in which he was sitting. But he remained forward on the edge, a cheap throwaway ballpoint poised over the open notebook on his knee. Beside him on the arm of the chair the cup of tea Mrs Hatton had pressed upon him stood untouched and cooling, with a biscuit soggily absorbing the liquid slopped over into the saucer.

'You're, er, how old?'

'Twenty-two.'

'You were educated at the local grammar school?'

'Yes.'

'And then... ?'

'I went to a training college.'

'And now you teach, what, domestic science? Why didn't you study a subject connected with writing?'

'I've always been interested in housecraft and so on. The writing thing's comparatively recent.'

'Even as a little girl Ruth was handy about the house,' Mrs Hatton put in. 'Of course I encouraged her and taught her all I could, purely for the sake of it. That kind of ability's never lost.'

'No, quite... So how did you become interested in writing?'

'I started going to a literary composition class in the evenings, just as a change. We were expected to do some writing of our own.'

'How long did it take you to write this novel?'

'Oh, about a year.'

'That would be working in the evenings?'

'And a few hours at weekends, when I could manage.'

'Did your family encourage you?'

'They didn't know what I was doing.'

'Oh?' The young man looked at Mrs Hatton, who tried an indulgent laugh.

'No, we had no idea until this morning when the letter came.'

'You preferred nobody to know?'

'Well, yes. I think when you've never done anything like that before it seems a very personal thing. You become rather self-conscious about it. I mean, it might just be self-indulgence.'

'But in your case, it seems the novel is good enough for publication.'

'Yes. Perhaps I've been lucky.'

'I think you're too modest, Miss Hatton. Publishers have their standards.'

'I think so too,' her mother said. 'We're all very proud of her.'

'By the way, what's the book called?'

'*This Day, then Tomorrow.*'

The reporter repeated the title after her, putting it in full among the shorthand symbols in his notebook.

'And can you give me some idea of what it's about?'

She had expected that question, and thought about it at odd moments in the day, but without much result.

'Well... that's not easy.'

'I don't expect you to tell me the plot. But is it a love story, a thriller, or an historical piece... you know.'

'It hasn't got much of a plot to tell. It's a love story, I suppose.' Oh yes, it was about love. And innocence. About the necessity for trust and the inevitability of its defencelessness in the face of betrayal.

'A romantic novel.'

'Oh no. It doesn't fall into that slot.'

The firmness of her reply quickened his interest. 'You mean it's too outspoken?'

'I'd prefer to say it's honest.'

'What about the main characters, and the background?'

'The main character is a girl who's away from home for the first time, at college.'

'You mean, like yourself?'

'No, not exactly.'

'It's not autobiographical, then?'

'No, look. A writer uses settings and the kind of life he or she knows well then adds observation and imagination.'

'I see. So you don't expect the reader to identify you with the main character.'

'I hope not. If you'd read the book I don't think you'd ask me that.'

'Oh, why not?'

'The girl in the novel has an abortion.'

And now she had gone too far, revealed much more than at this stage she had ever intended. Her mother's gaze was on her. Did it contain the first flicker of alarm?

Ruth said quickly, 'Look, I'd be grateful if you didn't mention that. It sounds so sensational out of context.'

'Well, of course not, if you say so.' The reporter looked disappointed at losing the spicy core of his story as soon as it had been revealed. 'But our readers aren't going to be shocked by the mention of a word like that.'

'I know your readers,' Ruth said. 'They've got the same proportion of the prudish, the hypocritical, the bigoted, and the just plain ignorant as any other community, and I don't think it's fair that either I or my book should be prejudged by mentioning such an emotive subject at this stage. I can justify what I've written in its context, but they'll have to read the book to arrive at a balanced judgement.'

'I think you could be wrong.' The young man frowned. 'A little bit of the right kind of publicity can help to sell books.'

'That's not the kind of publicity I want.'

'Certainly not,' Mrs Hatton said. 'We do have to live in this town.'

'Yes, of course. But Ruth could almost hear him thinking: but if that's the case you can't blame me if your daughter writes a book which she finds it embarrassing to talk about.'

She began to bring the interview to a close.

'Have you got as much as you need to be going on with?'

'Yes, I suppose so. Just a few more background

418

facts. Your father is Mr Hatton the dentist? And have you any brothers or sisters?'

'Ruth has an older sister who works for a firm of estate agents,' Mrs Hatton said, 'and my eldest daughter is married to an officer in the army, who's stationed abroad at present.'

'Righto, then. Thank you very much.' The young man stood up, almost dislodging with his elbow the tea-cup beside him. 'Sorry, I'd forgotten that.' He took the cup and in his eagerness to show that he'd really wanted the tea, drank the lot so quickly that drops spilled down the front of his anorak. The biscuit he left in the saucer.

'It will be in the paper this weekend?' Mrs Hatton asked.

'All being well. By the way, do you know when the book's being published?'

'I've no idea.' Ruth gave a little laugh. 'It's all a bit premature, really. I haven't even signed the contract yet.'

'Oh, that'll be all right, I'm sure,' the young man said. 'I'll look forward to reading it.'

She saw him out then went back into the sitting-room. Her mother was standing on the hearthrug.

'Don't you think it's time you let me read this book?'

'If you want to.'

'Well, of course I want to. I want to for its own sake; and after this weekend people are bound to stop me and mention it. I ought to know what my daughter's been doing, didn't I?'

Ruth said, 'I'll get it for you now.' She went to her room and brought down the carbon of the typescript. Her mother felt the weight.

'There seems to be a lot of it.'

'It'll be a normal-length book when it gets into print.'

'It's not the kind of thing you can read in bed, anyway. All that typing, and I never knew.'

'The typing's the least of it,' Ruth said. 'By the time you reach the final copy you're laughing.'

Mrs Hatton glanced at the first couple of pages. 'Ruth... it isn't... well, sensational, is it? I mean, there's so much stuff between covers these days that I wouldn't have in the house.'

'I've written a novel, Mother,' Ruth said. 'It's neither a fairy story nor something that exploits dirt for its own sake or for money. You'll have to make up your own mind.'

The young reporter rang up the next morning to ask for a photograph of Ruth. Mrs Hatton lent him a formal portrait taken while Ruth was at college. Ruth didn't like it. She wasn't unattractive, she knew. She had been told more than once that her legs were good and there had been a time when she would stop on catching sight of her naked body in a mirror and take in the fineness of her skin and the way her narrow back emphasised the plumpness of her breasts in a sensual reverie of self-love which was a reflection of another's professed adoration, an exulting in what she had to give and the way in which it was taken. Once upon a time... But all the camera ever showed was a pale bespectacled face with an insipid half-smile: the face of one fitted for nothing more passionate than studying, passing examinations, writing a book. There was, she supposed wryly, a kind of justice in it.

Her mother read the manuscript during the day, when she was alone in the house. Ruth found herself tensed for the reaction and tried to interpret something from her mother's behaviour. But there was nothing to be seen and no word passed between them on the subject until Mrs Hatton had finished the novel.

'I suppose it's well written. I don't know what other people will make of it, though.' Ruth was silent. 'It's not... well, it's hardly the kind of book I'd have expected you to write.'

'Oh?'

'Did you... did you know somebody at college who had an abortion?'

'You pick up all manner of information if you keep your eyes and ears open, if you talk to people, listen to what they tell you, and fill in the bits they don't.'

'But this girl that the book's about, who has the love affair. Was it necessary to go into so much detail?'

'I wanted to make it vivid and real.'

'Yes, but... I must say, I felt myself blushing more than once. Why, there are things in there I hardly knew about myself.'

'Oh, come on, Mother. You've had three children.'

'Well, I didn't know till after I was married.'

'Times change.'

'Yes. So I'm to take it – I mean, I can't do any other than take it – that you've already–'

'Mother,' Ruth said firmly, 'the book's the book and my private life is my own business.'

'All the same, when I think of the mortal danger you've been in. And I thought I'd brought you up so well, the three of you.'

'I'm sorry, Mother, but if you call bringing-up well teaching your daughters to bake and sew, seeing they're fed and clothed, encouraging them to go to church once a week, but telling them almost nothing about some of the most fundamental aspects of life, then you can't wonder they expose themselves to mortal danger the minute they leave the house.'

'Well, if that's what you think...'

421

'I'm sorry, Mother, really,' Ruth said. 'I didn't mean to hurt you.'

The words had, indeed, sounded shockingly harsh; but she was on the defensive, fearful of an attitude which could sap her confidence, turn her pride in something honestly achieved into a timid conformity with all those stultifying approaches to life that she most detested.

'I'm sorry if you think I've failed you in any way,' her mother said stiffly.

'Just so long as–' Ruth began, then stopped.

'So long as what?'

So long as you don't cripple me now by imposing your small-town sensibility on me, was that she wanted to say. But that would only force her mother further into injured pride.

'Mother, I know,' she said carefully, 'that I'm bound to come up against a number of people who'll put the worst possible construction on what I've done. But I hope they'll be far out-numbered by the other people who'll like and appreciate the book, or at least respect it for what it's meant to be. I want to think you're one of the latter people and that you're on my side.'

'I'm always on your side, you know that, whatever you do and I shall defend you to the last. I just can't help wishing you'd written, well, a nicer book, something more wholesome. I don't know what your father will make of it, I'm sure.'

'Doesn't it affect you at all?' Ruth said. 'Don't you find yourself concerned for the girl in any way?'

'Oh, yes, I'm sorry for her. All that sorrow and pain. And there's no doubt that the young man does treat her shabbily. But on the other hand, I can't help feeling that most of it's her own fault. And as for that awful mother, always putting her husband down...'

Ruth began to smile but her mother, not looking at her, didn't see. There was a silence, then Mrs Hatton sighed.

'I suppose it'll be all right in the long term.'

'A nine-day wonder,' Ruth said.

'All the same, I'm rather sorry now I was in such a hurry to ring up the paper. I could have had a little time to get used to it all if I'd read the book first.'

Ruth laughed.

'Never mind. Let's hope it makes a lot of money for me. That'll justify it in everybody's eyes.' *sarcasm*

Teacher at School

But oh, that damned self-consciousness!

It started at the beginning of her first class on Monday morning, with whispers in a group of junior-school girls.

'Saw your picture in the paper, Miss.'

'Have you really wrote a book, Miss?'

'Written,' Ruth corrected. 'Written a book.'

'Well, have you, Miss?'

'Yes, I have.'

'What's it about, Miss?'

'Are you going to be on the telly, Miss?'

'Now, look, let's all settle down, shall we? This isn't the time to go into all that. This morning we're going to make some biscuits...'

She met Arthur Debenham drinking coffee in the staff room during morning break.

'Ah, here's our own Edna O'Drabble. Or is it Margaret Brien?'

'What a lot of ignorance you pretend to, Arthur,' Ruth said. 'Have you really not read either of them?'

'You ought to know by now, Ruth, that only the literary dead have any chance of winning Arthur's grudging respect,' Lois Rayner said. 'His secret vice is lesser known women novelists of the Edwardian period.'

Ruth laughed. Lois was a toughie; a stocky, flat-chested spinster of about Debenham's age, with yellow in the roots of her grey hair and ferocious flyaway frames on her glasses.

'No, I wanted to congratulate you,' Debenham said. 'I suppose it's still something of an achievement to get a book published, even in these days. Perhaps it's expecting too much to hope that it might be readable as well.'

Ruth gasped and flushed heavily as he put down his cup and walked away. Even Lois was taken aback.

'Of all the miserable devils!' she said as the door closed behind him.

'I don't suppose he meant it to be taken like that,' Ruth said.

'If he knows so much about English Literature he should have learned how to frame his words at his age.' Lois's eyes flashed behind her glasses. She poured coffee and handed Ruth a cup. 'Here you are, honey. I think you'll learn more about stupidity than malice. Though they do say the literary world's riddled with it. That and back-scratching. You do my washing and I'll do yours.'

'I wouldn't know about that. I'm just a novice.'

'First steps,' Lois said. 'Who knows what they can lead to? Anyway, I hope you'll give me a signed copy for sticking up for you.'

Ruth smiled. 'I'll see what I can do.'

'They do say his wife gives him hell.'

'Oh?'

'Oh, yes. Makes his life a misery, by all accounts.'

From the members of the evening class she received an envy in which she basked, behind an outward demeanour that was quietly modest. The class met in an adult-education centre in a larger town some miles from Ruth's home, and the first some of her fellow students knew of her success was when their tutor, Jim Thomas, announced it at the start of the session.

'Our congratulations are due to Ruth Hatton, who's got a novel accepted for publication. And our admiration for her reticence in keeping the fact that she was working on one to herself until it was proved successful.'

Thomas shared the envy of the others. 'D'you know I've written three novels without one offer of publication?' he said to her afterwards.

'But you've published poems and stories.'

'Yes, just enough to reassure me that I'm not wasting my time entirely.'

'Oh, come now. I don't know how you can talk like that.'

'Don't you? It's one thing spouting in a knowledgeable way about the subject, and another doing it oneself.'

'But isn't there an awful lot of stuff published that you wouldn't put your name to?'

'Oh, yes. And quite a bit I'd give my eye teeth to have written.'

'Well, you don't know yet which category my book comes into.'

'No, that's true.' He looked at her reflectively for a second, then they laughed together.

'And now I shall be terribly self-conscious about your seeing it.'

'You won't have any choice, though. If you offer something to the world, the world has a right to express its opinion.'

425

'Yes.'

'Does the thought bother you?'

'A little.'

'The excitement must more than make up for it, though, eh?'

'Oh, yes!'

The sudden clear blaze of delight in her eyes made him laugh out loud again. He put his hand on her shoulder as they walked to the door.

'I wish you luck with it.'

Trip to London publishers

An antidote to Mrs Hatton's reaction, and the largely uncomprehending wonder of the family's friends and acquaintances, was provided by a trip to London to see the publishers. Half-term was fortunately near so Ruth was able to arrange to go within ten days of their asking to see her.

London was hot, the air heavy. After a short journey on the Underground she took a wrong turning and for a time was lost. When she rediscovered her direction she was late and had to hurry, arriving at the tall old house in a leafy square, near the British Museum, with the composure she had gradually drawn round herself on the train evaporated in the heat, and feeling her body sticky inside the suit which had seemed just right in the chilly morning at home, but which was far too heavy for the weather here.

Ruth had imagined vaguely, in her naivety, a place like a newspaper building, with glass-partitioned offices and the faint hum of printing presses from below; but here she was reminded of a solicitor's premises as, after waiting in the reception office for a few minutes, she was led up the narrow creaking stairs past the blank doors on each landing.

described] The room she was shown into had two tall paned
offce windows looking out onto the green foliage of the trees.
It had obviously been an upstairs drawing-room when,
in the time of a novelist like Thackeray, the houses in
the square were occupied by London's prosperous upper
middle class. She wondered how many distinguished
literary figures of today had been shown into this
room, offered a seat in this overstuffed armchair of
indeterminate age, and plied with cigarettes and sherry,
as she was now while polite enquiries were made about
her journey and small talk exchanged about London and
the unexpected warm weather. The cigarette she refused;
the sherry she accepted. The diversion of an incoming
telephone call allowed her a few moments to turn her
head to the books on the fronted shelves behind her: row
after row of the firm's titles at which she peered to see
the names of those writers published under the imprint
to which she herself would soon belong.

'Well...' Raymond Waterford put down the receiver
and smiled at her across his desk. He was the firm's
editorial director, the person with whom she had
corresponded, a bulky man in his middle forties with
untidy thinning wavy hair and a square fleshy face. He
wore a navy-blue pinstriped suit and, in flamboyant
contrast, a huge yellow bow tie with blue spots. He
fiddled with a new briar pipe but didn't fill it. He wasn't
a pipe-smoker, he'd already told her, but he was trying
any method he could think of to break himself of the
habit of an enormous daily consumption of cigarettes.

'We like your novel very much, Miss Hatton. All my
colleagues agree with me about its exceptional quality.'

'Thank you.'

'It isn't always the case. Are you working on
something else?'

'I haven't had the time since I finished that one.'

'You mean we're the first people to see it?'

'Yes.'

'What made you choose us?'

'You publish one or two writers I admire. If you're good enough for them you should be all right for me.'

Waterford laughed. 'Quite. And I think you'll find we're as good as anyone else in London at selling fiction. You are going to write another novel, though, I take it?'

'Oh, yes. I'm mulling over an idea now.'

'Good. A publisher likes to look to the future, you know. Most first novels don't make any money; it's with the second or third that the dividends start to come in. In this case, though, providing the reviewers can see what's in front of their noses, and the public respond in the right way, we might have a small success. But don't let me build you up too much. This business is full of people who've come unstuck with their predictions.'

Ruth hesitated. It seemed silly here in this room. But she asked just the same.

'You don't think it might be a bit too much in parts?'

'What? How d'you mean?'

'A bit outspoken.'

'Too graphic, d'you mean? Goodness me, no. Nobody here has suggested anything of the kind.' He smiled. 'Do you still live with your family?' Ruth nodded. 'I sometimes think,' he said 'that the only tenable situation for a writer would be an omniscient anonymity, knowing everything but not taking any part in it.'

'You mean something like a Catholic priest?'

He gave a guffaw. 'Yes, something like that.'

'Except that readers seem inclined to see it the other way round,' Ruth said. 'That it's the writer who's making the confession.'

'Yes...' His attention had wandered. He moved papers on his desk as though looking for something, then glanced at his watch. 'We ought to be going to lunch.'

He asked if she wanted to freshen up and, calling in the girl who had brought her upstairs, had Ruth shown to a small lavatory on the next landing. Then, a few minutes later, she and Waterford were walking across the square, he swinging a tightly rolled umbrella with which he pointed the way at each intersection. In the restaurant, a low-ceilinged room with oak-panelled walls, red velvet upholstery and quiet, attentive waiters who addressed Waterford by name, Ruth, her tongue loosened by a mixture of excitement and wine, became talkative, telling Waterford at his prompting, about her family, her career at college, her work now, and which writers she admired. At one point she recognised the face of an actor whom she'd seen in films at a nearby table and Waterford amused her by recounting a slightly scandalous anecdote about the man. Then Ruth switched to questioning him. When was her book likely to be published? How long before she would see the proofs...?

'You haven't got an agent, have you?' Waterford asked.

'No. Should I have?'

'Yes. You won't be able to handle the subsidiary rights yourself. A paperback sale is our province, but then there are all the other pickings: foreign rights, both in the United States and on the Continent; possible serialisation before publication; film rights, and so on.'

'Can you recommend anybody?'

'I should think so. It's a question of who'll be best for you. How long are you going to be in town?'

'Till tomorrow. I'm staying with a friend tonight.'

'In any case, he'd want to read the book before

429

deciding whether or not to take you on. Have you got a spare typescript?'

'Just one carbon.'

'If you could send that on to me as soon as you get back. You won't need it, will you?'

'I don't suppose so.'

'No. You forget this one now and get on with the next. In any case, if I have it you've a perfect excuse for preventing people from reading it before the proofs are ready.' He smiled.

'All right.'

'I fancy it's something that writers have to get used to,' he said, returning to the subject they'd begun to discuss in his office. 'I mean the question of saying in print what you possibly wouldn't discuss in so-called polite society. It's not easy to be honest. So far as I can gather the solution is to find an environment in which you can feel free and at ease, yet not cut off altogether from the sources of your inspiration – if we may use such a word. Your material, if you like. That's why so many young writers come to London after their first success. And why too many of them find that in doing so they've lost their basic nourishment. The other side of the coin is the danger in becoming too big a fish in too small a pond.'

'The pond may be small,' Ruth said. 'But I think it's very deep.'

'Well, then. We shall have to wait and see what you haul out of it with your next book. In the meantime, you won't really mind becoming quite well known and having your picture in the papers, will you?'

'No,' Ruth admitted. 'No, I don't suppose I shall.'

'No,' Waterford said, 'you'd be quite a rare human being if you did.'

In the middle of the afternoon, slightly muzzy headed *Staying with Monica* from the lunchtime wine, Ruth made her way by Underground to the flat of her friend, in Baron's Court. Monica Darrell had been in Ruth's year at college, but soon after qualifying she had given up teaching to go on the stage. After a year with a provincial repertory company she had landed a regular role in a television serial and now she was combining this with a part in a long-running West End play, which had been recast for the second time.

'I wish you'd write something decent for me,' Monica said. 'This play I'm in is a terribly creaky old thing; but the public love it and it looks as though it'll run forever. Why don't you write a super television play and tell them you simply must have me for the lead?'

'I'll have to think about that,' Ruth said.

'It's all a living, though. And God knows I shouldn't grumble when there are any number like me out of work. Anyway, it's lovely to see you, Ruth, and absolutely marvellous news about the novel. You are a sly boots, though, not saying anything about it before.'

Ruth gave the excuse she'd given everyone else. Not that she minded one bit Monica's reading the book. She was the kind of intelligent equal for whom she'd written it, and whom she expected to be her most perceptive audience.

'When is it coming out, then?'

'They're going to try to get it into the autumn list. That means before Christmas at the latest.'

'And do they seem pleased with it?'

'Yes, they were very flattering.'

'Let's hope you have a big success with it, get lovely notices and make pots of money.'

Ruth turned from the window. They were high up

under the roof of the house. 'That field's a bit of luck, isn't it?' she said. 'So totally unexpected when you're in the street.'

'It's the grounds of a church,' Monica told her. 'You can't see the building itself for those trees, but if you look past that wall you can just make out the tops of some gravestones.'

Ruth sat down on the bed-settee. 'You know,' she said. 'I've got the funniest feeling about the book. I think it's going to do very well indeed.' She was silent for a moment, then she laughed, breaking the intent seriousness of her features. 'Probably no more than wishful thinking.'

'Sillier things have happened, as my Aunt Amelia used to say. You just keep your fingers crossed, lovey, and hope for the best.'

Monica brewed a pot of tea and made some toast.

'Lucky I'm written out of the series for a couple of weeks,' she said, 'or I should hardly have had a chance to talk to you. When I'm rehearsing that and doing the play as well it's all go, go, go from nine-thirty in the morning till ten-thirty at night. I usually wait and eat properly after the show. Then if I'm lucky there's someone to pay for my supper too.'

'Is there anybody special?'

'No, not just now. And that reminds me.' Monica arrested the motion of the teacup towards her mouth. 'I saw Maurice Waring the other week.'

'Oh? Where?'

'In the Salisbury. I nipped in for a drink with a friend after the show and there he was.'

'Did you speak to him?'

'For a minute. He seemed quite pleased to see me. Glamour of the stage, and all that. I suppose he'll be

432

mad keen to read your book when he hears about it. Very fond of the off-beat success things, is our Maurice.'

'Did he say what he was doing now?'

'Teaching at a grammar school somewhere in the Home Counties. I forget just where he said. Ruth, he's not queer at all, is he?'

'Whatever makes you ask that?'

'Oh, I don't know exactly. Something about the way he was standing there eyeing people when we went in. Maybe my imagination. He was probably just looking out for celebrities.'

'Anyway,' Ruth said, 'I don't know that he is. Or I should say was.'

'You should know, I suppose,' Monica's gaze lingered on her for a second. Ruth felt it rather than saw, because stupidly she couldn't bring herself at this moment to look back at Monica. She had nothing to hide. Except, that was, the way her heart had lurched at the mention of his name, and the trembling hollowness just under her ribs now, which it seemed to her must show in an unsteady control of her voice.

'Is he married, or anything?'

'How can he be if I got the impression he might be queer? But then, I don't know. I didn't ask him and he didn't say.'

'Did he... did he ask about me?' She was impatient with herself for putting the question. She had thought herself in command of her emotions on the subject; that the long labour of the novel had purged her of bitterness, bringing her to the realisation that to keep her wounds open was to destroy the beauty of what she had felt at the time. She had come to terms with it, so she'd thought. But now she was undone again, jealous of Monica who had spoken to him, stood near him, only

433

a few weeks ago, when she herself had not seen him for more than two years.

'He asked about the old gang in general, then mentioned you. Did I ever see you. So I told him we wrote to each other, and what you were doing.'

'And that was that?'

'Yes. What else did you expect?'

'Nothing.'

'Ruth...' Monica said in a moment, gently chiding.

'I know.' Ruth poured herself another cup of tea. 'He'll get a shock if he does read the novel.'

'Oh? It's all in there, is it?'

'Well, I used it rather than recorded it. I mean, that's what a writer does. But it's close enough for him to recognise it. The girl in the book has an abortion.'

'Wow! You don't mean...? You couldn't have...'

'Not without you and perhaps some of the others knowing, no. But he'd gone away by that time. No, I just extended it all a bit, pushed it to a further extreme. I did think for a time that I was pregnant, you see.'

'And you never said a word!'

'No, I kept it to myself. Terrified out of my wits for nearly three weeks.'

'I don't think I was ever absolutely certain that you and he...'

'Had been sleeping together? Weren't you? It was bloody marvellous, Monica. The most stupendous uplifting experience of my life. Until it turned sour, of course.'

'I was never quite sure before how badly he'd behaved... So when he reads the novel he's going to wonder if you...'

'I expect he will.'

'Serve the swine right. If he's got enough conscience

434

for it. Of course, I've got to be honest and tell you that I never really did care for him myself...'

after (?)

In the early evening they set out for the theatre. While Monica was getting ready for the performance, Ruth wandered along Shaftesbury Avenue, looking into the shop windows. The play was, as Monica had said, a rather creaky, contrived piece and not the kind of thing she would have gone to on her own initiative. But Ruth had never seen her friend working on the stage before and was glad of the chance. Afterwards, she met Monica at the stage door.

'Is there anywhere special you'd like to go?'

'I don't think I've ever been to that pub you mentioned. The Salisbury, was it?'

'Oh, it's just a place in St Martin's Lane where you can sometimes find a few actors after the show.' Monica paused.

still in love

'It's not his local, you know, Ruth.'

'No,' Ruth said. She felt foolish, found out in something unworthy of her. 'Let's go and eat, shall we?'

return home

While still in London she could to some extent keep her main concerns at bay; but once on the train, with the thread which connected her to the familiar and the past drawing tighter over every mile, she gave herself to a brooding examination of her state of mind.

The conviction which had come to her yesterday, that the novel would be a success, was as strong as ever; and on its foundation she allowed herself to build the notion of a new life. She saw opening out before her prospects of which she would hitherto hardly have dreamed; saw them with a prophetic clarity, but soberly now, without elation. For she knew that whatever small measures of fame and

435

fortune came to her with this book would have to be justified by the long and continuous labour of the future; saw also that the task before her would provide no magic shield against the disappointments and deprivations of her life; rather would it, in its conscientious execution, expose her to a raw-nerved apprehension of reality such as she had never known before.

And, oh, that all this should have come to her so soon, while the joy was still fresh in her!

If she were not, therefore, to lose everything there was above all else the grave necessity of making something of *herself*: of learning somehow to hang on until she found, if not happiness, a strength of mind to endure whatever in its probing, analysis and self-questioning this new life could challenge her with, so that through it all she would in her basic purpose keep firm and true both to her talent and the memory of that exultant womanhood she had known when Maurice loved her.

Had she been a praying girl she would have prayed. As it was, she closed her eyes and addressed herself with stern resolve.

A little while later a white-jacketed steward slid open the door of the compartment and announced the first sitting for lunch. Ruth had not thought herself hungry but now she got up and made her way towards the dining-car, swaying from side to side as she balanced herself against the motion of the train.

symbolic action

THE GLAD EYE

For C.M.B.

Work in Progress

Otterburn had come to live in this cathedral city when he left his wife. He rented a room and kitchen, with a shared bath and lavatory on the next landing. He had never lived alone in his life before and from his window he could look down three floors at the river flowing between its stone banks and think that at least he hadn't far to go if he decided to do away with himself.

The river ran through the city under four bridges. Upstream was the bishop's palace, which Otterburn had not yet seen. The city was a great tourist attraction and at every season of the year, though more plentiful in summer, damp crocodiles of children and groups of visitors speaking many different languages could be found in the narrow streets and around the cathedral, whose walls of carved stone were just now free of masons' scaffolding for the first time in years. It sometimes seemed to Otterburn that every corner one turned gave fresh evidence of the city's beauty. He soon found also, as others who had come to live here before him had discovered, that the damp air gave him recurring trouble with his sinuses.

One day, coming into the house, he found an envelope addressed to him on the mat behind the door. It surprised him, for no one knew he was here. Yet this was an envelope with his name written on it in someone's hand. He took it upstairs and opened it in his room. There was a single sheet of rather good dove-grey writing-paper, folded once. On it, written in the same hand, was the message: 'I shall be in the Ferryboat at seven tonight'. Nothing more. No signature. No date. Otterburn could not decide whether it was a woman's handwriting or a man's. He looked at the envelope again. There was no stamp or postmark. It had presumably been delivered by its sender. And seven tonight meant just that.

The Ferryboat was a riverside pub a couple of minutes' walk away, a smart place with a colourful inn sign and well-kept white paint on the outside. Its rooms were small but cosy and always spotlessly clean. Its brass and mirrors gleamed. On cooler days wood fires burned in the grates. Small dishes of olives and tiny silver onions and potato crisps stood on the bar counter in the lounge. At one end of the counter at lunchtime joints of cold ham and roast beef rested on a white cloth and cuts of these were offered with jacket potatoes and a green salad or as the filling between slices of crusty bread. On warm days then, and sometimes on balmy evenings, the clientele would spill out onto the embankment, to drink at tables on the cobbles and watch perhaps a skiff with a lone rower speed upstream or a white pleasure boat glide by.

The Ferryboat was Otterburn's local but he had been in only a couple of times. Its food was expensive and its drinks always a few pence dearer than in the other pubs nearby, and Otterburn was being careful with his money. Otterburn's wife would not want, because her father had money. It was only when he had won a prize in a premium-bond draw that Otterburn had finally decided to break away from his wife. His windfall had been twenty thousand pounds. His idea was to live on it until he sorted himself out; but inflation would cut into its value, and with over three million unemployed the prospects of finding another job were not good. Not that Otterburn relished the thought of working for someone else again, but he would have to earn a living in some way when the money ran out. Unless he did do away with himself. There had been times when that had seemed the only way of freeing himself from Hazel. He had thought also of leaving her, but until his good fortune he had had no money.

Otterburn also had a daughter, but as she was a pupil at a boarding school he saw her only during the holidays. The combined influence of Otterburn's wife and the school had given the girl a distant manner and sometimes she would treat Otterburn as though she was not quite sure who he was and wondered why he should be there every time she came home. She had certainly always been made aware that it was her grandfather's money that, directly or indirectly, kept everything going. When Otterburn had finally fallen to wondering why Hazel had married him in the first place, he reached the reluctant conclusion that it satisfied something in her nature to be able to choose a potential failure, confirm him in that role and dominate him because of it. 'Thee stick by thi family an' thi job, Malcolm lad,' Otterburn's father-in-law had said to him early on, 'an' tha'll never want for owt. Is'll see to that.' That the rich little business in importing and exporting specialised foodstuffs that Hazel's father had created and built up could carry one passenger was the interpretation Otterburn came to put on the situation. 'Sufferance,' he had finally said to himself. 'That's what I'm living on. Sufferance.'

Otterburn looked again at the note. He thought on reflection that the writing was more probably a woman's than a man's. Then again, it had almost a childish look. If that were so, he told himself, it was not because it belonged to a young person but because its backward slope was a disguise.

He heated chicken soup for his lunch, the remains of the can he had opened yesterday. Otterburn had not been able to cook when he came to the house, beyond boil and fry eggs and grill bacon. Now he could scramble eggs and soon he would master the making of omelettes. He was determined, with the help of a basic cookbook, to learn how to feed himself on a simple but balanced diet. At present he fell back more often than he liked on expensive frozen foods, but he intended before long to be knowledgeable in buying the ingredients for casseroles and stews, the buying and preparation of his own fish and in making pancakes and vegetarian dishes which would cut his intake of meat. In the meantime he heated the soup and cut bread and thought about what he might have for his evening meal which would fit in with his visit to the Ferryboat at seven.

But who said he was going to the Ferryboat? Why in heaven should he take the slightest notice of a message from someone who couldn't sign his or her name?

Because it showed that someone was interested in him.

After he'd eaten, and drunk two cups of tea, Otterburn lay down on his bed which, with a woven cover over it, doubled as a divan. He had not done anything physically strenuous but he felt tired. He felt tired rather a lot lately. With no routine to shape and control his day, indolence took over. He should, he thought, make some kind of plan for occupying his time. Perhaps he might study in depth the history of the city, embarking on a programme of reading with the aid of the public library. With nothing to distract him, he could become an expert. From the trunk of the subject he could explore the many branches, political and economic, religious and secular. Perhaps he could eventually write some articles himself and publish them under a pseudonym. Or even a book.

Mildly excited by the prospect, Otterburn dozed off.

He woke to find himself wondering what he should wear this evening. He'd been accustomed to sports jackets and jumpers and slacks, and off-the-peg business suits of unmemorable cut and cloth. His shirts were in plain white or pastel shades, or with faint stripes on a white ground. He almost always wore a tie, feeling undressed without one unless he had on a sweater whose neck came up about his throat. He had no style. A lot of men who frequented the Ferryboat had style, even if it was only in the careless way they wore a t-shirt with patched and faded jeans. Otterburn did not want to go to that extreme. It only worked if you felt not the slightest trace of self-consciousness. But there was room for some improvement.

He looked at his watch. It was only the middle of the afternoon. There was still time for him to catch the bank open. Otterburn had stopped using his credit card for fear that when he informed the company of his change of address his wife would trace him. His prize from the premium bond he had kept secret from her. Somehow he had realised immediately the opportunity it gave him, so he had said nothing and deposited the money in an account at a new bank, transferring it yet again when he moved to this city.

Leaving the house, Otterburn walked briskly along the quay and up a sloping alley to emerge into the street. There were several men's outfitters of quality, some specialising in shirts and knitwear, some in suits of clothes, others in shoes, and a couple of department stores who could equip one from head to foot and from the skin out. He stopped as he passed the windows of one such and thought that he could go in and pay by cheque when he knew what his outlay was. But then, he might this evening find himself called upon to stand drinks, or even a meal, and it would be as well to have spare cash in his pocket. So he walked to the bank, made a withdrawal with three minutes to spare, then retraced his steps.

In the store he selected a two-piece casual suit in blue denim and took it into a cubicle. One thing, he thought as he appraised himself in the glass, was that though he was no longer a lad he still had a lean body that didn't need forcing into slim-hipped trousers. The cubicle mirrors gave him views of his profile and the back of his head. His first thought was that he needed a haircut, his second that he didn't. His hair at this stage in its growth waved quite becomingly in the nape of his neck. If left for another couple of weeks it would be long enough for a restyling by a barber who knew more than the short-back-and-sides Otterburn had always favoured, simply from long habit. Perhaps he could brush it forward instead of back and dispense with that neat parting he had fought so long to establish when a boy. From this, Otterburn went on to the question of his spectacles. He didn't think he needed to indulge in the vanity of contact lenses: the appearance of many men was enhanced by their glasses. What he should try was a more modern type of frame, with larger lenses. But these were longer-term considerations. For the present he felt and looked well in the denim suit. The effect would be complemented when he added a new shirt. He chose one of wide navy-blue and narrow pale-pink stripes, with a scarlet thread running through the pink, then paid for his purchases with cash. The suit he thought quite cheap, though the shirt cost more than he was used to paying. He left with the goods in a large carrier bag with the name of the store printed on it and walked back to his room through the warm and slightly hazy air of the afternoon.

Taking advantage of the quietness of the house, Otterburn went down and ran a hot bath. He lay in it for some time, watching, his thoughts in the same suspended state, his pubic hair and his limp penis floating under the surface of the water. Otterburn rarely indulged in sexual reverie. Though his intimate life with Hazel had consisted of an efficient but matter-of-fact once-a-week Saturday-night coupling, a routine relief usually initiated by her and never referred to out of the bed, it had been enough to keep him from fancying women on the street and from longing for some more intense liaison. He supposed he was undersexed. He thought, on the occasions when it crossed his mind, that he was lucky. It had seemed enough for Hazel and its absence had not preoccupied him since he had left her. Now he wondered if the letter were not drawing him to the beginning of a sexual adventure. The letter... He could still hardly believe it was real and he had opened it and read it again before coming down for his bath. The distant nudging of common sense told him he was being foolish in taking so much trouble to prepare for an assignation made in such a mysterious fashion. But is, it was distant. His mind was as languorous as his body, drifting, floating, waiting for whatever might happen.

Someone was interested in him...

The skin of his fingertips was wrinkled. He had not known that since he had played in his bath as a child. He pulled the plug and stood up, putting a quick steadying hand to the wall as a faint giddiness made his head spin. He had stayed in too long. He took his sponge and squeezed water from the cold tap over himself.

Back in his room, he pulled on pyjama trousers under his dressing-gown and tucked a scarf round his neck. The squeaking groan of an unoiled pulley drew him to the window. Some men were unloading bales into a warehouse from a barge across the river. Otterburn dragged a chair over and sat down to watch.

On his way to the Ferryboat, Otterburn strolled up the alley to the street and bought an evening paper. It would give him a prop with which to occupy his eyes and hands, should he have to wait. How would the approach be made? Would someone simply walk up to him, smile and say, 'Did you get my letter?' It was at this point that he wondered if he were about to be faced with some wrongdoing from his past. We could all, he told himself, feel the occasional touch of a nameless anxiety: that was a part of the human condition. Yet, as he cast his mind back over the dull march of his years, he could find no specific act of his that merited guilt. He had lived a blameless life. His trouble was that he could not imagine anyone being interested in him for his own sake.

He had decided that it would be better if he were a few minutes early; he could watch then who came into the pub, and it would save him from feeling that he himself was being observed as he entered. The pub was at the ebb of its evening trade. The after-office drinkers were already gone or about to leave. There were some tourists, who would not linger. The late evening customers had not yet appeared. Otterburn chose the lounge. He bought half a pint of bitter, and as two businessmen left a corner table he went over to it and sat down with his back to the wall. From here he could see the door at the far end of the room as well as that at this end of the bar, through which he had entered. Yes, he must be first, for by no stretch of the imagination could he picture any of those present as the author of the note. That group in anoraks were visitors, come to look at the sights. They in their turn, as they suddenly all laughed, were being given a quick once-over by the landlord who, in check Viyella shirt and yellow tie, his glasses hanging from a cord round his neck, had just come in to join the girl behind the bar. That elderly gent sitting alone, neat grey hair, well-cut navy-blue blazer, reading the *Financial Times* and drinking from a half-pint pewter tankard, lived in that big bay-windowed house farther along the embankment. And that middle-aged man and the much younger woman were too absorbed in each other even to have noticed him except as someone they needn't fear. An office romance, if he'd ever seen one. Soon they would go their separate ways, he to make his excuses at home, she to fill in her time somehow till the next snatched hour. The only remote possibility was the thin woman of indeterminate age, in tweeds, sitting at the bar, lighting a fresh cigarette within seconds of stubbing out the last, and ordering another gin and tonic, lemon but no ice. But Otterburn had seen her before too, and if she had wanted to know him she would have hailed him and drawn him into her company with the unself-conscious ease with which she chatted to the barmaid and the landlord and whoever of the regulars stayed long enough at the bar. You could find her counterpart, Otterburn

447

reflected, in pubs and hotel bars all over the country: the woman who gave the impression of having seen it all, who had settled for a secure but boring marriage to a dull but tolerant husband, to whom she would return each mid-evening, ever so slightly tipsy, after a couple of hours steady drinking.

In any gathering Otterburn merged with the background, but he prided himself on missing little. He observed and speculated and remained uninvolved. It occurred to him now that this was probably the ideal make-up of a writer. Except that he couldn't write. But how did he know that? There he went, dismissing himself before he had even tried. Wasn't that something else he might explore in his new-found freedom? Of course, while he might be good at noting people's appearance and mannerisms, his speculations about their character and their private lives could be wildly wrong. But did that matter? His guess was that, while a writer might use real people as starting-points, he very soon found himself casting their personalities into the mould of his own. And there was an obvious snag. Had he himself enough personality, did he care enough, to be able to draw characters who could make a reader care? Yet Otterburn felt excitement stir again at this second new prospect. He could do no more than try. It amused him, gave him even a strange feeling of power, to think of himself going about noting people not simply from a habit of his nature, but as a collector. If he couldn't think of plots all at once, he could at least keep a written sketchbook and train himself after each outing to record, as objectively as a painter or a photographer, what he had seen and heard.

Otterburn had lifted his newspaper and was looking past it with renewed interest at his fellow drinkers when he saw his wife coming into the room. Intensely startled, he raised the paper higher until his head and shoulders were hidden as Hazel glanced round the room then half-turned to speak to the man who was following her.

There was nowhere for Otterburn to hide. If he got up now, it was unlikely that he could reach the door before she turned again and saw him. But what was she doing here and who was that she was with? From his first startled glance Otterburn couldn't recall ever having seen him before, though he supposed he could have met him and forgotten. In which case the man might remember him, especially if there was something irregular going on.

Otterburn risked moving his paper slightly to one side. His wife had taken a seat at a table in the middle of the floor and now had her back directly to him, showing him a quarter-profile as she removed her gloves and spoke to her companion, who was ordering drinks at the bar. Hazel was looking particularly smart. She had on her best black suit and a white blouse with a jabot, black nylon tights and high-heeled black patent-leather shoes. Her hair was newly washed and set and she had had that blonde rinse which restored its fading colour. He supposed she was, to some eyes, a handsome woman. It was amazing the improvement brought to her legs by the right shoes and stockings. Her hips and her breasts were ample but still shapely, only hinting yet at the excess another few years might bestow. To his surprise, Otterburn felt his flesh stir; as though he didn't know all too well the briskness and lack of finesse with which she despatched sexual appetite. Not that he had had any direct experience to compare that with, but he did read, and today's explicit novels left him in little doubt that there were prolonged delights to which they were both strangers.

449

In his contemplation of his wife's back, Otterburn had, he suddenly realised, let the paper down until his face was completely visible. And at that moment the man Hazel was with turned with the drinks and looked directly at him. His stare hardened. Otterburn lifted the paper again. After a moment's consternation, he felt himself grinning broadly. Of course the man didn't know him. Otterburn had just been given warning that he was not to ogle his own wife! How rich! Whether or not Hazel and her companion were any more than just good friends, the man was obviously jealous and possessive. What a joke, Otterburn thought, if he were to stare at Hazel until the man felt forced to do something about it. How their faces would fall when Otterburn then went over and let Hazel see him. A pity it wasn't worth it. But it wasn't. Once Hazel knew where he was, she would give him no peace.

She was looking over her shoulder as she picked up her handbag. Her companion nodded to a sign on the wall. She got up and crossed the room without looking at anyone and went out through the door nearest to Otterburn. Otterburn knew where the Ladies was. He gave her a moment to find it herself, then stood up and emptied his glass. The man was staring again. Surprised at his own boldness, Otterburn grinned at him and winked before walking out through the same door.

There was a huge pale American Ford parked on the cobbles outside. For some reason it reminded Otterburn of an enormous double bed. He knew instinctively that it belonged to Hazel's companion. Ownership of such an opulent and extravagant car, parked where no one was supposed to park, fitted exactly that arrogant stare and that black moustache, so thick and neatly trimmed it looked like something glued to the fellow's upper lip. So, Otterburn asked himself, was Hazel having an affair, and if so was it one which had started since he left her, or had it been going on before? Further, did it help or hinder him in his new way of life? More to the immediate point was that Hazel's appearance had ruined his own assignation. And what could he do now except wait for them to leave? And by that time might it not be too late?

Otterburn strolled aimlessly along the embankment, tapping the rolled newspaper against his leg. He felt now like someone who has turned up to a party on the wrong night: to a party, in fact, that was already over. 'All dressed up and nowhere to go.' He turned up off the riverside and into the town. A few minutes' aimless walking found him outside the painted window of a pizza parlour. He looked at the menu. He was peckish. He went in. He'd always maintained that he didn't care for pizzas, but now he wanted something simple and cheap which would satisfy his sudden appetite, if not delight his palate. He ordered at random from the ten or more variations on the menu and asked for a half-pint of lager. The place was busy. There were even some families with quite young children. People were coming and going all the time and the waitresses in their green aprons and matching caps hurried between kitchen and tables without a moment to catch their breath. A young woman came in, stood looking round for a moment, saw that she hadn't much choice, then sat down at the next table. She took a small square of handkerchief from her shoulder bag and polished her glasses before reading the menu. Otterburn read his paper. His pizza came. It was enormous. He picked up his knife and fork, hardly knowing where to make the first incision. He cut a piece. The topping was still sizzling and he gasped, reaching for his lager, as it scorched his mouth. The outer door opened and shut again. A group crowded in.

'D'you mind?' a voice asked.

Otterburn looked up. The girl from the next table had half-pulled out the chair opposite him. He didn't understand at first but with a mouthful of pizza he couldn't yet swallow he made noises and waved his knife about. She sat down.

'If I sit here, they can all sit together,' the girl explained. Otterburn looked past her. Five young people had taken possession of the table she had left. He swallowed.

'Very thoughtful of you.'

'It's so very busy tonight.'

'Is that exceptional?'

'Well, no. They seem to do well most nights.'

'You've been in before, then?'

'Yes. It's simple and convenient, and not expensive.'

'Quite. That's what I thought.'

'What is that you've got, if you don't mind my asking?'

Otterburn turned the menu round. 'Er... it's a number eleven.'

'It looks good'.

'I'm not an expert on pizzas,' Otterburn said, 'but there's plenty of it and it's very hot.' He swallowed another mouthful. 'And quite tasty too.'

'Mmm.'

A waitress came and put a plate of spaghetti bolognese in front of the girl, then sprinkled grated cheese over it with careless haste. The girl put her fork vertically into the spaghetti, twirled it and lifted some to her mouth. Her light brown hair fell softly across each cheek as she bent her head slightly forward.

'You've done that before,' Otterburn said.

'Yes. I lived in Italy for a while. The only reason I eat this after what I got used to there is because it's cheap.'

'It's not a country I know,' Otterburn said. 'I've been

to Spain, but not Italy.'

'Do you live here?' the girl asked.

'Yes. Do you?'

'I do just now, yes.'

'What's your job?'

'Oh, I'm sort of in-between things.'

'I suppose a lot of people are like that just now.'

'Yes. What do you do?' Otterburn hesitated. The girl said, 'I'm sorry, if you don't want to tell me. But you did ask me.'

'I'm a writer, actually,' Otterburn said.

'Oh? That must be interesting. Would I have heard of you? Do you write under your own name or a pseudonym?'

'You won't have heard of me,' Otterburn said. 'My name's Otterburn. Malcolm Otterburn.'

The girl was frowning politely. 'No, I'm afraid I haven't. And it's quite an unusual name, isn't it? I mean, not one you'd forget.'

'Think nothing of it,' Otterburn said.

'I can see now why you hesitated to tell me, though,' the girl said. 'It must be terribly embarrassing to say you're a writer and people have never heard of you.'

'It happens all the time,' Otterburn said. 'But you haven't told me your name.'

Now it was her turn to appear reluctant. 'Promise me you won't laugh.'

'Why on earth should I laugh?'

'Because this is where I always get embarrassed.'

'You mean, you're somebody famous whom I ought to have known?'

'No, no, nothing like that. It's just my name.'

'Well...?'

'It's Dawn,' the girl said. 'Dawn Winterbottom.' Otterburn grinned. 'You did promise,' the girl said.

'No, no,' Otterburn said. His smile broadened. He could not suppress a chuckle. The girl's colour was up as she looked at her plate. Otterburn found himself reaching over to touch her hand.

'Please. Don't be offended. I'd probably have found nothing funny in it if you hadn't so obviously expected me to. Please,' he said again, when she didn't respond. 'Finish your spaghetti before it goes cold, and don't mind me.'

The girl took some more spaghetti onto her fork. 'I've thought of changing it,' she said. 'But after all it is my own name and I think people should make the best of their own names. They're part of them, after all. Aren't they?'

'Of course they are,' said Otterburn, who saw little logic in what she was saying.

'And after all it's the quality of the personality behind the name that counts, isn't it?'

'I suppose it is.'

'And there's nothing wrong with your personality,' Otterburn went on. He was enjoying himself. 'You're good-natured enough to do a kindness for strangers, like letting those people have your table, and unself-conscious and natural enough to sit with another stranger – a man, what's more – and make pleasant conversation without fear of being misunderstood. I'd say all those are qualities very much in your favour.'

'You seem rather specially nice yourself,' Dawn said.

'Oh, there's nothing special about me.'

'Oh, but there is. Writers are special. They must be or there'd be more of them about.'

'There are more than enough already,' Otterburn said. He was sure that must be true.

'Yes, the competition must be frightening. Tell me, do you actually manage to earn a living from it?'

454

'Well...' Otterburn looked a touch bashful. 'I wish I could say I did. But the fact is, I have a private income.'

'Lucky for you. I'm sure that must take a lot of the worry out of it. It means, I suppose, that you can write what you want to write and not just to make money.'

'You're really very perceptive,' Otterburn said.

'And what are you working on just now?' the girl asked. 'If it's not too personal a question.'

Otterburn emptied his mouth, took a drink of his lager, and said, 'I'm writing a story about a man who comes to live on his own in this city. One day he finds a letter pushed through the door with his name on it, which is strange because nobody knows he's there.'

'What does the letter say?'

'It says, "I shall be in the Ferryboat at seven tonight'."'

'Is that all?'

'That's all. No signature, no address, no postmark.'

'Is it from a man or woman?'

'He can't tell. The handwriting may be disguised.'

'And what does he do? I mean, does he just tear it up and ignore it, or does he take it seriously?'

'He can't help being intrigued by it.'

'No, I expect not.'

'Someone's interested in him, you see.'

'It sounds like something out of a spy story.'

'Yes, it does. But he's just an ordinary sort of chap, who certainly doesn't know any official secrets.'

'But he must have a secret of some kind. Perhaps a guilty one from his past.'

Otterburn looked at her with admiration. 'You know, you really are clever. But I'm afraid that's not the answer. He's led a rather dull and totally respectable life.'

'Hmm. So is it a man or a woman who's written the letter?'

'You asked me that before. I don't know.'

'Well, does he go to the... where is it?'

'The Ferryboat. Yes.'

'And what happens?'

'I don't know,' Otterburn said again.

The girl frowned. 'But you must know. You're writing the story.'

'But I don't know how it ends,' Otterburn said. 'Not yet.'

'You mean, you've made up this, this intriguing situation, but you haven't worked the rest of it out?'

'Yes.'

'You've set yourself a problem, haven't you?'

'Oh, it's happened before,' Otterburn said airily. 'It'll work itself out if I hang on and be patient.' He was sure he'd read this in an interview with a writer, somewhere. It sounded to him to have the ring of truth.

'Well, I wish you luck with it,' the girl said. She ate the last scraps of spaghetti, put down her fork and spoon and wiped her mouth with her paper napkin. Otterburn pushed aside the remaining third of his pizza. 'You've not made much of that.'

'It's very filling. Are you having a sweet, or just coffee?'

'What about you?'

'Just coffee, I think. I'd like to buy you a sweet, though, if you could enjoy one.'

'No, thanks,' the girl said. 'I'll accept a coffee, though.'

Otterburn signalled a waitress. To his surprise, one noticed him and came immediately.

'Well,' Dawn said, 'this is very pleasant.'

'I'm glad you think so. Tell the truth, I was feeling, well, a bit down, before you joined me.'

'Because your story's not going well?'

'Yes.'

'Are you married?'

'I was,' Otterburn said. 'Still am, actually,' he admitted, 'but separated. What about you?'

She shook her head. 'No.'

'Not had the time, with all that travelling?'

'I suppose so.'

She reached down and brought up her shoulder bag.

'I'm sorry I can't offer you a cigarette,' Otterburn said, 'but I don't use them.'

'Me neither.' She took the small handkerchief and touched it to her nose. 'There's only one thing wrong with this town. The damp air gives me the perpetual sniffs.'

'There's always a snag to everything.'

'Yes.' She put the bag down again. 'You must live alone, then?'

'Yes.'

'Like the man in the story.'

'Yes. What about you?'

'With an aunt. When I'm here.'

'It's good to have a base. Somewhere you can call home. Will you be off on your travels again soon?'

'It depends. You never seem to get anywhere; always moving about. You see a lot, but you don't get anywhere.'

'And with jobs so hard to come by just now.'

'Yes. My timing hasn't been so good, coming back to England in the middle of a recession.'

'You're young enough to see it through.'

'I'm perhaps older than you think.'

'I wasn't asking,' Otterburn said.

The coffee came. Otterburn, drinking through the froth, found scalding liquid underneath.

'Damnation! I'm either burning my mouth or scalding it tonight.'

457

'Do you feel better, though?'

'In what way?'

'You said you were down before.'

'Oh, I feel much better now.'

He did. He had never met anybody like Dawn Winterbottom before. Here they were, total strangers, chatting as easily as if they'd known each other for years. He was wondering how he might prolong this evening – could he venture to offer to buy her a drink? – when she said: 'I've just remembered. There is a pub called the Ferryboat, down by the river, isn't there?'

'Yes.'

'Do you always use real places in your work?'

'It depends.'

'But couldn't that lead to complications?'

'Not until someone reads it. Maybe I'll give it a fictitious name before then.'

'You said he went to the pub but you didn't know what happened when he got there.'

'Yes.'

'Hmm. I never knew writers worked like that. I thought they had it all planned before they started.'

'Well, now you know different.' An idea came to him. 'Look, if you don't mind my asking, what are you going to do now?'

'You mean when I leave here?'

'Yes.'

'I suppose I was going home. I was supposed to meet someone, but it fell through at the last minute.'

'Well, what I was wondering,' Otterburn said, 'was if you'd like to join me for a drink at the Ferryboat. It's just a stroll from here. Perhaps you could help me to see what happens.'

'In the story, you mean?'

'Yes. Being there with somebody else might just spark it off.'

She smiled. 'I must say, I've never been picked up with such an unusual come-on.'

'Oh, please,' Otterburn said. 'Please, you misunderstand me.'

'Don't worry. I've defended my honour in tougher places than this.'

'You're making it difficult for me,' Otterburn said. 'And it's all been so pleasant and natural, so far.'

'I was joking.'

'On the other hand,' Otterburn said, 'there are some strange men at large, and if you'd rather not.'

She looked at him. 'I think I'd like to.'

'You'll come?'

'Yes. Thank you.'

Their bills were already on the table. As the girl reached again for her bag, Otterburn picked up both of them.

'Let me get this.'

'Oh, I couldn't do that.'

'Of course you can. It's not a fortune, and it's my pleasure.'

Outside, as they strolled towards the pub, she slightly ahead of him on the narrow pavement, Otterburn could not bring her face to mind. It was, he thought, one of those faces which seem to change with the light, one whose features would fix themselves only after another meeting. While her clothes were neat and clean, like her hair and hands, she didn't dress for effect either. She was a tall girl and her heels were not high. Over her jumper and skirt she wore a lemon-coloured lightweight raincoat which she had not taken off during the meal. And what an awkward business it was, Otterburn reflected, simply walking along pavements like this with anybody one didn't know well. The naturalness and ease of the café had gone, leaving him self-conscious, casting about for something to say. She was silent too, now. He took her elbow and turned her as she would have passed the mouth of the alley which led to the river.

'Down here.'

The American car had gone. Otterburn hoped it meant that his wife was no longer inside. He went up on his toes and looked in through the small-paned window. He couldn't see her.

'What are you doing?'

'Looking to see how full it is.'

He would have to risk it. He went in first, then held the door so that she could pass him. The pub's evening was in full swing. All the seats looked taken. The girl followed Otterburn to the bar.

'What will you have?'

'What are you having?'

'I don't know. A Scotch, perhaps.'

'I'd like that. On the rocks, please.' She turned and looked round the room as Otterburn ordered. 'Is this your local?'

'It's the nearest.'

'You live here, by the river?'

'Yes.'

'Is that where the man in the story lives?'

'Er, yes, it is.'

'How many of these people do you know?'

'Just one or two I'd pass the time of day with.'

'Which one would you choose as the writer of the letter?'

'I don't know.'

460

'Is it a man or a woman?' she asked him, for the third time.

'I don't know.'

'It's really got to be a woman, hasn't it? Cheers.'

'Cheers,' Otterburn said. 'Yes, I suppose it has.'

'Unless you're building up to some kind of homosexual situation.'

'Oh, no,' Otterburn said. 'Nothing like that.'

'Why not?'

'I hadn't thought of that.'

'It might be worth thinking about, though, mightn't it?'

'Hmm,' Otterburn said. He thought about it now as his glance flickered round the room. Could the author of the note still be here, patiently waiting for him but unable to make a move now because he was with someone else?

'Your character's not gay, then? The one who gets the letter.'

'No.'

'You could always make him gay.'

'Hmm.'

'Perhaps he's got latent homosexual tendencies that he's never known about, or kept firmly suppressed.'

'Ye-es...'

'And the writer of the letter recognises that.'

Otterburn felt uneasy and offended.

'I don't think I'd like that.'

'Do you find it distasteful? I thought writers were men of the world.'

'It's just that I know very little about all that.'

'Did you imagine it as some woman who secretly fancies him?'

'I've told you, I haven't thought it through yet.'

'I'm only trying to help you, like you said.'

'Of course, but –'

'If it's a woman, why doesn't she simply make it in her way to bump into him and get to know him?'

'Perhaps she's shy and repressed.'

'She's going to be awfully disappointed if she arouses his interest with mysterious letters and then he doesn't take to her.'

'Perhaps she doesn't intend to reveal herself.'

'Then why make an assignation?'

'I don't know. He's only had the one letter. Perhaps she'll tell him more in a later one.'

'It's not much of a story, is it?'

'Well, not so far.'

'If you did it the way I suggested, you could make it really strong. You could bring in homosexual jealousy and revenge. Perhaps suicide, or even murder.'

'You've got a very lurid mind.'

'Do you think so?'

There was a glint in her eye. It occurred to Otterburn to wonder if she was pulling his leg.

'Anyway,' he said, 'it's not the kind of story I write.'

'Not so far, perhaps. But perhaps you should widen your scope. Perhaps that's why you're not better known.'

'I'll think about it,' Otterburn said. 'Let's have another drink.'

'Thank you.' She gave him her glass.

When he turned with the refills she waved to him from a table.

'If you don't know any homosexuals,' she said as he sat down, 'I could introduce you to some.'

'Here?'

'Yes. There are one or two in the company at the theatre, to begin with, and some others who live here. They're not all madly camp,' she went on, as Otterburn frowned.

'Some of them you might never guess at, unless you were that way inclined yourself.'

It would mean, Otterburn thought, that he could see her again. He had never met anyone like her. He couldn't read her. She seemed in control of every situation. He had seemed in charge for a time, in the pizza place; but not now.

'Well,' he said, 'I'll try anything once.'

She smiled. 'Be careful. I only suggested you meet them.'

Otterburn blushed. 'How long are you staying in town?'

'Until I get bored. Or the money runs out.'

'What do you do when you've got a job?'

'I've done all kinds of things. I was teaching English as a foreign language in Italy. But I was foolish enough to have an affair with the man who owned the school and when his wife found out he ran back to her bosom and I had to move on.'

Otterburn, flabbergasted by her candour, looked at her with renewed interest and said nothing.

'Then I've been a waitress and a barmaid. I've lugged a guitar about and sung at folk clubs and done seasonal work at holiday camps. I worked for six months as a secretary in Australia. I did a stint at a summer camp for children in America; your keep and some spending money and a chance to see a bit of the country.' She shrugged. 'Now I'm here for a while. Till something turns up.'

'You don't sound the type to bring a man his pipe and slippers in an evening.'

'Is that the kind of woman you like?'

'I suppose I've always been used to knowing where I am.'

'You left your wife, though. Or did she leave you?'

'Oh, I left.'

'Were you in a rut?'

'Yes. Yes, I suppose I was.'

'But with your work, and your private means, you could go anywhere you like.'

'I suppose I could.'

'Why don't you?'

'I suppose you think of writers like yourself: restless, always on the move.'

'Perhaps I do.'

'They're not all like that. Haven't you heard of the country cottage, with roses round the door?'

'I'd love to read something you've written. Could you lend me something?'

'I left everything behind when I moved out. It was rather sudden and I wanted to travel light.'

'Perhaps I'll look in the public library.'

'I doubt if you'll find anything. My early books are out of print and I've mostly published in magazines since.'

'You need a really good shake-up and a change of direction.'

'That's what I had in mind when I left my wife and came here.'

'It's a start, anyway.'

The whisky was going down very quickly. Otterburn thought he perhaps should have stuck to beer.

'Could you enjoy another?'

'Yes, I could,' Dawn said. She opened her bag. 'But let me get them.'

'No, no,' Otterburn said. 'I'll go.'

'You can go,' the girl said, 'but I'll pay.' She put a pound note on the table.

Otterburn hesitated, then picked up the note. 'Same again?'

'Unless you'd like something different.'

'I hardly like to mention it,' Otterburn said, 'but the prices they charge here, this won't cover it.'

· The girl laughed out loud as she put some coins on the table. Otterburn took to the bar the image of her laughing. Now he knew what her face was like.

'How do I get in touch with you?' he asked when he came back. 'If I want to take you up on your offer.'

'Are you on the phone?'

'No. Well, there is a communal phone, but it depends on someone answering it and I might not get the message.'

'I'll give you my number,' Dawn said. She wrote on a slip of paper.

They left after another round of drinks, which Otterburn bought.

'Well,' she said, 'I'm afraid I wasn't much help.'

'Oh, these things often take a little time,' Otterburn said. 'Perhaps I'll try thinking along the lines you suggested.'

'Just whereabouts do you live?'

'Along here.'

They strolled along the embankment. It was a fine night. The river slid by. Lights were reflected in its smooth broad surface. Here they were, Otterburn thought, walking by the river in one of the oldest cities in Europe. He felt elated, buoyed up by the beauty, the mystery, the boundless possibilities of it all.

'That's me, up there.' He pointed as they paused before the house. 'Third floor front.'

'Yes,' Dawn said. 'Well, you won't get your feet wet there.'

'Hmm?'

'The river comes up and floods these houses practically every year.'

'Perhaps I shan't be here long, anyway.'

'You're not settled, then?'

'Oh, no. Sort of in transit, really.'

She asked him the time. 'I'd offer to come up with you,' she said then, 'but I really must go.'

'My dear young woman!' Otterburn said.

'What's the matter?'

'I hope you don't say such things to every strange man you meet.'

'There you go again, thinking you're no different from anybody else.'

'You flatter me.' Otterburn said.

'I must be off, anyway. Thank you for a very pleasant evening.'

'Thank you,' Otterburn said. 'But won't you let me see you home?'

'No. I can get a bus just across the bridge. Goodnight.'

She was moving away from him, quite rapidly. He called after her. 'Goodnight.'

He let himself into the house and went straight to bed. He thought that he would lie awake for some time, but only a few minutes after he had started to retrace the evening from the moment she walked into the restaurant, he fell asleep.

He slept quite late. An idea had formed in his mind and he lay on his back, the house still around him apart from the hum of a vacuum cleaner somewhere below, and considered the sheer audacity of it. In a while he got up, breakfasted on cereal, toast and coffee, washed himself and dressed. He looked for coins, found the paper with the girl's number on it and went down to the wall telephone on the ground floor. He dialled. A woman's voice answered.

'Could I speak to Miss Winterbottom, please?'

'Just a minute. I'll get her.'

'Hullo?'

'Dawn? It's Malcolm Otterburn.'

'Oh, hullo.'

'I was thinking...'

'Yes?'

'What you were saying about broadening my scope.'

'Oh, yes?'

'I was wondering how far ten thousand pounds would take us.'

'You were what?'

'We could get quite a long way on that, I should think. Wouldn't you?'

'Pretty well all the way round.' She laughed. 'Are you serious?'

'Oh, quite.'

'Look,' she said, 'I was just going out. I'll see you in the Ferryboat at seven.'

'Will you think about it?'

'Oh, yes. And I hope you will too.'

'I've done that.'

'All right. But I'm late for an appointment so I must rush. I'll see you in the Ferryboat at seven.' She hung up.

Otterburn saw the envelope on the mat behind the front door as he turned from the telephone. He picked it up. It had his name on it. He slit it open and took out the single folded sheet of paper. '*I saw you,*' the note said, in the same hand, '*but you didn't see me. I like your new outfit.*' He folded it and pushed it into his trousers pocket. Checking that he had his keys, he left the house and walked along the embankment and up into the town. In a branch of W. H. Smith he bought a

467

pad of feint ruled A4 paper and some cartridges for his fountain pen.

Back in his room, he pulled the table over to the window and sat down with the pad of paper before him. He got the ink flowing in the nib of his pen, looked out at the river for a few moments, then rested his cheek on his left hand and began to write:

'Otterburn had come to live in this cathedral city when he left his wife. He rented a room and kitchen, with a shared bath and lavatory on the next landing. He had never lived alone in his life before and from his window he could look down three floors at the river flowing between its stone banks and think that at least he hadn't far to go if he decided to do away with himself.'

The Pity of It All

Wednesday afternoon, it was – as if she'd ever forget – half-day closing, and Nancy's mother was going on while she cleaned the house around Nancy, who was doing the week's wash. Since Nancy seldom went out in the evenings and couldn't watch television forever after she had put little June to bed, the house was near spotless before Nancy's mother started on it; but she had to occupy herself and Wednesday afternoon had become a ritual. Nancy's mother came and cleaned the house and went on about something.

What she was going on about now was what she had gone on about ever since Jim had been killed. Where was the sense, she asked, in Nancy tying herself to this house when there was a place for her at home, a garden for little June to play in instead of a short length of street and a deathtrap of a through-road at the end of it, and herself and Nancy's father to look after the child while Nancy went out and enjoyed herself?

Oh, and didn't she go on! Saying the same things,

week after week. She had decided what she thought was best, and wouldn't leave it alone.

'I like my independence,' Nancy always told her. 'I like to have a life of my own.'

'You bring June to me on your way to the shop,' Nancy's mother said, 'and you collect her on your way home. You can't go out on a night because she's got to be looked after. If you call that having a life of your own. You never get out and see anybody.'

She saw enough people in the shop during the day, Nancy always told her. She was happy enough in her own home when she'd done her day's work.

'A young woman like you, shutting yourself off,' her mother said. 'You'll never get anywhere if you don't get out and about.' She would never find another husband, Nancy's mother meant. Jim had been taken suddenly, and that was sad; but Nancy was a young woman, with time to have another two or three bairns, but not if she never went out and mixed with people socially.

It was the first week of the school holidays and children were noisy in the street. Some young ones had been and fetched June straight after dinner. June herself would be starting junior school in the autumn. Then, with Nancy tied at the shop till six in the evening, Nancy's mother would accept the extra chore of collecting June in the afternoon. All the more reason, Nancy could hear her mother saying, why Nancy should listen to sense and sell this house and move back home. But though Nancy had often spoken to Jim of 'popping round home' when visiting her parents' house, she no longer thought of it as such. Here was home, the house she and Jim had bought and done up together, talking of the day they would get something better: a semi, they thought, with a lawn at the back to sit out on and a vegetable patch where Jim could grow things. There had been no rush.

Then they had come to tell her about Jim, baffled themselves by the tragedy of it. In a safe pit with a low accident rate, and no fatalities for years past, he had walked alone into a heading, where a stone had fallen out of the roof, pinning him down and, so they told her as a crumb of comfort, killing him instantly. She was carrying the child and thought at first she would surely lose it. The doctors told her she was tough. Her mother had been known to call her hard. But Nancy had never paraded her feelings; she did not know how to behave to impress others. Her duty was to hang on and think of the new life growing inside her: a bit of Jim that he would now never see. Perhaps she would re-marry one day; but she would not go out and look for a chap, and he would have to be pretty special for her to notice him. That she had told her mother. It seemed to Nancy that she told her every Wednesday, while her mother went on.

Now she was telling Nancy that she'd had a reply from a guesthouse in Bournemouth, whose address a friend had given her, and they could have accommodation for the last two weeks in August. Nancy's mother thought the south coast would be a pleasant change, but if Nancy wanted to go elsewhere with a friend it would be no trouble for her and Nancy's father to take little June with them. But no, there was nowhere else that Nancy wanted to go.

Afterwards, Nancy found she could remember that moment with vivid clarity, though its components were all familiar ones. There was the attitude of her mother's body as she held the vacuum cleaner while she wound the flex on to the hooks; the sudden rush of water in the automatic washer as it performed its last rinse; the

471

sunlight on the step outside the scullery door. The voices of the children were no longer near.

'Just have a look out at June, will you?' she said, as she opened the washer and passed clothes over into the drying compartment. 'They've gone quiet.'

Then a minute or so must have passed, but it seemed like no time at all before Nancy's mother was calling at the end of the yard. 'June! June, where are you? Ey, you two, bring June back here. Don't you know how busy that road is? No, keep hold of her! Don't let her -!' And Nancy was out and running across the flagstones and into the street, as though she knew before she heard that awful screech of tyres and saw the car slewed round and the little legs in the blue and white Marks and Spencer socks, washed just once, and the stupid, older girls who had led her into it, standing petrified, soundless, and she herself making no sound – not yet – while her mother set up an endless moaning chant beside her: 'Oh! oh! oh! oh! oh! ...'

Nancy's father could not eat his food. Nancy had had nothing but cups of tea for over twenty-four hours. They talked behind her in low voices. 'It's the shock,' her father was saying. He couldn't take it in.

Nancy's mother was saying what she'd said ever since Jim died; that there had been no sense in Nancy living on her own with the bairn, when a good home had been waiting for them here. Nancy told her to shut up; let it drop.

'I don't care, Nancy. You could have come here and been as free as you liked. You can't stop living just because –'

'Just because what?' Nancy challenged her. 'What are you talking about? I don't know how you can fashion to bring it all up. You never let things rest; you just go on and on. You were sick to get me out of that house, and now you've got something you can hold against me for the rest of your life.'

'Nancy!'

There might have been a row then, because if what Nancy accused her mother of was not strictly true, her mother talking like that would not help Nancy to stop thinking that if only she had taken her advice little June would not have been in that road at the moment that car came along, and... And if Jim had not walked into that heading, or he had come out of the pit into a safer job, and if she had never met him and she'd never had the child...?

But the doorbell rang.

Nancy's mother, on her feet, went to answer it, coming back a few moments later to stand, curiously tongue-tied, inside the living-room doorway.

'Who is it?' Nancy's father asked.

'It's a chap, to see our Nancy.'

Nancy's father began to get up from the table. 'She can't see anybody now. Can't they leave her in peace? Some folk...'

'No, Cliff, wait a minute. It's the feller at...'

'Who?'

'He's come to see our Nancy.'

'Who is he?' Nancy asked.

'They call him Daymer. If you don't want to see him, just say so.'

'No. If he's come we can't turn him away.'

'Look, Nancy,' her father said, 'there's no law says you've got to see him.'

And she didn't want to, but he'd come and she must.

Her mother showed him in. 'This is a sorry house you've come to.' That tongue. It could spare nobody.

473

In the one direct look she could manage, Nancy saw that he was nicely dressed, still young. She wondered if his eyes always looked so hurt, or if it was only because of what had happened. Of what, she suddenly realised, had happened to him.

'Mrs Harper... I'm sorry to intrude on you at a time like this, but I felt I had to come. There's nothing I could say that wouldn't be hopelessly inadequate. You do understand that I hadn't a chance of avoiding your little girl? It was over in a flash.'

'Nobody's blaming you,' Nancy said. 'It was an accident. They do happen.'

'It was an accident that took her husband,' her mother told him. 'In the pit.'

His voice was shocked. 'Oh, I'm... It sounds worse than useless, Mrs Harper, but if there's anything I can do, anything at all.'

'You can't bring her back, can you?'

No mercy there. Her mother was, in fact, a good-hearted woman. But that tongue...

'Have you any family, Mr Daymer?' Nancy asked.

'A boy, Peter. He's away at school.'

'I expect he'll be well looked after there.'

'Well...'

'It wouldn't be easy for you to come. I thank you for it.'

'If there's any way I can help, any way at all, please let me know. I'll give you a card and put my private address on the back.'

Her mother took the card. 'Oh, you work at Ross's, do you? I used to know Mr Finch's wife, before she died. We did charity work together.'

'He's my father-in-law. I married his daughter, Elizabeth.'

'A lovely woman, she was, Mrs Finch.'

474

'Yes, indeed. And now I must go. Goodnight, Mr Frost, Mrs Harper.'

'Is he in his car?' her father asked when her mother came back from showing Mr Daymer out.

'Yes.'

'I don't think I could drive a car again, if anything like that happened to me.'

But, Nancy thought, you'd got to keep going. There were times when you thought you couldn't. But you'd got to.

They sold cigarettes and tobacco and cigars, sweets, and newspapers and magazines in the shop. Some of the magazines Nancy was not keen on selling. They had pictures in them of women with their legs open, showing all they'd got. Sometimes the women had their hands down there, as if they were touching themselves up. Not that she was prudish herself, but it embarrassed her when men were embarrassed by buying them. Some of them were. Some were really brazen about it, eyeing her up and down as they threw the book on to the counter, as though she chose them all herself and guessed exactly what they would like. Still, they were dear and the owner said they made a good profit. Marjorie, the other girl, younger than Nancy and not married, thought they were a giggle, and when things were quiet she would pick one out and read the letters, which were all about sexual experiences. 'They must make them up, Nancy. Don't you think so? Honest. It's dreamland. Hey, listen to this one!' Well, they knew what men were like, didn't they? Marjorie would say. Jim himself had not been averse to a look and a laugh, though when it came to the thing itself he'd been easily enough satisfied so long as he got what he called his 'night-cap' regular. He was always pretty tired and it didn't last long. It was all right. She'd loved him and couldn't complain, though just every now and then she'd find herself wishing for a bit of finesse, that they might linger, enjoy it for itself, not just for the end of it. And it had been a long time now… Marjorie had a boyfriend, a cocky lad called Jeff, who sometimes called in to buy a packet of fags and make arrangements with Marjorie. When Marjorie couldn't resist telling Nancy what a smashing lover Jeff was, she nearly always stopped at some place, cutting off the subject in a way which told Nancy she was sorry that she hadn't got anybody now. And Nancy wished she wouldn't, because she didn't want that kind of pity. It had been a long time… But she still missed Jim and could not bring herself to think of anyone taking his place.

Marjorie's big blue eyes brimmed with tears the morning Nancy returned to the shop. Nancy had to steel herself to accept this kind of sympathy. It was natural, but it threatened the defences she was building along the slow path to days in which there would be moments when her mind was not obsessed with what had happened. The nights were the worst, before she managed to sleep; then the mornings when she woke ready for a routine – the kisses, cuddles and chuckles, the dressing of a child's warm plump body – that was no longer there. It was why she was still with her parents: her own house had an atmosphere of expectancy, as though waiting for someone to come back from holiday, or a spell in hospital, and resume life as it had known it.

Sometimes Nancy took sandwiches to the shop – there was an electric kettle in the back room where they could make tea or coffee – but it was nice to get out for a while around midday, and she went for a snack then to the Bluebird Café, a clean place run by a Cypriot family, a couple of streets away. This particular day she had gone in perhaps a few minutes later than usual to find it full, and she was standing looking for somewhere to sit when a man she hadn't so far noticed spoke to her.

'Mrs Harper...'

It was Mr Daymer, at a table for two, with one of the few empty seats in the place opposite him. She said, 'Oh, hello,' and he asked how she was.

'I was just going to order,' he said. 'Perhaps you'd...' There was a newspaper on the other seat and one of those slim zip-up cases for papers, as though he'd been keeping the place for somebody. He reached over and moved them. 'Please,' he said. 'There's not much choice, anyway.'

She thanked him and sat down. As he said, there wasn't much choice, and she couldn't be rude.

'I haven't seen you in here before.'

'No. Do you come in much?'

'Yes, I suppose I'm a regular.' But he knew that. She somehow knew that he'd known. So what did he want with her that he had to pretend things and cap his pretence with a downright lie – she was sure he was lying – when he said, 'I had an appointment in town and just happened to spot this place.' He tried to smile, but it was a poor attempt. He wasn't easy. But how could he be? In his place she would have run a mile before meeting her face to face. So why was she so certain he'd been waiting for her, expecting her to come?

He handed her the menu. 'What do you usually have?'

'Oh, just a snack. Poached egg on toast. Something like that.'

'They've got what they claim is home-made steak and kidney pie, I see. What about joining me in that?'

She told him no, she wouldn't; that her mother would have a cooked meal waiting that evening. She didn't even want the snack now, just coffee, her stomach was all knotted, him sitting there bringing it all back so sharp and clear. But his eyes looked so hurt again she couldn't bring herself to get up and leave him.

'Are you living with your parents now?'

'For a bit. My mother thinks I'll stay for good now. She was always on about it before. I've got a nice home, though. I don't want to let it go.'

'I imagined you as an independent person.'

What did he know about her? He wasn't her class, though his voice was more careful than naturally posh. He was the head of a department coming down onto the shop floor in his nice suit and shirt and expensive tie, as at the firm she'd worked for before she married Jim. His fairish hair was just long enough, touching his collar, for fashion, but neatly cut. Like his fingernails. Neat hands: no oil, pit-dirt ingrained, work scars. A gold signet ring, heavy gold watch and strap. A Rolex. She'd seen them in shops, had once looked at some with Jim before he'd laughed and settled for something reliable at thirty quid with a face she'd thought rather smart. She had it in a drawer at home now. It was easy enough to look at his hands because it was too hard to look each other in the face.

He wouldn't have the steak and kidney pie when the waitress came for the order. No, he said, when Nancy said not to mind her, he wasn't really hungry and, like her, he would have a cooked meal this evening and he only ate a substantial lunch when he was entertaining firm's guests. And then, Nancy thought, he wouldn't bring them to the Bluebird, but somewhere like the Regent or the new motel. And when he had his meal

478

tonight it would probably be nearer eight then half-past six, with sherry or gin before it and a bottle of table wine to go with the food. Mr Daymer had married the boss's daughter, Nancy's mother had told her. Nancy's mother had looked up to the late Mrs Finch. Mr Finch apparently still lived in a big house on the other side of the park. She didn't know whether Mr Daymer was clever or not, but it probably didn't matter. He would be looked after in the firm because of who he'd married. He'd landed on his feet. He'd 'got it made', as Jim might have said. So what did he want with her? Oh, he'd done a terrible thing, but nobody was blaming him. Witnesses had said he hadn't a chance. June had been killed because silly young lasses had got her onto the wrong side of the road and then let her start to cross back on her own. They'd been taking care, had promised to take care, but their minds were too young to make them take care all the time. They knew, and they were sorry: everybody was sorry, but it was done. Mr Daymer was sorry, but, as her mother said, he couldn't bring June back.

Because they had just coffee there was an excuse not to linger. Besides, Nancy thought the management didn't like people taking up tables for coffee when there were others wanting seats for lunch. Mr Daymer asked her one or two questions about her job; did she like it, and did her employer look after her. Then he collected his belongings and went out with her.

'Goodbye,' Nancy said. 'Thank you for the coffee.'

'Please,' he said, 'don't forget. If there's anything I can do. Anything at all.'

'That's all right,' she told him, and then again, 'Goodbye.'

She had an idea that he watched her to the corner, but she didn't like to look back to make sure.

He telephoned her at the shop a week later. As it happened, she was on her own in the back room and answered herself.

'Could I speak to Mrs Harper, please.'

'Speaking.'

'Mrs Harper, this is Walter Daymer.'

'Oh, yes?'

'How are you?'

'Oh, pretty fair.'

'Is Wednesday your half-day?'

'Wednesday, yes.'

'Will you be doing anything then?'

A few weeks ago she could have answered him without hesitation: she would be doing the wash while her mother put the polish on a clean house around her.

'I don't know, really.'

'I wondered if you'd like to go for a drive with me.'

'Oh, well... I don't know.'

'We could run out into the country. It'd be a change for you.'

'I suppose it would. But you don't have to. There's no need for it.'

'I'd like to. We could have lunch on the way.'

She said, 'Just a minute,' and laid the receiver down, stepping away from the telephone, to think. She was standing like that when Marjorie came in from the shop.

'Are you still on the phone, Nancy?'

'Yes.'

'Are you all right? There's nothing wrong, is there?'

'No, I'm all right.'

The shop bell rang. Marjorie left her. Nancy heard Mr Daymer's voice, small in the receiver. She took a deep breath and picked the receiver up.

They had said they would meet in the market car-park, where Mr Daymer would be first and watch for her. Nancy hadn't wanted him to call for her at the shop; Marjorie might linger and, in any case, the proprietor always came in at the end of a working day. They were behaving, Nancy thought, like people with something to hide. But it was something better not talked about with others until it was over. Someone had told Nancy's mother that Nancy had sat with a man in the Bluebird. Nancy's mother had seemed pleased, probing for hints of a more than casual acquaintance, until Nancy told her it had been Mr Daymer.

Apart from anything else, Nancy's mother had said then, Mr Daymer was a married man. Nancy asked her if she thought his buying her a cup of coffee constituted grounds for divorce. No, said her mother, but it wasn't a big town and people liked to talk. Nancy had told her mother she might fancy the pictures this afternoon and her mother had said that might do her good, help to take her out of herself. Marjorie had seen the film in question and talked about it in some detail.

Mr Daymer took her into a white pub on a hillside on the way. He wanted to buy her a good lunch, but all she would have was a ham and salad sandwich and a glass of lager. When she asked him how he had managed to take the afternoon off, he told her that he would be driving up to Newcastle when he left her. They were building a factory there. She supposed he was important enough not to have to account for every hour of the day. He said he would also take the opportunity of calling to see his son, who was at a boarding school in North Yorkshire. Peter had been writing home about bullying in the school. Mr Daymer's wife, who had experience of boarding school, thought the lad was exaggerating; but Mr Daymer, who had not been away from home until university, felt that the boy was genuinely unhappy and wanted to get him transferred to a day school near home. He believed anyway, he said, that children should spend their formative years with their parents. Then he seemed to become embarrassed by talking about the boy, and changed the subject.

They drove on, arriving eventually at a hilltop from where, Mr Daymer told her, you could look into three counties. Or you could, he said, before local government reorganisation had changed so many county boundaries. He wasn't sure where they were now officially. It was very beautiful, though, and they were lucky with the weather.

'I remember,' Mr Daymer said, 'when I was a boy and I got my first bike. A secondhand "sit up and beg" it was. I attached myself to a local cycling club and they came up here one Sunday. It was a matter of pride with me to stay the course. Thirty miles here and thirty back. I slept for twenty-four hours solid after it. My parents thought I'd gone into a coma.' It sounded to Nancy as though Mr Daymer's parents had been no better off than her own. He was a poor boy who had married a rich girl, and there were things they didn't agree about. She wondered who most often had the last word. But now she had to get matters straight.

'Will you tell me something, Mr Daymer?'

'What?' he said. 'But look, I wish you'd call me Walter. Mr Daymer sounds so stiff and formal.'

She couldn't bring herself to do that, so she just said, 'Will you tell me why you wanted to see me again? Why you asked me to come out for a drive with you?'

'It's not an easy question to answer.'

'You must have a reason and I'd like to know what

it is. It seems to me I ought to be somebody you'd be best off forgetting.'

'It can't do you much good seeing me, if it comes to that.'

'No.'

'It's just,' he said after a minute, 'that I feel so... so inadequate. And sorry for you.'

'I don't need your pity.'

'It's not pity. Not in the ordinary way. Anyway, why did you come? You could have refused easily enough.'

She thought about that before she answered. 'Perhaps I'm sorry for you. You can't stop thinking about it, can you?'

'No, I can't,' he said. 'I want to help you and I can't. There's nothing I can do. You know, even a simple thing like a holiday. If you wanted to, I could arrange it.'

'I don't want your money. And there's nowhere I want to go.'

'No. Forgive me. It was a foolish idea.'

'What does your wife think about it? You've told her you've seen me, I suppose?'

'She knows about the other time. I told her what I've told you – that I feel helpless. I thought that first time that you seeing me as a person might help you to get some kind of perspective on it. That it might help you to forget the stranger – the instrument almost – who knocked down your little girl.'

She found herself looking at the interior of the car she was sitting in as a thought turned her suddenly cold. Was it the same colour? 'This isn't the...?'

'No, no,' he said. 'I got rid of it.'

She let her breath go. 'But you made it in your way to see me that other time, didn't you?'

'Yes,' he admitted. 'Yes, I did. And I wondered

afterwards; I wondered whether it had done either of us any good. Because–' his hands were trembling now: she felt that his whole body was trembling, and he was breathing like somebody who had just run up a flight of stairs – 'because,' he forced himself to say, 'when I think about you now I feel such an overwhelming tenderness and compassion, I can hardly hold it in.'

She began to cry then. He turned and shifted over in his seat as the tears came.

'Nancy...' He reached for her and pulled her close to him, his hand stroking her hair, and saying, 'Nancy, Nancy, please don't cry. I don't want to make you unhappy. That's the last thing I want. Please don't cry,' while, at last, she did cry; she cried and cried, as though her heart would finally break.

She cried because of what was past and because she saw with prophetic clarity what was to come. He needed her because of what he had done to her. He could not live with that without knowing her, and she could not turn him away until a time came, as it must, when he would have to go. She would move back into her own house and he would come to her there. Shyly, gently, with a romantic yearning, he would reach for her, and she would take him into her bed. He would be gentle there, too, soft with gratitude for the forgiveness of her body; and she would enjoy that, because it had been a long time for her. He would speak then of love, and the possibility of leaving his wife, disappointed at first, then grateful without knowing it, that she would not respond in kind. For something would happen. She did not know when; she did not know what. But something would happen and when it did she would tell him that he was not her man (he was not strong enough for her, though she would not tell him that). He need not be afraid she would cry for him; she had only ever cried for one man and he would never come back, and must he be hurt because she was not hurt again? Did he not want the peace of knowing that he had needed her for a time as she, she would say, had needed him, but that now it was done it was done? Was there no strength to be drawn from that, or was his heart one made for haunting? All this, she saw, would happen before she was alone again; though as she was the stronger and knew what was to come she would in that way be alone all the time.

They sat apart again. Perhaps, after all, she thought, as he did not speak, he would find the strength to draw back now. Unnoticed, a darkening sky had piled up behind the car. Rain suddenly lashed the windows. Nancy shivered. Mr Daymer put his hand in her lap. She answered its pressure with the pressure of hers. Then, knowing full well how it must, must end, she waited for it to begin.

The Glad Eye

When his wife threw Talbot out of the house because she suspected him of screwing around and he finally stayed out the best part of the night a couple of times as if to confirm it, he shrugged and told his friends he was sick of married life and had left her. Which in one way was true, since she had offered him the choice of changing his ways or going, and when he wouldn't promise, but denied everything in a defence that climbed from baffled innocence to blustering outrage, it ended with his packing a single bag and storming through the door.

Doreen thought she had handled herself extremely well. Though she was screaming inside, she had refused to be drawn into even raising her voice. All the same, he had gone. She had not expected that. She had seen herself shaming him, then, just possibly, in her own good time, forgiving. It couldn't be all that serious, because she could not understand what he was looking for outside that she didn't give him. Not that she was not bitterly hurt: all the time they had lived together while he was getting rid of his first wife, close and snug; and then, when they'd not been married two minutes, he started this, going out when she was on late shift at the petrol station and not coming home before dawn. The sheer barefaced cheek of it took her breath away. So, surprised but implacable, she let him go.

Talbot took temporary lodgings with a workmate, a married man with two children, who had a spare bedroom. Hollins's wife, a quiet woman, looked sideways at Talbot, but said nothing. Hollins himself, dismissing Talbot's initial explanation, told him he should either never have started playing away, or shown more sense in covering it up.

'Mick,' Talbot said, 'I got pissed a couple of times and kipped down here.'

'First I've heard about it,' Hollins said. 'Is that what you told her?'

'I tried, but she wouldn't have it.'

'And it's what you want me to say if she ever asks?'

'Would you?'

'Nay, lad, I might, but I can't speak for the wife. And where were you, as a matter of interest?'

But Talbot's face closed up.

He had met his first wife again after a long interval, running into her on the street in Leeds one day when he was buying discount spares for his car. They were face to face before either saw the other and then, though he might have gone on with a muttered word, she stood her ground and appraised him with that oblique dry look he knew of old, that look that said she had no illusions about him, so he needn't try it on with her. He'd liked that when they met the first time, when she let him see she

487

was interested. No pussyfooting about with her: she let you see what she wanted. And look where it had got her.

'How're you keeping, then?'

'I'm okay.'

'You've shaved your moustache off.'

He touched his bare upper lip. 'Aye.' He had worn it because he had such a baby face: that soft skin, those deep-set blue eyes.

'Grown up a bit, have you? Don't feel you need it to hide behind now?'

'It's a change.'

She had liked it. 'Got married again, did you?'

'Oh, aye. What about you?'

'Me?' She laughed and shook her head. 'Not me.'

'I wondered.'

'Did you? I heard you were living with her.'

'Oh, we were. Before.'

'It can't have been long enough to sort you out.'

'How'd you mean?'

'Before you put a ring on her finger.'

'She knew what she wanted.'

'If not what she was getting.'

'T'same thing.'

'Oh, no,' she said, shaking her head again. 'Never in this wide world.'

'There's no use you starting slagging me now.'

'No, it's got nothing to do with me now. Are you working?'

'Aye. What about you?'

'I am at present. No knowing how long it'll last, though, things being the way they are.'

'They'll pick up.'

'So folk keep saying. Voting Conservative now, are you?'

'Things are bound to pick up.'

'Because they can't get much worse?'

'I just bat on, get me work done.'

'You always were a grafter, I'll say that much for you.'

'Anyway, so you're all right?'

'Yes, I'm all right.'

'Got a chap?'

'Mind your own business.'

'Summat suits you.' With some of the old ease, he reached for and nipped gently the narrow roll of flesh under the T-shirt above the tight waist of her jeans. She took a step back.

'It's being rid of bother that suits me.'

'You're letting yourself go.'

'Not me. That can come off any time I like. Your ways kept me down to skin and bone.'

'There you go again with your slagging. Still can't admit there were faults on both sides.'

'Oh, I don't know why I waste my time talking to you. You'll never change.'

But he liked that extra flesh on her, that soft roundness.

'Anyway,' she said, 'I'm glad I bumped into you, because I've a bone to pick.'

'What's that, then?'

'You owe me some money.'

'How's that?'

'You had a maintenance order made out against you. I've never had a penny piece.'

He affected surprise. 'I signed a banker's order. You should have got it regular.'

She grinned. 'Banker's order. Whenever did you have a bank account? Cash in hand, that's what you always believed in.'

'Anyway, you're managing, aren't you?'

'Yes, I'm managing. And you can stuff your maintenance, for what it's worth. I only asked for it on principle.'

'Well then, there's no need to get bitter about it.'

'Bitter? You don't know the meaning of the word. You lead a charmed life. Folk let you get away with murder. Is she soft like that an' all?'

'She looks after me and I look after her.'

'Just like we were, eh?'

'We had some good times.'

'Were they worth it, though?'

'You didn't seem to think so.'

'No. You can only stand so much. Then you want to get rid and start clean again.'

'Where's it got you, though?'

'I'm my own boss. I can come and go as I like. And I don't spend half my time wondering what you're up to.'

'It must be lonely, though, isn't it?'

She caught the look in his eye and took his meaning.

'I don't have to have a chap at any price.'

'So you haven't got one at all.'

'Who said so? I told you before – mind your own business.'

She moved, stepped round him. He stood aside. They had exchanged positions when he said, 'Are you going straight home?'

'I might be, I might not.'

'Are you on the bus?'

'I shall be, when I'm ready.'

'I've got the car on a meter round the corner. I'll give you a lift.'

'You've no need.'

'It's on me way. Come on.'

With all the appearance of his old assurance, he

490

walked away from her and turned the corner without looking back. He was opening the passenger door of the old pale blue Ford when she came up behind him.

'How long have you had this?'

'A couple of weeks. I gave a bloke fifty quid for it. It was always letting him down and he couldn't knackle with it like I can. It misses a bit, but I'll get it right.'

He was turning the ignition key, but the engine wouldn't fire. He got out, lifted the bonnet and touched something under there, coming quickly back round and catching the engine on the throttle as it throbbed into life.

'Flooded.'

For some reason then he turned his head and gave her the direct open grin she remembered from the first time she had ever seen him, and for a second it was as though all that had happened between then and now had never been. But it would always be the same with him, she thought. As with his cars, so with his women. He would knackle and fiddle, patch and make do, and grin as he had grinned now, happy in the moment of temporary triumph. Something told her to get out now and leave him, but before she could translate it into desired action he had the car in gear and was moving off.

She began to direct him as they left the city and entered the built-up fringe which joined it to its satellite towns.

'I know the way.'

'No, you don't.' He looked at her. 'Not any more.'

'You've moved?'

He didn't ask where or why, but, driving where she told him to, changed the subject.

'What do you do with yourself?'

'What d'you mean?'

'Do you get out much? I mean to discos or pubs and such. You used to like your nights out.'

'Oh, yes. I'm not missing out on anything.'

'Aren't you?' This time as he twisted his head his look had in it more than idle curiosity.

'Watch the road.'

But it was there, in his mind, uppermost, unavoidable now, what he had wondered only moments after he'd met her, when he noticed that new and appealing fleshing out of arms and breasts. Who had she been with since they parted? How many? How often? Because he remembered how it had been with her, especially when she was at her best: soft, receptive, then mountingly demanding as giving joined with taking, after those laughing evenings round at the pub, and half a dozen martinis topped off with maybe a brandy and Babycham.

'I've been going to evening classes,' she said all at once.

'Evening classes? What to learn?'

'Conversational Italian.'

'What for?'

'I went on holiday to Italy, with a friend.'

'A friend?'

'A pal. I thought it would be nice to know a bit of the language for when I went again.'

'You liked it, did you?'

'Yes. All that sunshine. All them old buildings.'

'All them cheeky fellers.'

'Oh, they're all right. They reminded me of you.'

'How's that?'

'They're full of themselves. They think they can pull women like picking apples off a tree. Especially foreign women, on their own.'

'They specially fancy blonde women, an' all, I've heard.'

492

'Oh, yes. They're not above pinching your bottom to show it.'

'Cheeky bastards. Are they any good when it comes to the crunch?'

'What do you mean?' She asked, though she knew very well.

'I mean in bed.'

'You'll have to ask somebody else about that.'

'Will I?'

'I don't go abroad to get laid by somebody I've never seen before and won't see again.'

'You can get that at home.'

'I can get what I want at home and leave alone what I don't want.'

'Let's hear you say something in Italian, then.'

'*Vada tutto diritto.*'

'What's that mean?'

'Go straight on.'

'Hey, that sounds real!'

'*Prendo la prima a destra,*' she said after a moment. 'Take the first on the right.'

From the road by the complex of six-storey flats there was a view into the valley, and the estate where they had lived together.

'How long have you been here?'

'Six months. I swapped a three-bedroomed house for a one-bedroomed flat. There seemed more sense in it.'

'You didn't fancy going home to your mother?'

'Oh, no, I value my independence. What's your place like?'

'A two-bedroomed modernised terrace house.'

'Are you buying it?'

'It's hers.'

'She must be the thrifty type.'

'An aunty left it to her. But she's a good manager.'

'Lucky for you.' She spoke again with one hand on the door catch as he reached for the ignition key. 'You've no need to switch off, 'cos you're not coming in.'

'Did I say I wanted to?'

'Well, that's all right, then, because you're not. *La visita e finita.*'

'You mean you can't even thoil me a cup of tea, for old time's sake?'

'Not even a cup of tea. Your wife'll be waiting for you.'

'Oh, she goes out shopping with her mother Saturday afternoons.'

'Well then, you can go and be getting the tea ready for when she comes in.'

'You know,' he said, 'just because we couldn't hit it off living together doesn't mean we can't be friendly.'

'I haven't tried to scratch your eyes out, have I? I should say that's friendly enough, considering.'

His sigh was loud. 'We had some good times at the beginning.'

'And some bad times at the end.'

'It's a pity, though, when you think about it.'

'Look,' she said, 'we agreed to differ. We parted. I've picked up the pieces. You're married to somebody else. So what's your game? What are you after now?'

'There's no game. I'm only trying to be mates.'

'On your bike,' she said. 'On your bike, Des, lad.'

She opened the door, got out, left him, walking to the building without looking back. The lift doors were closing on someone else as she entered the vestibule, so she walked up the two flights to her flat. There she unlocked her door, put her bags in the kitchen and then, before unpacking them, walked into the living-

494

room and to the window which looked out onto the road. The car was still there and he was out with his head under the bonnet again. In his brilliantly white newly laundered shirt of the type he always liked to wear in his leisure hours, sleeves turned back, three buttons open at his chest, impervious to the chill in the day, he looked like someone meant for a warmer climate, and he reminded her once more of the Italian men and the saunter of their lightly clad bodies, at expansive ease in sun and air. Then, as though he were acting out the part for her benefit, he stood away from the car with his hands on his buttocks before looking up and, seeing her, spreading his arms in a huge gesture of resignation.

'Now what's up?' she said aloud, as he pointed first to himself, then to her, and began to walk towards the building. 'Oh God, he's coming in.'

He was on the landing, trying to get his bearings, when she went to the door.

'What do you want now?'

'I've sprung a leak,' he said. 'I can fix it, but I'll need a bucket of water to get me home.'

He advanced on her before she could speak, as though her allowing him in now was the most natural of courtesies and not even worth a request. She thought for a second of stopping him and telling him to wait; then, as he put his hand on her arm and turned her through the doorway, she went without protest.

She told herself afterwards that it was when she heard the door shut behind him she knew he was back in her life. A part of her was astounded that she couldn't resist, that she could not summon again the spirit with which she had first refused to ask him in; but that part could only observe now as the rest of her, as though hypnotised by the inevitable, waited for the clinching move. 'If it doesn't come,' she told herself, 'I'm safe. I can send him on his way and no harm done.' But she knew with a certainty she would have risked her life on that it would.

He crossed to the window and was standing where she had stood to watch him.

'It's all right here,' he said.

'I like it.'

'Doesn't it get the sun?'

'In the evening. I'm not bothered about during the day. I'm out then.'

'Aye,' he said, 'it's all right. Cheaper than the house?'

'A bit.'

'Aye,' he said again. 'Got to watch the pennies. No sense in chucking money away.'

'I don't know if I've got a bucket big enough,' she said.

'I can always make two trips. Just so's I can fill up and get home without boiling.'

He followed her into the kitchen. 'You wouldn't have such a thing as a length of insulating tape?'

'I don't think so. I'll have a look.'

She had put her yellow plastic bucket into the sink and was running water into it. Now she bent to a cupboard below and took out her box of odds and ends: screws, nails, curtain hooks, a small screwdriver.

'No, it doesn't look like it.'

'I'm sure there was a roll among the stuff I left.'

'Oh, I've had a clear-out since then. I threw a lot of stuff away when I moved here.'

'You should allus keep a roll of insulating tape. It's one of the handiest things about a house.'

'Like a man,' she heard herself saying, 'but I've managed without one of them.'

'Well, look; if you ever need a job doing 'at you can't manage yourself...'

'You mean I can ring your wife up and ask her to send you over?'

'I'm only trying to be friendly.'

'You said that before.'

'I meant it. I don't harbour any bitterness over what you did; all that's in the past.'

'Over what I did?' Her laugh was short and bitter. 'God! That's rich, that is. Watch your bucket.' She made to pass him and leave the confined space of the kitchen; then, a moment later, without any seemingly deliberate movement, but like something subtly choreographed and accomplished before the eye could follow, he had her trapped behind the door. 'You're a buggeroo, aren't you?' she said. 'A first-class buggeroo.'

'Sandra...'

'Oh, you remember my name as well now? That's the first time you've used it this afternoon.'

'Sandra... I've thought about you a lot, you know.'

'You're a bloody liar. You'd have walked straight past me in the street if I hadn't stood in your way.'

'Only because you took me by surprise. I was a bit... well, embarrassed.'

'I'll bet you can't remember the last time. And for God's sake watch that bucket. You'll have it all over the floor.'

He reached behind him without stepping away from her and turned off the tap.

'Sandra... there's no need for all this.'

'Oh, bloody hell,' she said as she felt his hands on her. 'God, I ought to have my head examined.'

497

Some time later she reached cigarettes from the bedside cabinet, lit two and handed him one.

'I shall have to get rid of some of this weight.'

'What for? Why do women no sooner get a bit of what a feller likes, they want to get rid of it?'

'It's this spare tyre, though. It bothers me.'

'Do some exercises for it, then.'

'Only solution. If I slim for it I shall lose it off my tits and arms as well.'

'You don't want to do that. They're just right now.'

'You noticed, didn't you? As soon as you saw me. You noticed and you thought, there's old Sandra all fattened up for a quick kill.'

'I thought nowt o' t'sort.'

'What did you think, then?'

'Well, I noticed. I hadn't seen you for three years, so o' course I noticed.'

'Then it struck you while we were talking that you fancied me, so you thought you'd see if there was anything doing.'

'I never really stopped fancying you.'

'You bloody liar. You lie like breathing.'

'Are you trying to kid yourself now you didn't enjoy it?'

'Enjoy it or not, I shouldn't be here like this with you.'

'But you did enjoy it, and you are here, so stop reckoning you wish it hadn't happened.'

'Won't she be wondering where you are?'

'I told you, she's with her mother.'

'You've not got her pregnant yet, then?'

'No.'

'Maybe it was you after all, then, the reason we didn't have any.'

'I'm not ready for a family yet. There's plenty of time for all that.'

'It'd be funny if you'd managed it with me, this time, wouldn't it? That'd be a laugh.'

'Why don't you relax and stop nattering yourself?'

'I can't.' Suddenly she was crying. 'Oh, God, all that time, all that trouble. I knew I should never have stopped when I saw you. You were walking on and I should have let you. I thought I'd got over it and now here we are again.'

'Give up,' he said. He slid his arm back under her head and turned her towards him.

'I don't want any more trouble.'

'There'll be no trouble.'

'There won't because you're not coming here again. I hope you understand that.'

'We'll talk about it later.'

He stroked her shoulder. Behind his closed eyelids he was stroking Doreen. He had watched her as she slipped off garments, seen the shadows as they shaped her body. In a moment she would be with him. She knew when he watched her like that and she slowed her movements as if deliberately making him wait.

He moved, twisted, then straddled and covered her.

'Oh, God, no!' Sandra moaned. 'Don't say you can do it again so soon!'

They were demolishing three blocks of old property in the middle of the town. There were two huge deep square holes with a tall temporary fence round them. Des stood by his lorry, taking a few minutes out for a smoke while the JCB turned on its caterpillars and loaded broken masonry from the third site. Everything around was thick in dust. Fresh clouds of it rose and settled each time the shovel dug and took its load. Hollins came up, crowbar in his hand, and spoke to Des through lips caked with it.

499

'You what?'

Hollins leaned in and raised his voice against Des's ear. 'I said isn't that your missus over there?' He motioned with his head.

Beyond the piled rubble two women were walking along the road between this site and the fence enclosing the next. One of them was Doreen.

'Haven't you seen her lately?'

'No.'

'I thought you'd been back to try and make it up.'

'You know what she did, don't you?' Des said. 'She changed the locks on the doors so's I couldn't get in.'

'She doesn't spend all her time in the house, does she?'

'No, but if she feels that strong about it I'll be buggered if I'll crawl.'

'Got another nest to keep warm in, anyway, haven't you?' Hollins stood beside Des and watched Doreen and her friend. 'Smart lass, though. You know how to pick 'em, if not how to keep 'em. Look, they're off in for a drink.'

The two women were going through the front door of the King's Arms.

'Look, Mick,' Des said, cover for me for five minutes, will you?'

'He wants this load away before dinnertime, doesn't he?'

'Get it filled. I'll be back. If he turns up, tell him I got taken short for a crap.'

He walked towards the pub and went in through the side door. The landlord came out of the Gents in the passage as Des looked at the signs on the doors.

'Tap-room for you, lad, if you're wanting a drink.'

Des went into the big room at the back, where there

500

was heavy linoleum on the floor and the stools and benches were covered in crimson leatherette. No upholstery or carpet for his clothes and boots to soil.

'Give us a pint of lager.'

He usually drank only tea during the working day and he swallowed a third of the cold liquid before setting the glass down again, feeling it cut through the dust in the back of his throat.

There was a way through from this bar to the one in the lounge and he could see chairs and tables, but no one who was in there.

'Are there two young women in yonder?' he asked the publican.

'Aye. Just come in.'

'There's one in a brown frock with like big yellow flowers on it. Tell her there's somebody in here wants to talk to her, will you?'

As the landlord went through he moved along the bar counter to where he would be out of view if Doreen looked across. He glanced round the room. There was no one else except two middle-aged men at a corner table, making up betting slips for the afternoon's races.

The door opened.

'Oh, it's you. I thought it must be.'

'Doreen. I saw you go by.'

'What do you want, then?' She turned her head and looked at the two men, her voice restrained, low-pitched. She hated scenes.

'I want to talk to you.'

'Get talking, then.'

'I can't here, like this. Are you working tonight?'

'What difference does it make to you?'

'Look, I've only got a couple of minutes before the boss is on me back. Can't I come round and see you?'

'What for?'

'I want my tool kit.'

'I'll leave it out for you.'

'I want to say I'm sorry.'

'So now you've said it.'

'Give us a chance, Doreen, love. Is this all it meant to you, two minutes' talk in a pub?'

'You know what it meant to me. But you didn't give tuppence for it.'

'Well, I do now.' He swallowed the rest of his drink. 'Look, I shall have to go now. If I lose this job I don't know where I'll get another. I'll come round tonight, about eight o'clock, and we'll have a talk.'

'I don't know what there is to talk about.'

'Give us a break, lass. I can't carry on like this.'

'You should have thought about that before.'

'Christ, you're hard! Have you no feeling?'

She hesitated, glanced at the two men once more. 'I'd made my mind up it was finished.'

'Well, if it is, it is. But at least let's talk about it like two grown people.' He looked at her, knew he was at his most abjectly appealing, and waited while she wavered before his direct conscience-stricken gaze.

'Come round if you want, then. But make it half-past seven. I've somewhere to go later on.'

Sluiced clean from head to foot and dressed in a newly washed shirt and his best fawn slacks, he arrived at the door ten minutes early and waited for her to answer his ring. She had changed into a sweater and cord jeans. Her make-up looked fresh and he followed her into the living-room on a hint of perfume.

'I haven't got long,' she said.

'Why'd you change the locks?'

502

'Because I thought I'd very likely come home one night and find you tucked up in bed.'

'It's a job when a bloke can't get into his own house.'

'My house. It was mine before you came and it's still mine.'

'Well, our home.'

'A lot you cared for our home, or our marriage.'

'Look, Doreen, I didn't come here to argue. We've had all that. I know I've been a rotten sod.'

'Oh, you're admitting it now.'

'Yes, I am. I've been a rotten sod and I want to say I'm sorry and see what we can work out.'

'You mean to say you're admitting you'd been with another woman?'

He sighed. 'Aren't you going to ask me to sit down?'

'Please yourself.'

He was carrying a four-pack of lager. 'Do you want a drink?'

'Not specially.'

'Do you mind if I have one? I'm not finding this easy.'

'Confessing your sins?' He didn't answer. 'You know where the glasses are.'

He went to the kitchen, took two glasses, opened one of the cans and poured into each.

'Here, you may as well join me.'

'Put it down.' He placed the glass on the low table in front of the sofa. The gas fire was on low heat. The room was warm to him. She had always liked more warmth than he did.

'I asked you a question. You didn't answer.'

'What was that?'

'I said, are you admitting now that you'd been with another woman.'

He shook his head. 'I can't deny it. I should have owned up before you threw me out.'

'Why didn't you, then?'

'Because I was scared you wouldn't understand.'

'What makes you think I will now?'

'I don't know. But I've got nothing to lose now, so I thought I'd chance it.'

She shook her head as he offered cigarettes.

'What was she like?'

He shrugged. 'She was nobody.'

'Was she a whore?'

'Hell fire, no! She was a divorced woman. She was a bit lonely and willing and, well, I was tempted.'

'What was so special about it?'

'Nothing.'

'Have I ever refused you?'

'No.'

'So what did you want from her that you weren't getting at home?'

'I don't know. Ask other fellers; they might explain better than me.'

'I'm not interested in other fellers. I'm asking you.'

'Doreen, love, look, listen.'

'I'm doing both.'

'Look, if a marriage is going to break down as easy as that, it's about time people stopped getting married.'

'A lot of people are. I only wish I'd been one of 'em.'

'I know I can't expect you to take me back straight away...'

'If at all.'

'...but I have said I'm sorry. I've come here tonight, cap in hand, to try to save our marriage.'

'You'd better tell me how you intend to do it.'

'Well, like I say, I can't expect us to pick up now

as if nothing'd happened, so what I thought was if we took a bit of time over it and saw each other for a while without living together, we might get things sorted out.' She reached for the glass in front of her, lifted it, then put it down again without drinking. 'I mean, we could find out how we felt about it after two or three months, or maybe six. P'raps it'd take a year. I don't know, but I'm willing to wait.'

'What do you mean, see each other?'

'I mean we'd be separated, but I'd come and take you out.' He got up and crossed to sit beside her. She moved along the sofa to leave space between them. 'I don't like to think of not seeing you at all, but I do see 'at you'll need time to get over it and make your mind up whether you want me to come back for good.'

'Where are you living now?' she asked after a moment.

'I'm using Mick Hollins's spare bedroom. His wife's a nice woman. I'm comfortable enough for the time being. I mean, I'm hoping it won't be forever.'

'I thought you might have moved in with her.'

'Hell, no!'

'I wish it had never happened.'

'So do I, love. But one mistake. We can't let it spoil everything.' He took her hand and slid his fingers between hers as she instinctively made to pull away. 'What do you say? Where's the harm in giving it a try?' He chuckled and squeezed. 'We can reckon I'm on probation.'

'You can talk,' she said. 'I'll give you that.'

'Somebody's got to talk for both of us,' he said, 'or else that pride of yours'll finish us for good.'

'I call it self-respect.'

'Whatever you call it, you can carry it too far.' He looked at his watch and went to fetch his glass. 'What

505

time are you going out?' he asked when he was beside
her again.

'Soon.'

'Is it something important?'

'Why?'

'Chuck it and come out with me. I've missed you.'

'You should have thought of that before.'

'I'm thinking about it now.' He pulled her gently
back till their heads were resting a foot apart. 'What
do you say?'

'I suppose I can be late.'

'Is nobody calling for you?'

'No. It's some women I meet round at the pub, after
bingo.'

'You've never taken up bingo,' he said. 'Not you?'

'No, I meet them after they've been.'

'Well, we could go to another pub and then I could
drop you off there for the last half-hour.'

'I don't want them seeing us together, thinking I've
turned soft.'

'All right. I can understand that. Till you know your
own mind. So let's just stop here and talk a bit more.'
He moved his face towards hers. 'Can you manage a
kiss on it?'

'You didn't say that was part of the bargain.'

'I didn't think it was till I got you near me. But, you
see, I've missed you and there's no reason why we...'

He sat up, twisting in his seat. He took a drink, put
down his glass, then hunched forward, his arms on his
knees. She waited without moving from where he had
left her.

'Well, I don't know whether it'll work or not, but we
are married, even if we shan't be living together, and
all I know is I don't want to be tempted to go drinking

506

and birding with the lads at the weekend. And I don't think you... well...'

'What?' she said.

'I don't think you want to live like a widder-woman either.' He shifted on the sofa and looked at her, taking her hand again, this time holding it between both of his. 'You don't, do you? I mean, let's face it – seeing you, knowing you like I do, it's more than flesh and blood can bear.'

They went, later that evening, to two pubs, neither of them where she was due to meet her friends. Des chose carefully, knowing the kind of place she liked – or tolerated – and the kind she liked to say she wouldn't be found dead in. He made her laugh a couple of times and for a moment then she could almost forget how he had let her down. For a moment, until her face clouded again and she toyed pensively with her glass while he sustained the conversation single-handed and kept a careful watch on every shift of her mood from the corner of his eye.

He left her a little after one. She awoke from a doze to find him dressing by the bedside. He leaned over to kiss her as he heard her move.

'I'd like to stop till morning,' he said. 'But a bargain's a bargain. Thanks for everything, and I'll be seeing you.'

She had been cold in bed ever since he had left. Now, as she heard the house door shut quietly behind him, she stretched her slack limbs into each warmed corner then, spreadeagled, fell into a deep sleep.

The clack of the letterbox woke her again. She had not slept so soundly for some while. Her body felt drugged with satisfaction. She was surprised that he had gone without argument and thought that she would not, as she'd felt then, have had the will to deny him had he insisted on staying. But this was how it should be. She would call the tune now, until she was sure he was sufficiently contrite and she could take him back. There was, as he had said, plenty of time to consider that. In the meantime, she wished there were someone to bring her a cup of tea.

Des had the Hollinses' youngest on his knee and was helping her with her reading. Bess Hollins, cooking and laying the table for the evening meal, watched them with that slow smile which lingered perpetually, deep in the jet-like lustre of her eyes. It was of a piece with her unhurried movements and her soft Devon voice. She was just beginning to show with her third child.

'I'm sure Uncle Des has had enough of that for now, Claire.'

'Nay, she's right where she is for a minute or two.'

'You're good with them. You should have a family of your own.'

'Not much chance of that, is there, with me placed as I am just now? Anyway, I've got a ready-made family here. What more could a chap want?'

'You're comfortable, are you?'

'As snug as a bug in a rug,' Des said. He squeezed the child. 'I bet you've never heard that one afore, young Claire – "as snug as a bug in a rug". Eh?'

'He is an' all,' Hollins said. He was kneeling on the floor near the sink, with parts of the vacuum cleaner laid out on a sheet of newspaper.

'But look,' Des said, 'I've been meaning to say. I'm taking a lot for granted. I don't want to get under anybody's feet. The minute you feel I'm a bother you've only to say the word.'

'Oh, no,' Bess said. 'Mick and I had a talk about that. You're no trouble to us. You pay your way and the children like you. You can stay as long as you like.'

'But when number three arrives you'll mebbe be needing the room.'

'Oh, it'll be a while before that one needs separate accommodation. And perhaps by then you'll have got your own affairs straightened out.'

'Aye, well. As long as we know where we stand.'

'Might you be going to see your wife tonight?'

'I thought I might pop over later on.'

'He's not saying which one,' Hollins said.

Bess had not heard. She wasn't meant to. It was between men. In the knowing grin that Hollins threw at him over his shoulder there was, with its just discernible glimmer of envy, an invitation to Des to share for a moment his surely understandable glee in the situation he was so cheekily and adroitly manipulating. But Hollins could never remember that cheek was a quality Des only ever recognised in others. For all he gave his friend was that characteristic little frown which Hollins finally understood as the look of one whose cross in life is to be perpetually misjudged.

And Hollins, turning back to his repairs, thought, 'Well, that must be it, then. That must be how it's done.'

Foreign Parts

He's doing it again. Those two girls passing the pavement table. 'I wonder where they disappear to when they get older...' I thought nothing of it when he first brought it up, but now that he's mentioned it again and he's watching them right into the crowd, I'm bound to own to a twinge of irritation. No, it's not jealousy: just that after I've agreed to come here and we're together so far from home I don't think he should be looking at other women. Not women yet, either, which is hardly designed to let me forget my own age and the flaws I see in the mirror every day or when I catch a glimpse of myself at that certain angle in a shop window. For I only have eyes for you, dear... Was that how I imagined it, wanted it? No, come on, Cheryl; we're mature people, worldly enough to plan and take this holiday together simply for the pleasure of it. But still...

'There seems to be a particular type of young girl here,' was what he said before. 'They have long legs, narrow hips and full high breasts.' But then, he said, all the grown women you see gossiping in doorways and carrying shopping-bags in every town and village on the island are short-legged, stocky, wide-hipped. So where do all the young girls go? That's like another song...

'Do you find them attractive?' I'm asking him now, careful to keep it light and neutral.

'Oh, I'm not really drawn to dark-skinned women. Especially women who don't mature well.' That grin he's giving me before he drinks. He's got the nicest, wickedest grin I've ever seen in a man. What drew my eye the first time I noticed him; and the way it drives out the sadness that sometimes lurks at the back of his eyes when his face is still.

I don't know what that wife he's separated from looks like, but I can make two compliments out of what he's said: me – the wrong side (if only just) of thirty – with my nearly white hair and my transparent white skin. I can't complain that I don't turn him on. 'You almost glow in the dark,' he said when he saw me on the bed in the heat that first night. Then he was all over me while I lay there, not stopping him but not giving yet, wondering if this was what I'd foreseen at the end of all the white lies and secret planning. But we were both fagged-out from the lateness and the journey and George was over-excited, he said, at that first-ever full sight of me and too quick at the end, for which he apologised. 'It'll be better for you next time,' though it wasn't much, though nice enough and I could see he enjoyed it so I pretended so he wouldn't feel let down.

'It doesn't matter unless you're thinking of something permanent, does it?' Then I chide myself because he could think I'm hinting at him and me.

'I don't follow.'

'Whether they mature well or not.'

511

'You mean chasing women at their best age? Not really my style.'

'No.' But I don't really know. I don't really know him, come to that. He could still be living with his wife, for all I know; him on one side of London and me on the other and only ever meeting somewhere in the middle. I'm perhaps only one of a string of women he makes up to on his rounds. Except he can hardly go abroad on holiday with all of them. Perhaps I'm just his choice for this year.

The pleasure boats are filling up for trips round Grand Harbour. We've talked about going later. That sea so blue it's almost fierce and the white light that sometimes turns to pink at sunset on the stone fortresses standing on this side of the point and right round the other side. I wondered, I must confess, what kind of place we'd come to that first night, driving from the airport through the dark and nothing to see but piles of white stone all round and the pot-holed roads and the bouncing, swaying minibus that quite turned my stomach over, and me congratulating myself that I hadn't felt a tremor on the plane. But then we woke to the sun...

I love the sun: day after day of settled heat without a sign of a thunderstorm or the clouding-over you get at home. But we should be somewhere else, away from this crowded corner of the island, where the streets are narrow and stifling and here on the promenade there's exhaust fumes from the endless traffic churning by. The buses, single-deckers, such as you've not seen in England for a lot of years; George says we send old buses here to die – like elephants all go to that secret graveyard – but the Maltese do them up, painting them in that pale green livery and putting them back into service. Scores of them, you can see, outside the main

512

gate at Valletta. Adaptable, the Maltese, George says. They've learned to be. If everybody at home worked as hard, the country wouldn't be in the mess it is in. Cheap and frequent, too, the buses. Perhaps we should have gone by bus and not bothered hiring the car. As it is, the island being so small, we've seen it all in the first few days, and now... No, we're not bored and you do want to relax on a holiday and not spend all your time dashing from place to place; but it does mean we're thrown more on each other.

Head back, the sun on my face, as George goes inside the bar for more drinks. I must be careful.

It's fiercer than I'm used to and I go lobster-pink before I brown. What was George saying about nude pin-ups of girls who've been sunbathing in bikinis? They're brown everywhere except the intimate parts and they look as if they've got leprosy in their breasts. Well, he'll have to put up with that, since there's nowhere on this island where you can take all your clothes off. They're devout Catholics here and the women keep covered, which was why when men first looked at me, like those two locals are doing from the table along the pavement, I thought I was perhaps showing a hint of nipple or a too natural bustline without my bra. Until I realised it's my colouring that's the chief novelty. They think I can't see them stripping me where I sit. But I can, and I don't mind as long as I've got my sunglasses to protect me. Maltese men are not as brazen as I've heard some Spaniards and Italians can be, so there's no feeling of danger in it. In times gone by, I suppose, I could have been some rich man's favourite and lived in one of those big secret houses in Valletta or Mdina, brought out occasionally to be shown off to his friends, and nothing to do but pamper my body, keep my skin white and not get fat.

At home, men hardly look at me twice. I'm just another face in the crowd.

Would I have taken to that kind of life, I wonder? Being kept as a favourite, I mean. I do like men. I like having them around to look after things, make arrangements, take me places. Funny to think I'd have been married to Ronnie now, and perhaps two or three kiddies growing up, if he hadn't got that rare disease they said rats carry. Swimming in that flooded quarry – he loved his swimming, Ronnie did; how he'd have loved all this clean blue water here – when he cuts his foot on a rock and in only a few days he's dead. Of course, I was shocked and I cried and everybody felt sorry for me as well as him, with the date already fixed and the bridesmaids' dresses made. I couldn't tell them – I never told anybody – when I realised a few months later I'd never really loved him, not as I always think people who marry ought to love each other, and I felt relieved that I'd not gone through with it and found out too late. Though perhaps I wouldn't have found out. Perhaps I should have grown to love him, settled into married life like all the rest, made the best of it. That's living for most people, after all, isn't it?

And as there's been nobody special since, people who remember think I've never got over him, that I must be comparing every eligible man with him and finding them lacking. Well, they are, or else it must be me, because it's never got as far as that since then. Oh, there have been men, and one or two adventures. That time with Mark, when he took me up to Leeds with him because he needed secretarial help, and after dinner and a nightcap he came to my room in his dressing-gown and pyjamas. I'm not on the pill, I told him, and it's the wrong time in the month and I wouldn't risk it like that anyway. And if he didn't have contraceptives in his pocket, ready. I

514

asked him, because I was put out, what had made him think I was such a sure thing, and he said he hadn't been sure at all but it would have been stupid to find I was willing and lose the chance because he hadn't taken precautions in advance. When he smiled, he made me laugh with his little-boy-caught-in-the-jam expression, and I had to admit the sense in what he said. It was nice, too. He was slow and gentle. Though it did cross my mind to wonder afterwards, when there wasn't another time, whether it wasn't consideration that had held him back, but rather when it came to it I wasn't all he'd hoped. But I'm liable to do myself down like that and he was awfully busy, always dashing here and there, and it wasn't long before I left for this other job.

George brought his precautions with him, this being a Catholic country and him not wanting the embarrassment of going into a shop and asking, let alone running the risk of being refused. Imagine finding ourselves here, on our own, with a room and a bed for the first time and not being able to do what we came for. Well, partly what we came for. I caught sight of the box when his case was open. Good lord, I thought, taking in the size of it, he can't be expecting it twice every day. But no, he was a bit eager the first couple of nights, then last night he just tucked his arm round me and went to sleep after a kiss. Trust me to lie there then, wanting him to wake up and take me. I nearly got hold of him in the night to bring him on, but I thought better not. If it happens that he can't till he's rested a day or two, it'll really embarrass him. After all, he's not a young man any more. Not an old man, by any means, but over forty. And men have their pride in these matters.

He's a long time coming with those drinks. He'll have got chatting to the barman. Likes to get to know

515

the natives, he always says. I hope those two men don't start thinking I'm on my own and waiting to be picked up. No, I'm obviously on holiday and waiting for someone. They're perhaps hoping it's another woman. I wonder what kind of time two women could have here, if they were that way inclined. Now, I didn't like that. Not the way that one looked then spoke to his friend and they both laughed. I'm not showing anything, am I? So what's the joke?

The joke is, it isn't me they're looking at now, it's this tall girl coming towards us. Blonde. Swedish or German, I'd guess. Nearly six foot, golden brown everywhere you can see. Straight, as though she's carrying a basket on her head, shoulders back, bosom out, free but firm inside her white blouse, and sauntering, sauntering for all the world as if she's on a beach, alone and miles from anywhere. Style. Oh, God, they don't half make you feel small and timid and provincial.

Come on, George, you're missing this one. She's not dark-skinned and she won't disappear as she grows older. She'll still have most of it when she's fifty. No, don't come out till she's gone, even though I want to spend a penny now and I daren't leave the table empty because there isn't another one free.

I'll write that card to my mother. She'll expect more than just the one to say I arrived safely. We arrived. Maureen and I. 'I've never heard you talk about Maureen, have I?' she said, because even though the office is miles away and she's never likely to meet any of them I somehow couldn't use any of their names. 'What's the matter with Mavis this year?' 'Oh, she's got a feller.' Which she hasn't. She wanted us to go away together this year like last. 'A friend who lives nearby,' I told Mavis. 'Maureen.' My mother doesn't know that George exists, though Mavis does of course, because him coming into the office every three or four weeks is how I met him. And then when he first asked me out it was when we were alone, naturally, and since he has no reason to tell the others his business, it was more or less left to me to tell them or say nothing. It was because I didn't know his domestic circumstances that I kept quiet. Then I went on like that. Maybe I've got a naturally secretive nature. Or I just believe in personal privacy. Anyway, I didn't feel in need of their advice about the wisdom of going out with a married man, even if he is separated. They'd naturally have thought we were having it off straight away, the minds they've got, and we weren't. We just went out for a meal every two or three weeks and, apart from a kiss or two and some touches a bit more intimate, that was it. No doubt things would have gone further faster if we'd had somewhere private to go, but we hadn't. It was hard enough finding places to park the car so that we could go as far as we did. Which was no doubt frustrating for him, though I liked him for his patience and the way he wasn't desperate to get there at all cost. Or didn't show it.

Then: 'I'm going on holiday, Cher. Like to come with me? To Malta?' And, to make sure I didn't misunderstand: 'We could go as a couple. The only place we'd have to show separate passports would be the airport.'

So he fixed it all. Simply booked a double room through a travel agency. We could have got a flat, which would have meant no fellow guests to size us up, but George didn't want the bother of self-catering and neither did I. Whose business is it besides ours, anyway? People do it all the time nowadays. I brought the cheap ring with me, though. George smiled but didn't rib me about it. 'If it makes you feel easier,' he said. And I have to admit it has. It's a modern world. You don't have to live like an old maid because you're not married. All the same, you don't have to shout it from the rooftops either.

'Here we are.'

'You've been a long time.'

'Did you miss me?' His grin, turning it into a compliment.

Don't nag him, Cheryl. You didn't mean to use that tone of voice. Or did you?

'I was just wondering why it was taking so long.'

'I was chatting to the owner. Likes the British. Makes a change these days. He says he had tears in his eyes as he watched the old Ark Royal leave Grand Harbour for the last time.'

'Do you know where the Ladies is?'

'Somewhere inside, I expect. Go in and ask.'

'I don't like to.'

'There's nothing to be shy about.'

'It's the way they look at you.'

'The men? It's your imagination.'

'Oh, is it?'

'You want it both ways.'

'What?'

'You don't like the men looking at you but you're offended when I say they don't.'

'I know when men are looking at me.'

And I do. Like he's looking now. Sidelong. Eyes everywhere but meeting mine. Him and the others. All alike. Not with me any more. Inside himself. Thoughts about me but not for sharing. Not with me, at any rate. Oh God, I wish I hadn't come. I wish I hadn't seen that look. It's gone now, but I saw it. He doesn't know. He doesn't know that I know he can talk about me to someone else. 'Went abroad with this willing piece I picked up on my rounds. Shared a bed in the sunshine. Nothing serious. All right for a fortnight, but don't want to get involved.'

I'm due to start my period. How can I stay so close to him for another week, share his bed, his bathroom, see him first thing every morning and last thing at night?

'Are you going, then, before we move?'

'Move where?'

'Anywhere you like.'

'I thought you must have somewhere in mind.'

'I'm easy. Where would you like to go?'

'Hampton Court, Kew Gardens, Richmond Park.'

Now why did I say that? He's looking at me now with a little frown.

'Don't you like it here?'

'I was just joking. You said anywhere I liked.'

'There must be something you'd like to see.'

'Haven't we just about seen it all?'

'In less than a week?'

'It's a little island.'

'It seems smaller to little minds.'

'Sorry.'

'Don't mention it.'

'I meant, what did you say?'

'It wasn't important.'

It was, though. And I did hear it. Is that what he really thinks about me? He's good at hiding his feelings. I mean, they don't show in his face. If I have irritated him nobody could tell from his face. But he did say it. Straight out. As good as telling me I've got a small mind. Now when did he come to that conclusion – before we came or since we got here?

He's bored with me, that's what it is. He's lost interest in telling me things. When he notices something now he keeps it to himself. He's saddled with me, all this way from home. He can't make friends, either, without including me. He's probably wishing he was on his own. If he's not now, he will be when I tell him the curse is due. A fat lot of good I'll be to him then. Because that's all he brought me for. It must be.

'Look, do you want me to go and ask?'

'Sorry. What?'

'Sorry or what – which?'

'Sorry?'

He's playing with me now. I always suspected he could have a clever tongue.

'Would you like me to go and find the Ladies for you?'

'No, thanks. I'll go.'

And, of course, like so many little things you think you'll find embarrassing, it's mostly in the mind. The man behind the bar hardly looks at me as he answers the question I don't finish.

'Can you tell me where the–?'

'Up the steps, madam.'

Yes, I shall probably start properly in the night. I must be careful about the sheets, and I shall have to tell George. Funny, I was half pleased that I wouldn't be bothered with it for a few days – that I had the perfect excuse – but now I'm fancying him, thinking about it, remembering what it was like – or what it would have been if I'd enjoyed it more. Suppose I said I wanted to go back to the hotel now and we went up to the room and I let him see what I wanted and I gave him a really good time, without one of those things, unprotected, nothing between us – surely I'm in the safe period now – he'd like that, wouldn't he? He'd be especially grateful for that.

He's got to be glad he came. He's got to remember it and me, not tip me out of his thoughts like Mark did after that time in Leeds. Oh yes, he did, Cheryl. We know he was here, there and everywhere and you left for that other job, but he could have kept in touch, spared you an hour or two for a meal, or just a drink, showed you that even if he hadn't enjoyed your body enough to want it again there should still be some tender feeling – or at least respect – between people who've been as close as that. Close? Mouth to mouth, skin to skin, flesh to flesh. How close was that, ever? You've been used, they'd say; the types who sit around in baggy frocks and talk and talk about sexist advertising and exploitation and men who look at them in the street, until you think they must live every minute of their lives close to screaming. So why can't I say I used them – Mark and George – that I had them for my enjoyment? I can't because I didn't. They had me, and I let them.

'You're easeful, Cheryl,' my mother says to me when I come home and put my slippers on and curl up near the fire with the telly. 'You never stir yourself. You let everything come to you.' And what doesn't come I do without. That's why she said what she said when I told her I was going abroad for the first time. 'Do you good. Take you out of yourself.' To where?

I wonder what he's thinking – George – as he sits there waiting for me. His bare arm's stretched out as his fingers hold the cold glass on the table. You think they're thin, his arms, but they're strong and the muscles hard under that down of hair that's almost auburn in the sun. He's lean and hard like that all over, like a board, and not the slightest hint of a paunch. Only in that touch of scrawniness about the neck can you see – oh, ever so clearly when you think hard about it – what he'll look like as an old man, when the adam's apple shows bigger and the skin pulls tight over his cheekbones and round his mouth. His eyes are the kind that will turn paler then and perhaps water at every touch of a cold wind.

Oh, George, who are you? Why are we in this strange place together? What do you want with me? Tell me, George, because I'm lonely.

'There, that couldn't have been so bad. Was it?'

'No.' His humour's back. Perhaps I misjudged him: my imagination reading things that aren't there.

'Shall we go back?'

'To the hotel?'

'Uh, huh. It's noisy and smelly here, with all the traffic. We can lie out on the roof.'

'If everybody else hasn't the same idea.'

Come on, George, let me surprise you. We'll call in the room to change and then I'll surprise you; and afterwards we'll talk, because it will have been different and you'll know that.

The cars they hire out to you, they're all the same make, George says, all the same colour, all with around 30,000 miles on the clock. And the tyres. George wouldn't accept the car the garage man brought him until that bald front tyre was changed.

'If I as much as drove out of the front gate at home with a tyre like that,' George told him, 'I'd be pinched on the spot.' 'But it's not raining,' the man said, oh so reasonable. Oh so reasonable is what they all are. 'What's the trouble?' they'll say if you find anything wrong. As though sensible men can reach agreement on any subject on earth. But George was firm and the man said to follow him and drove round to a garage in a back street where he took a wheel from an identical car and swapped it for ours. We both laughed when the

522

other car, with our bald tyre, turned up the next day for another guest. 'Are you going to tell him?' I asked, and George said, 'He's got eyes in his head. And, like Mr What'shisname pointed out, it's not raining.'

There are even more cars outside the hotel now and George says to go in while he finds a place to park. It's a relief to be out of that tin box in heat like this.

'Oh, Mrs Jennings.' The girl at the desk calling. 'Mrs Jennings.'

Nobody's addressed me by any name at all, except madam, so far, and I'm nearly to the lift before it dawns.

'International telegram for your husband. It came just after lunch and I didn't know where to reach you.'

'Oh, right. Thanks.'

It's confusion that carries me on into the lift and up to the room without waiting for George. Who knows he's here? The lift doors again. Sounds carry with all these bare tiled floors. His tap.

'The girl downstairs gave me this.'

'For me? A telegram?'

Turning away to give him a moment of privacy. The sea glinting between the white buildings beyond the dusty road. A family – mother in blue-flowered bikini overflowing with rolls of mahogany flesh, father in trunks, hair everywhere except on top of his head, two small children – crammed, with deck-chairs onto a sliver of sand. All the sand there is. Always there, every day, foreigners, rude; they stare if you go anywhere near them, as if you might march up and ask for your turn.

'It's Kathleen...'

Me: blank. Who?

'She's been taken ill.'

His wife, of course. Mrs Jennings.

'Is it serious?'

523

'I shall have to put in a phone call.' George looking round at the telephone as though he doesn't know how to start.

'Who knew you were here?'

'My father. I had to leave word with somebody.'

Because he couldn't cut himself off. He's still tied. He's separated but he leaves word where he is. If not who with.

On the phone now to the girl at the desk. 'Hullo... Yes, this is Mr Jennings. I want to make a call to England. It's a London number...'

Listening to the number he gives her. Could be anywhere in Greater London, except for the three or four exchanges I happen to know.

George sits on the bed, his back to me. The bed where I was going to give him a good time, something to remember. Why can't I feel for him, for her? Because I don't know her. Mrs Jennings. I don't know him; nothing of all that life of his, past and present, out there. Only a joke, a laugh, some figures of speech, the way he holds his knife and fork, chews food; his smell, his weight and touch in the dark, his spasm and his gasp.

He's telling me nothing. Sitting so still. 'Surplus to requirements.' That's one I've heard him use. Now it's me. 'Not wanted on voyage.' I won't ask.

'I'll be about downstairs.' If you want me.

Cool lobby with grey and yellow tiles. The girl's face turning from the switchboard, eyes behind huge dark glasses. She knows. They all know. Do they care? None of their business. But I've made it their business by wearing this ring. I care what you think, which is why I'm pretending. Mrs Jennings. No, I'm not Mrs Jennings. I'm me, Cheryl Green, on a dirty fortnight with Mrs Jennings's husband and what's it to you?

If it's serious enough for a telegram, he'll have to go home. Find an early flight and leave. And what shall I do? 'You stay on, Cher,' I can hear him saying. 'It's all paid for and you may as well have the benefit.' Of what? Curious looks? Questions from the bolder or kindlier ones? 'What a pity your husband had to leave.' 'Yes. He was called away on urgent business.' Still living that pretence after he's gone.

But what can I tell my mother if I arrive home a week early myself?

Well, I know what I'm going to do for a start. Get rid of this bloody ring. Not another minute will I wear that.

I'm standing on the rocks between the road and the sea when I hear him call. He waves as he walks towards me.

'Did you get through?'

Why am I asking? He'll tell me what he wants me to know. Just as much. Just as little.

'Yes.' A deep breath. 'She's taken an overdose.'

That quick flick of a glance as he said it, anticipating my reaction, which is something like three seconds of pure naked panic before, with my heart pounding, he says, 'She's all right. They found her in time.'

'Can you get a flight home?'

A shake of the head; something stubborn about the mouth. 'I'm not going. It was a put-up job. She never intended it to work.'

'How can you know that?'

'I know her.'

'All the same...'

'She's pulling the string, that's all. Letting me know she's still holding the other end. She didn't want me when she had me – not what I call wanting – but she just can't let go.'

525

George talking now, letting it all come out, everything he's never told me before. How he went for her quietness, thought she was different, ladylike; found she was just dull, didn't care, went through life in a trance; wouldn't think of a child, but let him take his occasional satisfaction till shame turned him off and he couldn't any longer. Now she was bleeding him dry of every penny she could, living in that expensive mortgaged house, never lifting a finger to provide for herself, just hanging around till he couldn't imagine what she did all day, what she thought about, how she passed her idle life: a kept woman with no obligation to provide his pleasure.

'She knew where I was. She'd get it out of the old man. He'd soften when she pleaded with him. He'd like us back together. Separation and divorce, they're all against his grain. I can't make him see what she was doing to me. She wasn't unfaithful, didn't drink too much. She liked money but she kept things going in a fashion. Why couldn't I make the best of things, look at people who had real troubles? Well, in twelve months' time I'll be legally free. And in the meantime I'm not going to let her spoil this.'

'All the same, it won't look very nice, will it? Your wife taking an overdose while you're abroad with your fancy woman?'

'Don't talk like that. Why do you say such a thing?'

'Because...' Shrugging. Because it's true, George. What does he want me to say?

'I can't tell you how much I've enjoyed this. This peace. It's early days yet, Cher, but I'd like to think...' Then he sees, as I move my hand. 'You've lost your ring. Have you taken it off? Where is it?'

'Down there.' And, as he looks puzzled: 'In the sea.

It floated. I watched it for a while. There's no tide here, is there? It could float there till somebody sees it and fishes it out and wonders how it got there.'

'Did you take it off because of the telegram?'

'Better an honest fancy woman than a counterfeit wife.' I like that: it's well put. I've surprised myself.

'Listen, Cher; I want you to understand. I'm not being callous when I refuse to run home to her. She does need help, but not from me. This is her last throw. When this doesn't work, she'll leave me alone.'

'Why is it so important, stopping on here?'

'Because it's not finished. Because if we go back now I don't think things will ever be the same. It's early days, like I said, Cher. I shan't be free for another year; but I hope when I am you'll still be around. Will you?' Taking my ringless hand, he asks again. 'Will you, Cher?'

And how easy it is once the question's put; once I know exactly what he wants.

'If you really want me to be, George.'

Because I do get lonely, and time is getting on, and I do like having a man around to look after me and take me places; and all the rest I can manage. It's what you give for what you get, and I'll be as fair as I can. There is something I ought to tell him if I were being totally honest, all the cards on the table, and that's that I feel I know his wife now, know her better than I know him (or how could I have been on the wrong tack all this time?). But it's a thing he'll never see just now and with a bit of luck perhaps it'll never dawn on him later. Because I'll be better than that. Oh I will, I will, I will...

Huby Falling

I was at school with Clifford Huby. He must be the most famous product of an establishment not given to turning out celebrities or even fitting its sons for much in the way of material success. Huby managed it on both counts: the wealth through a business acumen none of us knew he possessed and the fame through a taste for high living and a second wife who had taken off most of her clothes in a couple of minor films and whose breasts photographed well in a wet swimsuit on the deck of a yacht off the Cote d'Azur. Now notoriety...

We were a wartime intake, most of us scholarship boys from working-class homes, with just a few fee-paying pupils among us, of whom Huby was one. Secondary education in those days was limited to the bright and to those who had the cash to compensate for their dullness. Classes were small and everyone knew everyone else. But Huby was never in my set, whose activities often bordered on, and occasionally slipped over into, the criminal. Eddie Duncalf, who, the last I heard of him, was driving a lorry, once went to a party at Huby's house and reported that the guests were mostly boys from the snobbier and more expensive schools in the locality and their standoffish sisters; so I gathered that Huby's family had solid connections. Scholastically, Huby was a plodder. In his relationships he displayed a tactlessness which irritated some to the point of cursing him, and there were instances of reckless behaviour which endangered not only himself but others. Nor was it unknown for him to pick on someone smaller than himself in a manner not so much brutal as foolishly gleeful. 'You don't know your own strength, Huby, you daft bugger!' Well, he found out. And some of us had already found his soft centre.

Our headmaster was Dr Heathcote Jefferies, a fiery little jumping-cracker of a man whose voice when he was enraged – and he often was – could be heard halfway through the long corridors of the school. A stern disciplinarian, and remorseless pursuer of malefactors, he gave weekly addresses in assembly, remonstrating with us about our patriotic duty, which was to refrain from sabotaging the war effort by slacking, smoking, declining to disturb the brilliantined perfection of our hair by wearing the school cap, and chatting up the girls from the nearby high school at the bus stop. Jefferies had four sons: one had studied law, another medicine; there was one in the church, and one still at Cambridge. We never knew his real opinion of us – it was usually expressed in tones of blistering contempt – but we were not the stuff such achievement is made of; though we did eventually manage a parson and a handful of schoolteachers on top of the foundation of clerks and mechanics. Oh, and a couple of town councillors, one of whom once fought a general election for the Tories in a solid Labour constituency.

And, of course, Huby.

It was easy enough later to realise the foreboding that must often have gripped our elders during those first years of the war; but whatever fears did possess them either they hid them well or we discounted them. It seemed inconceivable to us that we could possibly lose. Some of us had fathers or brothers away in the forces, which brought it a little nearer home. There were evacuees among us who spoke of destruction rained from the skies, in queer southern accents which we cruelly mocked. And uniforms everywhere, austerity, rationing, the blackout. But either morale remained remarkably high or we were deplorably insensitive.

The blacked-out nights cloaked our after-school activities. What did we do during those long dark evenings when no glimmer of light broke the facades of houses, when you could not tell if a shop was open or shut till you'd tried the door and stepped round the heavy entrance curtain, when elderly women walked carefully along by the sparse glow of blinkered torches, armed with hat-pin and pepper for defence against the known enemy or that masquerading as daytime friend? We went to the cinema as often as our funds allowed, acquiring an encyclopaedic knowledge of the Hollywood film of the period; but there were hardly any school societies and no youth clubs, except the religion-tainted groups run by the local churches, which we were at pains to avoid. So we must often have been bored and in this boredom we sought and found the excitement of petty crime. But we were never apprehended by anyone vengeful enough to make an example of us and the taint did not spread into adult life. At least, so far as I know. One or two of those adolescent rogues standing where Huby is now would tempt me to hindsight and the smug satisfaction of having seen it coming all those years ago. But Huby was not in our gang.

A core of staff too old for military service held the fort among the comings and goings of men conscripted and released. We moved steadily up the school, some of us making the most of what was offered, others inexorably losing ground as they frittered away the advantage our scholarships had given us in a society preponderantly made up of those fated to leave school at fourteen for a life dominated by hourly wage-rates and the time-clock.

A changing awareness of the girls down the road brought vanity, which was expressed by a facsimile of adult smartness, in pressed trousers, polished shoes and slickly parted hair. The greater part of our time was spent in the ordinary pursuits of boyhood; but we sampled experiences such as smoking, gambling and fondling girls in the shelter of long grass or the darkness of ginnels with the curiosity and awakening appetite of anyone growing through one stage of life into another which seems more pleasureful and exciting.

There had been a firewatching duty since early 1940: a master and three senior boys sleeping in school every night – the master in the staff room, the lads on campbeds in an attic in the old building. They were supposed to patrol the grounds during an alert and tackle any fires with stirrup pumps until help arrived. The duty was voluntary, but most of us did it for the novelty of sleeping away from home and being in school but outside the discipline of the timetable. We read and yarned, played cards, had a dartboard until too many wild shots pitted the door with holes and it was taken away from us. Some of us smoked, too; always with an ear cocked for footsteps on the bare steps and a paper ready to waft the incriminating fug out of the window. It was an adventure and our activities, though some in violation of the school rules, were innocent enough. Until I did a duty with Eddie Duncalf.

I became aware in the early hours of the morning that Eddie was not in the room. He was absent for some time. The next day I asked him where he'd been. He grinned.

It turned out – and I was not the only one who knew about it – that Eddie had somehow obtained keys which gave him access to the pantry in the kitchen and the store cupboards there. From them he was helping himself to small amounts of the foodstuffs used for school meals: butter, sugar, cheese, tinned meat – anything, in fact, which was scarce or rationed. I went with him once, but creeping along those dark corridors in the night, expecting at every corner to bump into the master in charge, was too much for my nerves. I could never fathom anyway what Eddie did with the stuff. There was not enough for him to trade on the blackmarket, even if he had the contacts; and I couldn't imagine his mother accepting it without explanation. I could only assume he hid it and concocted treats for himself when he was alone in the house.

He made his last raid on a night when Huby was sharing the duty with us. As Eddie crept from the room and down the stairs, Huby spoke across the distance between our beds.

'He's a fool.'

'What?' I responded drowsily.

'Duncalf. He'll get nabbed one of these times.'

'What d'you mean?'

'Don't make out you don't know.'

I snored gently into the darkness.

But Huby was to be proved right; or partly so. For, although Eddie was not caught in the act, the outcome was the same. The cook had apparently known for some time that pilfering was taking place. This particular week she had taken an extra-careful inventory and when Eddie over-reached himself and stole more than usual she was able to pinpoint the losses with accuracy. There was an enquiry among the kitchen staff. No culprit could be found there. Then a cleaner remembered seeing currants and raisins on the floor of the firewatching room. Heathcote Jefferies questioned the masters first, then summoned to his study all the lads on that week's roster.

We lined up, jostling shoulder to shoulder, in an arc across the front of his desk. Jefferies, at the window, waited till we'd settled before spinning round and reaching for a list of names. He checked us off against this without speaking, then took his stance at one end of the mantelshelf.

'There's been some stealing from the pantry.' His gaze raked across the line of faces.

'The culprit is someone who has been on firewatching duty in the last week.'

No one spoke. Jefferies must already have selected the likelier suspects, for there were among us some members of swots' corner who would no more have robbed the pantry than smoke a cigarette or fail to do their homework diligently. Three of them, Tolson, Lindsay and Carter, did duty together and were standing at one end of the line. Jefferies began with them.

'Did you steal from the pantry?'

'No, sir.'

'Did you steal from the pantry?'

'No, sir.'

'Carter, did you steal from the pantry?'

'No, sir.'

'Did you steal from the pantry?'

'Oh, no, sir.' This was Billy Morrison, a good lad, who knew about Eddie but would never have dreamed of giving him away.

Jefferies paused here and changed his tactics.

'Do any of you boys know who did steal from the pantry?'

This was one of Jefferies's least likeable traits, his inviting you to shop someone else. Morrison spoke for all of us. 'No, sir.' I thought afterwards that it was a trick of the light, but I wanted to believe that his lip did visibly curl and that Jefferies noticed it.

Jefferies returned to the direct question.

'Did you steal from the pantry?'

'No, sir.'

'No, sir.'

'No, sir.'

'No, sir.'

'No, sir.'

Eddie: 'No, sir.'

'No, sir.' Me.

A stonewall defence. He couldn't break it. He had come to Huby, who was last in line.

'Did you steal from the pantry, Huby?'

'No, sir.'

We were through.

But Jefferies, stuck with all those monosyllabic denials, let his gaze linger on Huby for another couple of seconds. And Huby, unable to make do with that simple and unbreakable 'no', rushed in and sank the boat.

'I was in the room, sir.'

Jefferies pounced. 'Which room?'

'The firewatching room, sir.'

'How do you know?'

'I don't know what you mean, sir.'

'How do you know you were in the firewatching room?'

'I was, sir.'

'You mean it couldn't have been you who stole from the pantry because you were in the firewatching room at the time.'

'Yes, sir. I mean, no, sir.'

'So, if you didn't do it, it must have been somebody who was on duty with you. Eh?'

'No, sir.'

'But you've just told me that it happened while you were on duty, but it wasn't you because you were in the firewatching room.'

'No, sir.'

'So you weren't in the firewatching room?'

'I was, sir.'

'At the time the pantry was being burgled.'

It was no longer a question but a statement. Huby floundered. He went red. His mouth trembled. He was lost.

'Yes, sir.'

Duncalf came back to the form-room alone twenty minutes later, beaten and angry, and with a threat of expulsion hanging over him which, as it happened, was never carried out. 'You absolute blithering idiot, Huby. If you aren't the most useless sod I've ever met.'

But he wasn't, as he was not many years in showing.

It was working for the press that kept me in touch with Huby's early fortunes and made me aware of him again when he really started to rise into the big time. I ran into him now and then before I moved to a provincial evening paper from the local weekly. He was clerking for an uncle, marking time before he went off to do his National Service. When he came back he began to do

535

small deals in scrap metal and before long he'd branched out into war-surplus materials. He made quite a bit of money, married a girl from the town and moved into a new four-bedroomed house.

Then I lost sight of him until, subbing on a national daily in Fleet Street, I began to see news pars about him and, when his first wife divorced him and he married a girl fifteen years younger than himself, the occasional photograph. By this time he was going up fast; everything he touched seemed to prosper. His interests were widespread: mail order, unit furniture, domestic appliances. I don't know what quality he discovered in himself and nourished so successfully that he became a millionaire by forty, because, frankly, I don't understand that kind of talent.

It was the business editor who ran through the list of Huby's interests for me and who later, aware now that I'd known him once, warned me of the whispers which preceded the investigation into his affairs and the eventual bringing of charges. Facing the music with him are a couple of fellow directors and the secretary of one of his companies. I don't know, of course, whether Huby is guilty or not, whether his substance is solid or just a bubble blown by him or his colleagues. But a number of offences do seem to have been committed and it looks as though the real issue is who is going to carry the can.

What I'm wondering now is whether Mr Heathcote Jefferies Jr, QC, who is to open for the Crown, is as good an interrogator as his father was, seizing on any tiny slip to force, with the ruthless sharpness of his mind and the overwhelming power of his personality, a breach in a solid wall of falsehood. Does he know that Huby was one of his father's pupils years ago? Probably not, and it doesn't matter. The old man had no doubt forgotten the incident long before he died.

But I know what I'd be feeling if I were in the dock with Huby tomorrow, aware that the penalty this time will not be six of the best but more like a year or two inside and a paralysing fine. And waiting – oh, the sweaty-palmed, stomach-fluttering waiting – for Huby to be offered and succumb to that fatal temptation to enlarge.

Good

Caroline rang again that morning, at a quarter to nine, after Fred had left the house but before peak rate started. Jean accepted the transfer-charge call.

'Mum. Sorry about that, but I'm short of change.'

'That's all right, love. You must never let that stop you.' Jean put a smile into her voice. 'Mind you, your father did have a word or two to say about our conversation ten days ago. It was on the bill that came yesterday. Nearly four pounds' worth.'

'Oh, dear! Did you tell him what we were talking about?'

'No, I didn't. Time enough for that, if –' She stopped herself. 'What news have you got?'

'None, really.'

'You mean there's no change?'

'Hmm.'

'How's Alan?'

'Well... fretting a bit.'

'I expect he is. But from what you told me...'

'Oh yes. All the same, it's worrying.'

'This thing is going to be a worry in years to come as well, unless someone can do something about it. Have you seen a doctor or do you want to wait till you come home?'

'It could be too late then.'

'Don't be silly. I didn't mean that. I'm sure it's nothing now.'

'I've made an appointment here. I'm going tomorrow.'

Jean's younger daughter had irregular periods, a minor nuisance until she met a boy at university and began to sleep with him. Sleep with him! Ye Gods! What Jean's mother would have said to her! What Caroline's father would say if her education was put at risk. Not that it would come to that, but Jean did wish that Caroline was where they could talk face to face, taking as long as they needed, and not nearly two hundred miles away on the end of a telephone. Thank goodness, though, the child felt able to share her worry. She had always told all three of them – they both had, come to that – that if anything was wrong they should come to them first. Anything, she had said. Because even the nicest, best adjusted of children had to live in the same world as everyone else.

Stephen was still in bed. When she had finished her chat with Caroline, Jean took him up a cup of tea. He had shown no desire to go to university and so had not screwed himself to that extra pitch of effort to qualify for entrance. Now Jean rather suspected he wished he had: the three extra years of study would have kept him off the labour market. He did not know what he wanted to do. In better times he could have taken any old job until he found his path. But the better times had slipped into economic recession and there were no jobs; all he had now was this morale-sapping life on the dole. Fred said he had a school full of younger Stephens. 'What can I tell them?' he would say. 'How can I spur them on when I know full well that most of them are destined for the scrapheap at eighteen? Some of these kids may never work. I can't see whoever's in power getting three and a half million back into jobs. We shall reap the whirlwind of all this in ten or fifteen years' time,' he would brood at his most pessimistic, 'with an alienated generation that won't be integrated into a society that's shown such little regard for them.'

Stephen stirred under his duvet as she went into the room and spoke to him. She put the teacup on his bedside table and told him not to let it go cold. He had always been sluggish in the mornings. Jean had sympathised with all three of them in the amount of sleep they needed while they were growing. But this lying late in bed every day was not right for a young man of Stephen's age. Yet how could she blame him? What challenge did the days hold to get him up each morning? The world was wasting him.

'If you want me to cook breakfast for you, you'd better not be long because I've got to go out.'

'I'll see to it myself.'

'There are eggs and bacon and sausages in the fridge.'

'Naw. Mebbe I'll have them at lunchtime.'

As his head emerged, she noted again that he badly needed a shave. But she did not put that down to his present lethargy: an incipient beard seemed to be a mark of his age group.

'What will you do today?'

'Dunno.'

'You could start by cleaning this place up. It's like a tip.'

'Oh, Mum.'

Yes, Oh Mum. Afraid now of nagging, Jean mostly let things slide, thereby abetting him in his apathy. During the last depression, in the thirties, proud men had polished their worn shoes, snipped threads from fraying cuffs and collars and gone out each morning to haunt labour exchanges and factory gates, then shop-window gaze or linger in the reading-rooms of public libraries until it was time to go home and pretend for another day that they were still employed. Until what savings they had ran out and they had to face their families and own up.

Jean's mother had told her things like that. The bad times for her had had bad luck thrown in for good measure. Widowed when Jean and her brother were still young, she had turned her hand to any mortal thing that was legal and decent to bring them up and put them through grammar school. Jean's standards of fortitude had been set by her mother's example. You held on, never let go, worked till you could hardly stand, asked for nothing that was not your due and fought tooth and nail for everything that was. 'You know all about poverty,' Jean could hear her saying, 'but I'll see you're never familiar with squalor'. But that extra two years at grammar school – four earning years between her and Jack – had been the limit of what could be managed. No college or university for them. Jack might have become a civil servant, instead of settling for local government; she herself would surely have become a teacher; probably out of the house again and doing something interesting once the children had stopped needing constant care and attention. But that had become her role, the purpose of her life: to look after Fred and the kids, make a good home for them, see that they had everything she could provide.

Had she done it well? She could only measure that

541

against the failure she saw every day: surly, disaffected children; husbands and wives with hardly a good word for each other; others leading their own, separate lives, drifted apart, some of them split up. She had been lucky: the two who were away kept in touch, came home; all three confided. There had been that terrible time, quite early on, when Fred had become infatuated with that unmarried teacher from the school in Calderford. 'I can have a friendship, can't I?' he had pleaded, when even she had seen what couldn't be hidden any longer. And for months she had sweated through nights when he didn't touch her and others when he clung wordlessly to her, making love in a silent frenzy, as if to drive the demon of infidelity out of himself.

And they were still together. It was never spoken of, never brought up, thrown out. Yes, she had done it well and she had been lucky. All the same, there were times when... But never mind.

Stephen had not come down by the time she had drunk another cup of tea herself and washed up her and Fred's breakfast pots. She put on her coat, took her shopping bags and called from the foot of the stairs: 'I'm taking my key in case you want to go out. Make sure you lock the door and I'll see you for lunch.' She waited. 'Do you hear?'

She backed the car carefully into the street. She had the use of it during the day now that Fred, with a doleful recognition of his thickening waist, had taken to cycling the two miles to school. This was one of those mornings when she was glad not to have to wait for a bus: blustery, whipping the poplars of the garden opposite, with rain in the wind. Straightening the vehicle, she fastened her seatbelt, managed that stiff initial push into bottom gear and drove off to her first call.

'Was that your car making all that noise?' Millie Tyler asked, handing Jean her cup of coffee.

'I'm afraid the exhaust's gone. I heard it rasping a bit the other day but I quite forgot to ask Fred or Stephen to look underneath. It's nearly four years old. Stephen gets on to Fred regularly about part-exchanging it while he can still get a decent price. But Fred's having one of his periodic economy drives.'

'Oh?'

'I don't mean he's penny-pinching. But I know he'd like us to see Venice this year and he does feel the burden of Caroline's fees and having to subsidise Stephen. I mean, he's got to let the lad keep most of his dole if he's to have any life at all.'

'Oh, yes, you've got to give them their chance.'

'Well, Caroline, anyway. All Stephen can hope for at present is that things will pick up before all the stuffing's knocked out of him.'

Mollie's two daughters were living away, married to men with good prospects. Mollie herself, widowed twelve months ago, was only just recovering from having a breast removed.

'But how are you feeling?' Jean asked.

'Oh, pretty fair. I think they're just about ready to give me a clean bill of health.'

'Oh, that is good news, Mollie.'

'Yes, it could all have been a lot worse.'

'Is that a new dress?'

'Yes. I thought I'd treat myself.' Standing, Mollie drew herself up in the closely-fitting tweed frock. 'You couldn't tell, could you?'

'You'd have no idea. You look as good as ever.'

'Yes, I look all there,' Mollie said wryly, 'even if I know I'm not.'

Jean had always admired Mollie's figure and envied her ability to keep it trim yet shapely without the fussy regimen that so many women had to adopt. In her late forties, she was a woman with looks enough to choose her way into a good second marriage, if ever she wanted one. But what now? Jean wondered. At what stage did you tell a man that what he saw and liked was not all it seemed? And what were the chances of being doubly lucky and picking a man you really wanted who would also swallow his disappointment and accept it as part of the bargain?

'I've got a bit of shopping to do. I wondered if there was anything you wanted.'

'I'm all right, Jean. I can manage all that.'

'Well, you look fit enough just now, but you didn't sound it on the phone the other day.'

'Oh, that was just this bug that's going around. You're sick and on the run for twenty-four hours and then it leaves you. Have you managed to keep clear of it?'

'Well, so far, yes. There's been a bit of it among the staff at Fred's school.'

'He's all right, is he, Fred?'

'Yes, he's fine.'

'And how's Caroline? Still enjoying herself.'

'Oh, yes. She's settled to it nicely.'

'When are we going to talk about that coffee morning?'

'There's the flag day before then.'

'Yes, well, we ought to give people plenty of time, so's they've no excuses. Otherwise it'll be the same old story: leave it to Jean; she'll see that it's all right.'

'They usually rally round, when it comes to it.'

'Some do, some don't.'

'Don't make me out to be a martyr, Mollie.'

'That's your word, not mine. Whenever have I heard you moan?'

'What have I got to moan about?'

'There's not one of us who hasn't got something, at some time or other.' She looked up as Jean sighed. 'That came from deep down. Was it for something special?'

'I was just thinking that you shame me, Mollie. With all that's happened to you, what right have I to grumble?'

'If you've got something to grumble about, grumble.'

'That's just the point. I haven't.'

All the same...

The woman came back into the greengrocer's as Jean was transferring her purchases from the counter to her shopping bag.

'I'm just wondering if you've given me the right change...'

Jean only half heard as she lingered, thinking there was something else she needed. The customer went again. 'Sorry, my mistake.'

The woman behind the counter took coins from the still open till and handed them to Jean. 'There's your change, dear. Thirty-seven pence.'

Jean was outside before it clicked in her mind. Opening her purse, she checked the coins in there, then took those the woman had given her from her pocket. She went back in and to the head of the queue.

'Excuse me.'

'Yes, love.' The woman glanced up from her rapid serving.

'My change.'

'It must be catching today,' the woman said. 'I did give it to you, you know, love. What was it, now? Thirty-seven pence.'

'Yes, but you've given it to me twice. I know by the coins in my purse. I hadn't that much loose change when I came in.' She handed the money back.

'Well, thank you.' The woman smiled. 'I must have been dreaming.'

'Both of us, come to that,' Jean said.

'Aye, well, I don't know about you, love,' the woman said, 'but it's not dinnertime yet, and I could lose a small fortune by half-past five.' She put her head back, her fleshy throat above the neck of a shocking-pink jumper pumping uninhibited laughter out of her broad chest.

Mrs Rawdon stopped Jean as she reached the pavement on the other side of the street. Preoccupied, Jean would have walked past her.

'Mrs Nesbit.' She was a small deferential body in a worn tweed coat.

'I'm sorry. I hadn't seen you.'

'Oh, you've more to think about than me.'

Jean looked into the pale crumpled face and wondered, as she had before, how anyone without an ailment could nowadays age so much before her time.

'How is your husband, Mrs Rawdon?'

'That's why I stopped you.' The woman shook her head. 'I'm afraid...'

'I'm sorry.'

'We cremated him the day before yesterday.'

'Had he been in hospital?'

'Oh, yes. They had to take him back in the end. I'm glad I've seen you, though. I thought you ought to know, you having been so kind to us.'

'It was nothing,' Jean said. 'I happened to know about the Trust, that's all.'

'It made all the difference, though, having that holiday.

546

We both enjoyed it. It seemed... well, it seemed to bring us together again.'

'I'm glad. Are you all right now?'

'Oh, I shall manage, don't you fear.'

'Good.'

Jean had pleaded the woman's need for a break, more than her husband's. Should she, she had asked, be penalised for her loyalty to a man who had spent all on drink and gambling? They did like nice comfortable cases of hardship, these guardians of ancient funds, where all concerned were equally deserving.

'Are you all right yourself, Mrs Nesbit, if you don't mind me asking?'

'Yes, of course.' Mrs Rawdon was peering solicitously into her face. 'Why?' she found herself adding.

'Just my feeling. I saw you as you crossed over the road, and wondered.'

'I was miles away.'

'Yes. I expect you can always find plenty to think about.'

'It seems to find me, Mrs Rawdon.'

Surprising Jean considerably, Mrs Rawdon said, 'In an empty mind there's room for nothing. But you can always cram a bit more into a full one. But excuse me. I've delayed you long enough.'

It was on the tip of Jean's tongue to say, 'Let me know if I can be of any help,' but she held it back and let the woman go, not knowing whether she might be asked later for something she could not give. One had to be practical about these things.

Was she all right? Of course she was all right.

It was as she was scoffing at Mrs Rawdon's curious fancy that the feeling came upon her. She could not have told anyone what it actually felt like.

There was no sense of faintness or physical fatigue, but quite suddenly she realised that she could not make up her mind what to do next. Aware that she had not moved from where Mrs Rawdon had left her, she looked in through the big windows of the supermarket, saw the queues at the checkouts and knew that she could not go in. It was silly. The crush was unusual and would soon clear. There were things she needed, things she had left the house to buy. But she did not want to enter the place. The thought of doing so aroused in her something like panic.

She felt sweat break out on her neck and forehead. Well, at her age, she knew what her doctor or her friends would make of that. And yet, there was something more. What the devil was it all about? What was it all for? If she bought groceries now they would get eaten and she would have to come back for more. As when she cleaned the house or weeded the garden. The house got dirty again; more weeds grew. So it went on. Nothing was ever settled. You ate to live, to eat to live, to eat... Brought up a new generation to do the same. And what was ever accomplished?

Forcing her legs to work, she turned and went slowly along the parade of shops: jewellery and watches, shoes, meat, an optician's, magazines and newspapers... There was another supermarket, recently opened, round the corner. People she knew had shopped there. She had told herself she would try it some time and compare its range of goods and prices. She quickened her pace slightly, turning her head once as, after several seconds' delay, she fancied someone had given her a greeting.

The premises of the new store were not a conversion but entirely new, of raw red brick, built on the site of a demolished building. Jean entered, took a wire basket from a pile and went through the barrier. The layout of the shelves was strange. She looked at the hanging notices which offered general guidance and consulted the slip of paper on which she had made her list.

Special offers, new lines, loss leaders. So many pence off this and that, but be careful because now you were in here with everything to hand you could lose that advantage by paying over the odds for something else. She wandered, her mind still drifting, refusing to focus, while she picked things up, looked, put some things back, put others into the basket. She was buying more than she had come for. It was hard not to do that in a new place, with fresh brands, different labels. All set out to hand, so that you didn't have to ask. All set out to tempt you to second and third thoughts. Help yourself. Take what you want and pay for it. Or don't pay. Defray the rising cost of living by stealing a proportion of your weekly shopping list. They did it – some did, she didn't know who they were – and got away with it. Some did. They must, or there would not be those occasional reports of the percentages these big concerns wrote off. And it must be easy, so easy, to drop one thing into the store's basket and another into the open mouth of your own bag. To think that there must be people who came out every shopping day with that intention. Or was it more casual than that, more haphazard, tempted suddenly and taking a chance?

Jean was through the checkout and on the pavement outside before she felt the hand on her elbow and heard the voice that froze her to the spot.

'Excuse me, madam, but haven't you got something in your bag that you haven't paid for?'

Turning her head, forcing herself to look into the woman's expressionless face.

'I think you've made a mistake.'

'If I have, perhaps we can sort it out in private, inside.'

The hand tightened its grip slightly. Jean wondered what would happen if she refused, shook herself free, made off. People were looking. The beat of her heart was sickening. Was this how it always went? she wondered. Why couldn't the woman see that this was special, different?

The manager's office, a tiny room with a yellow wood desk, a filing cabinet and two chairs, was at the back of the store. The woman let Jean walk to it in front of her. The manager was a young man with sandy hair and an absurd little moustache. It was perhaps his first important appointment. He asked Jean's name. She told him. He wrote it down.

'What's the address?'

'Thirty-three Willow Grove.'

'Is that nearby?'

'Three or four minutes by car.'

'Have you shopped here before?'

'I usually go to Dunstan's.'

'But you thought we'd be easier to steal from?'

'This is all a mistake.'

'Mrs Nesbit, we have TV surveillance here, with instant playback. Right? Would you like us to show you what we saw?'

Jean said nothing. No, she would not like that.

They emptied the contents of her bags onto the desk top, separated the goods she had bought elsewhere and checked the rest against her till-slip. The manager sighed then lifted the telephone and dialled a number.

'Will you send somebody round as soon as possible.' He listened. 'Yes. Yes.'

'If I've got something I didn't pay for it's because I didn't know I had it,' Jean said.

'Whether you took it deliberately or not will be for the court to decide. Right?'

'You mean you actually intend to prosecute?'

'It's company policy. Out of my hands. We always prosecute. We're new here. One or two convictions to start with might stop it getting a hold. Right?'

'But over a little thing like that.'

'Little or big makes no difference.'

'Do you seriously think I'd risk my reputation for such a trivial thing?'

'I don't know about your reputation. For all I know, you might make a habit of it.'

'I've never done such a thing in my life before,' Jean said, adding quickly. 'I haven't done anything now.'

'I don't know why you don't just own up,' the manager said.

The woman who had apprehended Jean, youngish, straw-coloured hair cut short, was silent, standing with her back to the filing cabinet. Her glance kept lifting above Jean's head. Jean looked round. In the corner on the wall a closed circuit television screen flickered silently. She saw shoppers among the banks of shelves. 'I'd advise you to change your tune when you get into court,' the manager was saying. 'They don't like to have their time wasted. You can always plead a mental blackout. That's a steady favourite.' His voice was edged with sarcasm. Jean felt herself colouring afresh.

The police constable was young too, though with dark hair and a soft complexion. He glanced at Jean when he came in and looked round as though expecting to see someone else. He was visibly embarrassed as the manager spoke to him and held up the tin of pilchards.

'Is this it?'

'That's it.'

'Nothing else?'

'Isn't it enough?'

'You're sure there's no mistake?'

'Whose side are you on?' the manager asked.

The young constable bristled. 'There's no need for that, sir. It's just that I know this lady, and –'

'You know her, you say?'

'Well, not personally.' He looked at Jean. 'Your husband taught me at school.'

The manager pointed to the television screen. 'Look, I've spent enough time with this. Right? See for yourself?' He pressed switches.

Jean found herself wondering how long they kept tapes like that, if it would be destroyed when it had served its immediate purpose or kept on file to condemn her forever.

She got Fred on his own after their evening meal, when Stephen had left the house for some vague rendezvous.

'Fred, there's something I've got to tell you.'

'Yes?'

'Put the paper down. It's very important.'

'All right. I'm listening.'

'The police might come.'

'Here?'

'Yes.'

'Whatever for? Is Stephen in trouble?'

'No, it's me.'

'Have you clouted the car?'

'No.' Jean drew a deep breath. 'I'm being prosecuted for shoplifting.'

'You're what?'

'I took something from that new supermarket in Cross Street this morning. They called me back inside and sent for the police.'

'You're pulling my leg.'

'I'm not Fred.'

'But... What did you take? Did you really take it?'

'A tin of pilchards. I really did take it.'

He was incredulous. 'A tin of pilchards! You mean to tell me they called in the police over a tin of pilchards?'

'They said it was company policy always to prosecute.'

'My God!' He was speechless for some time. Jean poured herself another cup of coffee. 'You personally know half the Bench,' Fred said, lifting his hand in a gesture of refusal as she held the coffee pot over his cup. She was surprised at the steadiness of her hand.

'The ones who know me will have to stand down, I expect.'

'Will it really come to that?'

'They said so. They said they had to make an example of anyone they caught.'

'They'll let you off.'

'No, I'm afraid not.'

'The Bench, I mean. You're well known in the town. You're a person of... of standing.'

'All the worse, I suppose. I should know better. And it's not as if I were in need.'

'Of a tin of pilchards? Who needs a tin of pilchards? What made you take a tin of pilchards?'

'I saw them on the shelf and remembered that Stephen is fond of them.'

'Pilchards? Stephen likes pilchards? Buy him some, then. Buy a dozen tins and keep them in the cupboard.' He stopped, then looked straight at her. 'You're not ill, are you?'

'No. I don't think so.' She had not thought of that. No, that wasn't it. She must not let them make her out to be ill.

'You'll have to deny it. They'll believe you. They'll have to believe it's a mistake.'

'I've no defence, Fred. They have a television tape.'

'Christ! This is going to look fine in the *Argus*. And don't think the *Evening Post* won't pick it up as well.' He strained his neck out of his shirt, then loosened his tie. He needed a bigger collar size; she had noticed that before. 'How is it going to affect my position? I'm always having to chastise light-fingered kids. I can see their smirks now. They'll make a meal of it. They'll have me for breakfast, dinner and tea.'

He got up and went to the cupboard where they kept their small stock of drink. He took out the whisky bottle. 'Do you want one?'

'No, thanks.' She wondered when she would start crying.

He poured one for himself, then said, 'I'm sorry if I seem selfish; thinking about myself. But I'm trying to imagine all the consequences.'

'I'm not blaming you, Fred. After all, you didn't do it. I did.'

'Yes, and I still can't understand. I can't for the life of me understand what could have possessed you.'

'It was a feeling that came over me. That's the only way I can explain it.'

'What kind of feeling?' But she merely shrugged. 'You're not some crack-brained neurotic housewife trying to make up her bingo losses, or somebody who steals for kicks. You know better. You're as honest as the day's long. You're sturdy, dependable. People know you, respect you, look up to you.'

'A good woman,' Jean murmured.

'What?' Then he caught it. 'Yes – *good*.'

'Yes, I'm good,' she wanted to say to him. 'I *am* good. But how can I prove how good I *am*, unless I do something bad?'

She wanted to say it, but she didn't. She did not think he would understand that.

The Apples of Paradise

It was a dazzling morning. Though patches of frost still lay white in shadowed corners, the big winds of the past week had gone and it was possible with the warmth of the sun on one's shoulders to stand without feeling chilled.

Hare had slipped into a rear pew of the chapel just before the coffin entered and now he took a place on the asphalt path, a little way from the cluster of invited guests who would be returning to the house for refreshment.

Chapel and graveyard stood high on a hill. Wholesale demolition of old property had opened up a fresh view of the town and a wide green sweep of cropped grass bordering a new road had left the once closed-in Victorian building in a rather striking isolation. This had been a town of non-conformist churches in Hare's youth. Now the few left struggled on with amalgamated congregations, their one-time differences in Methodist doctrine submerged in their need to survive.

Hare felt one or two glances of half-recognition as the parson intoned, but Fell himself had his back to him and the two women whom Hare took to be Tom's daughters, standing arm in arm with their men, had been too young when he left the town to know now who he was.

Waiting, Hare assumed his demeanour to be one of sombre composure, but his stomach felt empty and faintly nauseous and he was not sure how he would react to Fell's quite proper and expected display of grief. Hare didn't think he could cope with Tom's tears, and Tom had never been afraid to cry when given cause.

Hare was perturbed by a sudden thickening in his throat. And they were finished. He must control himself. He stepped forward as Fell turned and walked towards him.

'Tom...'

Fell stopped and peered into his face. 'Gerald? You came, Gerald.'

Fell took Hare's gloved hand between both of his and they examined each other. The changes in the look of a friend one sees regularly are almost as imperceptible as those observed in one's own looking-glass, but these two had been apart and nearly thirty years masked for each the youthful face he'd known and kept as the only possible memory.

'You're looking very well, Gerald.'

And Tom, Hare thought, seemed uncharacteristically stoic in his self-possession.

Fell's daughters hovered for a moment, then proceeded slowly to the gate and the waiting car.

'I'm sorry, Tom,' Hare said. 'I truly am.'

Fell shook his head and looked at the ground. 'A bad do, Gerald. A bad do. We could have had another ten or fifteen year. But,' he glanced into Hare's face now with a regretful little smile, 'it wasn't meant to be.'

Hare was the taller of the two. His weight had increased

no more than a few pounds since his twenties and, apart from a small round pot-belly, hardly noticeable under his well-cut clothes, he was as lean and trim as then. His smooth dark hair showed a powdering of grey, with two white wings above his ears. Fell had always been the stocky one and now he was comfortably round, though, still, Hare had noticed, light on his small feet. A few strands of once fair-to-gingerish hair were combed across the totally bald crown of his round head.

'But come back home, Gerald, where we can talk in the warm. Have you got a car?'

'Yes, it's just down the road. But I can't, Tom.'

'You're not going back straight away?'

'No, but there's something else I must see to.'

Hare had not planned this refusal. It was just that now, watching the people leave the graveyard, he felt a sudden violent wish not to have to talk to anybody else and, as a focus of reminiscence, become a welcome diversion in the uneasy aftermath of the funeral.

'Will you be at home tomorrow?'

'Oh, aye.'

'What if I came round then?'

'Yes,' Fell said, 'come round when we can be quiet and on our own.' They settled on a time. 'You know where it is, of course?' Fell said with a flicker of humour.

'I think I can still find it,' Hare replied.

Hare could hardly remember a time when he didn't know Fell; certainly, he could not recall how they had met. It must have been at Sunday school. Both Hare's family and Fell's had been Methodist and rigidly insistent on the boys' attendance at chapel three times every Sunday. Fell's father was an ironmonger; Hare's had owned, in partnership, a furniture shop. Much of the furniture

Hare's father had sold was made on the premises by three craftsmen. It had a name for quality. Their steel-framed three-piece suites were said to last a lifetime, and in those inter-war years long before the coming of discount warehouses of the type Hare himself had ended up owning, when their main rivals were the cheap-jack city shops who attracted a different kind of customer anyway, their reputation spread miles beyond the boundaries of the little town.

Approaching their teens, both Hare and Fell were enrolled as fee-paying pupils at a grammar school; not the local one to which they could have won free places through County Minor Scholarships, but an older foundation in the nearby city with a better academic record. Fell was a year younger than Hare and in a lower form; but they continued together at chapel where at one period, in their early teens, they pumped the organ together for morning and evening services. It was felt to be a job for two lads as the pipes were not as sound as they might have been and keeping them filled with air called for considerable exertion. The one time Hare did it alone found him at the end of the service exhausted, his skin bathed in sweat and his heart pounding. It was unfortunate that Fell's absence had coincided with that of the regular organist and the appearance of a deputy notorious for the pace at which he dragged out hymns, as well as his seizing a chance of practice by launching on an extended voluntary as the congregation filed out. But Hare liked the duty because it allowed him and Fell, tucked away behind their screen, seclusion from the people in the body of the chapel during the services, with whose content he was becoming bored and disillusioned.

It was at about the time Hare was privately rejecting its teachings that the chapel played host to a two-week evangelical mission of students from a Methodist college who were being trained for the ministry. The mission culminated in 'conversions', when the erring, the strayed and the sore-at-heart were enjoined to come forward to the communion rail, there to kneel and be born again in Christ: to be 'saved'.

Hare sat through it with a mounting discomfort of spirit. It wasn't merely the small-minded rigidity that characterised many of the chapel's regulars which more and more alienated him. There were to him too many flaws in the gospel preached from the pulpit week after week: too many anomalies that his intellect could not accept and which his faith was not strong enough to overlook. He realised that, more than simply rejecting the teaching of his church, he was beginning to doubt the existence of God in any form he found acceptable. He had never discussed this with Fell or anyone else and when, to his mild surprise, Fell got up and went forward to kneel with the others at the rail, Hare decided to keep his own counsel until such time as he could reach a clear decision. That, he felt, would be when his reluctance to displease his parents was outweighed by distaste for his lip-service. In any case, war threatened. Chamberlain had averted one crisis, but Hitler was making more and more demands. A war would change a lot of things.

Fell started courting a cheerful fresh-faced girl from among those who had pledged themselves to the Lord during the mission. Hare decided that Fell's conversion had been less for its own sake than a way of making himself more acceptable, of showing himself to be serious, to Emily Schofield. In later years Hare could blame his inability to reconcile Laura Sherwood's chapel-going with his own hardening doubt for his failure to make sure of her when she seemed to welcome his attentions. Laura was neatly shod. Her hair was tucked under a little blue hat. The collar of a white blouse encircled her slim throat. The soft stuff of the blouse formed a V between the lapels of her plainly tailored costume-coat. The coat hinted at a gentle fullness of breast that stirred Hare to a tenderness which lodged under his heart in a weight of longing.

When he first saw her he did not know who she was; knew nothing about her except that she had emerged, bible in hand, from the nearest of the town's other Methodist chapels. A few days later she came into the shop while he was waiting on counter. She had a couple of chairs which needed recovering: would he show her some material and give her a price? Hare said he would call himself. She gave him her name and her address: The Cottage, Millbank Lane. He told her that he had seen her coming out of her chapel and she said she had chosen it because it seemed most like the one she had attended before they moved to the town. No, she had not been here long; less than a year. Her father had retired early from his business because of ill-health. He was a widower and she kept house for him.

There was about her a haunting womanliness, a gentleness and a natural grace which made the other girls he knew look either cheap or gawky and his thoughts seem shameful. He felt she would have been profoundly shocked to know of some of the things which flitted through his mind. He knew little of these matters and during the walks they began to take together in the long summer evenings of those months just before the war he avoided physical contact and any familiarity of speech. He did not know what she expected of him and was terrified of offending her. When war was declared, knowing that he would eventually be conscripted, Hare volunteered for the RAF and flying duties. 'I shall pray for you,' Laura told him.

He was sent for training to Canada and came back as a navigator to a squadron of Coastal Command on operational duty in the Middle East. It was when he had completed his overseas tour and was given a home posting that he met Cynthia. She was all that Laura was not: direct, pleasure-loving, passionate in her seizing of the moment. 'Life's short,' she reminded him as she took him into her bed. 'There's a war on.' It was his late initiation and he was grateful to her. She stripped him of his inhibitions and thoughts of her sustained him during the long patrols over the Atlantic. Periods of hazardous duty were punctuated by evenings of drinking and heightened gaiety and snatched opportunities of making love. Cynthia helped her father to run his hotel and sometimes she could entertain Hare in her room without fear of scandal.

He counted himself fortunate that he wasn't an infantryman slogging through the desert, or a member of the crew of one of those ships they watched over, heaving below on the ocean with no sight of home or a woman for weeks or months at a time. What Cynthia gave Hare became as necessary to him as a drug. For by this time he was losing his nerve. He thought his luck was bound to run out and he expected every patrol to be his last. The knowledge that he was at much less risk than Bomber Command crews operating over Europe was little consolation. Fear had seized him and wouldn't let go. They married by special licence. When he awoke sweating in the night as his aircraft plunged towards the grey swell of sea, Cynthia was there to be clung to.

Hare brought his wife home to an empty house. His father had died of a heart attack while Hare was overseas and his mother decided to go and live near Hare's sister, who had already married and moved away before the war. The speed with which the rift between himself and Cynthia opened surprised Hare. Peacetime marriage to a shopkeeper was different from a wartime one to an officer of RAF Coastal Command. She found it dull. It bored her. There was no sign of her conceiving and starting a family and she soon grew restless. Her manner took on a bitter edge, as though she felt she had been deceived. She had the house refurnished and still disliked it. She persuaded Hare to acquire a plot of land and start to build a new house. He also bought a flat at Scarborough, where she spent more and more time. She became friendly with a set there who hung around a hotel bar at weekends and drank cocktails. Hare found them brittle, living on their nerves, and left Cynthia to it.

Tom Fell had waited for call-up, failed the medical and been excused military service. He married Emily Schofield and, by the time Hare was demobbed, was the father of two girls. When the first post-war elections were held he stood for the Urban District Council and took his seat as an independent, benefiting from the belief of many working people in the town that while you might vote Labour in parliamentary elections, in local ones you were wise to choose men of substance who would look after the town's money while looking after their own. It was an argument whose logic made Hare smile; but when more seats became vacant he was persuaded by Fell to stand on the same platform. They were both important and respected men in the town, Fell argued, and it was right that they should have a say in what looked like being its new prosperity. They were, in any case, the kind of men who could attend council meetings held during working hours and it was their responsibility to guide the community's affairs.

'I hear you're building a house,' Fell remarked one day as they stood alone together at the window of the council chamber, before a meeting.

'It's Cynthia's idea,' Hare said. 'I'm happy enough with the old one.'

'I'll be glad of first refusal when you come to sell.'

'I'll remember.'

'Putting up something with a bit of style?'

'It'll be big enough, anyway.'

'Two or three kids,' Fell hinted. 'They'll soon fill it for you.'

'Nay,' Hare said, 'there doesn't seem to be much prospect of that.'

'I'm sorry to hear that, Gerald. My two lasses are a great joy.'

'We shall rattle round it like two peas in a drum,' Hare said gloomily. And, he added to himself, with as much likelihood of touching.

Where had all that gone to, he wondered, all that passion? How could Cynthia have lost interest to the point where pride stopped him from pressing himself on her? She behaved towards him now as though he had cheated her, as if he had promised her something he'd known he could never fulfil. He had even begun to harbour fears for her mental stability.

'She doesn't seem to want to mix much,' Fell was saying.

'Who, Cynthia?'

'Yes. Emily thought she perhaps ought to call and see her, but she doesn't want to push herself.'

It was an idea. There were activities Cynthia could share in, charities she could help support. People here tended not to make a fuss; they left you to yourself until you showed that that was not your choice.

'We don't see you at Chapel, Gerald,' Fell said.

'No. Cynthia's not a chapel-goer, and neither am I any longer.'

'That seems a pity.'

Hare didn't choose to discuss with Fell his loss of faith, but now he said, 'I wish Emily would call. Perhaps Cynthia's felt out of place, plumped down here in a town where everybody's known everybody since Adam was a lad.'

The chamber was filling, the chairman of the council about to call for order. 'Put her up to it,' Hare said. 'See what happens.'

He saw Laura Sherwood at a distance in the street and stepped into a shop as she walked towards him. There had been nothing spoken between them to account for the embarrassment he felt. They had corresponded spasmodically at the beginning of the war, but only on the level of news, hers from home, his, censored, from the other side of the world. She had been away during the leave given him between his training and his overseas posting, and when her letters stopped he told himself that they had either failed to find him or she had, more likely, formed some attachment. He had not seen or heard of her since his return: it was possible even in a small town to go for long periods without bumping into someone. Now a discreet enquiry told him that she was still unmarried.

She began to fill his thoughts, until he faced himself squarely and acknowledged the bitter mistake he had made. If only he had waited. If only he had kept up their correspondence and used that to begin the courtship he had been too diffident to press while they were together.

It was in the grip of this renewed longing and in

565

the thought that only she stood in his way that his attitude towards Cynthia began to match hers towards him. She seemed surprised that he had turned and, as though excited by the smell of battle, began to provoke open rows.

'How can a man change so much?' she said. 'That's what surprises me.'

'I don't know what you expected. You've got a good living in a comfortable house, in a pleasant town full of pleasant people.'

'That lot, looking at you sideways if you wear anything a bit out of the ordinary. That lot with their bibles under their arms, sticking their tupp'ny-ha'penny noses in the air.'

'You won't try to understand them. You never make one move to be friendly.'

'No, because they bore me rigid; and now you're back among them you're just the same. What happened to that knight of the air in his beautiful blue uniform, that's what I want to know?'

The way she could mock, her head back, dark eyes glittering with malice.

'He was something got up for the duration.'

'Well, I preferred him, even if he was shit-scared half the time.'

Hare flinched and coloured. He could never match the sheer wantonness of her tongue. 'You're fit for nothing but the bar of some pub,' he said, 'swapping dirt with your customers and taking whichever of 'em you fancy into your bed.'

'And what kind of satisfaction do you think you give a woman in bed?'

'It was all some kind of pretence, then, was it, all that at the beginning?'

Her chin came down. The blaze subsided. She seemed genuinely lost herself.

'I don't know what it was,' she muttered, 'except that I must have been out of my mind.'

Suddenly he found hope kindled that she would leave him.

'You'd better decide what you're going to do, then,' he said.

'Do? Do? What is there to do?'

'Clear out. Do what you like. We'll get a divorce.'

'On what grounds?' He saw the spirit flare in her again as she looked at him. 'It'll cost you a packet to get rid of me, Gerald. And that's on top of the scandal.'

He wondered if there was anybody in the Scarborough set with whom she went too far; if her behaviour there could give him a lever. Perhaps he ought to hire someone to watch her. He shrank from the thought.

Hare saw Laura again and this time did not avoid her. She looked at him directly, with a genuine friendliness that seemed free of resentment. He asked after her father.

'I'm afraid he's failing,' she told him. 'He doesn't go out any more.'

'You never come into the shop,' he said. 'You've become quite a stranger.'

'Circumstances change. And you don't buy furniture every other week.'

'True enough.'

'How is your new house progressing?'

'You've heard about that?'

'I saw the builders and someone mentioned your name.'

'It's my wife's idea.'

'How is Mrs Hare? I never see her about the town. Is she well?'

'Oh, she's all right in herself.' He found himself hoping she would detect the lack of concern in his voice.

The weight under his heart seemed to bow his shoulders as he watched her go.

He was standing outside Fell's new double-fronted shop and now the door suddenly opened and Tom came out wearing his khaki working-smock.

'Gerald...' Fell glanced along the street. 'Wasn't that Miss Sherwood?'

'Yes.'

'Pleasant woman. Keeps herself to herself. She goes to the Primitive Methodists, so we don't really know her.'

'Seems she's occupied in looking after her father.'

'And no chance of a match, I expect, till he's off her hands. Pity. She'd likely make some chap a good wife. Not a bad-looking woman. No raving beauty, but not plain either.'

His remarks irritated Hare. He felt there was even a hint of prurience in Fell's discussing in such terms a woman he hardly knew.

'Well, that'll be her business,' he said.

'Oh, aye,' Fell said. 'Hers and some single young chap's. Nothing to do with old married men like you and me.'

Hare was turning to go when Fell went on, 'By the way, Emily spoke on the telephone to your wife.'

'Oh?'

'Seems they've fixed up to go on a jaunt together.'

'A jaunt?'

'Yes. To a horse show, somewhere Wetherby way.'

Hare stood bemused. Well, if it worked and Cynthia made one friend in the town... It was no use his yearning for the impossible. He should try to build on what he'd got. And they had been close, in a way, he and Cynthia, for a while. Something, he told himself, must happen. They couldn't go on indefinitely as they were.

'Is she interested in horses, then?' Fell was asking.

'She used to ride a little at one time.'

'Well, that's where they're going. Let's hope they have a nice day for it.'

'I decided to take your advice,' Cynthia said, when Hare mentioned it. 'If she wants to be friendly I may as well give it a try.'

'Tom Fell's my oldest friend,' Hare said. 'And his wife's a straightforward warm-hearted woman.'

'Well, we shall see.'

'How will you go?'

'In my car. She doesn't drive.'

He felt himself softening towards her. 'Cynthia,' he said, 'we ought to be able to do better than this.'

'It's a poor lookout if we can't.'

Hare was dozing by the fire, a book in his lap, when the uniformed police sergeant came to the door. He was from the local station and on foot. There had been a bad accident on the Al. The driver of one of the cars was Mrs Hare. No, both she and her passenger were alive but seriously injured. Could Hare tell him who the other woman was?

'It's Tom Fell's wife.'

Hare gave the officer a lift round to Fell's house. Fell had to take the children to his parents before he could leave for the hospital. To Hare's astonishment, he told the girls, still drooping from their disturbed sleep, what had happened. He sat beside Hare on the journey to the hospital, already in a state of shock. 'Oh God, what a terrible thing,' he said over and over. 'Oh God, help us, what a terrible, terrible thing,' until

Hare's own nerves were jumping and he forced himself to drive with an exaggerated care that brought Fell to an almost frantic impatience. 'Hurry, Gerald. For God's sake hurry.'

Cynthia was in the operating theatre. Hare was told that she had every chance of recovery and since there was nothing he could do here why didn't he go home and telephone in the morning.

He came upon Fell in a corridor. Fell was leaning against the wall, his face hidden, his shoulders heaving as though he were trying to vomit. Hare touched him. 'Tom...' When he turned Hare saw that he was torn by great racking sobs. He got out his words as if they were choking him. 'She's dead, Gerald. Emily's gone. Oh, what am I going to do? Whatever can I do?'

Cynthia came home to her own bed after a fortnight. Hare employed a nurse to look after her while he was out at his business. She had some while ago demanded a room of her own, but now he moved a bed in beside hers so that he would be near her in the night. She became withdrawn, brooding, in a prolonged reflection on her situation. He woke in the middle of one night to find her lying still, eyes wide open, the lamp burning on the far side of her bed.

'Is there anything you want?'

'No.'

'Are you comfortable?'

'Yes.' There was a silence. 'I was just thinking.'

'Yes?'

'What a pity it couldn't have been me.'

'What?'

'What a pity she was killed and I was spared.'

'You're talking nonsense.'

'No, I'm not. Your troubles would have been over. You'd have been free.' A silence. 'And so would I.'

Hare took Laura's father's death as an excuse to call on her. She gave him tea.

'I feel quite... quite lost without him; without him to care for and think about.'

'Now you can think about yourself for a change.'

'Yes. He'd had a pretty fair innings. Not like poor Mr Fell's wife. That was a terrible shame. How is Mrs Hare?'

'Up and about now. She'll soon be quite her old self.'

'She had a lucky escape.'

'Yes ... You know that we don't hit it off, Cynthia and I?'

'I didn't, no. I knew she didn't mix much in the town.'

'We virtually live apart.'

'I'm sorry. But God moves in mysterious ways and you've got plenty of time to settle your differences and grow together again.'

'I made a terrible mistake,' Fell said. 'And all I can think now is, if only I'd waited. If only I had.'

'I don't know what you're trying to say to me, but I wish you wouldn't. It really is none of my business.'

'But it is, Laura. I should have waited and come back to you. Do you remember those times before the war, when we used to walk out together?'

'Of course I remember, but –'

'I said nothing then because I was in awe of you.'

'In awe of me?' She laughed. 'Never!'

'Oh, I was. And then the war came and separated us.'

'And then you married and brought a wife home.'

'I still want you, Laura. I want you more than I ever did.'

'You mustn't talk like that. You have a wife.'

'I'm ready to separate from her. I can't go on like this. I'll get a divorce.'

'Do you expect me to give her the grounds for that?'

'I'll find a way.'

'"Those whom God hath joined let no man put asunder." I don't believe in divorce.' She turned away and walked across the room. He could see that she was agitated, her face aflame. 'And I've told you, you mustn't come here and talk to me like this.'

'You still cling to all that, do you?' he said. 'The chapel, religion?'

'Of course. Don't you?'

'No. All that mumbo-jumbo was sticking in my throat before the war came, and nothing I saw while I was fighting changed me back. The clergy blessed both sides, you know.'

'You shouldn't blame God for the shortcomings of His followers. Besides, men who might be killed at any time need spiritual comfort, whichever side they fight on.'

'If God exists,' Hare said.

'You don't think he does?'

'They estimate that the Nazis slaughtered six million Jews. What loving father would let that happen to his children?'

'Suffering has always been a mystery,' Laura said. She came and took his cup. 'And now I think you ought to go.'

He got up. One thing, he thought, he would know before he left.

'Laura... I want to ask you and I want you to answer me truthfully.'

'You've said enough. Please go now.'

'I want to know... If I were free, would you... would you favour me?'

She sighed as she moved to rest one hand on the mantelshelf and look into the fire.

'There was a time,' she said finally, 'when I thought a great deal about that. But you're not free, so the question doesn't arise now.'

Cynthia had an older sister who had married and settled in Australia. She wrote to Cynthia in glowing terms of the new life and the glorious weather. Why didn't Cynthia wangle a trip out and recuperate in the sunshine?

'Why don't you go?' Hare said.

'Do you mean it?'

'Of course. Why not?'

'It'd be awfully expensive. And there's the new house.'

'It won't bankrupt me,' Hare said. 'And the house can be ready for you when you get back.'

'Suppose I don't come back?'

'That's up to you. Go by sea. The voyage will do you good.'

'Perhaps it'll give us both a chance to sort ourselves out.'

'Is there nobody else here who'll miss you?' Hare said.

'What do you mean by that?'

But when he shrugged and said no more she did not press him to explain.

Fell was having a hard time coming to terms with Emily's death. His eyes would fill with tears when he spoke of her.

'I still can't get over it, Gerald,' he said. 'Every time I hear the door open I expect her to walk into the room. You're without your wife now, but just imagine to yourself, just close your eyes and imagine that she's gone for good, and you'll have an inkling of what I'm going through.'

'It's no use my pretending that Cynthia and I are as

573

close as you and Emily were,' Hare said. 'You've seen and heard enough to know that.'

'No,' Fell said, 'and to think it was an act of good neighbourliness that brought it about. If only Emily hadn't made that offer. If only she hadn't rung your wife and agreed to go on that trip.' He turned away, choking.

Hare waited till Fell had himself under control.

'"If only", Tom. They're just about the saddest words we have.'

'She was one in a million, Gerald. Nay, in ten million. I'll never replace her. I can't even begin to think of putting anybody else in her place.'

'Perhaps not. But you ought to have some kind of help with the girls, you know. There's them to think about as well as you. They've lost a mother, and that they can never replace.'

Laura's cottage was a sturdy five-roomed stone building whose fabric her father had had renewed. It stood beside and at an angle to a steep unsurfaced lane, a vehicle's width, down which women from the town took a shortcut to the yarn-spinning mill by the river. On the town side it was almost hidden by an overgrown bank; on the other it looked across the wide valley of river and canal to low wooded hills.

On venturing to visit her again, Hare was glad to find her in the garden. It allowed him to seem merely to be passing and saved him the embarrassment of facing her across her threshold.

'Hullo, there,' he called to her stooping figure.

She straightened up and, momentarily dazzled, shielded her eyes with her hand so that she could see him standing against the sun.

'Hullo.'

'You know, you really have got a marvellous view here.'

'I thought you'd bought the best view in the neighbourhood.'

'You mean with the new house? Something ready-made like this would have saved me the bother.'

'Oh, but your new house will be much more splendid than this.'

'It's a folly,' Hare said. 'A pure grandiose folly.'

'Why did you go to the bother, then?'

'It was my wife's idea. I thought I'd told you.'

'But don't married people come to agreement on such important matters?'

'Some might.'

She was keeping her distance, standing where he had found her. He lifted the gate latch and stepped inside, seeing her head go back an inch.

'You know my wife's gone to visit her sister in Australia?'

'No, I didn't.'

'She thought the change would do her good.'

'After that terrible accident...'

'Oh, she's over that now. Quite recovered.'

She wiped a lock of hair off her forehead with the back of her wrist that showed between her gardening-glove and her sleeve. Then she looked down at herself, as if suddenly conscious of the old clothes she was wearing.

'You keep it nice,' Hare said, waving his hand at the garden.

'Father got it established. It was a wilderness when we came, and it would soon be so again.'

He saw that she was uneasy in his presence, but he motioned to the open door. 'I wonder if I might... for a minute.' And when she still did not move or speak. 'There's something I want to talk to you about.'

575

'I thought we'd had all that out.'

'Please,' Hare said. 'It'll only take a few minutes.'

He followed her, waiting while she removed soil from her flat-heeled shoes on the iron scraper outside the door. When he reached to shut the door behind them, she said, 'Please, I'd rather it were left open.' She didn't offer him a seat.

'I wondered how you were making out on your own,' Hare said. 'How you were managing.' She looked at him, not understanding. 'If there was anything you needed.'

'Are you offering me money?' she said at last.

'I didn't know how your father had left you,' Hare said.

'And what would I be expected to do for it?' She coloured then as Hare looked away. 'I'm sorry. I don't think you deserved that.'

'It would be foolish to be in need when I could help. I shouldn't like the thought of you wanting for anything.'

'It's kind of you. But quite impossible.'

'I don't know why it should be.'

'Oh, but it is. In any case, I might be leaving the district.'

'Leaving?' Hare was startled by the violence with which his heart lurched.

'I'm not destitute, but I must find a way of keeping myself. My mother had relatives in the south. I thought I might get work there.'

'What kind of work?'

'As a housekeeper. Looking after Father all those years has left me fitted for little else.'

'I could probably find you something in the shop.'

'No, please.' A little smile touched her lips.

Panic at the thought of losing her forever brought a thought to Hare.

'Tom Fell needs a housekeeper and a nanny for his girls.'

'Oh?'

'His wife's death hit him badly. He just doesn't seem to be able to reconcile himself to it.' He saw that he had her interest. 'Would you like me to speak to him about it?'

She looked round the room then crossed to the window.

'You don't really want to uproot yourself and go away, do you?'

'I do love this house,' she said eventually. 'I hate the thought of leaving it.'

She stood with her back to him. He went and turned her to face him.

'Stay,' he said. 'Please don't go.'

They had never been so close. Even in the old days he had ventured no more than a steadying hand over a stile. Now he lifted her hot face and bent his towards it. Was he wrong or could she really not hide a hint of softness in her lips before they closed hard against his?

'No.' She twisted free. 'Please go now.'

She went and stood in the open doorway.

'Will you let me speak to Tom?'

'If you like. But I can't stay unless you promise never to come here again.'

A woman passed along the lane, twisting her head to give them a narrow-eyed appraisal as they stepped out of the house.

'It takes only one person to start the tongues wagging,' Laura said.

The telegram arrived when Hare's wife had been away six months. 'Cynthia seriously ill,' it read. 'Letter following but think you should come at once.

Hare left the business in the hands of his partner and took a flight to Australia. He had nine days in a flying boat in which to wonder just what awaited him. As they flew across the eastern Mediterranean and put down at places he had become familiar with during his first operational posting, he thought, 'When I was here before I didn't even know she existed.'

Cynthia had cancer at an advanced and inoperable stage. There were some new drugs which might arrest it for a time, but she must not be allowed to make that long journey home. Hare was surprised and moved by the courage with which she suffered and fought during the months left to her. She kept active for as long as possible.

'I always used to say life was short, didn't I?' she said. 'Well, now I know just how short, I want to make the most of what's left.'

It was a time of reconciliation, with bitterness gone, and, for Hare, a strangely ennobling experience. It left him needing time to think and come to terms with himself and his memories. After the funeral he booked a passage home by sea. It was during the long voyage, keeping himself to himself, that he would do his mourning, bury the past and brood on the possibilities of the future.

He came off the train at his local station to find himself on the edge of some farewell party spilling across from the other platform. He recognised one of Fell's daughters. She greeted him shyly.

'Hullo, Elizabeth. What's all this about?'

Before she could reply, Fell himself came round the corner of the station-master's office. 'Elizabeth, the train's due. Don't wander away.' He stopped at the sight of Hare.

'Gerald! How well you look. Fancy you turning up just now!' Fell was dressed in a new suit, a carnation with fern in his buttonhole. 'Come round here a minute.'

He took Hare by the arm and led him along the end of the building. Laura, in a slate-blue two-piece and a hat with its veil turned back, was standing in a group on the other side.

'Laura, look who's here.' She turned her head as the train ran in beside her. 'We got married this morning.' Fell laughed, thumping Hare's back. 'You should have come home earlier and been my best man.'

Laura came to them. It was impossible to read any more in her smile than quiet pleasure. 'Welcome home,' she said.

'Thank you,' Hare said.

'We'd best get on, Tom,' Laura said.

'I hope you'll be very happy,' Hare said.

Now, on the morning after Laura's funeral, Hare was once more in that house through whose rooms he had wandered like a man demented. The weather had changed again.

'It seems,' Fell was saying, 'that we have one calm day for half a dozen blustery ones.' He put coal on the fire then reached for the decanter and topped up Hare's sherry glass and his own.

'It dropped right yesterday, anyway,' Hare said.

'Aye, aye. How does it feel to be back as a visitor in your old home?'

'Strange. Like a memory that won't quite focus.'

'It's been a good home for us. You know,' Fell went on, 'we thought about it afterwards, but that day you ran into me and Laura on the station, you were, so to speak, coming home from your own wife's funeral, weren't you?'

'In a manner of speaking, yes.'

'And you never said a word.'

'There was hardly time. And it wasn't a day to burden you with that kind of news.'

579

'No. But then, you always kept your feelings to yourself more than I did.'

'You knew that Cynthia and I hadn't hit it off for some time before she went to Australia. Though we were, in a way, reconciled during her illness.'

'Yes. I remember how I was when Emily was killed. Just as if the world had caved in on me. I didn't know where to put myself.'

But not this time, seemingly, Hare thought.

'And then,' Fell said, 'you sold out, pulled up stakes and went off without a goodbye. Whatever made you do that? Too many uncomfortable memories?'

'Something like that,' Hare said. 'I never really settled down after the war. Then that spell in Australia, when Cynthia was dying... I felt like a fresh start, where nobody knew me.'

'And you never got married again.'

'No.'

Why shouldn't I tell him? Hare thought. What harm can there be in it now she's gone? It might even give him some satisfaction to know the truth. His mind framed the sentences as Fell looked into the fire, silent, his thoughts elsewhere.

'I went away because I was in love with Laura. I should have made sure of her before the war, when it looked as if she was interested and we were both free. But she wouldn't entertain me while I was tied to Cynthia and she wouldn't hear of me getting a divorce. When Cynthia died I came home to claim her, but I was too late. So I left, rather than live in the same town, seeing her and being constantly reminded what a fool I'd been.'

That was what he thought of saying, but before he could start the other man turned from the fire and forestalled him.

'You know,' Fell began, 'we were real friends at one time...'

'Still are,' Hare put in, his spoken words followed by the immediate thought: *But did I ever really like him?*'

'Yes.' Fell turned his head and gave him an appreciative little smile in which there was a lurking sadness. 'I often think about those years just after the war. They were the golden years, Gerald. For me, at any rate. I know you had your troubles... Some men are lucky enough to have a time like that; and luckier still if they recognise it while they're living it. Well, that was my time, and it all fell to pieces when Emily was killed.'

'But surely,' Hare said, 'you've had compensations since.'

'Oh, yes,' Fell conceded. 'Oh, yes; and I'd be churlish not to admit my good fortune in marrying Laura. All the same... Well, we have known each other a long time, Gerald, and I can tell you what I wouldn't tell another living soul.'

'But what's wrong with the man?' Hare thought, and felt irritation move in him.

'She was a good wife,' Fell went on, 'a good woman and a good mother to the girls. And I shall miss her. But somehow, you know, though we were comfortable and never differed in anything that mattered, I sometimes found myself with this feeling of – well, I can only call it disappointment. A feeling that something, somehow, was missing. It was never the same as it was with Emily, you know, and perhaps I was a fool for ever thinking it might be.'

Wind suddenly buffeted the windows and tossed the bare branches of the lime trees in the avenue. Hot coals fell in the fireplace. The two old friends sat silently looking into the flames.

581

AUTHOR'S NOTE

The Apples of Paradise is a re-working of Thomas Hardy's story Fellow Townsmen. I had brooded for some years about an alternative denouement to Hardy's tale, whose irony he either did not see or chose not to use, but which appealed strongly to my own artistic temperament. At first I saw the writing of my own version as no more than an interesting exercise in which I retained some elements of Hardy's plot and planted other clues to its origin in the names of its chief characters. Hardy's are Barnet, Downe and Lucy Savile. Barnet Fair is rhyming slang for hair, or in this case Hare. Downe becomes Fell, and Lucy Savile's initials are retained in those of Laura Sherwood.

While this necessary acknowledgement of its source inevitably emphasises the similarities, and invites disparaging comparison, The Apples of Paradise, in its execution, acquired enough independent life to persuade me to offer it for publication.

The Running
and the Lame

There were people getting onto the bus before Mrs Brewster was safely off, and the driver was letting them. You got the odd one like that, careless, surly, as though they weren't lucky to have a job in times like these. Her walking stick and shopping bag slipped along the stretched arm whose hand clutched the rail while her foot felt for the ground. She wondered with a touch of panic if he would be heedless enough to close the doors on her before she was down and clear. The stick slid free and fell, coming to rest half on, half off the platform, as both her feet touched the ground and she stepped back onto the pavement and regained her balance. Then someone from behind nipped nimbly past her, grasped the stick and put it into her hand, his other hand supporting her elbow.

'You all right, Ma?'

'Thank you,' Mrs Brewster said. 'Thank you very much.'

She peered at him as she waited for her heartbeat to slow, but she had on the wrong glasses for recognising anyone at this range. All she could make out was a youngish man with dark hair, wearing a blue anorak with a broad yellow stripe down the sleeve. God! She was a mess these days: overweight, short of breath, arthritic in her joints, half blind. Fit for nothing but the knacker's yard, Randolph might have said. It had been one of his 'speaks' that he came out with whatever the company, asking what was vulgar about it when she chided him. She would have to stop coming into town if she couldn't get off a bus without danger. But her local shop had closed six months ago and the neighbours she'd been friendly with had lately moved away. She hated to be dependent on anyone, let alone strangers.

'It's Mrs Brewster, isn't it?' the man asked, and she peered at the pale outline of his face once more.

'Yes. Do I know you?'

'I know you.'

There was no clue in the voice. 'I'm sorry, but I can't place you.'

'That doesn't matter.'

'My eyes aren't what they were.'

She had known so many people in the old days, and many more had known her. Great heavens! She had been mayor of this town and a justice of the peace. All that had happened after Randolph had gone. While he was alive she had been content to back him up; then when he died the Labour Party had offered her his safe seat on the town council. She had taken the gesture as a great compliment, to Randolph as well as herself. How proud he would have been of her, and how distressed to see her now.

'You can manage now, can you?'

'Yes, I'm all right now.'

'I'll be getting on, then.'

'Yes. Thank you for your trouble.'

People weren't all bad, Mrs Brewster thought, as the man walked away. You could think otherwise from all that was reported in the newspapers and on television, and, of course, she had known a lot of cupidity and mischief while she was on the bench; but there was still some politeness and disinterested concern in the world. Helping lame dogs over stiles; helping fat old women off buses.

Mrs Brewster's first errand was to the post office, to draw her pension. On her way across the marketplace she was greeted a couple of times. Sometimes she didn't recognise people who spoke to her, but she always called out a cheery reply. Sometimes, she suspected, she responded when the greeting was not meant for her, but she would rather risk looking foolish than snub someone. 'I saw old Mrs Brewster in town this morning,' she could imagine them saying. 'Blind as a bat, but she still soldiers on'.

As she passed under the bulk of the town hall, the clock in its tower struck a quarter after eleven. Oh! but they'd had some times inside those walls: Mayors' Balls, Chamber of Commerce and Rotary Club dances; brass band concerts and choirs; the small parties and receptions she herself had held in the Mayor's Parlour during her year of office. She had met Randolph at a dance in there over fifty years ago. He had only recently come into the town to manage his uncle's foundry, which he later inherited. When they had been introduced and had danced together, he took her down to supper in the Winter Gardens. He didn't seem to want to leave her. She felt his gaze on her all evening and he came back to her every time she was for a moment unattended. He told her then that he fancied standing for the council and astounded her by telling her he was a member of the Labour Party. Men who owned or managed businesses stood as Conservatives, or Independents – which was the same thing under another name. Randolph overturned the natural order. Her father, himself a Liberal, said as much later when she wanted to ask Randolph to the house. Randolph had laughed. 'They don't know how to weigh me up. Even my uncle looks at me a bit sideways. "As long as you do your work and don't start wanting to hand the business over to a commune", he says, "I don't see as it makes much difference. Except, o' course, I shan't be able to put you up for t' Conservative Club."'

But the local branch of the party had thought him a catch and let him show what he could do in a ward held by a long-standing and popular Independent whom not even Ernest Bevin or Herbert Morrison could have ousted. He increased the Labour turn-out and its vote; then, when John Henry Waterhouse died, they gave him the prize of his safe seat, and she had inherited it in her turn.

Mrs Brewster needed a couple of postage stamps. She hesitated, then paid for first class. She owed a letter to her widowed sister-in-law, who lived in the south, and though what little news she had to write was in no way urgent, she felt that second class post for personal letters looked mean. The management of the Post Office irritated Mrs Brewster. She could understand their advertising on their own vans, but not their making long and costly TV commercials for overseas telephone calls, or taking quarter-page advertisements in the newspapers for services in which they held a monopoly. It was all a vexation – like the gas bill she went to pay through her bank when she had finished in the post office. She had expected it to be bigger than usual because of the extra heat she had used in the house during that prolonged spell of ferocious weather before Christmas. Bigger it had proved to be, but when she examined it closely and compared it with the equivalent quarter of twelve months before, she found that she had in fact used little more gas, and the extra cost was almost entirely due to increased charges. Oh, she could manage. The provision Randolph had made was, with her pension, sufficient to see her through the time left to her, which couldn't be all that long. She could manage; but there were others to whom the increasing cost of living was one never-ending fret, and she did not like to imagine what anxiety she might have had to live with were she, say, ten years younger.

From the bank she made her way to the outdoor market where she bought some greens and a small piece of fish. Then to the butcher for a lamb chop and some bacon. Enough to supplement what she kept in her small freezer – which she liked to keep in case she couldn't get out of the house – but not too much to weight her bag till it became a burden.

Now Mrs Brewster could address herself to her shopping-day treat: a bottle of Guinness and a pub lunch, followed, if she felt in the mood, by a glass of port. There was nearly always someone in the Bird in Hand whom she could chat with, though she almost always waited until she was invited before offering her opinion, for she did not want to become one of those boring old people who chipped into every exchange.

The old woman he had helped at the bus stop came into the Bird in Hand as he was sitting up at the bar counter enjoying his first pint of lager. She moved warily in from the door as though expecting traps for her feet, and the landlord called to his black labrador, which had flopped half under one of the tables. 'Now then, Satan,' the old lady said as the dog stood up in her path. He sniffed at then licked the hand which held the walking stick. Transferring the stick, she let the dog nuzzle into the bent fingers. 'Snottynose,' the old woman said. 'Old snottynose.' 'He knows you, all right,' the landlord said. He had already uncapped a small bottle of Guinness and was carefully pouring it as, casually wiping her hand on the rough tweed of her coat, she approached the counter. 'Oh, he knows me,' she said. Mrs Brewster. After all these years. She'd felt she ought to know him. And so she should.

'Will you be partaking of lunch?' the landlord asked as he picked out the money for the drink from the loose change she had spread on the counter and rang open the till.

'Steak sandwich and chips,' Mrs Brewster said. 'Ask Maisie to brown the onions. No hurry. Whenever she's ready. I'm not to ten minutes.'

The landlord went and called the order into the back and Mrs Brewster took her glass and turned to choose a seat, nodding 'Good morning' as she faced the man at the bar. There was no one else in the room.

'Morning.'

She peered at him, her eyes narrowing. 'Are you the young man who rescued my walking stick?'

'Yes.'

'You've still got the advantage of me.'

'You were well known at one time.'

'At one time, yes. Those days are over now, though.'

'Nobody gets any younger, Mrs Brewster,' the landlord put in as he came back and started to pull another half-pint into his own glass.

'You two have still a bit further to go than me,' Mrs Brewster said.

'That's something nobody can be sure of.'

'No, you're quite right,' Mrs Brewster conceded. 'And it wouldn't do for us to know such things.' She stood for a moment, turned in on her thoughts, before asking the man at the bar, 'Do you live here?'

'I used to.'

He saw that she was still no wiser. It would nag her now, but he thought she wouldn't like to pester him with more direct questions.

She turned away and moved to sit down as he looked past her and through the window to where Eric was getting out of the rusting L-registered Marina he had just driven into the yard. Eric ran his hand round the waistband of his trousers, tucking in his shirt, then hoicking the trousers up as he walked out of sight round the corner of the building. The man at the bar had emptied his glass and ordered a refill and was holding money when Eric stuck his head and one shoulder round the door.

'Now then.'

'How do, Eric. What'll you have?'

'Oh, the same as you.'

Eric was holding his hands as though he half expected to be asked to shake; then he employed them to go again through the motion of tucking down his shirt and pulling up his trousers which, like his jacket, were stained with engine oil.

'Been losing weight, or do you buy your suits secondhand?'

Eric rested one hand on his belly. 'Got rid of a bit o' beer gut.'

'Not much chance of a beer gut where I've been.'

Eric shot a quick glance at the landlord, who was at the till, as the other man took a deep swig of his fresh pint.

589

'You don't look too bad on it, anyway.'

'Like the tan, do you?'

Eric drank. 'What's on your mind, then?'

'Let's go where we can talk.' He got off the stool and led the way to a table down the room.

'It won't be as quiet as this for long,' Eric said, following.

'Perhaps it won't take long.'

Eric took out a green tobacco tin. He slipped a paper from its packet, laid tobacco along it and began to roll a smoke. The other man watched him fumble for a couple of seconds then reached across. 'Give it here.' His deft fingers evened the lie of the tobacco, then closed the paper into a neat cylinder. He held it out to Eric with the gummed edge free. 'Lick.'

Eric said 'Thanks' and pushed the box across the table. The other man pushed it back.

'Broke that habit long since.'

Eric lit up, inhaled, took a drink of lager, all with quick, restless movements. The other man sat hunched at the table, both hands lightly touching the cold moist outside of his glass.

'What made you come back here?' Eric asked. 'Been me, this is the last place I'd 've come to.'

'Been you, Eric, you wouldn't have been where I've been.'

'Been me, there'd 've been no need for any for it.'

'Still kidding yourself about that, are you? Still think if she'd married you first she wouldn't have taken somebody else on?'

'She's been all right with me all this time.'

'But she'd had the fright of her life, lad.' His gaze took in Eric's jacket. 'That's a good whistle and flute. Or it was at one time. Still like to dress nice, I see.'

590

'Never took in the jeans bit,' Eric said. 'I've spent enough time in overalls. I like to make an effort when I go out.'

'Does she still like her nights out?'

'Well...' Eric looked at his hands. 'You can't do all you might like when you've got young 'uns.'

'Oh, yes, the young 'uns. Two, aren't there?'

'That's right. Two lads.'

'Two lads. Happy families.'

'You had your chance.'

'What chance was that?'

'If you couldn't make her happy...'

'You self-satisfied bastard. You think you'd 've done any better? She'd have made mincemeat of you, the woman she was then.'

'Happen so. Happen not.'

'You got the leavings, mate. What was left after me and that other bastard.'

'You're still not sorry, I see.'

'I'd 've swung for the bastard. Her an' all.'

'There were plenty thought you should have.'

'Well, I didn't. And now I'm out.'

'So what's it all been for? What are you after, coming back here?'

'That's what I thought I'd find out.'

'It's all done with, a long time ago.'

'You'd know how long it's been if you'd lived every day of it like I have.'

'Me heart bleeds.'

'I want to see her, Eric.'

Eric shook his head. 'No. You can't.'

'Has she said so?'

'She doesn't want to see you.'

'Has she said so?' he asked again. 'Does she know I'm out?'

'We don't talk about you.'

'She must have known my time was about up.'

'We've never talked about it.'

'So you didn't tell her I'd been in touch with you?'

'No.'

'What are you scared of?'

'Raking up what's dead and buried.'

'Hasn't she got a mind of her own? Since when did you do her thinking for her?'

'I look after her now.'

'You're taking a lot on yourself.'

'If you think she's still pinin' for you, you're mistaken.'

'I'd like her to speak for herself, Eric.'

'After what you did? You must be barmy to think she'd give you the time o' day.'

'What's to stop me waiting on the street for her?'

'I can always set the police onto you. They'd make you leave us alone.'

'You'd enjoy that, wouldn't you? But she'd have to know then. Why don't you just do it the easy way and give her a message: tell her I'd like to see her.'

'What will you do when she says no?'

'I'll cross that bridge when I come to it.'

'Christ!' Eric said, 'but you do fancy yourself, don't you? All this has learned you nowt, has it?'

'I've done my time, Eric. I've paid for what I did.'

'Paid? They've let you out, but who says you've paid? Do you think she thinks you've paid?'

'That's up to her to say. You can't talk for her on that.' He paused while he drank, long and deep. 'You're taking too much on yourself, Eric. Tell her I want to see her.'

'You haven't even asked how she is. D'you think time's stood still for everybody while you've been inside?'

'Have her looks started to go, then? Do you make enough to give her what she wants, or has she been working her fingers to the bone for you?'

'We do all right.'

'I should doubt it, from the look of that clapped-out wreck you drove up in.'

'It happened to be the one in the yard with the keys in it. Tomorrow it could just as easy be a Merc.'

'Go on, Eric, impress me. You buy cars at auction, patch 'em up and flog 'em for a few quid more to suckers who don't know any better.'

'And what bright golden future have you come out of nick to? I don't know whether you've heard, but we're in a recession. There's over three million unemployed. What have you got to offer her, even if she wanted it?'

'Who says I want to offer her anything? Who says I want her?'

'What the hell do you want, then?'

'I want to see her. How is she?'

Eric took a deep breath. 'She's dying.'

'You what?'

'It's cancer.'

'Go on.'

'It started a couple of years ago, in one breast. They hoped they'd caught it in time.'

'I don't believe you.'

'Believe what you like. I never knew it was like that. Sometimes she's nearly like normal, except she's thinner and easy tired. Other times she has to stop in bed. Soon she'll be in bed for good – for what time there is left.'

'How long do they give her?'

'She won't see another Christmas.'

'Steak sandwich and chips, Mrs Brewster.' The landlady put the plate on the table with a knife and a fork wrapped in a paper napkin. 'I hope I haven't kept you waiting.'

'No, no. No hurry. I'm just nicely ready for it now. You're quiet today.'

'There'll be a few more in later. But it's the schools' half-term. We're always a bit quieter then.'

'Maisie...' Mrs Brewster leaned in over the table as the woman turned to go. 'Do you know that chap over there, the one looking this way?'

'Can't say I know either of them. I noticed them as I came through from the kitchen. They're not falling out, are they?'

'They're not bothering anybody else, if they are. No, he seemed to know me and I've this feeling I ought to know him.'

'Didn't you ask him who he was?'

'I gave him plenty of chance to tell me, but he didn't let on. It's these blessed eyes of mine lately; they miss so much they wouldn't have missed at one time. He said he used to live here.'

'Well, of course, we haven't been here long.'

'No, well...'

'Have you got everything you want? Would you like some mustard, or vinegar?'

'No, just salt and pepper. Thank you.'

He tapped his empty glass with a fingernail and waited for Eric to take the hint.

'D'you want another?'

'How much is brandy these days?'

'About the same as this.'

'Wouldn't want you to be out of pocket. I'll have a brandy.'

'Any particular brand?'

'I'm not fussy.'

He was feeling light in the head, as though dizziness might strike him if he stood up. Well, he was out of practice. But two pints of lager shouldn't have got to him like that.

Cancer. And they'd already had the knife into her.

Across the room Mrs Brewster was eating her food and wiping juice from her chin with her paper serviette. She twisted her head and looked at him. The sunlight through the window behind her turned her glasses into two impenetrable discs of reflected light, but he thought her mouth curved in a little smile.

She had not smiled that day he had faced her in the magistrates' court in the town hall, when they sent him up to the crown court on a charge too grave for them to try. Her mouth had worked then as the police gave the evidence and she heard just what he'd done. He'd thought she was having all on not to be sick. There was more than one in the room that day who would cheerfully have marched him out to the marketplace and topped him there and then. And now she couldn't place him.

Eric had got the drinks and paid for them. He left them on the bar and went through the door he had entered by. As the landlord stepped into the back room, the other man suddenly got up and walked to the bar. He took the brandy and threw it back in one; then, without looking at Mrs Brewster, he went out.

There were doors in the passage marked LADIES and GENTS. He walked past them and into the street.

Mrs Brewster tried to poke a scrap of lettuce from under her top denture with her tongue. She would have to go and rinse it. She drank the last quarter-inch of her

Guinness and considered whether or not to buy a glass of port. It was dull in the Bird in Hand today. Boring. She would have been better occupied in eating a snack at home while watching *Pebble Mill at One* on television.

One of the men came back, the one who had come in last. He went to the bar counter and only looked behind him at the table where he had been sitting when he saw the empty brandy glass.

'He went out,' Mrs Brewster said.

'Oh.'

This man remained standing at the bar. He bit at one of his fingernails before drinking.

'He must have gone,' Mrs Brewster said.

'Yes... Aye...'

'Should I know him?' Mrs Brewster asked; but the man was now in a study and seemed not to have heard her. Then he suddenly turned his head.

'Did you say something?'

'I said I thought I ought to know him.'

'Oh, he's nobody you'd be interested in, love,' Eric said.

The Middle
of the Journey

Dear Monica,

So you heard. I didn't want to alarm you or upset you without real cause so I decided I'd wait until I had something positive to tell you. I've always known how fond you are of Raymond, though it was believing your friendship for me came first that led me to unburden myself to you all those years ago and only afterwards did I realise that I'd not behaved with the last ounce of tact in choosing you as my confessor. But then, confession itself can often be construed as a selfish act, can't it, and what in the end are friends for was what you said to me yourself at the time. So here I go again, because at the moment you can only know what everyone else knows, not what else came out of it.

We were driving up the A1 to Yorkshire and I was telling Raymond that I couldn't remember travelling so far north in England since I'd visited my Aunt Lally, in Harrogate, as a child. But, of course, I could. 'I've passed through on the train to Scotland, but that hardly counts.'

Raymond said the trains are so frequent and fast nowadays he'd been tempted to suggest we should travel that way.

'You'd have had to pay carriage on the wine,' I reminded him.

'True. And they're just that bit off the beaten track, which would have put them to the trouble of meeting us.'

The man we were going to stay with has a house in the country, with a large cellar. He had put it to Raymond that with the number of free-house pubs and well-to-do families in the area an agency for quality wines could be run from his home, and Raymond, looking for a foothold in that region, had agreed to give it a try, though he had wondered aloud to me whether our host's immediate interest extended any further than the possibility of making enough profit to cover his own wine bill.

'Anyway, with the car,' I pointed out, 'we can leave when we like, should anything go wrong.'

'Wrong?'

'If we're bored by them, or they're bored by us; or the food's awful, or the beds are damp.'

'You're becoming a regular fusspot, Nora.'

'No, I'm not. But I do know the minimum I need to keep me comfortable and contented, and I can't throw myself into these adventures with the blithe abandon I used to.'

'Adventures! A weekend in the country with a potential customer? Blithe abandon? Whenever did blithe abandon win over your natural caution?'

'You'd be surprised,' I wanted to say, 'astounded if I confessed to you now.' I hadn't thought about if for years. Well, not let it preoccupy me for more than two or three consecutive minutes. It was only this journey to that part of the country which had brought it back. Not that we were going to the same part exactly, either: it was a good thirty miles away. I'd checked it on the map before telling myself that it wouldn't have mattered if we'd been bound for the same hotel: no one would have been likely to remember after all that time.

But I remembered: I remembered more than I'd known I could, giving myself the luxury of sitting down and letting myself remember; safe now at this distance of years.

Raymond was telling me what the country was like: 'Farming land; great sweeps of it. Rich. Well wooded in parts. It's not like the Dales, you know. People who don't know Yorkshire think everything outside the cities is barren moors and the Dales.'

Oh, yes, the Dales. The weather had been atrocious, but we had hardly cared. We had walked in wind and rain and exclaimed as occasional sunshine lit vistas we had resigned ourselves to not seeing. Four bracing days, three blissful nights. (Did I tell you all this? Enough of it, anyway.) It seemed to me like abandon, though I'd banished guilt by an act of will. Raymond was on a buying trip in France. Douglas and I were a long way from home, and he had chosen well: a place he'd called on a couple of years before and remembered. I'd tried teasing him, asking him if he'd brought someone else here, before.

'It struck me as a good place for a honeymoon.'

A honeymoon. Ah...

'Not for young people who need nightlife, theatres, bright lights,' he said, 'but for a mature couple who are content with each other.'

Yes, a honeymoon...

Douglas, as you know, had married and divorced young. 'It didn't take,' he said. 'Thank goodness we were both sensible enough to let go before any lasting damage was done.' He'd been bitten once and now trod warily. I was no threat to him. We didn't speak of the future – not then. The present was everything and life too short to deny ourselves the pleasure we gave each other. Many a lasting marriage has been under-pinned by a little outside excitement, I'd told myself. Douglas had seemed to understand; to want and expect no more than that.

Until he spoke of honeymoons, and then, the imagination being what it is, my thoughts began to reconstruct our affair as a trial run for a venture on which I knew we both would have happily embarked were there nothing in the way.

Only Raymond, of course. No children, and likely to be none. Not much passion, either, if the truth be told – and now was the time to tell it – but a gentle, companionable union which I'd thought contained all I should ever need for the rest of my life.

'Do whatever you think is best for you,' you said to me. 'Do it and abide by it.' And only much later did it occur to me how hard it might have been for you not to say straight out, 'Go with Douglas, if you want him so much.' For that would have freed Raymond so that you and he might... Well, not then, but later, in the fullness of time. (Am I imagining all that? Forgive me if I am. But you may never have allowed yourself to frame the thought so clearly.)

Raymond came back from France with tales of the wife of the vineyard owner he had bought from. 'She seemed to me to be a woman who had all a woman could reasonably hope for: good looks, three healthy children, a well-to-do and respected husband who obviously loves her. And what is she? A cold, arrogant shrew. If he didn't love her so much and hadn't his work, which is his passion, I suspect he would have to acknowledge that she does her level best to make his life a misery. All I could think of was how very, very lucky I am to have you and how very, very easy it must be to make a mistake that could ruin one's life.'

He wanted me that night and something in me responded so that I opened myself freely and worked to quicken our feeling. He was grateful. 'Well, old girl,' he said afterwards, 'I rather think you must have been missing me.'

Douglas said I wanted both of them. 'I want you,' I told him, 'but I can't hurt him.'

'You're going to have to choose.'

'Oh, why didn't you say all this at the beginning?'

'I didn't know at the beginning. But now you must choose.'

'Not yet, Douglas,' I said. 'Please, not just yet.'

And then one day, as you know, I went to where he should have been and he wasn't there. I waited for his message – I had to leave it to him. None came. It was over.

Perhaps you can see that for Raymond to tease me about my 'natural caution' was to tempt me, with the ache long gone, to diminish my sacrifice: to let in the small voice which insinuated that caution had indeed been my prime motive, that saving virtue of common sense which had told me, even in deepest thrall, which side my bread was buttered on.

Because I did get my reward, you know. I got what I'd always wanted as a girl: marriage to a gentle and totally reliable man and a civilised life in which I could read the books I wanted to read, see the films and the plays, take my seat at the opera, travel, tend my garden, entertain his friends, mine, ours, in a home where money was never a pressing problem.

601

So why was I feeling so strongly at this late stage (because of where we were going, because of the memories the journey had resurrected, because of his light-hearted jibe about my 'caution'?) the urge to tell him how it had all been bought and paid for?

I offered to drive for a spell, but I knew he didn't want me to. He didn't mind long journeys so long as he was at the wheel, but he was a poor passenger and soon began that tuneless humming that might have sounded to others like contentment, but which I knew as a sure sign he was ill at ease.

I, on the other hand, perfectly relaxed physically, felt sleep reach for me. As my head rolled and jerked, Raymond said why didn't I let the seat down and take a nap.

'Sure you don't mind?'

'Not a bit.'

'I always feel such a cheat, napping while someone else is driving.'

'And I always say I don't mind.'

'Well, if you won't let me drive.'

'Take your nap. I'll put the radio on.'

'We can stop for coffee whenever you wish.'

I knew in my sleep that the car had stopped, which was what woke me. I took in slowly as I stretched and yawned that we were not on a hotel or snack-bar forecourt, but by the roadside, as a massive container lorry whooshed by with a warning blare of horn, shuddering even the sturdy Volvo where it stood, and drowning for the moment the inane voices on a local radio phone-in programme.

I turned my head, starting to ask 'What... ?' and sitting bolt upright as I saw him.

He couldn't speak. I wasn't even sure he could hear

me. The spasm seemed to have left him; his hands still clung to the wheel and his eyes stared straight ahead, looking at God only knew what, out of a face bloated with a colour the like of which I'd never seen before and hope and pray I shall never see again.

There was no moving him to get to the wheel myself. I wondered how much warning he'd had and as I switched off the radio and loosened his tie and spoke to him again, I knew that I had no idea at all how to take the first steps in such an emergency; I mean what was dangerous, what might make the difference between life and death.

I made out what looked like a pub sign some way in front and opened the door. 'Raymond, I'm going to get help.' As I got out I thought to reach back, turn off the ignition and switch on the hazard warning lights. Then I ran, stumbling at first along the rough grass shoulder before I risked taking to the edge of the road itself.

The doctor was explaining to me: 'A lot of things – even familiar things – have become jumbled – scrambled, you could call it – in his mind. He couldn't get his own name right this morning.'

'Good lord!'

'He's not going out of his mind,' he went on quickly. 'You mustn't worry about that. It's quite a common effect of a seizure and in a day or two it should sort itself out.'

'He is going to be all right, isn't he?'

'Oh, yes; with treatment and rest he should be back to normal quite soon. I say normal, though you'll both have to regard what's happened as a warning and see that he adjusts his way of life accordingly.'

It was the first time I'd spoken with this man – the specialist. At first it had been the staff in Casualty, too brisk and preoccupied to tell me anything.

'You don't live hereabouts?'

'No, our home's in Surrey. We were on our way to visit some business connections of my husband's, in Yorkshire.'

'But you've found a place to stay?'

'I'm in a motel, just outside town. They have my phone number on the ward.'

I wanted to ask him more, but I guessed he'd told me all he could – or wanted to – for the present. His telephone pinged as though it was about to ring. He moved some papers on his desk. He was a busy man. I got up and left him.

Devilishly expensive it was, too, the place I'd booked myself into that first fraught day, taking the easiest course and choosing from the hotel guide that Raymond carried in the car. Comfortable, of course, with a private bathroom, colour television and a refrigerator stocked with enough drink to keep anyone paralytic for a week. And a drink was what I felt I needed, limp as I was with relief that Raymond was going to be all right, and suspended now in a kind of limbo, not knowing how long we must stay in this strange place halfway to our destination.

I chose whisky. I mustn't get drunk. A couple in my present state would make me tipsy. Oh God! Oh, thank God, thank God he was going to be all right (and he is, Monica, he is; I assure you). Just how much I needed him had been made plain to me on that roadside as the ambulancemen took him from the car and I stood, transfixed by pure terror at the possibility of losing him.

It was the weekend now. Raymond's office was closed and I couldn't remember the home telephone number of his partner. I must also ring the Ascoughs, who would be wondering what on earth had happened to us.

'I need some phone numbers, Raymond,' I'd said to him at the hospital.

His address book would be in his briefcase, which was now with our luggage, in my motel room. The case was one of those rigid-framed leather ones with numbered tumbler locks.

But all he'd done was smile, in a distant, dreamy fashion, as though he were far away, in a private place I couldn't reach. I'd hesitated to press him. And if, as the specialist had said, he couldn't unscramble his own name, how could his confused mind be expected to yield the six figures which would open the case?

I put the case on the low table and looked at it. With so many arbitrary combinations of figures assigned one in this computer age surely for himself he would have chosen a sequence he could readily recall. I tried his birthday. No. His office telephone number was seven figures. I tried the first six, then the last. I did the same with our home number, then I had a drink of whisky and looked out of the window. It was a lovely day. The land was green. I'd promised myself some country walks while Raymond did his business. What could the Ascoughs be thinking?

It was lunchtime, but I didn't feel like going to the restaurant. Ringing room service, I ordered soup and a salad sandwich. Coffee or tea I could make here in the room.

When I'd filled the kettle and plugged it in, then poured the rest of the whisky from the miniature and added another cube of ice, my gaze fell on the television set. I switched on and sat down opposite it. From where I sat I could see my reflection in the glass over the dressing-table unit. I wondered again at the face that had led a man to lead me astray and asked myself what Douglas

605

would have made of it now. Well, I'd experienced that. I'd known it, was the better for it, and no harm done. For now I'd something to measure it against.

There was a magazine programme on television. They were talking about a new picture biography of the Princess of Wales and showing film of her wedding day. It was when my food had arrived and I was thanking the waiter and looking for my handbag while wondering if I'd remembered aright that service was included, that a thought slipped into my mind.

I let the food stand and the kettle come to the boil as I rolled the tumblers of Raymond's case and clicked the locks open.

Then I was crying and choking as I tried to swallow what was left of the whisky. That he should have chosen that combination. That that should be the sequence he lined up every day when he opened the case. The date of our wedding.

'Oh God, but that's touching!'

I'd spoken out loud. Because he'd reached me. Not knowing, he'd reached me as surely as if he'd placed a gentle fingertip on my cheek.

His partner wanted to drive up straight away. I put him off. 'Don't trouble, Eldon. There's nothing you could do. Tomorrow or the day after they may let me take him home. The specialist seemed quite optimistic.' I said nothing about the scrambling of Raymond's mind. Eldon is a fussy and pedantic man and a careless word about that could lead him to wonder if Raymond would be capable of pulling his weight again.

The Ascoughs' phone was answered by a girl with a thick foreign accent.

'Is nobody here,' she said. 'All out.'

606

I spoke slowly and clearly. 'Will you give them a message, please. This is Mrs Raymond Hawkridge. They were expecting us. My husband was taken ill on the journey and now we must cancel our visit. I'll ring them later, when I have more news. Will you make sure they get that message?'

'Will do,' the girl said, and hung up.

My soup had gone cold but I didn't mind. Soup of the day, which I'd not troubled to identify, had turned out to be tomato, which always gives me indigestion. Munching my sandwich, I boiled the kettle again and made tea. Before very long it would be time to take the car and visit Raymond once more.

I must ask him, try to get him to tell me, if there was anything I should do. Before that, was there anything in his briefcase I might need? I hadn't closed it. Its lid stood open, held by brass hinges. A handsome case, which I'd given him myself, with a mock-suede lining and leather loops holding pens. Two folders lay neatly in the base; other papers were tucked into two pockets in the lid.

I told myself that it was not my way to pry; but until I looked I could have no idea what might be important and what not. Ludicrously, as it seemed then, the old saw came to mind that those who eavesdrop seldom hear good of themselves. And then a moment later colour was flooding my throat and face. They burned as though I'd been caught shamelessly delving.

I was holding an envelope drawn from deep in one of the pockets – an envelope already slit open, though addressed to myself. I found that I could still hear his carefully modulated voice (an old-fashioned actor's voice, I used to tease) as I read what was inside (and which you, Monica, since I've come so far, may as well hear too):

607

'My dear Nora, I knew you would know it was finished when I didn't come to our usual place, and I knew that after all we'd said you would make no attempt to contact me. I thought it best that way, but now I feel I must say a final word.

'I am oddly bitter that you were ready to throw away what we found together. You speak of duty and moral choices as if they were absolutes handed down from on high, when you don't believe that any more than I do. I can't for the life in me see what you owe someone who has left such a void in your life, you have had to snatch at happiness elsewhere. Yours isn't a nature that craves the excitement of an adventure, yet you haven't the courage to grasp what is being offered to you. I hope you won't spend the rest of your life regretting it.

'For myself, I shall be a long time forgetting. As a start, I'm going abroad. I had the offer of this job before. Had things gone differently I should have taken you with me. Now I shall go alone. Who was it said there was nothing like a sea-change for putting an unhappy relationship in perspective? We shall see.

'The "decent" thing now would be for me to thank you for the great joy you gave me. I would, but it's been too dearly bought. I always said your Raymond didn't deserve you. Now I think perhaps he does. Goodbye. D.'

I got up then and went to the window and took several deep breaths, until my heart stopped racing.

Of course, I wondered how he'd come to intercept it and why he chose then to keep it from me. Not that there was anything in it that I hadn't already known and come to terms with. But why, when he'd decided not to face me with it, did he not destroy it? Why keep it and carry it with him? To remind himself of the perfidy of women? That what you trusted most was least to be trusted? Or

608

did he find in that ever-present knowledge that I'd been tempted yet turned back to him his greatest solace?

Dear Monica, I'm putting all this down because I have to try to get it clear in my mind, and that's best done as if I were talking to someone: someone who knew. But I doubt if I shall post this letter. Not this one, but another, a simpler one, appreciating your anxiety and putting your fears at rest. It's really too late in the day for me to let myself wonder whether there was a moment when temptation led you to try to turn things to your advantage.

But how bitter for you, as well as us, if there was. Because for myself, you see now, I have to come to terms with the realisation that Raymond has been living all these years not with the woman I let him know, but with one he knew as well as she knew herself. And I'm going to have quite enough to think about learning to live with that.

Rue

He lived alone in the house after his wife died. They had not got on for years and he was vaguely surprised when he found that she had made no will, so that everything came to him: what was left of her father's money, his collection of snuff-boxes, all she had owned. He had often wondered what it would be like to leave her; but the loneliness in the house after she died was appalling. The silence was the worst; that and opening the door to a room and knowing she would not be there. Her absence was like the ache in an amputated limb.

He was the managing director of a printing firm, was paid a director's fee on top of a substantial salary and was given a new car every two years. Fifty-three years old now, he would retire at sixty with a pension and a block of shares in the company.

Always reserved, he had many acquaintances but no close friends. The people who visited the house had come to see his wife. They stopped coming when she died and he thought they must have been relieved when he did not take up the invitations to dinner parties and the like which they sent him in the early days of his widowerhood.

A woman had come in two half-days in the week to help with the cleaning. He gave her his wife's key so that she could let herself in, but after a short time she left a note to say she would not be coming any more. He went to see her, wondering if he had offended her in some way and ready to offer her more money. She did not express herself clearly, but he gathered that she did not like the empty house either, preferring company while she worked.

At night he lay awake in his bed straining his ears for every small sound as the house cooled.

He thought about moving. He could sell the house at a handsome profit, buy a flat and invest the rest of the money. But he dreaded finding himself at the mercy of neighbours, who might have children, might quarrel, might play pop music into the night. He had always prized the quiet of the house, but not this silence. It was as though what the house lacked now was the sound of his wife's breathing.

There had been one child, a boy, who died in a swimming accident in his early teens. His wife had blamed him for that, said he could have saved the lad. In time he came to believe it himself. He found that he could no longer touch her. From being a tired routine, their intimate life died altogether. He gave himself occasional relief and tried not to let the subject preoccupy him.

Now he thought about the new relationships his freedom made possible and began to take stock of himself. He had felt middle-aged for years, but though he was a little overweight (he had always inclined to tubbiness), he still had his teeth, most of his hair, and managed without glasses except for reading. He took note of the age of politicians and others who came into the news, looked at them on television and compared his appearance with theirs.

He took up jogging. He bought a tracksuit and the right kind of shoes and at first drove out of the neighbourhood and began with short runs which would not put too much sudden strain on his heart. As the nights drew in, he also started trotting round the local streets, last thing. This served the double purpose of giving him exercise and tiring him for bed.

One night, after dark, he was stopped and questioned by two policemen, in a car. They asked him his name and address and what he did for a living. There was a man going about murdering women on the streets. He had been doing it for five years. Jordan realised when they had let him go what a good disguise the role of a jogger could be. It was natural for a jogger to be seen running; he could carry his weapons on a belt under his tracksuit and remove any blood from the suit by putting it straight into the washer.

Still the nights troubled him. It was then that he felt his loneliness most. He tried comparing his loneliness with that of a man who was impelled to murder strange women. It did not help him much.

He tried taking a nip of Scotch before going to bed and gradually increased his consumption until one night, when he had drunk a third of a bottle, he realised he was talking to himself. His mind, calm and concentrated at work, slipped late at night into a turmoil. When he had had a lot to drink he felt that there was something that made sense of everything lying just beyond the grasp of his thoughts. That was what whisky did to him, and drinking alone.

He had never frequented public houses but one evening, having noted the warmly lighted windows of the local at the end of the street, he forewent his run and walked along there instead. About to order Scotch, he changed his mind and asked for a pint of bitter. It was cool and palatable, making a good mouthful. He stayed an hour, standing at one end of the bar counter, and drank three pints. He felt the tension gradually drain out of him. His thoughts drifted. He vaguely recognised several people he had seen in the neighbourhood. A couple of them nodded to him, but none of them struck up a conversation. The barmaid, whom he had never seen before, wished him goodnight as he left. Her hair was the colour of partly burned corn-stubble. Her top teeth protruded slightly and her tongue occasionally flicked saliva from the corners of her lips, which remained apart in repose. Her sudden smile as she reached for his glass and dipped it into the washing-up machine behind the bar remained with him as he strolled home and let himself into the empty house.

He thought about her as, too sleepy to read more than half a page, he switched off his bedside light; and again when his radio-alarm woke him out of a deep, unbroken sleep. His bladder was full and as he padded briskly along the landing to the bathroom he wondered how old she was and tried to remember whether she had worn a wedding ring.

He had a ticket for the opera that evening. It was his greatest interest outside his work. There had been a time when he thought his wife enjoyed it too. But when he played gramophone records from his considerable collection or tuned in to a radio broadcast, she found excuses to do other things, and he began to realise that she had little ear for music and that only the stage spectacle made it tolerable for her. Latterly, she had sneered at what she called opera's 'unreality' and people standing about 'bawling their heads off'. He had found solace in shutting himself in another room and escaping through music into the world each score conjured up. Yet since her death he could not concentrate for more than a few minutes. Without her unsympathetic presence in the house, his thoughts wandered and even those favourite passages which could start to sing in his mind at any moment of the day slid by only half noticed.

Tonight he saw a performance of Verdi's *Don Carlos* in a new production not yet run in, with small troubles that lengthened the intervals and kept the audience late. He had thought of calling at his local for a last drink, but by the time he had driven up out of the city the pub was closed.

Lights still burned inside where the staff would be washing glasses and clearing up. He wondered if the woman lived on the premises and, if not, how she got home and how far she had to go. His wife would have called her common, a millgirl, and pointed with distaste to the unnatural colour and spoiled texture of her hair. Yet he could not forget the direct genuineness of that smile, and 'genuine' as the one word he found himself applying to her.

When he went into the pub the next evening, there was a woman serving whom he took to be the publican's wife. He did not like to ask how often the other woman was on duty and when she would be here again. They might have several casual staff for all he knew, and he had no name with which to identify the woman with the corn-stubble hair and that appealing open smile. Nor was she there on either of the two crowded weekend nights. He was being silly, behaving like an adolescent.

She was no different from any number of the women employed at the works. He must have sunk low in personal resource if he could be so affected by a single friendly smile from a complete stranger. If the pub had been any farther away, he would not have returned. But it was so convenient. He had taken to the beer and he liked the atmosphere. But not at weekends. Then there were too many people, too much noise and tobacco smoke. He was constantly jostled at the bar as he stood aside to let people get served.

He had other things to think about. He must work out a way of living instead of drifting from day to day. The house was becoming neglected. Every Saturday morning he dusted and vacuumed, but knew that it needed more than that. He had pinned a typewritten postcard advertising his need of a cleaner to the works' noticeboard, hoping that one of the women would know someone who wanted the work, but there was no response. Now he redrafted it as a small ad for the evening paper: 'Widower (businessman) requires cleaner, two sessions a week (no heavy work). Old Church Road area. References. Telephone outside business hours.'

She rang on a payphone when the ad had appeared three times. 'Are you the man that's wanting a cleaner?'

'Yes, I am.'

'Can I ask you what two sessions a week means?'

'Two mornings or two afternoons, whichever is more convenient.'

'No evenings?'

'Well, no.'

'That's all right, then. I've got an evening job.'

'You could probably combine the two nicely,'

'Yes...' There was a silence, as if she were thinking, or trying to assess him from his voice.

'Are you interested?'

'It is a genuine advertisement, isn't it?'

'What do you mean?'

'There's some funny folk about these days. You've got to be careful.'

'My wife died six months ago,' Jordan said. 'Things have been getting out of hand.'

'Hmm. I suppose I'd better come over.'

'When can you come?'

'Would tonight be all right? I'm not working tonight.'

'That's all right. Where are you speaking from?'

She told him a district of the city that was about twenty minutes away by bus and he gave her the number of the house.

'Shall I give you directions?'

'Is it anywhere near the Beehive?'

'It's just round the corner. Five minutes away.'

'I'll find it, then.'

'I'll expect you.'

'By the way, what's your name?'

'Jordan.'

'I'll be seeing you, then.'

He supposed it would mean nothing to this woman, but he had very occasionally to remind people in whom his name touched a distant chord of memory that he shared it with the hero of a Hemingway novel. 'Except that you don't look like Gary Cooper,' a local academic – a lecturer in American literature at the university – had once remarked. 'And I've certainly never had the pleasure of sharing a sleeping bag with Ingrid Bergman.' Jordan had added.

That had been at a gathering in the neighbourhood he'd been taken to by his wife. He supposed they still went on, those Sunday morning or early evening sherry parties, but he was never asked to them now. You could live very privately in these tree-lined roads of stone houses in what had once been a village with a couple of miles of open land between it and the city. That had suited him: he was a private man. But that had been before the loneliness which assailed him after his wife died. Perhaps, he thought, now, if he could get some help in the house he would give a party himself, renew some acquaintanceships, meet some new people. He did not want to think about living much longer as he was doing now.

He had already eaten a light supper and now he washed his hands and face and brushed his hair, and, after switching on the porch light, settled down in the sitting-room with a glass of Scotch and *Cosi fan tutte* on the record player. Though he knew the plot and what the characters were singing about, he found that following the translated libretto helped his concentration.

She came when he had just put on the second record. He left it playing and went to the door. She was half turned away, shaking her umbrella, and the scarf covering her head hid her hair; so that it was not until she had stepped inside and they faced each other in the hall that he saw who she was. His surprise then was such that his voice lifted involuntarily in a second greeting.

'Oh, hullo!'

'Do you know me?'

'You once served me in the Beehive.'

'Did I? You weren't a regular, though, were you?'

'Oh, no. There was just the once while you were there.'

'I'm not there any more now.'

'Ah! That explains it.'

'What?'

'Why I hadn't seen you again.'

'Were you looking?'

Her directness was unexpected. 'I noticed.' He held out his hands. 'I didn't know it had started to rain. Let me hang up your coat.' He took it from her while she unfastened her headsquare, shook her hair free and smoothed the hem of her pastel-pink jumper.

'Come through.'

In the sitting-room he had to indicate twice that she should sit down, while he took the record off the player. She sat on the edge of the deep armchair, ankles crossed as she looked round the room. She had pretty legs, Jordan noticed, and she was probably vain about them because her tights were flatteringly fine and of a better quality than the rest of her clothes.

'They're big, aren't they?' she said.

'Beg pardon.'

'These houses. They're bigger than they look from the outside.'

'You'd soon find your way around. I'll show you, later.' He sat down near her. 'Have you done this kind of work before?'

'Not for other people, no.'

'Well, nobody asks for a diploma in cleaning.'

'No.'

'Just for thoroughness. My wife was very thorough.'

'Did she do it all herself?'

'Oh, no. She had a regular woman.'

'What happened to her?'

'She gave up coming when my wife died. I don't think she liked being in the house on her own.'

'Why? There's nothing strange about it, is there?'

'Oh, no. I think she just liked someone to talk to. Is that the kind of thing that would bother you?'

'If you're here to work, you're here to work.'

618

'Quite. But it's why I have to ask for references. I'd have to give you a key and the run of the house.'

'Oh, yes. You can't be too careful these days.'

'What's your name, by the way?'

'Audrey Nugent.' She was looking into her handbag.

'Mrs Nugent, is it?'

'It was. I was married once.'

'No children?'

'No. Just as well, as it turned out.' She shrugged. 'I picked a wrong 'un.'

'I'm sorry.'

He took the folded manilla envelope she was holding out to him. 'There's these.'

They were both from publicans she had worked for; one, recently dated, from the landlord of the Beehive.

'You say you're doing evening work now?'

'I'm at the Royal Oak, in Ridley.'

'Didn't you like the Beehive?'

'It was further to travel and only a couple of nights a week. I wanted a bit more than that.'

'Hmm.'

'Was that opera you were playing on your gramophone?'

'Yes. Mozart.'

'I used to like Mario Lanza.'

'A bit before your time, surely.'

'I was only a kid. I had some of his records, though. He got fat.'

'Oh, yes?'

'It just piled on to him at the back end. He got like a barrel. Have you got any of his stuff?'

'I'm afraid I haven't.'

'They all seem to get that kind of weight, the best singers. Look at Harry Secombe.'

'And Pavarotti.'

She frowned. 'I don't think I know him.'

'You'll have seen him on television, perhaps.'

'I don't get to see much TV, working nights.'

'No.'

She gave a sudden sigh, more like a catch of breath, clasping her fingers in her lap, then examining the nails of one hand. 'Are they all right?'

'The references? You seem to have given satisfaction.'

He didn't know. Employers sometimes gave a reference to get rid of someone. It was hard to refuse anyone who had not been downright dishonest. Whoever came to him without a personal recommendation he would have to take on trust. Was she the one? She seemed more subdued now than when she had arrived, different altogether here from what he thought of as her natural surroundings, in the lounge bar of the Beehive, at ease, efficient, chatting with the regulars, flashing on that smile which had so enchanted him.

He realised that neither of them had spoken for several moments and that he was staring at her. He wondered what he could say to make her smile. He shifted in his chair.

'Would you like to look over the house?'

'If you like.'

'You're still interested...?'

'I need the work,' she said bluntly. 'I can't make enough behind a bar at night. I was a machinist in ready-made clothing,' she went on, 'but everybody's cut back. It's all this cheap stuff coming in from abroad. They work for nothing there. It's not as if we were rolling in it.'

Jordan stood up. 'Come and look round.'

She followed him through the house.

'Of course, I don't use all these rooms now.'

'No.'

'But I like the privacy.' Not the loneliness, though, he thought. Not that.

The choice was his. He would have to decide soon.

'What were you thinking of paying?' she asked as they came back down the stairs.

He told her, having added a little to what he had found out was the going rate.

'How many hours?'

'Say three hours, two mornings a week. That should keep things spick and span.'

'You'd have to take my time-keeping on trust, wouldn't you?'

'My wife was very fussy,' Jordan said. 'She had a time-clock installed in the hall cupboard.'

Now she laughed. She put her head back and her lips drew away over her teeth, a thin skein of saliva snapping at one corner of her mouth.

He smiled with her. He felt committed now. He asked her if she would come for the first time on a Saturday morning so that he could show her where everything was.

It was as she was putting on her coat that he sensed an uneasiness in her.

'Is anything wrong?'

'I don't like to ask you, but it's dark outside and there's this maniac about. I wonder if you'd be good enough to see me to the bus stop.'

'If you're nervous, I'll drive you home.'

'Oh, no, no.'

'You're quite right to take care. There's no knowing where he might pop up next.'

'I'll be all right at the other end.' He went for his coat. 'I'm not usually timid, but you don't know what it's like to be a woman with him about. You begin to look sideways at every man who comes near you.

621

'There's one thing you can be sure of,' Jordan said. 'He isn't coloured green and he hasn't got two heads.'

'What d'you mean?'

'I mean, he'll look like a million other men. Like me, for instance.'

'Give over' she said.

'Sorry.' Jordan opened the door. 'Is it still raining? I'd better have a hat in any case.'

Her bus went from the other side of the main road. He saw her across and stood with her at the stop.

'I'll be all right now.'

'I'd rather see you safely on.'

'You can call for a quick one.' She nodded at the lighted windows of the Beehive, opposite.

He thought of asking her if she would like a drink before she went, but said instead, 'What's the pub like where you work now?'

'Different.'

There was a double-decker bus standing in a line of traffic at the lights. It swung towards them and pulled up.

'I'll see you Saturday,' she said, stepping on.

'Yes,' Jordan said. 'Saturday.'

One morning several weeks later he had to get out of bed to let her into the house.

'I'd forgotten about the bolt,' he apologised.

'I wondered, when me key wouldn't open it.' She looked at him as he stood in the hall, in his pyjamas and dressing-gown. 'Did you sleep in, or are you–?'

'I'm not very well,' Jordan said. 'I think I may have the flu.'

It had started yesterday, with a prickling sensation in the soft flesh behind the roof of his mouth. In the afternoon he had begun to sneeze. By evening, his bones were aching and he could not keep warm. He had been sweating in the night and now his pyjamas felt clammy against his skin.

'You get back to bed, out of these draughts,' Mrs Nugent said.

'I must just phone the office.'

She was carrying the vacuum cleaner and dusters from the cupboard under the stairs as he finished his call.

'Don't hang about here. Go back where it's warm. Shall I get you some breakfast?'

'A cup of tea would be welcome.'

'You get off up. I'll bring it in a minute.'

He had not seen her since that first Saturday morning. Every Thursday he left her money in an envelope on the hall table. The house shone and was fragrant with the smell of polish.

'Have you taken anything for it?' she asked when she brought in the tray. 'Can I fetch you anything from the shops?'

He dozed, hearing the whine of the cleaner from downstairs. He was not aware that he had fallen asleep until he woke to find her standing there again.

'How are you feeling now? Is your head thick?'

'No.' He could breathe quite freely.

'Perhaps it's not ready to come out yet. Perhaps it's only a chill.' She put her hand on his forehead in a movement that was totally without diffidence, as though she were a nurse, or someone who had known him a long time. It was cool and dry. He wanted her to leave it there. 'You don't feel to have a fever.'

'I really felt quite dreadful last night.'

'A night's sleep and a good sweat. They can work wonders.'

She sat down on the edge of the bed. He felt the

623

pressure of her buttocks against his leg. Jordan had to remind himself that he had seen her only three times. It was as though the time she spent alone in the house had given her a familiarity with him. Yet her voice remained level and impersonal.

'I expect you usually have your lunch out.'

'Yes.'

'What will you do today?'

'I hadn't thought about it.'

'What if I stopped on a while and got you something ready?'

'Oh, no, there's no need for that.'

'I'm not in any rush to get away.'

'I don't know what you'd find.'

'There's bacon and eggs in the fridge. You must eat, y'know.'

'Yes. Perhaps I will, later.'

She looked at him contemplatively, like someone about to make a diagnosis or recommend a course of treatment.

'I'll tell you what you ought to do.'

'Mmm?'

'You ought to get up and have a hot shower and get dressed in some warm clothes. Then come downstairs and have some bacon and egg.'

Jordan smiled. 'If you say so.'

She nodded and got up. 'I do.'

When, some time later, he was sitting at the kitchen table with a plate of egg and bacon and fried bread before him, Jordan said, 'Don't you want anything yourself?'

'Well, I...'

'You must have something. You can't stay behind to feed me and miss your own lunch.'

'All right, then.'

He was finished and drinking a second cup of tea by the time she sat down opposite him.

'You made short work of that.'

He had eaten with a good appetite. Odd, he thought, how different the same food could taste when somebody else had cooked it.

'I hope you're settled,' Jordan said. 'Happy in your work,' he explained as she looked at him.

'Oh, yes. It's easy now I'm on top of it. There's nobody to make much of a mess.'

'No.'

'I was thinking I'd wash some of your paintwork down.'

'Whatever you think.'

'Who does your washing for you?'

'You mean my clothes? I've been sending them to a laundry.'

'I didn't know there were any left. That must cost a bomb nowadays.'

'It's not cheap, but–'

'I don't suppose you've all that much. You could put a bundle through the launderette once a week and leave 'em out for me to iron.'

'If you're sure you don't mind.'

An idea came to him. He was silent for a time, not knowing how best to express it.

'I still have all my wife's clothes.'

'Oh?'

'She was about the same build as you.'

'Oh, yes?'

'I don't want to offend you, but she had some nice things. If there was anything you fancied...'

'What made you keep them?'

'I've just never bothered about them. I did wonder if I might donate them to an Oxfam shop.'

'Hadn't she any friends who might fancy something?'

'I've lost touch. Besides, some people don't like to –' He stopped.

'Wear a dead person's clothes, you mean?'

'Perhaps not somebody they've known.'

'I couldn't entertain anything intimate myself.'

'Oh, no, no, no,' Jordan said. 'I could put all that out for jumble. But why don't you look at the rest?'

'All right.'

'Come upstairs,' Jordan said. 'I'll show you what there is.'

A few minutes later he was taking suits and coats out of the fitted wardrobes in his wife's room and laying them on the bed. To them, he added woollens from the tallboy.

'Of course, he said, 'they might not be your style, but it would be a pity to let anything go that you could make use of.'

'There's some nice things,' she said. She was looking at the labels in the garments. 'Things I could never afford.'

'She was particular,' Jordan said. 'She always went to good shops. But, as I say, please don't be offended, and don't think you'll offend me. It was just an idea.'

She was holding a wool frock against her. It was maroon, with a belt. 'What was her colouring? Was she fair or dark?'

'Fair-skinned. Her hair was sort of nondescript. Mousy, I suppose you'd call it.'

'Like mine when I don't do anything with it.'

'Why do you do things with it?'

'I dunno. Makes a change. D'you think it looks common?'

'Oh, please...' Jordan said. 'I didn't mean to be personal.'

626

'Go on,' she said, 'say what you think.'

'Well, perhaps you could use a rinse or something to bring out its natural colour, without... without going so far.'

'Perhaps I could.' She had picked up another frock and was looking into the glass. 'Maybe I will.'

'What do you think, then?' Jordan asked. 'About the clothes.'

'Could I try some of them on?'

'Help yourself. I'll leave you.'

He wandered into his own room where he stood looking aimlessly round before pulling down the duvet and spreading it to air over the foot of his bed. Downstairs in the kitchen, he put on coffee, then, running hot water into the sink, he began to wash the pots they had used. He was standing there with his back to the door when he heard her come in.

'You should have left them to me.'

'I'm not altogether helpless,' Jordan said. 'And you're on overtime already.'

He had switched on the ceiling light which hung low over the table and as he glanced up the darkening window gave him her reflection. For an astounding second he was convinced that it was his wife standing there.

'What do you reckon, then?' she asked as he turned.

She had on the maroon frock, but over it she was wearing his wife's fur cape that she must have gone into another compartment of the wardrobe to find. She seemed suddenly unsure how he would react to this.

'Splendid,' Jordan said.

His stomach churned with a sudden desire to touch her. Looking away, he reached for a towel and dried his hands.

'Course, I know you didn't mean this, but I couldn't resist just trying it on.' Her hands were stroking the fur in long soft movements.

'Why not?' Jordan heard himself saying. Then, when he realised she did not understand: 'Why shouldn't I have meant that as well?'

'You can't,' she said, lifting her gaze to his. 'It must be worth a small fortune.'

'Not all that much,' Jordan said. 'And so what?'

'You can re-sell furs like this,' she said. 'Don't shops take 'em back?'

'I don't want to sell it.'

'You can't give it to me, though. I couldn't take it.'

'Why not? I bought it. Why shouldn't I give it to whom I like?'

'You'll want it for a lady friend.'

'I haven't got one.'

'You will have. You'll want to get married again, some time. Won't you?' she said after a moment, all the time her fingers moving along the lie of the fur. 'What is it, anyway?'

'Blue fox, I think,' Jordan said. 'Yes, blue fox.'

'It's beautiful.'

'Won't you let me give it to you?'

'Hang on a tick,' she said on a slight laugh, 'I'm just your cleaning woman. You don't hardly know me.'

'I don't want to embarrass you...'

'You are, though.'

'Sorry.'

'I'll have to think about it.'

'Was there anything else you fancied?'

'I'll take this frock. There's one or two other things I like.'

'Take anything you want,' Jordan said. 'And think

about the cape. It will still be there when you've made up your mind.'

She had taken off the cape and was standing with it over her arm, her free hand still moving in long strokes across the fur.

'I ought to be going, before it gets dark.'

'I've kept you late. I'll put it on your wages on Thursday.'

She laughed. 'Nay, I reckon I've been paid enough.'

'Would you like me to drive you home?'

'You stop in and keep warm. How are you feeling now?'

Jordan put the back of his hand to his forehead. 'I don't really know.'

'You get a few whiskies inside you and have an early night. You'll likely feel better tomorrow.'

He sat for a long time at the kitchen table after she had gone, while the light faded in the sky beyond the garden. She had left in a casual, almost offhand manner which had taken him by surprise after the near-intimacy of their talk about the clothes. 'I'll be off, then,' she had said, and before he could stir himself from the reverie in which he was peeling the maroon frock off her shoulders and freeing her breasts for the touch of his hands, the front door had closed behind her. He told himself that he had made her uneasy; that she lacked the social grace to handle the situation he had created. She would brood about its implications, wondering what his generosity implied, and – never crediting its spontaneity – from now on keep up her guard. Not that any of it really mattered, for they would not meet again unless he contrived it.

He asked himself if he could justify taking two more days off work so that he could be here when she came again, on Thursday. Could he risk scaring her off altogether by doing that? But he must, he told himself, build now on what had been started – on that curious apparently disinterested familiarity with which she had felt his temperature and sat on his bed; the way they had looked at his wife's clothes together; her coming down in the fur cape. Why had she done that if she had not coveted it and wanted to give him a chance to offer it to her?

At first he drank one cup of coffee after another, telling himself that if he did not move he could pretend that she was still in the house, moving about those empty rooms. Then he got up to fetch whisky and as he was coming back through the hall the telephone rang.

It was his secretary. He had not spoken to her earlier, but left a message in her absence. Now she asked how he was and if he thought he would be well enough to keep an appointment he had made for Thursday morning with the representatives of the unions.

Jordan's firm enjoyed good industrial relations, but increasingly sophisticated technology entailed keeping the unions sweetened. It was vital always that nothing should go by default.

'If I feel like I do now,' he told Mrs Perrins, 'I'll be in at the usual time tomorrow.'

The first thing he noticed when he came into the house after work on Thursday was her envelope lying on the hall table. With her wages he had slipped in a note saying, 'Do please think seriously about the coat.'

Wondering why she had not telephoned, it occurred to him that she probably did not know his office number. Perhaps she would ring this evening. Perhaps, on the other hand, she was ill and could not leave the house.

It came to him now how little he knew about her. He had never made a note of the address she had given him and his only clue to where she could be found was the name of the pub where she had said she was working. It took him a few minutes, while he poured himself a drink and began preparing his evening meal, to bring that to mind.

He looked it up in the yellow pages, then got out a street map of the city and its suburbs. He did not like to think of her being short of money over the weekend, nor of the possibility that she was too ill to get out to the shops.

There had been no call from her by mid-evening, when he got his car out again and drove across the city. The Royal Oak was a big, square, late Victorian pub with two floors of letting rooms above the tall windows of the public rooms on the ground floor. Its best days had obviously finished when commercial travellers abandoned the train for the motor car and no longer spent three or four nights in one place. Now its badly lighted and greasily carpeted bars served as a local for the occupants of the score of streets of three-storey redbrick terraces which climbed the hill beside the main road – and, Jordan thought, only the seediest of them. He detested everything about the place, from the smell of stale beer and the garish wallpaper to the few people he could see – the lads in motor bike gear round the pool table under the wall-mounted television set; the shabby, earnestly gesticulating men drinking in the passage by the back entrance; and the shirtsleeved landlord who put his cigarette on the rim of an already full ashtray before coming to serve him. Jordan wondered when trade here justified Mrs Nugent's wages. He ordered a Scotch and looked with distaste at the glass it came in.

'Does Mrs Nugent work here?' he asked when the man brought his change.

'Audrey?'

'Yes. Is she on tonight?'

'She should be, but she sent word she was poorly.'

'Does she live nearby?'

'Are you looking for her?'

'I'm a friend of hers from when she worked at the Beehive.'

The landlord had taken in his clothes and now an expression Jordan couldn't read flickered briefly in his pale eyes.

'She lives in Birtmore Street.'

'Where's that?'

'Second on your left going back towards town. I couldn't tell you what number. Happen the wife'd know.'

'I'd be grateful if you'd ask her.'

'You're sure you're not after her for something else?'

'I don't follow you,' Jordan said. Perhaps the publican did not know that Mrs Nugent had another job. How did Jordan know what compartments she chose to divide her life into? He had told the man enough of his business.

'Some folk round here, y'know,' the landlord said, 'they're no better than they ought to be.'

'I'm only enquiring about Mrs Nugent,' Jordan said. 'I'm not interested in anybody else.'

Jordan sipped his whisky. The man nodded at the glass as he put it down. 'Same again?'

Jordan looked. There was still some left. 'Go on, then.'

The man went away, taking the glass, and spoke into a house phone.

'She'll be down in a minute.'

'There doesn't seem to be enough work for a barmaid,' Jordan said.

'That's where you're wrong. We get the young 'uns in disco nights.'

'Is that the kind of thing you enjoy yourself?'

'Times is bad. You've got to move with 'em. When Audrey and the missus are on together, I get in the public bar and leave 'em to it.'

He went to serve a youth in a studded leather jacket whose head was shaved to the bone up to the crown, where the hair sprayed out in lacquered vermilion fronds. When a woman with wispy fair hair, wearing a yellow hand-knitted jumper with short puffed-out sleeves appeared, she spoke to the man, who nodded his head in Jordan's direction.

'Audrey, was it, you was asking about?'

'I'd be grateful if you'd give me her address.'

'From the social security, are you?'

'I'd have her address if I were, wouldn't I?'

'Does she know you're coming?'

'I thought I'd see her here.'

'You would have in the normal way, but she's poorly.'

'So your husband says. He says she lives in Birtmore Street. What number is it?'

'Twenty-seven.' She looked at him as though regretting the ready answer.

Jordan left the premises wondering if everyone who frequented them had things to hide. It depressed him to think of Audrey Nugent spending her evenings there, and depressed him yet more to reflect that she had probably more in common with that place and its clientele than she had with the Beehive, and even more so than with him himself.

He sat in his car for several minutes before starting the engine and considered the wisdom of what he'd set out to do. Would she welcome his visit or think he was prying? He did not, he admitted now, seriously think she was in need of the money – not in urgent need, or she would have taken steps to get it. Now that he knew her address, he could put it in the post. Yet if he turned back now he would only castigate himself for his indecisiveness. 'Be honest,' he said out loud. 'Own up. You've come because you want to see her.'

He drove in second gear back along the main road and turned up the hill when his headlights picked out the cracked nameplate on a garden wall. Some of the houses had been fitted with incongruous new doors and windows. Others showed neglect in broken gates and leggy, overgrown privet hiding the small squares of soil that passed for front gardens. One such was number twenty-seven, which Jordan found when he had traversed the length of the street and kerb-crawled halfway down again. A dormer window had been let into the roof of this house and a dim light showed through the frosted-glass upper panels of the front door.

The money was in his pocket, still sealed in the envelope he had left for her with her name on it. All he need do was slip it through the letterbox. Then, he thought, she might, in that occasional direct way of hers, rebuke him later. 'Why didn't you knock? What were you scared of? Coming all that way and going away without knocking and having a word.'

He got out of the car and approached the house, still undecided. He was standing there with the envelope in his hand when a shape loomed up between the source of the light and the door, and the door was suddenly flung open wide before him. A man coming out at speed stopped in his tracks as Jordan stepped back to avoid being shouldered aside.

'Are you looking for somebody?'

'I believe Mrs Nugent lives here.'

634

The man grunted, his glance raking Jordan in a quick appraisal. 'Number three, first floor back.' He half turned and bawled up the stairs. 'Audrey! Bloke to see you,' then plunged out past Jordan, leaving him facing an empty hallway, with an image of a strongly built man in his middle thirties, with close dark curly hair, a dark polo-neck sweater and a tweed jacket which Jordan, for some reason, was convinced had been handed on or picked up second hand.

He stepped into the hall and closed the door as a woman's voice called from above. 'Who is it?' He hesitated to call back and began to mount the stairs, hearing as he went up the creak of boards on the landing. 'Are you still there, Harry?' the voice asked. The woman's head and shoulders appeared over the rail and as she saw Jordan's shape she said sharply, her voice rising, 'Who are you? What d'you want?'

'It's all right, Mrs Nugent. It's only me – Mr Jordan.'

She straightened up and stepped back as he reached the landing and light fell on him from the open door of the room behind her.

'What the heck are you doing here?'

Her question was almost insolent in its phrasing and abruptness. He would have reprimanded anyone at the works who spoke to him like that. But she was on her home ground: he was the intruder, and he had startled her.

'I'm sorry,' Jordan said. 'I came to bring your money and ask if you're all right.'

'Oh, that could have waited.'

'And when there was no word...'

She had backed into the doorway of her room and was standing with a hand on either jamb, as though denying him entrance, or – it suddenly struck him – looking, in the creased, floor-length plum-coloured housecoat, its

635

neck cut in a deep V to a high, tight, elasticated waist which clung to her ribcage under her breasts, like a still from a Hollywood film noir of the 1940s.

'You took a bit of finding,' Jordan said, and wondered at his exaggeration. Perhaps it was all of a piece with his new image of her as the femme fatale of a Fritz Lang movie.

'How's that?'

'I had to enquire at the pub.'

'The Royal Oak, y'mean?'

'Yes. I hope you don't mind. They seemed a bit... a bit cagey.'

'They wouldn't know who you were.'

'No.'

'Did you tell 'em?'

'No. I didn't think it was any of their business.'

'You're right, it isn't.'

Jordan held out the envelope. 'The money's here, just as I left it for you. You might need it if you've lost your wages at the pub as well.'

'Thanks. You're very thoughtful.' Taking the envelope, she lifted both hands to rub at her upper arms. 'There's a rare draught coming up them stairs. Didn't you shut the front door?'

'Yes, I'm sure I did.' He went to the top of the stairs and looked down. 'Yes, I did.' He glanced back at her. 'Well, I hope you'll soon feel better. Can I expect you on Tuesday? I mean, don't worry if you're still not up to it.'

'Don't you want to come in a minute?'

'I mustn't disturb you.'

'Come in, if you want. I'll warn you, though, it's a tip. I haven't cleaned up today.'

Jordan followed her into the room. A sink, electric cooker and a small fridge occupied a curtained-off corner.

She cleared some garments and magazines off the seat of a wooden-armed easy-chair. 'Sit down.' She went and sat on the edge of a divan whose covers were crumpled as though she had been lying on it. 'See how the other three-quarters live,' she said. 'Cosy, isn't it?' There was a sardonic glint in her eyes as she looked at him.

'Is this all you have, just the one room?'

'That's all.'

'You rent it furnished?'

'If you can call this junk furniture.'

Jordan's was the only chair. He wondered where the man he had met at the door had sat, if he had been in the room.

Mrs Nugent was tearing open the envelope. As Jordan remembered that his note about the fur coat was still in there, she took it out, glanced at it and replaced it with the banknotes, without comment.

'You seem nicely back on your feet, anyway.'

'I had a couple of important meetings. It seemed to leave me as quickly as it came. I hope you didn't catch it from me.'

'No, mine's a woman's ailment. I wait every month, wondering if it'll be a bad one. When it is, it crucifies me. Fair cuts me in two. No wonder they call it the curse.'

'Surely nowdays there are things...'

'I was fine while I was on the pill. But then they began to get windy about keeping women on it too long.' She shrugged. 'So now it's back to codeine and cups of tea.'

'The chap I bumped into,' Jordan said, 'is he a fellow tenant?'

'My step-brother. He comes and goes. Works away a lot. Oil rigs and suchlike. Sometimes abroad, among the Arabs.' She got up. 'He brought some whisky. Would you like some?' There was a half-bottle of Johnny Walker on the draining board.

'Well, I...'

She was rinsing a tumbler under the tap. 'Have a drink. You like whisky, don't you?'

'Just a small one, then,' Jordan said. 'I had a couple in the pub.'

'Another one won't get you into trouble.'

He asked for water and she handed the drink to him, half and half.

'Cheers, then.'

'All the best.'

'And thanks for coming over with the money.'

'I had visions of you laid up without any.'

'I wonder you've no more to think about than me. Do you look after all your people that way?'

'I try to see they get a fair deal. But I have staff for that.'

'Are there any jobs going at your place?'

'I'm afraid not. We've enough on finding work for those we have. Perhaps when things pick up.'

'If they ever do.' She drank, her face suddenly sombre. Jordan wondered if she ever allowed herself to think about the future, or simply lived from day to day.

'Could I ask you,' he said, 'if it's not too personal. But do you manage to make ends meet?'

'Look at this place,' she said, 'and work it out for yourself.'

After the chill of the night outside and the draughty stairs, the heat in the room was beginning to make Jordan's head swim. An electric fire blazed at full a few feet from his legs. He would, he thought, have to take off his overcoat or leave. About, for the moment, to shift the chair back for fear of scorching his trousers, he paused in his movement and relaxed his weight as the orange glow of the fire's elements suddenly faded to a dull red, then to black.

'Blast!' Audrey Nugent said. She reached for a purse and poked her forefinger into its pockets. Then she got up and looked on the narrow mantelshelf.

'Is it on a meter?' Jordan asked.

'You bet it's on a meter. He could nearly let you live rent-free, the profit he makes on that.'

'Let me...' Jordan took change out of his pocket and counted out half a dozen tenpence pieces. 'Here...'

'If you can make it up to the pound, I'll give you a note for it.'

'There's not enough,' Jordan said. 'It doesn't matter.'

She knelt by the sink and fed coins into the meter. 'Lucky you came.'

As the fire began to glow again, Jordan said, 'I wonder you can breathe in such heat.'

'Happen you're right. I do overdo it a bit when I'm not feeling well.' She switched off one of the bars, then drew on a woollen cardigan over the housecoat. At once all the presence – the allure, even – bestowed by the coat was gone. 'I was going to make meself a hot drink and get into bed, anyway.'

'I'm being a nuisance,' Jordan said.

'You walk on eggshells trying not to offend people, don't you?'

'Not everybody,' Jordan said. 'Not by any means.'

'What's so special about me, then?'

'You're in my private employ,' Jordan said, and wondered what other, less pompous form of words he could have used.

She drew the cardigan together across her chest and fastened the top buttons. Then she felt about in the crumpled folds of the divan cover until she found a cigarette packet, which she shook before tossing it towards a wastebox by the sink.

'You wouldn't have a cigarette on you?'

'I don't smoke,' Jordan said. 'I'll go and get you some, if you like.'

'Don't bother. Harry 'ull bring some back with him, if he remembers.'

'He's coming back?'

'He's kipping down here for the time being.'

'Oh...' Despite himself, Jordan let his gaze take in once more the limits of the room. 'You mean...?'

'I mean in here. That's his sleeping-bag on the floor behind your chair. It's just till he finds a place of his own, or takes his hook again. It won't be for long. He says it won't, anyway.' She shrugged. 'It helps with the expenses.'

Letting his imagination run free, Jordan had been rehearsing in it an exchange in which he offered to pay her rent for the privilege of visiting her one evening a week and making love to her on that narrow divan. Only an idle fantasy, he told himself. But he was sick of cold women with pretensions; he wanted someone direct, earthy, warm. He tried to imagine her response should he venture the suggestion, and saw her laughing in his face before ordering him out.

An alternative began to form – one more drastic in its way, but an offer she could refuse without offence, while leaving him with room for further manoeuvre. While he was turning it over, wondering if now was the right time to put it to her, she got up with a restless movement and taking the whisky bottle held it out to him without speaking, her hips moving inside the housecoat as she shifted her weight from one leg to the other, like one waiting for some overdue event.

She probably wanted him to go, he thought, as he shook his head and she carelessly slopped another half-inch into her own glass; wondering why he was hanging about now that his errand was done. Yet although this single cluttered room with its cheap tat of fittings and furniture oppressed him, he was held by the intimacy of their being alone here. The material of the housecoat – some kind of thin stretch velvet, he thought – hugged her hips in a clean slim line, and as she sat again its weight settled into the V of her thighs at the bottom of her flat belly. She carried no spare weight and her breasts would be small, small and firm and white, high on her long white body.

'Aren't you sweltering in that overcoat?' she asked suddenly, when neither of them had spoken for a time.

Jordan realised how long his silence had been and that this might have brought on the nervous energy of her movements.

'I must go,' he said. 'I've taken up too much of your time.'

'You're not spoiling anything. But I wondered why you'd turned so broody.'

'I'm sorry,' Jordan said, 'but I –'

'I've never heard anybody apologise so much. What d'you think you've done?'

'Made you slightly uneasy, perhaps. I don't know you well enough to go quiet in your company like that.'

'Be my guest,' she said. 'Was it something important?'

'Yes,' Jordan heard himself admitting, and knew that he must now carry the thought through. 'I was just weighing the pros and cons of –'

'The what?'

He was thrown for a moment. 'I don't understand.'

'It's me that doesn't understand you. The pros and... what did you say?'

'Things for, things against,' Jordan said.

'For and against what?'

'Asking you to come and be my housekeeper.'

It silenced her. She looked quickly at him and just as quickly away. A small smile touched her lips – whether of amusement, embarrassment or gratification he could not tell.

'If you'll just let me explain,' he went on.

'I think you'd better.'

Jordan was struck by the panicky thought that the step-brother might return before he could say it all.

'The house needs a woman in it,' he said. 'I mean, more than you can give it by just coming in twice a week. And I'm tired of cooking for myself. If it comes to that, I don't like living on my own there, either. There's plenty of room. You could easily –'

'You are talking about living in, then?'

'Oh, yes,' Jordan said. It was not, in fact, what he'd immediately had in mind, but the idea had grown as he was talking. 'You could have your own, er, quarters. I could easily make one of the upstairs rooms into a bedsitter. But other than that you'd have the run of the place and be perfectly free to do what you liked with your spare time. You could carry on working in the evenings if you felt you needed the change and the company. You might think that what I could offer you wasn't a full wage. I'm sure we could work something out, though, and you would have a comfortable home and all found.'

'Wait a minute,' she said as he stopped talking. 'Hold on a tick. This is all a bit fast for me. It wants some thinking about.'

'You don't have to decide now.'

She had clenched the fingers of one hand and was pushing the fist deep into her abdomen. The sudden pallor of her face perturbed Jordan.

'Is there anything I can get you, Mrs Nugent?'

'It'll go,' she said. 'That's the only good thing about it.'

Jordan got up. 'We'll talk about it another time, when you can put your mind to it.'

'You're a fast worker, I'll say that for you.'

'Please,' Jordan said, 'don't get me wrong.'

'I mean, you know next to nothing about me.'

'Nor you me, if it comes to that.'

'Haven't you thought what a risk you'd be taking?'

He had. Yet he also knew that a desire to do something for this woman had been growing in him ever since she had first smiled at him, in the Beehive. Why, if she would only let him, he could transform her life: he could take her out of this squalor, put her into decent clothes, give her a security that picking up part-time work where she could had never offered her. He would become her benefactor, friend, protector. Gradually, she would learn that she had someone of substance to turn to.

He held in his excitement at the prospect and curbed the urge to press his offer now, though the spasm of pain seemed to have left her as she drew herself upright, arching her back and taking a deep breath which she let out in a long sigh.

'What if it didn't work out?' she said. 'Where would I go then?'

'Why not come for a week or two first?' Jordan suggested. 'Keep this place on in the meantime. Let your step-brother look after it.'

'When would you want to know?'

'There's no hurry,' Jordan said. 'Don't bother about it now. Think it over when you're well again.'

On his way home Jordan was stopped by the police,

643

who had put a barrier across the suburban road he had chosen on no more than a whim. They did not tell him what they were looking for, only that they were on a routine check, before they asked him who he was, where he lived, where he had been and how long he had been away from home. Then they requested permission to shine their torches over the interior of his car and to examine the contents of the boot.

Jordan guessed what had happened and the local news on his alarm-radio woke him next morning with the details. A girl had been done to death only two hundred yards from a busy main road. It seemed that she had been found more quickly than some of the others and that she must have died while he was talking to Mrs Nugent. There were no details of how the killing had been carried out, but there were the usual hints of appalling savagery. Women were once again warned not to go out alone after dark: the attacks were no longer confined to one type of woman and all women should now consider themselves at risk.

During the next few days he found himself fretting about Audrey Nugent's safety. True, she had her step-brother at hand, but Jordan did not know how responsible he was; and Mrs Nugent herself, though sometimes anxious, was unlikely to let her movements be restricted.

He wanted to go and see her again, to reassure himself and to warn her. But he dared not seem to be pestering. It was best that she be left to get used gradually to the idea he had planted. So he spent a restless weekend that only hardened the conviction that he was planning the right course for him, and contented himself by leaving a note for her on the Tuesday morning, which did not refer to his offer, but merely said, 'Do please take care when you are out.'

He returned from the works in the early evening and let himself into the house, his pulse suddenly racing as he saw the light in the kitchen and knew she was still there. He made no effort to keep the pleasure out of his voice as she came out to meet him.

'Hullo! Have you been here all day?'

'I came after dinner. Thought I'd stop on a bit.'

'I am glad. You've no idea how good it is to come home and find someone in the house.'

'Have you never lived on your own before?'

'As a young man, yes. I lived in a flat for a while. But that was different.'

'I expect you still miss your wife.'

He said, 'I miss her not being here. We were married for a long time. You get used to things. Even things you don't especially care for at the time.'

She frowned a little, turning that over, until she realised that he was frowning too as he looked at her, or at the clothes she was wearing under her pinafore: a skirt and fawn jumper, sleeves pushed to the elbow, that he vaguely recognised.

'I found something else that fitted me. I hope you don't mind.'

'Fine,' he said. 'Didn't I tell you? I couldn't quite bring them to mind. There were some things she stopped wearing when she put on a bit of weight. As long as you don't find them too conservative.'

'Conservative?'

'Plain. A bit dull.'

'Oh, I sometimes think I'm a bit too tempted by bright colours, myself. I like folk to see me coming.'

'You must trust your own taste in things.'

'All the same, you could mebbe pull me up when you think I'm going too far.'

Jordan was delighted. 'Would you let me do that? Wouldn't you mind? Really?'

'You're a gentleman. You don't want a housekeeper who looks like – well, a barmaid from the Royal Oak.'

He could hardly believe what she was saying. 'Does that mean you're coming? Have you made up your mind?'

'You said something about giving it is a try. Me bag's upstairs. I thought I'd stop for a day or two and see how it works out.'

At the end of each working day, Jordan sat for a few minutes after clearing his desk and basked in the pleasure of knowing she would be there when he got home. They would have a glass of sherry then, his the *fino*, hers something rather sweeter, and discuss their evening meal. She was a competent plain cook and all he had to do was unobtrusively add the spices and herbs whose uses she seemed unaware of. She remarked on their flavour with approval.

'You seem to do all right by yourself. I don't know what you need me for.'

'There's a difference between helping and doing it all the time.'

'I was wondering about your shopping.' They had so far used food from his freezer.

'Do you want to do it?'

'If you tell me what to get and how much to spend. You'll have to see to the fancier things yourself.'

'Perhaps we could do it together to start with.'

'If you like.'

'When, though? When could we fit it in?'

'What about Saturday morning?'

'That's all right by me, but –'

'You don't work then, do you, or go playing golf?'

Jordan laughed. 'Whatever made you think about golf?'

'I just thought you might play.'

'I did try it once,' Jordan said, 'but I couldn't take to it. No, Saturday's all right, but what about your weekend?'

'What about it?'

'Do you mean you're staying over?'

'If you want me to.'

'What about your job at the pub?'

'I told 'em I was going away for a few days. I'll mebbe pack it in altogether if things turn out right here.'

'I hope they will.'

'You're satisfied with it so far?'

'So far,' Jordan said, smiling.

His greatest fear was that, alone all day, she would become bored and begin to pine for the old life: the lights, the noise of crowded places, the kind of company she had been used to.

'You mustn't think you've got to stay in all the time,' he told her. 'Just be careful not to be alone on the streets after dark.'

'I'm all right,' she said, 'for now. I'm enjoying the change.'

She liked to bathe before she went to bed; he, in the morning. He wondered how often she had bathed before and suspected that it was not every day. But now each evening she made the most of the privacy of the bathroom, the huge soft unused towels he had got out for her and the abundant hot water. Going in after her, he would brush his teeth standing in the humid scent of bath oil and talcum powder and think of her long slim body lying in one of the two single beds in the guest room she had chosen to sleep in. Each morning, as his radio switched on, she brought him a cup of tea and quietly informed him that breakfast would be ready in fifteen minutes. He had not asked for this and was startled by her first appearance at his bedside in the plum-coloured housecoat he had seen her in before, though she performed the service in the same matter-of-fact way in which she had put her hand to his forehead when he was not well, and she was out of the room again before he had lifted himself onto his elbow. In everything it was as if she were striving to do exactly what he expected of her; in all but the smallest, most routine matters she waited for his cue. He, in turn, longed for a familiarity in which he would know instinctively how to please her, while savouring the novelty, the strangeness of her presence in the house.

On Saturday morning Jordan and Mrs Nugent moved slowly along the aisles of the best of the nearby supermarkets, he choosing articles from the shelves while she pushed the trolley beside him. His wife had loathed supermarkets and had patronised a number of local shops, where she was known by name and could ask for precisely what she wanted, and, in some cases, have it delivered.

'What shall we have for dinner tonight? There's tomorrow as well, isn't there? Are you fond of steak? Do you think as there are two of us we could run to a small joint? If there's anything left we can eat it cold – or I can – in the week. What kind of vegetable do you like best? No, you say; I really don't mind: brussels sprouts, cauliflower, whatever you fancy. Look, there's some asparagus. We could have it with the steak, or perhaps as a starter. Don't you like it? Oh, you don't know. Well, let's take some; I know you'll enjoy it when you taste it. I quite like fish as a change, too. I have one or two good recipes for fish. But if we want that we shall have to go to the fishmonger down the road.'

They were nearing the checkout when the woman – a friend of his wife's – whom he hadn't noticed, spoke to Jordan.

'Hullo, Robert. You're quite a stranger. Where have you been hiding yourself?'

Mrs Nugent turned her head to look, then moved on a few discreet yards and examined a display of tableware. Jordan made polite noises.

'How are you bearing up? Time does slip by, doesn't it? Henry and I were only speaking about you the other day and reminding ourselves that we ought to be getting in touch. But you're not alone, I see. I spotted you from over there, before I saw your friend. I've got to confess that it gave me something of a turn.'

'Mrs Nugent helps me in the house.'

'Oh, I see. It was the coat that did it. I caught a back view and I could have sworn it was just like one that Marjorie wore.'

'Do you really think so?'

'Perhaps I'm wrong. It wouldn't be the first time. Henry always says I'm just as likely to get hold of the wrong end of the stick as the right one. But then, he's not to be relied on in all things. You look as though you'll have quite spent up. I expect you like to get it all done in one fell swoop, instead of popping out for bits and pieces. That's more a man's way. And it was such a comfort to Marjorie's friends to know that you could cope. "Oh, he's quite capable, Robert," I remember telling someone at the time. "Robert can cope." And of course you never know just how much people prefer to be left to their thoughts at such sad times. Some people like to be taken out of themselves, others to be left alone with their memories. I did wonder, though, how long you'd be before you put the house on the market. A lovely house – a real family home – but I always thought it just a touch big even for the two of you. I know Marjorie loved it. She told me so once. "I like space to breathe and room to turn round without falling over Robert," she said. Just her joke. You've still got Marjorie's father's snuff-boxes, I suppose? Henry was talking about them the other day too. Always admired those. Not that he could afford to buy them, even if you wanted to sell. They must be worth thousands... Yes... poor Marjorie. I do still miss her, you know. But perhaps I shouldn't say things like that to you when you've learned to come to terms with it. And if you've got someone bobbing in and out and helping you to keep things spick and span – wasn't Marjorie the house-proud one? – you won't feel so entirely alone. I must say you've been very fortunate to find somebody. It's so hard to find help nowadays, even with all this unemployment. Reliable help, I mean, because you can't be too careful who you let over your doorstep. Did you find her through an agency, or... ?

'Recommended by a friend.'

'Oh, well, that's ideal... That back view. It gave me quite a moment. Do give us a ring and come round some time. We rarely go out now that Henry's retired, except for the occasional drive. And of course none of us goes out in the dark any more. We daren't. Terrible, terrible. What can the police be doing not to have caught him before this?'

Jordan walked unhurriedly after Mrs Nugent, who had moved out of sight. She turned to him as he rounded the end of the shelves. 'Silly bitch,' he said, and for a second her face retained its thoughtful gravity before breaking into that smile which, rare as it was now, always seemed to him like the sun coming out.

650

'Did you tell her who I was?'

'Of course. What is there to hide?'

Nothing. Except his thoughts. His occasional reveries. His projections of a future for which he could see no durable shape. 'Live each day as it comes,' he told himself, 'and be grateful for it. Build on whatever we're establishing.' She seemed content and he was happier than he had been in years: conscious of his happiness and trying not to spoil it by fearing that it would not last.

After supper, which they ate together, using the dining-room at her suggestion (and she had washed up, refusing his offer of help) he read for an hour while she watched television in another room. He wanted to join her, but as she respected his privacy so he must respect her free time. Perhaps later, if she stayed, he would hire a video recorder so that she would not be deprived of programmes by her evening chores.

At a little after eleven she looked into the room and said, 'If you don't want the bathroom for a while I'll go up now.'

'Okay. Isn't the late-night film any good?'

'It's foreign, and I'm tired.'

'Bed's the best place, then.'

'By the way, what time do you like breakfast on a Sunday?'

'Any time we both feel like it. I think you could lie in for an hour, if you want to.'

'I'll see. Goodnight, then.'

'Goodnight.'

He put a record of singing on the player and poured himself a Scotch. After a time he went across the hall to the room where she had been sitting to unplug the television set from the mains. The room smelled of cigarette smoke and there were four stubs in the ashtray. He left them. She would, he had no doubt, tidy in here in the morning and open the window briefly for fresh air. Before disconnecting the set he switched on. A man was speaking to a woman in passionate French. She answered him, accusing him of using her for his own devices. Jordan's French was not good enough for him to follow the exchange and a stilted moment in the translation in the subtitles made him suddenly laugh out loud.

Something woke him in the small hours. He lay there, trying to make out what it was. He had no recollection of a dream, yet his heart was racing as if he had surfaced from a nightmare. He turned onto his back and listened to the house as he had listened every night for a time after his wife had died. The feeling of unease persisted. Finally, he gave in to it and switched on his bedside light and threw back the duvet. Pushing his feet into his slippers, he got up and drew on his dressing-gown before stepping onto the landing.

He was standing looking over the rail into the darkness below when he heard the sound. It was like the soft, plaintive whimper of some small animal, trapped and bewildered; and it was coming from Mrs Nugent's room. As he moved to the door and put his ear to the panel, the animal-like plaint changed to indistinct words uttered in a rapid, low-pitched stream. When the voice all at once rose in a cadence of defiance, Jordan tapped lightly on the door and opened it. He had to step round the door before he could make out the shape of her lying in the nearer of the twin beds. For a moment then it was as though his presence had soothed her without her knowing it; then one of her arms began to thrash as she spoke again in a vehement outburst:

'No! No! You can't. I won't let you. You can't! You can't! You can't!'

'Mrs Nugent.' As he touched her shoulder, she twisted violently away from him, then back again. 'Mrs Nugent.'

She spoke as if still held in her dream. 'Who is it? What d' you want?'

'It's only me, Mrs Nugent. Don't be alarmed. You were only dreaming.' He knelt beside the bed now, one hand holding her hand that was free of the covers. With his other hand he found himself softly caressing her brow, then her cheek. 'You're all right now. Don't be afraid. You're safe with me.' There were tears on her face. He cupped her cheek and ran his thumb in the moisture under her eyes. She lay still now, allowing herself to be soothed.

Jordan raised himself and sat on the bed. She shifted herself to make room for him as she felt his weight settle. He began again to caress the pale shape of her face. Her hair was damp on her forehead.

'You're quite safe,' Jordan said. 'You're perfectly safe with me. I won't let them hurt you.'

In a few moments more her breathing was steady and deep. He wondered if she had really awakened.

He found her sitting at the kitchen table, drinking tea and smoking a cigarette.

'Good morning.'

'Hullo. You're up early. I thought you were going to sleep in a bit.'

'I forgot to reset my radio. It woke me at the usual time.' He got a cup from the cupboard and reached for the teapot, motioning her to stay seated as she made to rise. 'I can do it.' He nodded towards the thin plume of smoke which rose lazily in the still air beyond the tall

653

creosoted fence of his neighbour's garden. 'It must be going to be a nice day.'

'D'you think so?'

'He always makes a fire on the nicest days.' He joined her at the table. 'I thought you might have slept longer yourself.'

She drew on the cigarette. Her hand trembled slightly as she tapped ash into the glass tray.

'Did you come into my room last night?'

'Don't you remember?'

'Somebody was touching me.'

'You were dreaming. You woke me up.'

'I took a sleeping pill. I didn't know where I was.'

'You were frightened.'

'I must have been.'

'What was it about, can you remember?'

'Not much now.' She frowned. 'I was here on me own. It was different, somehow. Somebody came.'

'Who was it?'

'I don't know.'

'Do you often have nightmares?'

'I dream sometimes, but not like that. I haven't had one like that since I was a little lass. I mean as bad. They used to have to take me into bed between them.'

'Your father and mother?'

'Yes.'

'Were you an only child?'

'Yes.'

'Are they still alive?'

'Me mother died, after me dad ran off. I never heard what happened to him.' Jordan drank tea and waited, saying nothing. 'Do you want some breakfast?'

'There's no hurry.'

'Have you got any family?'

654

'My parents are dead. I have a married sister in New Zealand and a brother living in London,' said Jordan.

'Do you ever see them?'

'My brother came up for my wife's funeral. I hadn't seen him for some time before that.'

'You're not close, then?'

'No.'

'I think that's a shame. I pined for brothers and sisters when I was a kid.'

'You've got your step-brother.'

'Well... He's not really me step-brother. I just call him that. It's what he calls himself.'

'I don't follow.'

'Me mam was never married to his dad.'

'You all lived together?'

'For a year or two. Then me mam died. An auntie took me in. I never saw Harry again till we were both grown up. He come looking for me, one time. "Don't you know me?" he says. "It's your step-brother." I didn't know him from Adam at first. Then I begun to see it was him. He always calls me his step-sister. I don't mind, if that's what he wants. It makes things look a bit more respectable, I suppose, when he turns up and wants a place to sleep for a week or two. Not that that matters much. Nobody cares nowadays, do they?'

'Apparently not.'

'Does it bother you, then, that sort of thing?'

'Oh, I always say people can do what they like, as long as they don't do it in the street and frighten the horses.'

'You what?'

'Just an old joke. What did Harry think of you coming to live in here?'

'I don't really know.'

655

'Didn't he say anything? Did he think it was a good move or a bad one?'

'He said it was up to me.'

'Do you think you can still settle, after last night?'

'...Nothing happened last night, did it?'

'You were crying out in your sleep. I came in and calmed you.'

'Was that all?'

'Can't you remember?'

'I must have had another dream, after you'd gone.'

'What about? Her cup was empty. He reached for the pot and refilled it for her, not wanting her to start moving about. 'What was your other dream, then? You weren't frightened again, were you?'

'No.' She shook her head and lowered her face, one hand to her forehead.

'Do you mean I was in it?'

'It's too silly...

'Silly?'

'Embarrassing. It's best not talked about.'

'But you thought it might actually have happened. Is that what you mean?'

'Not really.'

'It was vivid, though. It must have been.'

'I told you, I'd taken a sleeping pill. I didn't know where I was.'

'If it wasn't frightening, was it curious or pleasant, or what?'

'Let's forget about it.'

'You brought it up.'

'I just wanted to be sure.'

'I don't know why you want to make such a mystery of it,' Jordan said. She lit another cigarette. He noticed that her hands were still unsteady. 'You smoke too much.'

'Only sometimes. Do you still want me to stop on here?'

'You haven't changed your mind, have you?'

'I was still making it up.'

'Is there anything I can do to help you decide to stay? I obviously can't guarantee to keep out of your dreams.'

'You won't get it out of me that way.'

Emboldened by her small smile, Jordan said, 'Well, at least tell me this much: did I seem to enjoy being in your dream?'

She got up. 'Shall I make another pot of tea or are you ready to go on to coffee?'

'Make which ever you prefer.'

'Say which you want.'

'I'll leave it to you.'

'You don't sulk, do you?' she asked. 'I can't abide people who sulk.'

'I don't sulk; I show my displeasure.'

'I wish I'd never mentioned it.'

'But you wanted to be sure.'

'There's no need for sarcasm, either.'

'Well, what did you want to be sure of, for heaven's sake?'

She banged down the full kettle, slipped home the plug, closed the switch.

'If you must know,' she said, 'I didn't want to spend the next couple of weeks wondering if I might be pregnant.'

'You mean to say,' Jordan said, on his feet now, 'that you think I'm the kind of man who'd creep into your bed and take advantage of you while you didn't know what you were doing?'

'What are you getting mad about?'

'I'm wondering what sort of a man you take me for.'

657

'You are a man, aren't you?'

'What does that mean?'

'If I invited you into my bed, what would you do?'

Jordan turned to the window. His neighbour's garden fire was burning well now. A sudden spring of breeze fanned out the smoke before lifting it over a nearby roof. He was astounded that things between them had come so far so fast. It was not the way he'd imagined it at all.

'Can't you answer?'

He tried to keep his voice cool and level. 'What makes you think I'm interested in you that way?'

'If you're not, you're not. But I want to know. I want to know if that's what you had in mind when you asked me to come and live here.' When he didn't speak, she went on, 'I reckon I've a right to know that much.'

'Which is the answer that will keep you here?' Jordan asked.

'Try telling the truth.'

Whatever happened now, Jordan thought, things could never be the same. He felt like a small boy caught in some shameful action. Yet if he denied what he wanted he was sure she would feel obliged to go.

'I want to make love to you,' he said.

She was silent for so long he thought she must have left the room. He forced himself round.

'Did you hear me?'

'I heard you.' She was pouring boiling water into the teapot. 'You should have said. You should have told me.'

He stepped towards her and put his hands on her shoulders from behind.

'Audrey...' But she turned and brushed past him to set the teapot down on the table.

'Don't be in such a rush,' she said. 'It's time I made

your breakfast. And then there's one or two things we have to talk about.'

'I'm scared stiff of getting pregnant,' she was saying to him a long time later that day.

'You won't.'

'You can get something, can't you?'

'Tomorrow.'

Reminded by his neighbour's activity, he had spent most of the daylight hours in his neglected garden, keeping away from her and trying through physical labour to curb his mounting excitement.

But images of her came again and again to fill his mind until, by nightfall, he was almost sick with longing and could only toy with his evening meal.

'You should have said. You should have told me.'

'I didn't know how. I didn't want to frighten you off. I hoped you'd come to the idea in your own time.'

'I don't know what it is you see in me.'

'I'd like to look after you. Do things for you. Nice things.'

'What for? I'm not your sort.'

'Perhaps that's why.'

'You're a gentleman. I'm nothing.'

'You're talking rubbish.'

'You know next to nothing about me.'

'You're what you let yourself be.'

'Seems to me I've nearly always been forced.'

'I won't force you,' Jordan said.

'No, you'd kill me with kindness.'

'Would I?'

'You will. If I let you.'

'Promise me,' she was saying to him now. 'Promise you won't go any further than I let you.'

659

'I promise.'

Her mouth moved against his as her tongue probed. She tasted faintly of tobacco smoke. He shuddered as her hand explored his groin. When his own hand slid down across her flat belly she took it firmly and led it to her breasts. He clutched them and gasped as the spasm started in him.

The papers were needed for the meeting. Mrs Perrins said she had searched high and low but could not find them. 'You took them home with you, didn't you? I remember you saying you'd take them home to read in peace.'

'I thought I'd brought them back.'

He was slipping. He forgot things. Yet he felt in bounding physical condition. She had noticed the difference in him and he had caught her once or twice looking at him in a mildly speculative way.

He had just returned to his office after lunch. The meeting was called for three-thirty.

'I shall have to go back and look for them,' he said. 'We can't manage without them, that's for sure.'

He left the car in the street and walked up the drive. The house was afternoon-still. Audrey got most of her work done in the morning. He supposed she could have gone out, though he knew she quite often took a nap after lunch.

He went straight upstairs, his feet moving lightly, two steps at a time. Her door stood ajar. It opened without a sound over the carpet as he stepped round. She was asleep, the sheet down to her hips exposing the long curve of her naked back. Jordan thought the man lying on the other side of her was sleeping too until, in the second before the closing door cut off his

660

view, a head lifted off the pillow and Harry's eyes looked directly into his.

The telephone in the hall began to ring as he got to the top of the stairs. He was down and reaching for it when he heard movement on the landing and she came into view, drawing a wrap about her. She paused for a second as she saw him and he noticed that she could not resist a quick look behind her.

'What are you–?'

There was something in her face beyond instinctive apprehension: something he couldn't in his present state define, and which was gone almost as soon as he had discerned it.

He waved her to silence, the receiver filled with the effusive apologies of his secretary. He listened, said a couple of words and hung up.

'How long have you been back?' Her voice was lifted, unusually carrying.

'I've just come in.'

'Is there something wrong?'

'I came to get some papers, but my secretary's found them.'

'I was lying down.'

'So I gathered.'

He felt suddenly as though he would fall. She took a step towards him as his hand groped for the wooden arm of the chair beside the telephone. He sat down heavily, bending forward to thrust his head between his knees.

'What's the matter? Aren't you well?'

'I'll be all right.'

'You look as pale as lard,' she said when he straightened up. Her hands fluttered at the stuff of the wrap, drawing it closer, smoothing it down.

'I just went dizzy for a second, that's all.'

'Shouldn't you rest for a while?'

She had to say that, he thought. She couldn't avoid saying that.

'I've got an important meeting. They can't hold it without me.' He got up and stood very still for a moment, checking his balance.

'Well, you just be careful driving.'

'I will.' He turned at the door. 'By the way, there's been a slight change in my plans.' Her eyes held his. He was the first to look away. 'I have to entertain a customer. I shan't be in for dinner.'

From his office Jordan drove into the city centre and found a place to park. He went into a pub and drank two large whiskies then walked across the street to a cinema. He sat in an almost empty auditorium until he became slowly aware that what he was looking at on the screen was what he had seen when he first came in. Then he went out into streets upon which night had fallen and drove home.

The house was in darkness. He went about the ground floor, switching on lights, before going upstairs to her room. The wardrobe and drawers were empty of her belongings. The suitcase she had brought them in was gone too.

Nearly two weeks passed before Jordan brought himself to drive across the city to Birtmore Street. Time after time he had conjured up the image of her as she had come down the stairs towards him, drawing the wrap around her nakedness. Again and again he had analysed and reinterpreted the expression on her face as she had seen him. Slowly, over the days and nights, the idea grew in him that her look had been that of one who realises she has committed perhaps the greatest folly of her life. Only when this notion became fixed in him did his misery relax its paralysing grip. Only then did some lingering vestige of hope tell him that, in spite of everything, all might not yet be lost.

When he had struck a match by the dark glass of the door and rung what he took to be her bell, he tried once more to rehearse what he might say, and once more gave up the attempt. He did not know what he would say until he saw her reaction. Perhaps he would need to say very little. He wanted her back. She would know that when she saw him.

He rang again, making a slow count to five as his finger held the push. More than likely she was at the pub, working. He had thought of looking in there first, but balked at the prospect of meeting her again for the first time in public. But better that than not seeing her at all. There was no need for a fuss. His appearing would tell her and if there was in her anything at all of what he had imagined – no, known – she would make it in her way to have a private word.

The voice challenged him as he reached the gate. 'Were you ringing my bell?' A girl stood in the now lighted doorway, a plump girl, as round as a bouncing ball. She took a couple of steps back into the hall as Jordan approached her. A deep lateral crease in her pale green T-shirt marked the division between belly and breasts. 'What d'you want?'

'I was hoping to see Mrs Nugent.'

'You were ringing my bell.'

'Sorry. I thought it was hers. Is she in, d'you know?'

'Who did you say?'

'Mrs Nugent.'

The girl's right hand had a firm hold on the edge of the door, as though she were ready to slam it on him.

663

'I don't know anybody of that name.'

Do I look like a woman-killer? Jordan thought. And yet, what did a woman-killer look like? He kept a reassuring distance as he said, 'She lives in the first floor back.'

'She doesn't, you know,' the girl said. 'That's where I live, as of yesterday. And I'd be out as of tomorrow, if I'd anywhere better to go. It's a right bloody dump.'

'She can only just have moved,' Jordan said helplessly. 'Are you sure you've not seen her?'

'What name was it again?'

'Nugent. Audrey Nugent. She was sometimes with a man called Harry. In his middle thirties, well built, dark curly hair.'

'There's nobody like that here now, mister.'

'Then I'm sorry to have troubled you.'

'If you say so.' As the door began to close, she added, 'Better luck next time.'

Jordan forced himself to enter the Royal Oak. It was busier than before and he had to wait to catch the landlord's eye.

'You might remember me asking for Mrs Nugent some time back.'

'Oh, yes?'

'Does she still work here?'

'Hasn't for some while now. I heard she'd gone to housekeep for a feller, somewhere the other side of town.'

'You've no idea where I might find her now?'

'Did you find her before?'

'Yes.'

'You shouldn't have lost her again, then. Scotch, wasn't it?'

'No, thanks,' Jordan said. 'So you've no idea where she is?'

'None at all, mate.' The man was already moving away.

Jordan called at the Beehive and drank a couple of pints. He had done that two or three times while she was with him. She had sent him. 'Walk on to the Beehive and have a pint while I watch the telly. Do you good.' He had stood at the bar, savouring the cool beer and recalling in his mind's eye the first time he had seen her and the extraordinary warmth and charm of her smile; his own smile, bestowed like a blessing on all who came near him, wrapped round the knowledge of just where she was, what she was doing, who she was waiting for.

The beer got to him quickly. He stood with his head down in his shoulders, both hands on the bar counter, thinking again of how she had looked as she came downstairs, with uppermost in her mind, the instant after seeing him, the realisation of all she had put at risk. 'I would tell you,' he said softly, aloud, 'if I knew where you were.'

He went home. He hated the place now and wondered how quickly he could sell it. But suppose he did sell it and, as he had with her, she came looking for him and did not know where he had gone? How his wife would have mocked him...

On a thought, he went straight upstairs to his wife's room where he opened the wardrobes. The fur cape was gone, as was her jewellery box from the dressing-table drawer. He couldn't think now why it had not occurred to him to look before. Downstairs again, he crossed the hall to the small sitting-room that his wife had used in the evenings, a room he had no more than glanced into for several weeks. The display cabinet housing her father's collection of snuff-boxes stood against the wall behind the door. A sliver of glass broke under his feet. It had needed only a small hole, just big enough for an arm to reach in. The heel of a woman's shoe could easily have made that.

When, a few weeks later, the chairman of the group that controlled his firm called Jordan to head office to tell him personally that owing to a major reorganisation in difficult times the board was compelled to ask him to take early retirement, but there was a sizeable golden handshake and his pension to see him through in comfort (and, after all, wasn't business these days full of younger men who had every intention of throwing off their responsibilities when they were little older than Jordan was now?), Jordan sat as though he was not hearing a word that was said to him.

'How did he take it?' a fellow director asked after-wards.

'How did he take it?'

'Was he surprised, shocked, resentful?'

'It's hard to describe. I can't remember his saying a single word. He was like a man who's given up altogether, a man who quite simply doesn't give a damn about anything.'

LATE STORIES

I Shall Get You for This

A schoolgirl vows revenge on the brutal man who beats her mother & killed her dog

The moment came when Louise saw clearly what she *return from holiday* must do.

Twenty of them had been to summer camp in the Lake district. She hadn't wanted to go because of Gravy, *the dog* her puppy dog. She hadn't had him long and was full of loving him and her duties to him. But that, she told herself was the way of a child, who couldn't appreciate more than one pleasure at a time and had to squeeze one dry before turning to another. He'd be there when they got back... Then when they did come back she could feel her reluctance to say good-bye to the happiness the trip had given her and return home. Because Gravy wasn't all that would be waiting for her and for two glorious weeks – once she had got over the fret of not being at home to care for Gravy herself – she had been free of it all.

By the time the bus had slowed at the corner of Lantern Lane Mrs Fordingly had said her cheery good-byes and got off and it was Mr Ainsworth who twisted in his seat and called, 'Isn't this somebody's stop? You. Louise, don't you get off here?'

'I'm not going straight home, sir,' she heard herself saying. 'I'll get off with Natasha,'

'When did you decide that?' Natasha, her friend, asked as the bus picked up speed again.

'Just now.'

'Will you walk back?'

'I expect so. It's not far.'

'I can't stop out long,' Natasha said. 'Me mam's got something fixed up for tonight.'

'It's all right,' Louise said. 'I'm not expecting to be asked in for me tea.'

There were cries of "So long, then. Behave yourselves. See you Monday. A-a-irgh! Don't talk about Monday!' as they alighted.

'What's wrong, then?' Louise's friend asked.

'Oh, same old thing.'

'A pity they don't fall out.'

'They do fall out, but it doesn't make him go. All it does is...' But that was enough. There was a frontier of confidence that she couldn't cross without demeaning her mother.

'He knocks her about, doesn't he?" Natasha suddenly asked, though she wasn't asking so much as telling Louise that she knew.

'Does everybody know?" Louise returned after a moment.

'Me mam does anyway.' Louise's friend hesitated, then blurted in a rush of candour that scalded Louise's cheeks, 'Tell you the truth, it's why I never ask you into the house. Me mam won't let me because she thinks your mam might feel obliged to ask me back and I've been told never to cross your doorstep. Me mam knew your mam quite well at one time, y'know, and she's still got a soft spot for her, even though your mam's livin' tally with a chap 'at brays her.'

So there, it was out. It must be common knowledge. Everybody knew and some would pity her.

Natasha had high apple cheekbones and a fair complexion, and she could blush as well as anybody when there was something to blush about. Now they both stood there with their faces on fire so that a woman passing by turned her head to peer at them.

'I'm sorry. I shouldn't have told you.'

'It's as well to know.' Louise hoicked her kit-bag into a more comfortable carrying position.

'I'll have to go. She'll be wondering.'

'Okay. See you Monday.'

They had separated by a few paces each when Natasha called to her:

'Ey, Lou...'

'Yeh?'

'Wasn't it real, though?'

'Yeh, real.'

Natasha lived in a semi-detached council house which her parents had bought from the Corporation. Louise lived in a twelfth-floor council flat in one of six blocks that stood three on either side of one of the oldest roads into the city: Lantern Lane, so-called because a long, long time ago, in the days of horse-drawn carriages, a spate of robberies had prompted men to set up in business as escorts to light travellers safely to their destinations.

On arriving back from last year's summer camp, she had found Gary in the flat a thin, hard-muscled man – younger than her mother – lolling, every inch at home, in jeans and T-shirt. He'd be stopping for a while, her mother said, an edge of excitement on her voice as she

671

looked from one to the other and watched their sizing-up. Something in the building trade. In and out of jobs, which these days you couldn't blame anybody for. Louise couldn't take to him however she tried, though; but if her mother needed a man she would have to get used to him being around, to the flat feeling smaller, to her loss of ease and privacy. Yet what woman needed a man who treated her like Gary had soon begun to treat her mother?

She knew as soon as she saw her mother now that something was amiss and ran her scrutiny swiftly over her for marks of violence. But he didn't need to strike her: he could shrink her with words. Once they had had rows that Louise could hear through two doors and across the lobby. But her mother rarely retaliated now and the performance was mostly solo.

'You had a nice time?' came in that bright false voice.

'Yeh, real. You all right?'

'Oh, yeh.'

'Gary not in?'

'No, no. He had to go out.'

'Where's Gravy, then? Don't tell me he's taken him with him.'

'No.'

'Where is he, then?'

'It's what I've got to tell you. Do you want a cup of tea or a drink of pop? I can make you a sandwich if you're hungry.'

'Mam, what are you rabbiting on about? Just tell me where Gravy is. Have you shut him in my room? You know he still chews things...'

She went and flung open the door of her bedroom. Everything in there was neat and tidy as she had made it before going away. 'Where is he?' There was panic now. It was bad, this. She knew it for sure.

[handwritten margin notes: "Gary with mother" and "the disappearance of the dog"]

672

'He's gone, love.'

'What d'you mean 'gone'?

'He's lost. He got out and we haven't seen him since. We think somebody p'raps picked him up and took him away.

'Stole him?'

'Yes. I mean, it's the most likely thing, isn't it – that he's safe an' comfy with somebody else?'

'Suppose it was little kids who took him and left him where he couldn't find his way back?'

Her mother stood rigid, drawn-faced.

'How the hell could he get out and down twelve floors?'

'That's what we don't know, love. He just disappeared. All the rest is... well... what else can we think?'

'When did it happen?'

'Thursday. No, Wednesday.'

'This week, y'mean?'

'No, last.'

'All that time since?' Why didn't you let me know? I could have come home and looked for him.'

'Don't get carried away, love. It's mebbe for the best.'

'What d'you mean 'for the best'? How can it be for the best with Gravy among strangers, God knows where?'

'I mean he chewed things, like you just said. He made his mess on the floor sometimes and whined when you were at school.'

'He only made a mess when nobody took him out.'

'That's what I mean. Who can keep a dog and exercise him properly in a twelfth-floor flat? He was growing as well. He wouldn't always have been a scrap. Remember them paws on him.'

'You should have said all this when I brought him home.'

'Well, I did. But it was a bit late, wasn't it?'

673

'He ran away 'cos somebody kicked him.'

'Now don't talk wild, Louise.'

'It's not wild. I'm just upset, d'you hear? Why couldn't you look after him? Are you good for nothing nowadays except... except a punch-bag for *him*?'

'Louise!'

'Don't Louise me. If I were a couple of years older you wouldn't have to bother with me any more. An' you won't have as soon as I can make me own way.'

Her mother broke then. She slumped heavily at one end of the table and put her face in her hands. 'Don't go on. Haven't I enough to contend with without you badgering me an' all?'

There were tears there. Louise took her own to the privacy of her room where she stayed till morning.

Somehow she slept. On Sunday she kept a sullen distance. At dinnertime her mother and Gary went to the Nut Tree, where her mother had a nine-to-eleven cleaning job five days a week. Gary went out again on Sunday evening, only this time he would look for mates in the city-centre pubs where Louise's mother didn't care to go. She wasn't much of a drinker anyway.

On their own, Louise and her mother sat some distance apart and shared looking at the tv for a while before Louise ran a bath and began to gather her things for the first day at school after the break. Her mother had washed her clothes but there were a couple of small sewing jobs which Louise did herself in her room.

She was still awake, reading, when she heard Gary come in and recognised the slur on his words. When she woke in the morning she could have dismissed the raised voice in the night as a dream until she came upon her mother in the kitchen where there wasn't enough room for her to hide the swelling under her right eye and the discolouration of a maturing bruise.

'Is he still in bed?' Louise asked.

'And fast on. Don't disturb him. We'll both be out of the house before he stirs.'

'What do you tell 'em?' Louise asked.

"What do I tell who?'

'At the pub, when you go to work and they see you like that?'

'They don't ask. They know better than to interfere.'

'I don't know how you stand it, Mam. It beats me why you don't throw him out. It's your flat, in your name. He's only here for a roof over his head and somebody to take it all out on. All the badness in him.'

'You're too young to understand,' her mother said. She poured tea. P'raps you will one day.'

'That's where you're wrong, Mother. I never will understand, because I shall never let a man treat me like that. Never.'

At the bus stop Roseanne Wilkinson from the block opposite was staring at her. Roseanne was three years younger than Louise and had told someone she thought Louise was marvellous. Louise didn't know why Roseanne thought that but knew that young girls sometimes got that way about older ones and tried not to think how creepy it was being stared at day after day by someone who seemed afraid of speaking to her and blushed every time she caught her eye.

This morning Roseanne suddenly appeared at her side.

'Louise...'

'Hi, Roseanne.'

'You've been away at summer camp, haven't you?'

'Yeh. Didn't you go away yourself?'

'No. Me mam's not been well.'

'Oh. I hope it's nothing serious.'

'I don't think so.'

There was an awkward pause. Louise wondered what she might say to fill in and hoped that Roseanne, who obviously had something on her mind, wasn't going to start telling her how marvellous she thought she was.

'Louise...'

'Yeh?'

'I want to tell you something.'

'Oh, yeh?'

'Can we... will you walk over there with me? I don't want anyone else to hear.'

'The bus'll be here any time, Roseanne. Can't it wait?'

'It's private.'

'Well...' To Louise's intense embarrassment she saw that Roseanne's eyes had filled with tears. Oh God, what was she going to say?

'It's about your little dog.'

Louise immediately took her by the arm and led her aside. 'You mean Gravy?'

'That little black pup you had.'

'He's gone missing. While I was away.'

Roseanne nodded. Her tears had spilled over. She couldn't hold her face straight.

'Me mam said not to tell you. She said I'd to keep out of it because he's a nasty piece of work.'

'Who?' Louise asked, though she felt sure she knew.

'That feller 'at lives with you and your mam.'

'What about him, Roseanne?'

'It was awful. Me mam'n me, we saw it all. We were looking out for me cousin Lawrence. He'd never been to see us an' we were looking out for him.'

676

'What did you see, Roseanne?'

'He...' Her voice rose uncontrollably into a high-pitched whine of distress. "He threw it out of the window. Your little dog. Me mam said "Good heavens above" and hoped I hadn't seen it as well. But I had, I had.'

Louise's heart was pounding up into her throat.

'I hope you're not making all this up.'

'How could I? Why'd I want to do that?'

Where was the body? Didn't anybody else see it? Why wasn't there somebody in the street to pick him up? She had hold of Roseanne's arm again and her grip tightened.

'They couldn't, Louise. Let go, will you, you're hurting.'

'I don't understand why—'

'There was a lorry passing by. It was full of old stone and bricks. It fell straight on top of that an' never moved. Then the lorry just carried it away.' Louise thought she was going to pass out. When she took hold of Roseanne again it was to keep herself upright.

Roseanne was sobbing, her face drenched.

'Oh, isn't it awful? What a terrible thing.'

The bus was approaching. It slowed.

'You'll miss the bus, Roseanne.'

'What about you?'

'I'll get the next one.' She gave the younger girl a gentle push. 'Off you go. I'll see you later.'

Louise turned and walked down the steps of the pedestrian underpass. She put her face on her forearms against the wall. She wanted to retch. She heard footsteps and the old voices, a man's first:

'What have you had for your breakfast, lass?"

She made no response.

A woman said, 'Been glue-sniffin' or summat. God knows what they get up to nowadays.'

677

They went. Their slow footsteps scraped on the concrete stairs.

Louise suddenly realized that she was living the most important moments of her life so far. As she slowly brought the horror under control she knew with the growing calm of clear resolve what she must do.

'I shall kill him.' she said aloud.

the determination

She told her mother what she knew as soon as she got back from school. Somehow she had got through the day and done her work without drawing attention to herself. Her secret had held her steady.

She would kill him.

'I'm sorry, Louise. I'd give *anything* for it not to have happened.'

'Oh, you don't mean that. Not anything.' It was the cause of it all that she would never give up. Not until she was released.

'I don't understand you.'

'Well, you don't have to bother, because I shall see to it meself.'

'Louise, what–'

'I shall get him for it. That's what I mean.'

'Love, for God's sake don't–'

'Face him? Oh, I won't. He's never knocked me about and I don't intend to start him off. But I shall get him for it, have no fear.'

'Oh,' her mother began, 'don't talk so...' But her faint patronising smile died with her voice as she gave her a suddenly uncertain sidelong look.

'Sooner or later,' Louise said. 'The time will come.'

Preparing for it, working out how, would steady her in resolve. No more railing. No more corrosive despair. She had a purpose now. All she had to do was keep cool, be patient, think of ways, while she sharpened her loathing into a deadly point of resolute steel. It would be the more satisfying if he could know about it when the time came.

For it *would* come. And she would know when it arrived – oh, yes – the day, the hour, the moment... when...

unresolved ending

Safe Journey On

Melanie and Heather were going down from the mountains to the coast, by coach, for the second half of their holiday. Heather's ex had tried to warn her off the entire trip because of trouble inside the country; but simply talking to him on the telephone had upset her so much she wouldn't have taken his advice on anything. Heather and Keith had not lived together for three years, but as soon as the divorce had become final he seemed to want to hold an inquest. Melanie's husband couldn't have cared less about any trouble they might run into; his own plans were all he was interested in. And although there had been empty seats on the aircraft and the hotel wasn't full, Melanie couldn't understand what the panic was about, because their week in the mountains had been quiet enough to be boring. There was no night life – even the bars closed at ten-thirty – and the hotel was deserted during the day while people walked in the high meadows and woods, or made lengthier excursions over the passes where there was still some snow this late in spring and reports of melting slides which closed the roads for a time. Somewhere up one of the passes was the chapel of the Russian prisoners who had built the road. Heather had read about it and kept letting Melanie know that she fancied a day out to look at it. But walking all that way was not Melanie's idea of a holiday pastime and Heather did not want to go alone.

Melanie's friend Susan had chosen and arranged the holiday then fallen ill, leaving a place which Heather, who needed a distraction, had been persuaded to fill. A bright idea of Melanie's to contact Heather, whom she had not seen for years. Or so she had thought. She wasn't so sure now. But that could be the deadening effect of this place, which Melanie was surprised Susan had chosen (and that she had allowed her to choose without checking), and everything would surely be better once they were on the coast. Melanie was going to sunbathe topless when they reached the sea and regretted that it did not seem the done thing here, because she spent most of each day lying in the sun on the hotel terrace while Heather sat nearby in the shade and read one paperback after another. Melanie had attractively firm breasts for a woman turned forty and had not been afraid of showing them on beaches in Spain and Italy. Seeing Heather stepping out of the shower one time, she had told her, in her usual candid way, that she had nothing to hide either, and why didn't she join in when they reached the coast. But Heather, trying not to look self-conscious at being caught naked, had said she did not enjoy lying in full sunlight anyway. A hospital almoner, Heather was used to hearing and dealing with people's difficulties; yet there was often a shy, almost vulnerable look about her.

Sometimes after dinner they chatted with the only two unaccompanied men in the place, a couple of Scots who left the hotel every morning straight after breakfast, wearing thick stockings and walking-boots and carrying knapsacks. They amused Melanie. 'Doch an' Doris' she had christened them as she and Heather saw them setting out on another twenty-mile tramp. 'They say it's wonderful above the snow-line,' Heather said. 'Another world,' Melanie murmured. 'Another worrrld.' She sighed. 'There's almost bound to be something more enticing on the coast.' 'Enticing?' 'Fetching, then.' 'They're all right,' Heather said. 'The younger one – Andrew – is quite good-looking in his own way,' Melanie allowed, 'but Gavin... well, I never did go for wiry little men with ginger hair on their legs.' 'You sound as if you've known a good many,' Heather said, and Melanie said, 'Oh, I've been around, Heather my girl, I've been around,' while she opened one eye behind her sunglasses to see how shocked Heather might be looking.

On the last night before the women left one of the men sniffed at Melanie's maraschino on the rocks as the bar was closing and said why didn't they come up to their room and have a farewell drop of malt whisky from their duty-free bottle. 'Just a wee doch an' doris,' Gavin said, so unexpectedly becoming the stage Scot that Melanie, glass at her lips, almost choked as she tried not to burst out laughing.

A quick conference in the ladies told her that Heather wasn't keen.

'I'd planned to pack and have an early night. The coach leaves at half-past seven.'

'Oh, come on, let yourself go for half an hour.'

'But what do they want?'

'It's not what they want, it's what we're prepared to give them.'

'In my case, that's nothing.'

'Not even a joke and a laugh?'

'Half an hour, then. I shall leave after half an hour whether you're ready or not.'

Melanie could not help, all the same, looking at Heather in slight puzzlement when she did get up to go as second drinks were being offered.

'I did say...'

'Well, yes, if you must.'

'You're not going yet, are you?" Andrew asked, flourishing the bottle. "Won't you have another? I thought we were just getting really relaxed.'

'I did say to Melanie.'

'You run along, then,' Melanie said.

'Shall I bring you back the key?'

'Just leave the door unlocked, can't you?'

'If you're not going to be long I shall probably still be packing.'

I really can't say how long I'll be, Melanie wanted to say. If you're going go, don't hover.

'We'll say good-night, then,' Andrew said, already pouring into Melanie's glass. 'And if we don't see you in the morning, safe journey on.'

They had been talking about the seaside resort where Melanie and Heather were heading for and Gavin had described it, a town of ornamental stucco on baroque villas, dreaming behind trees of their imperial past, when, a part of the old Hapsburg empire, they had been visited by lesser lights of the Austrian court and their women. Now Melanie realised that Gavin had gone. Where was he?

'I think he went after your friend.'

'Did he really?'

'He might be just seeing her to her door.'

'Or what?'

'Or I don't really know.'

683

'Do you two have some kind of signal?'

'What do you mean?'

'Meaning, now I want to be left alone.'

'What a suspicious mind you've got.'

Melanie smiled at him. She enjoyed this game. She had played it before.

'If you'd anything else in mind you've left it a bit late.'

'Have I?' He was, to give him his due, making a good job of looking puzzled.

'We shall be two hundred miles away this time tomorrow. I intend to have everything I came with. Nothing more; nothing less.'

'It's a pity. I think that next week could have been much more interesting than this last.'

'And now we'll never know.'

Andrew came with his glass and sat beside Melanie on the sofa. It was not a sofa really, just an extra built-in single bed, and not what you would call comfortable to sit on for long. He took her hand. She let it lie.

'You really are a rather attractive woman, Melanie, all the same.'

'All the same as what?'

'That we're not going to get to know each other any better.'

'Are you married? Tell the truth now.'

'Yes.'

'What about your friend?'

'Separated. What about yours?'

'Divorced.'

'And your marriage is...' His thumb moved the rings on her hand... 'is it in good working order?'

'Yes, it's all under control. And now might be a good time to tell you that you are holding the hand of a grandmother twice over.'

'I don't believe you.'

'Married for the first time at eighteen; daughter not much older and pregnant in the first year. Nothing to it.'

'What happened to the first husband?'

'Killed in a road accident.'

'And the second one believes in live and let live?'

'Something like that.'

'You know, I'd no such thought in my mind until you started to talk about it.'

'Which I wouldn't have if your friend hadn't left us alone tight on cue.'

'Have it your way.'

'Oh, I shall. And please don't kiss me, Andrew. I'm unusual for this day and age, but I do find it such an intimate thing.'

'Well then, I'll remove myself from temptation." He got up and went back to the bottle.

'No more for me,' Melanie said. "In fact, I think I should be toddling along,'

'And feeling grateful for your lucky escape,' Andrew said. He was looking at her with an expression of slight amusement. She felt herself flushing. It was not working out quite as it should have.

'Better luck next week,' she said as he opened and held the door.

He allowed her that and, she knew, stood to watch her till she had turned the corner.

Irritability was ready when she put her hand to the knob of her own door and felt its resistance. She knocked, wondering why Heather could not remember a simple request to leave the door unlocked. She knocked again, louder, and a third time hard enough to hurt her knuckles. Turning her hand she thumped the door with the bunched edge of it. 'Heather,' she said loudly, 'for heaven's sake open the door.' She looked round as a door opened behind her. A man in pyjamas looked out.

'Are you having trouble?'

'I think my friend must have gone off into a deep sleep.'

'The night porter downstairs should have a pass-key.'

'Yes. Thanks. That's a good idea,'

'It's the only idea, unless you want to wake the whole floor.'

What a dump it was, with everybody in bed by midnight and afraid of being disturbed.

Melanie went to the lift. A few dim bulbs cast a miserable light on the square of sofas and low tables which turned the inner part of the lobby into a lounge. There was a brighter glow coming from the room behind the desk, where the night porter sat. Melanie rapped on the desk until he looked round the door.

'I'm locked out of my room. I wonder if you have a spare key.'

He stood behind the desk in his shiny blue uniform, thick-set, square-featured, Slavic.

'Number, please.'

'Three-one-one.'

He turned and found the empty hook. He waved his hand at it.

'I know it's not there,' Melanie said. 'My friend has fallen asleep and locked me out.' She was about to mime sleeping when someone tapped on the glass of the entrance door. The porter turned and looked. 'A moment.' He walked to the door and opened it as Melanie made out two people. Heather came in with Gavin. The porter was pointing to the room key in Heather's hand. Heather's voice carried across the space. "I know I should have, but I didn't.' She came towards Melanie, looking apologetic.

'I must have wakened half the floor, Heather, thinking you'd gone to sleep.'

'I'm sorry, Melanie. I never thought.'

'*I* put it out of her mind,' Gavin said. He held out his hand to Heather. 'I'll say goodbye now.'

'We're on the same floor,' Heather said. 'Aren't you coming up?'

'In a minute. I want a word with the porter.'

'I'll say good-night, then.'

'Yes. Good-night.' He nodded at Melanie. 'Good-night.'

Melanie managed to keep silent until they were in their room, when she let rip.

'Really, Heather, you made me feel quite foolish.'

'I expect I did, and I'm sorry.'

'What were you doing out there, anyway?'

'I was keeping Gavin company until he felt he could go back to his room.'

'What was keeping him from his room?'

'I should have thought you'd be in a better position than me to know that.'

'Of course Andrew thought it all very convenient when Gavin left us alone.'

'Did he? Did he try something on?'

'They always try something on. How far they get is another matter.'

'So long as we know.'

'Is that what you take me for, Heather? Because if it is I'd better tell you before we go any further that I like men, I enjoy their company, but I'm not especially interested in sex.'

'As long as your husband knows it's general and not just something about him,' Heather said.

'Are you trying to be offensive?'

'I believe I am.'

687

'I don't know why. I've done nothing to you.'

'No, you haven't. I apologise again.'

'If we all looked at life the way you look at it, there'd be even more of us divorced.'

'Perhaps so.'

Melanie had rapidly undressed. Heather was taking things from the wardrobe that she wouldn't need in the morning and folding them neatly into her case. Packing the night before, Melanie thought, was one of the little ways by which Heather made you feel idle and sloppy.

'What did you find to talk about out there in the dark, anyway?'

'Oh, this and that. He's a pharmacist. He has a shop.'

'I thought you already knew that.'

'He was telling me about the Russian prisoners' chapel.'

'You know, I really do think you owed it to yourself to see that. Just because I didn't want to walk all that way...'

'Well, it's too late now. But Gavin told me this story about it. Do listen, Melanie. It's so beautifully sad.'

'Go on, then. I'm listening.'

'Well, the Austrians fought the Russians in the First World War and put some of the prisoners they took to building a road over those mountains. One day, in atrocious weather on the summit, a local girl got lost in a blizzard while looking for some goats that had strayed. One of the Russians found her and took her down to safety. She'd surety have perished if it hadn't been for him and her grateful family gave him shelter in return and a good fire to sleep by. Now, he was a trusted prisoner or he'd have been shackled like his comrades, and it was thought he'd made an attempt to escape. They wouldn't believe his story about the girl and the goats. They gave him fifty lashes and transferred him to an even worse place in another province. When the thaw came and the girl could climb up the pass to see him he'd gone. She never saw him again, but she spent the rest of her life grieving for him, because in that brief time she'd fallen eternally in love with him. Eventually the war ended, the prisoners were repatriated and the road was completed. In the meantime the goat-girl had come into an unexpected legacy and with the money she built a small chapel at the summit of the pass in memory of her lost love. One day she set out there alone and was never seen again. But people swear that at certain times, when all the conditions are right, she can be heard weeping by those engaged in their silent devotions.'

'Isn't it haunting?'

'I thought things couldn't haunt you till long after.'

'Well, don't you think it's the kind of thing you'll never forget?'

'I suppose it is. If you're as interested as you were to start with.'

Melanie was rubbing lotion into her brow and cheeks with both hands at once.

'Look, Heather,' she said, 'I'm glad you don't sulk, because there's one thing you should know about me. I say what I have to say, then forget it. Life's too short for bearing grudges.'

She opened her pyjamas in front of the long mirror on the door and looked at herself. She was beginning to show a tan and was afraid that her breasts would already look repellently white against it when she took off her bikini top on the coast.

On the coach Heather struck up a conversation with the stocky grey-haired woman sitting across the gangway. It was the first time they had exchanged more than a couple of words. She was one of those who had gone out every day in walking-gear and she had not lingered in the dining-room.

Now she told Heather, while Melanie listened also, that it was her first time in the country since her husband's death, five years ago. Before that they had come every year, sometimes more than once. He had, she said, been one of those parachuted in during the war, to make contact with the partisans, whatever that meant.

'You must know it intimately and have lots of friends,' Heather said.

'Well...' the woman waved a square, capable-looking hand, 'some parts better than others. And old friends grow old and fall away...'

The coach was climbing.

'I didn't know we'd be going over the mountains,' Heather said.

'It saves thirty miles if the pass is open.'

'This is the road the Russian prisoners built, surely.'

'Yes, it is. Near the summit is their chapel.'

That damned chapel!

'I heard a story about that,' Heather said.

'Oh?'

'You must know it already.'

'Perhaps not.'

'Well, it's about a girl who lost some goats in a snowstorm...'

Something made Melanie glance across at the woman as Heather finished. A little smile played on her lips.

'You hadn't heard it, then?'

'No. Who do you say told it to you?'

'A man at the hotel.'

'A local man?'

'No, a Scotsman on holiday.'

The woman's smile had broadened.

'Why are you smiling?'

'It doesn't matter. There's no harm in it.'

'You mean it isn't true?'

'What a pity if it isn't.'

'But you'd surely have known it if it were.'

Heather's colour was rising. The woman noticed it too.

'But it doesn't matter,' she said again. 'There's no harm done, is there?'

'No, but...'

But you don't know Heather, lady, Melanie was thinking. As Heather fell silent and looked distractedly away, the woman kept stealing little glances at her flushed face.

'I've upset you. I've made you feel foolish.'

'No, really...'

But she was upset. In a moment she began to mutter under her breath. Melanie felt impelled to break in on it.

'Heather... what on earth's the matter?'

'We couldn't stop, could we?'

'I shouldn't think so. We've hardly got started. Don't you feel well?'

'I'll be all right.'

Sweat had broken out on her top lip. Melanie found a scented freshener tissue and put it into her hand.

'Use this.'

The stocky woman had been to the front of the bus to speak to the courier. She smiled at Heather and Melanie as she returned to her seat and the speakers crackled. The courier cleared her throat.

'Your attention, please. I have been asked if we can stop at the chapel of the Russian prisoners on the summit of the pass. Such a stop is not on our schedule, but we can allow ten minutes. Ten minutes only, please, as we have a long way to go. First of all I will tell you a little about the place...'

It sounded to Melanie as if the courier had not heard the story about the goat-girl either.

The chapel, which stood on a level patch of cleared ground above a sheer drop of a hundred feet or more, was a small building of roughly dressed stone with a steeply pitched roof and a bell-tower. The walls had the same rough, unplastered finish inside. There were no seats. The single oblong room was bare except for a rectangular stone altar table on which stood a wooden crucifix and twin stone jars holding fresh wild flowers.

The cold in the place struck Melanie at once. 'God, they must have frozen.'

When she looked round Heather had gone. Melanie went out also. The sky had darkened. It felt less like early morning than approaching night. She wandered along the side of the building and was in time to see the stocky woman beckon to Heather as though she had been waiting for her. Heather stood beside her on the edge of the precipice. The woman took her finger from her lips and Melanie respected her request for silence as she herself approached them.

'Can you hear it?' the woman asked.

Heather nodded. The two of them faced the void and listened.

'Well,' the woman said eventually, 'any number of people would tell us that that is no more than a trick of the wind.'

'They would.'

'But I'd like to think I'm one of those who knows better.'

'So would I.'

And if that was what they wanted, Melanie thought,

where was the harm? She would have turned away then, except that the sudden tears in the stocky woman's eyes held her where she stood.

'Are you all right?' Heather reached to take the woman's arm.

'It's all at risk, you know.' The woman gestured with her free hand above the void. 'All in great peril. If we could hear the crying of the dead, the thousands upon thousands who spilt their blood for it, it would appal us.'

'It's too complicated for me to grasp,' Heather said.

'Perhaps for any of us,' the woman said. 'Perhaps it always was.'

The courier, impatient to get away, was calling them to the coach. As Melanie set off she heard the woman ask, behind her 'Will you be seeing your Scottish friend again?'

'I've no idea where he lives. I don't even know his surname.'

'A pity. He sounds like an understanding man.'

Almost immediately they began to descend. The road on this side was cut into the mountain in a zig-zag line, sometimes plunging into cuttings before emerging again to heart-stopping views of the plain below. Once, as they seemed to turn back on themselves, they could see for several moments the chapel on the summit against a livid sky.

'It's going to snow again up there,' the stocky woman said.

The words themselves seemed to chill Melanie to the bone. 'God, I'll be glad when we get to the sea.' Although she was wearing a windcheater she rummaged in her drawstring bag for her rolled cardigan. There was something under it which she offered Heather. A fat paperback book.

'This is yours.'

'Where did I leave it? I think I had it in the bar last night.'

'It was handed to me at reception this morning.'

'By the way," Heather asked, "did you get Andrew's address?'

'Whatever for?' She'd been tempted to ask 'Who's Andrew?'

'Oh, I just wondered.'

'All over Europe,' Andrew had said at one point, 'there'll be people like us, strangers getting to know one another.' And moving on in the morning, Melanie had thought.

'Is your book any good?' she asked.

'Quite gripping, if a bit long-winded.'

'I wouldn't mind having a go when you've finished.'

'Not much further now.' Heather riffled the pages, then asked, 'What's this doing here?'

'What is it?'

Heather held up the small piece of card and looked at both sides. She trembled suddenly, as if the same cold that Melanie had felt now touched her. Without asking again Melanie took the card from Heather's fingers. It was a business card with Gavin's name and the address of his shop printed on one side. On the other was a scribbled note which it took Melanie a moment to decipher:

'Dear Heather,
Should ever serendipity – or a lost goat – bring you to Perth I'd like you to look me up. G.'

The stocky woman was speaking to Heather across the aisle. 'Last view.' In the instant they looked up at the summit of the pass again the road swung, taking the coach behind a wall of rock and the chapel was finally lost to their sight.

Melanie was glad to see the back of it, and the mountain too. For as they emerged into the open again she saw on the horizon a rim of blue that common sense told her couldn't possibly be what she was so looking forward to, but which her eager imagination only too readily transformed into the sea.

WWW.THELIBRARYOFWALES.COM

PARTHIAN

Vic Brown, a young working-class Yorkshireman, is attracted to the beautiful but demanding Ingrid. As their relationship grows and changes he comes to terms, the hard way, with adult life and what it really means to love.

A cult classic, Stan Barstow's landmark 'Brit-Lit' novel of the sixties led the way for authors like Nick Hornby.

ISBN 9781906998356
£7.99

www.parthianbooks.com

PARTHIAN

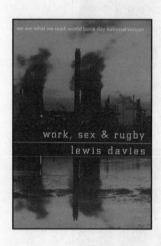

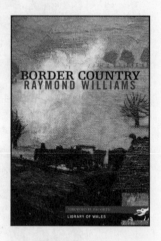

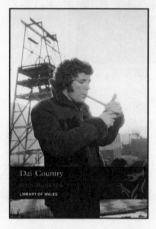

www.parthianbooks.com